BOOKS BY MACDONALD HARRIS

HERMA

HERMA

MacDonald Harris

New York Atheneum 1981

The photograph of Kitty Hawk is reproduced by kind permission of Culver Pictures.

Permission to quote from the following songs is gratefully acknowledged:

''Kiss Me Again'' by Henry Blossom and Victor Herbert, © 1915 by Warner Bros., Inc., Copyright renewed, All rights reserved

''There's A Long, Long Trail'' by Stoddard King, © 1914 by Warner Bros., Inc., Copyright renewed, All rights reserved

''My Buddie'' by Gus Kahn and Walter Donaldson, Lyrics © 1922 by Gilbert Keyes Music Co. (Pursuant to sections 04 (c) and 401 (b) of the U.S. Copyright Law)

''Minnie the Mermaid'' by Bud De Sylva, Copyright © 1930 by Leo Feist, Inc., Copyright renewed, Assigned to Chappell & Co., Inc. (Intersong Music, Publisher) and David Shelly Publishing Co., Inc. for the U.S.A. International Copyright secured. In Canada, Copyright © 1923, Copyright renewed 1951 by Leo Feist, Inc., All rights reserved

Library of Congress Cataloging in Publication Data

Harris, MacDonald, 1921–
   Herma.

   I. Title.
PS3558.A6468H4   1981   813'.54   81-66005
ISBN 0-689-11179-7   AACR2

Not having had ancestors like other people, I have been forced to invent them. This book is fearfully dedicated to them, in the hope of placating their spirits.

She was a genuine product of the far West—a flower of the Pacific slope; ignorant, audacious, crude, but full of pluck and spirit, of natural intelligence, and of a certain intermittent, haphazard good taste. She used to say that she only wanted a chance—apparently she had found it now. HENRY JAMES, *The Siege of London*

CONTENTS

I. SANTA ANA

1.

When all was ready, Papa called from the drive, and then Mama gathered Herma in her arms and came out, both of them in their Sunday best. Mama and Herma both wore white dresses, the one a tiny copy of the other. Mama's dress had a blue ribbon worked into the hem, and Herma's dress was trimmed with strawberry-colored ribbon. Mama had a broad straw hat of the same blue as the ribbon in her dress, and her parasol too was trimmed in blue. They all mounted into the buggy, Papa snapped the whip, and away they went.

As for Papa, whom Herma greatly admired—wondering what it was like to be so large and calm, so knowledgeable about everything, and so hairy and fragrant in a way that was more like that of horses than of women and girls—he wore his best dark-blue suit, a starched collar, and a necktie with stars on it. His coat was open and the glittering gold watch chain could be seen hanging across his vest. His hat was a gray derby with a brim that curved down in front and back. His face was rather pale, since he worked indoors and was not able to get outside very much, and his blue-eyed glance was steady and serious. His sandy, rather wispy mustache was neatly clipped. He looked like exactly what he was—a successful young newspaper editor and also a Baptist.

Everybody in Santa Ana was something—if not Baptist, then Methodist, or Presbyterian, or Episcopalian, or even Congregationalist—although these last were rather odd, since they had no church of their own and had to meet on Sunday mornings in a storefront on French Street. The Baptists, of course, had a proper church—white and neat, set in a green rectangle of lawn, with a sharp-pointed copper steeple on top of it. There were hibiscus bushes around it, their blossoms like red and orange flames in the glossy foliage, and a number of shaggy palm trees on the lawn. Here Papa pulled up and tied Delilah to a bush, and Mama and Herma got down.

Herma was at the stage where she was getting too heavy to carry, and yet so small that she might get lost, or be trampled on, if she were put down among that confused and stirring mass of adult legs. On the whole she preferred to be carried. Her sense of independence preferred walking on her own two legs, yet from her vantage high up in the hollow of Mama's bosom she could see about over the wide world, observing its customs and making mental notes about how she herself would behave later, when she was big. So down the aisle they went—Papa first, his derby off now so that the balding circle in his sandy blond hair was visible, and Mama followed with Herma, her white dress rustling in the silence. They sat down in a pew, a word that made Herma want to giggle. However Meeting was serious and Herma was not allowed to laugh, or make any other noise, otherwise she was subject to Papa's disapproval.

After everyone had sat down in their pews (don't laugh) there was a long silence broken only by murmurs and rustling of clothing, and then Brother Goff appeared carrying a book. He was not very much like Papa. He was tall and craggy and he wore a string tie around his turkey neck. He had bushy eyebrows, and since he had no hips his trousers sagged a little to show a gap between his belt and his vest. On days other than Sunday he was an orange rancher. He was only a lay preacher, Mama had explained, although what this meant Herma had no idea. He opened his book and began reading out of it, and Papa and Mama followed silently along in little books of their own, as if to be sure he was reading it right.

After this Brother Goff set the book aside, everyone else did too, and Brother Goff went on speaking without the book. He spoke of Sin and Redemption and Grace Abounding and Satan and Scriptures and Redeemer and Atonement and Eternal Torment and Calvary and Faith and Works and Total Immersion. As he went on speaking about these things he became quite agitated, his face turned red, and the little veins stood out on his neck. Herma was afraid he was angry, but Papa had told her he was not, or at least not at them or at anything specific, instead at a rather vague Thing in general. Brother Goff came to the end, still angry, and glared out at them, and everybody said, "Ah. Men."

Next came the Hymns, which were easy to understand, or took no understanding at all—they were just something to enjoy, like an ice-cream cone, or a strawberry from Gump & Blake's. Sitting in Mama's lap, Herma even piped away at the melodies herself, with a certain accuracy—she was precocious in this. Herma's favorite perhaps was *In the Garden,* because of the excitement of the hanging pause that seemed to shudder for an eternity before the chorus began in earnest, authorized by a birdlike and humming B flat from the Bell Pump Organ played by Mrs. Opdike:

> "And He . . . ."
> (Here the excruciating wait for the organ)
> "*walks* with me and he *talks* with me . . . ."

The longer this was prolonged, the greater the ecstasy of the moment when it finally broke loose. Mrs. Opdike had a knack of prolonging it extraordinarily—as though it were a warm and delicious lump of taffy that she was stretching into a string—longer—longer—until it seemed it must stretch onto the floor, whereupon she caught up the lump deftly and went on.

Along with this, there was *Rock of Ages, Cleft for Me* and *The Old Rugged Cross*—which had a rug over it, in Herma's vision, perhaps because it was old and they didn't want people to see it—and *Bringing in the Sheeps*, of which the words were almost as incomprehensible as Brother Goff's orations, but which had the most dashing and rousing tune of all, one to make the blood stir so that Herma bounced on Mama's lap—Mama didn't like that, but since Mama was kind it was Papa who told her to stop. It was only some time later that Herma grasped that the ''Sheeps'' were really ''Sheaves,'' but this didn't help in the comprehension very much—flour came from Fagel's in ten-pound bags, and since she lived in a land of orange groves and palm trees she had never seen a stalk of wheat in her whole life.

More complex—so much so that it was some time before Herma grasped its full intricacies—was *The Church in the Wildwood*, which had a different tune for gentlemen and for ladies, and yet was arranged somehow so that the two tunes worked mysteriously together. For a while everyone sang the same thing, and then the sexes divided, and contended with each other, so to speak, but in a friendly way. The ladies' voices were high and trilling, the gentlemen's gruffer and deeper, with a weight to them that Herma could feel in her breastbone.

(Ladies)   Come. Come. Come. Come.
(Gentlemen)   *COME. COME. COME. COME.*
(Ladies)   Come to the church in the wild . . . wood . . .
(Gentlemen)   *COME.   COME.   COME.   COME.*

Herma was introduced to the mysterious world of counterpoint, which was also a world in which ladies and gentlemen were different. What would happen, she wondered, if a lady went on singing ''Come, come, come'' instead of going on to the part about the wildwood? She tried, in her tiny treble which was no louder than a piccolo, but extraordinarily penetrating in the small church with its bare walls:

come. come. come. come. come. come. come. come.

Again it was Papa who told her to stop, not by saying anything, since this was not proper during Hymns, but with a glacial look and a frown whose meaning was unmistakable. Herma switched back to singing with the ladies, who declaimed that no place was so dear to their childhood as the little brown church in the vale. This was better anyhow because, as Herma now saw, the gentlemen's part was rather boring. Ladies were better at singing than gentlemen, and enjoyed it more, even though it was Brother Goff himself who led in his own gruff and gravelly baritone, a delivery in which the twang of his native Kentucky was clearly audible. Herma sensed that in Brother Goff's view of the matter, singing out loud was not really a suitable occupation for a grown-up man, but it was called for in the practice of his belief, so he did so, grudgingly, even though loud enough to shake the rafters, apologizing with a little clearing of his throat before each line began. And so they went on—Brother Goff's half-ashamed bull-roaring mingled with the trilling soprano of Mrs. Opdike at the organ, the bashful and not very musical duet of Papa and Mama, who sang under their breath so to speak, and the braying of a brassy carpenter named Farkuss, who sat directly behind Herma and whose warm breath smelled of something fragrant and medicinal like hoarhound drops—an odor so strong that it stung. It was a disgrace, Mama said afterward when they had come home, but Papa only twitched his mustache a little.

And perhaps Mr. Farkuss only liked to sing. Certainly Herma enjoyed singing, even when she was alone. Scarcely old enough to be out of her crib, she was able to amuse herself for long hours on end with labyrinthian sequences of melody which she had apparently invented—a kind of babyish singsong, going up and down, with syntax, semicolons, pauses for effect, and rousing climaxes which reached the C two octaves above the middle of the piano. It was not really music, perhaps, but a kind of vocalized mimicry, which at times touched the borders of the uncanny. Now and again she seemed to be imitating the cooing of the pigeons that strutted about on the back lawn; at other times one could recognize the oblique and weird intonation of Mah Song the Chinese vegetable man as he came down the street on his wagon—an oriental cadence which, through some mysterious penetrating quality, announced his coming a half an hour or more away, enabling each housewife to put down her list on a scrap of paper and collect together her coins before the two horses stopped (if all went well) at the curb in front of the house. "Children," said Papa distractedly, having no experience whatsoever of children, "are natural mimics." It was a long time, to tell the truth, before anyone paid any attention to this pastime or predilection of Herma, or noticed that there was anything out of the ordinary about it. Children were savage little animals, not quite human, who had not yet learned the niceties of excretion, table manners, and how and when to use one's larynx—this was well known, even if one didn't talk about it in quite those terms. So there was no accounting for their behavior—if they put beans up their nose, or poured out their mush on the floor, or looked inside their underwear, these were only instances of an imperfection inherent in their age, which would no doubt be self-curing with maturity—otherwise they would have to be confined in some institution or other. So Herma's singing, if that was what it was.

Yet what Herma was doing—still so young that she slept in, not a crib exactly, but a bed with a wooden fence around it that could be put down to take her out—in the end compelled attention. And so one day there was Papa, listening behind the door. The child was standing in her tiny nightgown, holding onto the bed fence to support herself, and singing, not loudly but persistently—she had been at it now for half an hour. She had been through *The Church in the Wildwood* with its iterated "Come, come, come" like an old English round, *Bringing in the Sheaves*, *The Old Rugged Cross*, and *Rock of Ages*. Now she had embarked on *In the Garden*, her favorite. A kind of shiver passed through Papa—a cool thrill in the presence of the uncanny. For Herma was singing it all. In her piping piccolo, two octaves above the rest of the congregation, one could nevertheless recognize the very intonation and personal stamp of Brother Goff's baritone—every Kentucky nasal, even the little cough before he began each line. The voice *was* that of Brother Goff, elevated by some laryngeal necromancy high into the region of the tiny songbird. And that was not all. Mrs. Opdike could be heard, too, trilling away at the "And . . . He . . ." that preceded the climactic *"walks!"* And even, in the pause that intervened, the resonant B flat of the organ that released the Niagara of voices. Like a tiny Victrola, Herma recorded the whole Baptist church. The machine being minute, it was like the Lord's Prayer engraved on a pin, but every nuance and throat scrape was there. The chill had left Papa now, but he felt dry-mouthed and a little faint. He went into the kitchen and drank a brassy-tasting glass of water.

Children, he told himself, are natural mimics.

2.

The house on Ross Street had a white picket fence around it, and a gate in front with a tinkly bell. Older now and able to range farther, Herma spent most of her waking hours outdoors. Her preferred and private domain was the backyard. The grass there was long and cool to the feet, and around it was a jungle of lush and profuse California vegetation, all more or less getting out of hand because Papa didn't have time to trim it: bougainvillea with flaring red blossoms, geraniums rampaging along the back fence, the hibiscus with its horn-shaped flower out of which emerged a long red pistil as stiff as a broom handle, the bird of paradise with its strange beaky magenta blooms that looked as though they might eat insects, and perhaps did. The lawn by itself was a wonderland to explore. A single square foot of grass, if Herma examined it with her nose on the ground and her rear in the air, was a menagerie of creatures as wild and queer as herself, even though tiny: plodding ants carrying packages, crickets, disreputable mealybugs, earthworms if she dug a little, bees sucking the clover, and a ladybug which she dispatched from her finger with a puff of air and the ritual valedictory: "Your house is on fire and your children alone." And perhaps the ladybug did have a house, and perhaps it really was on fire, and perhaps the children were all alone; Herma half believed this, withheld her sympathy, and accepted it in the natural order of things; she did her part by telling the ladybug the news. Standing up again with grassy knees, she picked a blackberry off the bush that stuck through the fence from the Sampsons' next door, turned on the garden faucet to irrigate her toes and stamp in the mud produced, ran around in tightening circles on the lawn until she fell down giddy on the grass, and threw walnuts onto the roof and waited for them to come down—finally a walnut struck her square on the head and this made her angry, and she stamped on the enemy and ate it with great satisfaction, even though it was rancid. Then she found herself all at once staring through the fence at Mr. Sampson's Delilah. They had their own buggy but no horse—there was no need for it, Papa said—although perhaps they would have one, he hinted, when he became Editor-in-Chief. As fortune would have it, the Sampsons were Adventists, so they went to Meeting (if that was what the Adventists called it) on Saturday, so that Papa was able to borrow Mr. Sampson's horse every Sunday and hitch it to their own Higgins buggy to go off to Meeting—in return, Mr. Sampson would sometimes borrow the buggy. Delilah was an old mare with rheumy eyes who took a melancholy view of things, and bared her yellow teeth as she cropped at the grass—what would it be like to have those huge yellow teeth, Herma wondered—what would it be like to be bitten by them? A sweet panic seized her, quite harmless since Delilah was on the other side of the fence, and she flew around the house and out the picket gate at the front, making the bell ping like a streetcar.

Ross Street was not paved; nothing was paved in those days, except the two blocks of Fourth Street in the center of town where the stores were. There were cement curbs—the optimistic founders of the town knew that one day Ross Street should and would be paved—but for now there was only warm, soft dust in the summer, and a smooth and sensuous mud, as fine as potter's clay, in the winter when it rained. But it was summer now and Herma set off, with this luxurious talcum sifting over her toes, under the sycamores that arched over the street on both sides and lent everything a dappled greenish light, wavering slightly like the sea. Three houses down, she knew, she would encounter the Hickeys' old English bulldog, Dr. Johnson, lying asleep in the dust squarely in the middle of the street—this was his place and everybody knew it—the boy with the milk wagon and Dr. Violet in his buggy would steer carefully around him. Drooling from the jaw, senile and pot-bellied, Dr. Johnson opened one red eye, no more, and regarded Herma as she passed. Yet even in his sleep Dr. Johnson, like everybody else, could recognize the distant incantation of Mah Song and would get up grumpily, in due time, and limp over to the curb to let the vegetable wagon pass—for like everybody else he knew that Mah Song did not understand horses and could not steer them, even to go around bulldogs.

Proceeding thus down Ross Street, past the house of the Kessler Girls who had never married and were as queer, people said, as Dick's hatband, past the sagging bungalow of Mr. Farkuss from which loud hymns could be heard even when it was not Sunday, she arrived in due course at Fourth Street—not yet paved here, but it was if she turned and walked east only a couple of blocks. Herma knew the names of the streets by heart—Ross, then Birch, then West, then Sycamore, then Main. At West the dusty street burst all at once into pavement and the stores began. Anything in the world could be bought in those two magical blocks of Fourth Street from West to Main.

Still too young to read, she knew the stores already, some on account of their odor or by the things in the windows, others because the proprietor whom she knew would be standing in the doorway. First came Feeley's Book Store, which in addition to books also displayed an Edison phonograph and a number of photographic devices—these latter strange machines with red bellows, gleaming rings and levers, and square or oblong black bodies. Herma stared down each of the Cyclops eyes, one by one, before she turned and went on. In the window of Hickey's Hardware and Plumbing there was a model windmill, no larger than Herma herself, the blades of which revolved by some mysterious force even though there was no wind behind the glass. From the open door of Fagel's Family Grocery came a tantalizing odor of chocolate, coffee, and spices. Next came the *Blade* office where Papa worked ("all day long," as Mama said, attempting to evoke Herma's sympathy; but Herma thought it would be better than languishing in the house all day as Mama did). Over the *Blade* and up a dusty stairway was Dr. Violet's office; but no one ever went there, since it was only a tiny cubicle with hardly room for a desk and Dr. Violet himself preferred to "come to the house." Dr. Violet had a number of silver instruments which he applied to various parts of the body when he examined Herma. He tickled, but not in a friendly way, instead with a malicious grin, and Herma didn't care much for him.

A few doors farther down was Paul's Undertaking Parlor, with its heavy red curtains drawn so that nothing could be seen from the street. Mr. Paul *took people under;* although Herma didn't know why he took them under, or what happened to them there. A little shiver passed through her at the sight of the red curtains, but Papa had explained that Mr. Paul only took very old people under, like Grandma Harris that Herma scarcely remembered, since she was still being carried in Mama's arms then. On the corner of Sycamore was Proper Procter's Dry Goods and Outfittery, with gentlemen's clothing in one window and ladies' in the other; then Gump & Blake's Luxury Fruitery—Mr. Blake, who was a friend of Papa and Mama, would invariably offer Herma some delicacy, a fruit never seen at home, like a loquat, or an alligator pear, or a guava. Next came Shakespeare's Cigar Store, which gave out a totally different smell from Fagel's, dark and druglike, so heady that Herma felt it might make you dizzy if you inhaled too much of it. Conwell's Bridlery next door to it sold harnesses, whips, and bridles for horses. One window was full of such things, and in the other was a tiny buggy pulled by a papier-mâché horse. Before each of these things Herma was accustomed to pause for ten minutes or more, so that an exploration of Fourth Street might take a whole afternoon—but Mama, in bed with her book, hardly noticed or cared, and Papa came home from the *Blade* office only at seven.

Finally, almost at the corner of Main, came the climax and best thing of all, Q. R. Smith's Palace of Drugs—a real palace, exactly like those in picture books, with a high ceiling of embossed tin, gleaming and gilded, and the great hall underneath stretching away so long that the end could hardly be seen from the street. On one side were white shelves mounting high up the wall, filled with rows of green canisters, bottles of colored fluid, phials, decanters, and ewers with blue lettering. On the other side were the ten thousand mahogany drawers with brass fittings, redolent with the odor of herbs and homeopathic remedies; and the clerks, Papa said, knew what was in every one of the drawers. Along the aisle were cabinets displaying the chemical aids employed by ladies to enhance their beauty; but it was not very respectable, Herma knew, to make use of such things. Or, if one did, it was well to follow the example of Mama, who applied a tiny dot of vermillion to her cheeks and rubbed it in so well that, in the end, nothing could be seen but the faintly flushed spot caused by the rubbing. It is not what one does that matters, Herma concluded, but what is seen by the eye. Because Mama was respectable; in fact, the very notion of the respectable was to be measured by Mama, and even to call this matter into question for purposes of information was enough to throw Papa into a frigid disapproval that might spoil an entire dinner. Once, also, Herma had seen Mama putting something dark on her eyelids. But by that time she was wiser and didn't ask Papa about it.

The most fabulous of all, in Smith's Palace, was the ice-cream fountain with its wire stools and marble counter, where a boy in a white jacket and cap, privileged above all others of his kind, presided over an elaborate apparatus of taps, spouts, handles, silver piping and tubing, tubs white with frost, alembics of multicolored syrups, and crucibles exuding the delicious odor of chocolate, butterscotch, and caramel. The cold, Papa had explained, was produced not by ice but by a machine with black intestines that could be seen if, by chance, the boy took away a panel of the wall to twiddle and adjust it. For Herma the very peak of ecstasy was to imagine herself perched on the stool before the marble counter in her white frock with the strawberry ribbon in it and a ribbon of identical red in her hair, the same dress she wore to Meeting, and before her one of those delights in three or more colors of the rainbow which the boy prepared in a silver cup misted with frost.

But only rarely did Papa and Mama (or more probably Mama alone, when Herma came to Fourth Street with her) allow Herma to mount onto the wire stool. The luxury of it, probably, was too sensual and oriental. More often, when they came to Smith's Palace, it was for Mama's bottle of Female Remedy. Gentlemen, it seemed, did not have a Remedy, and Herma pondered over this. Perhaps, she thought, it was because they went to work instead of languishing in a stuffy house all day like Mama. Yet some gentlemen, she had observed (although not Papa), possessed an amber potion in bottles which they sipped at when they thought no one was watching, and which made them almost as cheerful as the Female Remedy did Mama; and Mr. Farkuss, she now knew, was one of these.

* * *

At the corner of Fourth and Main was the Orange Empire Bank; grand, but not quite so grand as Q. R. Smith's Palace of Drugs. On the other side of Main the pavement ended and the town began to peter out. On the corner across from the bank was Hite's Feed and Grain, a large ugly building with the name painted on the side. After that there was not very much—some weedy vacant lots, then Polanski's Livery Stables. This was not a very nice place—whinnies and coarse horsy smells came out of the long iron-roofed shed. Here Herma had to push her way through a crowd of men who were standing around blocking the sidewalk, wearing derbies and vests, some smoking cigars, and others spitting on the ground and rubbing it out with their foot. The passage of Herma through their midst invariably produced various comments and inquiries, on the order of "Hey, is you Alice Ben Bolt?" and "Whatcha got there in yer drawers, kid?" Turning, she gave them a significant sign with her finger, as she had seen them do to each other, and passed on. That is some little girl, was the opinion at the livery stable.

Men were coarse beasts in many ways. Herma went on, walking in the soft dust of the street because the sidewalk was too hot for her feet. A block farther on, at the very end of town, was the Southern Pacific station, a small wooden shed with a ticket office in one end and a waiting room with benches and cuspidors in the other. It was here that you got on the train to go to Los Angeles—Papa had done that. In the ticket office there was nothing much to be seen but a man in shirt-sleeves with a green eyeshade. The waiting room was even worse—only an old man reading a newspaper, and a fat lady with a disagreeable child who stared at her. "Where is *your* Mama?" the child asked her pointedly. Ignoring him, she went outside and stood beside the two iron rails, supported by an endless number of tarry-smelling slabs of wood, and stretching far away into the distance down an open lane between the orange groves. If you listened carefully, you could sometimes hear a faint mumble and ringing from the rails, as though some genie or troll were crying weakly to get out—as in fact they were doing right now. The man in the ticket office didn't seem to notice, but the fat lady did, and led her child out, followed after a while by the old man reluctantly rolling up his newspaper.

The ringing and rumbling grew louder; the ground could be felt to shake a little under the feet. Then, down the tracks a mile or more away, the train burst into view. It came on with a certain magnificence, giving out a great throaty roar from its whistle and jetting white steam from its wheels. Growing larger and slowing down as it approached, it finally managed to bring itself to a stop in front of the station with a squeal of brakes. There it sat, black and panting, enormous, continuing to make a muffled bellowing sound and exuding waves of hot and oily-smelling vapor.

Yet Herma was not impressed with this. It was only a machine, of the kind that men hit with hammers and swore at when they didn't work right. What did provoke her awe and admiration was the long line of glass-windowed cars behind, into one of which clambered the fat lady and child, followed by the man with his newspaper. There was a magic here, some power that pulled deeply at a fundamental urge in the human soul—or at least in Herma's. The cars were like houses, snug and self-contained, but they were houses that could go off down the tracks and take you anywhere in the wide world. You could go anywhere in the train, and see everything. And someday she would, she resolved. All these meditations occupied only a few seconds, for the 2:23 from San Diego didn't linger very long in Santa Ana. The engine growled and hissed steam, and the great iron wheels clanked into motion. With dignity— with its own kind of dignity—it gathered speed and moved out of the station, drawing the line of glass-windowed cars behind it.

But at the very end was something that caught Herma's heart—a car different from the others, painted in a rich dark-blue enamel instead of shabby black, and with decorations cut into its spotless crystal windows. There was only one person in it. In the salon at the rear, an elegant parlor upholstered in gold and burgundy, sat a lady all alone in a gilded chair. Her dress, Herma saw in the instant it took the car to pass, was a marvel—a sheath of cloth-of-gold with buttons down the back, curving in at the waist and culminating in a swelling monobust in front. Her hair was piled in a diademlike coil on her head, and she wore a pearl choker about her neck. On the table before her was a bottle and a long-stemmed glass. And she was smoking a cigar. The blue car went by and Herma watched the passing, one by one, of the gilded letters she could not understand, only grasp the shapes as potent and mysterious hieroglyphs. A . . . R . . . D . . . E . . . N. Then the train was gone, scattering papers and dead leaves along the tracks. Herma watched it until it had disappeared around the curve toward the distant city.

3.

According to Mrs. Opdike, something had to be done about Herma's gift of music, before she became much older. For, she went on, as the Scripture warned, it was a sin to hide one's Talent under a Bushel. Setting aside her deficiencies in Bible scholarship, Papa was ready to accept Mrs. Opdike's authority as a musician, at least such as there was in a rather small town, and so he bent to her recommendations. Herma, still so small that a pillow was necessary on the stool, was set down before Mama's square Chickering. Mrs. Opdike herself came every Wednesday afternoon to give her lessons, and Herma had to practice for a half an hour every day. Mama from upstairs could hear her practicing and didn't have to get up from the bed where she lay reading. The initial repertory included Scales, *The Happy Farmer,* and even, suggested Mrs. Opdike bursting with confidence, an Etude for Little Fingers which she had copied years before out of a book.

But even Mama from upstairs could tell that things were not going right. The small stubby fingers were flaccid and recalcitrant; they wandered like wax and would not press onto the right keys. They bent like rubber; they seemed to have joints that worked the wrong way. They were intractable and would obey neither Herma nor anybody else.

And when matters improved, it was only to get worse. Herma, set to playing her Scales ("For," as Mrs. Opdike said firmly, "*discipline* is the basis of all the arts."), only pretended to touch the keys, and instead (as Mama ascertained by creeping stealthily downstairs to watch her) ran her fingers over them in the air while she sang the two octaves in an uncanny imitation of the piano: *ping ping ping ping* for the high notes, *dong dong dong* for the ones in the middle, and an unearthly kind of Chinese-gong effect for the low ones down at the left. It was amazing that a sound so deep could come from so tiny a chest. As if aware of Mama's presence on the staircase behind her, Herma ran through her whole dumbfounding span. The little hand floated like a fairy over the keyboard, and the voice, beginning with the Chinese gong, ran all the way up to the tinkle at the top. Her fingers were not even touching the keyboard.

This was too much for Mama. Before such phenomena, the authority and wisdom of Papa (even though he was not an expert on children) was called for. He was secretly made to come home from the *Blade* in the middle of the afternoon—an unheard-of event, almost a violation of nature—and hide behind the door to listen. It was time for Scales again.

peep
ping
ping

sang Herma, stretching out her tiny arm and not quite touching the high C with her finger.

That night after Herma was put to bed they discussed it, shutting the doors carefully and speaking in lowered voices. "That child," declared Papa distractedly fingering his mustache, "is deceitful, pretending to play the piano when she is not playing it at all." (He didn't ask himself whether it was deceitful as well to spy on a little girl from behind the door.) "She is also very strange, and in my opinion we ought to have Violet look at her to see if there is anything wrong." "Oh, that's nonsense," said Mama. "What does Violet know about it? Nothing is wrong, she's only very talented, as Mrs. Opdike said, except that perhaps we're trying to train her in the wrong way." "Indeed we are," said Papa, embarking on another subject altogether, "she's growing up far too queer, left unsupervised by herself in the house all day. She ought to get more fresh air." "That's nonsense too," said Mama. "She goes for a walk every afternoon." "Yes," said Papa, "Mr. Peebles" (this was the Editor-in-Chief) "saw her down by the livery stables the other day."

Clearly this was leading nowhere. In the end Papa washed his hands of the matter, and it was left for Mama to decide what to do. Quite obviously a change in the program was called for; Herma's dexterity was laryngeal and not digital. She wasn't able to learn to sew, either, although she, Mama, had roll-hemmed a handkerchief when she was hardly old enough to walk. Herma only pricked herself with the needle and, instead of crying, regarded the red spot on her finger with a kind of scientific curiosity and then licked it off, evidently with savor. As Mrs. Opdike said, "Of course she can't sew. It's her little *voice* that is talented; it's like a tiny perfect little flute." And also, thought Papa to himself, like a tuba, and the C two octaves below the middle of the piano, and a Chinese vegetable peddler, and a pump-organ, and Brother Goff coughing. But he kept these reservations or anxieties to himself, and it was agreed that Mrs. Opdike if she wished could attempt to teach the child Voice.

But, "For Heaven's Sakes," as Mrs. Opdike said, "I don't have to teach her anything; it's all I can do to keep up with her." Herma already knew every song in the hymnbook, as well as Mah Song's chant and *Old Dog Tray,* which she had heard a man singing on Fourth Street. Nevertheless, Mrs. Opdike instructed her in two-part harmony, and they sang duets together, Herma soon demonstrating her ability to sing either the tenor part or country alto, as it was called, in which the harmony ran along above the melody. "She is a whole little choir in herself," said Mrs. Opdike, who had an unbounded enthusiasm for the strange and prodigal and found it all a delight; unlike Papa, who had a tendency to be made anxious by anything that was slightly outside his ken. It was something like Darwin's Theory of Evolution; once you conceded that your grandfather might be an ape, or that a little girl might sing baritone, then there was no place to stop. Of course Herma did not really sing baritone; she simulated Brother Goff's voice but in her own timbre, as though you might imitate a bass viol with a violin by slackening the G string until it wobbled. But this nuance escaped Papa, who was even less a musician than he was a specialist in infancy and only felt that a little girl who sang when she was supposed to be playing the piano was, in some way that he could not express, committing an untruth. Yet how could you tell a lie merely by playing the piano? Was it possible that music itself was mendacious? Here his thought took alarm, and stopped altogether.

Mrs. Opdike was not so easily alarmed. "She is just doing grand," was her opinion. "She is a dear little girl, and some day she will be a famous opera singer. For Herma," she declared, "can do *any thing* that she wants. And she will."

For the moment, however, Mrs. Opdike's ambitions did not extend so far, and she concentrated on preparing Herma for an eventual role in the choir of the First Baptist Church. She also taught her the only two songs she knew that were not hymns, *The Last Rose of Summer*

and *The Little Lost Child*. Piping these to piano accompaniment, Herma
was a charm, and almost ready to be presented to the public, Mrs.
Opdike said; although Mama vetoed this. However, to give her due
credit, Mrs. Opdike was honest about her limitations as a teacher and
sincere in her concern for the full development of Herma's talent. "I
recommend," she said, "the purchase of a phonograph. For only the
greatest artists," she said, "are fit to serve as models for *this* little
voice." By which she meant, no doubt, that she herself had reached
the end of her string and that there was no one else in all of Santa Ana
who knew enough about music to teach Herma anything, she had got so
far by herself. And it was true that Herma sang not only the hymns
but *The Last Rose of Summer* and *The Little Lost Child* all in the manner of Mrs. Opdike, which was a rococo sort of style, all trills and
vibrato, with little philosophical depth to it or attention to expression.

Such things were costly and it was a weighty decision. Papa pondered for several days, pulling at his mustache and figuring, now and
then, on a piece of paper at the rolltop desk in his study. But in due
course he bought an Edison phonograph, on special order from Feeley's,
and brought it home to be set up on the parlor table. And in truth it
was a fine and impressive apparatus and an addition to any home. It
was a varnished mahogany box with a crank on the side, and a horn
like a large flower. The mechanism was mounted on top, and inside the
box was a drawer for the six wax cylinders. On the front were the
words "Edison New Duplex."

It worked—as he explained to Mama, conscious of the male obliga-
tion to understand all things mechanical, and first consulting the in-
struction brochure—through the rotation of the waxen cylinder at the
top. In reproducing the sound, the point of the needle ran over the eleva-
tions and depressions in the bottom of the groove cut in the cylinder.
Thus an increased pressure was transmitted upward to the diaphragm
when the point ran over an elevation, and a diminished pressure when
the point ran over a depression. The diaphragm was thus—as it were—
pulled inward and thrust outward with each vibration, but these
pushes and pulls followed each other so rapidly that the ear apprehended
only a buzz, that is, the music or other sound that was to be reproduced.
As for the horn part of it, he imagined that its purpose was to magnify
the sound. For some reason Mama blushed at this lecture, and he felt
it better to drop it. It might have been on account of the word reproduce,
or something about the shape of the horn. He understood women only
slightly better than he did phonographs, and perhaps she had detected
some nuance that escaped him. In short, he left it to the women—to
Mama and Herma and Mrs. Opdike—to concern themselves with the
practical operation of the thing. He showed them how to clamp on the
wax cylinder, and set the needle lightly and carefully into the groove,
and then he washed his hands of it.

And so Herma had an artificial singing master, one with a long neck
and a mouth like an Easter lily, one that scratchily grated out the most
celebrated voices of the age from its six cylinders: Patti in her famous

"Lassù in cielo" from *Rigoletto,* Madame Schumann-Heink intoning some songs of Schubert, Melba's "Mi chiamano Mimì," Tetrazzini trilling away at the Bell Song from *Lakme,* the great Jean de Reszke crooning Don Giovanni's Serenade to mandolin accompaniment (the only record he ever made), and Chaliapin booming away at the aria from the second act of *Boris Godunov*—this last came through the machine something like a large grasshopper grating its wings. Herma had no difficulty with any of these. Italian and Russian were equal to English, and she simply transposed De Reszke up an octave, and Chaliapin two —he sounded more like a cricket on the hearth, up there, than a grass-hopper. At first she even included, in her laryngeal acrobatics, the hissing of the needle on the wax, although Mrs. Opdike was able to cure her of this. Madame Schumann-Heink's Germanic profundities, even the little catches in her voice, were easy for her. One might have said "child's play," except that Herma was not playing, although neither was she working; she was simply opening her lungs like a tiny bird. Mrs. Opdike, in spite of her optimism, did not entirely approve of her mimicry of Madame Schumann-Heink. "A very *great* voice, my dear," she told her, "but one that you can hardly learn from now. You ought to wait until you are more *buxom.*" But it was Papa who had chosen the cylinders, or rather the man at Feeley's—they came with the apparatus. And so Herma learned Schumann-Heink, and Chaliapin too. She was the only singer Mrs. Opdike had ever encountered who could master that Russian sound with four consonants in it. Herma had no difficulty with it. It was like a rag with three raw eggs in it being dropped on the floor: *shtch.*

Papa, one Sunday afternoon, found that peculiar and slightly un-canny transformations had been going on in the sanctity of his home, or what he had imagined as such, while he was away working every day in the *Blade* office. He stopped reading, lowered the newspaper into his lap, and began listening more carefully.

"How heavy is the Hand of God in his wrath," Herma was in-toning in perfect pitch although two octaves high. Finding no answer to the Tsar in Russian, she could only reply with:

"Sì, mi chiamano Mimì,
ma il mio nome è Lucia."

The high F made the glass of the parlor windows ring. Papa stood up holding his newspaper, then he set the newspaper down and went into the kitchen to talk to Mama.

"Now it seems she's learned Italian."

"Russian too," said Mama with a little smile. "She learns it from the phonograph."

"I am not speaking about the phonograph. I am speaking about this child who is very odd and getting odder all the time." He twitched with his fingers at his mustache, as he always did when he was uncertain about something. "She leads an unhealthy life. She is in the house all the time.

She should be outdoors playing like other children. She needs more fresh air.''

''She's always outdoors when she isn't singing,'' said Mama. ''She roams around like a little savage. You yourself told me that Mr. Peebles saw her down by Polanski's. There are lots of worse places for her to be than right here at home, listening to her phonograph and singing. Besides, she may be a famous singer some day.'' At this Mama smiled and became a little excited, and a flush came into her cheeks. ''Mrs. Opdike says it would be a sin to hide her talent in a basket.''

''Under a bushel,'' Papa corrected her. ''I'm not sure it would be a good idea for her to be a singer. These people travel all over the world with dubious companions. Down at the *Blade* we've got a syndicated article about this Melba. It seems she has very free ways. Of course Mr. Peebles is not going to run it. If I were to show you the article,'' he said, ''you'd see what I mean. Although of course,'' he added quickly, twitching at his mustache again, ''there's no need for you to read it. It isn't suitable. But if you read it . . .''

But how had he got started on this blessed article? It was not what he had meant to talk about at all. ''My point is,'' he went on, attempting to recapture the thread of his argument, ''that we are not dealing merely with talent in this case. I am familiar with what talent is. My point is that we are dealing with a very odd child. She does not have normal interests. Little girls are supposed to play with dolls, help their mothers in the kitchen, and prepare themselves in turn for a life of motherhood and devotion to their own future families. That is the mission of women,'' he went on, speaking roundly in platitudes as he always did when he fell into the style of editorials for the *Blade,* ''as it is portrayed for us in the Holy Scriptures and the precepts of established society. Woman is charged with preserving all that is pure, innocent, and uplifting in our imperfect mortal existence, and with providing in the home a haven of comfort and solace for her husband and children. Music is all very well; a young lady should be able to play the piano and also to sing, if her inclinations lie in that direction. But it is not proper for her to sing like a Russian basso, or to learn foreign languages without having studied them. In short, what we have to deal with here,'' he concluded, pulling at the other side of his mustache, ''is not a talent but an aberration. She is not normal. She does not get outdoors enough. She needs some tonic or other. Or perhaps sulphur and molasses would be the thing. I don't know. Perhaps we should ask Violet.''

''That's nonsense,'' said Mama. ''What does Violet know about music?''

4.

So Dr. Violet was not called after all, and instead, the next Sunday, in the afternoon after Meeting, they went to the beach. To do this you walked down Ross to Fourth Street and along Fourth to Main, where the Yellow Dog was waiting in the middle of the street. There it sat, looking much like the horse-car that had previously trudged its way down the narrow tracks from Santa Ana through Angel Town to Balboa, except that the Yellow Dog went by electricity. For this strange substance Herma felt a fascination that had previously been evoked only by the forces of nature, like insects in the grass or Mr. Sampson's Delilah. It was invisible, and ran without a sound through a slender metal thread, but was capable of bursting out all at once in orange sparks that flashed from the trolley overhead and fell in a shower through the air, and then to make the Yellow Dog hum into motion and start off down the tracks. Something tingled inside Herma when she thought about it. It had many of the qualities of genies in stories, except that, since it never assumed the guise of a barrel-chested and half-naked eunuch, it was not at all frightening. It was an obedient sort of magic, and one capable of myriad powers and effects. Somewhere under the car the engine waited tractably until the motorman pushed his knob, and then, with a thrumming noise, it drew along the car with the people inside as powerfully as a pair of horses. It was a magic and delight, and the Yellow Dog itself was a thing to charm any child. It was like a little house on wheels, with a slanted mast at the top that ran along the wire suspended over the street. It was painted a bright canary with red trim. All along the side, from one end to the other, were the stretched-out words ''The Daniel O'Garritty Electric Traction Company,'' and on the front and rear, simply ''D. O' G.'' in elaborate red letters with square tops and bottoms.

They climbed on, Mama helping Herma up. The rear half was open like a kind of veranda, but the front end, where the motorman sat holding the brass knob in his glove, was a little room with glass windows and fringed curtains. Papa gave a coin to the motorman and they took their seats in the front. The seats faced sideways, so that Herma was by herself and Papa and Mama were facing her on the other side. Papa, in the same blue suit and derby that he wore to Meeting, carried a large wicker hamper which he set on the seat beside him. Mama wore her white dress with the blue ribbon in the hem, and her white parasol, with the point resting on the floor, had a blue ribbon around the edge. Her hat, her blue Sunday boater, was tilted a little to one side, a raffish touch which contrasted oddly with her seriousness and her pale complexion. Mama was delicate; this was the way people put it. She was not ill exactly, but she was not able to do very much and stayed indoors resting for the most part. As Papa said, the fresh air would do them all good; and Mama, while not putting much real faith in this, conceded to his opinion. A little smile played on her lips as she caught Herma's eye. Herma was wearing her Sunday dress too, the one with the strawberry-colored ribbon in it, and a ribbon of the same color in her hair. It was her fourth or fifth Meeting dress; when she outgrew one and needed another she always wanted it just the same. Her legs, which did not quite reach the floor, terminated in black patent-leather shoes with white socks. She was excited and slightly feverish, thinking of the sea, the wicker hamper, and the nickel in her pocket for a cone from Haroun.

Presently the motorman, who was believed by some people to be Mr. O'Garritty himself, settled on his stool and adjusted his greasy glove. He pushed the brass knob and the Yellow Dog hummed and started into motion, making a slow clacking sound as it went over the joints in the tracks. Herma looked out the window opposite at the houses slipping by. It was like the private car on the train; you were sitting in a little room with fringed curtains, yet the house carried you over the world while you sat and looked out the windows. The other passengers were a nervous-looking thin man in shabby clothing, and a brown woman holding a brown child in her lap. They were all minding their own business and paying no attention to her.

Herma, turning over the rich storehouse of her imagination as Mama might ruffle through the things in her sewing box, conjured up an imaginary wineglass and bottle on an imaginary table in front of her. Holding her fingers gracefully, she raised the glass for a ladylike sip, then set it down on the table again. Next she puffed at her cigar, which she held between her first and second fingers. Replacing the cigar in the saucer (it was majolica, she decided, with blue flowers on white), she was about to reach for the wineglass again when she became aware that Papa was watching her steadily and with an intent expression. Dissolving the table, glass, bottle, and cigar back into the insubstantial phantasm from which they had come, she gazed placidly at the people sitting opposite.

The brown woman, who was rather plump, wore a white dress like Mama's, but she had a rainbow-colored shawl with a fringe around her shoulders. Herma had never seen a shawl like that, and she was fascinated with this flamboyance. Did this mean that the brown woman was not respectable? She studied her with more care. The child, who was solemn but energetic, kept twisting about on his mother's lap to peer out the window, saying, "Mira, Mama!" and pointing at the most ordinary things, a schoolhouse with a flagpole or a dog passing in the street. It was true that everything looked different from the Yellow Dog, yet Herma, with her own self-contained aplomb whatever the excitement inside her, felt superior to this brown child who was constantly astounded. The mother, who seemed sad, said nothing.

A little farther on, as the Yellow Dog turned onto Myrtle, they passed a motorcar, which was stopped dead by the side of the street

while the driver lifted its lid to see what was wrong. It was the first
one Herma had ever seen except in magazines. It looked like a black
buggy that had lost its horse, with a coffin in front for the motor. She
peered curiously at it.

"I have written an editorial against those things," said Papa.
"But Mr. Peebles probably won't run it, because he has one of the infernal things himself. They don't work," he added, "and they smell
bad."

"And the noise," Mama added.

"They frighten the horses."

"And they might," Mama prophesied, "run over some child."

The brown woman with the child on her lap seemed not to notice
the motorcar. Beyond the windows the landscape moved by like a
painted canvas unrolling in a theater. The orange groves were behind
now and the tracks ran over a flat river-bottom land planted with sugar
beets. The sugar factory was visible in the distance, an immense yellow
barracks puffing smoke out of a chimney. The brown woman began
gathering her possessions—a tattered paper bag, a cardboard suitcase,
and the child which she sat upright on the floor in front of her. There
were some houses ahead in a clump of trees, gradually drawing closer.
The motorman applied the brakes and the Yellow Dog slowed down and
came to a stop before a tiny ramshackle station with a tin roof. This
was Angel Town, called Angelitos by the people that lived there. Here
the brown woman got off with her paper bag, her cardboard suitcase,
and her child.

Herma had time only for a glimpse. The town was set in a shady
grove of sycamores. It was like a miniature of Santa Ana, with the
streets crossing neatly at right angles, and yet different—something
about the smell or the colors. The houses were tiny, painted white with
trim of emerald green, blue, orange, or sometimes purple. They were
covered with flowers—twining myrtle, oleanders, roses, and geraniums.
An odor of fried food and chili hung in the air, mingled with the scent
of flowers.

Then the motorman pressed his knob and the Yellow Dog hummed
smoothly away, leaving Angel Town behind. The tracks ran along a
kind of bluff parallel to the river bottom, then abruptly they came out
onto a rise and the sea was visible ahead. The Yellow Dog curved
jerkily to the left and continued on with some low bluffs on one side
and the sea on the other: first the even parallel rows of breakers, then
a vast plain of emerald green dotted with whitecaps. It seemed to go on
forever. What was on the other side? She wasn't sure; China, perhaps,
or Paris where Madame Melba sang in the Opera. She had seen the sea
before but it still excited her. She stared gravely out the window at it
with a little pull stirring in her heart, somewhere between curiosity and
desire. Mama and Papa, on the seat across from her, hadn't even turned
their heads to look behind them.

But now, coming up at the edge of the water a little distance away,
was a curious building that Herma had never noticed before. It looked

like a beached ship, or a warehouse that had half decided to go to sea: long and rambling, with a higher part at one end like the cabin of a steamer. Except for that it was only a kind of long, low shed built partly on stilts over the water. There were three bicycles in front of it, and a horse tied to a hitching-post. On the roof was a long, narrow sign, painted red with tin letters nailed to it. The R at the end had half fallen off, but it could still be read—and of course Herma, much bigger, had learned to read now.

CANTAMA R

She wondered why it was called that—whether the sea sang there, or whether people sang about the sea. But some instinct told her it was better not to ask. The Yellow Dog came to a stop. There was no station, only a kind of platform of boards in the sand by the tracks. The nervous-looking man got off here and set off over the dunes in a furtive-looking way, without looking behind him, toward the ramshackle building.

Papa, who was sitting with his back to the beach, glanced around behind him. After a moment he cleared his throat and said, "I understand the authorities are not prepared to do anything about the problem." He said, "I have written an editorial on the subject, but I don't know whether Mr. Peebles will print it."

Mama turned her head even more briefly. She said, "It *is* tatty." Her glance, like a hummingbird moving to a flower, fell on Herma for an instant. She exchanged a significant look with Papa. Then they both fell silent and gazed out the window over Herma's head, at the plain brown bluff on the other side of the tracks. The Yellow Dog started up again and went off along the beach. Herma caught a glimpse of the nervous man disappearing into the ramshackle building.

They had the Yellow Dog to themselves now; everyone else had gotten off. For a while they continued on along the same landscape, with the sea on one side and the low bluff on the other. Then the bluff fell away and ahead was Balboa Bay, a thin sheet of water full of shoals, with the long sandbar of the Peninsula separating it from the sea. The Yellow Dog, jerking a little to the right, continued on down the Peninsula. A few houses were scattered along the tracks, clustered here and there into gap-toothed villages with many vacant lots. The Yellow Dog stopped at Newport, then at East Newport. Then, a mile or so farther on, it came to the end of the line. This was Balboa. The three of them got off, Mama helping Herma down after her and Papa carrying the hamper.

Even here, at its broadest point, the sandbar of the Peninsula was only a few hundred yards wide. The road from Santa Ana ended here and there was only one cross street, running from the Bay to the trolley station. At the Bay end of the street, built out on pilings over the water, was the Pavilion, a large blue and white building with a gray roof and a kind of belfry on top. People went dancing there on the upstairs floor, and underneath was a restaurant. Since Papa didn't approve of dancing, and they couldn't afford to go to restaurants, Herma had never been there. Along the short street from the Pavilion to the beach were the three hotels, the Surfside Apartments, the Netherlands Apartments, and the Hotel Balboa. Here pale lizardlike people from Los Angeles came to stay in the summer. That was all there was, except for Haroun's Mecca, a small kiosk on the beachfront where ice cream, salt-water taffy, and various polychrome forms of soda water could be bought.

With Papa leading, they trudged in a procession across the sand to a point almost at the edge of the water. Here Papa set the hamper down and took out of it a plaid steamer robe, which he spread out on the sand. There were only a few other people on the beach, most of them summer visitors from the hotels. Mama unfurled her parasol, and they both sat down. Papa crossed his ankles, pulling up his trousers carefully in order not to spoil the crease. Mama gazed out at the sea with a pleased look, her chin raised a little. The filtered light under the parasol gave her an ethereal and transparent look, as though her flesh was made of some substance like crystal. The light breeze touched and lifted the blue ribbons of her dress.

Herma glanced at Papa and Mama out of the corner of her eye. They were paying no attention to her. Kicking off her shoes and socks, she tore off across the sand, feeling to be sure the nickel was still there in her pocket. She didn't stop until she was standing in front of the gaudy red and white kiosk with its striped awning. The ice cream was dispensed by Haroun himself, a clever mahogany-colored man who might have been of almost any age; perhaps he was very old, or perhaps he was only wrinkled by the sun. Herma knew exactly what she wanted. First, however, it was necessary to go through the usual litany. She reached up to the counter, which she could barely see over, and put her nickel on it.

"Vanilla cone."

"Sure you don't want chocolate or strawberry or pistachio? Pistachio is very good."

"No."

"Some chocolate sprinkles on it?"

"No. Just vanilla."

"Okey-dokey," said Haroun. Seizing his scoop, he plunged it into the tub of vanilla and scrounged it around to form a ball. With the other hand he simultaneously slipped a cone from the bottom of the glass receptacle over the counter. With a flair he juxtaposed the two, the scoop above and the cone below, and pressed the thumb-lever so that the ball fell exactly into the mouth of the cone. Then he whipped a paper napkin dexterously around it and passed it across the counter. Herma had to stand on tiptoe to reach high enough for it. She licked it just once and then raced off across the sand with it.

A few yards away she stopped and examined it, with a solemn and intense concentration. The place where she had licked had virtually smoothed itself out, as ice cream will. In the warm sun it had already reached the preliminary stages of melting. The ivory hemisphere, sagging slightly as she tipped the cone to one side, seemed to tremble at its pores with a faint and evanescent perspiration. With a deliberate and excruciating slowness she raised it toward her mouth, watching it until at last it went out of focus and turned into a cream-colored blur. Her tongue came out and descended to it. The agile and moist little red snake aimed straight at the center, then at the last moment it turned and dodged the summit, and instead made its first quivering contact at the side. Round and round coiled the red tongue tip, skillfully skimming off what was liquid and leaving the soft but solid mass underneath. The pale and glistening mound gradually diminished. Only when it had sunk almost to the level of the cone edge did she allow herself, or more precisely her tongue, to dart directly at the center.

Now the game changed. The convexity had turned into a concavity, while losing none of its pale deliquescence or its sweet savor to the tongue. This organ now descended into a spiral and gradually deepening orifice the shape of a maelstrom. Deeper and deeper probed the flexible pink tip. The tongue was tiny, but in some way Herma managed to extend it almost to the bottom. Almost, almost! The pink snake quivered but couldn't make it. In the end she tipped the cone up to get the last of the melted sweetness. A circle of white was printed onto her face around the mouth.

It was ended, like all other pleasures. Yet she hardly minded. She had bought the ice cream and eaten it. It was hers—not only the ice cream itself, which no longer existed, but the savor and memory of it, which she might cherish in herself secretly for as long as she pleased. As for the slightly soggy shape she held in her hand—like an illustration for a geometry problem—it didn't interest her. It was only a concavity from which everything important had been removed. She looked into it. It was rather disgusting. She flung it away across the sand.

Looking up, she found herself confronted by a boy about her age in a sailor suit, who had somehow managed to procure a balloon and was holding it self-importantly on the end of a string. He stared at Herma and his aplomb gradually vanished. What was a balloon to an ice-cream cone! And how rich, how privileged, how profligate must be the child who could eat the ice cream and throw the cone away! Herma felt this, and so evidently did the boy. She trudged past him with hardly a glance. He gazed after her dejectedly, seeming to forget the balloon string in his hand.

The expanse of sand was wide, and Herma had almost lost her way. No, there was the steamer robe with the two figures on it and the parasol, everything trembling slightly in the sunlight. Herma, cleaning herself with her tongue as she went like a small animal, arrived with only a few sticky vanilla drops on her face. Papa glanced at her mildly. He was sun-warmed and somnolent, and his face was slightly pink under the rim of his hat.

"Before lunch?"

Mama said, "You yourself gave her the nickel for the cone."

"But I didn't tell her to eat it before lunch."

"You didn't tell her not to." And Mama added, "It won't do any harm. It's only a little milk and sugar."

"That's it," said Papa. "Only milk and sugar, and it cost five cents."

It was Mama herself, planting her parasol in the sand, who took out the lunch from the hamper. First came napkins, plates, cups, a jar of mustard, another of pickles, the salt and pepper, and finally the lunch proper: chicken sandwiches, potato salad with a star of sliced egg arranged on top, and Herma's favorite cookies, which had dates in a spiral of glossy brown emerging from the lighter surface. To drink there was a Mason jar of lemonade. Herma failed to eat her sandwich crusts, dropped potato salad on her dress, and mismanaged a cookie so badly that half of it fell in the sand. But no one seemed to notice; Papa gazed out to sea, and Mama nibbled at her sandwich in a ladylike way without allowing even a crumb to fall from her lips. Herma, disposing of the last of her lemonade, and inspecting the fallen piece of cookie but finding it hopelessly sandy, sprang up and ran away across the sand to the edge of the water.

A wave foamed up and coiled around her ankles. Pulling up the hem of her skirt, she ran after it and chased it back into the ocean where it belonged. But another one was rolling in, snarling and throwing up white feathers of spray. It seemed immense, but Herma knew it would get smaller as it approached her. She even advanced a few steps toward it. Then, as it swept up the sand, she fled—not in panic, but in a game she played with this powerful and playful monster the sea, a game which she knew the sea would finally win, as her audacity grew and the waves went on alternating in their eternal way, some coming a little farther up the beach and some not so far. Her ankles were soaked, then her knees, and finally the hem of her skirt. She tucked the skirt into the elastic bottom of her drawers—glancing around—but Papa was lazy and warm on the steamer robe and seemed not to notice her. Now, with her legs bare, she could chase the waves out farther. But finally— as was inevitable—the biggest one of all caught her with a slap, soaking her thoroughly. She splashed her way up out of the water onto the hard-packed sand and raced away along the edge of the surf, running, running, away from Papa and Mama, until she began to pant.

Then all at once she stopped. A mile away down the beach was a fantastic apparition: the tents of the Great Pacific Traveling Exposition, a bedraggled caravansary that for some reason had chosen a number of years ago, before Herma was born, to settle on this stretch of sunbaked California beach, putting up its canvas castles, erecting painted signs in the sand, and draping its banners and faded flags to the sea breeze. Although it called itself Traveling, it had been there for some time now and showed no signs of moving on.

Herma of course had never been down the beach that far. The Exposition was something that Papa and Mama didn't even discuss, something like Cantamar, although perhaps for different reasons. It was possible that, like going to restaurants, it only cost too much. But it was not this, Herma was sure. It was that there was something in the Exposition that was—not proper to see—not *respectable,* that was the word. The great tents, which sagged in some places and stuck up in points in others, had a certain tawdry magnificence to them. Some of them were made of a pale bluish canvas, splotched and faded, and others had once been black but were now an indifferent gray with dustings of white on their peaks, as though snow had fallen on them. Even from a distance the gaudily painted signs and posters could be made out. A curious odor came down the beach from it—a savory smell of things fried in lard, along with the scent of lotion that came out of the door of the barber shop, masculine and yet effete and decadent. She stood looking at this tawdry Araby for a few moments longer. Then she turned and ran back down the beach toward Papa and Mama.

5.

By the time the Yellow Dog brought them back to Fourth and Main it was almost five o'clock. The air was still balmy, with a yellow tinge as though there were specks of gold floating in it, tiny and almost invisible. Lazy in the warmth and going more slowly now, they walked the few blocks along Fourth Street and up Ross to the house. Papa still seemed pink and distracted, and Mama too seemed stimulated by this expedition to the beach, but it only made her paler than usual, as though she had shrunk like a flower from the sunlight.

When they were inside the parlor and the door shut behind them, Papa hemmed once, chewed his mustache, and glanced covertly at Herma. Then, staring at the Dresden doll on the mantelpiece, he offered his opinion that the sea air made one drowsy and the thing to do was take a nap before supper. At this Mama's paleness left her and a faint flush appeared on her cheeks. She said nothing. But she too evidently thought that a nap would be a good idea, because she went off with Papa into the bedroom. The door shut. There was silence, broken only by the usual clickings and groanings of the house standing warm in the late afternoon sun.

No one had suggested that Herma should take a nap, so she ran out into the backyard, banging the screen door behind her. Coming home after such an excitement—the hot sun and sand, the complex ecstasy of the ice cream, the kelpy water washing around her legs, even the distant and mysterious squalor of the Exposition—she felt surfeited with the vast richness and profusion of life. The world was kaleidoscopic, variegated, and infinitely meaningful. Nothing was uninteresting, nothing was without significance—nothing was boring or banal. Everything gleamed, like the individual stone in a bright Byzantine mosaic. The whole world of nature was full of curiosities, many of them charged with mystery. Snakes had no legs but could walk, for instance, and hummingbirds kissed flowers instead of each other as people did.

Flopping down onto the grass, she turned once again to studying the myriad life pullulating under the blades. Two black beetles crawled by, one on top of the other—that was a convenience, for the one at least. For some reason this reminded her of the whole matter that ladies and gentlemen were different sorts of people. Papa was certainly nothing like Mama. He was more severe, his voice was deeper, and he wore different sorts of clothes. He was stronger in all ways, able to lift heavy weights if necessary, even though it made his mustache perspire. The whole world, Herma reflected, was filled with the invisible structure of he and she. Mr. Sampson's Delilah was a she, God was a he. Ladybugs were she, and all dogs seemed to be he, although Herma was not quite sure about this. Men had big watches, which they pulled out on chains from their vest pockets, and ladies tiny ones. Perhaps even the flowers were she, since the hummingbirds kissed them with their sharp sword-like beaks. And sticks and stones, for all Herma knew. And clouds in the sky. The whole universe, it seemed, was split into this vast dichotomy, which Herma was now become aware of as its details were revealed to her one by one. Ah Sweet Mystery of Life, as the song put it—Mama sometimes sang it softly, tinkling along with herself with one finger on the piano.

But now Herma began to wonder what it meant that Delilah was a she. She had no children, nor did she have long hair or wear a dress. Getting up off the grass, she went to the fence and peered through the crack in an effort to seek out some evidence on this question. But instead she saw Boy Sampson.

Boy Sampson was exactly her age but he was not like her at all. He was not curious about things—at least not curious about them in the way that she was. He liked to break things, instead of looking at them intently as Herma did in order to understand them. There he was, just beyond Delilah's protruding tail, breaking off a branch from the lilac bush. He was a chubby neckless boy with small eyes and hair that grew only on the top of his head, although perhaps this was only the way his Mama cut it. He wore his usual summer outfit—cotton trousers cut off just above the knee, with the ends unraveled, and a white shirt with no collar. The shirt was not very clean and neither were Boy Sampson's bare feet—they were dirt-colored up to the knee. The Sampsons were Adventists, Mama said, as though this explained a good many things. This inferior condition, however, did not seem to weigh Boy Sampson down with any shame or modesty. He swanked around the yard like an Arab prince, dominating each bush and blade of grass to bend it to his suzerainty. Herma, with her eye fixed to the gap in the fence, was privy to all the antics that a small boy goes through when he believes that no one is watching him. The things he did were banal and yet significant, like the gestures performed by an actor. In this Theater of the World, she was the audience and he the unwitting but versatile performer.

First, still swaggering around with the stick in one hand, he stuck the fingers of his other hand into his bottom and scratched himself— that wasn't nice, unless you did it in your own room with the door closed. He threw away the stick, found something iron in the grass, brushed off the dirt, and tried to see if it was sharp enough to cut his initials on the door of the shed. It wasn't, and he abandoned it to chase a floppy butterfly that was staggering around in the air a foot or so above the grass. Trapping it in his hand after many failures (he was not very agile), he pulled off one wing and turned it loose to see if it would still fly. It wouldn't, and he stamped it out with his foot. He found a piece of lath, set it against the protruding root of the fig tree, and tramped on it with his bare foot; it broke with a satisfying snap. He looked for another stick, and found only the green lilac branch as thick as a cane; when he stamped on this it didn't break and he gave a small yelp of pain. Not angry, only coldly vindictive, he threw it over the fence, where it landed on the grass behind Herma.

What next? He disappeared down the cellar door and came out with a wooden sword fashioned of another lath, sharpened at one end and fitted with a cross-piece of the same material. With this he tried prodding Delilah in the same place he had scratched himself, but she didn't seem to appreciate this. She gave a whinny and a stamp. Boy Sampson left off and began cutting the air with his sword, satisfied with its menacing hiss; then he turned to slashing off the heads of the daisies along the fence. He made a little grunt with each slash. The yellow heads flew into the air and toppled down, giving off a sickly odor of things crushed. So much for the daisies. When they were all decapitated he turned to the irises and flags, in a flower bed bordered with stones. They too were quickly dispatched with the wooden sword. His Mama and Papa too, Herma thought, must be taking a nap; but presently they would come out and a terrible retribution would follow. This would be worth waiting for.

But in fact it did not happen. Instead, Boy Sampson, tiring of his sport and damp with exertion, advanced in an odd spraddle-legged way on the lilac bush. Spreading his legs apart, he began unbuttoning his trouser buttons. There appeared a little pink spout, evidently flexible and just the right size for the fingers so that it could be turned in whichever direction he wanted. This appliance began ejecting a yellow thread. Boy Sampson waved it from side to side, irrigating not only the lilac bush but the stones around it and a bee clinging nearby on a blade of grass. The accuracy of the thing was impressive. The bee fell off, drenched in foamy yellow wine, and staggered away to dry itself. Boy Sampson directed his aim back to the center of the lilac bush, which he was also able to drench with precision. At last the golden flow petered out; and now Herma knew what this rather coarse expression meant.

Boy Sampson replaced the small rosy faucet inside his trousers, after a good deal of hip-squirming. What a convenience! And apart from its usefulness it was a jewel in itself, like a baby's thumb with a little pink hood at the end.

Herma decided that she had to have one of those.

6.

Only once did Herma go on the Yellow Dog by herself. It was on a day in the autumn a few weeks after the Sunday at the beach. She remembered it for years afterward, not only because of the small thrill of the forbidden connected with it, but because of what had happened later that afternoon; and moreover, in the back of her mind, there was no question that the thing that happened—even though it didn't affect her directly—was connected in some way with the fact that she had done something she was not supposed to do.

Her transgression—if that was what it was—seemed a relatively minor thing in itself. Papa had given her a nickel "for being good" —specifically, for sitting quietly during Meeting without squirming, and afterward shaking Brother Goff's hand in such a dignified and adult way—this made everybody smile—and also because he, Papa, was feeling pleased with himself and expansive because he had just been named Editor-in-Chief of the *Blade,* Mr. Peebles having finally chosen to retire after so many years.

So Herma had a nickel, the first money she had ever possessed which was not to be spent for a specific purpose. The next afternoon as soon as lunch was over she dashed out of the house with the coin tucked into the pocket of her dress, and when Mama inquired where she was going, she said simply, "To spend it"—which was true, although the trouble was that when Mama called after her in her anxious voice, "All right. But don't go too far, dear," she had simply nodded— and there was where the untruth came in, because she knew that Mama would not have approved of where she was going. The fact was that, try as she would, Herma found herself unable to be totally truthful at all times, especially where adults were concerned.

At Fourth and Main she clambered confidently on and gave the coin to Mr. O'Garritty when he came around to collect it. Mr. O'Garritty, with his greasy glove and walrus mustache, his broad and mild red face, would surely take care of her if anything untoward happened. So she reasoned, while at the same time she was filled with the secret and sensuous knowledge that the things you were not supposed to do were always more interesting than the things that were approved. She settled into her seat and, carried away by the daring of the adventure, forgot to play her game of drinking wine and smoking her cigar on the private railroad car.

Her plan was simply to ride to the end of the line at Balboa, buy a vanilla cone from Haroun's, and come back—her grasp of finances at this time not quite encompassing the fact that, having spent the nickel for the ride on the Yellow Dog, she would no longer have it for the cone. She had not thought this out—perhaps deliberately—although the mathematics of it would not really have been too hard if she had applied her mind to it. But women were not really capable of understanding money—as Papa said, admonishing Mama for having spent too much of the household budget for a mauve party dress from Proctor's, so that he had to give her more at the end of the month—and Mama, her cheeks coloring, had said nothing, so evidently this was true.

All went well at first. There were a half-dozen other passengers and no one paid any attention to Herma, one set of adults probably assuming that she belonged to the other, and vice versa. But when the Yellow Dog stopped in Angel Town a sudden and inexplicable impulse struck her. It was something about the smell of chili and fried food, or the bright flowers flaring against the white houses. A pull of the exotic seized her, a strange and inchoate desire for the unknown and foreign. She got up and dashed to the rear, and stepped down off the iron step just as the Yellow Dog lurched into motion again. Mr. O'Garritty had not noticed, and none of the other adults paid any attention. As in a dream she walked away down the shady street.

The town seemed oddly deserted and quiet. The tiny houses, she now saw, didn't have lawns like the houses on Ross Street; the front yards were only weeds or bare dirt, but everywhere there were flowers—geraniums, roses, oleanders. Some of the houses had only beaten earth inside for a floor. The rooms inside were at ground level—there were no steps or stoops. Most curious of all was that there were no people, or almost none. Now and then she heard a murmur of voices in the distance, in the odd rhythmic intonation that went up and down like waves.

She passed a pair of children sitting in a yard with a dog. The dog barked at Herma and the children stared gravely. A little farther on, attracted by a sound as though someone were continuously and tirelessly slapping a child, she looked through a window and saw a woman patting a lump of bright yellow cornmeal between her palms. The lump spread and widened to the size of a dish; the woman turned it over, first one way and then the other, so that it grew perfectly round and as tough, apparently, as a dishcloth. When it was large enough she flung it onto the table and took up another lump without breaking the rhythm of her slapping. Herma stared entranced. A rich odor came out of the house, something like bread but tempered with the pungency of oil. At just that moment the woman caught sight of Herma and looked piercingly at her out of two burning shadows of eyes, without ceasing her slapping. She seemed very melancholy, and there was hostility in her expression too. Herma stared back for a long moment, and then she went on down the street.

There was not much to Angel Town. You soon came out of it into the open country, and here the road took a turn to the left and went off through the fields of sugar beets. The fields were all alike and there were a number of roads. Herma was soon confused—although not exactly lost, since she had no aim in mind and no desire to turn back. There were still a few houses along the road here and there—one with a crazy kind of pepper tree hanging over it like an umbrella, so that it was cool and shady underneath. Behind these small houses were patches of lettuce and celery. There was a pleasant muddy smell of irrigation, the smell of dry dust mingling with water.

She had come out now onto an unpaved road that ran along a bluff above the river, following its curves and twistings. Ahead there was a cloud of dust rising from the fields, and something happening under it. She stopped and tried to make out what it was. After a while the cloud of dust, drawing nearer, turned into a large crowd of brown men in white clothing approaching along the road in a ragged column. They were in a state of excitement, and flung up arms and emitted yells as they came. Herma climbed up onto a concrete irrigation pipe to let them pass.

The brown men were all dressed the same, in white cotton trousers and white shirts. Some were barefoot, and others wore dirty shoes made out of crossed leather straps. The only item of clothing they wore that was not white was the handkerchief that some had knotted around their necks. Some of these were blue, others orange or red. Some were bareheaded, others wore straw hats with wide flat brims. They hardly paid any attention to Herma. They yelled, "Huelga, huelga!" and raised their fists into the air. There was indeed a great crowd of them. They stretched along the road as far as Herma could see, and they filled it from side to side. "Huelga!" they cried. And some others, "Compañeros!" or "Lucha!" Still they gave the impression not of being angry, but of being defiant about something and at the same time a little astonished at their own defiance; they glanced sideways from under their hats across the fields, and one who caught Herma's eye looked away almost as though he were embarrassed. When they cried, "Huelga, huelga!" it was as though they were trying out the sound, rather gingerly, to see what effect it would have on the warm and still air.

There was another sound in the distance, a rumble or clopping of hooves and a jingle. Coming out on the road from Angel Town, Herma could see, was a column of horsemen riding three or four abreast. They too were all dressed alike, in khaki tunics, Sam Browne belts, and hats with floppy brims. They were exactly like the Rough Riders in the stereoscope views that Papa took out of the cabinet in the parlor on Sunday night, unloading their horses in Havana or charging up San Juan Hill. At their head, too, was a man something like the leader of the Rough Riders, broad-faced and heavyset, with spectacles and a large mustache. They didn't yell and wave their fists like the brown men, but they came on in an efficient and determined way as though they didn't intend to stop.

At the sight of the Rough Riders the brown men faltered. There was another single scratchy cry of "Huelga!" and the parade continued on for a few yards. The Rough Riders down the road broke into a gallop; the ground shook with the rhythmic sound of hooves. The column of brown men began to break up; some turned one way and some another, and a few ran off across the fields. From the horsemen came high-pitched whooping yells. Shots rang out. The riders stormed down the road past Herma, overrunning and mingling with the confused crowd of brown men. Except for their barrel-shaped leader, the Rough Riders were lean and wiry men with pale faces. They rode expertly, at full gallop with revolvers in their hands, steering their mounts with nudges of their knees. One of them yelled in a cracked voice, "Get them goddam Greasers!" and another, "Bully, boys! At 'em!" They went on firing their revolvers, mostly into the air but some level down the road.

There was a great confusion. The brown men ran every which way, some leaping across the irrigation ditch and fleeing past Herma into the fields. The Rough Riders galloped up and down the road, wheeling around to gallop back the other way, sometimes bumping into each other and cursing. There was a great cloud of dust in which things could be seen only imperfectly. One horse lost its footing and fell; the rider tumbled in an acrobatic roll, got to his feet cursing and kicking the still prostrate horse, and clambered back on when it managed to stand back up again. They rode off, the horse limping and the rider slapping the dust off his uniform.

It was over in a few minutes. The Rough Riders galloped back toward Angel Town, and the brown men for the most part straggled away in the other direction. Behind them they left a couple of bundles in the road, like dusty white rags. Near one lay a straw hat. There were spots of red on the rags, and under one a broad pool that spread and widened in the dust.

Herma stared at these two objects for a moment, and then she turned and ran as fast as she could back into Angel Town. The Rough Riders had disappeared in the distance now and the road was deserted. Even when she came into town there was no one in sight. Not a living creature was stirring; no woman slapping tortillas, no children with their dog. The doors were shut and everything lay in a heavy silence; the insects buzzed in the trees. Panting, she slowed to a walk.

Then behind her she heard wheels creaking and the slow clop of a horse. She turned. It was Mr. Farkuss in his wagon. There was lumber piled on the back, and a keg of nails. Mr. Farkuss was wearing his dirty overalls with no shirt under them. He was pink and perspiring under his straw hat, but he seemed quite calm.

" 'Lo there. Goin' for a walk?"

Herma went on down the road, saying nothing.

"Come out on the Yellow Dog, I expect."

When Herma still said nothing, he inquired, "Got another nickel to get back?"

She shook her head.

"Better clammer on then."

She got on, sitting on the keg of nails just behind Mr. Farkuss' shoulder. As usual he radiated a rich medicinal smell. In fact he had a bottle between his knees, holding it carefully to be sure it didn't fall over with the swaying of the wagon.

"Y'see," he told her over his shoulder, "I could give you another nickel for the Yellow Dog. But if I did, y'see, then you'd have to ask your Papa for another nickel to pay me back, and then he'd know all about it, y'see."

This seemed like excellent sense to Herma, so she continued to say nothing.

Mr. Farkuss took a sip from the bottle and replaced it between his knees. "Now I come down this way," he rambled on, " 'cause I've got a job of work to do for a fellow in a dance hall. But for somebody like you, it's not a very good place to take a walk. Them Spaniards, y'see, they don't mean no harm, but they might run right over a little girl like you, y'see, and not even notice you."

It seemed more likely to Herma that the Rough Riders would run over her, but she didn't say so. Mr. Farkuss took another sip. There was only an inch left in the bottle. He gazed at it, still cheerfully but with a fine calculation.

"Myself," he went on, "I've got nothin' against the Spaniards, y'see. Fact the fellow I'm doin' the job at the dance hall for is a Spaniard. Name is Buena Suerte. You know what that means?"

"Good luck."

"How come a lil girl like you knows Spanish?"

To her surprise Herma found that she had no idea how to answer this question. She just knew Spanish, that was all. It was as though she had always known it. She went on being silent, which seemed to be a good way to conduct herself with Mr. Farkuss and one that he seemed to find quite natural.

They came into Santa Ana along Sycamore Street and went on under the cool shade of the trees.

"If I was you," he said after a while, "I wouldn't tell your Papa about none of this."

Herma had no intention of doing so. Mr. Farkuss took a final sip, a little longer than the others, and held up the empty bottle to contemplate it with a philosophical resignation. Then he threw it away, in an unexpectedly violent gesture for so mild a man. It shattered, the pieces scattering like diamonds at the side of the road. Mr. Farkuss hummed to himself. His face was still pink and his hat pulled down to his eyes. He gazed out at the world with content, hostile to no one and accepting everything with a vast and encompassing benevolence. He smiled at a brown dog going by. They crossed Fourth Street and he smiled at a motorcar that had to stop to let him pass, while the driver shouted injuries. He let her off on Ross Street, a block or so away from her house so she could walk the rest of the way. Mr. Farkuss was not only kind, he was wise. Herma scampered home and went in the back door without anybody seeing her. The things she had seen in Angel Town—the melancholy woman staring out the window at her, the two children and their dog, the red-stained bundles of rags lying in the dust—were fixed indelibly in her mind. But her memory dealt with them on two levels. On the surface she soon forgot them, or pretended to herself that the bundles had been only rags. But deeper, in a dark corner of her mind that was safely tucked out of sight, this Day of Bad Things was one that long haunted her in her dreams. As for Mr. Farkuss, she had learned that there was good in evil, that the one could come out of the other; or that the two were so mixed up that sometimes it was impossible to tell which was which.

7.

Herma quickly reached that ungainly age when young animals seem all knees and elbows. Her short hair flopped in her eyes, and there seemed to be no curves to her. Yet, even if she shared the awkwardness of children of her age, she made it somehow into her own sort of awkwardness, and an oddly graceful one, like the awkwardness of a young giraffe. She climbed trees, fell out of them sometimes, scratched her knees, was stung by bees, got briars in her hair, and made herself sick by eating green plums. Yet with all this she retained her calm self-possession and her decorum; she was stoic while Mama with a comb tugged the briars out of her hair, and instead of crying she was only angry at the tree she fell out of, so that she turned and threw a rock at it and limped away with queenly dignity, bearing her purple bruises like jewels. She had the usual contempt of girls her age for boys; they were dirty, uncouth, slow-witted, clumsy, cruel, inarticulate, ungrammatical, destructive, and raucous; they were constantly in mindless and violent motion, they took things apart and couldn't get them together again, and they had no feeling for music. Boys in general couldn't sing worth two cents. It would be better, Mrs. Opdike said, if their Mamas and Papas didn't bring them to Meeting at all, because they only sat there in sullen silence like deaf-mutes, or worse, raised their voices in such scratchy and woofing cacophonies that it threw everybody off and nobody else could sing either.

As for Herma's own voice, it went on springing up like a weed, just as her body did. Its range was impressive, not to say phenomenal: from below middle C to a point two octaves or more higher, where it had the small but piercing quality of a whistle on a peanut wagon. It was either coloratura or dramatic, Mrs. Opdike said. It could go either way. Herma continued to sing both ways, and she had a repertory now of a dozen or more pieces. She was about ready, Mrs. Opdike said, to be presented to the public.

This debut, as carefully planned by Mrs. Opdike as though it were the première of a new Diva at the Metropolitan, took place at the Summer Social, an annual event always held on Fourth of July evening. The church itself was not large enough for this event, and it was held in the Oddfellows Meeting Hall, which was upstairs on French Street just around the corner from Fourth. The vast barnlike attic was decked with banners and rubber trees, a platform was contrived out of pallets from the Sunkist packing house, and there were trestle tables for the refreshments. After the obligatory fried chicken and potato salad there was, of course, ice cream. Herma consumed the hemisphere in her glass bowl lasciviously and yet with a studied economy, using exactly the same technique she had for the ice-cream cone at the beach—eating the melting parts first and going round and round the creamy lump with her spoon so that it diminished evenly on all sides and remained, as far as possible, firm and frozen in the center. When she was done there was not a trace of ice cream on her face or hands. And the bowl looked, almost, as though it didn't need to be washed. As a sensualist Herma had already learned to be neat. Papa hardly knew whether to commend her for this or not. Like many other things Herma did, it seemed unnatural and yet at the same time admirable. Papa himself had to take a napkin and wipe some ice cream out of his mustache. He himself was only human, he reflected, not without a certain admixture—not of malice exactly, since that would not be fatherly, but of something that might be called a metaphysical annoyance, directed not so much at Herma herself as at the general and universal State of Things, including not only Herma but himself as well, and the differences between them. Some people, he thought with a glance at Herma, seemed to have escaped the general human curse and to have been born, in some way, before the Fall. He wished that the child would cry, just once, or behave in some way that was identifiably childish. What was going to become of her? Never mind, he told himself, thrusting this thought away— from all evidence she would be able to take care of herself.

Then, the bowls put away and the trestle tables removed, the Program followed. It began with an invocation by Brother Goff, which droned on a little too long for Herma's taste. Following this, Mayor Kluckaus, who was not a Baptist but was invited as a courtesy, recited "The Man Without a Country." He was an accomplished orator and some of his effects were impressive—especially the gestures, defiance, contrition, stern inflexibility, and so on. Next some hands strung up a blanket on a rope, and when it was removed—after a good deal of shufflings and giggles from behind—there were three boys, Benjamin Karp, Arvie Larson, and McAllister J. Mullen, in a tableau of three Revolutionary soldiers marching all bandaged with fife and drum. Artistically and historically speaking, this was not a very great success —Arvie was supposed to keep one foot in the air and could not, and McAllister, who was supposed to be playing the fife, couldn't stop giggling. The tableau provoked mainly titters, followed by applause, but at least it broke the tension before the musical part that was to follow. Although Herma herself wasn't the least bit afflicted with stage fright—it was the Fennerman girls sitting next to her, waiting to sing their trio, who were all fidgety and kept swallowing.

The blanket and rope were taken away and the piano rolled into place. Mrs. Opdike herself sang first, accompanied on the piano by her daughter, a gawky adolescent a little older than Herma, who had ten thumbs for fingers and could barely keep up with her mother. Mrs. Opdike trilled through *The Lord's Prayer* in a version which repeated each line several times at different places on the scale, and concluded with an "Amen" so piercing, variegated, and prolonged that it provoked a ripple of applause, even though it was a sacred song. While Mrs. Opdike was coming down from the platform to take her place at the piano, and the last of the clapping died away, Beebie Fennerman punched Herma with her elbow.

"Look. There's Madame Modjeska."

"Where?"

Beebie pointed. A tall lady in a queenlike gray gown had just come in and taken her seat in the rear. She had a beautiful complexion, with dark eyes set in shadows, and her hair was arranged in a coil on her head. Since it was not polite to stare, Herma turned away.

"Well, who cares?"

"She's a famous actress," said Beebie, "and she has performed all over the world. She's very rich. She has a ranch in Santiago Canyon, and a castle in Poland."

Herma felt something dark inside her like a little knife. It was her first pang of professional jealousy. She said rather impatiently, "Yes, yes. I know who she is," and turned her attention back to the stage.

The musical part of the Program was continuing. A Mr. Felt, whom nobody knew very well, sang *The Lost Chord* in a vigorous baritone, and Gogo Larson, Alvie's brother, played *The Flight of the Bumblebee* or something like it on the xylophone. Next the Fennerman girls—their names were Aidie, Beebie, and Cecie—mounted onto the platform. After a certain amount of nervousness and shuffling they launched into *We Three Kings of Orient Are,* which was really a Christmas song, but it was the only song they knew—each sister took a different king in the verses, a rendition illustrating, if nothing else, that oriental kings are tone deaf. Mrs. Opdike ended the thing with an arpeggio in minor key from the piano. Now it was Herma's turn.

Hardly knowing how she got there, she found herself on the platform looking out over the audience. There was a soft dominant chord from the piano, resolved into the tonic. Herma began with *In the Garden,* followed by *The Old Rugged Cross* and *What a Friend We Have in Jesus.* After these token gestures to the ecclesiastical, she launched into the secular part of her repertory. On account of her exceptional talent, Mrs. Opdike had allowed her a longer program than anyone else, although nobody seemed to notice this. First came the Schubert lieder as sung by Madame

Schumann-Heink—these were easy, and Herma warbled the German ca-
dences while Mrs. Opdike plunked down the chords on the piano. Next,
the Bell Song from *Lakme* in the manner of Tetrazzini. In the middle of
these coloratura intricacies, which she trilled out as effortlessly as a bird
on a branch, she caught sight of Madame Modjeska at the rear of the hall
sitting up in her chair and gazing at her with a certain curiosity. Herma
came to the end of the bells, and Mrs. Opdike finished the thing off with
a single low G with her forefinger, like a period at the end of a sentence.

Herma and Mrs. Opdike exchanged a glance, and then Mrs. Opdike
performed one of her specialties as an accompanist—the infinitely delayed chord. This one was an augmented triad with an E at the top, just
above the middle of the piano. The chord hung there, trembling, until
finally Herma joined it, in her small and slightly hesitant soprano of
perfect purity. It was exactly the voice of Melba.

> "Sì. Mi chiamano Mimì,
>   ma il mio nome è Lucia.
>   La storia mia è breve."

Every inflection and catch in the voice was impeccable—even the very
faint hint, no more than a ghost, of an Australian twang in the stretched-
out i's and a's: ". . . *è loo . . . CHEE . . . aaah.*" There were three
people here mingled: Herma herself, then Melba, and then Mimì. They
all merged into Mimì, who was still hesitant and uncertain at this point—
she did not really know Rodolfo yet, even though he had told her frankly,
"Sono un poeta." But, taking courage as she proceeded into her auto-
biography, she repeated the five notes of the theme in a stronger tone—
rising, then falling to the lingering and tremulous D, as though resting
for a moment, before it soared upward again. The aria slipped magically
from one minor key into another, and then offered the listener unexpectedly, as a kind of gift, an enchanting tonic in the major—Puccini was a
sorcerer and did not need to take account of ordinary harmony. Herma's
voice was no longer tiny or hesitant. It drove with force and accuracy
through the aria; it had become that of the exultant Mimì, discovering
love in herself as she told her own story. It was lyric, lyric in the extreme,
it was the epitome of lyric. But there was death in it too, the melancholy
echo of the minor—for Mimì would die. This the voice knew, but it was
also moved by love, and it plunged and soared, exulted or lapsed into
the minor key, as the two impulses moved it. The high A at the climax,
almost two octaves above the middle of the piano, was of such a piercing
purity that it made the old hall tremble slightly. Herma held it for an
exquisite moment—it seemed as though her larynx must break, but it
poised on the note effortlessly—before she slipped down, almost regretfully, to the A flat and then to the E three notes below it. Mimì concluded
her story by remarking to Rodolfo—in a flat recitative, almost as though
she were speaking it—"Altro di me non le saprei narrare."

Herma stood waiting for the applause to end—patiently and without affectation, as though the long rattle of clapping in the hall were for
somebody else. There was a moment of silence while people coughed and

shuffled in their seats. Then, glancing at Mrs. Opdike and rising in a silver note from the G-seventh chord of the piano, she began in a slow tempo *The Last Rose of Summer*. After the Italianate complexities of Puccini this was simpler and more suited to the audience. The self-pitying catch in the voice was gone, and the song was direct and fresh—even though it had its own kind of pathos, an evening sadness that was enhanced by the virginal, half-tremulous, and yet confident sweetness of the voice. When it lifted to the high C in the first line it did so effortlessly, yet the soaring up of the thin girlish voice seemed almost more impressive, and more affecting, than the great A of the Puccini almost an octave higher. And this simplicity, with its faint note of the pensive, was exactly suited to the evocative twilight melancholy of the words.

> " 'Tis the last rose of summer
> Left blooming alone;
> All her lovely companions
> Are faded and gone;
> No flower of her kindred,
> No rosebud is nigh,
> To reflect back her blushes,
> Or give sigh for sigh.''

During the second stanza Madame Modjeska, sitting in the rear, shifted in her seat a little and Herma was able to get a good look at her for the first time. She recognized her now as the same lady who had sat with such queenly dignity in the private car—years before, when Herma was only a tiny girl—as it paused briefly at the S. P. station. The regal posture, the coiled diadem of hair, the watchful eyes were exactly the same. But Madame Modjeska had not turned to look at her then—or had she? Now the steady glance was fixed on Herma as she finished the second stanza and started on the third. And watching, Herma saw a hand come up slowly with a square of white cambric in it and touch at the corner of the eye. The hand with the handkerchief disappeared, and the face went on looking—the dark watchful eyes with the pattern of spiderwebs around them, a glance penetrating and yet thoughtful, as though it had not yet made up its mind about what it was seeing. The clear dulcet, nearing the end, slowed to follow the ritardando of Mrs. Opdike's chords.

> "When true hearts lie withered,
> And fond ones are flown,
> Oh! who would inhabit
> This bleak world alone?''

Who indeed? The audience seemed moved by the question, so melancholy and yet posed by one so young, and applauded it with a ragged clattering that went on for a long time. Madame Modjeska kept her eyes fixed on Herma. When the clapping had not quite died out she stood up and gathered her reticule, with a little smile on her lips. She had an odd way of smiling. It was not that she smiled spontaneously, but as though she had *decided* to smile, because she wished to indicate something to the person at whom she was looking. And that, Herma told herself with a little thrill, is because she is an actress.

Madame Modjeska lingered a little at the rear of the hall, while the others came forward to pump Herma's hand and Papa hung back shyly, chewing his mustache. Then she advanced in a dignified way, her chin slightly raised, until she stopped without a word a few feet from Herma. With her, behind and a little to one side, was a scholarly looking gentleman with a high pale forehead whom she did not introduce. And Madame Modjeska herself didn't say anything for quite some time. Then, simply and in a slight foreign accent, she said, "I am Modjeska."

"I am Herma."

Madame Modjeska smiled again at this. Then she said, "Tell me something about yourself, my dear."

"I live on Ross Street. My Papa is editor of the *Blade*, and Mrs. Opdike gives me lessons. I have been singing since I was five years old, and I hope to be an opera star. Altro di me," she concluded, "non le saprei narrare."

"And what does that mean?"

"I wouldn't know what else to tell you about me."

"Your Italian accent," said Madame Modjeska in a suggestive tone, as though she were asking a question, "is flawless."

Herma said nothing.

Madame Modjeska made her little smile again, only for a second.

"Are you acquainted with Nellie Melba, my dear?"

Herma shook her head.

"But you are."

"No, I'm not."

Madame Modjeska hesitated while she studied her a little longer. "Well, you are a curious little thing. You must study hard and pay attention to your teacher." They both glanced dubiously at Mrs. Opdike, a large and pale cloud in a flowered dress, who stood nearby simpering at this attention paid to her pupil. "Some day, of course, you must go away to a larger city, where you can receive proper training. But for now," she concluded, "let me only thank you for having given me a moment of pleasure." She reached into her reticule for something, and pressed it into Herma's hand, in the most natural way in the world. It was a twenty-dollar gold piece, Herma perceived as she opened her fingers and folded them again over the coin.

"I can't." She held the coin out to Madame Modjeska.

"Let me tell you something, my dear. Always take money when it is offered you. Give what you like in return for it, but only what you like. That is what I have done, and I have become rich and famous. Also, many men have loved me, and a few, perhaps, unselfishly." Here Herma caught the eye of the pale man standing behind Madame Modjeska, and he chewed his lip and looked the other way.

"If you take money," said Madame Modjeska, "it is only for Art. And Art," she went on, "is never paid highly enough. So whatever is offered you, it is only your due. Tonight you have made Modjeska get out her handkerchief, and that is not easily done. So put the money in your pocket and be careful with it.'' Here she stared without a word at the pale man, and he offered her his arm. She let her glance linger for a final moment on Herma. She said, ''Do widzenia, my dear.'' Then, turning in her queenly way, she allowed the pale man to lead her from the hall.

8.

As everybody agreed, Mama was not well, but not in any way that excited pity or even sympathy. Instead it was simply that she was tired and ''didn't feel up to things,'' so that she languished all day indoors in her own way, something like an odalisque in a harem—and in fact there was something Persian about the pale and perfect complexion, the dark eyes, and the aureole of dark hair that framed her face like a veil. However, Mama's lord and master was not a Pasha, but instead only Papa, who labored long and earnestly to support his little family in the office of the *Blade,* where he composed homilies on the day's events, obituary notices, squibs about weddings, and remarks about unusual phenomena of weather, such as hailstones or spells of unprecedented warmth. Whatever journalistic event he commented on—a mad dog on Fourth Street, or the excessive water bills charged by the County—he seldom failed to conclude by recommending that we place our trust in the hands of Heaven. He was solidly embedded in his Baptist faith, yet there were signs in him of a vague and unspecified anxiety or melancholy, that dread of empty spaces noted by Pascal. He did not understand the new century very well. He hoped, through his modest efforts as Editor-in-Chief of the *Blade,* to arrest these alarming changes and steer society back into the safe Eden of his youth, where Darwin was hardly heard of and ''workers'' were people who strove in the Fields of the Lord, serving as deacons or baking cakes for socials according to sex. He attributed Herma's wild-animal qualities—her roaming about with short hair, climbing trees, swinging upside down from branches with her drawers showing, even her uncanny and slightly weird gift of music—to the influence of the new era, without being able to explain very precisely what he meant by this. As he told himself more and more frequently, he didn't understand children very well. He himself did not remember being a child, and none of his relatives, as far as he could recall, had ever been children. He was aware that there were children in the world, but the custom, as he understood it, was that they were taken care of by their Mamas until they were old enough to launch out into the world for themselves. But Herma's Mama (her name was Dell, but Papa, out of some modesty or embarrassment, never pronounced this vocable, calling her ''you'' when he spoke to her directly, and referring to her with Herma as Your Mama) had barely enough energy to see to the minimum household tasks, preparing the meals and touching the furniture languidly with a feather duster, without supervising some wild creature who tore from one end of the town to the other as though possessed by demons. In short, both Papa and Mama were embodiments of the previous century—he representing Victorian rigor and morality, suspicion or anxiety about science, vague religious doubt, and she the wan, dark-eyed, sweetly melancholy notion of Victorian beauty—and so, in the new century, she began little by little to fade away, as though she were only an image in a magic lantern with a defective bulb.

As for Herma, he had for some months now been observing her in secret, with an anxious if somewhat distracted eye. She still roamed about and swung from trees, but now he began to note other and even more disquieting phenomena, certain sprouts and swellings the meaning of which was unmistakable, and yet which seemed to him surely premature —even though Herma was almost as tall as Mama now, and her head came up to his chin when he kissed her chastely goodnight on the brow. He knew little about the physiology of the tender sex, but he was vaguely aware that the menarche was a perilous gateway through which, nevertheless, God had willed that every female child must pass. It was terrible for the thing to happen, but it would be even worse if it did not happen. And, even if it did happen, many things might go wrong. There were women who—Sapphic love it was called. There were the Kessler Girls who had never married and were as queer as Dick's hatband. And there was a child at the other end of town—Papa knew about it only because he worked at the *Blade*—who had deposited an unspeakable tiny parcel in a trash barrel and then went off to Los Angeles, never to be seen again. Of course he never mentioned such things to Mama, but perhaps she had heard hints of them anyhow. How could one protect one's family from this sea of peril, this Knowledge of Good and Evil that lapped all about like a Noah's Flood that was rising to engulf them all? Gazing sidelong at Herma and stroking his wispy mustache, he reminded himself that in all things we must place our trust in the hands of Heaven. Yet another authority, he considered on reflection, might do no harm.

"I wonder," he suggested to Mama, "whether we ought after all to call in Violet."

"Dr. Violet?" she repeated, slightly pale, as though alarmed.

"To look at Herma."

"To look at her?"

"Because of the age she is." This with a fixed and significant stare.

"Well," said Mama vaguely, and yet with a faint flush of color in her cheeks, "I suppose it wouldn't do any harm. The child is growing rather fast. Although," she added, "Violet does charge two dollars."

"Money is of no account where matters of health are concerned," he told her. "I would appreciate it if you left the financial worries of the family to me."

*   *   *

Dr. Violet wore the same costume on all occasions: an old-fashioned frock coat like a stage magician, a shirt with a wing collar, striped trousers which he appeared to have slept in, and a pair of disgraceful shoes. His pockets were stuffed with a miscellaneous and random collection of objects: papers, medical journals, a brown bottle of cough medicine, wooden tongue depressors, a *Blade* of two or three days back, a mauve female stocking which was part of a blood-pressure apparatus, and a kind of long-dead octopus with metal fittings that passed for a stethoscope. With the help of these pockets he got along without the usual black bag; or perhaps he had lost his.

He dyed his mustaches—they were a glossy black, but the rest of his hair was gray. His teeth were eaten away like an unevenly melted honeycomb. He had a mannerism of lifting the disarrayed hair from his brow and pushing it aside with his pale, long-fingered hand with its not quite clean nails. He looked around the parlor with his gimlet eye, seeming to ignore the three people in it and instead appraising the furnishings. After a while he said, "I will have to examine the patient privately."

"Privately?" Mama exchanged a glance with Papa. "But before when you used to come . . ."

"She was jus a lil girl at that time. In this case, we have a young woman."

This was exactly the point. "Still," suggested Mama, "perhaps I might just . . ."

"Where can I examine her?"

Mama glanced at Papa, but he was looking the other way out the window.

"Very well. Dear, go with Dr. Violet."

"No."

"You had better take her into our bedroom," said Mama, for what reason she was not quite sure, except that it didn't seem quite proper for Herma to receive Dr. Violet in her own bedroom. She indicated the door at the end of the hall.

"It will jus take a lil while."

Herma's mouth was set. "No," she said again.

"Herma," said Papa firmly.

"Herma, go with Dr. Violet," Mama encouraged her. "And perhaps afterward," she added with a false cheerfulness, "we can go to Q. R. Smith's and . . ."

Dr. Violet, not a great talker under any circumstances, took her hand. There was a tussle. Herma was a good-sized girl now, and strong. Papa stood by helplessly, fingering his mustache, and Mama hovered over the two of them with conciliatory hands, not quite touching them, as though she hoped to conjure them toward the bedroom with her gestures. They went down the hall, Herma twisting like an eel, Dr. Violet lurching only slightly as Herma's jerks ran up his arm into the frock coat. The door closed.

Papa and Mama exchanged a glance, but neither said anything. Mama sat down in the bentwood rocker and pretended to take up her work, and Papa remained standing by the window. There were sounds of violent tumult from the bedroom. It was as though heavy objects were being flung against the walls, with grunts and small animal cries. Now and then a whistle, as of breath sharply intaken. Some small glass object broke—probably nothing of any great importance, since it made only a small tinkle. Then there was silence for quite a long time, broken only by an occasional bumping. Papa gazed out at the lawn across the street, where the Biemeyers' old gray cat was ineffectually stalking a robin, and Mama pushed the needle through her work and drew it out on the other side. The door opened.

Violet came out first, stuffing things into his pockets, and Herma followed after, her hair disarranged, chewing her lip. She was fully dressed but her clothes gave the impression somehow of having been put on in the dark; her dress was askew, one shoe unbuckled, the stocking twisted. She did not meet Mama's or Papa's eye. She strode straight to the sofa and plunked down on it, glaring out the window.

Papa and Mama said nothing.

Violet sucked his hand, inspected it, and then lowered it to his side. "Well," he said, "this lil girl is growing right up. Her height and weight are bout normal for her age. The larynx is well developed, and all the reflexes"—he took a small rubber hammer from his pocket and tapped it in his hand as if to show what he meant—"all the reflexes work quite nice. She might put on jus a lil bit more weight. Maybe some cod-liver oil."

There was a pause. Papa chewed his mustache. "Her—development is normal?"

"Oh, yes. She's coming right along. She is a real lil woman. Of course," he added, "each individual is jus a lil bit different." He seemed to stress these last words slightly, as he stuffed the mauve stocking and the stethoscope back into his pocket, and even repeated them. "Jus a lil bit different."

But Mama and Papa never did find out what he meant by this, for Dr. Violet, stuffing the two dollar bills down into his pocket along with the newspaper and the cough medicine, inspected the parlor once more, as though he were looking around in it absentmindedly for some object he had lost, and went out the door without another word. It was perhaps only Herma who knew what it was that Dr. Violet had referred to. "I bit him," she said quite simply.

9.

Boy Sampson (who still had no other name in popular parlance, although officially by this time it was Delbert) had grown into an oversized and awkward adolescent, all elbows and knobby knees, without losing his neckless quality or the querulous fixity of his glance. He was tall and gangly now, but he still had the same funny haircut and the same soft and babyish, somehow invertebrate look about him. He was hopelessly in love with Herma, although he himself wasn't aware of this and was conscious only of a sort of warm and limpetlike urge when he was in her presence. An urge to do *something,* he didn't know what; he associated it not with her but with the various other perturbations and dislocations that were going on in his body at this time, so it remained perfectly innocent.

For her part, she had a contempt for all boys, and this contempt was centered with a particular vehemence on Boy Sampson. He really couldn't do anything properly. He wasn't good at sports and he couldn't drive a nail with a hammer, as she saw watching from her backyard through a crack in the fence. He sucked his thumb and then mouthed an obscenity she was clearly able to decipher. He couldn't even climb a fence as well as she could. Impeded as she was by a white dress that came below her knees, she shinnied up and seized the boards in her hands, groped with her bare feet like a young monkey, pulled herself up until she lay in prone position on top of the fence, and dropped easily down to the grass on the other side.

"What do you want?"

"I need Delilah. I'm going to my Aunt Minnie."

With hardly a glance at him she went directly to the shed and began backing the old mare out.

"You'd better ask Pap."

"You know," she told him with dignity, "that your Papa lets me ride Delilah whenever I want."

This being true, he could only watch her sullenly as she bridled the mare and turned her around to face the gate. When they were smaller they had often ridden Delilah together.

"Let me go with you."

"No," said Herma, "I won't, because you always make that noise."

"What noise?"

"You know the one. The one you make with your bottom. You always make it when we go riding on Delilah together."

"Well, I can't help it."

"I don't care. It's not polite and I don't appreciate it, so I don't care to have you go riding with me, and that's all there is to it."

She mounted while Boy Sampson watched. Grasping Delilah's mane in her fingers, she pulled herself up and landed on her stomach on the mare's back. Then, sitting upright, she stuck her legs down. There she sat on her underdrawers, with the white dress pushed up on either side and her long legs showing above the knee.

Boy Sampson stared at her. She started up Delilah with a nudge of her bare heel, came to the gate and unlatched it, and rode out, leaving the gate open behind her. He watched, with the air of someone seeing something precious slip irretrievably and hopelessly away.

Delilah was old and fat but diligent. She clop-clopped along in the soft dust of the street under the shade of the sycamores. She was so broad that Herma's legs, as long as they were, stuck out with her knees protruding at an angle. Delilah had been to Aunt Minnie's many times before and almost knew the way by herself. Only once or twice did Herma have to remind her of a turn, with a bare heel nudged into her large warm stomach as soft as a balloon. The way went up Ross Street to Seventeenth, across town on Seventeenth to Main Street, and then out of town through the orange groves that stretched away endlessly toward the mountains.

Main Street very soon turned into a country road. There were no more sidewalks, and the glossy dark-green orchards went by in even rows like soldiers, separated every so often by eucalyptus windbreaks. There was a smell of orange blossoms and eucalyptus, a buzz of gnats in the air, a distant sound of someone chopping stove-wood. Now and then Herma passed a white ranch house gleaming in the green trees, with a barn at one side and a windmill behind it. There were lemon groves as well as oranges. The lemons you could tell because the leaves were a different color, a lighter green with pale streaks of yellow. They smelled different too—a keen bitter essence like some savage perfume from the Orient. It was hot; there was no shade except when Herma passed now and then under a tall row of eucalyptus. The road went straight on, the air over it shimmering slightly in the summer heat.

About three miles out of town she turned right on an unpaved lane. It had no name; it was called "the road to the Harris place." Aunt Minnie's ranch was a quarter of a mile or so down the road, which continued on another few hundred yards beyond it and then ended in the river bottom. The ranch was much like the others, except that it was smaller and more carefully kept. The house of white clapboard was only two rooms wide, and the steep roof and gables made it look like a dollhouse. There were fruit trees and a large walnut with wide-spreading limbs, ideal for climbing. Between the house and the unpainted barn was a yard with chickens scratching in it. Behind the barn was the strawberry patch, and beyond it the even glossy rows of lemon trees began. In the yard a chicken was trying, in vain, to peck open a dried-out walnut. Herma tied Delilah to the apricot tree and went in.

Aunt Minnie was Mama's great-aunt by marriage. She had been born, years and years ago, in Castellamare di Stabia, that sun-drenched, dusty, squalid, and half-starved suburb of Naples, a town of flat roofs, dirty children, and spaghetti with sour tomato sauce. She was christened Gelsomina, which means Jasmine—Mina for short. With her husband, an ambitious young shoemaker who had saved a few lire, she embarked for America. But in Boston the bridegroom died quickly, of homesickness perhaps, or quinsy from the unaccustomed cold; and Mina went to work for rich people on Beacon Hill as a maid. Until the son of the family, an impulsive youth named Bertram who wished to be a poet and modeled his life on that of Byron, ran away with her and married her in Albany, New York.

But Bertram came to realize, first of all, that Byron did not run

away with housemaids, second that Byron would never have settled in
or even visited a place like Albany, New York, and finally that he,
Bertram, probably had very little talent as a poet anyway. So with his
bride (still almost a child-bride, she was only eighteen) he went West,
like so many other failures, dreamers, idealists, embezzlers, uncaught
horse thieves, poètes manqués, disinherited sons, and other victims of
the American Dream.

There was no railroad in those days beyond the Missouri, and so
Bertram and his bride joined a wagon train at Council Bluffs, with
very little to offer except that Minnie—as the pioneers soon American-
ized her name—could make sourdough bread. Bertram played the guitar
a little, and believed he could fire a revolver, but was not judged capable
of holding the reins leading to a span of oxen, so for the most part he
trudged moodily along beside the wagon with his eyes fixed on the
horizon. All went well until the company reached the Great Desert of
the Utah Territory. There a bunch of Paiutes came out from some red
rocks and began riding in circles around the wagon train, whooping
and firing off their antiquated and not very effective rifles. The pioneers
picked off several of them, but this didn't seem to discourage the others.
The train stopped, somewhat in confusion; there was no time to form
the wagons into the traditional circle. Finally the Indians' horses grew
tired of going round and round like a circus, and slowed down, and this
made them easier targets. If the pioneers had not planned their defense
very well, the Paiutes had not planned their attack at all. They gave up
and trotted away, leaving several dusty corpses behind them. On the
pioneers' side, only two oxen were killed, and a small boy named
Owen B. Smith; and Bertram.

They camped where they were for two days, near the little town of
Saint George, while they ate the two oxen and buried their dead. Then
they went on. Another month of creeping across the desert under an
excruciating white sun—two more oxen died, and a woman named Mrs.
Peebles—and they came at last over the pass and down to San Bernar-
dino. Everything was green and prosperous. There were alfalfa fields,
fruit orchards, and wells of sweet water. Continuing on to El Monte,
only a day's journey from Los Angeles, the company stopped, and there
disbanded.

Minnie had no money, no friends, and only the clothes that could
be packed into a wooden box. So, coming somehow or other to Santa Ana
—no one was sure about the details—she married Uncle John Harris,
who was the brother of Mama's grandfather. Uncle John was already
fifty, but he had two great merits as a bridegroom: he was a widower
who was said to have cherished his first wife with perseverance and
affection, and he owned a lemon ranch. His first wife was called Aunt
Miranda; a ghostly figure in the family annals, since she died before
the age of photography. Uncle John himself was a craggy thoughtful
man who somewhat resembled Abraham Lincoln, except that he had no
whiskers and let his hair grow long. Although he was slow-moving and
abstemious, he was a man of deeply concealed passions, and one of his

passions was for Minnie. He knew as soon as he caught sight of her that he must have her; and he did have her, only an hour after their wedding, in the cool and darkened bedroom of the ranch house while the white afternoon sun blazed outside. His passion was thereby satisfied, and he never touched her in lust again to the end of his days.

What Minnie thought of all this was not clear. She never complained, and she told little about herself. At the time of her marriage, as shown in the primitive Daguerreotypes of the epoch, she was a small and slender young woman with dark eyes and glossy black hair, not pretty exactly but with a shiny and intense vivacity, like a blackbird. There she was in her gray silk wedding dress with a single rose pinned to it. Her face was thin and her whole body narrow, her shoulders no wider than a ten-year-old boy's. But she gazed into the glass eye of the apparatus with an Etruscan calm, an assurance that was highly sensual. Studying these antique brown images, it was possible to understand Uncle John's need. Since the need was so quickly satisfied, however, they lived together thereafter in chastity like an uncle and a niece, and had no children. Minnie never complained of this either. As for Uncle John, he was kicked to death by a horse at the age of sixty-two.

Now Minnie was far older than that herself, of course—brown and wrinkled like a dried apricot, with a thatch of white hair, and thin and hard as a fence post. But her eyes were live, and she had the abrupt quick motions, the alert sidewise glance, of the blackbird that she came to resemble more and more. From the long habit of solitude she talked to herself as she worked in the kitchen, and sometimes even sang, in a voice that was a kind of raucous scratching.

"Sit down, Girl. Where are your shoes?" Her voice was scratchy and creaked like an old well pump. "You smell like horse sweat. You've been riding that old mare without a saddle again, and it's summer. No man will marry you, Girl, if you smell like a horse. Sniff me. What do I smell like?"

She seized Herma and pressed her face against her own chest, which was enclosed in an old-fashioned linen blouse with a high neck. For the rest, she wore a long straight linen skirt, brown stockings, and men's shoes.

"Lemons," said Herma, pulling away from the linen blouse.

"A man will marry you if you smell like lemons. Three of them have married me. But nobody will marry you if you smell like a horse."

"I don't care to get married yet."

"No, you don't think you do, but you're getting to be old enough. Let me see you, Girl." And she not only looked at Herma but she felt her through the top of the white dress, where there wasn't anything in particular to be felt, to tell the truth. Herma didn't care for this.

"I didn't have any either, until I was twenty, and hardly any then. Some men don't mind that. There are men who like all kinds of different things. There are some men," she said, "who like girls who look like a boy."

"There are some men who like boys."

Aunt Minnie gave her a blackbird glance. "You *are* getting old enough to be married. There are some men who like boys, and there are also some women who like women. But you're too young to bother your head about such things, and besides it would make your Papa unhappy if he knew you knew about them. What do you want to eat?"

"A prairie biscuit."

They had been called that, in the family, since Mama herself was a child. Aunt Minnie's sourdough biscuit was a recipe she was never able to explain to anyone else—a handful of this, a lump of that—but above all the morsel of starter dough that was pressed into the rest and kneaded until it dissolved, and then put aside to rise overnight. There was no other starter like Minnie's—perhaps it was the same one she had brought across the Plains in the wagon train. So no one else could make sourdough like hers.

Aunt Minnie found a still-warm sourdough biscuit, separated the top from the bottom, and spread the two halves with home-churned butter. Herma ate this to the last crumb, retrieving a fallen fragment of butter with her fingers.

"Now what?"

Herma said nothing. It wasn't necessary. Aunt Minnie knew what she had come for.

The old woman sighed. "Go to the Cool Room for some ice."

Herma took the old-fashioned wooden bucket and went off with it— out the door, across the beaten-earth yard, and down into the room under the water tower. Like most people in the country, Aunt Minnie had her own well. It stood at the edge of the yard by the vegetable garden, with a tall windmill erected over it on an iron tower. On top of the tower the blades turned with a creak, working the pump down below, and the water came up in a pipe and was pushed into a tank on the water tower. This was a square building higher than the house, with a tank on top built out of slabs of wood, unpainted and damp with water leaking through the boards. Down below under the tower, slightly below ground level, was the Cool Room with its stone walls.

It had no windows, and you had to leave the door slightly ajar so that you could see. Potatoes and onions were kept here, fruit like apples, and even milk, although it soured after a day or two. In the far corner, under a wooden cover like a cellar door, was the ice. It was packed in sawdust, and Herma had to dig down through the damp yellowish mass with its resinous odor to find it. When she came to a chunk of ice she chipped away with the ice pick until she had enough to fill the bucket. She brought back the cream too; it was in a brown crockery pitcher on a low shelf just above the ice.

When she got back to the kitchen Aunt Minnie was already beating the eggs, cutting a lemon in two and squeezing in the juice, and adding the sugar. She took the pitcher of cream from Minnie and put this in the bowl. She didn't need to measure; she knew just how much. The cream was so thick it wouldn't pour and had to be dipped out with a spoon. There was one more ingredient. She took the squeezed-out lemon rinds and scraped them with a grater into the bowl—the tiny yellow particles glittered on the surface of the cream like gold dust. Then she began whipping the mixture with a thing that looked like a tiny carpet beater.

Herma only watched. She had seen Aunt Minnie do this many times, but she was never allowed to help. There was only one thing she was allowed to do, and that would come later. Aunt Minnie bent down into the cupboard and took out the large oaken freezer, with metal fittings and a crank on top. It was slightly damp and smelled like a boat. It had to be kept damp because, like a boat, if it dried out the wooden boards would shrink and it would leak. Aunt Minnie, with surprising energy for so old a woman, rapidly chipped up the ice into sharp and gleaming shards. These she sifted down into the space around the metal cylinder in the center of the freezer, alternating the ice with layers of salt. When it was full she carefully wiped the inside of the cylinder, to be sure there was no salt in it, and then spooned in the mixture from the bowl. It filled the cylinder exactly to the top, although she had measured nothing. Then the crank was fitted onto the top, with its long rotating paddle that stuck down into the mixture. The whole thing was set onto a chair, and another chair put next to it. Aunt Minnie wiped her hands. She was done.

Now came Herma's part. She had to sit in the chair turning the crank for a long time. It was easy enough at first, but after a half an hour the mixture in the cylinder began to thicken and the cranking got harder and harder. However you couldn't stop. That was when it was most important to keep cranking. Herma sat on the chair in her white dress, turning the handle until her arm ached.

Meanwhile Aunt Minnie busied herself in the kitchen, washing the bowl she had mixed things up in, rinsing off the beater, finding the whitened lemon rinds on the sink and throwing them away. She never stopped, all day long, and she never seemed to be tired. Some Spaniards came to cultivate the grove, and pick the lemons in the winter, but for the rest she ran the ranch herself—milked the cow, picked the apricots, and groped through the hen coop for eggs. When there was nothing else to do there was always some work in the kitchen. She found a broom and swept up a little sugar that had spilled on the floor, wiped the sink with a rag, and poured water from a glass onto the geranium on the windowsill. While she worked she sang in her blackbird voice. The song came from the same place as the recipe for the ice cream, the sun-baked Neapolitan town of her youth.

"Chist' è 'o paese d' 'o sole . . ."

Herma knew the song by heart, even though no one had ever taught her Italian, let alone Neapolitan; she knew it just as she knew Spanish, because languages came to her without effort and she breathed them in as easily as she breathed in the warm and clear California air. This is the land of the sun, the song went. This is the land of the sea. This is the land where all words, be they sweet or bitter, are always words of love.

Aunt Minnie's voice was only a kind of a croak. And yet the tune could be made out; that is, she didn't exactly sing the tune, but you could make out from the sound she made what the tune was supposed to be. The song was like a piece of fence wire that had been trampled on and needed straightening. Sometimes Herma hummed it along with her, in an effort to straighten out the fence wire, but Aunt Minnie paid no attention and didn't seem to notice. She put away the broom and began scrubbing the sink with some cleanser out of a can with a newborn chick on the label. She sang another little bent piece of the song: ''Sò doce o sò amare . . .''

She looked around to see if Herma was still turning the crank, rinsed out the washrag and hung it to dry, put away the ice bucket and the ice pick, and stood on a chair to replace the rock salt in the cupboard. Herma had to wait a long time for the last line.

''Sò sempre parole d'ammore . . .''

. . . with a lingering on the double m and the whole word stretched out in a long ritardando—it was a G, Herma knew, although Aunt Minnie only wavered around the edges of this note, never quite hitting it.

Herma had been cranking for the best part of an hour now. Her arm felt as though it were about to break. Aunt Minnie took the heavy freezer away from her and set it on the sink—even though she was slight she lifted it without difficulty. She unfastened the crank and pulled out the paddle, scraping the ice cream that clung to it back into the cylinder with a spoon. Unlike most people who made ice cream, Aunt Minnie didn't lick the spoon or the paddle, or in any way sample the exquisite confection she had made. She seemed to have no interest in it for herself, and only made it as some Giotto might make an altarpiece for a Pope, without covetousness and with total artistic objectivity. In fact, it occurred to Herma, she had never seen her eat anything at all, not even a prairie biscuit with butter. Still scratching away at the dimly remembered song out of her childhood, she rinsed off the paddle and left it in the sink. Then, getting onto the chair again, she took down from the cupboard a long-stemmed crystal goblet, the only one like it in the house. In fact, Herma thought she must have brought it with her from Boston, or perhaps from Italy, for there was nothing like it to be seen in Santa Ana or anywhere else in Orange County. There were acanthus leaves on the stem, and around the bowl were cut pastoral scenes of fauns pursuing nymphs, capering goats, and youths with wild hair playing pipes.

Setting the goblet on the table with a lace doily under it, she found a spoon and scooped out a perfect hemisphere of the ice cream from the freezer. It was a pure and virgin white, with only a faint tinge of gold from the lemon juice and the grated lemon peel. It liquefied slightly at the edges, while the thin glass of the goblet frosted. Herma waited, knowing that what Aunt Minnie was making was not finished yet.

Aunt Minnie bent over and found a box of strawberries under the sink, selected the largest one, plucked off the green leaves, washed and dried it, and set it base down in the exact center of the ice cream. Then, from the cupboard over the sink, she took down a jar of thin and translucent apricot glaze. She held a spoonful of this over the goblet and turned it. The amber fluid fell slowly over the strawberry, thinned, and spread until it covered the whole hemisphere of ice cream. The lemon-white was transformed to a delicate flesh tone; the pale dome gleamed through the thin golden membrane that clung to it and covered it, with the strawberry, its dappled red now also lightly touched with amber, in the exact center.

Aunt Minnie handed Herma a spoon which she had chilled in a little ice she had saved from the bucket. She said, "Eat, Girl."

Herma ate, while Aunt Minnie stood in the kitchen a little distance away watching her. She spooned around the edges first, dipped away delicately at the glaze, and saved the strawberry for last. Then she raised the goblet and finished the job with her tongue. Aunt Minnie didn't care about manners: it was not like at home.

When she was done Herma offered to wash the goblet, but Aunt Minnie told her, "No, Girl, you shouldn't wash the goblet. Aunt Minnie will wash the goblet. A person who eats something shouldn't have to wash the dishes from it. It spoils it that way. And besides you might break the goblet. It's fragile and it's very old." She took the goblet away from her, washed it and dried it, and put it away in the cupboard. Then she seemed to forget Herma completely. Turning her back on her, she got some blacking and a rag and began scrubbing rust spots off the wood-burning stove. As she worked she took up the song again, such as it was, in her scratchy thread of a voice.

> "Chist' è 'o paese addò tutt' 'e parole,
> Sò doce o sò amare,
> Sò sempre parole d'ammore."

10.

Outside in the bright sunshine Herma untied Delilah from the apricot tree, mounted, and nudged her with her heel. When she came to the road she hesitated. Then instead of going off toward town she turned to the left, the other way. After a hundred yards or so the road dwindled away to a kind of rocky trail and descended to the river, such as it was in this part of the world; at this time of the year it was almost dry. Delilah picked her way along the sandy river bottom littered with large round boulders. She knew the way almost as well as Herma did. Herma, feeling warm and content in the sunshine and with the ice cream inside her, began humming the old words about the land of the sea and the sun. When she got to the last line she broke out into full song, with all the Neapolitan flamboyance and florid tremolo in the voice:

"Sò sempre pa-ro-le d'am-more . . ."

A little abashed, she looked around. But the river bottom was deserted. The trail went on, skirting the larger boulders and passing now and then through a patch of willows so that the branches brushed against the sides of the old mare. A mile or so farther on down the river bottom was the Old Quarry. The granite had all been dug out years ago, for tombstones, cornerstones for banks, and county courthouses, and now there was only a great oblong hole in the river bottom that stayed filled with water even in the summer. With a little thrill of anticipation Herma imagined herself pulling off her dress, kicking off her drawers, and slipping into the cold and slightly stagnant water with its faint tinge of green.

But as she approached the quarry she caught a glimpse of something up ahead—something moving. There was another patch of willows at this place along the riverbank, and she urged Delilah up to it with a nudge of her foot and looked through a gap in the branches.

On the sandy beach by the quarry were five or six men and their horses. They had ridden down to the quarry to go swimming, and now they had come out and were drying themselves in the sun. One man, sitting on the back of a white horse, was wearing a cotton singlet and nothing else. He was young and fair, and his forehead was pink from the sun. Another was a boy about Herma's age, with damp drawers that came to his knees. His wet hair was plastered to his head. Near him was a man clad in nothing but his shirt, hopping on one foot to put on his shoe; but he was wearing his hat. Another one was stark naked. He had his side turned toward Herma, and he was scratching his head thoughtfully, as if trying to decide whether he was dry enough to get dressed yet. He seemed to decide that he was, for he turned to the place where his clothes were, a few feet from him on the sand. In doing this he turned directly toward Herma, so that the front of his body was visible. He seemed to stare at her for a long time. But she was sure he couldn't see her; only her eyes showed through the gap in the branches. She remained motionless, watching him with fixity.

This man, after staring at the trees for a while, seemed to remember that he had been about to put his clothes on, and advanced toward them with a flat-footed and apelike kind of dignity. He picked them up. The shirt was still buttoned, and he raised it over his head and pulled it down, shaking his arms so that the hands would come out. Something in the middle of his body shook too, and swung back and forth.

Herma pulled at the bridle and touched Delilah lightly with her heel, and they climbed up the riverbank with hardly a sound. At the top was an orange grove. The old mare's hooves, which she set down in a leisurely fashion one at a time, made only a kind of whisper in the soft dirt. But a little farther on, when she came out onto the road, she showed an unexpected burst of energy and broke into a trot, so that Herma had to hold on to the stiff mane in order not to fall off. The trot continued down the long road through the orchards. Herma stared at Delilah's ears, one of which was flopped over and the other upright. She was thoughtful, or not so much thoughtful as reflective, although she hardly knew what she was reflecting about. It was a very general and yet strong and profound kind of reflection. The oddly serene and pastoral, almost Homeric scene at the quarry stuck in her memory. The young man astride the white horse had the air somehow of a warrior out of a fable, clad only in the light singlet as though it were a piece of armor. There was a negligent and kingly air too about the others. The men were strong and calm. They were prepotent. Even though naked, they moved easily through the world and met its gaze with confidence, knowing it was theirs. Herma, still looking at Delilah's flopped ear, had forgotten where she was. She came into town. It had an odd look, as though a new house had been built, or as though somebody had died in one of the houses and they had pulled the window shades. But everything was exactly the same.

Arriving home, she turned Delilah loose in the Sampsons' backyard (Delilah ambled obediently into the shed and stopped there, swishing away flies with the tail), then climbed over the fence into her own yard and went into the house. It was the middle of the afternoon. Papa was away at work, and Mama was ''lying down,'' as she always said, although she slept so soundly after lunch that it would have taken a cannon shot to awaken her. Barefoot as she was, Herma made no sound as she went upstairs to her room. She took off her clothes—which was a simple matter, since there were only two of them, the white dress and the drawers—and then took a bath; because even she could tell now in the closed bedroom that riding a horse bareback in the summer made a person smell. There was no sound from the bedroom across the hall. Herma splashed in the tub for ten minutes or so. Then she pulled the plug and got out, dried herself carelessly, and went back to her room trailing the towel.

There was no mirror in the bathroom. That would not be proper, according to the notion of Papa and those of his generation; for what would there be to see in a mirror in the bathroom, except one's own unclothed body? Papa had never quite worked this thought out even to himself, and yet that was why there was no mirror in the bathroom.

There was one, however, in Herma's room. It was an heirloom, inherited from Grandma Harris, and who knows who had owned it before that—it was very old. It was a very large mirror. If it was not in Mama and Papa's bedroom it was because there was no room for it there, cluttered as the room was with the big double bed, the large chest of drawers with its swelling double bosom, Mama's dressing table with its collection of bibelots, and a dozen other pieces of medium-sized and small furniture that were deemed necessary for the proper operation of Mama and Papa's conjugal life. In Herma's room, which contained only a small iron bed, a kind of chiffonier in which she kept her clothes, and a small square table with wicker legs to put the lamp on, there was plenty of room for the mirror. It dominated the far end of the room opposite the window: a large and massive object with square feet, and a frame something like a picture in a museum. The glass was badly tarnished; there were silver-gray splotches all over it, a long streak at the side like rain falling from a roof, and in the right-hand corner another darkish outline that looked like a spider crawling over a hand. Things looked different in the mirror than they did in the real world—that is, on Herma's side of the glass. The world on the other side of the mirror was an identical but reverse world in which one's right hand became the left, the calendar on the wall opposite was written in Chinese, and so on; but even odder than this was the trans-formation wrought on the *atmosphere* of the world beyond the mirror by the darkish splotches and discolorations of the glass—a world with a dark enticement to it, a thrill of the unknown and perilous, that could hardly be accounted for by the mere optical facts of reflection.

Herma looked at the other Herma standing only a few feet away from her in this other world. She saw an adolescent who, as yet, had scarcely any feminine characteristics to her body except for its lack of masculine features, such as she had observed on the men at the quarry. In her right hand (the left hand in the mirror) she was holding the towel, with the end trailing on the floor. Her short hair was still damp from the bath; drops of water gleamed on her narrow shoulders. The skin was as white as alabaster, except that the face and forearms were pink from the sun. In a frontal view such as this the two small bumps on the chest were invisible. The hips were straight as a board, and the feet large, as in all young animals. The mysterious and silvery image in the mirror, if a single thing were only added, might have been that of a boy.

Herma turned away from the mirror and went to the door. It was closed but not latched. The latch was a screwed-on sort of affair, a small metal box with fluted knob fixed to it. But the screws that held it to the door were loose—they had been for some time—and the latch wouldn't work. Herma tried to screw them in with her fingernail, to no effect—she only broke a nail. She said, ''Oh, drat the thing!'' She went to the chiffonier, found a slipper, and jammed it under the bottom of the door. Then, trying the door to be sure it wouldn't open, she went back to her position before the mirror.

She looked. There she was, the silly thing, with her narrow shoul-ders and hips, and a slight frown of concentration marring the smooth-ness of her brow, staring at her other self as though it were an enemy. She spread her feet slightly on the carpet, and put her hands on her hips. Herma had a strong will, as everybody had noticed. And now she *willed strongly,* as one might struggle to wrench a heavy stone out of the earth with a crowbar.

For a while nothing changed; the image in the mirror was the same. She strained once more, with all the force of her body and will. There was a tickling between her legs, a crawling and creeping sensation at that particular hidden place people didn't talk about. And then it happened. There was an odd slow sound, a kind of soft plop, and a part of Herma turned inside out in exactly the way that you would turn a stocking out. The thing that appeared was about the size, in fact, of a small child's sock, although as heavy as though it were full of sand. At first it was damp, dark, and purplish like a newborn baby, but after a minute or two it began to fade to a pale rose. And rose was the right word for it too, because the rounded and conical sort of cap on the end was exactly like a pink rosebud about to burst.

It was an exalted moment, a moment of keen triumph and exultation; and yet calm. He went on looking in the mirror a little longer, with a deep curiosity. He saw a thin-shouldered, handsome, and slightly frowning youth who might have been a twin of Herma. His hair was a little long for a boy, but some wore it that way. The feet were big— boys have large feet. He had Herma's look of determination, her fine hands and features, even a certain roundness of contour here and there. But he was unmistakably a boy, a slim and good-looking young man. He was satisfied.

Coming to himself, he found the towel at his feet and wrapped it around his middle. He looked around him. He took the slipper out of the door and flung it across the room. Then he opened the door cautiously. There was still no sound from the bedroom across the hall. But from downstairs he heard an unmistakable tiny noise: the chink of china against a saucer. Mama was having a cup of tea to restore her spirits, which were always somewhat slow to waken after lying down in the afternoon. He pushed the door the rest of the way open, strode across the hall, and entered the large bedroom.

The bed was still unmade and the blinds pulled down. The room was filled with a dim shadowy light. He crossed rapidly to the closet and pulled it open, still holding the towel around himself with one hand. It was hard to see anything in there, but after a little groping he found Papa's Sunday suit. He laid it over his shoulder—all with one hand, because he had to hold the towel with the other—and found a shirt and socks as well. He tried Papa's derby, but it was far too large and came down over his ears. The shoes were too large as well but they would have to do. Draped with his plunder, he stole out swiftly and went back to his own room.

Up the stairway came a little sigh. Mama, sitting at the kitchen table, had taken her first sip of tea. He dressed rapidly. Everything was too large, especially the trousers, but luckily they were fitted with braces so there was no danger of their falling down. When the shirt and coat were in place there was only a certain empty region of air around his middle, between his body and the clothes, which perhaps would not be noticeable from the outside.

He looked at himself in the mirror; in the clothes far too large for him he looked like a second-rate clown in a circus, except for the thin and intent seriousness of his expression. Still looking in the mirror, he felt in his pockets. There was nothing much except an old train ticket and, in the side pocket of the coat, a small gold penknife with a folding blade.

He turned away and went to the chiffonier. In the tumble of underdrawers, hair ribbons, handkerchiefs, mismatched stockings, hairpins, pictures of actresses cut from magazines, and dried flowers half crumbled to dust—Lord love us, but she was untidy!—he groped for and found Madame Modjeska's gold coin. He dropped it into the left-hand coat pocket, and took the knife out of the other pocket. With this he went to the door and dexterously tightened the screws to the latch. Girls, he thought, never were any good at fixing things. He tried the latch to be sure it was working properly, and confidently went out.

With the over-large shoes it was a trick going down the stairs without making any noise. The hallway at the bottom of the stairs was arranged in such a way that it was necessary to pass briefly by the kitchen door, but it was almost shut and he accomplished this quickly and without incident. The screen door at the back of the house he was careful to close silently. In another minute he was out on Ross Street, walking briskly, and with as much assurance as he could muster in his odd costume, down the sidewalk toward Fourth. No one, as far as he could tell, had noticed him leaving the house.

No one on Fourth Street paid any attention to him either. It was late afternoon and the town lay in a heavy warm somnolence. A buggy went by, leaving little specks of dust quivering in the slanting light. There were only a few people out on the street. He went directly along the sidewalk to Proper Procter's, through the double door, and to the right toward the men's section.

As ill luck would have it, instead of a clerk in the men's section it was Mr. Proper Procter himself, a suave and rather unctuous individual with a pince-nez and a small mouth. Not only did he know Papa but he probably knew who Herma was too. However, he showed no sign of recognition, neither did he seem to pay any attention to the awkward and ill-fitting clothing that had obviously been made for somebody else.

"May I help you, young man?"

"I would like a suit. And the whole outfit—shirt, shoes, socks, braces, a necktie, and so on." He strove to master the adolescent quaver in his voice.

"Certainly. If you will step this way."

He led him through the glass cabinets gleaming with shirts, belts, braces, and neckties to the rack of ready-made suits. Procter's was the first store in town to offer ready-made clothing—the end of all gentility, according to some, but in the opinion of the more modern-minded a great convenience and economy. In fact Procter's suits, ready made as they were, were faultless in construction and of the latest cut and fashion. Mr. Procter deftly whipped a tape measure around his waist, and measured him again from crotch to foot—he almost flinched at that, but controlled himself. Then Mr. Procter pulled out and displayed on top of the rack (a) an alpaca summer suit with green pipings around the lapels; (b) a conservative blue serge, so dark it was almost black, much like Papa's own suit; and (c) a light brownish-gray suit with pin stripes of darker brown, a nipped-in waist, a vest with a watch pocket, and narrow tubular trousers.

"It all depends," Mr. Procter told him, "on the taste"—glancing as though for the first time at what he was wearing now.

"Exactly. I'll take this," pointing to the gray pin-striped suit.

"It's sixteen dollars. It's the latest thing that young fellows are wearing in the city. You need a chocolate derby, a white shirt with a low collar, a plaid necktie, and shoes the same color as the hat, only we call 'em cordovan and not chocolate."

He saw that in fact this was exactly what he needed. Mr. Procter was not only highly tactful but faultless in his choice.

"Just as you say."

"Fine. I'll have the suit fitted. Mr. Rubenstern!" he called up the stairs.

"Fitted?"

"Yes, fitted."

"It isn't necessary. I'll wear it just as it is."

Ah, explained Mr. Procter, but that wasn't possible. The sleeves were too long and the trousers too large—and anyhow, as he pointed out in a final and irrefutable argument, the cuffs of the trousers weren't finished and had only been cut off with pinking shears. By this time Mr. Rubenstern, a stout and discouraged-looking gentleman with a bald head, was coming down the stairs with his own tape measure draped around him. He went off to a dressing room and put the suit on, and then came out while Mr. Rubenstern jerked and tugged at it and slashed away making marks with a thin piece of chalk. He was growing more and more impatient. He hadn't really anticipated all this.

Mr. Procter had out a ticket with blanks on it, and groped in his vest for a pencil. "Name?"

With no particular hesitation he said the first thing that came into his head: "Fred."

"Last name?"

This time he was a little at a loss. A second or two passed before a vision of the Feed and Grain store came to him, a little further down on Fourth.

"Fred Hite."

"Address?"

"Liberty Hotel."

"Ah, you're a guest in our town. You'd like the suit sent to the hotel then?"

"I don't think you quite understand. I want to wear it. And right away."

Ah, but that too was impossible, Mr. Procter explained with his polite air of infallibility. He could have it in a day or two, or if there were a rush, tomorrow morning at eleven.

"Out of the question. Can you see me going around like this?"

This was the moment, if Mr. Procter had ever felt the impulse to do so, to ask *why* Fred was going about like this. But he was too tactful, or too familiar with the manifold sartorial eccentricities and deviations of the world, to make a comment. Evidently he saw the point, and agreed if only silently that Fred could not go about like this, but the most he would concede was ''Perhaps tomorrow morning.''

''I'll pay extra.''

It was not necessary to pay extra, Mr. Procter assured him. At Procter's every service and courtesy were provided the customer, and the price was only that indicated on the garment. He looked with some fixity at Fred's thin adolescent face, with its shock of dark hair and its intent and determined expression. Then he turned to the tailor.

''Mr. Rubenstern, are you very occupied?''

''Not vurry.''

''Perhaps,'' Mr. Procter conceded, ''if you could come by again in an hour or two. We close,'' he warned him, ''at six. Do you think we can accommodate the young gentleman, Mr. Rubenstern?''

Mr. Rubenstern seemed plunged into a fit of gloom. He said, ''I'll stop everything else.''

It was settled. Fred went back to the dressing room, took off the suit, and passed it out to the still dejected Mr. Rubenstern. He dressed and came out. Then there was no help for it; he was banished out into the street again in the baggy black suit and loose shoes. After he had tried on the new suit and taken it off, the outsized clothes felt wretched, and worse, conspicuous. He gritted his teeth and raged inwardly. Staring down the passersby and forcing them to avert their eyes, he strode down Fourth to the S. P. station and back again on the other side of the street, and found by the clock on the bank that he had used up only five minutes. He forced himself to slow his pace, even stopping now and then and pretending to look in a shop window. In this way he was able to stretch out his circuit of Fourth Street, up one side and down the other, to fifteen minutes. Each time he passed Procter's he looked in to see if Mr. Rubenstern was by any chance waddling down the great walnut staircase with the suit over his arm. *An hour or two* might mean one hour, might it not? To make sure, he took another trip up and down Fourth Street, and then strode into the store with his chin jutting out, saying nothing.

Mr. Procter, finally, seemed a little impatient with him. But as a merchant it was not his policy to have emotions, and he was almost successful in concealing his irritation. ''I don't think it would be ready yet,'' he said firmly. He called up the staircase. ''Mr. Rubenstern!''

The bald head appeared over the balustrade. ''I'm not able to do miracles yet. I'm only human.'' But he was able to do miracles, for he appeared almost immediately on the staircase, holding the suit over his arm.

The suit fitted like a motorman's glove. Miracle or not, Mr. Rubenstern knew his trade. Fred had to have Mr. Procter's help in tying the plaid necktie; Mr. Procter stood behind him and guided him in the mirror. The cordovan pumps were so elegant that Fred had the impression he could fly, if he pushed himself upon his toes a little. The shirt had French cuffs, and Mr. Procter had provided imitation-jewel links, evidently as a gift. Mr. Rubenstern, standing at one side, put the hat on him as though he were helping to dress a mannikin. Mr. Procter, meanwhile, was wrapping up the old clothes in a brown-paper bundle.

"Wait!"

Fred took the clothes away from him, groped in the pocket of the black coat, found the Double Eagle, and handed it to him. Mr. Procter glanced at it reflectively, as though he were interested in numismatics, and then turned away without a word to put it into the cash register. He gave Fred a handful of change—no paper, just a half-dozen or so coins. Fred slipped them into his pocket without looking at them.

"Thank you. And good day."

"And the package?" inquired Mr. Procter, still placid.

"I'll call for it later."

11.

       Out in the street Fred walked along with a springy step. He felt himself a different person, and in fact he was. In the well-fitting fashionable suit, the neat white shirt, and the brown shoes that seemed winged, he launched out into a world that seemed all at once gleaming and marvelously simple, and his for the taking. The first thing he took from it was a cigar. He stepped into Shakespeare's and ordered, "A Guantanamo."

These, popularly called Nickel Guanos, were the local favorite. They were long and thin and if tended with care would last for an hour or more. Fred put down his nickel.

"A light?"

"Thank you."

The clerk lit the cigar, and Fred sidled out into the late afternoon sunlight again. He took a puff. He was uncertain what to do with the cigar when he was not smoking it. Certainly you didn't leave it in your mouth. Only the men standing around at the livery stable did that. But it seemed awkward holding it in his fingers, as though it were a firecracker that he was about to throw away as soon as he found a place to throw it. Trying several different grips in succession, he finally stuck it between the first and second fingers of his right hand, then held the hand behind him with the wrist gripped loosely in his left. This seemed casual and had a devil-may-care air to it. Fred walked down Fourth to Main, looked around to see if anybody were watching, and got on the Yellow Dog.

Smoking was permitted only in the rear half which was open to the

air. At this time of the day he had it to himself. There were two or
three passengers in the closed section in front. He sat comfortably with
his legs crossed, drew at the long, thin cigar, and expelled the smoke in
a leisurely way. Like a millionaire, like a young prince, he savored his
Guantanamo while the landscape rolled past him in the gray twilight
air. The sugar factory went by, then the beet fields with men working
bent over in the long, narrow trenches. Some day, he thought, he might
own all this. Anything was possible for a clever young fellow with ambition and a cool head. He might sell it to a combination of bankers from
the East, or he might keep it in order to speculate on the world sugar
market. He took another pull at his cigar, and the Yellow Dog slowed
for Angel Town with its brakes squeaking.

When it started off again it was only five minutes to the beach.
The car made its jerky turn to the left, ran along between the bluff and
the beach for a mile or so, then clacked to a stop by the half-broken
wooden platform lying in the sand. Fred got off and threw away his
cigar.

The big building lay like a stranded ark at the edge of the sea, only
a hundred yards from the tracks. A boardwalk led out to it across the
sand. As he drew closer he got a good look at it for the first time. It was
constructed, evidently, out of odd scraps of lumber of all shapes and
sizes, with a piece of tin or corrugated iron nailed over it here and
there. On top of it was the sign with the R almost fallen off at the end.
Only the front side facing the shore rested on the sand; the rest of it
was built out over the water on pilings. The left end of the building was
long and low, with dusty windows and an unpainted wooden door in the
middle. At the other end was a structure that was entirely different. It
seemed to be three stories high; at least it had three rows of windows.
Although it was built of wood like the rest of the building, it affected a
kind of pretentious mock-classic style; there were fluted columns with
the paint peeling off them, wooden niches with carved wooden vases,
and along the top a jigsaw frieze like a kind of tawdry Parthenon.
There seemed to be no separate entrance to this part of the building.
But as Fred came closer he saw that there was a sign on it too, or at
least that someone had affixed a small board high up on it with the
crudely painted words: "Hotel Dolores y Sueño." There was no sign
of life from any part of the building; the only sound was a gentle crashing now and then as a wave broke through the pilings underneath.

The unpainted wooden door at the left end was slightly ajar. He
pushed through it and entered, leaving the door open behind him. At
first he could see almost nothing. It was early evening now and the
place was dark. Finally he began to make out some details. This part
of the building was a long dance hall. At one end was a small platform
for the band, with a music stand and some chairs on one of which was an
abandoned saxophone. Behind the platform, for some reason, a piece of
faded red velvet was hung on the wall. At the other end of the hall was
a larger raised floor, stretching across the room from one side to the
other. On it were a half-dozen tables and chairs with wire legs. The

tables had not been cleaned; there were bottles on them, some lying on their sides, and brownish pools of liquid. Behind the tables was a tiny bar, and over the bar was a mirror with a picture painted on it, an improbable romantic scene of lovers and moonlight. Underneath were the words "Cerveza El Brujo." To the right of the bar, at the very end of the hall, was the door that led to the hotel.

This door had a curtain hanging in it of the same red velvet as the drapery behind the band. The curtain was half open, and there was someone standing in the opening. She was half the length of the dance hall away from Fred, and it was some time before his eyes adjusted to the gloom enough that he could make out something of her. She seemed very young, perhaps no older than he was. But her body was full; she was a miniature woman with breasts that were already large enough to sag. Her black hair was parted in the center and fell away on either side like ravens' wings. She wore a slightly tawdry red dress like a Spanish dancer, with slits to the knee, and there was a red paper flower in her hair. Her small round face had no expression whatsoever. Her glance, moving in a leisurely way from one part of him to another, took in the thin adolescent form, the stylish suit, and the pale but resolute face.

"It costs a dollar," she said, "but for you it will be twenty-five cents."

12.

Fred came home in a high state of exhilaration and managed to sneak into the house without being observed. He went upstairs and into his room, securely latched the door, took off his hat, looked into it as if to see if there was some message there, came to himself and put the hat away in the closet, walked around the room, and looked at himself in the mirror, opening the coat and sticking his thumbs experimentally into the vest. Then he went to the chiffonier and dropped the last of his coins into the drawer, which was a terrible mess, with underclothing, crumpled magazine pictures, and soiled ribbons sticking up out of it. He found a scrap of paper, wrote something on it, and stuck it into the frame of the mirror. Then he began undressing and hiding the various items of clothing away in dark and inaccessible corners of the closet.

When all the clothes were off he went back to the mirror. For some time he gazed intently at the image in the grayish splotched glass. It was just like everybody else's all right. He felt pleased with himself. It was even superior to the average, according to the girl at Cantamar, who told him that length didn't matter but the diameter and what she called "hard here and soft there" were the important factors. Right now it was soft everywhere, and looked very much like those of the men swimming at the quarry, and a good deal more impressive than Boy Sampson's in his opinion. Of course, that had been many years ago. Fred stood before the mirror for some time, conscious of the simple and functional beauty of this new thing he had acquired, but not in any egotistical way. He was simply satisfied, with *it* and with himself.

But of course he couldn't go around like this for the rest of his life. Even Papa and Mama, as dense as they were—innocent, it would be better to say—would eventually notice. He began concentrating again, gathering all the force of his will at that place at the center of his body. In, in, he strained with every nerve. Five minutes or so he stood, pulling upward and inward with all his will, while the thing tickled and crawled slightly as though in protest. He wasn't quite sure whether what he was attempting would work or not. But at last it succeeded.

When it went up and in, it made a sucking sound like water going down a drain, not a very pleasant sound to tell the truth. It was very quiet in the house. From downstairs, now and then, there was a faint sound of pots and pans as Mama prepared dinner. The square mirror, in silence, reflected back its silver-gray and slightly sinister image. Herma stood before it for a little while longer examining herself. She was exactly as always. Then she noticed a piece of paper stuck into the frame of the mirror. On it was scrawled in blocky letters, "Clean up your chiffonier drawer." She pulled this out, crumpled it angrily, and threw it into the wastebasket. Then she went to the closet, took down a white dress with eyelets, found a clean pair of drawers and some stockings in the chiffonier, and dressed. She put on her shoes by first standing in them and then wiggling until the heels went into place. A final check in the mirror. Was that a smudge by the side of her mouth? No, only a shadow. She went down to her supper only a little late. Neither Mama nor Papa paid any attention to her. Papa didn't look up from his soup.

The next day, while Mama was lying down, Fred went to Procter's for the brown-paper package and brought it home. By suppertime Papa's clothes were put away in their place in the closet. No one noticed this either, since Papa only wore the suit on Sunday, and it was still only Thursday.

13.

Herma dug around in the top drawer of the chiffonier to see if Fred had left her any of Madame Modjeska's Double Eagle at all. Oh, what a peacock! Almost twenty dollars for clothes! Not to mention a quarter for the other filth. After searching for some time she found another quarter and some odd coins. These she put into her small reticule along with a handkerchief. From the drawer also she took a strawberry-colored ribbon for her hair, not very clean as a matter of fact, and tied it while she looked at herself in the mirror. Above the white dress she saw a pale and thin face with watchful eyes, a mouth that looked as though it were listening, with faint irony, rather than preparing to say anything. She looked like a young lady in a story and not a child at all. The dress was cut so that one hardly noticed her thin and rather boyish figure. She hummed to herself:

> "Sì. Mi chiamano Mimì,
> ma il mio nome è Lucia."

With her hair so short it was hard to make the ribbon stay in place; she gave it a firm tug as though she were a sailor tying a knot. Then, taking her white parasol with the strawberry ribbon around the edge, she went out.

The place she was going was not entirely respectable. It wasn't on Fourth Street with the other shops but a few doors around the corner on Main, near the place where you took the Yellow Dog. First came a tumbledown shack where an old man sharpened knives, and a Chinese laundry. Then there was a vacant lot, and beyond it was the Electric Theater, which had a two-story false front on it, as though it were trying to pretend that it was a real building on Fourth Street. The front was painted in odd colors—pale pink with a tinge of violet, a chrome yellow on the green side, and a purple that was almost black. The doorway was a kind of large elaborate portal. In the center of it was a square column of mirrors not more than six inches on a side. From a hole in this column, enclosed by a kind of velvet sock, an arm emerged and took your nickel, and passed out a ticket in return. But this was only an optical illusion; if you looked more closely you could see that the column was only half a column and set into a whole arrangement of mirrors, behind which the person attached to the arm was concealed. This piece of magic in itself, Herma felt, was almost worth the nickel.

The theater was smaller inside than it seemed from the street; it was a narrow windowless room hardly larger than the parlor of Herma's house. A large goggled machine with wires coming out of it stood at the rear. In front of the machine and filling the rest of the room were rows of chairs of all different kinds; no two were alike. At the other end of the room was suspended what appeared to be an ordinary bed sheet, although it was more probably a square of canvas. Herma took a seat. There was only one other customer, an old woman Herma had never seen before, with a wisp of gray hair sticking out and a cat on her knees. Very probably she was a witch. There was something witching about the whole place, and perhaps she belonged to it in some way as a permanent fixture.

Herma had taken a chair almost in the last row, so that she could not only see the show on the white screen but could watch the operator of the projecting machine as he worked. He was a serious young man with a mustache that was just starting to grow. He wore a white shirt and necktie, and he had put on black velvet sleeve-protectors to keep his shirt from being soiled by the machine. His arm, Herma saw, was the same one that had come out of the mirror column outside to take her nickel. The projectionist seemed unaware of her presence and went on adjusting his machine as though he were alone in the room.

He fastened on a large reel of film and threaded it through the goggle. The arc lamp was separate from the rest of the machine, like a hurricane lamp except that it had two black wires coming out of it. He started up the lamp, filling the room with a white glare, and then inserted it into the projector. There was a kind of clucking noise. At first a square of blank light appeared on the screen. Some spots, blotches, and letters of the alphabet flashed by, and then there appeared on the screen the black and white image of a horse, tossing its head and agitating its feet in an exact simulacrum of galloping. This went on for some time. Another horse appeared, this one drawing a buggy the wheels of which really went around, although for some reason backward.

There were more images, some of moving people, or faces talking. Herma sat in delight, not moving a muscle, hypnotized by these dancing shadows that were somehow more real and more vivid than life. The ghostly white figures against the black background seemed to exude a pale fire around their edges. And that was not all. The projectionist, once he had set his machine in motion with the arc light sputtering, was free to do other effects. As the horse galloped across the screen, for example, he knocked together a pair of coconut shells to simulate the clopping of hooves. Two lovers appeared on a marble balcony in the moonlight, and he dexterously lowered the needle onto a Victrola at his elbow. The saccharine strains of Schumann's *Traümerei,* only slightly scratchy, filled the room. But the needle was removed when a droll, pale, serious man, with a lock of hair falling over his brow, appeared at the head of a stairway and started to go down it. In absolute silence he set his foot into a scrub pail on the landing. It was a pregnant moment. The pale man took another step. As he fell down the stairs with marvelous violence, the projectionist thrust back his foot and kicked over a row of bowling pins on the shelf behind him. Herma turned to glance at him; he was just as serious as the man falling down the stairs. In spite of his gravity, and his conscientious attention to his task, he was remarkably dexterous. He could clack together coconut shells, adjust the arc lamp, and twist the lens of his machine for a finer focus all at once, without losing his air of modest but competent aplomb.

Now came a young woman in a flowing dress running slowly through a field of flowers, and the projectionist, reaching behind him, seized an atomizer and sprayed something into the air. A soft vernal perfume filled the theater, while the young woman reached her lover, who sprang from his horse into the flowers and embraced her. The projectionist had other atomizers for coffee (while breakfast was served in a boardinghouse), for a salty smell like seaweed (a ghostly schooner with silver sails crept out to sea), and a heady aroma of wine (some peasants, barefoot and the women holding up their skirts, climbed into an enormous wooden tub and began treading around on the grapes). There were no bad smells, Herma noticed. All the odors were pleasant ones. There was a scene in which a wisp of a man in baggy pants got Limburger cheese on the bottom of his shoe, and looked around to see where the smell was coming from. But the projectionist didn't have a perfume for this, and probably he valued his own dignity, and that of his theater, too highly to do so.

The winy odor gradually dissipated in the darkness. The Victrola needle descended again and there was Madame Schumann-Heink, singing the same lieder that Herma had memorized from her own Edison phonograph. The full-busted Diva faded spottily from view, and then reappeared as Brünnhilde in the climax of *Götterdämmerung*—singing the soprano role even though she was a contralto, perhaps because the Victrola ran a little too fast and made everything sound higher. The set was magnificent, even though it could be seen only indistinctly in the mass of shimmering black and white shapes. The vassals placed Siegfried's body on the pyre. Brünnhilde applied the torch, and the flames shot up. "O Wotan, hear me," she intoned through the horn of the Victrola. "On him, the hero who wrought your will, you laid the curse which fell upon him! Yet he must betray me, that all I might comprehend! Rest then, god!" The flames consumed the screen, while the orchestra thundered its apotheosis. To the strains of the Valhalla theme the light gradually faded.

The projectionist removed the arc light from the machine and set it on the table. A white illumination as bright as daylight filled the room. The spectacle was over. There was a wet sound like someone slapping two fish together. It was the old woman with the cat on her knees, clapping.

Herma got up and moved toward the exit. The projectionist was still at his place, making some adjustment to his machine. Even though he was intent on what he was doing, he glanced up as she passed. Their eyes met for an instant.

Herma paused. "Do you have many other operas? I'm fond of operas."

The young man hardly smiled at all. He was very serious. "Not at present. I'm expecting some from Los Angeles." After a moment in which he seemed to hesitate, he inquired, "Which do you prefer?"

"I'm fond of Puccini. Also Mozart."

"Next week I may have *La Bohème*. And also *The Marriage of Figaro*."

"The whole operas?"

"Oh no," he apologized. "Just the better-known arias. The reels we have at present last only for twenty minutes."

"Perhaps they'll invent a machine that will show a whole opera."

"Perhaps. In any case I can change the reels quickly. You'd hardly notice unless you turned around to watch me." Here he stopped, and seemed on the brink of a question. "If you could come back next week . . ."

"I'd love to."

She smiled; he remained serious. He seemed on the point of saying
something else, but evidently changed his mind. He stood with one hand
on his machine watching her as she went out the exit.

In the dazzling sunlight outside Herma paused. Everything was
exactly as before. The peasants treading grapes, the man falling down
the stairs, and the *Götterdämmerung* had all dissolved into the air; they
were only shadows, in fact, even though they were shadows ingeniously
and magically charged with electricity. She turned back to look at the
theater once more. She was only a few steps from the mirrored column,
the velvet stocking of which now began to stir and agitate as though
something was working its way through it. A hand appeared with out-
stretched fingers, then the arm in its sleeve-protector. Herma allowed a
pleased smile to creep over her face, since the owner of the arm was behind the mirror and couldn't see her. She took the hand and shook it.
The fingers didn't insist; they released hers after only a second. The arm
disappeared back into the column. Herma walked back up Main Street
and turned the corner onto Fourth.

It was still only four o'clock. Papa came home from the *Blade* office
only at seven, and supper would be at seven-thirty. She had a quarter
and a nickel left in her reticule. She went into Q. R. Smith's Palace of
Drugs and seated herself on the high wire stool in front of the marble
counter. The boy, who was polishing the marble with a damp rag, stopped
and looked at her questioningly.

"I would like," she said, "a scoop of lemon vanilla, in a goblet, with
a strawberry on top and apricot glaze."

The boy adjusted his cap and turned to the row of frosted tubs
behind him. "Lemon vanilla?"

"That's right."

He inserted the scoop of ice cream deftly into the goblet, set it on
the counter, and took out the jar of apricot glaze, thrusting a spoon
into it.

"No," said Herma. "First the strawberry."

"First the strawberry?"

"The strawberry first."

He took out the strawberry in his fingers.

"Point upward," she instructed him.

With a glance at her he set the strawberry onto the dome of ice
cream point upward, then poured the thin translucent varnishlike glaze
over it until it covered everything. He added a spoon and a paper napkin.

"Anything else?"

"That's all. Thank you very much."

Forgetting to mop the counter, he watched her as she ate it. This
Herma did in a leisurely but systematic fashion. At first she only brushed
the spoon lightly around the edges of the ice cream, barely touching the
amber glaze that clung to it. When she had gone around the goblet several
times in this way she dug in more deeply, crushing one side of the dome
so that the strawberry tipped and slid toward the spoon. Still she was

skillful and righted the strawberry again by digging a hole on the other side. The mixture in the goblet gradually turned to a pale luminous substance as soft as honey. In the middle was the strawberry, exactly the same color as the ribbon in her hair. Herma was careful to stretch out the climax as long as possible. At the last moment, with a confident gesture, she descended on the strawberry and devoured it. Then she scooped out the last of the melted ice cream and licked the spoon.

The boy was still watching her. "Say, that looks good," he said.

14.

Dr. Violet got his chloral and other medications that were necessary to him from Q. R. Smith's in wholesale lots, under the allegation that he passed them along to the various patients under his treatment. He was thoroughly familiar with pharmaceutics and had made a special study of calmants, sporifics, and stimulant tonics. Chloral, a clear and limpid fluid discovered by Liebig in 1831, was to be particularly recommended as a valuable agent inducing sleep and quieting stages of excitement. However, if taken regularly it induced melancholy in the patient, along with enfeeblement of the will, muscular lassitude, and inability to secure the sleep it promised, making necessary a progressive increase in the dose. Ten grains a day was said to be a prudent limit.

Dr. Violet had gone far beyond this point. He took sixty grains a day, an enormous dose, so that in the summer he sweated chloral from every pore. And he did not restrict himself to this single pharmaceutical, otherwise his good friend Q. R. Smith might have become suspicious. Dr. Violet had learned to vary his diet. A grain of digitalis now and then did no harm, and if necessary he injected a little caffeine into himself, which produced on the nerves the effect of an electric battery. In this way addiction to any one medicine was unlikely, and he only became addicted to them all in a general way, which was perhaps less harmful, or at least a less pointed and immediate problem for him to think about. Not that he spent a great deal of his time thinking; even though he had possessed, in his youth, a powerful intellect. At times he was so full of chloral, veronal, bromide, opium, paregoric, laudanum, and morphine that he could scarcely focus his eyes on the phial to see what he was taking next, and had to stick himself with pins in order to avoid slipping away altogether—and permanently—into the shadows. "For," as he told himself, "just as morphine is an antidote for pain, so pain is an antidote for morphine."

Yet even under these conditions he retained a keen intelligence and awareness of what he was about, so that he seldom made a mistake in a diagnosis or a course of treatment. If a certain number of his patients died, well so did everybody's. Man was mortal, his stay on earth was short, nasty, and brutal, and he was born to suffer as the sparks fly upwards. In Dr. Violet's own opinion he was far too conscious most of the time; unnecessarily so. There was very little to be aware of in this part of the world anyhow, and most of the time he lay under the burden of an excruciating and crushing boredom. It was a cruel stroke of fate that had condemned him to live out his life in this sun-kissed backside of the world, where everybody went to bed at nine o'clock and the chief entertainment was singing hymns on Sunday. There weren't even any interesting diseases. In such a one-horse town what could you expect? Nobody had enough money to get sick, and besides they were all as healthy as oxen. Violet had missed his destiny. He was born out of time in an alien land, condemned to wrest cornflowers out of a soil that should have provided him with orchids. In the Paris or Vienna of the epoch—or better yet in some place like Shanghai—he might have fitted in and flourished, giving full rein to his talent for the most exquisite and refined forms of decadence. One could imagine him, in such a stimulating milieu, another Wilde or Sade—an oriental Caligula—a necrophile of genius like Poe. As it was he took chloral, examined schoolgirls, and read medical books. He took down a dusty and battered volume of pathology and opened it to the chapter on tumors. There were illustrations in color, which was entertaining. He had examined them for only a little while when there was a knock on the door.

He opened, and a thin, pale, but determined-looking youth came in. They examined each other for some time in silence.

"I'm Fred Hite."

Violet nodded abstractly, as though it were a thing he knew perfectly well but didn't wish to be impolite by saying so. Fred began unbuttoning his trousers.

"Bin to Cantamar I expect."

Fred said nothing. He went on taking off his clothes, except for the shirt which he left unbuttoned. Dr. Violet gazed at him with a detached curiosity, as though he were something displayed in a medical theater. He seemed not surprised by what he saw, not even particularly interested, just observant. "Each individual is jus a lil bit different," he said after a while. "Come over here by the sink."

Without bothering to take off his coat, he first dipped Fred's manhood into a searing basin of permanganate. Then, grinning maliciously and taking up some kind of medieval torture instrument, he injected some other fluid, perhaps sulphuric acid, far up into the thing.

"That ought to do it. Although," he said, "you might have to have a nother treatment in a week or so." He seemed to reflect, and then he said, "You got a beauty there all right." It was not clear whether he referred to the afflicted member or to its malady. He told him, "I used to get quite a bit a pussy when I was your age. My experience is you don't necessarily have to pay em. And furthermore," he went on, "you sometimes get more when you don't pay em than when you do. And then too," he said, thinking further, "you're not so likely to get something nasty like this. Although that sometimes happens too."

Except for his name, Fred had not said a word from the time he entered the office. Now, his teeth clenched, he gritted, "Spare me your reminiscences. Is that all?"

Violet gazed again at the now-empurpled genitals. "Usually," he repeated, "you get more when you don't pay em than when you do. But even when you pay em, you've got to watch out. The thing is, don't let em work on your sentiments. They're good at that. If you let em," he continued, "they'll turn you into a lil baby. That's what they really like, lil babies. And they try to turn all men into em if they can. But," he concluded, "if you keep up a good line, and let em know who's in charge, you can get an awful lot a pussy for free."

"I'll remember that," said Fred, still suffering the agonies of the damned. He put his trousers on; even this was painful.

"That will be one dollar seventy-five."

"I thought it was two dollars."

"No, for office it's one seventy-five."

Fred gave him a dollar and three quarters, put on his hat, and headed for the door.

"Don't let em work on your sentiments," Violet reminded him.

Fred slammed the door without answering. His footsteps could be heard rapidly descending the stairs to the street. Violet stood for a while as the buzz of a vast and grayish world played over by his only too keen consciousness. Going to the desk, he poured a half inch of colorless fluid from a phial into a not very clean glass and drank it off. Then he settled into the chair again with his book. This time he turned to a chapter explaining, with photographs, how to identify badly burned cadavers by their teeth.

15.

The dollar seventy-five in Fred's pocket had come from the chiffonier drawer, where he had earlier found Madame Modjeska's gold piece, rather than from any income of his own. By this time Herma was singing at weddings and other social events, and earned a dollar here and two dollars there—"a real professional," as Mrs. Opdike said. It wasn't long before she had saved twenty-five dollars, planning, rather vaguely, to buy herself a party gown with it, or to use it on a shopping expedition with Mama to Los Angeles. But Fred found the money in the chiffonier drawer, and spent it on a bicycle.

It wasn't just an ordinary bicycle. It was a Paramount Custom Racer, with a spring-mounted frame and a Parson saddle so small that it was hardly larger than a glove. The handlebars were underslung, so that you rode the thing as though you were bent over looking for something on the ground, and the grips were wrapped with tape. The actual price was twenty-three fifty, but Fred also bought a French racing cap and a pair of gloves with the fingers cut out. The Paramount came from Vico's Cycle Works, on Spurgeon just around the corner from Main. There were two bicycle shops in town, and Vico's dealt exclusively in specialty and custom machines. Vico himself, a morose and fiery Italian who had once been a racing cyclist, explained to him how to take care of and adjust the Paramount.

The front sprocket, attached to the pedal crank, was large. It drove the chain which, at the rear end, transmitted the driving force to a light-weight planetary transmission, with drums and bands for shifting. This gearshift mechanism was temperamental, even though it was an elegant piece of design. The bands had to be just so tight, and you could only get them right by trial and error. Then too, the rear wheel alignment was not done simply by loosening the axle and sliding the wheel in and out of the work, as on other bicycles. The chain tension was critical for proper operation of the planetary shift. So the whole affair—rear wheel, sprocket, and shift-box—was aligned longitudinally by an arrangement of shims so that it could be adjusted to a tolerance of five-thousandths of an inch. Fred was provided with a feeler gauge, a collection of wrenches, and a small can of oil. Vico shook his hand. He put on his racing cap with its violet and white squares, turned up the visor, and rode away.

Fred's attachment to his machine was immediate, intimate, and powerful. It gave him mobility, and an exhilarating sense of speed, but this was far from all. There was something to it of the mystique of the mechanical, a thing which he had a feeling for, and understood instinctively, from the beginning. He meditated on the matter as he raced down the back roads of Orange County, shoulders bent low and rear end high, with the dirt flying by underneath in his frame of vision. The power and fascination of the bicycle, he eventually concluded, came not from its speed or lightness, or any of its qualities taken singly, but from a complex and interworking mélange of qualities that made it, in the end, more than the sum of its parts and elevated what was only a mere machine into the realm of mystery. These qualities were as follows:

1. No other machine is divided into sexes. It fits intimately into the human body, as though designed for it.

2. It stays up by magic. One might *dream* of riding a bicycle and staying upright, but it seems impossible in real life.

3. The sprocket goes round, and the rear wheel goes round, but they are not partners in the task but master and slave. The rear wheel, the slave, is compelled to go round because it is fastened by a chain to the sprocket, its master. The rear wheel goes round much faster than the sprocket, which is only showing the rear wheel how to do it. The sprocket (the master) can stop whenever it likes, but the rear wheel has to go on turning.

4. As for the front wheel, it only chooses the direction the bicycle is to go, not the speed. The front wheel applies no force. It is a kind of free agent, an artist. If it should turn too sharply, the whole thing will fall down. But if it doesn't turn a little now and then, the whole thing will fall down anyway.

5. It is strenuous and yet restful. You run while you are sitting down, and yet you go ten times as fast with the bicycle as you would without it.

These reasons were not mechanically exact, perhaps. That is, they didn't really describe the bicycle in terms of the laws of physics. They were akin to the reasons one gives for being in love with a certain person and not another. They meant nothing in the end, but they accounted in Fred's own mind for the attachment he felt for his machine. Soon he was spending most of his afternoons on the bicycle, which he hid in the thick shrubbery of the backyard on Ross Street when it was not being used. From there he pitched it over the fence into the alley, and he was on his way. His thigh muscles ached at first, then grew stronger, then ached again, and finally hardened until he was driving the Paramount faster and faster and yet feeling no fatigue.

After a few weeks he had explored the whole county on the long roads through the citrus groves, most of them unpaved. In one of his favorite routes he pedaled the three miles up Main to Chapman Avenue, then east on Chapman through the small town of Orange, and on into the foothills to the County Park, a sylvan grove of live oaks with a creek running through it. This route continued on to Santiago Canyon, on a narrow road that was hardly more than a trail through the hills. The Paramount with its spring suspension flew easily over the stones and potholes. Coming out of the hills at El Toro with its prim white-painted schoolhouse, he raced back through the orange groves and into town again along Santa Clara Avenue—as it was called, although at this time it was really only a cow path full of ruts.

Or, alternatively, he might ride in a half an hour or less to the beach. This route started down Main Street, angled off to the right on Maple for a while, then continued on past the sugar factory and Angel Town along a dirt road that came out onto the coast at Newport. Here he would park the bike to walk out on McFadden Wharf and watch the schooners unloading lumber from Oregon and taking on lemons and bags of sugar so that (one could imagine) the lumberjacks in Oregon could drink lemonade. The beach route came back through Fairhaven—a land boom that had gone bust, and now consisted only of six dusty houses and a collection of unpaved streets—and so into town along Main again.

A third route took him ten miles or so to Anaheim, another small town even sleepier and more dusty than Santa Ana, since it had not had the good luck to be made a county seat. This town had been founded a half-century before by German settlers, who gave it its rather naive and homespun name. There was a Lutheran church and an odor of Apfel-küchen, and men in collarless shirts looked at Fred dourly. Anaheim had its own S. P. station, which looked something like a Hansel and Gretel house in a storybook, with gingerbread trim and an arbor with an ancient grapevine growing over it to shade the waiting passengers.

Here, on one memorable occasion, Fred found the 3:22 from Los Angeles just pulling out on its way to San Diego and raced it a little way out of the station; for a mile or so the tracks ran parallel to the road.

Through the glass windows he could see the passengers looking out at him, in idle curiosity, or some perhaps in admiration. He was conscious of the audience as he bent low over the handlebars. For a while he was able to accelerate faster than the heavy train; he passed it up and left the locomotive far in the rear. But as it gathered speed, it quickly began to eat up the distance that separated them.

Glancing around, Fred saw that it was only a hundred yards behind. Ahead was the place where the road turned and crossed the tracks diagonally. He bent over and pedaled with every ounce of his strength. By this time the Paramount was doing perhaps twenty miles an hour. The iron monster behind him was capable of sixty or more. He felt a keen excitement, enhanced by the very real sense of peril. His heart pounded and the blood shot through his veins like wine. Live dangerously, as some German philosopher had advised! The Paramount flew like a shot across the tracks and an instant later the train, still gathering speed, thundered over the crossing, missing him only by a few feet. The white faces of the passengers watching him fled past and were gone.

The locomotive, drawing the cars after it, racketed away down the lane between the orange groves. Fred stopped, putting down a foot, and looked after it. With his interest in all forms of machinery he felt a considerable admiration for the train as a technological accomplishment. Through his ingenuity, man was no longer at the whim of a horse or the wind. He trapped the wind and put it into the boiler of his machine, paved the road with iron bars, and it darted over the countryside, carrying with ease not only crowds of people but the heaviest loads, from barrels of flour to elephants. As the newspapers were fond of pointing out, it ushered in a new age of prosperity, carrying citrus fruit from Santa Ana to Weehawken and Baltimore and bringing back manufactured goods from the East, thus improving the standard of living of the local ranchers and eventually himself and his family.

But what was a train to a bicycle! For one thing, it was not capable of staying upright on two wheels—that magic permitted only to the one vehicle fitted intimately to the human form. But far more important, in Fred's estimation, was the fact that the train, for all its power and prepotence, was condemned to follow along meekly wherever the tracks led it. It could be switched from one track to another, if the men who controlled it chose, but once on the track it was locked helplessly to the rails by the grooves in its own wheels. Like the rear wheel of the bicycle, it was a slave. Whereas the bicycle itself, guided by its owner, was free to go wherever his will or whim led him—effortlessly, at lightning speed, and with an intense sensation of pleasure exceeded only by one other thing. With two feet on the ground he was only mortal. The Paramount enforked, he became a god—if not to others, at least in his own mind. And that was all that mattered.

But that was before he found out about aeroplanes.

16.

Fred was an avid reader; Herma was not. When he was not riding his bicycle he spent a good deal of time in the Santa Ana Public Library, a small Spanish-style building with a tiled roof, on Sycamore at the corner of Fifth. Inside it was cool and quiet; usually there were not very many patrons in the daytime. There he sat, one spring afternoon, lost to the world and poring over a recent issue of *The Scientific Gentleman.* An aeroplane, the insight struck him with the force of a revelation, was only a bicycle redivivus—the Apotheosis of the bicycle. The Wright Brothers were bicycle mechanics. An aeroplane was only a bicycle with a set of canvas sails sticking out of it on either side, a gas engine such as could be found in any garage, and a whirling screw to propel it through the air instead of pedals. It was even driven by a bicycle chain. He studied the article more carefully, going back over it to read it again from the first.

Our correspondent has informed us of the successful test on December 17, at Kitty Hawk, North Carolina, of the flying machine constructed by the two young Dayton inventors Wilbur and Orville Wright. Four flights were accomplished in a single morning, against a twenty-one mile wind, starting from level with engine power alone. The average speed through the air was thirty-one miles an hour, and the longest period of remaining free of contact with the ground was fifty-nine seconds.

The machine is driven by a special four-cylinder gas engine envisioned and constructed by the Wrights themselves. The cylinders are four inches in diameter and the piston travel is four inches. The propulsion mixture is ignited by means of a magneto, and the rotating motion of the engine is transmitted to counter-rotating air-screws through a chain and sprocket arrangement. The operator controls the machine in prone position. Extending rearward from the center of the car is a double rudder of canvas stretched upon a frame of wood. A forward elevator-vane is provided for guidance, and the machine is tilted to effect turns, in the manner of a bicycle, by an arrangement of cables which warps the air-planes. Our correspondent has been able to provide the photograph below showing the machine rising from its monorail.

In the manner of a bicycle. A machine which does things possible only in fantasy, a machine which is controlled by lying down and gripping the crucial parts with the body, a machine in which the force of imprisoned fire makes effort unnecessary, and a machine which finally rises effortlessly from the ground and mounts into the air, exactly as in a dream. Fred became aware of moisture in his palms; he was getting the magazine damp. There was a film of sweat on his upper lip, too. He looked around to see if anybody had noticed. The room was empty except for

the librarian Miss Elmira Cliff, a spinster with a bun who was pasting cardboard pockets in books. Leaving the magazine open on the table, he got up and went out in a kind of trance.

Outside the sun was shining brightly. After the cool shade of the reading room it made him blink; the mundane reality of the small dusty town pressed down upon him and drove away, almost, the fabulous memory of the picture in the magazine. Feeling a little odd, he mounted his bicycle, but when he put it in second gear it slipped. He got off patiently, propped it against a tree, took his wrenches and his feeler gauge out of the tool kit hanging behind the tiny saddle, and spent a conscientious ten minutes adjusting the bands. Then, leaving the tools on the grass, he rode around in a circle to test it. Shifting into all gears, he found them properly adjusted. He went back to pick up his tools and put them away in the tool kit, then he rode off at high speed down Main Street in the direction of the beach.

He passed the Yellow Dog, swerving around and cutting in ahead of it easily, and sped on past the sugar factory and the flower-spangled houses of Angel Town. His legs drove like pistons. He didn't slow at Newport, or at East Newport where he made a spectacular curve around a wagon that was backing up to unload some barrels at McFadden's Wharf, and he kept on going past the Pavilion. In only a little over a half an hour after he had left the library he braked to a stop before the Great Pacific Traveling Exposition, with its sagging blue and gray tents and its signs in gaudy colors.

He leaned the bicycle against the Kotton Kandy booth and locked it. Then he went in. Pulling down the visor of his violet and white racing cap and sticking his thumbs in his back pockets, he strolled around through the gaudy booths and concessions as though he were wandering at random. There was only one thing he had come to see, and he knew what it was. But the Exposition was laid out in a confusing pattern of circles and crisscrossing lanes, and it was easy to get lost. It was impossible to get a view of the whole thing at one time, and the concessions resembled one another so that you might look at the same thing twice and realize only after you had been standing there for some time that you were repeating yourself.

Besides, some of the concessions were distracting, and he found himself standing before them, bemused, and forgetting what he had come to see. There was the Underwater Ballet, Mr. Revery the photographer who made you look like anybody you wanted, and the Villes Imaginaires, a magic-lantern show of cities that never were and never could be. The Eye Collector had the largest collection of glass eyes in the world, three thousand four hundred and nine. It was not clear where he got them. Did he have them made expressly? Did he murder people to get them? It was more likely that he obtained them from undertakers, for a price. Fred was not very interested in this exhibit.

There were many more things to see and Fred didn't have time for them all. He passed by the Musical Vegetable, a man with no arms and legs who played the violin, and Madame Titicaca, the Lady Who Was Tattooed on the Inside. Professor Roentgen Mirador, who claimed to hold a diploma from the Sorbonne, presided over a Hall of Mirrors that hummed like an electric streetcar. When people went into it you could see their internal organs and even clear through them. Rumor in Santa Ana had it that there were those who had gone inside and never returned; they had dissolved into the mirrors. Fred didn't believe that, but he wondered what happened to you when you were inside and what it felt like when people were looking through you. But the Hall of Mirrors was the most expensive of all the concessions, fifty cents, and anyhow it wasn't what he had come to see.

It took him some time to find it, after he had wandered back and forth on the crisscrossing lanes of the Exposition for some time. It was at the end of a lane, a kind of a dead-end street, with nothing but the sand of the beach behind it. It was odd that he hadn't noticed it before; it was certainly conspicuous enough. In shape it was like a silo of canvas on a framework of poles, twenty-five or thirty feet high and open at the top; from the outside nothing could be seen, and there was only a racket from behind the canvas, a hissing and heavy thumping as though someone were subduing a great serpent. The sign said simply

FLYING MACHINE

in large block letters, and below, in smaller letters, ''F. Gambrinus, Prop.'' The canvas was covered with pictures of legendary and fanciful flying apparatuses, and a kind of mast or derrick projected from it at the top.

Fred walked around looking at the pictures. There were fantastic flying machines of all sorts: ornithopters, inflated footballs propelled through the air by screws, carriages with balloons supporting them, a man in a black dress suit and top hat shooting skyward on a steam rocket. Another contrivance had a boat body with wheels and hinged wings, with an arrangement of cords to make them flap. From his reading in *The Scientific Gentleman* Fred recognized Le Bris's Artificial Albatross,

Cayley's flying carriage with its bird body and whirling disks, the orni-
thopter of De Groot, Henson's Aerial Steam Carriage, and Von Siemen's
gunpowder-powered rocketcraft. The circular display, he now saw, was
arranged according to historical principles; beginning with improbable
machines belonging entirely to the world of fantasy, carriages drawn
through the air by swans and so on, it progressed through Cayley, De
Groot, Henson, and Von Siemen to Chanute's glider, which actually
existed and had carried a man aloft, even though at the caprice of the
winds and only for a short distance. At the end was Lilienthal's expensive tandem-winged failure, which had collapsed into the Potomac and
almost drowned its operator.

When he came around to the front of the canvas structure again the
noise from inside had stopped and Gambrinus himself was now standing
by the ticket booth. He bore himself with great dignity even though he
was only about four feet tall. He was dressed in a frock coat, striped
pants, and an old-fashioned beaver in the style of at least a half century
before: a gray furry hat, somewhat cylindrical in form, but tapering
outward so that it was wider at the top. On his small applelike face was
a mustache and a short Imperial. His copious eyebrows were turned up
at the ends, giving him a cunning and slightly Mephisphelean look in
spite of his kingly bearing. In the ticket booth behind him was his
daughter Marmora.

"How much is it?"

Gambrinus turned, as though noticing him for the first time, and
contemplated his thin and intent face, his knickers, and his bicycle cap.

"A quarter. Twenty-five cents. A fourth part of a dollar."

"Can I look at it first?"

"No."

"I just want to look at it."

"I am not a philanthropist, my friend. I am a businessman."

"How does it work?"

"You'll see that after you've paid your quarter."

"Is it like any of the machines in the pictures?" Fred pointed to
the painted canvas behind the dwarf.

"No. It's more modern. It's in accordance with the latest scientific
developments. Also," he added, "it works, which none of these did."

"It works by steam," suggested Fred, guessing from the sounds and
odors that proceeded from behind the canvas.

Gambrinus said nothing.

"Does it maintain controllable free flight?"

Another silence.

Fred gave up. "All right." He reached in his pocket for the quarter
and held it out. But Gambrinus stepped aside, not deigning to soil his
hands with money, and it was Marmora who took the quarter, giving him
in return a piece of cardboard with a hole punched in it and the words
"Flying Machine." She was taller than her father, but still came only
to Fred's shoulder. Her face was heart-shaped, with large fawnlike eyes
and a small chin. Her face was pale as marble, but with a touch of color

flaring in the cheeks, as though she were slightly feverish. Everything was childish about her except for her mouth, which was round and full as a woman's. A strand of her long silky hair had strayed down onto her shoulders. She wore black tights, a close-fitting black jersey with a low neck, and dancing shoes. Hanging from her neck was a small golden heart on a chain so fine it was almost invisible.

She said nothing. Fred took the ticket and followed Gambrinus in through the canvas.

As it happened two other customers were waiting. Gambrinus evidently collected three or more of them inside the canvas before he started up the machine. This was because, as Fred had surmised, it was steam-operated and took a certain time to set in motion. The contrivance in the canvas silo was made, for the most part, out of a Stanley Steamer motor-car engine and an old iron chair. A length of gas pipe was welded vertically to this assembly, and at the top of the gas pipe was a pair of large fans like those used to discourage flies on a ceiling, except that the blades were ten feet or more in diameter. Through the gas pipe ran a fine steel cable, attached at the bottom to the floor and at the top to a derrick thirty feet or more in the air. There was a crackling of wood burning, and a medicinal smell of steam and oil—the boiler was fired with eucalyptus logs, which accounted for the odor. From the boiler to the flying machine ran a rubber hose with a valve in the middle.

The first customer, a young man in a shiny black suit and clerical collar, got into the chair and was buckled fast. Gambrinus verified the pressure gauge on the boiler and checked the safety valve. Then he picked up the hose and turned the throttle valve in the middle of it. The two fans began rotating in opposite directions. They whirred and turned into a blur. The engine emitted steam and a noise like a ripsaw. The machine bumped and bounced, then uncertainly moved upward, in fits and starts, until it reached a point some halfway up the wire. The young man in the clerical collar looked somewhat alarmed; he stared down from the chair to see how far away the ground was. But there was no turning back once you were strapped in the chair and Gambrinus had the valve in his hand. Gambrinus, dropping the valve temporarily onto the floor, threw another log in the boiler. The young man in the clerical collar was made to mount almost to the top of the wire, his face paler and paler. Then he came down in jerky fashion, plunging three feet or so down and then bouncing upward again before descending another step. The landing, however, was gentle; Gambrinus with fine touches of the valve brought the whole heavy business to the floor like a feather.

Next it was the turn of a serious gentleman in a pince-nez, who had the air of someone subjecting himself to a scientific experiment rather than treating himself to an amusement, and was perhaps an engineer interested in keeping up with the latest developments in aerolevitation. In view of his maturity Gambrinus did not take him up quite so high. The machine reached a point approximately halfway up the wire, and wavered there for three minutes or so while the gentleman in the pince-nez, evidently, took mental notes. The business of bringing the thing down was not as easy as it looked at first. This time Gambrinus' hand slipped on the valve, and the machine fell heavily to the ground from an altitude of perhaps a foot. The pince-nez fell off and the gentleman turned red. Gambrinus did not apologize, any more than a surgeon might for an unsuccessful operation. He hardly even glanced at the gentleman in the pince-nez. Instead he turned to Fred, with a small and distant bow.

Fred sat down in the iron chair. Gambrinus buckled him in and then went back to the valve. The eucalyptus fire was crackling hotly now. Fred felt himself rising, and to his surprise was hardly conscious of the noise of the Stanley engine. There was a great rushing and thrumming from the vanes over his head, and a powerful down-draft. The engine was under the chair, the iron seat of which it warmed considerably. A jet of steam shot out from between Fred's ankles, which he was careful to hold apart. And yet the whole contrivance gave the impression of lightness, of grace, in spite of its iron weight and the roaring of boiler and engine. To his surprise Gambrinus didn't take him very high, hardly higher than he had the gentleman in the pince-nez. Fred felt a sense of disappointment as the machine descended in its jerky way and touched down onto the floor.

Gambrinus left the valve partly open, however, and the fan blades went on turning overhead. Fred now saw that Marmora had left her post at the ticket booth and was standing at the entrance to the canvas. Her ankles crossed, one hand on the canvas, she licked her lip at one side with an air as though she were waiting for something—like a dancer, perhaps, waiting in the wings for her cue.

Gambrinus did not unstrap Fred. Instead he seemed to look to Marmora for advice. A three-way glancing of eyes took place: Gambrinus looked at Marmora, Marmora looked at Fred, and Fred looked from one to the other. Fred was not sure what was happening. Finally Marmora nodded very slightly; her chin moved a fraction of an inch and then came upright again. Gambrinus picked up the valve, but instead of turning the lever he handed it to Fred.

The hose was quite long; it snaked around the edges of the canvas structure for fifty feet or more before it reached the boiler. It was more than long enough, Fred now saw, to reach to the top of the derrick. He moved the lever. The blades over his head slowed. It was the wrong way. He turned it the other way, and the rushing of wings over his head mounted to a higher pitch. This time the machine stirred, bumped once or twice, and rose into the air. With the valve partly opened the thing rose to about the middle of the wire before it slowed and hovered. When he himself held the throttle, Fred found, the sensation was entirely different than when Gambrinus had worked the valve. Before there was only the moderately exhilarating sensation of mounting into thin air; now he had all at once the sense of controlled flight, of power and freedom, of transcending the mundane laws of physics that limited other men. A touch of his fingers and he mounted; another touch and he settled. The warm seat and the trembling iron pipe at his back gave the impression that the machine was a living creature, or more precisely that *he himself* was the living creature whose powers had been miraculously extended by this contrivance of iron and fire. His own body trembled with the vibration of the thing, and the jet of steam hissed from between his legs. He and the machine were one. It was an extension of his body, but instead of making the body heavier it made it light as a feather and at the same time enormously powerful. If it were not for the wire fixed to the crane at the top, Fred felt, he might soar away until he became only a speck to Gambrinus and the others watching him from the ground.

Gambrinus showed no impatience, and made no gesture suggesting that he should bring the machine down. He only watched, tilting his beaver backward to look at the steep upward angle. Fred descended several times, practicing landings. The first two or three were rough and he was afraid he might damage the machine. But it was stoutly built; it only emitted little puffs of steam as though it were protesting at this treatment. Finally, barely touching the throttle as though it were the key of some musical instrument, he settled onto the floor so imperceptibly that he hardly realized it had happened. Gambrinus didn't smile exactly, but his Imperial tightened and a wrinkle appeared at the sides of his mouth.

Fred tried a few more landings, then he decided to climb to the top of the thing and see how high he could go. There seemed to be plenty of pressure; out of the corner of his eye he could see the gauge on the steam boiler. He opened the throttle carefully, lifted past his previous stopping place at the middle of the wire, and continued on upward. Gambrinus watched him imperturbably. It was possible, Fred thought, that if the machine went too high the whirling blades might become entangled in the mechanism of the crane above, but surely Gambrinus would have warned him of this. With one eye on the dwarf he went on opening the throttle. He had passed the point now where Gambrinus had stopped the young man in the clerical collar, three feet or so short of the top. The edge of the canvas structure seemed to plunge up and down before his eyes. There were kaleidoscopic glimpses of the tops of tents, the Pavilion in the distance, and McFadden Wharf sticking out into the ocean. Finally he managed to steady the machine at its maximum height, well clear of the canvas screens.

He could see everything. Far in the distance, extending its snowy back into the sky, was the Sierra Madre. There were orange groves, hills, a cluster of trees that was Santa Ana, a smaller one that was Angel Town, and the stranded hulk of Cantamar where the ocean met the land. And then for some reason the machine did something it had never done before. Perhaps *he* did it in some way, by some adjustment he made, or some act of his will, but he was not aware of it. He felt himself turning, slowly and with total control. The horizon rotated like a clock. He saw in all directions. This was the world. He was above it, mastering it. It was all his.

Of course, it was necessary to uncoil in the other direction in order to free the machine of the twisting steam hose. This too he did without much difficulty. Then, finding himself lined up as he had been before, he closed the throttle slightly to descend. He looked around for Gambrinus, but he seemed to have disappeared. Marmora was still standing by the entrance to the canvas. As he settled onto the ground their eyes met, and she made a little smile. Then she looked away.

17.

As she had promised, Herma came back to the Electric Theater again the next week. She had been singing at weddings again, and she had a five-dollar bill and some change in her purse. But there was no one at the ticket office; that is, no arm came out of the mirrored column in the doorway to take her nickel. She went in and found the projectionist working with a frown of concentration at his machine, adjusting and oiling it. He stopped and wiped his hands carefully on a piece of waste. Then he introduced himself as Mr. Earl Koenig. He apologized for having taken the liberty of a handshake on the occasion of their previous meeting.

"It's quite all right."

She looked around the theater, which was totally empty except for the projector at the rear staring into the darkness like some kind of mechanical Cyclops.

"Do you have the operas?"

"Yes. I have obtained *La Bohème* and *The Marriage of Figaro* from Los Angeles, as I indicated to you last week." He had a rather formal way of speaking, perhaps simply out of shyness. He looked at her uncertainly, stroking his mustache at the side. "Would you like to see them?"

"Yes, I would."

There was a certain amount of awkwardness between them. But Herma's quick and cheerful acquiescence, her total lack of coyness, seemed to put him at his ease. There were no other customers. Mr. Koenig, in fact, shut and latched the doors and abandoned the ticket office so that from the outside the theater appeared closed. They smiled at each other. Herma took a chair immediately in front of the projector, and Mr. Koenig deftly ignited the arc lamp and inserted it into the machine.

There was a rhythmic clucking sound, and the usual fleeting white letters ran down the screen. Then the attic scene from *Bohème* appeared, and at the same instant Mr. Koenig lowered the needle onto the Victrola record.

The Parisian garret was almost dark. A shaky and indistinct Rodolfo touched the hand of a Mimì barely visible in the gloom. Then the moonlight shone from the window and the two figures could be seen more distinctly. "What a frozen little hand!" sang Rodolfo with feeling out of the Victrola horn. "Won't you let me warm it?"

Herma's hand strayed onto the Victrola table at her side. To her surprise—or rather, to tell the truth she wasn't surprised at all—another hand softly touched her own. It remained there throughout Rodolfo's rather lengthy explanation of who he was—"Qui son? Sono un poeta." Then Rodolfo fell silent, the orchestra played a few chords, and a soprano like a tiny squeezed thread began to come out of the horn.

> "Sì. Mi chiamano Mimì,
> ma il mio nome è Lucia.
> La storia mia è breve."

The flat a's, with just a hint of head voice, contrasted with the perfect silken and liquid roundness of the o's and u's. It was a pretty voice, even though it was so thin that it scarcely seemed able to force itself out of the Victrola. After a few bars Herma joined in and helped it. Her own youthful soprano, even though it was undeveloped and lacked body, easily overwhelmed that of the shaky Mimì on the screen.

A moment later she felt the other hand lifted from hers in the dark. She went on singing, a little disappointed. But Mr. Koenig had only taken away his hand to lift the needle from the Victrola record. The soprano and the orchestra were cut off, and there was only Herma's own thin and fluted voice working its way through the Puccini harmonies. She watched the screen, synchronizing her singing exactly to the movements of Madame Melba's lips. From time to time she darted a quick glance at Mr. Koenig; she could see his face outlined in the dim reflection from the screen. He was watching the screen intently, with an occasional glance at his machine to see if it was running properly. He seemed to have forgotten she was there, or perhaps he was embarrassed over having touched her hand. "Altro di me," she concluded on a clear and lingering D natural, "non le saprei narrare."

It was the end of the aria. Mr. Koenig, reaching to the Victrola, lowered the needle into the groove again at the exact place to rejoin the orchestra and the figures on the screen. Herma smiled to herself. She liked shy, gentle men who knew how to do things; she liked them because they knew how to do things, and because they were shy. The orchestra resumed its tinny imitation of Puccini's chords, and Rodolfo and Mimì embarked into the "Soave Fanciulla" duet. But Herma didn't join in with the Victrola anymore, and Mr. Koenig's hand didn't touch hers again in the darkness. The two voices blended together in the last strains of the ecstatic love duet. Then the last of the film flapped its way out of the projector.

She turned to watch Mr. Koenig deftly changing reels and lowering the needle into the groove again. Now it was the turn of Mozart. It was quite a different matter from the tawdry Paris attic. The setting was a magnificent palace in the baroque style, with rich hangings and elaborate bric-a-brac. Ladies and gentlemen in eighteenth-century costumes stood about singing with their hands on their hearts. Figaro sang his "Se vuol ballare" with great sarcasm, grimacing with narrowed lips out of the screen. The Count and Countess quarreled. People changed costumes, disguised themselves, and fell in and out of love from one aria to another. It was very elegant. Herma was fascinated by the graceful and girlish figure of Cherubino, in his tight-fitting breeches and his embroidered coat which swelled a little in the front. He had a short wig, well-fitting white stockings, and slippers with buckles. He took the coat off, however, to sing his Canzonetta, which Herma knew by heart as soon as she had heard it once. The pretty page begged the ladies to tell him what love was.

> "Voi che sapete
> che cosa è amor,
> donne, vedete,
> s'io l'ho nel cor."

The ladies evidently knew a good deal about the matter and offered him a number of suggestions. Herma now recognized Cherubino as the same Nellie Melba who had sung Mimì. But how transformed in her tight-fitting breeches and wig! It was difficult to make very much sense out of the plot from only twenty minutes of imbroglios and arias. But evidently everything came out all right. Susanna and Figaro were reunited, and the Count begged his wife forgiveness ("Contessa, perdono!"). Once again the end of the film flapped through the projector and the small theater turned white.

Herma stood up. Mr. Koenig was busy subduing the sputtering arc lamp. When it went out the theater was left in a kind of crepuscular half light. Mr. Koenig set the extinguished lamp on the table.

"Was my little hand cold?" she inquired with only a faint malice.

He didn't respond to this. He only colored a little. He cleared his throat and said nothing for five seconds or so. Then he said, "I wonder if I might proffer an invitation. If it is inappropriate, please say so and pardon the importunity."

Herma smiled. She wondered if he would ever be able to extricate himself from this elaborate language and speak to her naturally.

"Proffer?"

"Yes, proffer." He blushed again.

"What sort of invitation?"

Another pause. She waited gravely for him to speak.

"I have a small motorcar, and I thought we might perhaps take a spin around town. Or somewhere else," he added, as she went on looking at him with her slightly unsettling composure.

When she didn't answer he led the way out the rear door of the theater and into the alley. There, in an open shed, was standing a vehicle that looked something like a small buggy without any shafts for the horse. It had a certain elegance about it. The seats were of quilted leather; the body was polished mahogany, and there was a single acetylene headlamp in front.

"A Waverley Electromobile," he said.

"But where's the motor?"

He pointed out a kind of metal box on the rear axle.

"The motor is very small. The batteries are in a box at the rear. As you see, there's a rheostat by the operator's hand to control the electric current. The motor delivers five horsepower, which gives a road speed of from three to sixteen miles an hour."

Herma understood nothing of this, but went on looking pleasant. "How far will it go before . . ."

"Before the batteries are exhausted? Twenty or more miles."

It occurred to Herma that "a spin through town" might not be such a good idea, since Brother Goff or even Papa might happen to be out on Fourth Street and see them whirring silently by. It was not that there was anything improper about being with Mr. Koenig, but—Papa didn't approve of motorcars.

"Then will it go as far as the beach?"

He reflected for a moment. But he seemed to be reflecting not so much about the capabilities of his machine as about Herma. He gazed at her with a certain air of surmise. After a moment he said, "Of course."

They both smiled again. After another slightly awkward hesitation he handed her into the left side of the machine, where there was a little brass step for the foot. Then he got in on the other side and began fussing with the various levers and controls. There was a hum and the Waverley began moving backward. Once out of the shed he turned the rheostat the other way and they slipped smoothly forward, down to the end of the alley and out onto Main Street. In a few moments they were out of town on the country road to the beach.

The thing was steered with a tiller like a boat. Mr. Koenig kept one hand on the tiller and the other on the rheostat, which he adjusted when the Waverley mounted a slight rise or slowed to pass around a hay wagon. He seemed intent on his driving and kept his eyes fixed on the road ahead, without turning to look at Herma at his side.

It was a little after five. The sun had just set and a clear and warm, grayish air flowed over them as they rode along. The Waverley was so quiet that Herma could hear insects buzzing in the fields as they passed. She glanced at Mr. Koenig. In the transparent light of the dusk she was able to examine him carefully for the first time. There was a classic fineness about his profile. The brow was large, the other features even and symmetrical. His fine, rather sparse hair was the color of wheat, and it was exactly matched by the eyebrows and by the mustaches that drooped slightly at the corners. Although she hadn't noticed it before, he had put on a leather motorist's cap with a visor as he came out of the theater.

Although he kept his eyes fixed on the road he seemed aware that she was looking at him. "The tires are solid rubber so there's no danger of a flat," he said without turning his head. "The brakes are an improved kind, worked by friction pads pressed to the rear axle."

"It's a lovely motorcar."

"We're now going at about fifteen miles an hour. I don't have a speedometer, but I plan to have one installed."

This was his notion of how to make conversation with a young woman. However, like all conversations between two young people who

are alone for the first time—like the duet between Rodolfo and Mimì—
it had the air of really being about something else. Herma felt pleased
with herself. They had passed the sugar factory and Angel Town now
and were running along the road parallel to the beach. Ahead the spidery
legs of McFadden Wharf stuck out into the ocean, and the houses of
Newport and East Newport went by. Then, so quickly that Herma was
hardly aware of where they were, they came to the short cross street
with the beach at one end of it and the Pavilion at the other. Mr. Koenig
turned into the street and parked his machine at the side.

"Shall we get out?"

She smiled, and he came around to her side and handed her out onto
the wooden sidewalk.

He seemed uncertain. He looked about him, up and down the street
with its three hotels and the Pavilion at the end. Some of the windows in
the hotels were already lighted. In the gray twilight air everything
seemed altered and slightly enchanted.

"What would you like to do now?"

"I don't know."

"We could go for a walk."

Herma took thought and decided to be daring. "What I've always
wanted to do," she told him, "is dine at the Pavilion."

At this he looked alarmed. "I believe it's quite expensive."

"I'm sure it is."

He cleared his throat. "It's a little embarrassing. You see, if I had
anticipated it, it would be a pleasure . . . But the fact is, at the moment
I don't have enough with me."

"Well, I have."

"But I couldn't possibly—"

"Yes, you could. Anyhow," she pointed out blithely, "you didn't
charge me for a ticket at the theater. So we're friends, aren't we?" She
added playfully, "They always say it's the woman who pays."

"I don't think they quite mean that."

Still, he allowed himself to be led down the sidewalk past the hotels
to the large blue and gray building with the cupola on the top. Around
the line of the roof, high in the air, a row of electric bulbs shone like a
magic necklace. She slipped her hand into Mr. Koenig's elbow. He didn't
seem to notice.

A broad stairway at the center led upstairs to the dancehall. They
walked around this and into the restaurant. Inside the enameled double
doors a maître d'hôtel of great dignity was waiting, in a white jacket
with gilding on his sleeves like an admiral. He showed them to the table
by the window, and they were seated.

The large room overlooking the Bay was decorated in white enamel
boiseries with gilded trim. The chairs were in wine-colored velvet, and
the tables glittered with white linen and silver. On the walls were bracket
lamps in the forms of arms in classic drapery. Each arm held out a
candelabrum of small, dimly glowing Edison bulbs. The filaments shimmered slightly, lending the room and everything in it an insubstantial

or fairytale quality. In the distance a few lights shone on the other side of the Bay, sending broken beams to play on the black surface of the water.

Mr. Koenig was provided with a menu. He studied it for some time, and then inquired politely whether she cared for Poulet Reine Margot. Since he gave the impression that he perhaps didn't know what this was himself, she helped him out by remarking, "Yes, I'm very fond of chicken." He did know, however, that white wine went with fowl, and ordered a Moselle, which came in a silver bucket so cold it was veiled with frost.

At the sight of the bottle with its foreign label—she had never drunk wine in her life—a sudden thought struck her. "Excuse me," she said. Setting her napkin aside, she got up demurely and went to the maître d' standing at his post by the door.

"Is there a telephone?"

"Of course." With a bow he pointed down the corridor in the direction of the kitchen. There she found the telephone mounted on the wall, with a white enameled plate giving instructions for operating it. She picked up the receiver and held it to her ear.

"Number please."

"Santa Ana 131."

The telephone at home had been installed only a month or so before. Papa was not yet home from the *Blade,* and it was Mama who answered. She was still uncertain with the apparatus, and her voice came through only thinly and as though weakened by the distance.

"I've just had my lesson with Mrs. Opdike," said Herma, "and she's asked me to stay to supper."

"I see. Well, that's nice," said Mama vaguely. Then, thinking further, she said, "But Mrs. Opdike doesn't have a telephone."

"I'm calling from Q. R. Smith's," said Herma, plunging further into the lie.

"Well, that's fine, dear. Have a nice time, and be sure to offer to help Mrs. Opdike with the dishes."

Herma hung up the apparatus, feeling a little feverish. What would happen to girls like her, who went off on escapades with young men, and told lies to their mothers? Never mind; Mr. Koenig was a perfect gentleman, and the Pavilion was innocent enough. It wasn't as though it were something like Cantamar. Men! She made a little moue of disgust to herself. But Mr. Koenig, she was sure, would never go near such a place.

The dinner was a great success. They had a demitasse afterwards. When they had finished the tiny cups of coffee Mr. Koenig didn't get up. He sat there as though he were wrestling with a great moral problem which he wished to conceal from her. Herma saw that what afflicted him was the bill for the dinner, which was lying in a saucer on the table between them. As though it were the most natural thing in the world she reached into her purse and set a five-dollar bill in the saucer.

"I really . . ."

"No, *I* really."

With the wine inside her she was in excellent spirits and slightly audacious. The waiter, passing the table, spirited away the saucer and brought it back with the change. Mr. Koenig, after a moment's hesitation, left a quarter in the saucer. Then he pocketed the rest of the coins and they left.

Out on the sidewalk they had a friendly argument—he attempting to hand her back the money, and she refusing and pressing it back on him. Finally she stuck it in his coat pocket, her fingers as they came out brushing against the lean and pointed bone of his hip.

"Thank you for the dinner, Mr. Koenig," she said gravely.

"I wish you'd call me Earl."

"All right, Earl."

Their eyes met. With difficulty Herma suppressed a smile. He glanced around for possible spectators. Then, as they went on down the wooden sidewalk, his hand came out in the darkness and enclosed her fingers.

They passed the Netherlands Apartments and the Hotel Balboa with their lighted windows. Herma wondered what she would do if he invited her to go into one of the hotels. She hardly knew what she would have responded. But he seemed to have nothing of the sort in mind, or if he did he subdued the thought firmly. In fact, once they got back to the parked Waverley, he seemed more intent on his machine than on her, although perhaps this was only to cover his awkwardness. He pushed the tiller to one side, maneuvered out of the parking place, and then turned up the rheostat so that the Waverley glided off smoothly down the beach road back toward town.

When they reached Newport, however, he slowed.

"Perhaps you'd care for a little walk before we go back?"

"That would be lovely."

They got out. This was Old Newport, so called because it was the first town on the Peninsula, even though it had been built only about twenty years before: a small community of tents and wooden buildings clustered around the foot of McFadden's Wharf. They crossed the tiny square lined with storefronts. Everything was pitch dark. Across the square was the wharf with a double row of railroad tracks running out into it. Holding hands, they made their way along the tracks in the dark. There was a subdued crashing from the surf underneath. Far out ahead, at the end of the wharf, was a single white light.

Then the surf was behind them, and it was quiet. There was only the subdued murmur of the breeze, raising the ribbons on Herma's dress. The sea was black, almost invisible, only a wavelet flashing white here and there. A schooner from Oregon was tied at the wharf, but it was dark and there was nobody aboard. They continued slowly on past it.

Earl had taken her hand again in the darkness. Each time he did this absently, as though he were hardly noticing what he was doing, and when they came to a difficult place where they had to climb over the tracks he would release it again. It was a curious sensation. Something warm and sensuous flowed up Herma's hand and into her body, like a little current that was broken when the fingers separated. Once, when he seemed uncertain, she reached out for the other hand herself.

The wharf stretched far out onto the sea; it was, as Earl informed her with his command of figures, a quarter of a mile long, sixty feet broad at the end, and nineteen feet above the water. At the end there was a wooden post with a cross-brace at the top and a wire dangling from it. Suspended from the wire was a single large bulb the size of a fruit jar. A cloud of moths and other small insects bumped against the glass. The bulb swung slightly in the breeze, so that the white circle of light under it drifted and wandered on the planks.

They stopped exactly under the light. In the slightly rocking white glare they could see nothing of the shore; it was as though they were on a ship far out at sea. There was the sound of water washing gently underneath. Earl still held her hand. Then he turned toward her, taking her other hand too. She saw his serious face half in shadow from the light flooding down over it. It was a magic moment. A great romantic breeze blew through her, suffusing her blood with an excitement that was at the same time a quiet joy. She waited for him to make some sort of declaration or speak of his feelings. But Earl didn't seem to be romantic at all; instead he seemed to be struggling in the grip of a powerful animal urge. He wished to subdue this beastly part of him, and probably would, but only after great effort.

"Herma!"

"Earl . . ."

Evidently he took this first word as a question and the second as an answer, because he gripped her by the shoulders and kissed her fiercely. Herma moved forward and her body joined with his. The beast was there all right; it was even harder than his hipbone. An electric tingle, similar to the one produced by hand-holding but greater in intensity, passed from his lips to hers. When she allowed her lips to part, however, he broke away abruptly.

He got out in a muffled tone, "I respect you too much."

"Do you?" she said, seething inwardly.

18.

Fred stood naked before the mirror, examining himself intently, with particular attention to the chest to see if there were any signs of incipient hairs on it. It was a masculine form that he saw before him in the glass, but just barely. No hair on the chest; the body was slender and the hips almost straight. He was still pleased with himself. Herma, he thought, was more boyish than he was girlish. And besides, some intuition told him, there were women in the world who were attracted by this touch of grace, this slight suggestion of the androgynous.

Then he noticed a scrap of paper stuck into the mirror frame. On it, in a spidery feminine hand, he read, "Fred, the door latch is loose again. The door comes open and Mama and Papa are going to see you."

He glanced at the door behind him; in fact it was an inch or two ajar. Crumpling the note and dropping it into the wastebasket, he went to the bottom drawer of the chiffonier and took out a screwdriver, a tack hammer, and a small rat-tailed file. Then he went over to look at the latch.

It was a very simple mechanism. A square metal box fitted onto the door, with a fluted knob that you turned to set the latch. The steel tongue fitted into a slot in the door jamb, or more precisely into the striking plate with an oblong hole in it. But when the screws came loose the tongue wouldn't stay in place and slid out sideways. The trouble was that the screw holes from long overuse had become enlarged.

Still naked, he unscrewed the whole business and set the latch and the four screws on the chiffonier. Then he crossed the room to the nightstand and got a half-dozen burnt matches from the saucer under the oil lamp. He tapped these into the screw holes with the hammer, broke them off, and tapped in the broken ends as well. He chipped the ends smooth using the screwdriver as a chisel. Then he fitted the latch back into place and drove in the four screws, which now held tightly. The slot in one of the screws was badly chewed and he smoothed it off with the file. He also tightened the screws in the striking plate, which were only slightly loose. He closed the door and tried the latch. It worked perfectly.

Putting the tools away and going back to the mirror, he dressed himself in a white bicycle jersey and knickers and put on his French racing cap. With a final glance at his reflection in the glass, he went out, closing the door softly behind him. There was no sound from the bedroom across the hall where Mama was lying down. Outside he went to the bottom of the yard where he kept his bicycle, threw it over the fence, climbed over after it, and rode off to the library. Miss Elmira Cliff was used to him now and didn't even look up.

In the new issue of *The Scientific Gentleman* there was an article by a British engineer named Frederick W. Lanchester giving more details on the Wright flying machine, including drawings and precise dimensions. There was also more information about the control mechanism. The matter of the exact function of wing warping, which had puzzled Fred before, was cleared up.

Unlike previous machines such as the Voisin, which are designed to be automatically and inherently stable, in the Wright machine the lateral stability is under the direct control of the aeronaut. It is desirable to correct a false impression that is current on the action of the wing twist. It has been supposed by some that it is used to give the cant required by the machine when turning, but such is not the case. If the rudder is used, the machine almost immediately gets a cant owing to the greater pressure on the wing that in turning is moving faster through the air, and this cant becomes, if unchecked, far too severe. The twist is then used to check the cant, the wing on the outer circle—that is, farthest from the center of curvature—being 'feathered,' and the inner one having its angle of incidence increased. The wing twisting is effected by a system of cables, as illustrated.

The drawings showed how the operator, lying prone on the lower wing, controlled the cables by shifting his body left or right against a harness. With one hand he held the rudder stick, with the other the lever that adjusted the forward elevator. Fred studied all this intently. He imagined the sensations of lying down on the wing, fitting one's self into the harness, and gripping the two levers. Then, with the roar of the engine vibrating through it, the machine soared off into the wide and limitless sky. He slid his body back and forth on the library chair and imagined it pushing against the warping harness, left and right. On the table before him were the two levers, the rudder stick, and the elevator control. If you turned the rudder stick too sharply, the cant would be excessive and you had to correct by shifting the warping harness the other way. Miss Cliff stopped her work at the desk and looked at him sharply over the top of her Franklin glasses.

He shut the magazine with a snap, flung it onto the table, and went outside. A hot silence hung over everything; the trees were dusty, a cat was asleep on the library steps. He paced up and down on the lawn for a while. The details of the Wright machine swarmed in his head like bees, each one distinct and buzzing. Every word of the magazine article, every detail of the drawings, was fixed lucidly in his mind. At the same time he felt himself filled with an odd and powerful desire. It was very strange. At first the notion struck him that this urge might be satisfied with a visit to Cantamar. But this wasn't exactly it, and besides he remembered Dr. Violet's treatment. He felt in his pocket; he had a couple of quarters and a few other coins. He got onto his bicycle and rode off furiously down Main Street in the direction of the beach.

A half an hour later he parked the bike against the Kotton Kandy stand at the entrance to the Exposition. This time he knew his way through the maze of concessions and exhibits and made his way directly to the Flying Machine. But as he approached it he saw that something was changed. It was unusually quiet, and he had the impression that something that had been there before was missing. After a moment he realized it was the ticket booth.

There was no sign of anyone around. He started to push his way through the canvas flap to the inside, and met Gambrinus coming out.

"It's closed."

"Closed?"

"Yes. I have another business now."

Fred, still winded a little from the bicycle trip, felt a sense of cutting disappointment that surprised him in its intensity. He waited for Gambrinus to say something more, but the dwarf only stood there half in the canvas silo and half out, as though he were trying to block Fred's view of what was inside. There was no sign of Marmora.

"What is the other business?"

"It's an extension of my former enterprise," said Gambrinus with a Machiavellian craft, "only somewhat more technically advanced."

With similar stealth, Fred attempted to draw him out. "Is it a flying machine?"

The dwarf gazed at him narrowly.

"Are you able to keep a secret?"

"I believe so."

"I am not interested in your beliefs. You must swear."

"Very well. I swear," said Fred, a little amused.

"It is the first one of its sort," said the dwarf, "in this part of the world."

Fred waited for him to go on and explain more. But Gambrinus still seemed suspicious of him—or not suspicious exactly but dubious—or not dubious exactly but reflective, as though he were sizing him up and deciding whether he would do for some purpose or other. Evidently he decided he would, for after another moment of staring at him in silence he turned on his heel and led the way outside the silo and around to the rear of the canvas structure. Whatever it was, thought Fred, it was very small, because there was nothing there but a shed about the size of a piano case. Fred began to feel disappointed again.

The ticket booth was nearby, lying prone on the ground. Gambrinus opened the shed. After some fussing he led out a small dogcart; and in this case the appellation was no mere joke or metaphor, for in fact it was drawn by a sturdy and oversized Saint Bernard, who was called, with a singular lack of originality, Bernard. As for the cart, it was made out of wicker and resembled the gondola of a small balloon. It had brass fittings, ropes wound around the edges, and a polished wooden floor, but no place to sit. It was very old and worn; it gave the impression of an antique of some sort, or a ship in an old print.

They got in, Fred sitting on the wooden floor of the basket and Gambrinus standing with the reins in one hand and a gnarled old black stick in the other. With this he beat the dog, who paid no attention. He was about the size of an ordinary Shetland pony, and he seemed to have no will of his own; he was eternally cheerful, he was strong and tireless, and although he did not subsist on hay, he seemed in every other way to be under the impression that he was a horse. When he dunged, he did so not in the undignified way of a dog, but quite calmly like a pony, standing there between the shafts of the cart. Whenever he did this Gambrinus beat him with the stick, but Bernard paid no attention to this either.

They went off down the beach at a trot, Gambrinus steering the car out to the very edge of the surf where the sand was hard. It was only a little more than a mile to the end of the Peninsula. It was a lonely, deserted, and windswept beach. There were no houses this far down, although across the sea channel, on the bluff of Corona del Mar, someone had built a hotel which had finally collapsed and was abandoned.

However, as they drew closer Fred saw that there was a structure of some sort on the beach almost at the end of the Peninsula, one that he had never noticed before. The dogcart approached it rapidly. It was a kind of low barn or shed, shaped like a T, with large sliding doors on the front. It faced toward the sea, into the wind. In front of it a long wooden plank with an iron rail on top of it ran down the sloping sand toward the water. Fred's heart began to thump a little.

Gambrinus dropped the reins, clambered out, and unlocked the doors of the shed and pushed them open, grunting and straining at the task. He would not let Fred do anything. In any case Fred was too fascinated to do more than stand and look. He had already guessed what was inside the shed from its shape. But the thing was larger than he expected. The great wings, made of varnished linen stretched over beautifully fashioned frames of spruce, were more than six feet wide and forty feet long. Between them was an intricate spiderweb of bracing wires. The canard elevator stuck out in front so that the doors of the shed would barely close over it. The four-cylinder gas engine was mounted neatly on the lower wing, a little to the right of center to allow a place for the operator. Behind, in the gloom, he made out the eight-foot airscrews, cocked at an angle to fit under the roof of the shed.

He went inside and walked around it. Although Gambrinus would allow him to touch nothing, he was able to examine the controls at short range. The harness that enclosed the operator's body was a kind of wooden belt, with cables leading away on either side toward the wings. In front, at the edge of the wing, were the rudder stick and elevator lever. The whole thing smelled of varnish, of fine wood, and of engine oil. Fred made an effort to suppress his excitement. He took a breath, put his hands in his pockets, and came out into the sunlight again. He began interrogating Gambrinus with a studied casualness.

"What's this?"

"You can see what it is."

"Yes, but what's it for?"

"It's for anyone to fly who wishes."

"Anyone who wishes?"

"Yes. It's fifty dollars."

"Fifty dollars?"

The dwarf straightened his beaver hat and strutted around on the sand with an angry expression. "I'm a businessman, young man. I'm not a philanthropist. I earn my living by my enterprise. This machine is very expensive. And then I had to have it shipped out from Ohio, first by railroad to San Francisco and then by schooner to Newport. I am not an aeronaut. I have bought it on speculation, with the idea that the enterprising, courageous, adventurous youth of this part of the world will want to try their hand at it." Here he stopped, his angry expression disappeared, and he fixed his glance steadily on Fred's face.

"I'm interested, of course."

Gambrinus waited for him to go on.

"I think I could fly it. I'm familiar with the way the thing works. In theory at least."

"No doubt."

"For the steam machine you only charged fifty cents. For this you ask fifty dollars. That's a hundred times as much."

"It's very expensive, as I told you. I'm not a philanthropist."

He said nothing more, and there was a silence between them. While Fred stood watching with his hands in his pockets, Gambrinus pushed the big doors shut and fastened them with the padlock.

They got back into the dogcart and Bernard drew them rapidly away across the sand.

Gambrinus turned to him. "I don't suppose you have fifty dollars?"

Fred said nothing.

19.

Herma stood naked before the mirror, examining herself intently, with particular attention to the chest, to see if she could see any signs at all of swellings at the places where two small aureoles, the size of berries, were fixed on the flat and narrow surface. She thought she could make out a pair of slight convexities, if she stood at just the right angle, although perhaps they were only shadows. It was a boyish kind of figure. Still, she liked it.

Then she noticed a scrap of paper stuck into the frame of the mirror. In square blocky letters it said, "Tough titty. Your dude can project everything except what you want."

Crude-minded brute! She tore the paper off and threw it into the wastebasket. She found another piece of paper and wrote on it in her spidery hand. "O, Bird-Man. There's no money in the top drawer. So don't get your hopes up."

Still stark naked, she stuck this into the mirror. Then she went to the chiffonier for her drawers, flung on her white dress with the strawberry-colored ribbons, tossed her hair to shake the tangles out of it, glanced one last time into the mirror, and went out.

She went down Ross and turned left on Sixth, then right again on Sycamore. It was only five minutes to the tiny bungalow with the screened porch running across the front of it, shaded and cool under the trees. Mrs. Opdike's cat Amadeus was sleeping on the glider in the screened porch. Herma pushed open the door and went in without knocking.

Mrs. Opdike was at the piano, tinkling away at some Chopin or other. She was not an expert pianist, or musician of any sort, and didn't claim to be. "For," as she said, "all my heart and soul goes to my pupils, and it is through them that I give to the world my art." Still there was nothing pretentious about her, and she spoke of her music as another woman might speak about her cooking. There was, in fact, a housewifely quality about her attitude to music. She produced music as other women produced apple pies. She did her best, dusted the flour off her fingers, so to speak, and set it on the table. If anyone liked it, so much the better. She concluded the Chopin with a single plump finger on the E flat and said, "Hello, dear."

There was a placid and capacious quality about Mrs. Opdike. She wore flowered dresses and her face was pink, her hair pink too, so that she gave the impression of a large floral cloud sitting at the piano— where she almost invariably sat, unless someone else was playing it. To imagine Mrs. Opdike in bed, or eating dinner, or doing anything else than music, was unthinkable. Mrs. Opdike was a floral cloud at the piano.

"We must buckle down today," she told Herma, "and work like a trooper." (One of her favorite expressions.)

"The Bell Song from *Lakme?*"

"No."

She was spreading another score out on the piano, a very large one. It was as thick as a book.

"Today instead," she said, "I want you to try something new. As you know," she went on, "the new French's Opera House is now being built, at Fourth and Bush. It will be a great contribution and it will enrich the cultural life of the community. And for the opening, which is only a few months away now, there will be a gala première, and do you know what the first performance will be?"

Herma didn't, so she told her, "*The Marriage of Figaro,* by Mozart. And the news, dear, which is not announced officially yet, is that a great Diva from the Metropolitan Opera in New York will be engaged for the lead, and people are contributing to a fund for bringing her here. I can't be sure yet, but it's possible it will be Albertina Moellendorf. She's the prima donna of the Metropolitan, and she receives two thousand dollars for a performance. Or so they say. Perhaps it will be somebody else, but it will certainly be a great soprano from the Metropolitan. Anyhow," she said, realizing that she was getting distracted in these dreams about La Moellendorf, "the other parts will be sung by artists from San Francisco or Los Angeles, except that local singers may be used when others aren't available, or if they cost too much. Do you know what that means, dear?"

Herma didn't know what it meant.

"It means that you must begin working right away, and practice night and day, and work like a trooper. Because some of the parts," she explained, "will be cast by audition."

She opened the score and flapped it out onto the music stand.

"W. A. Mozart
LE NOZZE DI FIGARO
Opera Buffa in Quattro Atti"

"And," she went on, "do you know the part you are going to sing? The part of Cherubino."

She flipped the pages over to the second act. "Tra, la la la la. Voi che sapete, che cosa è amor. I can't really do it because it's a mezzo part. Cherubino, my dear," she said, "is a boy. It's called a breeches part. Mozart often composed male parts to be sung by women. He liked curiosities of all kinds. He once met a singer called Lucrezia Agujari who was called La Bastardella. She could sing coloratura up to C in alt. That's a whole octave above high C, which is already a nightmare for most sopranos. He wrote the role of Queen of the Night for her and made her sing even higher, up to F in alt."

But she was getting distracted again, she realized. "Tamino in *The Magic Flute* is often sung by women. Now then, dear, this is the Canzonetta, which is the main aria for Cherubino in this particular opera. It isn't really very difficult." She struck a chord and, bending forward to peer at the score, embarked into the continuo accompaniment.

Herma pretended to look over her shoulder at the music, which she knew perfectly from hearing Madame Melba sing it at the Electric Theater. She slipped easily through the song.

"Voi che sapete
che cosa è amor,
donne, vedete,
s'io ho nel cor."

"Why, that's splendid, dear. It's as though you already knew it. You'll make a perfect Cherubino. If you were a boy, you'd be a counter-tenor. But since you're a girl you're either a soprano or a mezzo-soprano. You can do either, dear. Your versatility is prodigious. I've never contended that you have a great voice, Herma dear. It's a good voice, but the tessitura is prodigal. In this case," she said, "it's a mezzo part, so you'll have to sing mezzo. But that will be easy for you."

"Will I be dressed as a boy?"

"Of course. With a wig and tight breeches, and shoes with buckles. Pretending to be a boy is easy." And here she got distracted again and went off on one of her detours. "Men," she said, "make such a fuss about being a man. According to their view, nobody can do anything but them. But all they do is go around the world with all that hair on their faces, sticking their—noses into everything. The silly creatures."

"Have you tried it?"

"What, dear?"

"Being a man."

"No, but anyone can tell it's easy by watching them do it."

Herma had got to the point where she wasn't sure what they were talking about anymore, and neither, evidently, was Mrs. Opdike. She brushed it all off and flapped the score back to another place. "But you'll have to work like a trooper. You haven't got the part yet. There will be *many* fine voices at the audition. But you have perfect pitch.

And as I've always told your Mama," she said, "Herma can do *any thing* that she wants. And she will."

She tried her next on the little aria in Act One. "I no longer know what I am, what I do, now I'm all fire, now all ice." Herma read it blithely off the score, staying very slightly flat on the high notes to indicate the melancholy, but suffusing the melody nevertheless with the pure and sweet fervor of love. As she sang it seemed to her that she stood with Earl on the wharf with the sea washing underneath.

> "Non so più cosa son, cosa faccio;
> or di foco, ora sono di ghiaccio;
> ogni donna cangiar di colore,
> ogni donna mi fa palpitar.
> Solo ai nomi d'amor, di diletto
> mi si turba, mi s'altera il petto,
> e a parlare mi sforza d'amore
> un desìo ch'io non posso spiegar!"

Mrs. Opdike blossomed. "That's *very* nice. One might almost think you were a man who wanted to—love somebody. You are a prodigy, dear, and I've always said so. Someday you are going to be a famous opera star. But first you must work like a trooper on the part of Cherubino. Do you know why, dear?"

Herma thought she did, but she said, "No."

"Because, if you win the part in *The Marriage of Figaro,* it may be your one big chance. And even a person with talent, dear, may have only one Big Chance, so you must be sure to be prepared for it when it comes, and make it into a triumph. Even though," she went on, "it may mean that you will leave Santa Ana and go on to bigger things. For," she admitted, "we are getting to the point where there is very little more that I can teach you. Although to tell the truth, Herma dear, I have grown very fond of you through the years, and I would be very sorry to see you go away. For you are the *best* pupil I have ever had in my entire life." Here, carried away by her emotions in a way that Herma would never in the world have expected, she wiped her eye with the back of her hand. Then, regaining control of herself, she reiterated, "You must work like a trooper. The thing is, at two different places in the opera Cherubino puts on girl's clothing. So then you will be a girl pretending to be a boy pretending to be a girl. Do you think that will be too hard for you, dear?"

"No," said Herma.

20.

Mrs. Opdike was a dear creature, who knew a good deal about music but rather less about life. And she knew nothing at all about Herma, and Herma's secret. And yet, the odd thought occurred to Herma that she herself hardly knew more about men than Mrs. Opdike did. They were indeed rather vain, gross, and silly creatures. There was nothing much about them to understand. And yet—did she *know* Fred? No, because she had never seen him and never been with him. He was only a wraith, a fleeting and elusive memory—a being who was present only when she wasn't, and never present when she was. One does not know one's self, even the odder parts of one's self, in the way one knows others—someone that one loves, for instance. If only, she imagined, she could step through the mirror, like Alice through the looking glass, and touch and clasp the person on the other side—then perhaps something might be different. Of course there was Earl. Here her blood gave a little warm jump inside her, and she smiled. But it wasn't the same—she didn't exactly *love* Earl, at least not in that way—even though she was very fond of him. Suppose, she thought—her reverie falling into a conventional and romantic vein—suppose it were really possible to love only one other person in a lifetime. And if that person were on the other side of the mirror—he was forever denied to her. The thought left her with a kind of empty longing, really a silly feeling, since what was the point of it? Unless—she smiled again. The idea occurred to her that Fred could have his photograph taken and give it to her, so that she could carry it in her purse. She could show it to people and tell them it was her sweetheart—here she laughed out loud, crumpled the note she had been about to write to Fred, and threw it at the mirror.

21.

Fred arrived, as he had planned, just at nightfall. Turning off the road, he pedaled his way carefully along the rickety boardwalk through the dunes to Cantamar. He locked the bicycle and stood it against the building, and inspected the place again from the outside for a moment or two. Then he went in.

The long dance hall inside was only dimly illuminated, so that the great spaces of the ceiling overhead remained in shadow. At one end a band of three or four musicians was playing dance music in a thumping tempo. No one was dancing. At the other end, on the raised platform, a dozen or so people were sitting at the tables. It was still early in the evening. The barman leaned on the damp mahogany surface in front of him, bored. Buena Suerte was sitting at one of the tables with three or four other people.

Fred went up to the table. Buena Suerte looked up, regarding him with composure. He was still a young man, perhaps only thirty, dressed with a kind of cheap dandyism in tight-fitting black pants, a black shirt, and a broad leather belt. He was clean-shaven except for the sideburns that came down in a narrow line almost to the corners of his chin. He didn't seem surprised that Fred recognized him. Everybody who came to Cantamar knew who Buena Suerte was.

"May I talk to you for a moment?"

Buena Suerte lifted his shoulders in a noncommittal gesture.

"Alone."

"These are all my friends."

Somebody brought up a chair, and a place was made for Fred at the table.

"A beer?"

"All right."

Buena Suerte summoned the waiter with a motion of his head.

"Dos Brujos."

The two bottles with glasses upside down on them came in an instant. Fred took his glass and poured it half full of beer. Buena Suerte left his where it was. The waiter stood with his napkin over his arm.

"Algo màs?"

Buena Suerte moved his head sideways a fraction of an inch, and the waiter disappeared. He seemed to be able to run the whole place with little motions of his head without removing his hands from the table.

Fred reached into his vest for a pair of Nickel Guanos and offered one across the table.

Buena Suerte smiled politely. "Please have one of mine."

It was an excellent Havana, a Fine Hortelano. They lit them and went on studying each other across the table for a while. Then Buena Suerte smiled again in his reserved way and introduced the others. The lean and wiry individual with catlike eyes on his right was Ocho Veces. On his left was Paco, a boy not more than fourteen who imitated Buena Suerte as well as he could in his clothes and manners. The last to be introduced was Evelyn, who was sitting next to Fred. She was evidently a little older than Buena Suerte, with a narrow face and a thin elongated body. She wore a short black dress with lace at the hem, and narrow strips over the shoulders like a piece of black underwear. On the neck at one side was a soiled embroidery rose.

"Are you Spanish?" she asked Fred.

She knew he was not. Even though he spoke Spanish, and fairly grammatically, he spoke it with a strong English accent.

"No."

"You have the body of a Spanish. You're slenderer than most Gringos. I'm slender too."

Buena Suerte caught her glance and gave her a single stare. She lapsed into silence, with nothing showing on her face. Presently Ocho Veces got up without saying a word; she rose too and they went off together toward the dance floor.

This left only Fred, Buena Suerte, and the boy Paco at the table. Buena Suerte allowed another silent minute or so to elapse. Then he said, "Y pues. You want to talk to me?"

"Do you know where a person could get fifty dollars?"

"Get fifty dollars?"

"Yes. I mean earn it."

He studied Fred for a moment with his lazy dark eyes. Then he said, "That is very difficult. It is a lot of money. Do I have fifty dollars?" He smiled. "What do you think?"

"I think you have it."

Buena Suerte only smiled again and said, "Es muy difícil." The conversation on this subject seemed to come to an end. They turned to look at the dance floor, where Ocho Veces and Evelyn were swaying around to the rhythm of a syrupy Malagueña. Ocho Veces was an excellent dancer. He carried Evelyn around with him like a doll. His left arm, holding her wrist, was stuck out with the elbow bent; his right arm clung along her back. With each step he thrust his leg in between her legs, skillfully, and left it there for a second. It was clear that for him relations between the sexes dominated his life but he personally did not consider them important. They were gestures to be learned, in order to be competent at your trade. Evelyn followed him woodenly.

"Perhaps there might be something," said Buena Suerte.

Ocho Veces and Evelyn came back to the table. Evelyn sat down next to Fred and put her hand on his. He pulled his hand away. Immediately, however, he became aware that her knee was touching his under the table.

"What kind of work can you do?"

"I don't know."

"There isn't much work to do around here." Buena Suerte glanced around at the almost empty dance hall. "Certainly not fifty dollars worth."

Under the table Evelyn slid her hand onto Fred's thigh.

"No hay mucho trabajo," repeated Buena Suerte. "Business is bad."

He seemed to consider, drawing at his Fine Hortelano. He hadn't touched his beer.

"Still, I can imagine ways in which a man might obtain that sum of money. There's your sister, for example."

"My sister? I haven't got a sister."

Evelyn's hand had now reached a point where it could verify for itself the effect it had made. Fred pushed it away. Evelyn sat back and resumed her former impassive expression.

"Everybody knows about your sister," said Buena Suerte. "She sings." He drew at his cigar and set it down on the table. "If she were to come here . . ." He glanced at Fred to observe his reaction. "Perhaps that might be worth fifty dollars. Even though it's a lot of money."

Fred stared back at him. "Come here!"

"You know. Just to be friendly. Just to sing a song and entertain the people who come here."

"Just to sing a song?"

Buena Suerte met his glance evenly. "Yes, of course. What else?"

"You shouldn't drink beer," Evelyn told Fred. "Beer isn't good for love. It only makes you go to the latrina."

She glanced at Buena Suerte. He made one of his almost imperceptible nods.

She went on, "Do you like a sweet wine? Muscatel?"

Under the table she had put her hand back on his thigh again. Fred pushed it away.

"In my room," she said, "I have muscatel, which is better to drink than beer. Also I have better music. Soft music, better to dance to."

She got up, and Fred stood up too.

"So," said Buena Suerte. "It's settled then?"

Fred met his glance for a moment. Then, without replying, he turned away and went off with Evelyn. She led him through the curtained door with a small brass plate over it: "Hotel Dolores y Sueño." He followed the black dress up a flight of stairs. The dress was short, and the hollows of her knees were visible in the slightly wrinkled black stockings. For the first time he noticed that she was wearing soiled pink bedroom slippers instead of shoes.

They reached the top of the stairs. In some way, although the hotel on the outside was rectangular, the corridor inside was curved. This, along with the sound of water washing underneath, contributed to the expression that the whole place gave somehow of a ship. Everything was painted a soiled white, and the fittings on the doors were brass.

Evelyn went on slowly ahead of him. The doors along the corridor were all identical, and each one had a small metal card-holder on it. Most of these were empty, but some had scraps of paper stuck in them with various markings: a crude drawing, a pair of initials, an awkward monogram. On one card there was simply a penciled circle with three lines extending from it: ☿ . Evelyn's door was the last on the corridor. On her scrap of paper was a square of E's facing all ways, with a crudely drawn torch in the center.

She translated for him: "Evelyn is hot four ways." Then she

opened the door and went in.

A sick-looking light bulb hung from the ceiling on a wire. The room was full of all kinds of junk. There was an old-fashioned high bed, which lacked a headboard and had a large lace mantilla tacked up on the wall behind it. The other three walls were lined with dressers, chests, and shelves. All the horizontal surfaces of the room were covered with an indescribable clutter of objects: dolls in costume, yellowed letters, pencils with the points broken off, a man's bow tie with an elastic ribbon, bottles with an inch or two of liqueur in the bottom, a small revolver with the cartridge chamber missing, a cosmetic box filled with faded ribbons, a partly used package of a well-known brand of condoms, a glass bowl containing a nutpick and some empty shells, a bag of caramels, an unstrung mandolin, various salves in tubes from which the caps were missing, a pink bird-of-paradise feather, and a styptic pencil. There were also countless photographs in cheap silver frames, mostly of actresses, politicians, and young men in slightly old-fashioned clothes. He recognized a photo of Ocho Veces and another of Paco, this second when he was perhaps seven years old.

He shut the door behind him. Evelyn was standing with her face fixed in a childish imitation of a knowing smile. Her black dress with the straps over the shoulders, he now saw, was not very clean; the hem was gray with dust. The embroidered rose was stitched in place with thread of a different color, and in the light from overhead the thread threw a tiny but clearly visible shadow onto the clay-brown of her chest.

She went to the dressing table and poured a half glass of amber wine into a tumbler. She handed it to him, saying, "A sweet wine. Muscatel. You shouldn't drink beer. If you drink beer, you start making love but right away you have to go to the latrina."

Behind the dressing table, he saw, was a mirror even worse than the one in Fred's own room. It was like gazing into a gray ocean, with ripples of breeze passing over it now and then. He said, "Thank you." He took the wine and set it back down on the dressing table.

Evelyn began disrobing; not rapidly, instead with a leisure that was evidently intended for a tantalizing seductiveness. Her dress came off with a series of little rotary jerks which were prolonged for some time. Then it was the turn of the stockings and some black underwear. She lay down on the bed.

Her body was extraordinarily lacking in curves. The shoulders, waist, and hips were all exactly the same width. One could have laid a board along her side and touched it at every point. The tuft of hair between her legs, black and glistening, ended in a point like a goatee.

"Aren't you coming?"

"No."

"Why not?"

"Just no."

She looked disappointed. She sat up and looked at him. Then she lay down again.

"For nothing then."

"Thank you. But it's still no."

She sat up again, thought for a moment, and then went to the bureau. She opened the drawer and took out a wrinkled bill. "I'll pay you."

Fred looked at the dollar bill in her hand. "No, I'm sorry. It's nothing personal. I just don't feel like it."

She gave him one more look, regretful and at the same time professionally appraising. Then she began putting her clothes on again. As he turned to leave she said, "Take the dollar anyhow." She tucked it into his back pocket, and he went out, shutting the door behind him.

22.

When he came back to the place a few nights later Fred had to take the Yellow Dog, since he had a suitcase with him that was too large to carry on a bicycle. He met nobody as he made his way across the dunes in the darkness. Arriving at the big stranded ark of a building, he opened the door cautiously and went in.

He stood for a moment in the shadows at the end of the dance hall. It was Saturday night and the place was crowded. The tables on the platform were all occupied. At the other end of the room the band was playing a tinny waltz. Nobody noticed Fred standing in the doorway. Carrying the suitcase, he pushed aside the velvet curtain that led to the hotel.

In the corridor upstairs he tried several doors. Some of them were open and some locked. In general, the ones that were unlocked were empty, or were used for storing various kinds of junk. One contained a collection of riding boots, harness, and other equestrian paraphernalia. Another seemed to be a storeroom for ship's hardware; there were pulleys, hooks, and shackles of the kind used to secure rigging. In another room everything was covered with dust and there was only a bare mattress on the floor. There were no mirrors in any of them.

He had to have a room with a mirror, even if there were a certain amount of risk involved. He went on to Evelyn's door, the last one on the corridor. Setting the suitcase down on the floor, he stood before the door listening. There was no sound from within. He tried the door cautiously; it was unlocked. The room seemed to be empty. As he slipped through the door with the suitcase he caught a glimpse of the boy Paco, at the other end of the corridor, watching him out of his blank brown face.

When Herma came out there was no sign of Paco or anybody else. She drew the door carefully shut, so that it latched almost without a sound. The building was silent except for occasional creaks from the old

planks and the rhythmic washing of the surf under the pilings. She
went down the stairs at the other end of the corridor, pushed through
the velvet curtain, and came directly out onto the dance floor.

Buena Suerte, sitting at his table, caught sight of her and drew
his breath in sharply. She was wearing a red dress slit to the knee,
black stockings, and black dancing shoes. In her hair, in lieu of a
flower, was a cluster of green strawberry leaves with a ripe strawberry in
the center of them. There were no other ornaments; her wrists and
throat were bare.

He got up from the table and came toward her. He said, ''Welcome,
guapa.'' After that he seemed to be at a loss for words. He stretched
out a hand to take her arm, but she evaded him and went on ahead
to the table. A place was made for her and everybody sat down.

Buena Suerte was very polite, even respectful. Everyone else was
silent. Evelyn stared at her impassively out of her brown face.

''Will you take something? A glass of wine?'' He pushed away
the bottle of El Brujo beer at his elbow.

''No thank you.''

''But what will you have? You must take something.''

''A cup of tea.''

This was quickly brought. Herma asked for a slice of lemon and the
waiter ran off and brought this too. She sipped a little tea from the cup
and set it down. Everybody watched her. Nobody said anything for the
ten minutes or so that it took her to drink the tea.

Herma looked out at the dance floor. It seemed slightly wavy, as
though it reflected the shape of the sea under it, although perhaps this
was only some sort of optical effect. The room was thick with smoke,
and there was an odor of beer and cheap perfume. The dancing couples
moved about aimlessly, like flowers caught in an eddy; the men were
mostly in black with white shirts, the women in gaudy-colored dresses.
There seemed to be a shortage of girls; at the far end of the floor two
men were dancing together.

Evelyn and Ocho Veces got up and danced once, to something that
the orchestra evidently intended for the ''Habañera'' from *Carmen*,
and then came back and sat down without a word. Evelyn seemed to be
in a bad mood. She fussed with the soiled imitation flower on her dress.
Then she stared in a sulky way at Herma's strawberry.

Buena Suerte waited for Herma to finish her tea. He waited a
little longer, drumming his fingers slowly on the table. Then he said,
''Y pues?''

''Y pues what?''

''Do you remember what you came here for, guapa?''

Herma smiled, in an artificial and conventional way. She got up
and went off across the dance floor. At the other end she bent over to
confer briefly with the bandleader. The three or four musicians were
installed in a kind of shallow pit set into the floor, so that they were
visible only from the waist up. The bandleader nodded. Then she herself mounted onto a tiny platform that looked as though it might be

half of an apple box, except that it was made of polished hardwood.

By this time the dancers had all left the floor and were waiting at the other end of the room. The band, as well as it was able, launched into a slow and sentimental music-hall waltz. Herma, her chin raised, still smiling faintly, sang with the ease and grace of a bird. The song told of one who, although she lived in a grand mansion and had riches at her command, was not as happy as she seemed, for a shame lay at the heart of her wealth and beauty. If Herma was touched by this it was only in a detached and artistic way. A vein of melancholy clung to her voice, with the slight catch of a tear now and then, but her expression remained quite blithe. The second time she embarked on the chorus with a slight ritardando, lingering on the key words, ''sad'' and ''wasted.''

> '' 'Tis sad when you think of her wasted life,
> For youth cannot mate with age,
> And her beauty was sold for an old man's gold,
> She's a bird in a gilded cage.''

Still slowing a little, she soared grandly to the high E on ''gilded,'' then came down to the A to finish.

She waited for the applause to end. Then, pausing and glancing at the bandleader with her little stiff smile, she sang *After the Ball* in the same key. But—this was more difficult—still watching the bandleader with her eyes, she slipped up a half note to do the second chorus in B flat. The lift, the slight effort she pretended to rise to the higher key— for in fact it was effortless— intensified the gentle and restrained pathos of the song. Many a heart was aching, if you could read them all—she could almost see them aching at the tables at the other end of the room.

Every eye was fixed on her. She exchanged another glance with the bandleader, and this time the slow melancholy waltz began even higher, in C.

> ''You made me what I am today,
> I hope you're satisfied;
> You dragged and dragged me down until
> My soul within me di - ed.
> You've shat - tered each and ev'ry dream,
> You fooled me from the start,
> And though you're not true,
> May God bless you,
> That's the curse of an ach - ing heart.''

The ''aching'' in the last line rose to an incredible and yet effortless high G, and held it for a long moment before it dropped down to the C. There was no applause. Everyone was transfixed, as though they were in a church. The band too stared at her. The trumpeter examined his trumpet, as though to verify that it had really played G above high C.

Herma waited for a moment to savor this effect. Then, with the band feeling a little more sure of itself, she sang several Spanish songs with plenty of *lágrimas* and *corazones*. The songs were about waifs who wandered about the world with no place to lay their heads, about lonely swallows and lovelorn doves, about lovers who sailed off on the sea and were never seen again, leaving suns that never set and rose. Her accent was perfect, since she had learned them on Victrola records made in Guadalajara. The trumpet player had tears in his eyes, although this was perhaps only from the effort of trying to play the two parts of the mariachi style on his single instrument. Herma concluded with one that everybody knew.

> "Ay, ay ay ay,
> Canta y no llores,
> Porque, can-tando,
> Se alegran,
> Ci-e-lito Lindo, los cor-a-zones."

The audience sat stunned. They had not expected this invasion of the Gringa into the complicated sentimental web of their own cultural heritage. It moved them at a place too deep to be reached by mere music. For a few moments they sat silent. Then they broke into heavy applause. It went on for a long time, the hands banging together with vigor and insistence. Someone cried, "Brava, Herma!"—the first brava of her career. A lady wiped a tear from her eye, it was not clear whether for the one who was dragged down until the soul within her died or for the thought that Cielito Lindo, in singing, might forget her sorrows and be happy.

When Herma came back to the table Buena Suerte was standing by it, staring at her fixedly. Before she could sit down he reached out and stopped her. With a toss of his head down the long room he got the orchestra started again. After a few vacillations, and a thump from the percussionist, it launched into a slow Andalusian dance.

"Come, guapa."

She was conscious mainly of his eyes—dark and drooping, with long, almost girl-like lashes. They never left her own eyes, except to flick upward now and then to the glossy fruit in its bed of green leaves. He held her two hands as lightly and deftly as though he were a musician holding his instrument or an assassin his weapon. He danced in a different way from Ocho Veces. There was a flamenco dignity and elegance to it. He remained always a foot distant from her, never touching her except with his arms. Steering her to one side, he marched a few steps pushing her backward. Then reversing—she following him—he moved backwards himself with the grace of a panther, while his dark eyes burned into hers. He held her hands high, so that when they switched in this way their elbows touched lightly. In between, while he marched backward and she forward, or the other way around—nothing moved above his hips. Only his lean legs in their tight-fitting black trousers slipped past each other like snakes.

He was only a little taller than she was. He was not a large man, although he was lithe and seemed to have muscles of steel. He held her hands lightly, but she felt that freeing herself from him would have been more difficult than escaping from the strongest shackles. Switch—she was going forward again. Switch—she was going backward. Each time they crossed in this way, with elbows touching, their faces almost brushed. His small and even white teeth appeared, but not in a smile. His head bent forward a little, and the next time they switched his teeth snapped.

She straightened a little and lifted her chin. But this gesture, intended as defensive, only gave her a proud and arrogant Spanish air that seemed to excite his passion. The orchestra went on thumping out its slow and smoky Andalusian rhythm. They switched directions again. This time the burning eyes and white teeth passed so close to her face that they were out of focus. She heard a sharp animal click. When she was able to see him with clarity again, from a foot away, he had a tiny piece of strawberry leaf in his mouth, which he spat out in disgust.

The next time surely the teeth would close on the small and glistening fruit. The moment came—with a small stamp of his foot he switched her body to the other side. But it was in the middle of this maneuver, as her hands turned in his grasp and the positions of the four hands changed, that his hold on her was least secure. She lowered her head and twisted like a wrestler, and the grasp broke. Slightly above her she heard the teeth click in empty air. In a second she had turned and eluded him, and was moving swiftly toward the door with its velvet hanging.

He was like a panther that, feeling the flesh of a gazelle firmly under its claws, finds in the next moment the prey inexplicably slipping away unscathed. His face darkened. He came after her across the dance floor in a long pounce.

But Herma was quick. Flying away over the uneven floor, she faltered once, almost tripped, and left one of her light dancing slippers behind her. But the other slipper had no heel and she was able to run as swiftly as before. She was conscious of something behind her; not an odor or a sound, or the feel of a hot breath, but a twang of desire like a tensed steel spring that penetrated all the senses at once.

For some reason Buena Suerte didn't follow her through the velvet curtain. Perhaps he was too conscious of his own dignity, and his worth as a man, to engage in an unseemly chase up the stairs. Herma went rapidly down the corridor to the last room, pushed the door open, and entered.

Panting a little, she locked the door firmly behind her. Then, to make sure, she jammed her remaining slipper under it at the bottom. Opening the suitcase onto the bed, she turned to the blotched and shadowy old mirror and began taking off her clothes. First the strawberry in its bed of leaves—a small crescent bitten out of one. She set it carefully into the suitcase. She pulled off the red gown over her head, folded it, and put it in the suitcase too, and the black silk stockings, and lastly her underwear, which was linen and had an oddly virginal look after the sensuous costume she had worn over it.

Then, her arms at her sides and her feet together, she stood for some time before the mirror. Her will, seeping through the nerves of her slim and curveless body, concentrated gradually at its center. Watchful, with a slight and sibylline smile, she waited for it to happen. It took rather a long time. Perhaps she was thinking about something else rather than concentrating. She forced herself not to smile. Out it came at last, with its faint and slightly prolonged plop. The other clothes were waiting, folded neatly on the bed.

Fred came out the door with his suitcase, shutting it behind him. He went down the stairs at a leisurely pace and pushed through the curtain into the dance hall. Buena Suerte was standing by the doorway, still holding the slipper, as though he hoped this Cinderella story would work out the way it was supposed to. When he saw Fred he threw it away. It rolled off across the dance floor, a dozen or more yards away.

"Well?" said Fred.

"Well?"

"Is that all? She was just to sing a song, isn't that right?"

Buena Suerte smiled.

"For the entertainment of your guests."

"That's right."

"And there's nothing more?"

"No. Just sing a song."

Buena Suerte remained silent for a long moment. Then, without taking his eyes from Fred, and still with his little smile, he reached into his back pocket and took out a folded lump of banknotes. Most of them were twenties, Fred saw, but at least one was a hundred. Without looking at the bundle he extracted a fifty and handed it to Fred.

"And so," he said, "good evening, my friend."

"Be seeing you."

"Yes," said Buena Suerte evenly. "Hasta la vista."

23.

The bright daylight burned on the sand. Off in the distance the sea shimmered in little points. Fred, in cycling knickers and a sweater, parked his bicycle against the Kotton Kandy stand and went down the lane to the Flying Machine concession. There was no sign of Gambrinus. He pushed aside the flap of canvas and entered. There was nobody in sight here either. The steam flying machine was gone. A few leftover parts were scattered around; a black rubber hose lay on the ground like a dead snake. He kicked this away and turned over a steam valve with his foot. A faint scent of burning eucalyptus wood still clung in the air. That was all.

Inspecting the inside of the canvas silo more carefully, he saw a flap or improvised door he hadn't noticed before. He pushed this open and entered. In a small room with canvas walls Gambrinus and Marmora were sitting at a little table drinking camomile tea. The dwarf got up with ceremony as he entered. Marmora took another sip from her tiny cup, then she stood up too with her hand resting on the table. She seemed to be looking not at Fred but at a point on the canvas wall behind him, with an expression that had something pleased about it.

"So," said Gambrinus with diplomatic tact, "you have obtained the . . ."

"Yes. I have the sum you mentioned."

"Excellent. We can go to the shed immediately." He took a napkin from the table and touched it to his lips. Then he found his beaver hat and put it on. "If you don't mind, Marmora will accompany us. She is . . . interested in these things."

"I don't mind at all."

The dwarf motioned him toward the door, in a kind of majordomo gesture with both hands. Fred went out, Gambrinus and Marmora following him. Out in the rear Gambrinus walked around the dead ticket booth and led Bernard out of his hut with the wicker car following behind him. It occurred to Fred for the first time that either Gambrinus kept the dog constantly hitched or was able, through some perception, to get wind of his arrival and prepare things in advance. Bernard stopped and waited patiently, his mouth open and panting a little since it was a warm day.

They got in. Gambrinus stood holding the reins as usual. The sides of the small wicker basket came approximately to his waist. Fred crouched down on one side and Marmora on the other. There was hardly room for the three of them. Fred's knees were pressed against Gambrinus' legs, and his hand, which he set on the bottom of the basket to steady himself against the jolting, was only an inch from Marmora's feet. Gambrinus clucked to the dog and they started off.

Marmora smiled faintly. In the tiny basket she was only a foot or two from Fred. He examined her closely for the first time. Her complexion was so pale that it seemed made of some artificial substance. She had perhaps a touch of the albino, although her large eyes, the eyes of some nervous animal like a fawn, were pale green rather than pink. The feverish spots on her cheeks stood out sharply against this pallor. She was dressed exactly as before: black dancing tights, a black jersey curving low at the throat, slippers with ribbons around the ankles, and the gold heart on its fine chain around her neck. Her small breasts, clearly visible through the jersey, were like the halves of an undersized apple. Yet they were perfectly formed, and evidently mature. She was a child. However her childishness was like her father's shortness. It was not something that was temporary. It was a permanent quality, the way she *was*. She would die a child, just as he would die a dwarf. She was older than he was, Fred saw now, perhaps twenty-five or more.

Bernard galloped along the sand at the water's edge. Gambrinus held his knotted black stick at the ready, but it wasn't necessary to use it; evidently Bernard felt like running today. In ten minutes or less the T-shaped shed drew into sight, and Bernard pulled up and slowed in the softer sand.

Gambrinus leaped nimbly out and drew open the doors. Fred got out too, and Marmora, with the grace of a ballerina, lighted on the sand like a bird. She stayed by Fred, behind him and just at his elbow, instead of following her father, who was fussing with the doors and clambering off into the inside of the shed.

Fred went inside after the dwarf, conscious of Marmora still following behind him. When his eyes became accustomed to the gloom he examined the launching apparatus, which he had only glanced at the previous time. The rail was an ordinary piece of railroad track leading out of the shed and down the sloping sand in the direction of the water. Mounted onto it, inside the shed, was a carriage consisting of a wooden frame with two small wheels mounted in tandem. These, he saw, were modified hubs from the wheels of a bicycle. On this carriage the flying machine simply rested and was held in place by its own weight. For landing there were skids shaped like the runners of a boy's sled. After landing, of course, it would be impossible to take off again without the carriage. You would have to land near the shed and then in some way lift the whole contrivance back onto the carriage so it could be launched again, or rolled in backwards through the doors. However Fred wasn't concerned with this problem at the moment.

He went back out into the sunlight, and Gambrinus followed him. They stood looking at the machine. Marmora paused just inside the door of the shed in her graceful dancer's pose, her fingers touching a strut of the wing.

Fred said, "I believe you said fifty dollars?"

Gambrinus pushed back his beaver hat. It was hot and he was perspiring. "That's right. It's fifty dollars. That's a great deal of money. But I'm a businessman and not a philanthropist. In addition to the cost of the machine, you wouldn't believe the expenses I incurred in shipping it out from Ohio. Fifty dollars, young man, if you knew the capital I have invested in this enterprise and from which I must extract a profit, is a very modest fee."

He took off his hat and wiped his brow with a handkerchief. Then he put the hat back on again.

"However," he said, "on the other hand Marmora would like very much to fly in the machine. She has never flown. And if you were to take Marmora with you in the machine"—he got out the handkerchief and mopped his brow again—"some special arrangement might be made."

"Special arrangement?"

"If you were to take Marmora with you," said the dwarf, "then it would be gratis. There would not be any charge. For," he said, "it makes all the difference whether the person who used the machine were just an ordinary customer, or someone who was a friend of Marmora. Such a person would not be a stranger but something like a relative, so to speak," he went on, looking not directly at Fred but just past his left ear into the air. "Just as I don't charge Marmora for the food which she eats at my table, so there would be no charge for the machine if the person flying it were, in a way, a member of the family." Here he stopped, still perspiring, and they gazed together at the figure of Marmora standing in the gloom of the shed.

Fred was conscious for the first time of her odor. It was the aroma of some immature fruit ripening in the sunshine, with a tincture of perspiration because of the black jersey and tights; but it was not real sweat, only baby sweat. As the two men stared at her she shifted her feet and looked down at her slippers. She had not spoken, and she still wore her faint mysterious smile.

Fred saw now that it was possible for two persons, the operator and a passenger, to lie together on the broad wing with the engine next to them. He said nothing, and Gambrinus began vigorously tugging the flying machine on its carriage out into the sunshine. But he was unable to do this by himself. With Fred behind pushing, and Gambrinus ahead pulling, the great wings came out of the shadow into the air. Marmora, still demure, stood aside. When it got onto the sloping track the thing started rolling and was hard to stop. Gambrinus reached onto the wing for a wooden wedge and jammed it under the carriage.

Fred left the fifty-dollar bill where it was in his back pocket. He pulled himself up onto the wing, lay down on it, and adjusted the cradle to his body. He supported himself with his elbows. Just ahead of him, at the edge of the wing, was the rudder stick. A little to the left was the elevator control, a small metal bar mounted on a pivot. There was no throttle. The four-cylinder engine ran at full blast, and there was simply an interrupter on the magneto to shut it off. The only other control was a gas cock in the fuel line. This he turned to open position.

Marmora mounted up nimbly, without a word, and lay down next to him. There was a small space between Fred and the engine, not more than two feet wide, and she fitted neatly into it. Gambrinus, standing upright in his dogcart, himself turned one of the airscrews to start the Wright gas engine. The bicycle chains clanked, the engine gave a wheeze and a cough, and then it caught. After a bang or two it settled into a steady roar, shaking the wing under Fred's body. There was another loud noise, a whir like a thousand birds' wings beating. He glanced around at the left airscrew behind him; it had dissolved into a blur. There was a smell of oil and heated metal. Fred glanced at Gambrinus and nodded.

The dwarf bent down and nimbly pulled the wedge away from the carriage. At first almost nothing happened. The machine moved forward slowly, as though reluctantly. Gambrinus went round to the rear of the wing, carefully staying out of the way of the spinning airscrew, and pushed. Now the carriage started down the track. Gambrinus ran after it, still pushing at the back edge of the wing. His hat came off and tumbled over the sand. He gave a final lunge, fell behind, and stood panting to watch it.

Fred was not sure the thing was going to take to the air. It reached the end of the track, hesitated a little, and then bumped upward. He had no time to see what was happening to the carriage, and in any case it was hidden by the wing under him. He could see nothing but waves, and the canard elevator sticking out ahead of him. Cautiously he pulled back a little on the elevator lever, and the double vanes out in front tilted. The wing seemed to press upward against his chest. The horizon ahead disappeared, and he and the machine and Marmora were alone in the sky.

The thing gathered speed; there was a whistle of air through the baling wire that held the wings together. Fred's sensations were curious. It was something like going very fast on a bicycle with the wind whistling past your ears—turning corners, soaring over rises—except that it was effortless, and that the two dimensions were converted to three. Yet oddly enough this did not make things more complex; instead in some way it made them simpler. You were no longer obliged to *take account* of the earth and the irregularities in its shape; you were freed from it and you could go any place you pleased, without bumping over potholes and with no danger of running off the road.

That is, provided you managed to steer it. Fred had not yet tried to turn the thing. All of itself—perhaps on account of the wind coming a little from one side—it was tilting to the right and the horizon was slowly circling. Through the effect of centrifugal force you had no sensation of turning or of tilting; it was the earth itself, the horizon underneath, that tilted and began rotating like a dish. This phenomenon was dreamlike and exhilarating, but it also constituted a great peril. For, if you lost any sensation of whether the machine was flat to the earth or tilted, you might turn completely over sideways, and then the thing would fall like a stone. And the earth itself, Fred saw, was the instrument that told you whether this was happening. Like some immense sundial or compass, it tilted, straightened, or rotated from horizon to horizon, and it was from this that you knew what you and your machine were doing. He moved the rudder stick cautiously to the right and at the same time shifted his body in the cradle to warp the wing ends. The horizon tilted and began rotating slowly to the left. He was getting the hang of it now. Rudder stick at center. Wing warp neutral. The horizon settled down and, after some reluctance, came to a stop. He smiled over his clenched teeth.

Ahead of him the horizontal canard elevators trembled in the rushing air. He was hardly conscious of noise, or he had become so accustomed to it that it seemed a sensation of his own body. Any conversation, of course, was impossible, and in any case Marmora was not very talkative. He glanced at her. Her chin cupped in her small hands, she gazed straight ahead into the wind. The silky strands of her hair whipped back and flogged her bare shoulders, but she hardly seemed to notice. Fred was still practicing turns. This too was much like steering a bicycle. He simply tilted the rudder stick and at the same time inclined the weight of his body in the direction he wanted to go, and the cradle fitted to his waist took care of the rest. When he turned to the right his side touched against Marmora's small firm dancer's body, and when he turned to the left he curved away from her. After that he worked out a way of circling always to the right, so that he could feel the slim form constantly pressed against his own.

Up to this time he hadn't paid very much attention to the axial stability, or up and down orientation, of the machine. He had touched the elevator lever only once, to make the thing rise off the carriage. Now he perceived that although he was racing along at a good speed he was still at the same altitude he had reached with that first soar, perhaps fifty feet above the water. He cautiously pulled the lever back. The horizon ahead disappeared and at the same time the whistle of the wind in the wires sank down a note. Climbing made the thing slow down. Glancing to the side, he saw that he had doubled his altitude to a hundred feet. Encouraged by this, he climbed in little increments, still circling, until he had reached the height of a good-sized hill.

Now he could see everything. Visibility was not very good lying flat on his stomach in this way, but when he tilted and circled he could see first the coast stretching off to the south toward San Diego, then the empty sea with an island on the horizon, then the sandy Peninsula—the tents of the Great Pacific Traveling Exposition about halfway down it were a violet-purplish blot—and the northern coast leading off toward some hills in the distance. Still turning, the horizon revealed the valley stretching away toward the Sierra Madre, filled with the green mass of citrus groves, a town sticking up here and there. The Bay was below— pale green with veins of darker color where the water was deeper. Its shape was complex. It was like some illustration in a medical book, except that everything was in white and various shades of green.

He climbed a little higher. It was hard to say what his altitude was, but it might have been five hundred feet or more. The Bay ran off to the north, narrowed into a kind of a creek, and then widened again. Along it ran a high bluff, almost vertical. In the late afternoon sun the bluff cast a shadow out onto the Bay. Far below him white birds were visible against this shadow, turning in graceful curves. Now and then one would dip into the shadow and disappear, and then reemerge an instant later like a spirit out of the night. It was a scene of extraordinary beauty: the water a pale lucent green against the sand, the islands in the Bay dotted with an emerald moss, the shadow of the bluff and the white birds turning against it. Fred imagined dipping down himself to disappear into the dark shadow under the cliff and coming out again into the sunshine. But that was too risky.

He had no idea how long he had been in the air. He wasn't tired; in fact the longer he went on flying the more energy seemed to pulse into his body from the wing vibrating under him. Or perhaps from the small tight body of Marmora touching his at the side. It was all part of a complex and powerful mélange of sensations: the whistling of the wind in the wires, the blatting of the unmuffled gas engine, the buzzing whir of the two airscrews spinning behind him.

So far he had climbed only cautiously and at a shallow angle. Now he experimented with climbing more steeply. Pointing straight ahead with the rudders, he pulled back more sharply on the elevator lever. The canards lifted as usual and the horizon disappeared. The note of the engine grew more labored. The wing pushed strongly against his chest. The whistling of the wind in the wires sank lower until he could hardly hear it at all. This was ominous. Just as a bicycle can only stay upright as long as it moves forward, so can a flying machine remain aloft only as long as the air continues to rush over its wings. The Wright seemed to hang poised by its nose for a second or two. Then it dropped, pointed almost directly at the Bay underneath.

There was a sickening swoop that made Fred's stomach touch against his backbone. Luckily he had a good deal of altitude, three hundred feet or more. Some sandbars and a stretch of green water rushed up rapidly. He pulled back gradually on the elevator as the machine gained speed again. It wasn't enough—the Bay was tilting back to the horizontal but still staggering up toward him at a dangerous speed. Clenching his teeth, he pulled back on the lever with all his strength. The wings with their wire supports groaned like a ship in a storm, and there was a sound of something snapping. Yet it held. Forty feet above the Bay, gaped at by a dumbfounded fisherman in a skiff, the machine came to the level, curved away to the right, and began gaining altitude again.

Fred now remembered about this phenomenon, which the Wright brothers had called a stall. Orville had all but broken his neck in this way, or perhaps it was Wilbur. Oddly enough it had not frightened him. He had been ready to die and in a part of his mind expecting to die, but it was all part of the same exhilarating and unreal, somehow transcendental quality of what was happening. He felt elated, in fact, in having accidentally encountered and mastered this most dangerous maneuver in flying. Just at that moment the engine stopped.

The sudden silence was shocking; it was like a great rush of angel wings. He had perhaps a hundred feet of altitude. He looked quickly around him. The fisherman in his skiff was a mile away. Ahead was the narrow neck of water, and then the Upper Bay with the cliff looming over it. If he held the controls just right, he found, the Wright would glide at only a slight downward angle. The only sound now was the hissing of the wind in the wires.

He glanced at Marmora; she was still placid, her chin in her hands, watching the pale green water rushing up toward them. The water wasn't very deep, and also there were a number of flat mossy islands. Fred picked one of these, close under the cliff. For a moment it seemed to him that he couldn't make the Wright go that far. But a breath of wind, coming from somewhere, lifted the wings a little. The edge of the island whirled by only a few feet underneath. What looked like moss from a higher altitude was now revealed as a thick tangle of reeds, water plants, and lilies. The bent-cane skids brushed over this vegetation, the whole machine waggled, then it slid with a prolonged crackling noise through the reeds and came to a stop. The rudders behind tilted up and then settled to the level again. It was very quiet. In a curious philosophical mood, Fred reflected that he had not asked Gambrinus how long the machine ran before the fuel gave out.

He unstrapped himself from the cradle and clambered down into the reeds, then he helped Marmora down. He looked around him. They were on a flat island a hundred yards or so long, shaped like a large comma. The tail of the comma was only a mud flat that trailed away into the water, but the round head, where they were standing, was like a miniature South Sea island, or something out of *Tom Sawyer*. Growing on it was a tiny jungle, coming only to their waists. The chief plant was an odd-looking exotic reed with a kind of tassel on top; perhaps it was papyrus. There were ferns, vines, wild succulents, and water plants of all kinds. One of the more curious was a kind of wild tidewater narcissus that grew in those parts. The leaves were the same pale and lucent green as the shallow water of the Bay; they grew in a profuse tangle that formed a kind of arabesque floating on the water. The flowers were extraordinary. They resembled daffodils, except that their white purity had something odd, barbaric, innocent, and self-contained about it; they gave the impression that their cup-shaped coronas had not yet opened up and perhaps would never fully open up. Perhaps they opened up at night. They emitted an extraordinary fragrance: babylike and yet powerfully sensuous. They exactly resembled, in fact, Marmora herself.

He turned and found that they were in each other's arms. They were like two children on a desert island; not fearful, simply inquisitive about this odd place in which they found themselves, and about each other. As though he were removing the petals from a flower he disrobed her. Then he did the same for himself, with her help. They lay down on the bed of narcissus.

Her lips were exactly what he had expected: a woman's lips attached to a child. As for her breasts, the prophecy that they would be young apples was also exactly fulfilled. They were almost as hard, and they were exactly hemispherical, not sagging off at all to the sides through the effect of gravity. When touched at certain places her slim form gathered and contracted, like a sea anemone, or a flower that captured insects. With her legs extended straight and her feet together, she twinkled her toes like a dancer.

After some time, becoming aware of an intense and keen sensation of pleasure at the center of his own body, he realized that he had slipped into her without noticing the moment when it happened. Her thing, the place where Fred now found himself, was extraordinary. It was like a little fluted pipe, lithe and strong, yet one had to be careful not to damage it. Some time passed. Fred was aware of the shadow of the high cliff a hundred yards or so away, creeping gradually toward them. Then all at once there was a little ripple, as though a trout had broken in the water of their common minds. Fred almost cried out; it seemed to him that the odd white blossoms of the narcissus around him stretched and opened. The ripples gradually died away, widening in circles, as ripples will. After that, there was no point lying there thinking. Marmora was not a thinker, nor did she particularly induce thought in someone who was with her. Fred extricated himself and sat up.

The shadow of the cliff was only a few yards away. In a few moments it would reach them. An ungainly looking bird was plopping around in the shallow water nearby, lifting its feet to clamber over the narcissus. It was large, almost as big as Marmora, and it had an awkward jerkiness about the way it stabbed its beak into the mud searching for food. The thing gathered together in itself, in a kind of caricature, all the ungainliness of earthbound creatures and their endless and tedious search for sustenance. It was, as Fred recognized from his rudimentary knowledge of ornithology, a Blue Heron, a rather rare bird in this part of the world.

It stopped jabbing its beak in the mud and stared at Fred. The tiny eyes were fixed on him. Then, evidently disapproving, it began sprinting away to windward across the shallow water. The motion was ludicrous, as though a person were trying to run on stilts and splashing in the water as he went. The big wings flapped: a-woo, a-woo. But then the heron managed at last to get clear of the water. He pulled up his legs and trailed them to the rear of his body. He assumed a soaring configuration, and became beautiful. No longer was he earthbound and limited. He turned into a flying machine, one perfectly designed, far finer than the Wright. He mounted effortlessly, turned away toward the cliff and into the shadow, and came out of it into the sunshine again. It was hardly necessary for him to move his wings. Taking advantage of every air current, he turned and banked, flexing the long feathers of his wing tips. He was nothing but two immense wings with a slim body between them, shaped to slip frictionless through the air, and a keen intelligence in the small tapered bulb on the front. Fred watched him for a long time. Not once did he move his wings till he was out of sight.

24.

Sometimes after they had dined at the Pavilion or simply gone for an evening spin in the Waverley, Herma and Earl drove back to the Electric Theater, and there he would put on a private showing for her. He ordered many different pictures from Los Angeles—comedies, melodramas, acrobats and circuses, fragments of opera, even newsreels of strutting Balkan soldiers or earthquakes in Armenia. The one she remembered most clearly, however, was the time she had quite unexpectedly seen Madame Modjeska appear on the wavering silver screen in front of her.

They had come back from the beach on a warm night that seemed to hold the promise of something special in it, a particular sensualism that seemed to hang in the dark air with its faint scent of orange blossoms.

Earl parked the Waverley behind the theater and helped her down from the machine. He was particularly courtly this evening. He opened the door of the theater also for her, and helped her off with the velvet cloak she sometimes wore over her gown in the evening. As he did this his hands touched the strawberry bouquet in her hair and disarranged it. She laughed. Reaching up, she pulled off the bouquet, took the strawberry out of the leaves, and offered it to him. At first he hesitated. Then he opened his mouth and she popped it in. After a moment he chewed it slowly and swallowed. Then he smiled, not quite understanding why she was behaving so oddly.

Once he was behind his projector his assurance returned, and he busied himself with the reel and the arc lamp with the deft gestures of a professional. He seemed really at home only in the theater and at the tiller of the Waverley. As soon as he was away from his machines, a bumbling male shyness came over him, and he was tentative and unsure of himself. It was this quality of him, as much as his skill with things mechanical, that Herma liked. She took her seat, and the projector started with its clucking whir.

This evening the program was chiefly dramatic. Bernhardt, propped on her cane, recited a scene from Racine's *Phèdre* in French. The Victrola seemed a little flustered by the foreign language and sometimes missed a word. "Tout a changé de face," the Divine Sarah intoned hoarsely,

> "Depuis que sur ces bords les Dieux ont envoyé
> La fille de Minos et de Pasiphaé."

But this last word came out "possibly;" the best the Victrola could do. Herma was also a little mystified by the fact that this speech was supposed to belong to Hippolytus, and was a reference to Phèdre herself, that is, to Madame Bernhardt. But perhaps the Diva was able to do all parts, including the male ones, which she therefore spoke hoarsely. Her Comédie Française accent, with its elegant grasseyement, was a marvel, except of course for the last word.

There followed several trifles, including a piece of *East Lynne* delivered by somebody or other and a rather confused scene from Belasco's *Girl of the Golden West*, all blurry and covered with scratches. "The film is rather worn," Earl apologized.

Then he threaded another film, and unexpectedly there wavered onto the screen the familiar queenlike figure with the alert expression, the dark patches under the eyes, and the restrained smile. She was visible only in half figure, wearing an elegant gown sprinkled with sequins. She began speaking, although nothing could be heard at first, because Earl was intent on setting down the needle at exactly the right place on the record. Then, after a little grating scratch, Madame Modjeska launched into her most famous part, that of Rosalind in *As You Like It*. "Am I not your Rosalind?" she inquired archly; and, hardly waiting for an answer, she went on to explain the true nature of love. Following that—she had a whole twenty-minute reel to herself—she did the Epilogue, and then, backing up to the middle of the play again, she engaged in a dialogue with Orlando in which she was clad in boy's garments and pretending to be Ganymede the amorous cupbearer.

ORLANDO: Are you native of this place?
ROSALIND: As the cony, that you see dwell where she is kindled.
ORLANDO: Your accent is something finer than you could purchase
            in so removed a dwelling.

Flickering slightly at the edges, he gazed in amorous surmise at the pretty youth, wondering perhaps whether the cony could be kindled. This ambiguity Herma found deeply exciting. She watched intently, a restrained little smile on her face.

"Love is merely a madness; and, I tell you, deserves as well a dark house and a whip as madmen do," the youth on the screen concluded with a meaningful lowering of his eyes. Orlando and Rosalind disappeared, to the sound of flapping celluloid. The screen turned white. The sputtering arc lamp was removed from the machine and extinguished.

Herma stood up. She and Earl were standing only an arm's length apart in the darkened theater. Taking resolve, she flung herself into his arms, but did so—with her thorough understanding of male pride in such matters—in a way that gave him the impression it was he who had seized her. They stood for some time enfolded in love's rapture, as in the wings of an enormous bird.

"What was that play anyhow?" asked Earl, a little mystified by the course of events.

"*As You Like It.*"

He managed to mumble, "I like *this* fine." He was thoughtful for a moment. "It's too bad," he said in a muffled tone, "that there isn't. You know. Some place we could go."

A most interesting idea struck Herma.

"Could we . . . do it . . . here?"

"But there's no place to . . . gee . . . it's impossible."

Herma pulled away from his grasp and went to the front of the theater to get eight or ten chairs. Even though they were all different, she selected those that were upholstered in one way or another. She arranged them in the narrow space in front of the projecting machine, front to front, so that the backs formed a kind of rail to keep them from rolling out. "There," she said. "You see, it's almost like a bed."

He stared at her dubiously. Still, he allowed himself to be pulled down on the improvised couch next to her. It was quite comfortable, more than one might expect.

Herma had another idea.

"But you have to start the projector."

"The projector?"

"Put in the film and start it. Put in the same film," she told him, "that you showed me the first time. You know, the horses, and the lovers on the balcony, and the Götterdämmerung."

"But why?"

"Because otherwise I'll get up and go home."

He sat up, crawled out of the bed of chairs, and searched around feverishly among the cans of film under the table. Finding the right one, he threaded it hurriedly and started up the machine. Then, with a long sigh, he stretched himself out beside her again.

Of course there were no sound effects. Earl couldn't be expected to get up from this precarious bower and knock together coconut shells, start the Victrola, and kick over bowling pins at every other moment. All the sounds had to be imagined. But this was not very difficult for a person with the gift of absolute auditory recall. Herma heard every coconut shell and note of music in her head, through a kind of willful and controlled hallucination. And even the odors were not too difficult to evoke, through this same sort of voluntary memory. The horses began galloping. Earl began—what? he was not quite sure what he was doing. He had the impression, somehow, that it was she who was showing him what to do, that it was she who knew better than he what it was that he wanted. He was also bewildered and pleased by the fact that most of their clothes seemed to have come off in some way without his noticing it.

As for Herma, she was transported—and now she knew that this expression, so often used in describing the effects of love, was no mere metaphor. She *was* the horse galloping; although perhaps the sound she heard was only that of their two hearts, the beats slightly staggered, pounding in syncopation. The lovers appeared on the balcony, and Earl gathered his courage and kissed her full on the lips, to the strains of *Träumerei*. This scene went on for some time, although neither was impatient for it to end. Earl effected his penetration, not without a certain awkwardness, just at the point where the sad man put his foot into the bucket and fell down the flight of stairs. It was all a little frantic but still quite nice, and it didn't hurt anybody, as things don't in movies. Herma felt that *she* had fallen downstairs, in a floaty and dreamlike way, and it made her spine tingle with an electricity that trickled out to her very toes and fingers. Earl seemed to be catching on. He learned as he went, and he gave the impression that he was entering a new epoch for him, one in which he transferred his skill with things mechanical into a more spiritual and sentimental realm.

The young woman in the floating dress ran through the field of flowers. The lover sprang from the horse and embraced her. They disappeared, and the peasants climbed into the tub and began treading on the grapes. Now the mood was not sentimental at all; it was earthy and Dionysiac. Herma was even more drunk than she had been after the bottle of wine at the Pavilion. Still, a part of her mind was clear, regarding everything with a piercing attentiveness. The celluloid whirled through the reels; one spool shrank and the other grew larger. Herma watched the ghostly schooner with silver sails creeping out to sea. It seemed to her that she too was embarking on a mysterious voyage, one that would take her to far lands, through perils, to joys and ecstasies that remained for the moment nebulous; although what she was feeling just now was perhaps a premonition. If this were true. . . . The screen fluttered white again, and then darkened into the Götterdämmerung scene.

The portentous Wagnerian strains pulsed in Herma's inner ear. Madame Schumann-Heink as Brünnhilde, wearing gold snake bracelets around her ample arms and a helmet with wings, called upon Wotan in a heroic mezzo. Siegfried's body was laid on the fire, and the large-bosomed heroine herself set the flame to it. Earl could hardly contain himself. The torch from the screen flared inside Herma and spread until her whole body felt feverish.

Madame Schumann-Heink was inexhaustible. Raising one arm, then the other, she frowned out of the screen and opened and closed her mouth. Herma heard the great high C of her "Siegfried, Brünnhilde greets you in bliss!" This ringing note made the flames leap up around the pyre. And just then, inside Herma and simultaneously at the very prick of Earl's desire, all pandemonium broke loose. The two of them became one, a one in which a great Lost Chord trembled and shook from the organ. The very central being of Herma, or of the one being they had both become, was lost in a vast fortissimo. A red glow spread on the horizon, to the accompaniment of the Valhalla theme. At last the flaming tremulo inside the two of them, where they were joined, died away. It was a good thing, because a mortal frame could only sustain so much.

There actually was a smell of fire. Herma came to her senses and sat up. The last of the film had flapped through the projector, but the screen was not white as usual. Instead it was smoking and little tongues of flame had appeared at the edges. As she watched, a piece the size of a hand turned black and peeled from the middle.

She hurriedly began putting her clothes on. There was a pounding of feet on the sidewalk outside, and a few seconds later the distant sound of a bell clanging. Where, oh where were her slippers? She found them, under the projector table. Earl was also having trouble finding his garments, some of which were under the bower of chairs. It was amazing how easily these things had come off, and how hard they were to find when you went to put them on again. Earl wore suspenders, which she hadn't noticed before. She seized the light cloak, threw it around her shoulders, and fled. There was no one outside in the alley, except that it was full of smoke.

The roof of the Electric Theater, which up to now had only been sizzling, burst into an orange-colored fountain. All the houses along Main Street, clear up to the corner of Fourth, were illuminated in the pinkish glow. A number of pigeons, awakened by all the tumult, flew in and out of the red smoky haze overhead.

Some people ran one way on the sidewalk, some another. Through the smoke she discerned Earl, quite calm to all appearances except that he had not been able to find his necktie, backing the Waverley out of the alley and steering it away to safety. Herma hurried up toward Fourth Street. No one paid any attention to her. Just as she turned the corner a magnificent fire-engine—a brass boiler set upright on red and gilded wheels and drawn by four galloping white horses—came down the street and careened around the corner onto Main.

25.

After the great excitement of the burning down of the Electric Theater, the next chief event to attract public attention in Santa Ana was the première of the new French's Opera House. It was a large and impressive edifice, built of solid brick with elaborate ornaments somewhat Moorish in effect, at the corner of Fourth and Bush. From the street entrance on Bush the doors led into the ticket office. At either side of this you went up a flight of stairs and came out, through a portal copied from the Alhambra in Granada, into the theater itself. A vast terrace of seats, five hundred and seventeen of them, sloped down to the stage, and there were boxes along the sides. For the artists there was also a stage entrance on the alley off Bush Street. The lighting was by Edison bulb but also by gas, in case there should be some difficulty with the newfangled electricity. On the front of the building, for two weeks in advance, the posters had been plastered.

Grand Premiere
THE MARRIAGE OF FIGARO
an Opera by Mozart
starring the celebrated
MADAME ALBERTINA MOELLENDORF
of the Metropolitan Opera Company, N.Y., N.Y.

Herma, arriving well ahead of time and with a keen sense of excitement at the stage entrance, went up the stairs and along the corridor to the door with her name on it. She had her own dressing room, since Cherubino was almost a lead part. In front of the small mirror—but a brand-new one—she donned her flamingo-colored breeches, her burnt-umber coat with gilded sleeves, her short wig, and her stockings. The breeches fitted like a glove. They were almost too tight; it was as though they were painted on her. Luckily the coat came well down over her fork, as some people called it. Pleased with herself, she went out and down the corridor to the stage, where she waited with the others in the wings.

After the short overture, the curtain went up and Figaro and Susanna embarked into their recitative arguing whether the Count had the droit du seigneur over his wife's maid. Figaro did his aria predicting that he would make the Count dance a tune, singing through his teeth, with expert sarcasm, "Se vuol ballare, signor Contino." This was repeated several times with da capos.

Herma could scarcely contain her impatience. She tugged at the scenery and breathed deeply. At last came the moment of her entrance as the amorous page. Running out confidently to center stage, she trilled, "Susanetta, sei tu?" wheeling so that the coat swung open to reveal the well-fitting breeches. She felt quite at home, basking in the flood of light from overhead and from the footlights at the edge of the stage. She felt no trace of stage fright, any more than she had at the church social, years before, when she was a little girl. It was here on the stage that she belonged! She felt as though she had always known that. She was moving forward now into her real existence, the life for which the years in the house on Ross Street, and in the small provincial town sleeping in its orange groves, had been only a preparation.

To tell the truth she didn't have much to do in the first act. However there was her charming little song, her I'd-like-to-know-what-love-is aria. She (or rather he, Cherubino) introduced just the right note of the plaintive, with an underlying gaiety just below the surface.

> "Non so più cosa son, cosa faccio,
>   or di foco, ora sono di ghiaccio . . ."

This was easy; not only had Mrs. Opdike drilled her in it over and over again, but she had heard Melba do it on the flickering white screen. When she finished there was even a trickle of applause from the audience in the vast black space out in front of her.

After that there was not very much for Herma in the first act, although there was a fine piece of stage business. Cherubino, dallying with Susanna, was surprised by the Count and took shelter behind a chair. The Count in his turn began courting the maid, but Basilio came in; so the Count sprang behind the chair, while Cherubino slipped adroitly under the cloth covering it. He sat there for some time with his head making a bump in the cloth. The Count emerged and began explaining how on a previous occasion he had discovered Cherubino hiding in just such a chair. "Like this!" he sang, whipping away the cloth. And there was the amorous page again. Coup de théâtre, leading to a four-part ensemble. Everyone sang away at exclamations of astonishment, dismay, and cynicism about the female sex. Cherubino didn't bother to defend himself. He only smiled, turning again so that the coat swung open to reveal the flamingo-colored breeches. This gesture so charmed the audience that a little rattle of applause broke out, right in the middle of Basilio's attempt to explain that all the trouble was due to this Cherub of Love. His black look told her: *that, Mademoiselle Herma, is called stealing a scene.* But Herma didn't care. The tenor who sang Basilio was only from San Francisco and not from New York; besides, he forced some notes and sang high B in falsetto. She smiled winningly at him. The curtain came down for the act.

But this was nothing to Herma's triumph in the second act. It was here that she had her most important piece, the long Canzonetta which she sang to the Countess while Susanna plucked the guitar. "You who know what love is, ladies, see if it's in my heart." She delivered the short lines, one after the other, with a bell-like clarity. The voice was youthful and naive and yet vibrant. It rose to the higher notes with an effortless grace, resting lightly, as it were, on the fragile guitar continuo. It floated, trembled, and sank from one note to the next in an arching legato, always in perfect control. When the oboe and then the full orchestra swelled in behind the guitar it was an entrancing moment.

> "Voi che sapete
> che cosa è amor,
> donne, vedete,
> s'io l'ho nel cor."

When she concluded on the B flat of *cor,* chin raised and mouth slightly rounded, the pure and viola-like clarity tempered with just a hint of head voice, there was a silence for a few seconds. Then a kind of storm broke out in the dark gulf in front of her. Beginning with a loud clatter, it swelled until the individual impact of palm on palm was no longer audible and there was only a vast roar, making the windows vibrate and hurting one's ears a little. It went on for quite a long time. Finally the Countess, breaking in over the last of the claps, was able to sing her "Bravo! Che bella voce!" with a quite evident note of irony.

For the Countess this whole business of Figaro's marriage was not a happy affair. The best she could hope for was a mild revenge on the Count for his philandering and the restoration of the status quo ante. It was not really a demanding role, in fact, although the Countess was supposed to be the star of the opera. No one paid much attention to her through the whole complicated imbroglio, and the only fine aria she had was her "Dove sono" in the third act.

But this was her moment. Alone on the stage, the Diva from New York, otherwise La Moellendorf, advanced to the footlights and stood for a moment dominating that great dark beast the audience, her antagonist. Then, with a silken skill, she embarked into the aria.

> "Dove sono
> i bei momenti . . ."

Since she had been singing this for thirty years, she knew it thoroughly and ran through it with impetus and verve. The orchestra, consisting of all the violin, viola, flute, horn, and cello teachers scraped together from the corners of Orange County, struggled valiantly to keep up with her. But before the end of the aria they met their nemesis. The Diva went through it the first time, from "Dove sono" down to "ingrato cor." Then there was a kind of da capo; she went back to the top of the aria and started over. With the orchestra silent, she climbed gradually up to the beginning with a cadenza of mounting oh's in sola voce. At a certain point the orchestra was supposed to rejoin her.

<pre>
                    o-o-ohhh,   DO - ve so - no
               oh,
       oh,   (ORCHESTRA)
     Oh,
</pre>

But at this point the orchestra and the Diva faltered a little, like two polite persons trying to go through a door at the same time. She glared at the conductor. He looked up. After a few jerks, Diva and orchestra came to agreement, and they finished the aria together, or almost so. But this little contretemps had thrown the Diva off badly. She was not used to such things. Even if one were paid two thousand dollars for a single performance, what did it avail if one were accompanied by cripples and paralytics with tin ears collected from some asylum? She had gone too far out west; far too far, in her estimation. She bickered with Susanna rather than conniving with her. "I've folded the paper, now how shall I seal it?" "Here, take this pin," gritted the Countess. Susanna jumped as the pin went through the paper into her thumb. Encountering Cherubino in girl's clothing (imagine, how fantastic and improbable, Cherubino pretending to be a girl), she inquired with throaty sarcasm, her voice having left her entirely, "And tell me, who is that lovable girl with such a modest air?"

She made it up a little with the orchestra in the fourth act, although by this time Susanna was seriously annoyed with *her* on account of the pin. Only Cherubino was imperturbable, seeming to have noticed nothing. Figaro, Susanna, the Count, and the Countess sang their quartet. The Count attempted to cuff Cherubino, but the blow landed on Figaro instead. Then Susanna took her turn at slapping Figaro, evidently dispersing in this way her hostility toward the Countess, whom the libretto didn't call for her to slap. Figaro winced. Everyone sang to be pardoned by the Count.

<pre>
          Susanna: "Perdono, perdono!"
          Figaro: "Perdono, perdono!"
          Count: "No, no, non sperarlo!"
          Tutti: "Perdono, perdono!"
</pre>

In the end, since everybody including the Count himself had been kissing the wrong lady, the Count agreed to pardon all. Everyone joined together in the Tutti finale, and they went off to celebrate the double marriage. The curtain came down to reveal the significant word "Asbestos."

There was a sound like Niagara Falls from the dark chasm out in front of the stage. It went on for some time. The Diva took several curtain calls, then the whole company came out. They stood holding hands, bowing and smiling toward the bright footlights. There were more calls of "Diva, Diva!" "Bravi tutti!" added some linguist in the audience. The Moellendorf from New York didn't care as much for that, putting her as it did on the equal with the others. But then another call began too, collecting and swelling as more voices took it up.

> "Herma!"
> "Herma!"
> "Herma!"

After that the various calls were mingled: "Herma!" "Diva!" "Bravi tutti!" This made the Diva extremely annoyed; she was unable to suppress a scowl as she went on smiling, all teeth, over the footlights. The combination was not attractive. It made every line show in her face. The smile became mechanical, a kind of corpselike rictus. She bowed once more, deeply, but the applause was already dying away.

The house lights went on, and the black animal turned into an audience in which individual faces could be made out. In the middle of the fourth row was Mrs. Opdike in her flowered dress, one huge smile. Mama's face glowed, and Papa went on clapping like a marionette long after everyone else had stopped. People began putting on their coats. In her box at the left-hand side Madame Modjeska collected her gloves, smiling in her own faint and controlled way, and left inconspicuously.

Herma went back to her dressing room to take off the gilded coat, the flamingo-colored breeches, the lace shirt with the ruff, and the white silk stockings. There was a note stuck into the mirror in the familiar blocky hand: "Don't forget The Last Rose of Summer."

26.

At Arden, Madame Modjeska's ranch estate in Santiago Canyon, a few friends had gathered to celebrate Herma's triumph. The house, which from the outside seemed only a simple bungalow standing in the moonlight, proved on the inside to be full of endless rooms and corners, unexpected turnings, stained-glass windows like a church, large paintings covering the walls, glassed-in bookcases full of books, an immense stone fireplace, and, in the main salon, an ornate table with carved lions serving as legs. The painting on the wall opposite was a life-sized portrait of Madame by Bastien-Lepage. Another painting, sitting on the floor, was a pre-Raphaelite tryptich depicting nymphs fleeing through the woods trailing flimsy scarves. There was no electricity in the house; the lamps were expensive china, with stained-glass shades. The chairs had long fringes like piano scarves.

Madame Modjeska took her by the hand. "This is Mr. Paderewski, my dear. The famous pianist," she added, as though there were danger of confusing him with some other Mr. Paderewski. He was a man with a pale, serious face, a noble nose, and a slightly bony and protruding chin.

His most prominent feature was the shock of blondish hair which stuck up, curly and unruly, on all sides of his head. He also had a mustache and a small Pan-like lip beard. He wore a dark-gray frock coat, a white shirt, and a white cravat. Nearby was a lady who was declared to be Mrs. Paderewska. Finally, there was Madame Modjeska's own husband, who for some reason was called Mr. Chlapowski. Herma recognized him as the scholarly looking man with the pale forehead who had accompanied Madame to the church social, years ago. "My Karol," said Madame. There was another person, a wisp of a man who stayed in the rear of the room, whom Madame did not introduce. He gave the impression that he was trying to hide behind a chair.

"And who is that?"

"Oh, that is just Henry, he is nobody in particular."

"But Pani Helena," objected Paderewski, "Mr. Sienkiewicz is not just anyone. After all, he has won the Nobel Prize only last year."

"Ah, but for us he is only our Henry," said Madame placidly. "And now where is the champagne? Have Oliver bring in the champagne."

Oliver proved to be the same wooly-headed coachman who had brought Herma to Arden, and who also served as butler, and seemed in all respects to be one of the family. "For," as Madame said while Oliver was right there in the room, "in America it is only the Irish, the Chinese, and the Negroes who know how to serve." Oliver nodded vigorously. He seemed to agree thoroughly with this judgment. He allowed Mr. Chlapowski to open the champagne, and then he, Oliver, accepted a glass himself. They all held up their glasses.

"To a new star that has appeared in the heavens tonight," offered Madame.

They drank. Herma, aware that you were not supposed to drink when the toast was to yourself, left her glass untouched. Instead she gazed speculatively at Madame. From across the room she gave an appearance of youth; at closer range it was clear that she was well into her sixties. Her heavy gray hair was coiled in a chignon, leaving the bottoms of her ears and her pale perfect neck exposed. She wore a simple black dress enclosing her to the neck, with a necklace from which some sort of badge was suspended; no other ornament. In spite of the dark patches under her eyes, it was her face that gave the impression of youth. She had an alert expression, merry eyes, and a restrained smile. She talked constantly, not listening very much to what other people said in return.

"Play something, Ignace. Play, play. We must have wine and song."

With a glance at Herma, and a humorous shrug, Mr. Paderewski sat down at the piano and spun his way effortlessly through a few nocturnes of Chopin. He sat bolt upright, with his elbows straight and hands high, glancing around ironically at the others—a kind of parody of a concert pianist's stance. He seemed to be a person who was easily amused. After the Chopin he did a few trifles of Gounod and Massenet.

Herma and the others clapped, and Paderewski, in the Slavic tradition, turned on the bench and clapped too to thank his audience. All this with his waggish expression, and his lip-beard like a dignified goat.

"Does Mr. Paderewski often play for you?"

"Whenever I ask him. He has to. For," explained Madame, "it was I who launched him on his career. Isn't that so, Pan Ignace?"

He smilingly agreed.

"He is my creation," she went on in her theatrical and slightly mocking voice. "He was only a waif, a vagabond, stealing hungrily through the streets of Warsaw. And finding him, I took him under my protection, I arranged for his first concert, and I introduced him to the most famous composers and conductors of Europe."

"Not exactly a waif, Pani Helena," he objected mildly. "More precisely, I was a music student."

"You were nobody. I found you. And now you are the most famous pianist in the world."

He made no objection, only smiling to himself. They had finished the champagne, and Mr. Chlapowski opened another bottle. They all filled their glasses again, except for Oliver, who set his glass on the piano and left the room with another friendly nod. Perhaps he had to clean the carriage, or bed down the horses.

"And now you, Pani Helena," suggested Paderewski. "Recite something."

Becoming at once mock-serious, she drew herself up. This was her stage manner—standing bolt upright or even rearing a little aft. She advanced to the center of the room and announced, in a parody of her light accent, "Becawss of my defectif English, I am going to recite in my native languish."

She launched into a long and dramatic speech of some sort. The succession of incomprehensible consonants, as prickly and agile as porcupines, ran through the whole gamut of emotions: suspense, drama, and pathos. The liquid voice, with only a slight scratchiness of age in it, was by turns melancholy, gay, impassioned, and tragic. At one point she laughed rather frenetically, and at another broke into sobs. She finished with her arms spread wide, in a peroration so magnificent as to seem Shakespearean. Mr. Chlapowski sighed, and Paderewski and Mr. Sienkiewicz for some reason were laughing.

"But what is it?"

"Only the alphabet in Polish, my dear. I often recite it in order to make fools of Americans. For," she said, "everyone should know Polish. It is the most beautiful language in the world. On a number of occasions," she said, "I have played Lady Macbeth in Polish, while the others only piped along in English as best they could. And at the end, whom do you imagine the audience acclaimed?"

No answer was needed to this. Madame finished her champagne, and threw the glass into the fireplace. But not wildly, instead with all the dignity of a countess. "Not only can I recite," she declared, "but I am also capable of acting, even though I am an old woman."

Arms akimbo, she broke into a kind of jig, or rather she seemed to be imitating the walk of various kinds of persons.

"Tak jedzie pan,
    Tak jedzie pan,"
(showing the way a lord walks),
    "A tak chlop,
    A tak chlop,"
(and the peasant walks so),
    "Tak Zyd na jarmark,
    Tak Zyd na jarmark,"
(and the Jew walks to market this way).

Recovering her breath, she said, "Like most Poles, I am afraid I am a little anti-Semitic."

"Oh no, my dear," Karol reassured her, "you are only realistic."

"What you are really saying, my great and good friend, is that you are the anti-Semitic one, and I am not."

"I am pro-Semitic," said Paderewski, "on account of the many sufferings of Jews which I saw in my youth."

"Bravo Ignace!"

"And also on account of Rubenstein, who is a friend of mine."

"But if you have a Jewish friend, that doesn't count."

"How, doesn't count?"

He and Madame began arguing this point in Polish, and Karol went out to the kitchen to see if there was any more champagne. Herma was left alone with Mr. Sienkiewicz, who seemed to have recovered some of his presence at least and had come out from behind his chair to stand by the fireplace.

"I am pleased to meet you, my dear. Pardon me, I don't know how to address you, I am a foreigner."

"Is it true that you won the Nobel Prize only last year?"

He stared back at her out of his pale eyes, and after a moment admitted shyly, "Yes."

"And what for?" Herma pressed him.

"It was on account of a book that I wrote called *Quo Vadis*," he said almost apologetically, as if he wanted to defend himself against any suggestion that his importance could be equal to Herma's own.

Herma: "Oh."

Mr. Sienkiewicz: "You have perhaps . . . heard of it?"

Herma: "No, I'm afraid I don't read very many books."

"I expected you wouldn't have read it," he said. "My dear, will you accept the congratulations of an old foreign man? I mean on your performance this evening."

"Ah, you were there?"

"I worshipped with the others."

"Anyhow, you're not such an old man." She smiled. He was another of the sort of men that Herma liked, gentle, shy men who knew how to do things, in his case write books.

He said, "I was born in the previous century," which was really not to the point, since so was Herma herself, and Boy Sampson. Back came Karol from the kitchen with another bottle of champagne, and filled all the glasses. But at this point there was a diversion. The wind had been blowing all evening, roaring in the oak trees and shaking their branches, and now Oliver came in to report that there was a fire.

They all went out to look at the fire. Standing on the lawn under the oaks, they watched while a river of bright orange crept across a hill in the distance, now and then throwing up a shower of sparks. The fire was to the west, and the wind was from the north, said Karol, so there was no danger of it burning down Arden. Still, they always had several fires like this in the windy season. "Which," he said, "is from January to December, with a day off for Christmas."

They went back into the house and finished their champagne. Paderewski seemed nervous. "These hills are one vast tinderbox," he said. "And if we caught on fire, who would help us? No one." He stared out of the window into the blackness, where a thread of orange was still visible on the hill opposite. "It's barbaric. One might be in Patagonia, or the jungles of Brazil. Pani Helena, I don't understand how you can bury yourself in this remote corner of the world."

Madame Modjeska: "Because we like it here, Ignace. It's a new land! When we came to California, there was not even the railroad. We carried our possessions from Los Angeles in carts. We are pioneers!"

Paderewski: "You who have played before the crowned heads of Europe, in the most famous theaters of Vienna and Berlin."

Madame Modjeska: "Well, it's pooh to all that, because I'm an old woman now, Ignace, and I like it here, as I said. And do you know, there is a coyote who comes into my garden, and also a rattlesnake."

Paderewski: "Oh, perfect."

Madame Modjeska: "Besides there are my begonias. If I left who would take care of my begonias?"

Paderewski: "You know that all Europe would fall at your feet if you returned to the stage."

Madame Modjeska: "On one leg like Bernhardt?"

Paderewski: "You have two legs."

Madame Modjeska: "I can hardly walk on either. My acting days are over, Pan Ignace, my dear friend. I am going to buy a little island in Balboa Bay and live out the rest of my years there, like a hermit."

"You are already a hermit here, Pani Helena."

Madame Modjeska: "Ah, fine. Stop and think what you are saying, you precious imbecile, my dearest Pan Ignace. We have dined like Lucullus this evening, and then we went to the opera, and now here we are surrounded by books and fine paintings and drinking champagne and you are telling me I am a hermit. I am old, old, but I draw my strength from youth. I must constantly have youth. Herma," she said, "you must sing. Sing your Canzonetta. Ignace, to the piano."

"I am a person of the city," he continued to complain while she led him to the piano, "and too much open space disconsolates me."

"No one is interested in your disconsolation, Pan Ignace. Play the piano. Music," she explained to Herma, "is good for the soul but bad for the character.'' And, perhaps in order to show that he did not have a bad character, Paderewski did in fact cheer up as he straightened his elbows and embarked into an improvisation of Susanna's guitar continuo.

Under the circumstances, and after the champagne, it seemed quite natural to Herma that she should have so distinguished an accompanist. With her hands clasped at her waist, she lifted her head and sang.

> "Voi che sapete
> che cosa è amor . . .''

The Canzonetta was so familiar now that she could have sung it in her sleep, under water in the bath, or hanging upside down on a trapeze. She lilted through the short lines with her young voice at its sweetest and most pleading. She could act too; a little wrinkle of pathos appeared in the immaculate and unmarred brow, belied by the smile in the eyes. And she concluded confidently: ''Ladies, see whether I've love in my heart.''

Everyone clapped politely. Madame Modjeska was wearing her restrained little smile, with an ironic look in her eyes. After a little conference with her accompanist, Herma went on to some other things. First the Bell Song from *Lakme,* to demonstrate her coloratura, and then ''Mi chiamano Mimì,'' as an example of her mastery of the more intricate and modern harmonic effects. The greatest pianist in the world, in fact, wrinkled his brow a little as he worked his way through Puccini's modulations. The clear young voice, dodging the harmonies deftly, came to its simple recitative statement at the end. ''Altro di me non le saprei narrare.'' Another polite patter of applause.

Herma glanced at Mr. Paderewski. He nodded. After a review of the chords, and a fragment of melody for a cue, the piano paused. Herma slipped softly into the song.

> '' 'Tis the last rose of summer
> Left blooming alone;
> All her lovely companions
> Are faded and gone;
> No flower of her kindred,
> No rosebud is nigh,
> To reflect back her blushes,
> Or give sigh for sigh.''

These were three stanzas, as Herma, and Madame Modjeska herself, very well knew. The clear and slightly thin voice lingered over the lines with a skillful pathos, coming up to the high notes a little flat and then gliding to the pitch, in the style of the sentimental song of the period. In the dulcet tone of angels, who pity and yet are unmoved, it described the gems dropping away from Love's shining circle, and advised the Rose to go to sleep with the lovely who lay scentless and dead. Herma's expression was placid except for the small wrinkle of sadness in her brow. She came to the last line, slowing to the ritardando in a clear and perfect pitch: ''Oh! who would inhabit this bleak world alone?''

The piano chord died away and the room was silent. Madame Modjeska couldn't help herself. Out came the handkerchief and she dabbed at the corner of her eye. It was so flagrant a device that she laughed while she wiped a tear from her eye; but still she wept. "You young witch. You knew—didn't you—that that song touched my heart?" Still laughing, she wiped the other eye and put away the handkerchief.

The others applauded, the shy Mr. Sienkiewicz in what was evidently the Polish manner, holding one hand horizontal and bringing the other down on top of it. "Not a great voice but a good voice," said Paderewski. "I see you have studied with Nellie Melba, who is a friend of mine."

Herma said, "No. My teacher's name is Mrs. Opdike."

"There is a mystery here about Melba which is yet to be resolved, my dear Ignace. However, I believe it is more than a good voice. It is a remarkable voice. Her character is another matter. I warn everyone to beware of this creature. She is a crafty little thing."

"In your days, Pani Helena," said Paderewski respectfully, "you were as crafty as a fox."

"Yes. That's why I like this one. My dear, let me tell you something about myself. No, no!" she protested to the others, who were smiling, "let me tell it to her, even though you have all heard it before. I have played in the Staatstheater in Berlin, the Opera House in Vienna, and the Odéon in Paris. Also I am very rich, I have this house which is called Arden after my *As You Like It*, and which was designed by Stanford White. I have an estate in Poland near Krakow. And I have a private railroad car which is also called Arden. When I travel about the world, everyone crowds to see me, and they pay large sums of money to see me walk on the stage. I have played with Booth, I have played with Mr. Otis Skinner, I have played with La Duse, who," she put in, "is a very conceited creature, I can tell you. My acting has been photographed with cinema machines. They even named a ship after me. And I am married to a count—Karol is a count, aren't you, Karol?" Mr. Chlapowski smiled. "And," continued Madame, "do you know how I got all this?"

"No," said Herma, since this seemed to be the vocable called for at this point.

"First of all I work very hard, and second I do not trust anyone to tell me what is right for myself. Managers agents critics no one, not even my beloved husband Karol." (Herma caught Mr. Chlapowski's eye; he raised his brows and sighed.) "I myself decide what is right for myself. I trust no one. Particularly not men. But this includes everyone, because as the world is presently organized, all the decisions are made by men. But not," she added, "those which I make for myself. Do not," she reiterated as though afraid that Herma had not grasped the point, "trust men to tell you what to do. Because they will advise you first of all," she concluded, "to get in bed with them."

"Oh, Pani Helena," sighed Paderewski, "you make it sound as though it were all our fault."

Madame seemed a little exhausted after this speech. Mr. Chlapowski was lighting another long thin cigar. "For me too, my dear friend, if you please." He extracted another from his coat pocket, passed it to her,

and lighted it. She drew on it and turned to Herma. She still seemed
tired. "You've never seen a lady with a cigar before, have you? But
in my country we have a saying: Break bread with an Arab and smoke
with a Pole. Don't be alarmed." She laughed. "I shan't ask you to
join me."

Herma was rather hoping, in fact, that someone would offer her a
cigar, since the customs at Arden seemed to be so free. She said, "I've
seen you smoking a cigar before."

"Have you?" inquired Madame archly. "And on what occasion, if
you please?"

"It was in the S. P. station in Santa Ana, when I was a small girl.
You stopped there for a moment in your private car."

"It's fate," said Madame, throwing up her hands. "We were destined to be flung together, you and I. And now, my dear, let's leave these
gentlemen, who probably want to tell unseemly stories to each other, and
go into the study."

She led Herma into a small room with books and musical scores on
one wall, an escritoire, a small round table with a scarf and a lamp on
it, and two chairs upholstered in tapestry. She herself sat down at the
escritoire and Herma took the other chair. It was almost daylight.
Through the window the sky was beginning to lighten in the east.

"My dear," she said fixedly, "have you obligations in the world?"

"I don't understand."

"What do your Papa and Mama wish for you in the world?"

"I'm going to become a singer."

"H'mm," said Madame. She regarded her reflectively out of her
dark, melancholy, and yet somehow humorous eyes. Then she smiled, but
this time as though to herself.

She opened the drawer of the escritoire, took out a piece of monogrammed notepaper, and dipped her pen into violet ink. "Dear Mr.
Larkin," she wrote. "I have something for you. And I think you will
know how to appreciate it."

27.

Fred went down Ross Street under the sycamores, which
were leafless now in the bright winter sun. In his right hand he carried
a large tapestry portmanteau, with brass fittings and leather reinforce-
ments at the corners, and in his left hand an equally large horsehide
suitcase, oblong in form. In this way balanced, like a whale ship hoisting
two whales, he managed to stagger down the sidewalk. As luck would
have it, after only a block or two he met Mr. Farkuss, who was coming
the other way in his wagon. The carpenter, who as usual had a grizzle
of gray on his red face, pulled up on the reins.

"Git in," he invited.

Fred threw the suitcases into the wagon and climbed aboard.

Mr. Farkuss got the horse going again with a slap of the leathers. He turned and stared at Fred in a rather blurred way, attempting to focus his attention.

"Goin' to the station?"

"Yes."

"Leavin' town?"

"Yes."

"That's a smart thing," said Mr. Farkuss.

He took the bottle from between his knees, tipped it up, and swallowed half a cupful or so. He sighed and wiped his mouth with the back of his hand.

"Care for a drink?"

Fred accepted, first wiping the mouth of the bottle on his sleeve and then taking a good-sized swig. He barely managed to avoid choking, but he maintained his aplomb. He handed the bottle back.

Mr. Farkuss picked his nose. "Last time I picked you up," he said, "you wasn't no bigger than a grasshopper."

Fred met his glance steadily. "I don't believe you ever picked me up before."

Mr. Farkuss examined him more carefully, in his blurry and yet fixed way, for quite a long time. One eye did not look in quite the same direction as the other. "No," he said after a while, "I guess I never did."

At the S. P. station he stopped to let Fred down. He watched while Fred pulled the suitcases off the wagon and balanced them one at the end of each arm.

"Them Spaniards," he said, "didn't mean no harm, but they might of run right over a little fella like you."

"Bye," said Fred. "Thanks for the ride."

Mr. Farkuss stared after him fuzzily, still trying to focus his attention. Then he shook up the reins and drove off slowly.

Fred carried the two suitcases into the station. He sat on one and put his feet on the other. In only a few minutes the morning train from San Diego appeared around the bend in the orange trees, rushed with a clatter into the station, and slowed to a stop with squeaking brakes. Fred pushed the two suitcases into the nearest car and then climbed in after them. There were no other passengers for Los Angeles. The conductor, out on the platform, consulted his watch. Then he yelled "Board!" to himself and clambered on. The train jerked, groaned, and launched into motion.

It gathered speed little by little down the track. Fred looked out the window. Over the roofs he could see the top of French's Opera House and the steeple of the First Baptist Church, the ragged tops of palm trees, a red flare of bougainvillea blossoms in a patch of green. A sort of hard walnut appeared in his throat, and he swallowed it with difficulty. Farewell, Santa Ana! With its rows of orange trees baking in the sun, and the sea crashing nearby on the white beach—nevermore, croaked

some raven. It was a childhood he was leaving behind, or was it two
childhoods? He was a little muddled on this point, but the walnut was
still there in his throat. For some reason, perhaps remembering Aunt
Minnie and her Neapolitan song, he cried inside himself, addio!

Then he saw something else. Down Fourth Street, and turning left
in front of the station, came Gambrinus in his dogcart. He was dressed
as usual in his frock coat and beaver. He was going at a mad pace, and
there was a furious look on his face. The train was still gathering speed,
and the dwarf overtook it until he was even with Fred's car. They stared
at each other through the glass and Gambrinus shook his fist.

"Thief! Seducer! Despoiler! Kidnapper! Assassin!"

He was beside himself with rage. Fred gazed at him, safe behind the
glass. Whipping up Bernard, the dwarf galloped him along the platform,
off the end of it, and on along the dirt right-of-way that paralleled the
tracks, kicking up a storm of leaves and dust. But more and more the
train outpaced him, and finally he was left behind.

28.

Las Flores, which was about thirty miles east of Los
Angeles, was on the Pomona line of the S. P. Fred had to transfer at
Los Angeles, and it was a ride of about an hour after that. The station
was a small rococo building covered with scrollwork and ornament,
painted a gleaming white with green trim. The sign on the roof was
almost as big as the station:

L A S   F L O R E S

in large ornate letters. There was no town anywhere near it. The S. P.
had built the station for the sole convenience of Mr. Larkin, and no one
ever used it except Mr. Larkin or his guests.

Here Fred was met by a coachman driving an elegant coach, a
tallyho drawn by four splendid bays. The two bags were loaded and Fred
got on top of the tallyho next to the coachman. They went off along a
broad avenue lined with oleanders in bloom. Presently they crossed
through the gate, a kind of Trajan's Arch imitated in carved wood and
scrollwork, and entered the ranch. It stretched as far as the eye could
see in all directions, with the foothills of the Sierras behind it. There
were woods and lakes, what appeared to be an enormous horse barn,
fruit and nut trees, grapevines, and fields of grain. Prize beef cattle
stood about in aristocratic poses. In the distance, on a pond, Fred caught
sight of a pair of swans.

The coachman seemed to have metamorphized out of a novel by
Dickens. He wore a short frock coat and breeches, which he was almost
portly enough to burst, and a porkpie hat. His beefy face was clean-

shaven. Quite possibly he was genuine and had been imported from England along with the tallyho. When he began to talk, however, it was in a pure western twang.

"You a friend o' Mr. Larkin's?"

"Nope."

He peered sideways at Fred out of his piglike but friendly eyes. Quite patently he liked to talk, and just as obviously he was a man of insatiable curiosity about his fellow human beings. He was favorably inclined toward Fred from the start, since he had chosen to ride on top of the tallyho, where they could have a little friendly conversation, rather than inside.

"He must know who you are. Sent me to the depot to pick up somebody off the 3:20. That's you, ain't it?"

"Yep."

But after a moment, not wishing to seem unfriendly himself, Fred remarked, "This is quite a place."

"I'll say it's quite a place. Ole Lucky, he made it all in the gold fields, y'know. Come out here in the fifties, at the time o' the Rush. But he didn't dig it out with no pick and shovel—not him."

"Not his style, eh?"

"Not ole Lucky. Didn't care for blisters on his hands. He lent 'em money at twenty percent. That was his style. And he snooped around and bought up claims that nobody thought was worth anything, and they made him millions. That's how ole Lucky got rich."

He was silent for a moment, allowing Fred to observe the wonders of the ranch as they passed.

"That there's the horse barn," he resumed after a moment. "Over a hundred prize Ayrabs in there, and some ridin' horses for the ladies. Horses and women, that's what he likes. Yep," he went on, "in his time old Lucky was a great one for actresses. That's why he built the Larkin Theayter in Frisco. Cause if you got a theayter," he explained in case Fred didn't see the point, "you got lots of actresses around.

"Course," he said after a pause, "all that was a long time ago. He still has a hotel and the theayter in Frisco, but he don't go up there much anymore. He sticks pretty close to the ranch. He don't need to go anywhere. He's got three houses right here on the ranch."

He pointed out the Big House, a kind of rococo wooden palace in the curlicued style of the seventies, painted white with green trim like the station, and the Cottage, in the same style but in miniature. Even so, it was as big as the largest house in Santa Ana. The Cottage, he explained, was used for guests of special importance, or those who brought an entourage with them. Lily Langtry had stayed there, Mr. Leland Stanford, and more than one President.

"And that there," he pointed with the end of his whip, "is the Adobe. First house built on the ranch. That's the only place where ole Lucky really feels comfort'ble. When there's no guests he likes to set around in the Adobe and talk to the boys. Me, and the hostlers, and them Spanish vaqueros he has to chase the cattle around. It's more homey there. He can set and drink whiskey, and tell stories with the boys, and fart when he feels like it. The Big House is for his lady friends. The Cottage ain't much used anymore.''

''Where are you taking me?''

''To the Big House.''

''I'm not a lady friend.''

''That's where he tole me to bring you.''

The tallyho drew up before the Big House, and Fred got out and set his suitcases down. He turned around. On the steps of the house he was confronted by an old man with a pale face and a wispy and dangling mustache. He wore a Stetson, a black suit with fine stripes, a white shirt, a black bow tie, and high-buttoned shoes, these last immaculately polished. Fred took a deep breath. This was it. Now he had to worm his way around this old codger who looked as wily as Proteus, and almost as wiry and tough—a man who had outwitted the shrewdest bankers of San Francisco and tricked people out of whole railroads. Still, he was getting a little senile now. At least Fred hoped so.

Larkin stared at him suspiciously. ''Where's the little gel?''

''I'm Mademoiselle Herma's manager. She'll be along afterward. I'm seeing to the arrangements. Where are our rooms?''

''Your rooms?''

''Yes. We require two rooms, but with connecting bath.''

''Connecting bath,'' Larkin repeated heavily, as though he hadn't understood.

''And a mirror.''

''When did you say this little gel is coming?''

''She'll be arriving after a while. And she'll be coming down to dinner.''

''She a pretty little gel?''

''She's a singer,'' said Fred, meeting his glance firmly. ''She sings opera and other things.''

''Modjeska said in the note she was a pretty little gel.''

''She said nothing of the sort.''

''Yep. Well, I'll spect to see her at dinner.''

''Right,'' said Fred.

Chewing his mustaches, evidently disappointed, Larkin disappeared. Fred was taken in tow by a Negro majordomo, who led him through the door into an elaborate Corinthian vestibule and up the stairs. Another servant, a boy with Spanish features, staggered after them with the two suitcases. This procession continued on along the upstairs hall, which was immaculately varnished and had pedestals every so often with Roman busts on them. Halfway down this long hall Fred met somebody coming the other way: a lady, rotund in form and no longer in her first youth, wearing a white silk gown that sparkled in some way with tiny silver points.

He stopped, forgetting for the moment to breathe. He was in the presence of what was surely the world's most magnificent bosom. In the upper part of the white gown—Fred was unaware of anything else for the moment—all of nature's bounty was displayed, wonderfully proportioned and straining at the silk. Every detail was, not visible exactly, but suggested through the contours of the ingeniously contrived gown. What in women of more modesty and discretion was a single and undivided monobust was here wonderfully bifurcated, the two convexities delightfully and excruciatingly distinct. Nor were they hemispheres, as in the case of very young girls or women of more modest development. They were lightly pendulous, semicircular at the lower edge but curving at the top into a catenary of the most symmetrical and geometric perfection. They were like two large and soft orbs of the most fragrant balm, suspended in faery film. At the center of each was something that resembled nothing else in the world so much as the tip of a baby's finger.

She stopped too and confronted Fred with one hand on her hip. They examined each other for a few seconds. Then she smiled. "I'm Ernestine Lalange. I'm a—friend who stays with Mr. Larkin."

Fred was still staring at the bosom. "Are you?"

"Yes. I just said I was. Are you hard of hearing?"

"No. My hearing is fine. Eyesight too."

"I can see that."

She stood there a moment longer, her hand on her hip and the upper part of her body thrust forward slightly. Then she said, "Your room's down there."

"We require two rooms, with connecting bath."

"You are a funny one."

She swept on, looking back at him once over her shoulder.

Herma, in her white dress with the strawberry-colored ribbons and the skirt that ended just above the ankle, came down a half an hour or so before dinner, while it was still light. When Mr. Larkin caught sight of her his mouth worked a little and his mustache tipped back and forth. He was wearing his Stetson in the house. But perhaps this was because he had been waiting to take her out to show her the grounds and outbuildings.

His eyes were a pale blue, the color of the sky after a dust storm. "Like to show you the place," he told her a little louder than necessary.

"I'd love to."

The horse barn was first. This was his pride. His carriage horses and prize Arabians were fed on the choicest grain in stalls of mahogany and walnut with fancy brass fretwork. The architecture and trim were identical to that of the Big House.

He lit a cigar and puffed it. "I know horses," he asserted. "Bought my first when I was only twelve and made a profit on it." He showed her the tack room, where his racing silks were on display, along with an extraordinary amount of expensive saddlery and the various trophies he had won. His comments were a kind of litany. They were evidently those he made to all visitors. "Never lost a race I didn't intend to lose," he told her.

They went on to the greenhouses, the pump house for the irrigation system where all the piping was polished brass, and the pressing room where wine was made from his own vineyards in October. The wine was served on the tables of his San Francisco hotel. He showed her a bottle. The label with the words "Las Flores" was in the same design as his racing silks, gold with a green Maltese cross. Herma was getting rather bored with all this. She examined the bottle and smiled patiently.

The tour of the grounds was somewhat more interesting. The whole central part of the ranch was one vast park. In the endless vistas of English lawn, oak trees were scattered about, along with magnolias, rare flowering eucalyptus, and coral trees. Mr. Larkin attempted to break off a branch of coral blossoms for her, but his hernia attacked him when he stretched upward for it and he had to desist. He pointed out the croquet court, the rose garden, and the Temple d'Amour, a kind of gazebo of solid marble in the classic manner.

He was very courtly, at this stage at least. However his mustache still tipped back and forth when he looked at her, an inauspicious sign. As they skirted around the large pond in front of the Big House he attempted to take her arm, but she eluded him. "You're a funny gel," he said.

The pond was very fine. It was full of lotus and rare water lilies, and there were genuine Egyptian papyrus along the edges. Swans glided over the surface in the gray evening air, and white egrets stood about in water up to their knees. Mr. Larkin threw his cigar into the pond. They went up the path from the pond to the Big House, challenged on the way by a peacock who threatened to spread his tail at them, but retreated when Mr. Larkin threw a rock at him. "Demned beasts. You know," he told her, perhaps through some devious association with the peacock's tail, "you're a pretty little gel."

He did take off his hat before they sat down at the dinner table. With the Stetson off he had an aureole of white hair that gave him an odd and quite spurious saintly look. The hair stuck out on all sides, around a bald spot that began at his brow and continued up to the center of his head. The straggly mustache was only partly gray. His nose was long and fleshy, with a bump in the center, and ended in a reddish bulb. He shook out his napkin and began eating, not waiting for the others. Also present at the table was Madame Ernestine, still in her white gown with silver spangles.

Following sherry, the dinner was expertly served by Chinese waiters. First came a trout from the trout pond, which was not the same as the big pond with the swans; then Chateaubriands carved from Mr. Larkin's own steers, along with asparagus, pickled cherries from the ranch, and wild rice brought in from Minnesota. The dinner wine was Las Flores Reserve, which was "fruity" as the saying goes and tasted like grape juice with bubbles in it. Mr. Larkin popped cherries into his mouth and expounded his financial principles—this too was evidently part of the lecture invariably delivered to guests. "Nobody ever collected a bill from P. J. Larkin without a court judgement," he said. "By the time I was as old as you are,'' he told Herma, ''I was married and a businessman, and making a fortune racing my own horses.'' He stared vacantly at the wall opposite. ''That was in Missouri,'' he added as though he had just recalled it. Seeming to remember that Herma was still there, he glanced at her, his mustache twitching a little, and ate another cherry. ''I was a millionaire,'' he said, ''by the time I was old enough to vote.''

While he went on staring at her and eating cherries, Herma examined Madame Ernestine. With feminine pitilessness she summed up her assets and faults. Once, it was said, she had been an actress. Now she was lightly fanée, not the Last Rose of Summer perhaps, but at least one getting on well into August. Her eyes were slightly puffy and there were lines around her mouth. But the bosom was superb, and this made up for all the rest. It was entirely a natural phenomenon and owed nothing to artifice; and neither, as far as Herma could tell, was any corset necessary for the trim and narrow waist. Herma felt a little twinge of envy. Her own waist was about the same size as Madame Ernestine's, but there was nothing much either above it or below it to accentuate the slimness so eloquently. Madame Ernestine said nothing during the meal, or very little. Mr. Larkin continued his monologue.

''When I was your age, I crossed the plains in charge of my own wagon train. Fit the Indians.''

''So did my Aunt Minnie,'' said Herma a little crossly.

''I was a crack shot. Still am. Fought a duel once with a fellow in Frisco that didn't like the way I bought his bank. Shot off part of his ear. Buying that bank was a smart business. Soon as I bought the bank, I foreclosed the mortgage it held on the Garnet. Those fellows were behind in their payments. It was supposed to be a secret, but I found out about it. Old Colis P. Huntington himself he said to me, ''P. J., a fellow has to get up pretty early in the . . . in the . . .'' He seemed to have trouble remembering what time in the day people got up. ''Get up pretty early to get ahead of you. He always called me P. J.''

''Is that so?''

''Him, and Mark Hopkins, and Leland Stanford, and Mackay and Fair and Flood and O'Brien. I knew all of 'em. I bought and sold 'em.''

''Did they all call you P. J.?''

''Everybody did who knew me well.''

''But that seems like a rather odd thing for women to call you.''

This seemed to fuddle him. He searched in his memory. ''But women didn't call me that.''

''What did the women call you?''

''Well, let me think. I don't know that they called me anything. I guess,'' he said, ''that they called me Mr. Larkin.''

There followed elderberry liqueur. Mr. Larkin's doctor had forbidden him coffee so nobody had any. Everybody got up from the table, and he led them into the largest and most ornate of the salons, which he called the sitting room. There he sat down at a square pianola the size of a wagon. Pumping this contrivance vigorously with his legs, he pushed the levers and played them first *If Your Foot Is Pretty Why Not Show*

It?, then *Champagne Charlie, Saturday Matinee, Kiss Me Mother, Kiss Your Darling,* and *The Cat Came Back.*

He seemed pleased with himself. He was still in fairly good physical condition, that was clear. Pumping the pedals of the pianola took a certain amount of vigor. He didn't ask Herma to sing. Perhaps he had forgotten she was a singer. But he remembered after all, because he turned and stared at her all at once in a fixed and portentous manner.

"And now, young leddy," he said, "let's go and have a serious discussion about your career."

He led her away to the library. There he sat her down in a chair and pulled up another chair so close that their knees were touching.

"I'm not a man that likes to waste his time," he said. "Now, I've got an opera company in my theater in Frisco. It's the best in the west," he said, although Herma knew that the Grand Opera Company was far more distinguished than the Larkin Theater Company, which confined itself chiefly to operettas and other trifles of no very great weight. "Yep," he said, "I pay all their salaries even when they're not working. Them singers," he said, "don't work one week out of three."

"Probably they're rehearsing."

But Mr. Larkin had a metaphor. "It's like a stable of racehorses," he said. "They go on eating hay even when they're not running." His hand was resting on her knee, perhaps out of absentmindedness. However, the serious discussion of her career seemed to consist mainly of his touching her knee as he made each point. As he went on there were fewer and fewer points, and more and more touching.

"There's a manager of the opera company," he said, "but he takes orders from me. He doesn't like that sometimes, but he does it."

The hand on her knee was strong and sinewy. It was the hand of a frontiersman, but a very old one. It was the color of antique parchment and the nails were not very clean. There were brown liver spots on the back of it. Never, never, and never in the world could she allow herself to be touched by anyone who had brown spots on the back of his hands.

She stood up, slipping the knee adroitly out from under his hand. "Maybe he thinks he knows more about music than you do."

Mr. Larkin stood up too. He followed Herma around to the back of the chair, where she had taken shelter. "That may be," he said, "but I'm the one that's got the money."

Herma circled a long walnut table with a lamp and a shawl on it. One could keep this up indefinitely. It was like a children's game. She went around the table one way, he the other.

"It's my theater," he said. "It's called the Larkin after me."

"No one," said Herma in a matter-of-fact tone, "can possess the soul of an artist."

He lunged around the table at her like a mountain lion. Herma turned deftly away between two chairs and out the door of the library. He followed.

"I buy 'em and sell 'em," his voice echoed in the corridor, evidently apropos of the souls of artists. She glanced back. He was a few yards behind, staring not exactly at her but over her shoulder in an oddly distant way, as though there were a ghost down the corridor behind her.

"I never lost a horse race I didn't intend to lose," he mumbled as though to himself.

Herma ducked out of the corridor and into a room that proved to be the dining room. There was no sign of Madame Ernestine. She went out through the door on the other side. The old gentleman, who was beginning to totter a little, chased her from room to room, knocking expensive vases from their pedestals as he went. When he saw Herma heading across the vestibule toward the front door he stopped and searched around on the hat rack for his Stetson, which he set firmly on his head. When he got it on he realized he had lost sight of her. It was out the door she had gone, the little witch. He went on across the marble tiles of the vestibule, groping in the air ahead of him like a sleepwalker.

Outside, Herma went down the steps into the night. A slice of moon as yellow as a melon hung in the sky to the west. It lightened the sky a little, but the park, the trees, and the pond were as black as ink. Her white dress glowing in the darkness, she went on down the path around the pond, not running exactly but at a quick walking pace. The old gentleman was somewhere behind her. She heard footsteps on the gravel, heavier and at a slower rhythm than her own.

On the far side of the pond the path divided. And here Mr. Larkin took a wrong turning. Instead of following Herma he went on around the pond in pursuit of an egret, which he mistook for her white dress in the darkness. He realized his mistake only when he was up to his knees in water. He stopped, watching the white shape take to the air with a beating of wings.

Coming back around the pond the other way, Herma regained her room without difficulty and latched the door. "What a donkey," she said. She went into the bathroom, turned to the mirror, and set her hands into her hair to push it back from her brow. She looked into the glass with a faintly sibylline, searching expression. Her fingers reached behind her for the hooks on her dress.

When Fred came downstairs it was after midnight. Mr. Larkin had gone to bed, and Madame Ernestine was wandering around aimlessly through the series of connecting varnished salons. When she saw Fred she found a servant and had him bring two tiny cups of coffee. The Chinese boy served them in a kind of breakfast room lighted with a pair of oil lamps. There was no electricity in the house, Fred noticed for the first time. It had been built in the seventies and Mr. Larkin had kept to his old-fashioned notions. They sat down at a small round table no bigger than a hat, so that their hands almost touched as they reached for the cups. Fred had difficulty removing his eyes from Nature's Bounty across the table and keeping his attention on the conversation.

He said, "Mr. Larkin seems very vigorous for his age."

"Oh, that pig. He has cast me aside, contending that I'm too old to interest anyone any more." She spoke in a slightly theatrical way, drawling the words as though it were a part she was taking only half seriously.

"I can assure you he's mistaken."

"He says I'm too heavy. He likes young girls. Skinny little things. He always has. However," she went on in her vein of mock pathos, "he allows me to go on living here."

"That's generous of him."

"Very generous. Or perhaps only absentminded. And then too, from time to time, when he gets hard up . . . It's humiliating," she concluded, not filling in the details.

"H'mm," said Fred.

"He's as horny as an old stallion. Few men can boast, as Lucky Larkin can, of having been sued for breach of promise at the age of seventy by a nineteen-year-old girl."

"Remarkable," said Fred.

If there were two moons, Fred thought, still entranced by the spectacle across the table, they would shimmer thus side by side in the soft summer sky. "It sounds like an exciting life."

"Oh, that sort of thing doesn't happen much anymore. I think he's getting more careful. Perhaps," she said, "someone will still shoot him in the end. But he's a tough old bird. He survives. Everyone else from his time is gone, but he survives."

"You sound as though you have a certain affection for him."

"I just ply my trade. Once I was an actress, and now I do this. It's not much of an existence. Do you suffer from myopia," she asked him, "or is there something wrong with the front of my dress? Perhaps I'm coming unbuttoned?"

"No, worse luck," Fred managed to mutter.

Up to now she had been chattering away without, apparently, paying him very much attention. Now she seemed to study him for the first time. A little smile gradually formed, quite contrived—the smile of an actress.

"I imagine you've already been taken on the obligatory tour of Mr. Larkin's possessions?"

"In a manner of speaking."

"Still, I imagine there are one or two you haven't seen. And I'm sure they would interest you."

From the bodice of the white gown she produced an object and held it up in her hand.

"What's that?"

"The key to the Cottage. However," she cautioned with a mock grave expression, "that is only for Presidents and very important persons."

They stood up, and she led the way out the door into the dark. It was only a short distance around the pond and across a stretch of lawn to the pretty bijou-like house with its elaborately carved ornaments. The moon had set now and it was very dark. The white-painted Cottage gleamed as though it were phosphorescent, or in some way exuded light of itself.

Ernestine opened the door in the dark, then lighted a single oil lamp with a rose-colored shade. Perhaps it was all part of the stage-craft; at least the lamplight did wonders for her complexion. Then she turned without a word and folded him in her arms. He felt himself sinking like a shipwrecked mariner into the world's most magnificent bosom. Hardly knowing how it had happened, he was surrounded by silk, softness, and warmth. He was no longer conscious of standing on his feet. Perhaps he wasn't standing anymore.

He began negotiating in a muffled tone. "There may be a misunderstanding here. This is all very pleasant, but really the only reason I am visiting Mr. Larkin is to serve as Mademoiselle Herma's manager."

"And so?"

"You see, Mademoiselle Herma wants to sing in an opera company, and an opera company is precisely what Mr. Larkin has."

"Then everything is fine."

Fred had two difficulties. The first was that he was being held so tightly that he couldn't breathe, and the second was that Ernestine's mouth pressed constantly onto his own in a way that made conversation difficult. "The trouble is," he managed to get out, "that Mr. Larkin can't seem to keep his mind on business. His attention strays," he explained, "onto other things."

"Leave it to me."

"Are you sure?"

"I guarantee it."

Fred, breaking out of the encompassing white silk, came to the surface and drank of a heady air containing perfume. They fell together onto a large sofa of baby-blue velours, decorated with ostrich plumes and bird-of-paradise feathers.

The white gown soared into the air like an egret. Fred too divested himself, if not so dramatically yet still with an equal skill. After that the drama proceeded rapidly from exposition through climax to dénouement. In spite of his youth, Fred already knew a good deal about the art of pleasing women. He was diligent, he had sensitivity, and he appreciated the feminine point of view. "Bravo, Fred!" cried Ernestine.

II. SAN FRANCISCO

1.

Herma woke up only very slowly. She chose deliberately in her sleep to do so, in order to savor every detail of the delicious sensations she knew she would find surrounding her as she awoke. First of all, there was motion. She lay in a medium-sized bed with yellow satin sheets, but the whole room and everything in it was dashing across the landscape at a dizzying pace, smoothly, with only a faint hum and a sound of rushing from the air going by outside. Now and then there would be a series of rapid little clicks, as though from a friendly insect, then silence again except for the hum and the faint rush of air.

She opened her eyes. The ceiling overhead was of hammered gold and silver, embossed with a design of morning glories. The room was paneled in satinwood, inlaid with ebony, gold, and amaranth. Directly before her eyes, facing the foot of the bed, was a mirror with beveled edges, only faintly gray in places where the silvering had begun to tarnish a little. On one side was the door to the corridor; on the other a window with a curtain drawn over it. The curtain was the same canary yellow as the bed sheets, embroidered in a fine gold thread. On the wall next to the window was an oval portrait of Madame Modjeska, and opposite it on the other wall was a kind of medallion with an intricate letter M and morning glories twining around it.

Pushing down the canary-colored sheet, she put her legs out onto the floor and stood up. On the carpet by the bedside with a leopard skin. The head was still attached to it and it looked a little like Mr. Paderewski. On the whole it was a friendly-looking leopard. Standing on the luxurious, slightly scratchy pelt, Herma looked into the mirror at the other end of the room.

She saw a girl in a long white nightgown that came to her ankles. The light cambric was translucent enough so that a pair of small, slightly protruding dots were visible on her chest, and the faintest hint of a little triangular shadow between her legs. There was a strawberry-colored ribbon worked into the neck of the gown, and the ends of the sleeves which came a little below her elbows. With the curtain drawn over the window, the bedroom was illuminated in a dim golden light reflected from the sheets and the canary-colored carpet. The face in the mirror, with its short hair and its frank and open, slightly amused glance, was tinged with this same gold. With the light from below the eyes were shadowed and slightly mysterious; they seemed older than the rest of her. The shoulders and the rest of the body were narrow; the gown fell straight to the ankles without touching the flat boyish hips. Herma smiled. She thought: if I were a man I would fall in love with this girl. Then she thought: no, if I were a man, I would be a beast like the rest of them, and I would only desire her. She smiled again.

She pulled the nightgown off and flung it onto the bed. Then she went into the bath, through a tiny door so narrow that you almost had to turn sideways to pass through it. The tub was carved from a single piece of Carrara marble. The washbowl and other fixtures were of this same rich and mottled, slightly iridescent stone. Herma sat down and tinkled—as Mama always called it when she was a child—into the Carrara toilet. Then she splashed water onto her face and hands and dried them on a pale gold Turkish towel with an HM monogram in the center. The elegant cut-glass vial by the marble basin, held in a silver ring so it wouldn't fall when the train swayed, probably contained cologne. Women who were no better than they ought to be used it, she knew, to arouse the lower instincts in the opposite sex. She applied a little, here and there. Then, totally naked and smelling like a magnolia, she went back into the bedroom to dress.

She chose a modest blouse, a long tubular skirt, and a strawberry-colored scarf tied loosely at the side with the points resting on her shoulder. Although the car rushed along smoothly with only a pleasant clicking from underneath, it did sway a little. Standing up after putting on her shoes, she almost fell and reached out to steady herself. Next to her hand was a brass plate with two white buttons, one marked "Butler" and the other "Galley." She pushed the first.

In only a few seconds there was a discreet tap.

"Come in," she said as though it were a game.

The door opened, revealing a portly middle-aged man with a bald head and gray sideburns. He was elegantly clad in a morning coat with a striped waistcoat showing under it. He said not a word.

"I would like some breakfast."

He inclined his head very slightly and gestured with his hand to show the way. Herma followed him down the corridor. In the parlor the place was already set at the small mahogany table. Everything was monogrammed: the linen cloth, the china plate and cup, and the silver service. In the center of the plate was a fine linen napkin in a silver ring chased in gold.

The butler spoke for the first time. His accent was English, authentic as far as Herma could tell.

"What would you like for breakfast, Miss?"

Herma felt she was being tested. "What would you recommend?"

"I would recommend smoked salmon with scrambled eggs, black coffee, and toast with quince preserves." As Herma considered, he added, "This is what Madame always takes."

Herma inclined *her* head, in the same discreet way. She could hardly keep from smiling. They were both behaving perfectly. She, Herma, had played her part at least as well as he had. He disappeared, leaving Herma to regard various replicas of herself in the mirrors which seemed to fill every part of Madame's private car which, Herma now remembered, was called Arden like her ranch. There was also a hand-carved piano to match the rest of the ornate woodwork, and a couch with satin pillows. Here in the parlor the curtains were opened and the sunlight flooded in. There were four windows, with ornamental etchings in the glass depicting the four seasons. Through these decorations the outside world penetrated only with a certain amount of distortion. Herma made out a grassy pasture rushing by, and some hills in the distance. But why concern one's self with the world outside, when what was inside regaled the senses so exquisitely? The ceiling overhead was the same hammered gold and silver as the one in the bedroom. Its design portrayed four nymphs, trailing scarves, being pursued in a circle by four shepherds similarly clad. A gold chandelier hung from overhead on a chain, and in some mysterious way was made not to swing as the train swayed its way around curves. At the end of the room, by the door to the galley, was another portrait of Madame Modjeska by Sargent, this one life-size and depicting her in her well-known role of Rosalind. Surrounded by the monograms and portraits, catching herself reflected in the dozen mirrors, Herma felt that there was perhaps a tiny trace of egotism in Madame. Still, she was very kind. It was probably simply a trait of actresses. Herma was uncertain whether she ought to guard closely against the appearance of this trait in herself, or encourage it in order to become like the others. She inclined toward the second idea. Very gravely, watching the images in the mirrors, she imitated the expression in the portrait: arch, slightly arrogant, the chin lifted a little.

In the middle of this pantomime, in place of the butler there appeared the cook himself with the breakfast. He was a pleasant black man, clad all in white, including a starched and immaculate chef's toque which for some reason he removed and set on a side table before he served the breakfast. The eggs and salmon were so hot they were still steaming, and so was the coffee.

Herma felt it was necessary to declare her independence a little from Madame, and from the butler, as polite as he was, by varying the breakfast slightly.

"I don't really care for black coffee. I'd like some cream."

"All right, Miss."

"And instead of quince preserves, some strawberry."

"Very good, Miss."

"What's your name?"

"My name Morton, Miss."

"Is that your first name or your last name?"

"That both my first name and my last name."

"And what's the butler's name?"

"The butler's name Mr. James. That his first name."

"You may call me Miss Herma."

"Very good, Miss. That your first name, Miss?"

"That's both my first name and my last name."

They both smiled at this. The cook grinned. Pouring the coffee, he inspected her sideways. "Madame," he said, "she sure can pick the lookers. All the young girls she let ride in this car, they could win prizes. The gentlemen," he said, "they not lookers quite so much. They incline to be older. They important gentlemen of various kinds. Some of them Polish gentlemen. The young girls, they in a different category."

"Does Madame let very many young girls ride in this car?"

"You the first."

They both laughed. Then there was a silence. Herma said, "So you think I could win a prize?"

"I was the judge, you could. Eat your eggs now fore they get cold."

"Do you have a lady friend, Morton?"

"I have two. One in Oakland, and one in Los Angeles."

It was one of the oddest conversations that Herma could remember having. On the one hand he retained the respectful and considerate manner called for by his condition, on the other hand he seemed to fall effortlessly into this intimacy as though they were old friends. After a moment, refilling her coffee cup, he inquired, "Do you have a gentleman friend, Miss Herma?"

"No. Or rather, yes," said Herma, a little confused. "That is, he isn't exactly a friend . . ."

"I understand perfectly," said Morton, although this could hardly be so. When Herma didn't quite understand it herself! But Morton, pressing a little way into her personal life and encountering this fluster, showed no sign of wanting to push further. He was the soul of discretion, in spite of his questions which would have been quite indiscreet in anyone else. "Reason I have a lady friend at both ends," he said, going back to his own life, "is that way I keep two persons happy. That very generous of me. Don't you agree, Miss Herma?"

"I would think," she told him, "that a person would be very fortunate to be your lady friend, Morton."

He had no comment to make on this. Perhaps she had been untactful. "We now passing through San Jose," he said. "You better hurry and finish up your breakfast, so you have time to spruce up a little fore we get to Oakland."

This remark, including its mild admonishment, he delivered with extreme politeness too, but in another manner. It was a fatherly manner; that was the only way she could think of it. He was advising her. He knew that young ladies are often dilatory, and she ought to be looking her best when she stepped off the train. She dug into her scrambled eggs and salmon, which were still warm, and finished them rapidly. Then she sighed with content. She looked around. Morton was still waiting to see if she wished anything else.

"How much more time do I have?"

"Half an hour. 'Cluding your sprucing up."

"Send Mr. James to me."

"Very good, Miss Herma."

Mr. James appeared and inclined his bald head as before, in his slightly superior way.

"I would like a glass of wine and a cigar. A Fine Hortelano," she added.

"Wine, Miss?"

"Champagne."

"Very good, Miss. And a Fine Hortelano."

He withdrew, returning in only a moment with a silver tray on which was a single goblet sparkling with pale amber fluid, the cigar, and a folded napkin. He showed no surprise. Perhaps he was used to such eccentricities. She had the impression that he would have behaved the same if she had ordered, perhaps, a leopard on a leash and a pipe of opium. He set the glass on the table, lit the Hortelano for her, and withdrew again with a bow.

The wine before Herma trembled faintly with the motion of the train. She drank only a little of it. It was not important that she should drink it. It was important only that she should sit this way, with the landscape unrolling behind the etched windows and draw at the cigar while the wine before her vibrated in its fragile tulip of crystal. It was not even necessary for anyone to see her. She saw herself, a little girl standing on the platform of the station in Santa Ana, gazing in dumb and hopeless admiration as this same railroad car had passed and disappeared down the track, scattering autumn leaves in its wake. As a matter of fact no one was paying any attention to her. It was rather early in the morning and the train was passing through San Leandro, a rather dull suburb of Oakland. Herma finished the cigar, stubbed it out in the saucer, and went off to her tiny bedroom to spruce up, as Morton put it.

2.

Exactly on time, the train drew in to the dim barnlike terminal out on the Oakland flats and stopped with a gassy wheeze of its brakes. Herma stepped down onto the platform in her neat skirt and blouse, with a light cape around her shoulders. After her came Mr. James carrying the portmanteau and the horsehide suitcase.

But Herma now saw a disadvantage to traveling in a private car. Since Arden had its own observation platform at the rear, it was necessarily at the end of the train. The ferry waiting in its slip was far off at the other end of the platform, beyond the engine. Mr. James kindly carried the two bags down to the head of the train, although this made him perspire in his morning coat and waistcoat. There he set them down, looking uncertainly at the ferry which was rocking in its slip and already half full of people. He seemed to have lost a good deal of his aplomb and calm command of the world once he left his own domain of the private car. In the sooty light of the train shed his morning coat was a little ludicrous; most of the other men were in work clothes, or in shiny serge suits and derbies.

"I'm sorry to say, Miss, that the train will be leaving in only a few minutes, to go off to the car barn where we'll be uncoupled. So . . ."

"I can do quite nicely from now on," Herma told him.

"Are you sure, Miss?"

She was quite sure. He left her, with a final little bow, and hurried back down the train. But after he was gone she was not so sure. She stepped between the two suitcases and tried them. She could lift them, but it was a kind of athletic feat. The muscles in her slim arms bulged like walnuts, and her knees showed signs of bending. She doubted whether she could take a step. She began to realize that in order to do so one had to remove the weight from one foot or the other, and this resulted in all the weight being transferred to the other leg, the knee of which crumpled.

"Help you with your grips, Miss?"

It was a young man, a rather nice-looking one, she observed with a second look, wearing the local costume which seemed to consist of a blue serge suit, a white shirt with a celluloid collar, a gold watch chain, and a derby. He had a bony face with a milky moonlike complexion. When he spoke he bent slightly forward, as though to bring himself an inch or two closer to her, all the while regarding her fixedly. His whole person was osseous and sinewy. There was something lightly sinister about him, in fact, although Herma could not quite lay her finger on what this was. In every outward way he was a pleasant enough person, and quite polite.

"It's only a few steps onto the ferry."

"Allow me."

In a masterful way he lifted the two suitcases. He hadn't anticipated their weight and they made him stagger a little. His pale face became slightly paler, and a film of sweat appeared above his mustache. He began lugging the suitcases down the ramp and onto the ferry, while Herma followed at his side.

"You've got a lot of luggage," he couldn't help saying.

"One belongs to my—manager."

He gave her a sidelong glance. "You're an actress?"

"A singer."

"Where's your manager now?"

"He'll be along."

He didn't seem to care for this idea very much, although he went on being outwardly pleasant. It was precisely this, Herma now saw, that made him seem lightly sinister: he smiled and spoke politely, but one had the impression that these were not natural impulses but only contrived means to an end, which might be quite other than smiling and polite. It was a crocodile smile. Yet he seemed to be a very respectable person. His serge suit wasn't shiny like those of most of the other men on the ferry. He set the suitcases down next to a polished wooden bench with a curving back. Then, still smiling in spite of his perspiration, he raised his derby to her and took his own seat—not next to her as she expected, but on the bench across from her, so that he stared directly at her from a distance of only five feet or so. Herma smoothed her skirt and sat primly with her hands in her lap, one suitcase on either side of her feet.

Although the ferry was more than half full now, there were only two other passengers on the pair of facing benches occupied by Herma and the bony young man. One was a weary female who looked as though she might be a charwoman going to work, and the other was a policeman in a blue uniform with brass buttons, not wearing his helmet but holding it resting on his knees, perhaps as a symbol that he was not yet on duty. The policeman had a broad red face and small suspicious eyes. The part of his forehead covered by the helmet when he was wearing it was white. He had one of the most inexpert haircuts that Herma had ever seen. It looked as though it had been done with a butcher knife by a child. The policeman stared from Herma to the bony young man and back again. It was clear that he saw that Herma and the bony young man were not yet friends, but that the bony young man hoped for them to be. He disapproved of this. He fixed his little eyes on them beadily. The charwoman also observed the drama, wearily.

"Your manager has evidently missed the ferry."

"I don't think so," said Herma.

It was true that the ferry was trembling and humming underneath now. The walls of the long shed were slowly beginning to move backwards, and the great paddle wheels, as high as a two-story building, were turning slowly. Then they increased their pace until the spokes blurred, throwing up two torrents of white water behind them. The ferry gathered speed out into the Bay. Here on the Oakland flats the water was still shallow and muddy. A few fish traps went by, consisting of reed fences held up by poles stuck in the mud. The bony young man leaned forward from his bench. He crossed his legs, in a manner indicating that he was about to speak again.

"He did miss the ferry, so I'll have to help you on the other side."

Herma said nothing.

"I'll be glad to do so. Where are you going?"

Herma averted her glance, caught the tiny eyes of the policeman, and looked in the other direction.

He bent toward her. "It's difficult for a young lady in a large city. I'd better accompany you to—to where you're going. I can see you settled. You see, I'm a clerk at the Crocker Bank, but the boss is a friend of mine and I don't have to be there before ten. My name," he added at the end, still leaning toward her confidently, "is Mr. Riemer."

The red-faced policeman wrinkled his nose. Herma had the impression that he was taking note of the name. Perhaps, she thought, he had a kind of imaginary notebook in there behind his nose, and the name Mr. Riemer went in there and was recorded until he had time to write it down.

"And I'm off at four o'clock," continued Mr. Riemer, "so perhaps, if you have nothing better to do, we might take tea at the Palace."

The policeman took another nasal note. The charwoman chewed the inside of her lip and regarded Herma thoughtfully.

From this point Herma resolved to say nothing to Mr. Riemer at all, neither did she meet his glance. She simply pretended he wasn't there.

"And afterward, dinner at Delmonico's. It's very discreet. They have private rooms." If he leaned forward any farther, Herma thought, he would fall off his bench. "So that your manager, in case he ever happens to catch his ferry, would never find out about it." Here he uncrossed his legs and crossed them the other way. "Oysters," he proposed in a kind of a croak, "and champagne." Before he had only smiled, but now he grinned. His lips parted. His teeth were slightly yellow.

Herma stood up and seized the two suitcases. She found that she could lift them after all, with a little extra effort. Swaying a little and supporting them an inch from the floor, she made her way to another bench. Unfortunately the only free places were in the row exactly behind the one Herma had been sitting on, so that the policeman and the charwoman, by looking over the tops of the benches, could still stare at her.

Mr. Riemer got up, came around the benches, and sat down opposite her, between a mother with her little girl and a businessman reading the *Chronicle*.

"I'll bet you haven't got any manager at all," he said. "You just made him up. Or if you have," he conjectured further, "he's given you the slip. He's a cad, is what he is. He's left you in the lurch." A trace of moisture appeared at the two ends of his smile. "I'll bet he's got some money of yours, hasn't he? I know these managers. I can tell you for certain, he's got a flossie in a flat in North Beach. That's where your money's going. He didn't meet you in Oakland because he's in North Beach with his flossie."

At this point his tongue came out and lapped away the moisture, which was on the point of slipping down the corner of his mouth. Then he was able to smile again. He did so very slowly, without taking his eyes from her.

Herma stood up and wrenched the suitcases off the floor again. With a feeling as though her arms were being stretched by some torture machine, she made her way around the kind of island that filled the center of the ferry, with machinery clanking inside it. She passed one door that said "Captain," another that said "Employees Only," and a third that said "Gents." Mr. Riemer, she saw, was following behind her. Moist and intent, leaning slightly toward her, he had a hand ready to take one of the suitcases in case she permitted. She came to a third door marked "Ladies."

The door was very narrow. When opened, it had a tendency to swing closed again, owing to the very slight and gentle rolling of the ferry on the waters of the Bay. Herma managed to get the large tapestry portmanteau inside. While she was doing this, she was unable to prevent Mr. Riemer from helping her with the other. He passed it to her through the door, leering significantly at the brass sign "Ladies" and at the porcelain fixtures quite visible inside the tiny compartment. She shut the door brusquely, almost amputating his smile.

When Fred came out a quarter of an hour later there was no sign of Mr. Riemer. Carrying the suitcases, he went to the empty bench across from the policeman and the charwoman and sat down. He was wearing a smart checked jacket, a pair of beige pants, and yellow pigskin shoes. On his head was a stylish derby with a curved brim, only a little bent from being packed into the horsehide suitcase with socks stuffed into it. The policeman, without moving a muscle, stared at him even more beadily than before. His eyes seemed to contract, and the well-developed sphincters drew his mouth tightly against his teeth. Fred, glancing down, saw that a piece of pink satin was protruding from the opening of the tapestry portmanteau. There never was a woman, he thought, who knew how to pack a bag.

He considered going off to buy a cigar, but decided it would be better not to leave the suitcases. At this point he caught sight of Mr. Riemer. He was roaming around the deck of the ferry, circling the machinery island in the center, bent slightly forward and rising on his toes with each pace. His keen unwinking eyes swept around like a searchlight. He had gone around three times, in this identical manner, before he caught sight of the two suitcases on the floor in front of Fred.

He stopped, but continued to lean forward. He had a remarkable and in fact unique sort of equilibrium, Fred thought. It was as though he were immune to the laws of gravity, or had the center of weight in a different part of his body than other people. He was able to lean forward at the angle of a stepladder without falling or losing a trace of his aplomb. Perhaps he had some kind of trick shoes. But he could do it sitting on a bench too.

Poised upright in this diagonal way, he stared at Fred and the suitcases. They were the same two grips, no doubt about it. Did he notice the scrap of satin sticking out of the portmanteau? The policeman certainly did. He hadn't taken his eyes off it since Fred sat down. But Mr. Riemer was more interested in Fred. The crocodilelike glance was not now that of a crocodile fixed on some succulent morsel like a baby, but that of a crocodile warily studying another crocodile.

The great paddle wheels slowed. Fred could see the city coming up now across the water, only a half mile or so away. The Ferry Building with its famous tower, an image included in every family's collection of stereoscope slides, was directly ahead. Fred stood up and lifted the suitcases. The policeman stood up too, holding the helmet upside down as though it were some kind of ceremonial vessel. His eyes flicked rapidly from Fred to the scrap of satin in the portmanteau and back again, eight or ten times. Slowly and heavily, he began moving in Fred's direction.

Fred went nonchalantly off with the suitcases, turned the corner, and opened the door with ''Gents'' on it. He threw in the two suitcases, followed himself, and shut the door. After he had opened both suitcases there was no place for him to stand, or sit, but on the toilet. He rearranged things, putting the opened portmanteau on the toilet and the leather suitcase on the floor in front of it, leaving him room enough to stand. Luckily there was a mirror, just as there was in Ladies. The two facilities were identical except for a urinal in this one, which decreased the available space even further but gave him a place to set his hat when he took it off. He packed everything away in his suitcase, the hat last with the socks in it. Then, stark naked, he projected his willpower into the mirror.

The thing was accomplished at last, but with some difficulty. Herma, with distaste, began taking her clothes from the portmanteau on the filthy toilet. As much as possible she avoided looking at the other fixtures in the tiny cubicle. She dressed hurriedly in the plain skirt and blouse. There was a lurch and a bump, and the sound of the engines stopped. The ferry had arrived in San Francisco.

She straightened the skirt around her waist, passed a comb briefly through her hair, and turned her attention to the portmanteau. It wouldn't shut, naturally, since it had far too many things in it. And, resting as it was on the top of the toilet, she couldn't stand on it. There was a noise of shuffling feet; people were leaving the ferry. She tried sitting on the portmanteau and bumping up and down with all her weight. The clasp still refused to shut; the two brass parts were half an inch apart.

She slid the thing down off the toilet onto the floor, which was also not very clean. In this way she was able to stand on it if she bent her head a little under the low ceiling. The place was tiny and hot and smelled like the lowest corner of Hell. The two halves of the clasp met. She bent down rapidly and snapped them.

She opened the door and pushed the two suitcases out onto the floor outside. When she came out after them she found the policeman contemplating her from twenty feet away. He had his helmet on now. He was in San Francisco and he was on duty.

She stared back at him pertly.

''How do I get to the Larkin Hotel?''

''Yer want to get a whore scab,'' he growled.

3.

The horse-cab was easily found. There were a dozen or more of them waiting out in front of the Ferry Building, and the driver even helped her with the two bags. He was a round-faced fellow of forty or so, wearing a battered top hat with a greenish sheen to it. He hardly even seemed to give her a glance; he snapped his reins to turn the horse around and set off briskly up Market Street. But he must have noticed her, because as soon as they were on their way he said without turning his head around, "First trip to town?"

"Yes."

"Where you from?"

"Santa Ana."

"Never heard of that one. Must be one o' them Spanish towns down by L.A. How do you like Frisco?"

"I just got here."

"Beautiful, ain't it? We've got the finest climate in the world." It was in fact a beautiful morning. The sun was shining brightly through the last remnants of a fog that was dissolving in little wisps over the hills to the west, and there was an exhilarating crispness to the air. He went on pointing out the sights, as the cab clop-clopped its way up the busy street filled with people and vehicles and lined with buildings taller than Herma had ever seen.

"That's the Wells Fargo Bank there on the right. Biggest bank in the west. And that there's the Crocker Bank." Where Mr. Riemer worked, Herma thought, gazing at it with a distant little smile. "That there's Newspaper Row. Chronicle Building on the corner. That there's the Grand Hotel, and right there next to it's the Palace. Cost seven million dollars, covers two and a half acres, and took five years to build. Has eight stories and one thousand four hundred and twelve rooms. Each room has its own fireplace, clothes closet, and private toilet, and every two rooms has a bath. Seven hundred bay windows. Special drawing room for ladies, and it's got its own fire system that holds six hundred and thirty thousand gallons. Where you puttin' up, by the way?"

"The Larkin."

"Oh. Well, that's a nice hotel too. Time was when it was the best hotel in town. That was before the Grand was built, and the Palace. Still," he added, "it's a nice enough place to put up. If you can afford it."

"I can afford it."

"That there's the Call Building," he said, pointing it out with his whip. "Tallest building west of Chicago. Ain't a brick in it. Made of poured concrete reinforced with iron rods. It would take something, I

tell you, to bring that building down. It's solid as the Rock of Gibraltar.''
It didn't look much like the Rock of Gibraltar. It was a high square
tower with a dome on the top perforated with many windows, so that it
looked like a saltshaker. ''Nothing like that down in Santa Ana, I'll
bet. Right up there on yer right is Union Square. City o' Paris Department Store. Plenty of skyscrapers up there and they're buildin'
more. That's the Press Club and that there's the U.S. Mint, and we're
just comin' to the Larkin Hotel.''

This whole travelogue had taken only ten minutes, since the pony
had trotted briskly, even though they had come halfway up Market
Street and the Ferry Building was lost in the distance behind. The
Larkin, as the cabman had said, was elegant but a little old-fashioned.
A boy in a pillbox hat appeared and seized her two bags. Herma gave
the cab driver fifty cents, which seemed to please him. He advised her
not to take any wooden nickels, told her she was a real looker, reiterated that Santa Ana must not seem like much now that she'd seen
Frisco, and wheeled off down Market Street toward the Ferry Building
in search of another fare.

The bellboy had the same breezy and informal air as the cab driver.
Chattering a mile a minute, he led the way into a lobby decorated with
red plush upholstery, velvet hangings, and gilt scrolls and filigrees.
''Even got our own theayter. You can go in it from inside, right through
that door there, or around the corner on Tyler. First trip to town? What
do you think of Frisco? Take a look at that clock there. Built by Tif-
fany's of New York. Not only tells the time of day in hours, minutes,
and seconds but the turn of the tides, the phases of the moon, and who's
got yer umbrella. Cost twenty-five thousand dollars. What name, please?''

''Miss Herma.''

''Room for Miss Herma!'' he bawled at the top of his voice, flinging
the bags down by the desk.

''What name?'' said the clerk.

''Herma.''

''What other name?''

''Just Herma.''

''See what I got here.'' He thumbed through a bunch of cards in a
box on the desk. ''First trip to town? Sure are a looker, I'll say that for
you. Where you from?''

''My room, please.''

''Well, don't fly off the handle. I've got your reservation right here.
Who's Fred Hite?''

''My manager.''

''Well, he made the reservation all right. Boy! Number 602.''

''Just a moment, please.''

He looked up from the registration card on which he was scrawling
the number 602. ''H'mm?''

''What kind of a room is it?''

''Sixth floor, Market Street, with a bath and its own bay window.''

"I require two rooms, with separate entrances and a connecting bath."

"Connecting bath?"

"A bath which can be entered from either room, each room with its own entrance from the corridor, and both rooms on Market Street."

"A bay window in both?" inquired the clerk with light sarcasm.

"That doesn't matter."

"Well, we ain't got it."

"You mean you have no such rooms, or you have no such rooms for me?"

"From your point of view, what's the difference? We ain't got it. Tell you what. You take 602 for the time being. I get off at five o'clock, and we'll have a cosy little supper in the Las Flores room and talk about it. That appeal to you?"

"I want to see the manager," said Herma.

The clerk sighed and motioned to the bellboy. "Go get the Sheeny."

Mr. Dickran Khatchanigherian was one of the features of life in San Francisco and had been for as long as anyone could remember. He had been an employee of Mr. Larkin since the days when the hotel was built. In person he was imposing: over six feet tall, bulky in the middle, with small hands and feet, but a head too large for his body. His nose was one of the wonders of creation. It was too large to fit between his mouth and his eyes, even in the oversized head, so it began somewhat above the eyebrows in the middle of his forehead, descended at a diagonal for three inches or so, came to a bump like an elbow, and continued on a distance farther to end in a bulb like a cab man's horn. Among the employees of the hotel he was invariably known as the Sheeny, although he was of impeccable Armenian lineage.

There he stood with many gold rings on his fingers, pointing his nose at Herma and working the muscles around his mouth, which was rather small. After a while he opened the mouth and said, "I am Khatchanigherian."

"I am Herma, and I require two rooms with separate entrances and a connecting bath."

The Sheeny took the reservation card out of the clerk's hands and looked at it.

"We have reserved number 602 for you, my dear young lady. It's a very nice room and has a bay window overlooking Market Street."

"It's not what I require."

"It has a private bath."

"I require two rooms, with separate entrances and a connecting bath."

"But I don't understand, my dear young lady, why you, being only one person, require two rooms, and in such an unusual arrangement."

"The other room is for Mr. Hite."

"Who is Mr. Hite?"

The clerk silently pointed to something on the card he was holding.

"Ah yes. Mr. Hite. And when will Mr. Hite be arriving, if you please?"

"Shortly."

"Mr. Hite will arrive shortly," pondered the Sheeny in a silken and slightly viscous voice. "And you require two rooms with separate entrances and a connecting bath." He worked the muscles of his mouth some more. "Is Mr. Hite a relative of yours?"

"That's none of your business. Do you have such rooms or not?"

"Oh my yes, my dear young lady, we do have rooms like that, we just don't have one reserved for you, that's the trouble. And besides," he went on in his syrupy voice, "I'm not sure Mr. Larkin would approve of this arrangement. It seems exceptional. It seems unusual. It seems . . . an arrangement at which one might lift an eyebrow."

"I'm a very good friend of Mr. Larkin."

This was not entirely truthful, but Herma said it and persisted, standing there between her two bags with her mouth firmly set.

"Well, the old fellow is getting on in years. He doesn't remember what he's done from one day to the next. If I were to telegraph him now, he might very well not remember you."

"My manager, Mr. Hite, is a very good friend of Madame Ernestine. Do you know who Madame Ernestine is?"

"Oh yes I do, my dear young lady." The Sheeny seemed impressed by this arrangement of friendships. If Herma was a good friend of Mr. Larkin, and Mr. Hite was a good friend of Madame Ernestine, then perhaps their sharing a suite wasn't so much a matter to lift an eyebrow at. "Yes indeed I do." Clearly Herma was a formidable opponent. She was well armed, and deft with her weapons. "Well, dear dear. Let me see what I can do. There's 401 and 403—no, that won't do. The Greek bishop is in there. 301 and 303. I was saving them for an important banker from the East who is arriving next week with his secretary, but I'll put him off in some way. 301 and 303." He motioned to the clerk, who got out the keys and slid them across the desk. "They are both on Market Street, my dear young lady, and both with bay windows. There is a connecting bath with the latest French arrangements. 301 has a fireplace, and 303 does not. Which would you prefer for yourself, and which for Mr. Hite?"

"I'll take the fireplace."

"Very well. The rate is thirty-seven dollars for both rooms, or two hundred dollars if taken by the week."

"The rooms are to be free."

"Oh dear dear dear. What are you saying, my dear young lady? The rooms to be free?"

The clerk called his attention to something on the card. In the lower corner, in small letters, was the word "Gratis."

The Sheeny worked his mouth around one last time. "The rooms, my dear young lady, are at your disposal," he told her, more greasily than ever, in an effort to smile. "Show the young lady to 301 and 303," he told the bellboy without raising his voice.

Herma went off, following the boy carrying the two bags.

"Dear dear dear," said the Sheeny. "What a pain in the ass. How long are we to have this nuisance around, I wonder? And I have no doubt that her so-called manager, Mr. Hite, is even worse."

"She's a looker, I'll say that for her," said the clerk.

The Sheeny said nothing, only snuffed contemptuously. As was well known, he preferred boys, if possible under the age of twelve. He was a personal friend of the police chief and had never been arrested.

The bellboy came back down. "I put her in 301, and the dude goes in 303. Miss Herma says she needs a piano in her room."

"A piano?"

"For rehearsing."

"Rehearsing what?" said the Sheeny.

4.

Herma arrived ganz rechtzeitig, as Mr. Speidermann put it. Women were in short supply in the repertory company of the Larkin, as they were in every realm of San Francisco life, with a single obvious exception—there were plenty of ladies of the night. In this the city conserved an aspect of the rough frontier town it had been only a generation or two before; its population was preponderantly male, and women of any sort were a novelty. Herma was not only a woman, but a young and pretty one, and one who could sing, and she was seized upon avidly—almost with a little pounce—by the director of the theater.

His name fitted him exactly—he was a slightly undersized, mild, rather insubstantial man, with spindly arms and legs, and a slow and deliberate way of moving (until he pounced), but a sharp beak that looked as though it might poison you if he bit you. If there was a bitterness deep in Speidermann, he had his reasons—beginning with the fact that he, a Viennese, a musician to the core, and a graduate of the Staatsoper conducting school, was treated as no more than an employee of the hotel and subordinate in all things to the Sheeny, who despised him, since he was neither a Greek bishop nor a wealthy Eastern businessman, and because the hotel had to put him up gratis as it did Herma. Going on through his list of troubles, he suffered from hemorrhoids, his salary was low, his exile from his beloved Vienna was evidently permanent, the Larkin Theater was inferior in all respects to its rivals the Grand Opera House and the Tivoli, and he as its manager was plagued by a chronic shortage of good musicians and of female singers of any sort, good or bad.

So Speidermann, hardly believing in his luck in finding this young and gilded fly in his net, quickly incorporated her into a production that was just going into rehearsal at the Larkin Theater—*Feminissima,* a revue starring Liane de Pougy, ''Straight from the Casino in Paris, France'' as the marquee out on Market Street had it. In the immemorial tradition of provincial theaters, everything that played at the Larkin was straight from somewhere, but never from San Francisco. And it went without saying that, while the star was imported, the musicians and the rest of the cast were local—so that Speidermann, in addition to his other troubles, had to find singers who could at least pronounce the French language well enough to convince an audience of San Franciscans.

Liane de Pougy, perhaps the best-known French music-hall star of her time, was a spectacular redhead, no longer in the first blush of her youth, it was true, but still shapely and energetic. Her voice was a kind of hoarse vibrant contralto exactly suited to her material and its traditions. It was the voice of a woman who had *lived;* this was what struck every member of the audience. In fact, she herself so declared: ''Moi, j'ai vecu bien,'' she sang in a smoky tone in her second-act finale. In the third act, finishing her song against a background of persimmon-colored peacock feathers, she was negligent enough to let slip a corner of her costume so that a round white fruit with a pink dot in the middle of it was momentarily visible, to the enthusiastic acclamation of the audience, nine-tenths male, and the hypocritical and simpering confusion of the star. In this spectacle, based on a ''poem'' by Jancel with music by Gaston Lemaire, Herma sang among other things a trifle called ''Si tu m'aimes comme je t'aime, tu m'aimes.'' Since she didn't drop any part of her costume, and there would have been nothing in particular to show on her chest if she had, there was no wild burst of applause when she finished. A notice in the *Evening Call* reported that the star ''was ably assisted by Irma, a young artist newly arrived from the south.'' As a junior member of the repertory, Herma was paid two hundred dollars a week. Since there were six performances a week and she had a song in each of the three acts, this worked out to eleven dollars and eleven cents a song, or slightly more than she had been paid for singing at weddings in Santa Ana. She took out a savings account at the Wells Fargo Bank, avoiding the Crocker because of the risk of meeting Mr. Riemer.

Feminissima lasted three weeks, and was followed by *The Merry Widow* by Franz Lehar (''The Latest Sensation Direct from Vienna''), which Speidermann perhaps felt he owed himself to compensate for his exile in this remote part of the world. This Teutonic confection didn't please, and the Sheeny himself ordered it stopped after a week. For a while the theater was dark, while Speidermann pondered what to do next, glancing nervously at the door through which the Sheeny might come at any moment, ordering him perhaps to put on a vaudeville with Scotch comedians and a dog act. Finally he bethought himself of Herma, who seemed to have a supple little voice and was already on the payroll, and also of an operetta performed in New York the year before called

Mlle. Modiste with music by Victor Herbert. No more imported stars, the Sheeny had said; the Pougy had cost too much, and so had the piece of Viennese pastry who had sung the Lehar. Herbert was at the peak of his popularity and the rights would be expensive. But on the other hand Herma would be free. The thing was, could she do it? Nobody had ever heard of her. She had a figure like somebody's younger brother. There was no place in it to let her dress fall down like Pougy, the plot was trifling, and there was only one good song. But he would have to do the best he could with what he had! At least the thing pretended to take place in Paris, there was that to be said for it. He telegraphed to New York for the score, despairing, as he came back along Market, to see on a poster that Tetrazzini was singing *The Magic Flute* at the Tivoli.

In the empty theater, with a single Edison bulb hanging over the stage and the rest of the place dark, Speidermann spread out the score and began explaining it to Herma and the accompanist. Three acts. Lyrics in English. The setting, Mme. Cecile's hat shop on Rue de la Paix in Paris, where Fifi was employed. Fifi had a talent for singing. An American millionaire financed her singing lessons. She married a Captain Etienne de Bouvray whose uncle had a castle. About in the middle of the thing, Fifi sang her waltz *Kiss Me Again*. The rest of it was a lot of whipped cream. Still, they had liked it in New York.

The accompanist, a veteran cynic in shirt-sleeves and a derby, slapped it out onto the piano. He tried a few chords. "Dum de dum dum. Oh dear one how often I think of the past. You gonna do the verse first? The verse ain't much. You better do the chorus first and then switch back to the verse."

"Pardon me, my friend," said Speidermann in his heavy Viennese accent, swallowing the R's. He turned the page to the chorus, pointed out the place to the pianist who began jabbing his fingers into the keys, and broke into a falsetto that bore a corpselike, thready, and catarrhal resemblance to a soprano.

He broke off and said, "Lovely. Ve'll start there and then svitch to the chorus," ignoring the fact that it was the pianist who had made this suggestion.

"But look here, Maestro, it's too hard for the little lady. She starts way down here below the middle of the piano, then she has to go way up to G on top of the roof."

"It's only an octave and a half," said Herma scornfully.

"Yeah, but you have to start down too low for a soprano, honey. It's for a more experienced voice."

"Horsefeathers."

"Okay, let's see you do it if you're so smart."

He played the D seventh, held it, then struck the G chord and Herma sang. Starting powerfully, with a slight throaty tone, on the B, she mounted up in an arching legato to the F and then effortlessly lilted through the rest of the line.

The accompanist took his hands off the keys. "You got a friend behind the piano or you doing all that by yourself?"

"Fantastisch," breathed Speidermann. "But meine Liebe, meine Liebchen, do the rest of it please, in case what you have just done was only some accident."

Herma sang the rest of it, while Speidermann clasped his hands and the accompanist watched her with a kind of cynical interest. It wasn't the low B of the opening that caused the trouble, it was or might be the difficult legato from high G to middle F, toward the end, which might be difficult to carry off without an unseemly swoop. But it was only musical comedy, Herma told herself.

"*Ten*-der-ly pressed . . ." she dropped to the F as easily as a bird alighting, "close to your breast . . ." By this time the accompanist had left off dallying with one-hand chords, and the full piano came in behind and under the voice. Herma swept on. There was nothing to it, it was easy! After this there was only the climax with its reiterated *kiss me*'s, swelling, pressing, soaring in its lyric exultation toward that final

high G which she rose to and held with perfect pitch and an effortless vibrato.

And, as the youthful voice died away, the rush of descending octave chords from the piano, as though tactfully withdrawing from the scene of so much lyricism and so much emotion—the final arpeggio—and the accompanist was left staring at the fermata marks at the end of the song, like two small eyes with eyebrows over them.

Speidermann's word was carefully chosen. It was not that it was so great a voice as all that, but that it was fantastisch in the way it coiled around the song and seemed to be able to do whatever it wanted, without effort, with perfect pitch and legato.

"Meine Liebchen, have you ever sung this song before?"

"No."

The accompanist: "Ever been kissed?"

Herma had no comment on this.

Accompanist: "Well, I think the kid will do all right."

"All right! But it's fantastisch! Wunderbar! Zauberhaft!"

"Well, I don't speak Dutch. But the kid's got a classy little voice there. A little more training and she could sing grand opera."

"I've already sung grand opera," said Herma with slight hauteur, "at French's Opera House in Santa Ana, California."

"Oh, pardon me."

After only ten days or so of rather frantic rehearsal—a dark house ate up money, as the Sheeny reiterated heavily—the Larkin opened with *Mlle. Modiste,* Comic Opera with Music by Victor Herbert and Book and Lyrics by Henry Blossom ("Straight from the Regency Theater in New York," declared the marquee rather ambiguously), with Herma as Fifi, Henry Wollantz as Etienne, and a nondescript middle-aged baritone whose name nobody could remember as the American millionaire. This time both the *Evening Call* and the *Examiner* sent critics, although the *Chronicle,* the aristocrat of the city's three papers, seemed never to have heard of the Larkin, or to have forgotten it in the long years during which it had slowly moldered and sunk in artistic esteem. The *Call* got Herma's name right this time, and the *Examiner* critic, a youth of twenty on his first assignment, lost his head completely and waxed so ecstatic that he had to be restrained by the city editor. As the review finally appeared, considerably toned down, it spoke of "a new star in the firmament" and "a youthful nightingale" and predicted, correctly, that in a week everybody in town would be humming *Kiss Me Again.*

And in fact it was the simple little waltz that drove the show to success, even though Herma had a clever little coloratura passage in the second act and Etienne pumped the maximum of emotion into *The Time, the Place, and the Girl.* At the Sansome Street firehouse the off-duty firemen harmonized on "Safe in your arms, Far from alarms," and there were numerous parodies—*Kiss Me in French*—*Kiss My Behind.* In this strongly male city with its smell of sea breeze, freshly cut lumber, and stale beer, the fad soon spread to the Mission Street saloons, whose habitués seldom went to operas, even comic ones. "I don't get it. What's her other name?" "She ain't got any other name. It's because she's French." "She ain't French." "Then how come she kisses you in French?" "She don't kiss you in French. She kisses you a-gain. And a-gain and a-gain and a-gain." These artistic discussions usually ended in the same way, with the musician of the place seating himself at the battered piano.

> "Kiss my behind,
> And you will find,
> Dat I will soon kiss yers too-o-o . . ."

Barbarians, breathed Speidermann. But what did it matter, since the dollars continued to roll in? But if they rolled in, they also rolled out—Wallantz, who had a certain celebrity, asked for and got five hundred a week, and here came that pesky Hite, Herma's manager, to demand more for her too.

"I've been reading this review in the *Examiner*."

"Ja, prachtvoll."

" 'A new star has appeared in the musical comedy firmament with the local premier of Victor Herbert's *Mlle. Modiste* at the Larkin. While Henry Wallantz performs capably as always, and Boris Krumpf' " (this was the baritone's name) " 'is at least competent, it is Herma in the part of Fifi who makes the show. This refreshingly youthful voice . . .' "

"I know, I know, please, I've read it."

" '. . . youthful voice, with an almost boyish charm, emanates from a person no whit less charming. Mlle. Herma is distinguished above all for her versatility, her easy command of a by-no-means modest vocal range, for the grace, above all, of her rendition of the simple but haunting waltz *Kiss Me Again*. One is hard pressed to say . . .' "

"Don't bother, I know it by heart."

" '. . . hard pressed to say whether it is the mastery of Herbert himself or the verve and flair, the innocence, of this youthful nightingale . . .' "

"So come to the point. Vat is it you vant?"

"Two hundred a week is ridiculous."

"She is in the repertory. That is the vages agreed on."

"Yes, but that was before she brought gold raining down on the theater."

"Some silver dollars, perhaps," muttered Speidermann. "No gold."

"Three hundred."

"Oh my. You are out of your head, young man. She has a contract. Two hundred."

"She might get sick. Sopranos often do."

"Vat are you saying?"

"If she were unhappy, she might get sick. A sore throat or something. I've seen it happen with sopranos more than once."

"A sort throat?" Speidermann wrung his hands. "Two fifty."
"Two seventy-five."
Speidermann sighed.

5.

Late night in the city. The streets were silent, rats
scuttled among the garbage cans, a slice of moon hung over Twin
Peaks. In the suite of connecting rooms at the Larkin, with separate
entrances but connecting bath, one slept. But which one?

Fred usually slept fitfully and had dreams, and had to get up frequently in the middle of the night to relieve himself. He was a restless
sleeper and made a wreck of the bedclothes. Herma on the other hand
slept like a baby. So after he discovered this, he made a habit of converting himself into Herma every night before going to sleep. Sometimes
he forgot this, and had to get up in the middle of the night to do it. It
was a queer business on the whole. Fred hardly knew what to make of it
himself. Through consulting the encyclopedia at the public library
under a certain heading, he found out a number of more or less gratui-
tous pieces of information—for instance that the ancient seer Tiresias,
having surprised some goddess at her bath, was punished by the gods
by being converted into a woman. Later the gods relented and changed
him back. For this he was supposed to be particularly wise. The myth
didn't say why; perhaps because, having been both man and woman, he
knew the secrets of both. After Tiresias the article ended and the encyclopedia went on to other subjects: Hermeneutics, Hermetic, Hermes,
Hermits, and Hernia.

Bah, Fred thought. Why so much bother about a piece of tissue that
popped back and forth from concave to convex every so often? Still, in
the whole matter he detected hints of a fundamental meaning which
eluded him, that sort of profound but vague significance we seem to
perceive now and then in the confusion of the world around us. There
was one question in particular that puzzled. How much did Herma
know of Fred, and vice versa? He pondered: awake, does one know
what one is asleep? Yes, in a way. And asleep, does one know what one
is awake? Yes, but only dimly. Asleep, one thinks: I would like to be
awake, so that this particular nightmare would be over. And awake: I
would like to be asleep, where perhaps in a dream I might meet *that
person* again. Of course, in the case of Herma and Fred, you were
awake in both cases. Yet the sensation was the same as that in a dream,
or like it.

Herma slept like a baby, without dreams. And Fred when he was
awake, to tell the truth, didn't spend very much time pondering over
these abstract and metaphysical matters. He was too busy with other

things. Not that managing Herma's affairs took much of his time. But he had his own concerns—after all, he had his own life to live—he couldn't spend it haggling with Speidermann over twenty-five dollars. Here he was, by some arrangement of destiny, living in this vital and bustling city which had the best climate in the world, as everyone kept saying. All life was open to him, in its myriad attractions and fascinations. His mornings were free. He spent them, for the most part, exploring the city on foot, with occasional recourse to cabs or to the Powell Street cable car. Everything was intoxicating—the climate, the tall buildings, the whole energetic and stimulating busy quality of the life about him. And the women—it was true they were outnumbered by men, but there were still a good many of them out on Market Street at ten o'clock in the morning, in fashionable clothes and carrying with them a faint scent of perfume as they passed. The sight of some pretty girl or other in the street was enough to make his heart twang like a harp string. And they were available! For, in at least a part of his mind, Fred always believed in the possibility that *any woman* might unexpectedly offer herself to him, resulting in a brief but intensely poignant episode, lasting only a quarter of an hour perhaps but never after forgotten. No obligations and no regrets. It would be beautiful. It would be exquisite. It would be poetry.

For Herma, this was only another instance of colossal male egotism. Every one of them, no matter how ugly or aged, imagined himself in a part of his mind to be irresistible to all women. Each one thought that there was something there in himself—some fierce and virile splendor, partly hidden—but some day the most dazzling beauty of all would detect it and hold out her arms saying "Come." The vain pigs! In the end they were the same, all of them—a lot of sweaty meat with a red prong attached to it. And they imagined that every Lillian Russell, every stage or opera star, every anyone at all, wished for nothing better than to have this thing inserted into her immediately. But a girl who would give herself in such a way was—a shameless thing. If she would do it for one, she would do it for all. That was what they ought to remember.

That wasn't it at all, Fred knew. One didn't imagine one's self irresistible, even to a beggar woman. It was simply that one always believed, or imagined in a kind of reverie, that such a thing might or could happen—not on account of one's own qualities, even though one was confident of them—but through a kind of incredible luck, a gift, unexplained and gratis, in the way that an unpredictable God may offer Grace to even the most hopeless sinner. And if it happened! It couldn't happen, one knew in one's rational moments. Yet it might. Such things have been known. And so one had to look carefully at all attractive women, to see if perhaps this one . . .

The crude brutes! For them, Herma thought, all women were just walking receptacles. Nothing else, and always. The trouble with being attractive to men, she thought, was that you couldn't turn it off and on. At times it was delightful. But at other times, when you were thinking about something else, or wanted to do something else, it was just a nuisance. But that was all they wanted from you, if you were just a little bit pretty. It was a perplex. On the one hand a pretty woman wanted to be pretty, and on the other hand—if she were intelligent at all—she didn't want to be only an object. And it really got rather boring being followed around by people who were lustful toward her, whatever else they might pretend to be interested in, or whatever else they might be talking about. When there were so many other interesting things in the world that you could do. Of course, the exception was Fred. *He* wasn't interested in her in that way. And nevertheless, he annoyed her more than all the others. His smug notes on the mirror! His failure to wash his hands after—you know what. And the way he spent money, which she earned. In short, Herma wished to be regarded as more than a kind of human Victrola and endless source of dollars, which was what Fred regarded her as.

Oh grand, Fred thought. Now that we are on the subject of vanity —there was that famous voice of hers. As her manager he was obliged to vaunt it. The clear vibrancy and force, the mastery of the true artist, and so on. But in his heart (even though he was not, he admitted, a musician) he knew she didn't really have a great voice. She had a clever voice, a voice that was apt at mimicry. A range of three octaves, it was true. And she was quick. She was clever. Her musicianship was instinctive and unerring. But a great voice? In any case, it wasn't as though she *made* something. She was just born with it, as though she had six fingers. So there was nothing to be vain about.

Fred, to tell the truth, did not have a very great respect for the vocal art. He thought: women like to talk, and the epitome of talking is singing—a loud, uninterruptable, very beautiful noise. Opera is a woman's world. Every opera centers around the soprano. It is always the woman who is the star—even in *Otello,* where the whole story is about Otello and Iago, and Desdemona is a shrinking little thing who hardly sings for five minutes. But she is the soprano and it's she who gets the bravas.

The female is the Creature of the Mouth, Fred thought, and the male is the Creature of the Hand. She has her orifice, he has his tool. The point about a woman, whether she was singing or making love, was that the orifice came open and provided pleasure. Tra la la la, Mi chiamano Mimì. But with a man, the thing, whatever it was, the hand, the tool—was *outside*—you did things with it. You raised skyscrapers, flung railroads across the prairie, or built flying machines and lifted yourself into the air.

Splendid, splendid, Herma thought. Also the Maxim gun and the cuckoo clock. Boys and their toys! The ability to utilize a screwdriver, in their minds, was a clear demonstration of sexual superiority. Thus their tendency to regard women too as machines—mechanical dolls that could be manipulated if you pushed the right buttons. Je m'en fiche de leurs machines! she told herself.

And then there was the matter of languages, Fred went on, following the logical sequence of thoughts. Both he and she were skillful. But he had to think before he spoke. Herma did not—if in fact she was capable of thought at all, as this process was conceived by the opposite sex. If it had been necessary to think in order to learn languages, probably she wouldn't have learned them. Instead she spoke like a parrot. He like a mathematician—in correct grammar, but haltingly, as though he were working out an equation. Yet he had a *feeling* for languages— he was interested in etymologies, fond of turns of grammar. Did she even know what an etymology was? She probably thought it had something to do with bugs.

Take your prong and go out on Market Street, Herma thought. Only don't catch another nastiness, the way you did at Cantamar. It was a very incompetent Deity, a male one no doubt, who had decreed that only through this folly could the human race reproduce itself and go on existing down the centuries. The beast with two backs! Fiercely she resented being the half that was underneath. And yet—and yet—with the right person—with Mr. Earl Koenig, or some other shy and gentle man who respected her—it could be beautiful. It could be exquisite. It could be poetry. The thing was, it had to come of itself. You couldn't just roam up and down Market Street looking for it. It was magic. It was a piece of luck, a Grace, as though an unpredictable god . . .

Which was just what Fred himself said, if she would only understand. But she would never listen.

6.

When there were no rehearsals, or other business at the theater like fittings, Herma had her afternoons free. She spent them, for the most part, exploring the city on foot, now and then taking a cab. But the city tucked into its hills was compact enough that you could get to almost any part of it with a half an hour's walking. The city, only a half century old and still growing and flexing its muscles like an adolescent, was already various, myriad, and richly cosmopolitan. There were art galleries, bookstores, specialty shops offering fine imported foodstuffs, stores where you could buy anything from Persian carpets to English Spode china. In the City of Paris Department Store alone there was enough to occupy Herma for a month of afternoons. She wandered with a thoughtful expression through the displays of imported lingerie, glass cabinets of French scent, expensive soaps shaped like apples or pomegranates, hats with bird-of-paradise feathers, shoes made from crocodiles, and mother-of-pearl combs. She didn't really care for buying things; she simply enjoyed drifting from room to room in the store, passing her fingers lightly now and then over a Spode cup or the feather of a hat.

Yet it wasn't really this part of the city—Market Street, the elegant shops on Montgomery, and Union Square—that interested Herma the most. The humbler parts of the city were full of unexpected discoveries. She liked to wander down back streets more or less at random—*flâner* was the French word. She didn't know where she wanted to go until she saw where she was. And when she got there, there was always something interesting. An old man playing a violin. A suicide being carried out of a house. A cab man beating a horse, and a lady beating the cab man with her umbrella. On Eddy Street, not far from the hotel, she found a shop that sold nothing but dolls—Chinese dolls, Dresden dolls, English dolls, old American rag dolls, commedia dell'arte sets from Italy with Pulcinellas and Columbines. There was even a Liane de Pougy doll in white india rubber, with a costume that came off piece by piece to reveal, finally, two breasts the size of pearls and a tiny mons veneris. She wasn't sure she cared for *that*. She was tempted, however, by a Chinese mandarin only six inches high, with a black satin gown and a mustache of genuine hair.

Funny, I've never had a doll, she thought. She took up the mandarin and examined him, with an odd pleasure at holding him in her fingers. Tiny as he was, the doll was calm and dignified, and the miniature mustache was immaculately groomed. There was something complex and mysterious about him, perhaps lightly sinister—she thought of the word *chinoiserie*. After a moment she put him back on the shelf. No, she told the clerk, she didn't care for anything. Yet it was the mandarin she coveted; if she had bought a doll at all it would have been him.

And in fact, of all the quarters of the city, it was Chinatown itself—from Kearney to Stockton and from Bush to Columbus Avenue on the north—that drew her back again and again. She was content to spend whole hours prowling along Dupont Street, stopping to look in the shops of a hundred kinds, and all different from anything she had seen before—spice shops, stores where you could buy bizarre vegetables like mandrakes and taros, fish markets with fish that existed only in Chinese paintings. Portsmouth Square was full of old Chinese gentlemen who had nothing to do all day, apparently, but sit on benches and chat in the sunshine. There were almost no women; the preponderance of males was even more striking than it was in the rest of San Francisco. And the women you did see were—it was easy enough to see what they were. They wore tight-fitting gowns slit to the knees, and their faces were whitened with rice powder, the slender eyebrows traced and blackened. Their glossy black hair was drawn up at the back in elaborate chignons to show their pale and fragile necks. Some of them seemed hardly older than Herma. She exchanged a glance with one once—the girl looked back at her boldly, appraisingly. Flat-chested like herself, Herma thought. Suppose she spoke to her—it might be interesting. She might . . . find something out.

But instead, after a moment, she turned haughtily away with her chin lifted and went on. Since there were no women in Chinatown, or only this kind, there were also no children. Only men—the old men in

Portsmouth Square, the young men endlessly smoking and reading the wall posters, and the clerks in the stores, who looked sad and bored, as though they never hoped to earn enough money to go back to their native Kwangtung until they finally died and were shipped back in boxes—a steamer had left the other day for Canton with two hundred such crates in its hold, the *Examiner* said.

Walking one day on Dupont Street, she strayed down a side street and found herself standing before an odd-looking building like a kind of pagoda, with stone lions guarding its entrance. After a short hesitation she went in. Beyond the vestibule was a large chamber full of the smell of incense and objects that seemed vaguely ritualistic. It was some time before her eyes adjusted to the dim light. Then she saw, across the room, a gentleman doing something mysterious in front of a statue of a plump man with crossed legs.

He turned and stared at her in a bland and not unfriendly way.

"Am I allowed to come in here?"

"Oh, yes."

"Am I interrupting you?"

"No, I am just paying homage to my various ancestors. You see," he explained, "we don't have gods as you do. Instead we make our ancestors into gods. In that way, perhaps, we can have a little more influence with them."

"Does it work?"

"I can't say for sure. A good many of the good things of life seem to have come my way, for one reason or another."

At this point he smiled. She studied him, able to see him properly for the first time now that her eyes had adjusted to the gloom. He was not exactly a young man; perhaps forty. He wore a tunic like the old gentlemen in Portsmouth Square, except that his was an elegant pearl gray instead of black. Below this was a skirt, both garments evidently of silk. His face was smooth and unwrinkled; only the faint pattern of creases around his eyes revealed his age. His soft mustache, neatly trimmed and drooping at the ends, was exactly like that of the mandarin in the doll shop. His English was excellent. He spoke without a trace of accent, although with a slightly clipped flavor that was perhaps British in place of the American drawl. He had a perpetually amused expression about him, or perhaps ironic was the proper word; yet there was the faint quality of the melancholy about him as well.

Since he continued to regard her, smiling, without feeling it necessary to say anything, she turned and began looking at the objects in the temple. Her attention was caught by the seated statue, which was perhaps not that of a man at all.

"Is that a Bodhisattva?"

"Not exactly, although you can call it that if you want. It's a representation of Kuan-yin, who is called in his female form Tara. Such statues are Buddhistic. However we are not narrowly sectarian. Over here, as you see, various people have hung up tablets to their ancestors. This practice is Confucian, although you don't have to be a Confucian to hang up a tablet. It is only necessary to have ancestors, and everyone has them. Perhaps you have some yourself. In which case, you are welcome to hang up a tablet.''

''What did you mean when you said that Tara is the female form of Kuan-yin?''

''Every man has a female reflection, and every woman has a male reflection. For Kuan-yin, his female aspect is called Tara. As you see, this figure is not particularly man or woman, or it is both at once. And here,'' he went on quickly, although Herma would have liked a little more explanation on this point, ''is the altar of the Great Luminary, or sun, and the Night Luminary, or moon. Farther to your right are the tablets to the Chua-tien or All Stars, to the Urh-shih pat Suh-sing or Twenty-Eight Constellations in the Ecliptic, to the Peh-tan Sing or Ursa Major, and to the Muh, Kin, Sui, Fo, and Tu, or Five Elements—wood, metal, water, fire, and earth. And across the room are the shrines to Siueh-sz', Yü-sz', Fung-sz', and Lui-sz', the superintendents of snow, rain, wind, and thunder.''

Here he stopped, and looked at her more carefully. ''But you are perhaps not interested in all this. Would you care for a cup of tea?''

Only a short distance away, in a narrow lane off Dupont Street, he led her into a shop with gold lettering on the window: ''H. T. Ming. Fine Porcelain and China.'' In the front at least the shop was very small, only wide enough for a door and the window with gold lettering, with a single vase in the showcase behind. But inside, beyond the small room with its display of porcelain much like the others in Chinatown, it widened out into an elaborate chain of apartments that wound their way through the intricacies of the building and even descended to the level below, on the hillside overlooking the Embarcadero and the Bay. At the center, on the upper level, was a walled-in garden with a very old fig tree. ''Perhaps it was here before the city.'' There was an enormous stone lantern with carved dragons and lions' feet, odd-looking plants in stoneware pots, and squares of stone for pavement, cool and mossy. The whole garden was perhaps only ten feet square but exquisite.

She followed him back into the house again. Facing onto the garden was a room where more porcelains were displayed, but it resembled a museum or a private gallery more than an ordinary shop. Only fifteen or twenty objects were displayed, on enameled pedestals or in crystalline glass cabinets. This room evidently served too as a kind of parlor. There were things to sit on—mats, and a kind of low silken couch with cushions against one wall of the room—but Mr. Ming didn't invite her to be seated. Instead he left the room abruptly. A bell could be heard tinkling in some other part of the house.

After a moment he came back. ''Tea-boy will come in a moment with the tea. He comes from the restaurant downstairs. The restaurant is downstairs,'' he explained, ''because it is in the next street over, and everything is on a hill here.''

He seemed to lose a certain amount of his aplomb now that he had succeeded in enticing Herma inside his house. Perhaps this very success was something he had hardly hoped for, so that he had no very clear idea what to do with her now that he had her here. Whenever he didn't know what to say, he smiled. His complexion was as fine as a girl's, Herma thought. Its color was difficult to describe. It was as pale as her own, and yet it was not exactly white. It was as though there was a subtle cast of some other color below the surface, perhaps mauve, or a pale lemon like that of polished gold. There was something—she hardly knew how to put it. There was something orchidaceous about him, some quality of the hothouse flower.

To break the slight awkwardness she turned and began looking around the room. ''So your name is H. T. Ming?''

''Not exactly. It is Ming Hang-Tze, but I have anglicized it for the purposes of the sign on my window. My name is also the name of a dynasty. But that is only an accident; the word *ming* simply means bright.''

''And you are a dealer in porcelains?''

''I have been, although I do very little business now. The only goods I have for sale are those in the outer shop. As you can see, the shop is very small. And I open it now only for special customers. You see, dear child, I have been many things. I have been a teacher of English in Canton, I have been a dealer in porcelain and an importer, and now I am a landlord and I own this building and also the building in the street below, with the restaurant and a number of shops. I have become so wealthy that I no longer have any need to work, so now I have nothing to do but live here with my beautiful things and enjoy them with my friends.''

''Do you have many friends?''

''Not many,'' he admitted, still with a smile. ''Only a few are interested in the things I'm interested in, and know how to appreciate them. Each of the things you see in this room,'' he told her, ''is precious beyond value.''

He unlocked a glass cabinet and took out a vase of white Ch'ing-pai ware of the Southern Sung dynasty. Flowers and birds were molded with incredible lightness in the thin porcelain. The glaze lent a cast to the white underneath that was perhaps blue, or perhaps only a slight intensifying of the white itself. ''The test of true porcelain is that it is slightly translucent. This one, as you can see, transmits not only light but shadows as well.'' He demonstrated by inserting his finger into it. ''Porcelain of the best quality is smooth and yet not glassy. It has a very faint texture, slightly unctuous. It has been said that it has the feeling of uncooked macaroni. But I prefer to think that it is like the skin of a young girl, hardened in the kiln so that it remains forever youthful.'' He smiled, and slid two fingers lightly along the vase. ''The Arabs believed that Ch'ing-pai ware would shatter if poison were put into it. That is not true, of course. Still this piece is very fragile. You could shatter it with a breath. Yet it is immortal if not broken. The color, the tone and translucence, will last for a million years.''

''Is it for flowers—or to hold wine—or what?''

''For nothing. Only to hold in your hand. If I collect porcelain and not bronze or stone it is because it is very fragile, and thus an analogue of life. And yet immortal, like life itself.''

He put the Ch'ing-pai piece back into the glass and locked it, and turned to the next cabinet. ''These are a pair of vases in white with underglaze blue, dedicated to a temple in Kiangsi in 1351, in the Yüan dynasty. This, of course, is the celebrated Chinese blue and white, the inspiration of the pottery of Delft and other European factories. Such Ch'ing-hua ware is quite common. However this pair is unique. The two vases are not identical, but complementary.''

Herma could see that, although the decorations of both involved dragons and other mythological creatures, along with botanical speci-mens, the decorations were not precisely the same. Mr. Ming contended that even the shapes of the two vases were not identical, although hours of study were necessary to perceive the difference.

''Exquisite.''

The aesthete in him was always mingled with the merchant. ''If I sold only one of these porcelains every ten years,'' he told her, ''I could live like a prince.''

''Would you sell me something?''

At this he was amused. ''Would you like to buy this house, including the restaurant next door? However,'' he added, ''sometime I may make you a gift of something.'' He went on to show her a few of the other pieces in the room. A tripod incense burner of southern Kuan ware, a rare three-color Ming vase with underglaze blue. A delicate celadon jug of the T'ang dynasty, beige with a cast of very pale green, and violet bands. There were only two others like it in the world, he told her, one in Dresden and the other in the Victoria and Albert Museum in London. Next, a Sang de Boeuf vase of the K'ang Hsi period. It was perfectly plain, of dark brownish-red with a bloodlike texture that seemed to glow, as though illuminated from the inside. Herma was a little afraid of this one.

''You are right, dear child. That vase is about Death.''

An odd spark of memory came to Herma, like a flash from a distant storm: the blood-red curtains in Mr. Paul's Undertaking Parlor. After a pause, during which Mr. Ming reassured her with a little smile, he went on. ''The color of the Sang de Boeuf vase is obvious. But there are also Secret Colors. Such ware is called Pi-sê Yao. It is a porcelain or china which seems white but has a sheen or cast, an almost invisible shadow which is not apparent to the ordinary person, or someone who has not been initiated into its secret. In the language of porcelain there are many metaphors for this—'like a bright moon, cunningly carved and dyed with spring water,' or 'like a curling disk of the thinnest ice, filled with green clouds.' A Secret Color may be a grayish or olive green, that is what we call celadon, or occasionally a brownish yellow without any green. At times we may find just the palest suggestion of a rosy tinge, but this is very rare. Can you tell me, dear child, the Secret Color of this piece?''

He stopped before an exquisite Blanc de Chine figurine, translucent, with faint marbling so that it resembled white jade. It was the figure of a standing gentleman in a white robe, perhaps a priest or a mandarin, with a fawn at one side. The hands were held out in a gesture of admonition or blessing, each tiny white finger perfectly formed.

Herma looked, for a long time. But it seemed perfectly white. She shook her head.

"Some day you will see it," Mr. Ming promised her, "if you pay attention, and go on looking. Ah! here is Tea-boy."

He was not exactly a boy, to tell the truth; he was almost as old as Mr. Ming himself. He came in with the greatest respect, set down the tea and the tea things on a tray, and left without a word.

The tea was on a lacquered table in front of the couch. The teapot had a kind of ear on it instead of a handle. The tiny handleless cups were to match. Along with the tea there were almond cakes and small wafers with sesame seeds. Herma made an effort to eat these without dropping crumbs. Mr. Ming ate nothing; he only sipped his tea.

"And so, dear child, you are a singer?"

Herma, her mouth full of almond cake, nodded.

He asked her, "Is it true that a high note by a singer might shatter porcelain?"

"I don't know. I've heard it might shatter crystal, but I've never tried."

"If it were not for this danger," he said solemnly, "I might ask you to sing something."

They smiled together at this small joke. The whole affair of meeting Mr. Ming and coming to his house seemed to Herma something out of a fairy tale. The odd encounter in the temple, his easy acceptance of her, his shyness and yet his adept skill and erudition with porcelain—even the curious way he had been foreshadowed by the tiny mandarin in the doll shop. It was the way things happened in stories, not in real life. Yet Mr. Ming was quite corporeal, sitting on the couch with his legs crossed oriental fashion and sipping his tea with care not to dampen his mustache.

"I like you better than a doll," she told him over her tea.

"Dear child, I have no notion what you are talking about."

"Do you live alone?" she asked him abruptly.

"Yes. I have a number of friends, as I told you."

"But you are not married?"

"Married?" He smiled. "How could I be married, dear child? There are no women in Chinatown, except . . ."

"Yes."

"Singsong girls. And that doesn't interest me. I have never known the embrace of an affectionate woman, dear child," he went on in a quite matter-of-fact tone. "When I was younger, in Canton, I was too poor. And now—I'm no longer young."

He stopped and seemed to be gazing at something across the room. She followed his glance and saw that it was a wall hanging: a painting on silk, Chinese red and umber on a beige background.

"The concubine Yang Keui-fei being assisted to mount her horse, by Ch'ien Hsüan." He smiled a little. "She was a concubine of the T'ang Emperor Hsüan Tsung, who became infatuated with her in his old age."

The costumes were red and beige, the horse a rich umber. Three servants were assisting the lady onto the back of a plump horse; stirrups didn't seem to have been invented in those days. By the horse's head stood the Emperor, a corpulent old man with a grizzle of a beard. You saw him, clasping his hands, peeping lasciviously at the glimpse of tiny bound foot that became visible as the concubine mounted the horse.

"A great monarch," said Mr. Ming. "A connoisseur of the arts, and a just magistrate. Yet when he loved he was only a foolish old man."

Here he stopped, as though hoping perhaps that she would make some comment. But she only looked around the room. It was getting late, the thought occurred to her. There were no clocks anywhere in the room.

As if guessing her thought, he said, "I was hoping, dear child, that you could stay for dinner. Tea-boy could bring up some simple dish from the restaurant. And you haven't yet seen my library. A precious collection that I show only to my most select friends."

It was time to go. But, having fallen into this fairy tale, she was determined not to lose her mandarin doll, since there was probably not another one like him in the world. Like Scheherazade, she deftly sought about for a way to extend the story into another night.

"I'd like to see your library. I sing every night at eight o'clock, and I have to be at the theater by seven, to dress and put on my makeup. But the theater is dark on Tuesday nights."

Mr. Ming seemed uncertain how to rise to this suggestion. He was not very familiar with theaters and not sure what was implied by the fact of their being dark. Perhaps he feared that in some way he was supposed to come there, to the dark theater. "You mean that . . ."

"There is no performance. So that next Tuesday evening I would be free."

He seemed reassured. His air of calm and wise aplomb returned. "Then on Tuesday," he told her with great formality, "I should be honored to have you as my guest for dinner."

"I'll be delighted. And so, good-bye for now."

She rose, with a certain awkwardness since the couch was very low, and he showed her out into the outer shop. He unlocked the door, and seemed almost ready to offer his hand or—make some other gesture. She was not quite sure what Chinese did when parting from friends. And anyhow, was she a friend? She wasn't quite, and yet she was more, in a way. She sensed this, and so evidently did he. Standing no more than two feet from her, he half raised his hand, then dropped it. The color came into his cheeks, and he managed to smile a little to cover his confusion. Herma smiled too and left, shutting the door behind her.

7.

When she came back, on Tuesday evening, the sun had already sunk into the fog behind Twin Peaks and darkness was beginning to filter over the city. A transparent gray light with a touch of gold in it seemed to hang over everything. The street door of the shop was unlocked. Perhaps he had unlocked it a few minutes before, knowing she was coming, because he was too shy to come and open the door for her. She went in, making a little bell tinkle.

Mr. Ming was waiting to greet her in the gallery, wearing this time a gold satin tunic with trousers to match, and elaborately embroidered slippers.

"You're very elegant. The door to the shop is unlocked. Aren't you afraid . . ."

"Of thieves? No, everything is protected by the Tong. You see, everyone in Chinatown, or at least every person of substance, belongs to one Tong or another. These are like associations or lodges, and in this way Chinatown governs itself. Members of different Tongs will assassinate each other, sometimes, but they will never touch possessions belonging to someone of another Tong."

"Or of their own Tong."

"Exactly. So in short there is no theft, or if there is it is quickly punished." However, he took the precaution of shutting the door of the gallery itself and locking it with a great bronze dead-bolt; but perhaps this was only so that he and Herma would be undisturbed.

"And now, since you have already been shown these trifles"—he was referring to his porcelains, any one of which if sold would enable him to live like a prince for ten years—"perhaps you would like to see my library."

There were no corridors in the house—which was not really a house, but a series of connecting apartments which seemed simply to have accumulated in the labyrinth of the building, without ever having been planned—so that it was necessary to pass through several rooms to arrive at the library. One of them seemed to be a dining room; Herma caught a glimpse of a low black lacquered table with two places already set on it. Mr. Ming passed on, into a room that was evidently around the house on the other side of the garden. It was entirely windowless. The walls were lined with bookshelves, some of them with locked glass doors. In the center of the room was a table piled with more books. On the table there was a pair of matching lamps in the grayish-green celadon ware of the Sung period. He lighted these with a long perfumed match and began showing her the books.

Since Herma was not a great reader and not a scholar at all—and some of the books were very scholarly—this was slightly boring. However, Mr. Ming was so nice a person, and so amusing when he fell into his shy and pedantic way of explaining things, that she repressed both her yawns and the slight smile that kept trying to form on her face. She listened while he explained the Five Confucian Classics, which he took with care from a locked glass case.

"These are the basis of all Chinese thought. First there is the *Yih King* or Book of Changes, then the *Shu King* or Book of Records, then the *Shi King* or Book of Odes, including poems, national airs, and sacrificial odes. There are many commentaries on this," he put in. "Next, the *Li Ki* or Book of Rites, and the *Chun Tsiu* or Spring and Autumn Records, which is a chronicle of Confucius' time attributed to the sage Kung-fu-tse himself. As you can see, my manuscript editions are very old and date from the tenth century."

"Are there any poems about love in the Book of Odes?"

"No, but there are a good many in Chinese literature, and most of them are in this room. I don't suppose you have heard of Li Po?"

"No."

"He was born in 701, in the T'ang dynasty. Listen to this."

He opened a small satin-bound book and began reading in a flat voice, almost without intonation.

"She, a Tung-yang girl, stands barefoot on the bank,
He, a boatman of Kuei-chi, is in his boat.
The moon has not set.
They look at each other—brokenhearted."

"But it's so sad."

"Most Chinese poetry about love is sad, for some reason. If someone wishes to be happy, it isn't recommended that he become a poet."

"Perhaps he just shouldn't become a lover."

"Perhaps," he agreed, a little sadly himself. "Li Po is said to have died through falling out of a boat into his reflection in a lake, while under the influence of wine."

"That *is* sad."

"Perhaps not. I think it is quite beautiful, since everyone has to die anyhow, in one way or another. Furthermore, many of us plunge at such evanescent reflections in the water, usually with fatal results. It is a question whether it is more of a folly to plunge at one's own reflection, or that of another." She wasn't following this part of his rambling discourse at all. He closed the Li Po and put it away. "I am not sure how many of these books you would like to see."

To Herma's surprise not all of them were in Chinese. He showed her a fine morocco-bound copy of *Marius the Epicurean,* a first edition of *The Anatomy of Melancholy,* a *Kamasutra* in a French translation, a first edition of *Lyrical Ballads* (he knew "Kubla Khan" by heart and insisted on reciting it for her), a Leopardi, and a Tasso in a seventeenth-century binding.

He took down another volume in an old binding and searched for something. Then he read it, or rather recited it with his finger on the passage but looking straight at her, with a slight expression of amusement.

"You are the reflection of Heav'n in a pond, and he that leaps at you is sunk.' "

She laughed. "Who said that?"

"Congreve."

"I don't know who he is."

"There are a great many things you don't know, dear child."

"And a great many that I do."

"Yes, I'm afraid that's true. But you must pardon me. These are only dusty old books, and I forget that you are a healthy young person whose dinner has been delayed."

"Not at all."

"This way, dear child." He indicated the door to the dining room for her, and allowed her to go ahead.

The reference to forgetting was a courteous formula. Mr. Ming forgot nothing. His invitation to dinner was a matter of precise timing, and Tea-boy was in the very act of setting the dishes on the table as they entered. They took their places, Herma tucking her legs in under the low table. The dishes were simple but exquisitely prepared. First came scented shellfish cooked in rice wine, then goose with apricots, and pimiento soup with mussels. There was no wine, except for the fine amber nectar the shellfish was cooked in; only tea. The table service was a fragile Yung Lo porcelain of the Ming dynasty, white with an underglaze pattern of bamboo leaves.

"What a beautiful teacup."

Mr. Ming remarked, "In ancient times it was said that the ideal size for a teacup was that of the breast of a young maiden." Then he stopped, feeling perhaps that in the light of Herma's own modest endowments the remark was not tactful. He was embarrassed. How had he got onto this subject anyhow? But Herma, relentless, refused to let him off. "You could try this one," she suggested, "on one of the singsong girls in Pike Street."

"Dear child, please be serious," he begged her. "I would have given my rarest porcelain not to have made the remark I just made, because it is exactly this subject I wished to talk to you about, but not at all in the tone into which we have fallen in talking about it. As you know, I am a bachelor and I live entirely alone. I have no one to share the beautiful things I have acquired, or with whom to exchange my thoughts. It is all wasted. Youth is wanted here, youth in my own life, and youth in this house. All of it I offer you, my dear. You may be the mistress of it all, if only you would agree to share my life."

Herma repressed a smile. "The mistress of all?"

"I might add that the proposal I am offering is entirely honorable. It is true that according to California law we cannot be married. But a marriage according to Confucian law can easily be arranged, and I can assure you that it is equally serious and far more binding. I will be a good husband to you. And I will demand of you," he said, embarrassed again, "nothing which you do not freely want to give."

Herma hardly knew what to say. She sipped the last of her tea and gazed at the fragile cup in her fingers.

"Perhaps you think I am only a foolish old man, like the Emperor Hsüan Tsung."

"No," she said after a pause, as though considering, "you are not foolish, you are not old, and you are not at all like the Emperor Hsüan Tsung."

"It is too much to ask that you should feel affection for me. I ask only your presence, and your acceptance of dominion over my house."

"But you see, Mr. Ming," she explained gently, "I have my career as a singer, and that must come first."

"I would make no claims on your time, dear child. You would be free to do as you please. Possibly I can even help you in your career. I have even," he said, with a slight air of chinoiserie that might have seemed sinister if she hadn't known him better, "certain influences in the world, of a kind that would perhaps surprise you."

"And where would we live?"

He pointed about to the vast luxurious chambers, with their rich Oriental tapestries, their porcelains, their works of art.

"But don't you see, Mr. Ming, in my career I must travel about the world, from place to place."

He smiled a little sadly. "Perhaps I could follow you. Or, if that is not possible, you could be my wife whenever you came to San Francisco, even though I should greatly miss you when you were gone."

"I am not sure," she offered as her final riposte, "that it is good for a singer's voice to be married."

Mr. Ming said cautiously, "I have heard that the conjugal act is said to reinforce a man's vitality, his Yang being recharged by his partner's Yin. Perhaps it is the same with singers."

She smiled at him indulgently, and set her teacup down. "Mr. Ming, you haven't shown me the rest of your house."

The bedroom, like the library, was a good-sized room without windows, somewhere around on the other side of the garden. Mr. Ming lit a lamp. On the walls were paintings on hanging silk scrolls, depicting for the most part fantastic landscapes with flora found only in the world of dream. He told her the names of some of them: *Gentlemen Conversing in a Landscape* (the gentlemen were hardly visible down in one corner), *The Coming of Autumn, A Thousand Peaks* and *Myriad Ravines,* and *Autumn Landscape,* this last by the famous K'un-ts'an of the Ch'ing dynasty, the most eminent brush painter of the classic period, according to Mr. Ming. Most of the subjects were autumnal, she noticed. It was not clear whether this was a reflection of Mr. Ming's taste, or was character-istic of all Chinese painting.

For the rest, the room contained a number of tapestries and wall hangings, a luxurious Persian carpet, a single moon-white Ch'ing-pai vase in a kind of shrine (he asked her to guess its Secret Color, but she was unable), and a most peculiar bed. It was a spacious affair with wicker walls and openings hung with curtains, more like a small room than an ordinary bed. Inside it was a stand with toilet articles, a mirror, a frame on which to hang clothes, and a bronze censer for scenting the quilts. A padded silk mattress covered the whole bottom, which was per-haps ten feet square. Herma opened the wickerwork door and looked inside. A tiny lamp was burning on a shelf. Next to it was a book. She started to examine it, but Mr. Ming told her she was looking at it from the back. Chinese books began at the other end from English books.

"What is it then?"

He took it from her, coloring slightly. "It is called *The Book of the Bridegroom*. This is a book in which the young man is instructed how to —care for his bride."

"May I not look at it?"

Although he still seemed a little embarrassed about it, he allowed her to take the book from him and examine it. In the thousand and one woodcuts in the text, couples were shown in every imaginable position, and a few that were unimaginable. She leafed on, fascinated. Evidently the Chinese were a nation of acrobats, or perhaps the amorous impulse for some reason developed in them abnormal resiliences. In one woodcut it appeared that the lady had divided her lover in two with a sword before embracing him, but on closer examination she found that the two halves of the gentleman were still joined, although in a roundabout way.

He took the book from her again. "It is possible to get the wrong impression by looking only at the illustrations. There is also a text, which in many cases is quite poetic." He leafed through it until he found the passage he wanted. " 'A slow thrust should resemble the movement of a carp caught on the hook; a quick thrust should resemble the flight of birds against the wind.' "

He smiled at her a little uncertainly.

"Oh, Mr. Ming," said Herma. "All that is so unnecessary."

Herma, who was in an excellent mood, stood him before her exactly as though he were the small mandarin from the doll shop and began un-buttoning his satin-gold tunic. The satin trousers he removed himself, hardly daring to look at her as she took off her own clothes. They were both very neat. They hung their clothes on the frame provided inside the bed, exactly as though they were an old married couple. Then they lay on their sides and discussed each other's bodies.

"Do Chinese people blush?"

He blushed. "Sometimes."

"I don't see how that's possible, because everyone says they are yellow."

"That's not true. The Chinese say that western people are red, but that's not true either."

"Are you sorry that my breasts are not larger?"

In fact, he seemed to have trouble finding them. He looked about on various parts of her body for a while.

"No. Chinese women in general have small breasts too. The Chinese regard western women as bovine. As a matter of fact, I have a slight inclination toward boys, and for this reason I find you particularly attractive." Herma didn't know whether to take this as a compliment or not. "Of course, I have never put this impulse into practice, and I have never revealed it to anyone but you. But for some reason, I find it easy to tell you everything."

"You're thin too." She reached out to touch the elegant, slightly translucent bone of his hip.

"Yes. Our bodies are much alike."

In fact, with her long dress removed, and his bulky tunic, it was remarkable how much the two bodies resembled each other. Not only were they exactly the same height, but the proportions were the same: thin shoulders, narrow hips, finely modeled limbs, matching oval faces with delicate, slightly androgynous features. The two bodies coiled together on the silken mattress and interwound like a pair of precious metal serpents, his silver and hers gold.

"*The Book of the Bridegroom* is on the shelf," she heard him saying in a muffled tone, "but I can't reach it from here."

"Mr. Ming, don't bother."

Mr. Ming himself, she reflected, was like porcelain. Even to his member—which was as hard as porcelain and a pale smooth white with just a touch of—what? A faint cast of mauve, she decided. Mauve was his Secret Color—not only of that part of him but of his whole body. She wondered if she too had a Secret Color and if he had noticed it. Perhaps, she thought, it was just the faintest touch of strawberry, under the lemon vanilla. His arms and shoulders, all of him, seemed as hard as porcelain too, and yet in some way soft and resilient—a rare and unctuous body quite different from her own and yet unmistakably human. It clasped hers tightly, in a way resembling none of the woodcuts in *The Book of the Bridegroom* but in a way unique to the two of them. Mr. Ming was evidently not ready yet for the flight of birds against the wind; he confined himself to gentle motions like a carp on a hook. Yet, somewhat to his surprise, and to the intense pleasure of Herma, the birds took flight anyhow, and soared off with a beating of wings that lasted for some time, and only gradually attenuated.

If Mr. Ming was not asleep, he was only perhaps too embarrassed to open his eyes. He resembled a Blanc de Chine figurine, pale and moonlike, faintly shadowed with mauve. And that reminded her of something.

Stealthily, watching him to be sure he didn't wake up or open his eyes, she crept on her hands and knees to the edge of the bed and lowered herself to the floor. Glancing around once behind her, she crossed the room to the Ch'ing-pai vase in its alcove, with a tiny lamp before it. She studied it for a long time. She tried closing her eyes and slowly opening them again. After she had done this several times, the last time opening her eyes very slowly as though she herself was wakening from sleep, she seemed to make out in the bone-white translucence of the vase a faint greenish shadow, like a reflection from the thinnest possible slice of sea water.

She crept back to the bed, clambered in, and hung close over Mr. Ming with care not to touch him.

"I've discovered the Secret Color of the Ch'ing-pai vase," she said. "It's celadon."

Mr. Ming awakened from his dream, if that was what it was. He looked about him with an air of solemnity, at his own naked limbs, and at hers.

"I am not sure how all this happened. I believe we have both been possessed by demons. However, any wrong will be righted as soon as I have made you my wife. Tomorrow I will discuss the matter with a magistrate I know. He is a member of my own Tong and a very respected person."

"When I am finished with you," she told him, "I'll take you back to the doll shop."

8.

Fred had a quick breakfast in the coffee shop, then he left the hotel at nine and set off briskly down Market Street. It was a busy day and the city was already buzzing with activity. The climate slightly intoxicated him. There was a vitality to the city, an electric snap in the air, lacking in the sun-baked and indolent South. The shop windows glittered with expensive merchandise, much of it imported. Spanking new green and white cable cars rattled busily up and down Market, from the Ferry Building to Twin Peaks. There were almost as many motorcars as carriages in the streets. A large Locomobile discharged a lady in furs, with a wolfhound on a leash, in front of the Palace Hotel. Fred stopped to watch. She was young and pretty, with a long and pale aristocratic face. The furs swathed her to the chin, although it was not very cold. The harp string in his blood went *twang,* as it always did at the sight of a pretty girl. She handed the leash to the doorman and drifted imperturbably through the glass doors into the hotel.

He came to himself and noticed the clock on the Chronicle Building just across the street: nine-fifteen. It was only a short distance to the Hyde Street cable car at the corner of Powell. The crewmen, assisted by the passengers, were just pushing the car around on its turntable to head it back up toward Knob Hill.

Fred got on, next to a girl in a middy blouse and a pleated skirt who seemed to be an art student. She was carrying long rolls of paper, a folded easel, and a portfolio with splashes of paint on it. Her heavy brown hair was piled in a coil on her head, which called attention to her perfectly white and smooth neck. She turned and gave Fred a bold glance. He was wearing his checked jacket, beige trousers, and yellow shoes, and he had managed to press out most of the dents in his derby caused by its being packed in a suitcase. She seemed to be examining this headgear with interest.

Fred felt the color coming into his face. *Ziiiing!* It happened again: an electric shock that made his nerves stand on end. It was a sheerly mechanical reflex, he thought. It probably had something to do with the climate. San Francisco was a stimulating city in all respects, and full of opportunities. The motorman pulled back on his long lever and the car started with a jerk.

As the car swayed, the elbow of the art student nudged gently against his side. Union Square went by, then the car started up Knob Hill. The Stanford Mansion went by on the right, then the Fairmont Hotel. At the top of the hill the car made a jerky turn to the left, went down a couple of blocks, and then turned right again.

The art student got off at Broadway and went briskly down the hill toward North Beach. Fred watched her retreating form with regret. Like everybody else in this busy city, she had something to do. The car went steeply down Hyde Street now. In the distance there were clouds over the Golden Gate, but here in the city a thin sun warmed Fred's knees. The car came down onto a flat stretch and rattled along toward the terminal only a block or so away. The Ghirardelli chocolate factory loomed up on the left. The motorman jerked back on his brake and deftly slid the car into the turntable that would turn it around, always provided a few volunteers were found to help push.

Here Fred got off and walked a block to the E car, following the directions given him by the hotel clerk. The streetcar, a large green affair with gleaming windows, came along presently. It took him along Bay Street, angled to the right on Cervantes for a while, and then continued along the waterfront for a mile or so until it came to a stop in a pasture with the Bay on one side and the Presidio up on the hill to the left. This was the end of the line; from here Fred had to walk.

The pointed yellow shoes weren't really suited for walking. Still, it wasn't very far. A half a mile or so across the meadow he could see a barnlike building with a curved roof, and near it a pair of insectlike shapes standing in the grass. At this sight his heart began to pound a little in his chest. Forcing himself not to hurry, he went on down a narrow beaten path toward the hangar and the two machines standing in front of it.

The brand-new corrugated-iron hangar looked as though it had been rather hastily flung together. On the front of it was a homemade sign saying "Curtiss Flying Service." There was no one in sight. Fred turned to look at the two flying machines parked in the grass. One was a Voisin monoplane in rather poor condition; the wire was rusty, and the short mast that held up the struts looked rather shaky. The other machine was a Farman. It was similar to the Wright Flyer, with a canard elevator and a combination of wheels and skids for landing. The engine was an Antoinette—heavy and, as Fred had heard, prone to throw its connecting rods through the cylinder wall. He turned and went back toward the hangar.

The large sliding door was open enough for a person to slip through. He went inside. There was a certain amount of light from openings up under the eaves of the iron roof. As his eyes adjusted to the gloom he made out a machine like nothing he had ever seen before, or even read about. It was a pusher biplane with midwing ailerons. Twin bamboo tail booms led back to the tail assembly. Between the wings was mounted what appeared to be a four-cylinder motorcycle engine. The wings were braced by a complex maze of horizontal, vertical, and diagonal wires—a rigger's nightmare. In place of the crude skids of the Wright, there was a tricycle landing gear with cut-down motorcycle wheels about a foot in diameter.

But what interested Fred more was the control system. Instead of lying on his stomach the operator sat comfortably in a kind of wicker seat like a Morris chair. In front of him was a stout metal yoke, hinged at the bottom so that it could move freely back and forward. At the top of the yoke was a wooden steering wheel like that of an automobile, except that the spokes were wire. Glancing around to be sure there was still nobody in sight, he tried the controls. To bank left or right you turned the wheel; to climb or descend you pulled back on the wheel or pushed it forward. The operator's feet fitted into a rudder bar which controlled the large rudder in the tail assembly. There was no canard elevator. Pushing on the yoke raised or lowered a large elevator surface at the rear, integrated with the rudder. The whole thing was ingeniously simple and beautifully designed. Obviously this was the control system of the future. Where was the throttle? There it was, just by the operator's left hand.

Some premonition made him turn. Unexpectedly a small man was there, with his thumbs in the back pockets of his overalls, stock still and watchful.

"Whatcha lookin' for, Buster?"

"I'm just having a look at this machine."

"Well, don't touch it."

"I'm not touching it."

"I know what you're doin'. I been watchin' you ever since you walked on the field. Who are you anyhow?"

"I'm Fred Hite." He went on recklessly. "You've probably heard of me. I'm a flyer from Southern California. They have Wrights down there. I'm living up here now, and I'm interested in flying this Curtiss."

The mechanic said nothing for a while. He took in the checked jacket, the well-cut beige pants, and the yellow shoes. He still had a look as though Fred was trying to sell him a gold brick. His attention was caught by the long hair sticking out from the rear of the derby.

"That's a funny haircut you've got."

"I'm in show business."

"You an actor?"

"No, a manager."

He said all this with such confidence that the mechanic didn't inquire why a manager in show business had to have long hair.

"That there," he said, "is an experimental model. Only one on the West Coast."

"Yep," said Fred. "A beautiful design. Ailerons mounted between the wings. Good airflow there. I like the tricycle landing gear." He walked around to the rear to inspect the engine. "That's a motor off a Harley, it looks like. Except it has aluminum cylinders." He set his hand on the engine confidently. "How much does it weigh?"

"I told you don't touch it. Two hundred and ten pounds. The whole thing weighs six hundred and fifty with nobody in it. How come you said you was a flyer, if you're a manager in show business?"

"I'm a gentleman flyer. Do you rent these things?"

"Sometimes. You got a license?"

"You mean they have licenses now?"

"Well," he admitted, "I ain't never actually seen one. Mr. Curtiss says we got to ask for licenses. You need a piece of paper from somebody sayin' you've had a lesson or two."

"What's the rate?"

"Twenty an hour, for the Farman and the Voisin. Like I say, you got a license?"

"I've had . . . quite an experience with the Wright," said Fred, thinking in a part of his mind of Marmora. He walked around to look at the controls of the Curtiss again. "This is a beautiful control system. It's a heck of a lot better than the Wright. The wing warping on the Wright doesn't work very well, and you can't see anything lying flat on your stomach. And the canard elevator," he went on, "is a rotten idea. It's an inherently unstable design. A touch too much and you stall or go into a dive."

"That's the trouble with the Farman," said the mechanic, pointing his thumb over the shoulder at the pasture outside. "Now this machine here," he said with calm satisfaction, "I helped Mr. Curtiss to build it. I practically built that control system myself." It was obvious that, with the influence of a little mild flattery, his mistrust of Fred was vanishing like fog in a sunshine.

Fred said, "The Wright doesn't have a throttle either. Just a make-or-break arrangement." He looked at the throttle on the Curtiss, a neat metal bar with a black knob on top of it. "What's the RPM at full power?"

"Runs about twelve hundred. Depends on the pitch. This here," he explained from the rear of the wing, "is something else you probably never saw before. It's an adjustable airscrew. You set it on the ground. The flatter the pitch, the higher the RPM, but you have to be careful, because if it goes over fifteen hundred the thing flies to pieces.''

Fred closed his hand on the throttle, observing the ingenious linkage that opened and closed the throats of the four carburetors. This time the mechanic didn't reprimand him for touching something. "That there's the mixture," he told him, "just under your left hand."

On the Wright, to adjust the mixture, you had to reach over and turn a plug on top of the engine, at the peril of catching your hand in the whirling bicycle chain.

"You say twenty dollars an hour?"

"That's for the Farman or the Voisin. This here is an experimental model. Mr. Curtiss don't want no one to fly it unless they're expert flyers. I ain't supposed to let you have any of them without a license."

"Let's say thirty."

The mechanic surveyed him doubtfully for a long moment. Then he said, "All right. You goin' to fly in that outfit?"

Fred took off the derby. Then, after some thought, he took off the checked jacket too and hung it on a nail in the hangar wall. "Maybe you could lend me some goggles."

The mechanic thought this over for a while. Then he went away into the office and came out with a pair of goggles, along with a leather cap which Fred put on backwards.

"Where's the thirty?"

Fred dug around in his pockets and came up with a twenty-dollar gold piece and a ragged paper ten. The mechanic put the coin in one pocket of his overalls and the bill in the other. Evidently he was scrupulously honest and never mingled his own money with that of his employer.

"My name's Kinney by the way. Pleased to meet you." He pushed open the sliding door of the hangar, with surprising vigor for such a small man, and then he and Fred began pushing the machine out into the sunshine. "Mr. Curtiss calls this here the June Bug," said Kinney, panting a little. "Now we get it. Headed. Into the wind."

He lifted up the front wheel of the thing and turned it around as though it were a child's toy, heading it into the sea breeze streaming in over the Golden Gate. Fred lifted himself up into the wicker seat and buckled his helmet, leaving his goggles up for the moment. He set his yellow shoes onto the rudder bar.

Kinney went around to the rear and set both hands on the airscrew.

"Set the mixture to rich. That's the ignition contact there to your right. Be sure it's off."

"Contact off."

Kinney swung the airscrew a half-dozen times. From the engine behind Fred there was a rich smell of gasoline. He turned the wheel and watched the ailerons moving, one up and one down. He pushed it back and forth; the elevator at the tail went up and down. He saw a disadvantage to the Curtiss design now; a canard out in front was constantly in view, but you couldn't see the angle of the rear elevator without crooking your head around. He set it to neutral and memorized where the yoke was: just even with his knees. He waggled the rudder with the rudder bar.

"Okay, contact now," said the voice from the rear.

"Contact."

Kinney swung the airscrew again. The engine gave a kind of a cough and there was a smell of half-burned gas. The second time it caught for good. The racket was terrific; the unmuffled motorcycle engine sounded like a string of firecrackers going off. On the grass ahead a few dead leaves and scraps of paper were sucked magically toward the aeroplane and flew by underneath.

"KEEP IT RICH FOR ANOTHER MINUTE," yelled Kinney.

Fred nodded without turning his head. He pulled down the goggles.

"WATCH OUT FOR GOPHER HOLES OUT THERE IN THE FIELD," Kinney went on yelling. "KEEP TO THE TRACK WHERE YOU SEE EVERYBODY ELSE'S BEEN TAKIN' OFF. WAIT TILL THE FRONT WHEEL GETS LIGHT, THEN PULL BACK AND YOU'RE ON YOUR WAY. LEAN NOW."

Fred leaned the mixture. He opened the throttle and the June Bug began to bump over the grass. Kinney ran along beside, still offering advice.

"DON'T GIVE IT TOO MUCH AILERON," he yelled at the top of his voice. "BECAUSE THE AILERONS SLOW IT DOWN. PARTICULARLY IN A TURN." He began to fall behind as the June Bug gathered speed. "WHICH IS MOSTLY WHEN YOU USE AILERON!" he yelled. "WATCH THE . . ."

The rest was lost in the din of the unmuffled engine. The grass raced toward Fred and fled by underneath. The thing bumped so much that it was hard to tell when the front wheel got light. He saw now what Kinney meant about gopher holes. He had forgotten to get onto the track in the grass where everybody else took off. Finally, judging that he had reached about forty-five miles an hour or so, he pulled back on the wheel. The June Bug rose but immediately began to slide off to the right. This was the torque effect, one of the disadvantages of the single airscrew. He corrected, a little too much in fact, and the thing slewed off the other way. This was bad for his airspeed and he was still only three feet off the grass. There was a fence ahead that was just about that high. Pushing the throttle all the way forward, he inched back gingerly on the wheel, wary of stalling when he still didn't have full speed. The fence shot by underneath.

When he came gliding back in, exactly fifty-seven minutes later, he was almost over the edge of the field when it occurred to him that Kinney had told him nothing about how to land the thing. Probably assumed he knew. Full throttle, half, or shut? The hangar was over on his left, and up ahead was the fence he had barely managed to clear when he took off. At fifty miles an hour everything happened very quickly. Fred had perhaps three seconds to perceive that he was coming in too high, and another second to decide what to do about it in order not to slam into the fence at the other end of the field after he landed. Of course there were no brakes on the murderous thing.

There is nothing like a certain amount of danger to hone the wit and stimulate fast thinking. In the split second remaining, Fred rapidly reviewed all the qualities of the Curtiss including Kinney's advice not to give it too much aileron because this slowed it down. He wrenched the wheel back and forth. The June Bug waggled in the air as the ailerons tipped one way and then the other. This slowed it down all right. It sank abruptly, causing Fred's stomach to rise against his ribs. The ground was coming up far too fast. Fighting the instinct to pull back on the wheel, he pushed it forward and at the same time gave the throttle a nudge. The June Bug fell in a swoop, then leveled out until the grass was only three feet or so below. He waited for the moment to pull back on the wheel . . . *now*. The thing dropped to the grass as lightly as a sparrow. When he came to a stop the fence at the edge of the field was about twenty feet ahead.

Kinney came running across the grass. Fred pushed up the goggles and shut off the contact.

"Nice landing, Mr. Hite. I forgot to tell you how to lose altitude case you came in too high. But I see you already knew that."

Fred clambered out, with nothing much to say for himself. "Torque effect is a little tricky." He walked around stiff-legged on the grass.

"Yep, well I guess you was used to the twin airscrews on the Wright. Help me turn this thing around, will you?"

They lifted up the front wheel and pointed it back toward the hangar. Then the two of them pushed it back across the grass, one on either side of the engine. Fred was still in a state of exaltation from his hour in the air. He hardly knew what he was doing. He still felt the trembling of the machine vibrating in his blood, the wind that sang in the wires and pushed against his body like a powerful hand, he saw the dizzying spectacle of the Golden Gate tilting back and forth and then settling to level as he turned. He hardly paid attention to what Kinney was saying; still something about the torque. "It don't cause no trouble. Long as you know it's there." The June Bug bumped over a hole; they were almost to the hangar. Kinney was panting again. "Mr. Curtiss thinks. Maybe you can. Bias the ailerons. To counteract it."

"No doubt," gasped Fred, short of breath himself.

They left the June Bug in front of the hangar. Fred went into the hangar for his jacket and derby. When he came out, still panting, Kinney was refilling the fuel tank with a bucket and a funnel.

"You're quite a flyer, Mr. Hite," he said, tipping in the last of the gasoline. "You know, next Sunday we're havin' an air show here. Mr. Curtiss, he's held up in the East and he can't make it. There's a sweepstakes for private aviators. We'd sort of like the Bug to win. It's for the publicity," he explained in case Fred didn't understand.

"That so?"

"That Frenchman will be here, Paulhan. A lot of people will be comin' out to see him. We charge a dollar for admission. He's goin' to fly a Farman. Not this piece of junk here," he gestured with his thumb. "A new one. It's comin' out by rail. Course the Bug is a much finer aeroplane. Fly rings round that Farman. Trouble is, it's an experimental model and there ain't many flyers round here that know how to handle it.''

Fred's heart began pounding again. He said nothing and remained outwardly calm.

''You could enter the Bug if you wanted. Course you'd have to pay the usual rent. And there's also an entry fee. Fifty dollars.''

''That's a lot of money.''

''First prize for the sweepstakes is a thousand dollars,'' said Kinney laconically.

''I'll think about it.''

''So long, Mr. Hite. That was a nice landing you made.''

Fred walked the half mile back across the grass to the end of the trolley line. He felt in his pocket as he went. He still had a dime for the trolley and another one for the cable car. He calculated how long it would be until Herma's next payday. Wednesday till Saturday: three more days.

9.

The cable car came to a stop at the corner of Powell and Market, and Fred got off. It was a few minutes before noon, and the sidewalks on both sides of Market were crowded with clerks and office workers going to lunch. It occurred to him for the first time to wonder where he himself was going to have lunch. For a while he had eaten at the Larkin and charged it to his bill, but the Sheeny had put an end to that. With no particular aim in mind, he set off in the opposite direction from the hotel, down Market toward the Embarcadero.

The crowd on the sidewalk was thick. People were coming both ways, streaming against each other like two rows of contrary ants. Fred went along at a leisurely pace, now and then dodging around someone coming the other way. The sun was shining warmly and people were beginning to perspire. There was a friendly odor of sunshine, humanity, and cheap whiskey in the air. Directly ahead of Fred was a bizarre obstacle: a glazier's boy carrying a kind of trestle or framework that fitted over him like a sawhorse. On the trestle were pieces of glass of all sizes and shapes. Fred moved to the left to pass the glazier's boy, working his way with difficulty through the stream of pedestrians coming the other way. He bumped against a pair of workmen, threaded his way around the clerk from a bank, and pushed past a yokel in a greasy hat, perhaps a miner from the gold country, who was gazing around at everything in a curious way. Then, framed in an opening in the collection of glass plates ahead of him, he caught sight of something that made him catch his breath.

It was the upper part of a persimmon-colored dress with two perfect and slightly pendulous globes in it, swaying up and down as their owner walked. Separating the two shapes, down the middle of the dress, was a row of buttons and a trim of lace. There could be only one bosom like it in the world.

Fred wheeled about, dodged around the glazier's boy, and set off the other way up the sidewalk. He caught up with her in only a few seconds.

"Ernestine! What are you doing here?"

She gave him a bright smile. "I'm walking up Market toward my rooming house, which is on Howard Street, not a very savory part of town, I'm afraid."

"But—Mr. Larkin?"

Her ironic, lightly theatrical manner was still the same. "Mr. Larkin, I regret to say, is no more. And that's a whole story, which I'd be glad to relate to you over lunch, if you'd be good enough to invite me."

Fred fell into a kind of babble. "No more? You mean he . . . Ernestine, what are you saying? Lunch?" The clock on the Ferry Building indicated a quarter after twelve. "It would be a pleasure, but the fact is . . . I'm just a bit short at the moment . . ." He stuck his hand into his pocket, a silly gesture that immediately made him color. "However . . ."

"Oh, if that's all it is, I can foot the bill. I've still got a few pennies. You'll just have to invite me, that's all."

She was quite blithe. Fred understood nothing. Together they went up Market another block and then off on Bush to a kind of rathskeller he knew where you could get a nourishing lunch for half a dollar.

They sat down and waited for their Würstel and hot potato salad to come. Fred stared across the table at her, his glance locked about a foot below her face. He was feeling a little numb. He was like a man who had found a chest of gold on the sidewalk and was, first of all, afraid that somebody would steal it from him, and second, trying to cast about for a way of opening it. With difficulty he removed his eyes from the persimmon bodice.

"You said that—Mr. Larkin—"

"He died in the most inconsiderate way imaginable. I take it you have never been called upon to unclasp yourself from a corpse."

"H'mm," said Fred. "Then he . . ."

"He was tenacious, the old goat. Even after having passed on, he was determined to let nothing escape from his grasp that he felt belonged to him."

"It can't have been pleasant for you."

"No, and that was only the start. He had hardly emitted his dying gasp when the house was full of lawyers. It was amazing. They seemed to spring out of the walls, and they began taking inventory of everything before the undertakers had the old man out of the house. I was ordered to vacate the premises forthwith."

"Vacate the premises?"

"My contention that I was Mr. Larkin's niece was laughed out of hand. I was escorted to the station with only the clothes on my back.''

Fred murmured, ''It's a beautiful gown.''

''You don't seem to be able to keep your mind on the subject. I'm up here, just a little higher than where you're looking. The point is that I have been cast off like an old shoe, and I have no place to lay my head except Mrs. Morbihan's rooming house.''

She still, however, gave the impression that she was acting a part rather than taking this personal disaster seriously. There was a little tragic arch of wrinkles in her forehead, but it was a mock stage despair. There was even a little smile on her lips. She rattled on blithely in her actressy voice. ''So you see me, victim of a cruel fate, a homeless child tossed about aimlessly on life's waters.''

The waiter arrived with their plates and two steins of beer. Ernestine drew a long sip from the stein, leaving a rim of foam on her lips which she delicately removed with the napkin. Then she attacked the potato salad. Fred left his lunch untouched.

''Then what are your plans?''

''I have no choice other than to resume my career on the stage or— something else. At the worst, it seems that bought embraces still fetch a good price. This is not the most pleasant way to earn one's living, but it is hardly worse than being incessantly chased through a drafty mansion by a senile saturnalian.''

''Ernestine, don't be ridiculous. If I can help with a little some-thing—'' He stuck his hand into his empty pocket.

''Oh, I'm not quite reduced to that yet,'' she said pleasantly. She raised a hand with a large diamond ring on it and touched a brooch in the middle of her bodice. It had a ruby in the center and was set with tiny diamonds around the edge. ''I managed to make off with a bauble or two when the lawyers were looking the other way. So for the present, instead of applying to a bordello, I can merely pay a visit to Uncle once in a while.''

''And after that?''

''It's in the lap of the gods, dear Fred. All fortune hangs by a fragile thread. And when it is cut, poof.'' She held the napkin a foot in the air and let it drop onto the table.

Fred could not account for the fact that he had not noticed the brooch before. He had been looking straight at it. Apparently it was a phenomenon of parallel vision: the left eye looked at what was on the left, the right to the right, and neither noticed what was in the middle.

''Perhaps there might be something for you at the Larkin Theater.''

She gazed at him oddly. Then she said, ''Perhaps.''

She had finished her lunch, wiping up the plate with a piece of bread which she also ate. Fred had only dabbled at the potato salad.

''And now I'll be on my way.'' She got up, setting down the money for the meal and the tip. ''Thank you for the lunch.''

''Ernestine, for God's sake. Isn't there some place where we can discuss this more . . . privately?''

She observed the direction of his glance. Then she looked back at him and made her fixed little smile. "Unfortunately my rooming house is presided over by an ogress of rigidly puritanical views. She has arms like an Irish policeman, and she has already pitched more than one swain out into the street. Not mine, of course," she hastened to add.

Fred stuck his hand into his pocket again. It was an unconscious reflex. He pretended that he had only meant to put both hands into his pockets, in a casual way. Saturday, he remembered, was Herma's payday.

"Are you free on Sunday?"

"Free to some," she said playfully. "For others, it's negotiable."

"You don't seem to be taking all this very seriously."

"It's only the problems of the world that are serious, dear Fred," she told him. "Our solutions to them are always a little ludicrous."

By way of Kearney Street they made their way back to Market. Here they parted, she turning to give him a final "ta-ta" sign with her fingers from twenty yards away. He watched her disappear across the traffic of Market and down Third Street. From the rear the persimmon-colored gown was a symmetrical hourglass, the lower half of which formed a callipygian structure of perfect proportions. This view was also nice. There were those, he knew, who were connoisseurs of such, but it didn't happen to be his specialty.

He got back to the Larkin a little after two. When he took his key at the desk the clerk stared at him significantly.

"Sheeny wants to see you."

"What about?"

"Can't say."

"Where is he?"

"In his orfice."

Fred wound his way around the desk and into a small cubicle with no windows to it except a transom over the door. A light bulb hung on a wire from the ceiling. The Sheeny was sitting with his feet on the desk, shuffling through a pile of papers. He hardly looked up.

"I have unfortunate news for you, my dear gentleman. Mr. Larkin, your benefactor, has passed on to his reward. The circumstances are touching. He was found in his favorite armchair with an open Bible in his hands, with his finger on the Twenty-third Psalm."

"Yes, I've already heard."

"Dear, dear, dear. You don't seem very crushed by the news. I'm afraid it's quite serious for you. You may vacate your rooms at your earliest convenience, or start paying for them, whichever you prefer. It's a matter of indifference to me."

"And the theater?"

"Ah. Miss Herma's position in the repertory is also terminated, I am afraid. Dear dear dear."

"We'll see what Mr. Speidermann says about that."

"Mr. Speidermann," said the Sheeny, exploring a nostril thoughtfully with his little finger, "will also be looking for a new job, as well as new lodgings."

"But everyone in town is singing *Kiss Me Again*."

"Yes, that's just the point, my dear Mr. Hite. Everyone in town already knows it, so there is no more reason for them to come to the Larkin."

"But the house is sold out for two more weeks."

"Exactly. I see you are well up on the affairs of the theater. You have a sharp head for business and you will go far. The point is, I have here a telegram from the executor of Mr. Larkin's estate, instructing me to put both hotel and theater immediately onto a businesslike footing. From the point of view of the hotel, this means no more free rooms. From the point of view of the theater, this means that in two weeks' time the opera company will be replaced by a vaudeville straight from the Orpheum Theater in New York. There will be the Tumbling Torricellis, a Scotch comedian, a dog act, and a family of Swiss bell-ringers."

"What a blow for the arts."

The Sheeny removed the little finger, examined it, and put it in the other nostril. "What will you, Mr. Hite? It's what the public wants. Sic transit gloria, and so on, if you will see my point, my dear gentleman. So that, as I say, it will be necessary for you to vacate your rooms, with separate entrances but connecting bath, in two weeks' time at the very latest."

"I imagine all of this must have saddened you terribly."

"Dear, dear, dear, it's a melancholy turn of events for us all. That our benefactor and friend, Mr. Larkin, should have been taken from us so suddenly. I won't conceal that I have sometimes been exacerbated by Miss Herma's—artistic temperament. She demands a great deal for herself. But I am not a man without a heart. I cast about in my mind in search of something for this talented young lady to do, at least on a temporary basis. And I think of the following. There is in the vaudeville company a certain Count Proxissimo, who throws knives, and requires an assistant. The only requirements are that the lady be pretty, and also that she be able to smile under all circumstances. The lady assistant wears silver trousers. Miss Herma will like that. The assistant wears trousers because some of the knives go between."

"I don't think she'd be interested."

"It pays twenty dollars a week. Of course," the Sheeny went on, examining the finger a second time to see if there were any news on it, "the rate for your present suite of rooms is two hundred dollars, so you could hardly go on living in them, even if Miss Herma does decide in favor of becoming the Count's assistant."

"We'll move to the Palace."

"Ah, you young people," sighed the Sheeny. "Full of ambition and blind hope." He seemed to fall into reflection about his own youth, when he was a shoe-shine boy in Smyrna and dreamed of coming to America and becoming a hotel manager.

10.

On Sunday morning Fred dressed with care, in a pair of corduroy knickers, boots, and a whipcord jacket and cap he had bought the day before, after he came into possession of Herma's pay envelope. The goggles, presumably, Kinney would supply as he had before. Putting on the cap, he gazed at his pale and intent face in the mirror. There was an astuteness to it, a foxlike keenness and confidence, that more than counterbalanced its soft youth and girlish quality. The Sheeny was right. He would go far. He would *have* to go far in the next two weeks or everything would fall down like a house of cards.

Then he noticed a scrap of paper in the mirror, with something written on it in the usual spidery hand. "Fred, you're crazy. We can't spend so much on aeroplanes."

He pulled it off, crumpled it, and threw it into the wastebasket. Then, going into Herma's room and rummaging around until he found another scrap of paper, he scrawled on it, "You sing, I'll spend the money." Sticking this into the mirror, he found the keys and went out, carefully locking the doors of both rooms.

Since there was still a good deal of Saturday's pay left, he engaged a horse-cab to take himself and Ernestine out to the Presidio. When they got to the field they found it covered with other cabs, private buggies, and motorcars. More than a thousand people had gathered, the ladies in white dresses and the men for the most part in black suits and derbies. On the road along the field there were posters on the telegraph poles.

GRAND AIR SHOW

Sunday, April 8th

Farman, Blériot, Wright, Curtiss,
and Voisin Aeroplanes

Admission $1. Free demonstration
Flight to Holder of Winning Ticket

See the Famous French Aeronaut Louis
Paulhan at the Controls of his Farman

Aeroplane Races

Grand Sweepstakes $1000 Prize

Presidio Meadows, at Noon. Transportation
by E Car or Geary Avenue Omnibus

Pushing through the crowd, Fred searched for the participants' entrance, but there didn't seem to be any provision for one. In the end he had to buy tickets for himself and Ernestine. He peeled two dollars off the lump of bills in his pocket. There were still quite a few of them left. A good-sized grandstand had been erected in the field near the hangar. The tickets for the seats were another two dollars, and he paid this too. Here he installed Ernestine with her parasol. She was wearing the same persimmon-colored gown she had on the morning he met her on Market Street, along with a matching Eugénie cap; perhaps it was the only gown she had. At any rate it was just as spectacular as it had been before. The parasol was white silk printed with red roses.

"You'll be all right here?"

"Just fine. My brave aviator! I had no notion you were such a hero."

Unfortunately everything Ernestine said had a faint flavor of irony. Furthermore, her brightly-colored dress and spectacular figure were already attracting attention from the crowd, and as might be expected the unattached males far outnumbered the ladies. He bent over her in an effort to kiss her cheek, but she parried and offered her hand instead. Still, in returning the hand to her, he managed to brush his own against the Incomparable Bosom. She colored lightly, then laughed. "Only the brave deserve the fair," she told him. He left, turning once to see her make her "ta-ta" sign with her white manicured hand.

There were a dozen or more aeroplanes on the field. He identified several Farmans, a new Wright Flyer, and a Roe triplane. The June Bug had not yet been brought out of the hangar. Fred went in. Inside the hangar, in addition to the June Bug, was Paulhan's Farman and a Blériot monoplane to be flown by the Frenchman Lecornu. Kinney was checking the magneto of the Curtiss and changing the plugs.

He turned and glanced at Fred, saying nothing. When he had finished tightening the last plug he said, "Let's have a talk in the office."

"Anything wrong?"

"Nope. Everything's just fine. Bug's in great shape." He stuck the wrench into the rear pocket of his overalls and picked his way through the other machines in the hangar, with Fred following him. "Magneto puts out a spark like a bolt of lightning. I changed the pitch on the airscrew so it goes to about fourteen hundred now. But you don't want to run it that fast for more than a few minutes, or it'll throw the rods out like a monkey spittin' nuts."

He led the way into the tiny office, which smelled of grease and had more engine parts in it than papers. "We'll let you have the Bug for thirty, same as last time, Mr. Hite, even though you'll be in the air more'n an hour mostly likely."

"I thought this was a promotion stunt for the Curtiss."

"That's right. But it's a private entry. Companies ain't allowed to enter the sweepstakes. Then the entry fee for the race is fifty, and the insurance is another fifty."

"Insurance?"

"Mr. Curtiss don't want nobody racin' without insurance. He ain't got but two June Bugs, this one and one on the East Coast."

Fred took the bundle of bills out of his rear pocket and peeled off the money. Herma's two hundred and seventy-five dollars was melting like an iceberg in summer. He had spent over a hundred on clothes. Renting the cab for the day was five dollars, and then there were the tickets.

Observing the much-thinned bundle going back into Fred's pocket, Kinney said, "Course all you got to do is win that thousand-dollar sweepstakes. Then you won't have no problems."

"Sure," said Fred. "What about Paulhan?"

"In that Farman?" Kinney had a mechanic's contempt for any machine other than his own. "Molasses in January. Got that water-cooled Voisin engine. Weighs a ton."

Fred wasn't so sure. He went out to look at the Farman in the hangar. It was a solidly built machine. There were four landing wheels mounted in a transverse line under the wing, with auxiliary skids to keep you from ground-looping. The pusher airscrew was keyed directly to the shaft, as on the Curtiss. Sensing someone behind and at his elbow, he turned. He found himself being inspected by a small, quiet Frenchman, with gray eyes and a little smile.

"Belle machine, n'est-ce pas?"

"Are you Paulhan?"

"Oui."

"Heavy engine."

Paulhan had no reply to make to this. He seemed amused at something or other about Fred. He went on looking at him for some time with the quiet little smile.

The machines were wheeled out into the sunlight. After a good deal of delay—the whole thing was badly managed and everything went behind schedule—a long, lanky flyer from Illinois took off in a Voisin and did some "aerial acrobatics," which consisted of a few rolls and wing-overs, followed by a long dive ending only a few feet from the ground, which produced a great gasp from the crowd. He glided down onto the grass with both hands held in the air, staring woodenly at the grandstand, to show that the thing would land itself.

Then it was the turn of a certain Mrs. Baker, who had drawn the lucky number for the free flight. She was strapped into the Roe triplane, behind the engine and ahead of the pilot, and flown around the pasture two or three times. She got out intrepidly, saying "Land's sakes" for her only comment. Following this, a gas-balloon race took off and dwindled away into three small silver balls, far off in the distance over Angel Island.

The sweepstakes was announced. The crowd—several hundred in the grandstand and a thousand or more standing in the grass on either side—grew silent except for a little murmur.

The five machines were lined up in the pasture. After a certain amount of foot-stamping and delay, the flyers got in and were strapped into place. In addition to Fred and Paulhan, there was Lecornu in his Blériot, similar to the Voisin but a more powerful machine, its single wing held up by a stubby mast with bracing wires extending to the wing tips. The others were the lanky middle-westerner in the Roe triplane, and a stocky young eastern amateur named Matsen in the Wright Flyer, which had a special monorail laid out in the grass for its takeoff. Matsen, in place of a helmet, wore his cap turned backwards, and disdained goggles. The rest of them were in proper flying rig.

The five mechanics strove to get the engines going. The Curtiss started on the first pull after contact, as did the Blériot. The Farman required another couple of pulls, while Paulhan waited patiently. There was a deafening din, and the air around the five machines filled with blue smoke. After a moment or two the Roe, powered by a four-cylinder Alouette, caught, faltered, and broke into a steady roar. The Wright was last; the sweating mechanic swung at the left-hand screw a dozen times until the bicycle chains rattled into motion and began spinning.

According to the rules, the five machines were to take off in sequence starting with Paulhan. Fred was next; the Curtiss took to the air easily and he tilted it into a long bank to the right. Then they were to fly around the field clockwise until the last one was in the air. At that point a large white flag, hoisted from the grandstand, would signal five minutes to start. A blue flag would be raised at one minute, and a red flag for the start. At that point all five machines were to be to the west of a rickety wooden pylon standing in the grass across from the grandstand.

Fred, with his throttle cut back, followed Paulhan around in a slow oval. Below on the ground the Wright was having difficulty getting into the air. A number of spectators were helping to push it, in danger of being decapitated by the airscrews or getting caught up in the flying chains. Finally it slid down its improvised rail, bumped once or twice, and managed to get a few feet into the air. The white flag went up. Fred and Paulhan, who were flying close to their stalling speed, caught up to the lumbering Roe triplane and lapped it. The thing seemed to be going only about forty miles an hour. Probably, Fred thought, it wouldn't provide very much competition. As for the Wright, its operator seemed to have his hands full just keeping it up off the ground. It went straight off over the field in the wrong direction, across the fence. Evidently Matsen had not found out how to turn the thing either.

The blue flag was up now. Then it went down, and Fred banked around to the right to get to the west of the pylon. Together the pylon and the grandstand formed a rough starting line two hundred yards or so long. Paulhan was above him and to the right. He caught a glimpse of the Frenchman's face; he was still wearing his little smile. Then they both turned to head back toward the starting line.

Fred kept his eyes glued on the empty flagstaff. He was a little ahead of time; he throttled back as much as he could. He was going to cross early—no, the red flag flapped its way up the staff just as the pylon went by under his wing. Paulhan was only a second or two behind him. It was a beautiful start. The others were not far behind, except for the Wright which was still struggling to turn around over the meadow in the distance.

Fred climbed to five hundred feet, enough to take him over the hills. The first leg of the triangle ran across the city to the tower of the Ferry Building at the foot of Market. It was a warm cloudless day, with only a little mist lurking along the beach and clinging to the top of Twin Peaks. The whole city lay below and ahead of him, swirling around the feet of its five hills. The thousands of housetops gave the impression of countless numbers of children's blocks, laid out in geometric lines and shapes. He made out the diagonal line of Columbus Avenue, running along the valley between Russian Hill and Telegraph Hill. His eye roamed along the waterfront looking for the Ferry Building. Trying to remember the map, he had the impression that the course to it lay approximately across Telegraph Hill. He had expected to see the characteristic tower as soon as he was in the air. But evidently it lay behind the hill from this angle. Then he noticed that Paulhan was not flying the same direction he was.

At the same moment he caught sight of the Ferry Building. It was considerably to his right, and Paulhan was flying directly toward it. He had made a bad blunder; it came from not studying the map carefully enough. He banked to the right, pushing the throttle wide open. The steady roar of the engine mounted a little. He had no way of counting the RPM except by the note of the engine. With the throttle wide open it was presumably Kinney's fourteen hundred, which would send the rods through the cylinder walls like a monkey spitting nuts. He held it for a while until Paulhan was only a few yards ahead, then throttled back so that the engine dropped a note or two on the musical scale. He was confident now that he had more speed than the Farman.

The two machines converged on the Ferry Building tower, the Farman still a little ahead. A rule of the race was that you had to round all pylons, including the tower, at an altitude less than their height. This was tricky because you could easily lose speed in a turn, if you didn't pay close attention, and drop like a stone before you knew what had happened. Fred throttled back a little, not too much, and sighted over his wing.

Ahead of him Paulhan went around in a wide bank. Fred turned inside him and much tighter. For a fraction of a second he caught a glimpse of the faces in Market Street turned up to watch him. The tower swam up rapidly, seeming to lean toward him as he banked. As he expected, the Curtiss slowed in the turn as the air dragged at the ailerons and rudder. He gave it full throttle again. Then he was arcund, kicking back on the rudder bar and straightening the wings to level.

He allowed himself a quick look around. To his surprise the Farman had gone wide on the turn. It was a hundred yards or so to his right, and gradually falling behind. Evidently Paulhan knew he didn't have the speed to beat the Curtiss and was counting on Fred making another mistake, or blowing his engine.

The Blériot with Lecornu aboard was just rounding the tower. The Roe triplane was far behind, lumbering along over Telegraph Hill, and there was no sign of the Wright Flyer. The Blériot was his competition now. The two machines were of about the same speed; the Blériot was perhaps a shade faster. Fred had a lead of several hundred yards, and it was three miles to the Alcatraz pylon. One thing at a time. For the moment he concentrated on getting to the Alcatraz pylon first. He could worry about the final leg later.

He allowed himself another quick glance behind. The Blériot was still gaining. The throttle was wide open; nothing to be done about that. He checked his controls to be sure they were all exactly flat, to cause the minimum of air drag. He even bent over a little, drawing his head into his shoulders to reduce the resistance of the wind. Not for nothing, he thought, was he an expert bicyclist. The long rocky outline of Alcatraz came into view, like a ship pointed out toward the Golden Gate. The pylon on top of it was a rickety structure of timbers and canvas with an "A" painted on it. The blasted thing was only about fifty feet above the rock; it didn't leave you much margin for error. He throttled back slightly; Lecornu couldn't get past him from this angle anyhow.

As he banked for the turn he looked around again. That infernal Lecornu was inside him now and coming on fast. Apparently he hoped to turn tighter and go by inside the Curtiss. It was a dangerous maneuver for both of them. If he didn't make it he would go sideways straight into the other machine, unless he managed to slide by above or below. But with a fifty-foot pylon there wasn't much room. The damned idiot! Gritting his teeth, Fred kicked the bar and swung the wheel over. The island, the rickety pylon, and the Bay with flecks of foam on it staggered drunkenly under him.

He was around. While he was still leveling out he turned his head for a quick look behind. The scene behind him was fixed and frozen, as precise as in a photograph. The pylon, a corner of the shabby canvas fluttering in the wind, stood bolt upright. Only a few yards from it the Blériot was in a steep bank; far too steep, almost vertical. A little below it the left wing had separated and was suspended in the air, canted at an angle, a piece of sky clearly visible between it and the rest of the machine.

A second later, without seeming to have moved from this odd position in the air, the Blériot struck the rock. There was a ball of flame which instantly turned into an expanding blossom of smoke. Fred had time only for a glance, then he had to turn forward again. He felt cold. Everything seemed unreal and for a moment he hardly realized where he was. Mechanically he reached out and reduced the throttle. He saw the Presidio coming up, out beyond it the Golden Gate, and over on his right the Sausalito hills. He went on flying like a mechanical man. He flew quite well, in fact. He made out the pylon and hangar in the Presidio meadows, and adjusted his course slightly to head for them. He found he had cut back the throttle a little too much and nudged it a hair ahead. The next time he looked around Alcatraz was far behind, with a pencil of smoke hanging over it in the sky. Paulhan had already rounded the pylon and was coming on a quarter of a mile or so behind.

The hangar was about a mile ahead. He could make out the grandstand now, and the clutter of people around it like black and white ants. The Bay was perhaps a hundred feet below him. At this low altitude the flecks of foam shot by with a dizzying speed.

He cut back the throttle again and pushed the wheel forward. The Curtiss put its nose down in a flat glide. Coming in this way from the east, the landing machines passed directly before the grandstand and landed only a few hundred yards farther on. Probably this was arranged on purpose to give the spectators a good view of the landings. It also gave the landing flyer a good view of the people in the grandstand, if only for a moment. Fred glanced to the left, hoping to glimpse the persimmon-colored gown in the crowd.

A moment later he turned his attention to the grassy field racing up below and ahead. He instantly saw that he had overshot the field. He was coming in too high and moving too fast. Ahead was that infernal fence he had barely stopped short of the time before. He twisted the wheel sharply to left and right, rocking the Curtiss like a boat in a seaway. Losing its grip on the air, it dropped so that his stomach came up against his ribs. He had overdone it a little. He pushed the wheel forward to pick up speed again. But it was too late; he was only about twenty feet in the air now. The machine, far below its stalling speed, behaved like a kite with a cut string. It came down tottering and swaying, hesitated, and seemed to hang fixed for a moment. Then it struck the earth with a solid thump, almost a splat, the tail surface and nose together.

There was a heavy smell of gasoline. The tank on the wing overhead had ruptured and the back of Fred's clothing was soaked with it. As for the tank, the wing, and the other parts of the machine, they were scattered about on the grass more or less in the shape of an aeroplane, but in a disarranged pattern as though some child had scattered the parts of a puzzle with his hand. The engine had rolled out and lay smoking in the grass a few yards ahead. It was lucky, he thought, that it hadn't struck him square in the back. There was nothing left of the wicker chair or the belt that had strapped him into it. He stood up, stiff-legged, and walked calmly but rapidly away from the wreckage.

After only a few yards he fell down. He wasn't sure why. Perhaps his leg was broken. Or perhaps he had only stepped into one of those infernal gopher holes. Lying on his side with an unidentified but not unpleasant buzzing in his ears, he watched while an odd-looking bug floated down past the grandstand, grew larger, and at last touched lightly onto the grass, setting its tail down only when the four transverse wheels were firmly on the ground. Gunning his motor in little bursts, Paulhan blatted and tottered the Farman around in a wide turn toward the grandstand.

People were running up toward Fred. Some of them pulled him up, others insisted that he sit down again. Kinney arrived, without haste. He had his thumbs in the back pockets of his overalls. He inspected Fred.

"You okay, Mr. Hite?"

"I think so."

"What was you daydreamin' about as you went past the grandstand? I saw you lookin' around in every direction except forward."

"I think my ankle is broken. Anyhow I beat Paulhan."

"No you didn't. You got to land the machine to finish."

"I thought any landing you could walk away from was a good landing."

"Not in racin' it ain't. Anyhow you didn't walk away. You fell down in that there gopher hole. And look at that machine! What am I goin' to tell Mr. Curtiss?"

"He says his ankle's broken," said someone.

"No, it isn't," Fred decided. "Somebody help me up."

Two spectators got him upright and helped him off toward the motor-ambulance at the edge of the field, Kinney following along behind. The ambulance attendants got his outer clothing off and inspected him while he sat on a folding camp chair. He had an ugly bruise on his right cheek-bone, a stiff neck—he experimentally wagged his head to left and right, and then backward and forward—and another set of bruises on his left ribs. Both knees were abraded; little pinpoints of blood appeared on them and slid down his shins. He had a gasoline rash on his back, and his left ankle was slightly sprained.

"I feel fine," he said.

He watched while the Roe triplane lumbered down through the gray air like a condor, bounced on the grass two or three times, and finally managed to bring itself to a stop.

Fred had almost forgotten the Alcatraz pylon. The frozen photograph formed suddenly again in his mind.

"What about Lecornu?"

"Monoplanes never was any good," said Kinney. "No way you can brace just one wing."

11.

Once installed with Ernestine in the horse-cab, and clopping back along Bay Street toward the city, Fred felt—not exhilarated exactly, but in a state of bodily grace, and somberly and metaphysically pleased with himself. There is nothing like a narrow escape from death to sharpen the consciousness and all the senses. And a few bumps and bruises, too, give one a sense of the exquisite intricacy and value of one's body. No matter that he had spent all Herma's money, and failed to win the thousand-dollar sweepstakes. He had savored the keenness of life, in this one afternoon, in a way beyond the imagination of any bank clerk or staid office worker. He felt the sting of the two bandages on his knees.

His ribs hurt, and so did the bruise on his face. When he waggled his neck something inside it gritted like broken glass. Never mind! He lived, he was still alive, and next to him in the cab was the warm and curvaceous presence of Ernestine, jammed close against his own side.

"My aeronaut! Poor wounded hero!"

"Careful of my neck."

"Tell me where else it hurts."

"Everywhere. You can kiss me though."

"Like this? And this, and this, and this."

"My right arm works okay." He wrapped it gingerly around her.

"Oh, I'm so glad of that."

"Hey! there's a telegraph office," said Fred, unwinding his arm from her. "Stop! Ernestine, do you by any chance have a half-dollar for a telegram?"

Sighing, she got out her purse and gave him the coin. He limped in, took a form from the desk, and scrawled on it, "Speidermann, Larkin Theater. Miss Herma is indisposed and won't sing Fifi tonight. Hite."

The clerk snatched it away from him. "Right away. Say, is that the Herma that sings *Kiss Me Again?*"

"You'd better hurry. It closes in a week."

He went out and got into the cab, somewhat gingerly. His knees were beginning to stiffen up a little now.

"Why don't we have some dinner?" he suggested to Ernestine.

"Some Würstel at the Rathskeller?"

"Is that the best you can do?"

She looked into her purse again.

At Gobey's Ladies and Gents Oyster Parlor on Sutter they regaled themselves on boiled terrapin and crab stew, along with a high-shouldered bottle of Sauterne in a silver ice bucket. Ernestine ate efficiently, mopping up the last of her stew with a piece of bread and holding the wine bottle upside down over her glass to get the last drop out of it. After the coffee Fred ordered pousse-cafés, consisting of ingeniously arranged layers of different-colored liqueurs in slim crystal goblets. They lingered over these confections for some time. Ernestine, her chin propped on her hand, toyed with the glass in her pale and perfectly manicured fingers. When the bill came Fred slipped it tactfully over to her side of the table, half hidden by the wine bottle.

She considered it languidly.

"Alas, I haven't got it, dear boy."

"How much do you lack?"

With a sigh she straightened up and consulted her purse again. "A dollar and a half. About. I'm not very good at figures."

He managed to find a dollar bill, three quarters, and an assortment of nickels and dimes in his own pockets. They left his money and hers on the table and stole out, waiting for a moment when the waiter was away in the kitchen.

Out on the street, of course, they had no money for a cab or for anything else.

"Tomorrow," said Ernestine, "it's to Uncle to hock the shiner. But he's not open at this hour, unfortunately. Where's your hotel, dear boy?"

"I'm not on very good terms with the management just now. What about your rooming house?"

"There is Mrs. Morbihan. She is quite formidable. However, it's possible that she is momentarily inattentive, or has gone down the street to the gin mill or something. We can go and see."

There was nothing for it but to walk: down Dupont Street, a little way along Market and across it to Third, and then a short distance up Howard to the rooming house. In all truth it was not a very appetizing-looking place. It was on the wrong side of Market Street—south of the Slot, as people said. The street was full of filth, and there was a gang of idlers loafing around the front stoop. The tall, narrow house itself was three stories high and the shape of a guillotine; the open door at the bottom was the hole where you put your head. In the window was a placard: "Morbihan's Residential Chambers."

They stopped a little way down the street and looked the situation over, as well as they could see in the dark. "It's not the Palace but it's cheap. Fifty cents a day," whispered Ernestine, "and I have the best room in the place, second floor front. She's there all right, the old reptile. Sitting in her room with the door open, where she can see everyone going up the stairs."

The curtains were drawn in the room on the ground floor. But inside Fred could make out the door of the lighted parlor, and a pair of large knees in a black taffeta skirt. There was no way to get up the stairs without going past that open door.

"I don't understand her prudery about her guests having visitors," he whispered. "It doesn't look like that part of town."

"Her morality is sheerly economic. It's a way of renting more rooms. Wait now while I think what to do."

She gazed speculatively at Fred, his torn clothes, and the bruise on his cheek.

"Come on."

Fred, still limping, allowed himself to be led down the sidewalk and across the curb into the street. They were directly in front of the rooming house. The gang of idlers watched with interest.

"Lie down."

"What?"

"Just do as I tell you. Lie down on your back in the street."

He lay down on the filthy pavement. His joints were getting stiffer, and he had to lower himself gingerly, limb by limb.

"No, wait. Sit up again."

He sat up. She pulled off the torn whipcord jacket and threw it a few feet away on the pavement. Then she ripped open his shirt, making the buttons fly away like bullets in the darkness. The bruises on his ribs were clearly visible in the glow from the gas lamp a few yards down the street. The idlers on the front stoop watched in a lackluster way, without changing their position on the steps.

"Now don't move. Shut your eyes. Fling out your arm in a death-like way."

Each muscle in Fred ached more than the other. The uneven paving stones pressed into his back. He heard Ernestine's footsteps withdrawing and mounting the sidewalk. "Evening, boys," she said genially. "Mrs. Morbihan! Help! A man's been run over by a carriage! He's dying! Police! Help!"

Fred opened one eye slightly to see a bull-shaped woman bolting out of the door in her black taffeta dress. "Begorra!" she cried fiercely. He closed his eye again while Mrs. Morbihan inspected him. Then she ran off toward the police post at the corner of Fourth.

Fred heard wheels going by on the pavement in one direction and the other, some only a few feet away. If he lay there much longer a carriage *was* going to run over him. He opened his eyes.

Ernestine had appeared at the second-story window. "Fred! Come on, now. Run! you precious idiot."

Ernestine soon had the clothes off him. The whipcord jacket still lay in the street below. It was torn anyhow and it smelled of gasoline. The others—the corduroy knickers, the boots, the shirt, and the silk under-wear from the City of Paris—she removed with a combination of moth-erly care and undisguised concupiscence. When she was done she threw off her own clothes, sending the persimmon-colored gown sailing so that it caught on the chandelier overhead. They sank together into a large feather bed.

Fred could hardly breathe. He ached in every bone. His knee ban-dages had come off and his raw knees scraped against the sheets. He allowed himself to be swept away into a Wagnerian sort of ecstasy in which pain mingled with the most intense of pleasures. Solicitous was the word for Ernestine. She was nurse, mother, and mistress all at once, the last of these in a nurturing sort of way in which he lay passively in the feather bed while she put this part of him here and that there, exactly as he would have done himself according to his most passionate desire.

"My wounded aeronaut! Fred! My own, my treasure!"

"Careful of my knee."

They rolled over, putting him on top. Up to now, he realized, it had been the other way. This was harder on his knee but it restored his sense of male dignity to a certain degree. Through the partly opened window they could hear voices from the street.

"He wuz here just a minute ago. Here's his coat."

"You sure you ain't bin drinkin', ma'am?"

"Sure and I've bin drinkin'. What's that got to do with it? I'm tellin' yez he wuz here a minute ago."

"Well, he picked up his bed an' walked."

"A Christian Scientist," said the other cop.

"Begorra, I never heard of sich a thing. His frinds must of carried him off. Look, here's a blodestain on the pavement."

"Tell you what, Ma'am, you sleep it off tonight. In the morning, if they's any more dyin' men in the street we'll come an' take 'em away."

"Fred," said Ernestine.

"What?"

"Nothing. Oh. Fred. Oh, oh, oh, oh, oh."

The feather bed went on tremoring for some time. When Ernestine finished, it was Fred's turn. When they came to themselves the voices in the street were no longer audible.

Getting out of bed stark naked, Fred prowled around inspecting his jail cell, as it effectively was. A cautious opening of the door proved that Mrs. Morbihan was back at her post by the stairway. He put on his clothes and assayed the situation more carefully. In addition to the front window there was another on the side, giving onto a tiny alley you could almost reach across with your hand. Leap across onto the roof of the other house? No, it was a good six feet higher and unattainable. Perhaps he could just dash down the stairs and into the street before Mrs. Morbihan had time to get out of her chair. But that wouldn't be fair to Ernestine.

"Ernestine?"

"Mm."

"Ernestine. Wake up a minute."

"Um."

Not much help to be derived there. He went back to the window on the alley and inspected it again. Tentatively he stuck one leg out of it. When he straddled the sill and felt around in the darkness outside his hand encountered a tubular shape running vertically down the wall, probably a drainpipe. It didn't offer much of a grip. He tried his weight on it, cautiously, and found a kind of bracket to dig his fingers into. No help for it. He launched out into the narrow space, dangling from the bracket.

Climbing up a drainpipe is an athletic feat, but sliding down a drainpipe is not as difficult as it might seem. Fred felt with feet and hands, and here and there encountered another bracket or a slightly projecting grip. The drainpipe itself scratched upward along his bruised ribs. Six feet or so from the bottom there was a joint in the pipe. The thing was old and rusted and it was already coming apart. Sure enough, when he got past this joint the thing broke and drainpipe, Fred, and all the rest of it fell the last few feet to the bottom of the alley.

Anxious not to make any noise, he turned like a cat in the air so that he hit the pavement on his back with the drainpipe on top of him. A whole network of pains shot through him, radiating from his back through all of his various bruises and wounds. He lay for a moment panting and trying not to yell. Then he got up, disengaged himself from the drainpipe, and stole cautiously out of the alley into the street.

The light was still on behind the curtains in Mrs. Morbihan's room. Fred straightened out his clothing and brushed the worst of the filth off him, then walked down the sidewalk past the idlers on the stoop, who followed him wordlessly with their eyes.

In a half an hour he was back at the Larkin. The night clerk made no comment on the torn knees of his knickers, the missing shirt buttons, or the fact that he was coatless. He slid the key across the counter, with only a glance at the bruise on Fred's cheek. Fred went upstairs, unlocked the door of his room, and let himself in. Without bothering to light the lamp he took off his clothes, dropped them on the floor, and flung himself into bed with a groan.

He was so sleepy that he could barely keep his eyes open. But in no position could he manage to get comfortable. When he curled up under the covers, knees drawn up and the pillow over his head, his bruised ribs tweaked at every breath. He tried the other side: no better. Flailing and tossing under the bedclothes, he arranged himself half on his side and half face down, with his weight supported by one knee and his chest. This was even worse. The slightest movement made little pains shoot from his bent knee and from his ribs, whether he lay on his left side or sprang around to the right. By this time the bedclothes were a wreck anyhow. He flung them off and got up.

In the bathroom he groped around for the small night-lamp and lighted it. Then, taking a breath, he stood with his feet together, quite motionless, and stared at himself in the mirror. It took about ten minutes, a little longer than usual. This was because he was tired. Still, Fred had found a good reverie to pull off the trick now. He imagined that he was going swimming naked and that a fish was about to bite him between the legs. This thought in itself produced a kind of retractive reflex that pulled the thing up a little. He imagined himself, through an act of will, pulling *all* his limbs into himself—arms and legs, too—and converting himself into a kind of fish. But if this really happened, he thought, he wouldn't be able to stand in front of the mirror to convert himself back again. He was definitely in a strange mood. Such thoughts had never occurred to him before. *Back inside, you little worm,* he willed forcefully. *I'm done with you for a while.*

As another device, he imagined himself sucking soda from a straw, but not with his mouth, instead with *that* part of his body. In, in. Finally the thing rose, contracted, and disappeared with its usual sucking plop.

Herma sighed. It was an ugly sound. She blew out the lamp, then she went into her own bedroom, opened the dresser drawer in the darkness, and took out her nightgown. A faint starlight seeped into the room around the edges of the window curtain. She pulled the gown over her head and drew it down, shaking out the creases from the silk. Then she turned back the bedclothes neatly and crept in, drawing up her knees with another little sigh.

She was lying on her left side. Something throbbed just at the point where her ribs ended. She rolled around gently, stretched out her legs, and tried lying on her stomach. This resulted in two sharp pains from her kneecaps. She drew the knees up again and tried the right side. This was a little better. But when she had almost fallen asleep she forgot and stretched out her legs again. The two sharp telegraph messages from her knees awoke her instantly.

She flung the covers back and got out of bed. In the bathroom she lighted the lamp again. She took off the gown and hung it on a porcelain hook on the wall. Then she stood before the mirror and looked at herself.

The bruise on her right cheekbone was the size of a plum and about the same color. On the left side, the three bottom ribs were outlined with delicate streaks of purple. The knees were really pretty. They were scraped like those of a small boy who has run too fast and fallen down on the pavement. There were reddish-purple circles on them, dotted with little spots of congealed blood, now almost black. Herma seethed. She controlled herself only with difficulty. She had an impulse to stand there before the mirror, gritting and willing until she pushed the obscene thing out again. It would serve him right to let *him* sleep with all these wounds. But he was such a rotten sleeper.

Instead, she opened the small drawer under the washbasin, took out a round pink tin of face powder, and opened it. Holding the powder puff in her fingers, she dabbed it at the plum on her cheek. Then, carefully and skillfully, she blended around the edges, added a little more powder in the center, inspected her work, and gave a final delicate touch with the powder puff at one edge.

Solemnly and without expression, she stared at the image in the mirror. The bruise was hardly visible. If you knew it was there you could see it. If you didn't, you might take it for a slight and barely perceptible color in the cheek, a touch of rouge.

She slipped the gown over her head again, with care not to smudge the powder on her cheek. Then she went into her room, lit the lamp, and rummaged around until she found a scrap of paper and a stub of a pencil. Setting her teeth, she wrote on it, "If I could get my hands on you I'd scratch you like a mandolin." She stuck this into the mirror. Then she blew out both lamps and got back into bed.

But she was still seething. Thoughts raced through her head. From the street below came the sound of carriage wheels, footsteps, the murmur of voices, a distant police whistle, the vast breathing of a busy and vital city that never slept.

She got out of bed again and lit the lamp in the bathroom. Taking the scrap of paper from the mirror, she scrawled at the bottom of it, "The Met is in town. Get out and hustle." Then she got back into bed and fell asleep instantly.

12.

Fred stood before the grandiose façade with its Greek columns rising up three stories to end in massive Corinthian capitals. In the center of the building, between a pair of caryatids bearing lamps, was a marble stairway leading to the two broad doors of gold-plated iron and glass cut with decorations depicting the nine Muses. To one side of the entrance was the ticket office. On the other side was a glass frame with a large poster in it.

C O M I N G
To the Grand Opera House
April 16, 17, and 19
The Great
E N R I C O   C A R U S O
of the Metropolitan Opera Company
in
L A   T R A V I A T A
By Giuseppe Verdi
with
A L B E R T I N A   M O E L L E N D O R F
And Company and Chorus

Fred studied this reflectively for a while. He chewed his lip. He took a leisurely turn up the sidewalk and then came back and looked at the poster again. He scratched his head, pushing his derby up in back and then carefully readjusting it. Finally, taking resolve, he went down Mission to the corner, up the side street, and around to the rear of the building on Jessie Street. As he expected, there was the usual door marked "Employees Only" and the usual watchman propped in the doorway on a rickety wooden chair.

Fred went up to him briskly with his thumbs in his vest.

"Vorrei parlare col Signor Caruso."

"Whatcha say?"

"Scusi, non parlo l'inglese. Sono un grand amico del Signor Caruso. Un amico d'Italia. Sono appena arrivato di Napoli."

Another man appeared in the doorway behind the watchman, younger and smoking a pipe. "What's this?"

"Some Dago. Wants to talk to Caruso."

"They're rehearsin' now, Mister. Capeesh? Busy. Can't see."

"Ma sono un grand amico. Enrico mi vederà, me ne sono certo."

"Amico, eh?"

"He looks like a Dago all right," opined the watchman.

"Scusi, signori. Vi prego . . ."

"Go on in," said the younger man, taking the pipe out of his mouth and waving with it. "They're rehearsin'. Don't bother 'em. They'll take a break after a minute."

When Fred didn't seem to understand, he made an encouraging motion with his pipe toward the door. Fred, smiling profusely and throwing off grazies behind him, went off down the corridor. It led to a stairway and, mounting this and opening a door with QUIET painted on it, he came out into the wings of the theater.

The stage was almost dark except for a pair of small Edison bulbs hanging on long wires from the flies overhead. A pianist was invisible in the shadows. In the circle of light under the Edison bulbs a half-dozen people were sitting around on stools. Two others were standing: a middle-aged man with a mane of gray hair, and a youngish, rather pudgy man in a black suit, an immaculate white shirt, and polished black shoes. This last person paced back and forth restlessly.

"It seems," he said in a strong accent, "that our Albertina is not in possession of her low notes today."

"Rico, don't be nasty. If the accompanist could do it a little higher . . ."

"Try it in B," the gray-haired man suggested.

With one hand the pianist shifted up in sixth-chords from G to B. He played a chord or two and La Moellendorf tried it again.

> "Flora, amici, la notte che resta
> d'altre gioie qui fate brillar."

She broke off. "Oh, stop, stop. What an inferior pianist you are. You can't even transpose, and you're trying to play my accompaniment."

The pianist waited.

"Would you like to try it in C, carissima?" suggested Caruso after a pause.

"No, B is all right," she sighed.

She set off into it again, only a little husky on the bottom notes this time. Flora, friends. Make the night bright with more joys.

> ". . . qui fate brillar."

"Molto bene, but when we come to our duet, what then?" inquired Caruso, still pacing back and forth but in a composed way, as though he were breaking in a new pair of shoes. "Then I will have to sing two notes higher, and what about my high B?"

"You do the duet in G and I'll do it in B," suggested La Moellendorf.

"Ah bello. That will sound like a fine dog fight. And our friend the pianist will need three hands."

"I can do it with my teeth," grated a voice from the darkness.

"Rico," suggested the gray-haired man, "everyone is out of sorts. Why don't we take five minutes for a cup of coffee. Then perhaps Albertina might like to try the second act instead."

"Magnifico! We are only five lines into this great opera by Giuseppe Verdi which goes on for three acts, and we stop to drink coffee."

"These things always start slowly, Rico."

They broke up, La Moellendorf heading for her dressing room and the others gathering around a small buffet where a Chinese waiter was pouring coffee from a silver urn.

Fred saw his moment. He sauntered forward out of the wings, came up to the buffet, said "May I?" in a polite tone, and held out a cup to the waiter.

Caruso stared at him, said "Buongiorno," and turned back to the gray-haired man.

Fred touched his elbow. "Excuse me," he said even more politely.

"Well, what is it?"

"I have an important matter to communicate to you."

"Bene. Go ahead. Ma presto. We have only got five minutes."

"It's extremely confidential."

"Who are you anyhow?" inquired Caruso.

Nevertheless, he allowed himself to be led away by the elbow over into the shadows of the wings.

"I understand the company is short of sopranos," said Fred in a low voice. "I happen to know," he went on rapidly before Caruso could contradict him on this point, "of a first-rate soprano who happens to be available through a chance set of circumstances. She—"

"Who?"

"Herma."

"Never heard of her."

"She would make a magnificent Violetta."

Caruso seemed not at all offended by this aggressive attack. He gazed at Fred curiously. He seemed interested not only in his well-cut clothes, his handsome face and long glossy hair, but in his suave and confident, not to say cocksure manner.

"But you see, my dear young friend," he explained with elaborate politeness, "we already have got La Moellendorf. So we have no need of another Violetta."

Fred: "Perhaps she needs an understudy."

Caruso: "Moellendorf never gets sick."

Fred: "She doesn't seem very well suited to the part. She isn't exactly a young girl anymore."

Caruso: "Ah, but neither is Violetta."

Fred: "Still, Alfredo is passionately in love with her. With Madame Moellendorf, one can hardly imagine . . ."

Caruso: "You seem very confident. Are you a singer yourself?"

Fred: "The furthest thing from it. Still, as a connoisseur of voices, I'm aware . . ."

Caruso: "You're very young to be a connoisseur."

Fred: "Madame Moellendorf is very old to be a demimondaine."

Caruso (smiling): "Where has this girl come from, this slip of a child you want me to listen to?"

Fred (deciding not to say from Santa Ana) : "From La Modjeska."

Caruso : "Ah, vero?"

Fred : "Sì. La celebrata diva polonese l'ha acclamato in una rappresentazione delle *Nozze di Figaro*, qui da noi in California."

Caruso : "You speak Italian well enough at least."

Fred : "E poi dopo a San Francisco, al Larkin Theater . . ."

Caruso : "Ah, that one. I've heard she tinkles along attractively enough. Kees Mee A-gayn, nevvero?"

Fred reached into his waistcoat for a card. Caruso took it and examined it politely.

> H E R M A
> S O P R A N O
> *Fred Hite, Manager*

"We're staying at the Larkin," said Fred.

"She sings lyric, or dramatic, or what?"

"She sings everything."

"Ah, I see. Another one of these acrobats of the larynx. You say she knows Violetta?"

"No, but she's a quick study."

"Oh dio," said Caruso. "Well, have her come around this afternoon and sing a little something. Perhaps I can find her a place in the chorus."

"To the theater?"

"No, to my room at the Palace." He scribbled a note on his own card and handed it to Fred.

"Ladies and gentlemen, for God's sake," said the gray-haired man, "let's get going. Shall we try the second act?"

13.

Herma dressed with the score of *Traviata* spread out on the washbasin before her. "Flora, amici," she hummed. "Dum de dum dum. D'altre gioie qui fate brillar." She put on her white dress with the strawberry-colored ribbon in the hem, and tied another ribbon of the same color in her hair. She applied a dab of the magnolia cologne to her elbows and throat. As a last touch, she took the powder puff and tapped it lightly around the bruise on her cheek, inspecting it in the mirror afterward to be sure that nothing showed. Then she collected her white parasol and went out, leaving the score of the opera lying open in the bathroom.

Having thrown herself on the mercy of Speidermann for another ten dollars, she was able to take a cab to the Palace. There she alighted, with great elegance and grace, assisted by an aloof doorman. At the desk she showed the card, and in only a moment she was being escorted to the elevator by a bellboy in a red uniform and a pillbox hat.

The bellboy knocked on the door of the suite on the sixth floor. From inside a voice intoned "Entrare" on a single clear tenor note—E above C. The bellboy tried the door. It was locked.

Presently the door was opened by Caruso himself, in a wine-colored dressing gown with his white shirt and tie underneath. He had changed his polished black shoes for a pair of Turkish slippers. "Ah, scusi. I keep my door locked because of obnoxious persons who might come here wishing to be in my opera."

Herma was not sure how to take this. She went in. Caruso closed the door and inspected her.

"So you are the new diva who is to astonish the Western world?"

"I don't know about that. I'm a soprano."

"So says your energetic manager Mr. Hite. We will see. Come over here, Mademoiselle—Herma, is it?"

The suite was immense. It seemed to occupy an entire wing of the sixth floor. In the parlor there was a view out over the Embarcadero, the Bay, and the Oakland Hills beyond. The furniture was mahogany upholstered in emerald plush. By the window overlooking the Bay was a Bechstein grand with a score spread out on it. Caruso sat down on the stool. He gave her an appraising look, without any particular expression. "You don't have very much chest for a soprano. What can you sing?"

"Puccini. Verdi. Anything."

"Try this."

Setting his stubby manicured fingers into the piano, he played a few chords of "Un bel di vedremo." She sang this effortlessly, and also "Mi chiamano Mimì."

He turned on the piano stool and folded his hands in his lap, looking at her with a little more interest.

"*Bene.* I see you have studied with Melba."

"No. Everyone says that, but I haven't."

"H'mm. Perhaps your old nurse was an Australian. Try this."

He turned the score on the piano to the first act. He played a G chord, then a C, and resolved to the tonic. Then, in mezza voce, almost as though he were talking, he sang the couplet of the chorus part for a cue.

"Giuocammo da Flora,
e giuocando quell'ore volar."

Herma replied, also in a light tone but in a voice that was almost full.

"Flora, amici, la notte che resta
d'altre gioie qui fate brillar."

He singing the chorus and she the soprano part, they continued on down to "La vita s'addoppia al gioir." Then he took his hands off the keys again.

"I thought your manager said you didn't know Violetta."

"I'm a quick study."

"Well. You have a nice little coloratura. But the question is whether it can fill a real theater. Now we will do the Drinking Song. And you see whether you can make tremble that flower in his vase."

With his head he indicated a single long-stemmed rose in a crystal vial on the piano.

"Are you sure we won't disturb anybody?"

"If we disturb anybody, bah, I am Caruso."

He played the cue chords. "Libiamo, libiamo ne' lieti calici," he sang, still in his conversational half-voice.

When he finished the chorus Herma joined in. This time she sang full voice. Caruso, playing the accompaniment, gazed at her narrowly, as if curious to see how all that sound could come out of such a slim and boyish chest. "E un fior che nasce e muore," she threatened the flower on the piano. When she came to the high G of "FER-vido" at the end of the song, in fact, the water in the slim bud vase trembled a little.

Caruso substituted piano for the four lines of the chorus. She sang her single line:

"La vìta è nel tripudio."

And he answered, with a little smile,

"Quando non s'ama ancora."

He closed the score and turned toward her on the piano stool, folding his hands in his lap again. After a moment he said, "So you are now singing in some trifle at the Larkin?"

Herma, with a parody of a stagy music-hall smile, sang through her teeth, "Kiss-s-s me a-gayn . . ."

"Yes, I know. You mustn't sing too much of that cheap spaghetti or it will ruin your timbre. Allora. It has been pleasant making your acquaintance, Mademoiselle."

On some impulse she said, "What charming slippers you're wearing."

He glanced down at the Turkish slippers. "Ah, you like them? They were made for me expressly in Constantinople. I am very fond of shoes. Come, I will show you my collection."

He led her through a white and gold doorway into the bedroom. There was an enormous bed with a satin cover and three pillows. Masses of American Beauty roses stood about in vases on various tables. The dressing room adjoining was almost as large as Herma's room at the Larkin. Caruso took an atomizer of Caron perfume from the dressing table and sprayed it into the air; a mechanical gesture. Perhaps he did it every time he came into the dressing room. He set the atomizer down and opened a trunk sitting vertically on its end. In each side were velvet boxes, four to a row and ten rows high, and in each box was a pair of shoes: eighty pairs in all.

"Why do you have so many?"

"Two reasons. First, I like them. Second, the public likes for me to have so many shoes." It was probably only because he had small feet, Herma thought; a harmless vanity. He showed her another trunk with fifty suits in it, and a third reserved for the various gifts and mementos sent him by the public: gold pens and pencils, a pair of binoculars with his initials on them, Havana cigars, canes and umbrellas, solid silver shoe-horns, matching hairbrush sets inlaid in silver and gold. On the table was an autographed photo of President Roosevelt in a silver frame. There were several bottles of expensive wine on the table. An unopened case of Krug Sec champagne sat on the floor.

"I drink very little wine. Before leaving San Francisco, I will give it to the bellboy."

The dressing table was cluttered with bottles of mineral water and various medicines. Following her glance, he explained, "To keep the bowels open, every night I take half a bottle of Henri's powdered magnesia in water. Also, I brush the teeth."

He held up a can of tooth powder.

"Samson was strong because of his hair. My strength is in my teeth. When one tooth goes, I will go too and Caruso will be finished." He made a mock smile to show her the teeth. They were perfect.

He put the tooth powder down and almost, but not quite, set his hand in the middle of her back to guide her out of the dressing room.

"Very well. I will see to it that you have a part in the chorus. Go and see Mr. Beckworth, the manager." He scribbled a note on a card and gave it to her. "Listen and observe everything, and perhaps one day you can become an understudy. Although Moellendorf," he was quick to add, "never gets sick."

The card smelled of Caron perfume, as did his whole person, but in a faint and attractive way.

"That's all there is to it?"

"I beg your pardon?"

"I can go now?"

He followed her glance to the bed with its gold satin cover. "What did you expect, my dear?" A little smile. "In my villa of Bellosguardo near Florence, I have a woman who is the mother of my two sons, and to whom I am perfectly faithful. We have been discussing art. I have devoted my life to my art, to my music, and you should do the same. You have a pleasant little coloratura voice. You must work hard to develop body and resonance. To sing the great parts, more power is required."

"I've already sung Violetta for you."

"Ah, but only the first act. The first act is coloratura, the second act lyric, and the third act soprano spinto, all without losing the congruity of the vocal line. You have not sung the other two acts. The duet with Germont in the second act—that is something else."

"Perhaps I will sing it sometime."

"Perhaps. But you must gain body and resonance." Briskly and impersonally, but still with great courtesy, he showed her to the door and held it open for her.

She smiled. "Arrivederci."

"Arrivederla," he replied, a slightly politer form.

14.

At the Larkin Herma demanded a piece of paper from the desk clerk and scrawled on it recklessly: "Dear Mr. Speidermann. I am resigning from the repertory and will not be singing Fifi anymore, since I now have a role with the Metropolitan. Perhaps you can get Mr. Khatchanigherian to sing the part. He has such a sweet voice. Herma."

But up in her room she was less confident. Role was saying too much. She was to be allowed to trill "Giuocammo da Flora" along with the rest of the chorus, that was all, for twenty dollars a week or so.

She was restless and didn't know what to do with herself. After pacing around the room aimlessly for a while, and looking out the window, she decided to change. Changing your clothes was always good if you wanted to change into a new mood, or have a new thought. Off came the white dress with the strawberry ribbon. She replaced it with a simple gray satin gown that fell to her ankles, beltless and without ornament except for a touch of lace at the throat. Standing in front of the mirror brushing her hair, she was still aware of a trace of her own magnolia scent, and of Caruso's Caron, this last no doubt from the card in the handbag in front of her. She hummed into the mirror: "La vita è nel tripudio . . ." She tried it in English. "There's naught in life but pleasure, when one does not yet love." No one ever talked like that. Opera, she reflected, was extremely artificial and had nothing much to do with life. And yet Caruso said . . .

She put on a gray hat with lace around it, tilted it slightly forward and to one side, and examined the angle in the mirror. A little more to the front. Then, still on impulse, she went out, sliding her key across the desk toward the clerk with a little smile. He stared after her phlegmatically.

Walking along the broad expanse of Market toward the Embarcadero, she felt exuberant and alive, and yet pervaded with a kind of bittersweet and unresolved longing. It was an odd sensation—not really unpleasant. Perhaps, she thought, she was in love. But with someone unknown and elusive—not with anyone she had yet encountered in the visible world around her, as various and fascinating as it was. It wasn't Earl in Santa Ana. Or Caruso. (Here a little smile at the thought of the atomizer of Caron, and the satin bed.) It wasn't even Mr. Ming. Dear Mr. Ming—she was very fond of him. Perhaps she would meet someone sometime—the real Other—and she would recognize him instantly. As Violetta had recognized Alfredo, from the moment she laid eyes on him. But for her this Other was still concealed—he was still only a shadow in the other elusive shadows of the phenomenal world. And was it really true that for each person there was only one Other? So the songs said. And so it was for Violetta, who gave herself only to mindless debauchery and feasting, until at last she found Alfredo and left her trivial life of pleasure behind her. Of course it ended badly for Violetta—Alfredo was her ecstasy but he was also her sorrow and death. It was too late—she had sinned and was sick, and could only sacrifice herself for the happiness of another. Still, this was only a story—opera was not life. *I have given myself to art,* said Caruso, *and you should do the same.* But for her this wasn't really enough, she reflected. She was resolved to give herself to Life—a life in which art played an immense part, but only a part. And all the rest of it lay around her—keen and glittering, copious in its variety and richness, its infinite possibilities of experience—dark and light, good and evil, pleasure and pain, sensuality, friendship, the joy of possession, the world of the spirit, the life of the mind. And it was all hers, she had only to choose.

She caught a glimpse of herself in the window of a store. In the gray dress with its lace she looked like a Parisian midinette—a pretty shop girl. "O soave fanciulla . . ." But Mimì too died of her love, and her lungs. This thought gave her a little chill. She forgot the shop window, strode off along Market another block, and turned left on Dupont Street.

In the narrow lane on the hillside overlooking the Bay she knocked on the door of the shop. For a long time no one answered. There was a bell, too; she found the string and pulled it, and there was a small bronze tinkle from within. She waited for some time, but without impatience. It was a fine day and there was a scent of pine from a tree overhead in the street, warm in the sunshine. Finally, through the glass, she saw Tea-boy appear at the rear of the shop. He came instantly to open the door for her.

"Is Mr. Ming in, please?"

"Massy, no. Go temple."

"I'll wait."

"Tea-boy go temple. Tell."

"If you think it won't disturb his devotions."

"Massy velly love Missy."

Herma smiled at this. After Tea-boy had disappeared she spent a few moments looking at the merchandise in the shop, then went on into the gallery with its porcelains and its low silken couch. She wandered about, looking at the porcelains, some in glass cabinets and some on pedestals. It occurred to her that she had never touched any of the porcelains, even though Mr. Ming had permitted himself to touch them and had commented on their texture and feeling to the fingers.

She knew where the key was, under a red lacquer tray on the shelf behind her. Taking it, she unlocked the cabinet and removed the white

Ch'ing-pai vase with the fragile birds and flowers under the glaze. She inserted two fingers into it and held it to the light to test its translucence, then took the fingers out and ran them over the surface of the vase. It was true that it had the slightly slippery feeling of uncooked macaroni. But she preferred Mr. Ming's poetic opinion that it was like the skin of a young girl. Of course, the one ought to be soft and the other hard. And yet, when she touched her own cheek and then the vase, the softness of the one and the hardness of the other were not apparent as a difference. It was important, she decided, to touch porcelain very lightly.

Hearing the rustle of a garment behind her, she turned and found Mr. Ming watching her from the doorway of the room.

"Perhaps I've done something I shouldn't. Do you mind if I touch the vase?"

He smiled in his reserved and controlled way. "If you like it, I will make you a gift of it. If you will allow me a little time to have it packed safely, it will be delivered to your hotel."

"But it's very valuable."

"Very."

She put the vase away in the cabinet. "Sometimes I don't know whether you're serious."

"I am always serious, my dear child, and always amused. If we are helpless in the hands of life, we can at least pretend it is a joke. Please make yourself more comfortable."

He gestured toward the silken couch. Herma sat down on it, and Tea-boy appeared almost instantly with tea and tiny fragrant cakes. For some reason Mr. Ming remained standing.

"I am very honored," he said, sipping his tea, and examining her as though he was not yet quite sure why she had come.

"No, the pleasure is all mine. Just to look at your beautiful things . . ."

"And it is for this that you have come?"

"That, and something else."

"And what is the something else?"

"I'll tell you, if you'll sit down and not go on standing there in that exaggeratedly respectful manner."

She laid her hand on the couch beside her. Setting his teacup on the table, he sat down, not where she had indicated with her hand but a foot or more from her, very correctly, with his back rigidly upright. She grasped that, with his infinite courtesy, he did not wish to presume on anything that had happened on the occasion of their previous meeting.

"You told me once," she began, "that you had certain influences in the world. I believe that's the way you put it. It was apropos of your proposal of marriage to me," she added, coloring lightly.

"That is true. But they are influences of a rather obscure sort. In general, they are not influences that can be made to operate in . . . your world. Yet, as a wealthy man and a member of an important Tong, I am in contact with"—he seemed to hesitate—"certain powers of a secret sort, whose services are available to me.''

''You mean your friends are magicians?''

''Not exactly. Something akin to it, perhaps.'' He gazed at her speculatively. ''Am I right that you wish to avail yourself of my influence in some way connected with your career?''

It seemed all very crass. But she said, ''Yes.''

''Then please explain, and I will do the utmost. I cannot promise the impossible.''

''The Metropolitan Opera Company,'' said Herma, ''which is on a tour of the West, is about to present *La Traviata* at the Grand Opera House.''

''Ah. *Traviata.* A touching story.''

''So you go to the opera?''

''No, I have never been to the opera. It's not the custom for us,'' he explained with a restrained sarcasm. ''But there are books in which one can read about such things. The *Traviata* of Verdi is adapted from *La Dame au camélias,* a novel by Dumas fils.''

He got up quickly from the couch, disappeared into the library, and came back with a book. ''This is a first edition, signed by the author and bound in genuine morocco.'' He opened it to the title page, which was spotted and yellowed with age, and passed it to her. ''There are novels on similar themes in Chinese. The figure of the noble courtesan is a familiar one in classic literature.''

Herma closed the book and set it down impatiently. She didn't care two figs for Dumas fils. ''The point is that, in this production, the part of Violetta is being sung by an antiquity called Albertina Moellendorf. The public must be protected from this incompetent person. She can't sing the low notes in the 'Flora, amici' and has to have it transposed a third higher. She is a dreadful old nuisance and everyone in the company is trying to think how to get rid of her.''

Carried away by jealousy, her occupational disease, she became quite heated. Mr. Ming evidently saw the point.

''H'mm,'' he murmured. He touched his mustache thoughtfully. ''And I gather that you . . .''

''It so happens that I can sing the part, by coincidence.''

''Well, my dear child.'' Mr. Ming seemed very dubious.

Herma added, ''She is staying at the Palace Hotel.''

Mr. Ming was silent for a moment. Then he said, ''And takes all her meals there?''

''Presumably.''

Another thoughtful silence.

''Well, let us think what to do,'' he said after a while. He hesitated for some time, seeming to choose his words with care. ''There is a member of our Tong who is by profession an herbalist and homeopathic pharmacist. And, by coincidence, he has a nephew who is a culinary worker at this same Palace Hotel. But it is not really a coincidence, because everyone in Chinatown has a relative who works in the Palace Hotel. Among the Chinese it is known as the Nine-Storied House.''

"An herbalist?"

"A very skillful man. One might almost say a necromancer in his knowledge of the countless strange, rare, and powerful substances to be found in the vegetable world."

"But I don't want to poison the lady."

"My dear child, who is speaking of poison? The tea you are drinking is an herb. It produces certain changes in the human body, in this case a feeling of energy and alertness. There are many other such herbs and potions, each with its different effect. It is in this, and a thousand other such things, that my friend is skilled."

They had finished their tea. Herma glanced at the companion on the couch beside her, with a speculative little smile. The tea had produced in her, just as he said, a feeling of energy and alertness.

"Mr. Ming."

He waited for her to go on.

"What will you do with the rest of your afternoon?"

"Why, I don't know," he said as though alarmed. He touched his mustache. "Read a book perhaps."

"Suppose I stay for a little while," suggested Herma, "and we could read another chapter from the *Book of the Bridegroom.*"

Herma lay in the large wicker bed, content and thoughtful. Mr. Ming had fallen asleep afterward, as he seemed to do on such occasions. He breathed evenly, turned on his side away from her, and she looked upward onto the ceiling of the little wicker room which was covered, she now noticed, with an elaborately embroidered tapestry depicting a pastoral scene. The strangeness of the situation impressed her. How was it that she—once a little girl hunkered down with her rear in the air, looking at two beetles coupling in the grass in Santa Ana—had arrived at this enjoyable but very odd juxtaposition? It would not seem plausible, even in a story, for Herma, the little girl so carefully nurtured by Papa and Mama, to be lying in a Chinese gentleman's bed in a house off Dupont Street, watched by a Ch'ing-pai vase in a shrine. And further —she pondered while the recollection of her pleasure still trickled warmly through her limbs and clung in a little honeyed place in the center of her body—was it wrong to do this with someone you didn't love? Violetta did, until she met Alfredo. It seemed to do her no harm, and it gave pleasure to a great many people, as well as to herself. It was only when she encountered her great love in Alfredo that she began coughing and then died. If this were so, then perhaps love was really a sickness, as a Viennese doctor contended in a book she had heard about.

Herma, gazing at the oriental shepherds and shepherdesses dallying on the tapestry over her head, concluded that, while perhaps for her as for everyone else there was a single fated love waiting in the wings, she felt no need for it at the moment. For love, of the fated or Liebestod sort, was something that carried you away, something over which you were helpless. And she didn't care to be swept away or made helpless.

As matters went now, it was *she* who chose and she who gave—even though this wasn't the role of well-brought-up young ladies as her age understood. It was possible that she was headstrong, and even that that was wicked. She was ready to accept that. Still, it gave her satisfaction to be the one who chose.

And who could ask for a warmer or more satisfying experience than that of giving pleasure to Mr. Ming? That kind, intelligent, sensitive, learned, unassuming, shy, passionate, and beautiful person, who, incidentally, seemed to have acquired a certain expertise in the matter in question since their last meeting—either he had been reading the chapter on ''The Means for the Coming Together at the Same Instant of the Pleasures of the Bridegroom and the Bride'' or he had been doing some thinking of his own on the matter. She turned to look at him, affectionately, with a little smile. He was still sound asleep.

Herma, with care not to disturb him, opened the wicker door of the bed and slipped out of it. She stole across the room to the Ch'ing-pai vase in its niche. The only light in the room came from a small lamp burning at the foot of this alcove, so that the vase itself, with its alabaster clarity and translucence, seemed to shed its own effulgence into the shadowy air of the chamber. Taking the vase carefully in her two hands, she returned to the bed. Then she lay down again beside Mr. Ming, who remained just as she had left him, lying on his side with his legs slightly apart and an arm over his face.

Gently, gently, with care not to awaken him, she brought the vase into juxtaposition with Mr. Ming's body. It was as she had thought. The colors of both were the same, except that the Secret Color of the one was mauve, the other celadon. She ran her fingers over the one and the other. Both were silky and cool, slightly unctuous to the touch, hard as jade and yet delicate and fine in substance. It was this, finally, that woke him up.

He turned and gazed at her, his eyes still heavy with sleep. In some way that he could not quite fathom, he found himself in bed with the two most precious objects of his universe, his beloved and his most valuable vase.

''You are a strange child,'' he sighed. ''Sometimes I think I have only dreamed you.''

''If so,'' she said, ''Chinese gentlemen have odd dreams.''

15.

The cab with Fred and Ernestine in it jogged along Mission, turned left on Second Street, and came out into Market with its busy traffic of motorcars, cabs, and wagons piled with goods. The double row of cable cars rattled along in both directions down the center of the pavement.

"It's only for a few days," he explained awkwardly. "You see, by then Herma . . ."

"I don't care to hear about Herma. It's not for Herma that I do it, dear boy, but for you."

She seemed quite cheerful, as always. There was perhaps a certain pallor to her complexion, and she seemed a little thinner. It would be a shame, Fred thought, if her figure were damaged by an inadequate diet.

"It's very kind of you, you know, Ernestine. I never expected such a—generous sacrifice." Although of course he had expected it; that was why he had come to the rooming house to see her—on foot, since he hadn't a coin in his pocket—and delivered his little speech in the parlor under the stern eye of Mrs. Morbihan. He had no choice. They were going to be evicted from the Larkin that afternoon.

"Everything I have is yours, brave Fred. My hero!" This with her usual trace of irony. Crashing the Curtiss pusher really wasn't much of a feat. Perhaps she was referring to his sliding down the drainpipe; or sliding halfway down and then falling the rest of the way with the drainpipe in his arms.

"Where is this—place you know about?"

"Oh, I know it well. It's on Jackson, just off Montgomery."

He gave the order to the cabman. The cab went up the hill through the financial district, past the great banks and the busy and animated Montgomery Block. A few blocks farther on it drew up on Jackson in front of a dusty-looking shop with the traditional three balls displayed over the door. Fred looked about warily. It was not one of the more elegant parts of the city. It was on the edge of the Barbary Coast with its three solid blocks of dance halls, saloons, and honky-tonk joints, and the usual street loafers were standing around with one foot on the wall behind them, spitting on the sidewalk.

Ernestine got jauntily out. Fred came around the cab and took her arm. "Wait," he told the cabman.

Inside they were confronted by a skeptical-looking Jewish gentleman with his arms spread and both hands flat on the counter. He wore a black vest, a yarmulke, and a pair of gold-rimmed Franklin glasses over which he peered at the world with suspicion. On the finger on the hand spread on the counter was a large and plain gold ring.

Ernestine unpinned the brooch from her dress and set it on the counter without a word.

He turned it over in his hands. Nothing changed in his expression. Taking off the Franklin glasses, he donned a loupe and examined the ruby through it. Then he put his glasses back on and weighed the whole brooch in an old-fashioned brass balance.

He set it back on the counter.

"Two hundred."

"There are the little diamonds around it too," Fred pointed out.

"Grainss of sand."

"But the ruby itself—"

"The ruby hass a flaw."

Fred took the loupe and inspected it himself. There was a tiny pinpoint inside it with spreading rays, as though it were about to crack.

"That's a star. It makes it more valuable."

"Star sapphiress I haff heard of. Not star rubiess."

"Two hundred and twenty at least."

"A hundred and eighty, now that I think of the flaw."

"All right, two hundred."

Unlocking the cash drawer, he set the coins out onto the glass counter one after the other: ten Double Eagles.

Fred looked dubiously at the coins on the counter. Then he turned to Ernestine. "What about the ring?" he asked, with a significant glance at the diamond on her finger.

"Paste," she told him, giving him a brilliant smile.

Well, he had to take her word for it. Rather awkwardly he began picking up the coins one by one, then swept them off the counter into his hand and put them in his pocket, along with the pawn ticket. He started toward the door with Ernestine. Then he turned and came back.

"Some change for the cab, please."

The pawnbroker took back one of the Double Eagles and counted out twenty silver dollars. All this weight of metal made a considerable lump in Fred's pocket, and he distributed some of it to the other side. The pawnbroker watched him disposing of it.

"If I had known you did not haff money for the cab," he said with what was perhaps a touch of dry humor, "I would haff said one eighty absolutely."

"Good day," said Fred.

Back in the cab, he ordered, "To the Larkin."

"Larkin Hotel."

"No, the Larkin Theater."

"Ain't nothin' goin' on there this time o' day."

"You're very knowledgeable about the world of the theater. Just take us to the Larkin. The stage entrance on Turk."

"Well, don't get heated." He snapped the whip and the cab clopped off rapidly down Kearney. "How do you like Frisco?"

"We live here."

"Finest climate in the world. That's Nob Hill over there on your right. The Flood Mansion. The Huntington Mansion."

"Fred dear, where are we going?"

"Don't worry, Ernestine. Everything is all right."

"I'm sure everything is all right, but where are we going?"

"Just for a little outing in the cab. It's a lovely day, isn't it?"

"Union Square," said the cabman without turning his head. "New Saint Francis Hotel. City o' Paris Department Store."

She said, "We're going to the Larkin, which is presided over by that reptile Khatchanigherian. This bodes no good, dear Fred, for either of us. I thought you said you were being evicted from the Larkin."

"What's that over there?" asked Fred, falling in with the game.

"That's the Call Building. Tallest building west of Chicago. Made entirely out of poured concrete. Ain't a brick in it."

"I'll bet it's as solid as the Rock of Gibraltar."

"You'd win your bet, Mister. U.S. Mint on your left."

"What's your horse's name?"

"Dolores. Say, didn't I pick you up a month or so ago down at the Ferry Building?"

"I don't think so."

"You was with a young lady had two great big suitcases with her. Just up from L.A."

"Nope."

"Well, mebbe not. That there's the Larkin, and where'd you say you wanted to go?"

"The stage entrance around on Turk."

"Like I say, there ain't nothin' goin' on there this time o' day."

"This is Miss Lily Langtry. I am Mr. David Belasco. We are going to discuss her contract in my private office."

"Oh *well* then."

He drew up before the grimy doorway on Turk. The fare was eighty-five cents. Fred gave him a silver dollar and told him to keep the change. He watched while Fred handed Ernestine out of the cab.

"See you later, Mr. Belasco."

With a snap of his whip he wheeled around briskly, and the cab clop-clopped its way back toward Market.

"Insolent rascal," breathed Ernestine.

"Harmless," said Fred. "An entertaining fellow, really."

They went in, past the watchman who knew Fred and hardly looked up from his chair propped in the doorway. He led Ernestine through the labyrinth under the stage, up a flight of stairs, and along a dark corridor. Nothing much was stirring. The dimly lit stage was visible at the other end of the corridor. Fred knocked on a door. After a moment, when there was no answer, he opened it and went in.

A slender but muscular man in his fifties was sitting with his feet on the dressing table, reading a tattered French novel. He had a complexion like fine parchment, dark glossy hair, a mustache with twisted points, and a neat Van Dyke. He was dressed entirely in black: tight-fitting trousers, a black shirt, and a black tunic decorated with silver embroidery. On the dressing table in front of him was a bottle and a glass with a half-inch of wine in it.

"Count?"

Without putting down the novel he looked up and nodded.

"I don't believe for a minute that your name is Proxissimo."

"Bergonzi, at your service."

"Or that you're a count."

"What did you wish to see me about?"

"I believe you have need of an assistant."

For the first time the Count seemed to notice Ernestine. The four legs of the chair came down to the floor. He put away the novel.

"Might. Who'd you have in mind?"

"This is Madame Ernestine Lalange, the well-known actress and celebrity of the international theater. She's temporarily between roles."

The Count surveyed Ernestine with professional expertise, with particular attention to the more obvious and salient aspects of her figure.

"She'd have to get into the costume."

"She can get into the costume."

"It pays eighteen a week."

"Mr. Khatchanigherian said twenty."

"That's because he takes two for himself."

"Make it twenty-two then, and Madame Ernestine will still have twenty."

"Who are you anyhow?"

"Her manager."

"Oh, Fred."

"What about your cut?"

"I'm generously waiving my commission in this case, because of my interest in Madame Ernestine's career."

"I'm bowled over," murmured Ernestine.

"The main thing about this job," explained the Count, "is that the lady has to smile. And smile. And smile. No matter what happens."

"Madame Ernestine is very cheerful."

"Try on the costume, honey."

The count crooked his finger negligently toward the wall, where something silver and glittering was hanging on a hook.

Ernestine took down the costume and looked about her in the small dressing room. "Where can I put it on?"

"In the entertainment business," said the Count, "we aren't very fussy about such things."

She looked at Fred uncertainly. He shrugged.

After another long glance at the Count, she began unbuttoning the snaps of her gown and pulled it off over her head. She was revealed in her chemise and drawers, the latter of which were visibly mended in several places. The Count examined his fingernails.

She put on first the narrow and glittering silver trousers—they were so tight she had to take her shoes off and then put them back on again—and then the tunic to match. Finally, there was a small pillbox cap of the sort worn by bellboys at the Palace, in the same silver with glittering sequins. The tunic buttoned in the front and mounted to a high collar fastened with a silver clasp.

Ernestine smiled. She seemed pleased by the costume.

The Count finished the wine in his glass, lifted the bottle, and found it was empty. He turned his attention back to Ernestine.

"Have to let that costume out a little."

"I'd recommend that you get a good tailor and have him fit it exactly."

"That's a good idea. Turn around, honey. Now turn back again. That's fine. Don't try to sit down in those trousers. You'll split them.

They cost me eighty-five dollars. Who else do you handle?'' he asked Fred in an easy and professional way.

''Singers mostly. Mademoiselle Herma, for example. She's with the Met just now, at the Grand Opera House.''

''Is that so?'' He got up from the chair and lifted a large wooden case with a handle. ''I'll show you my act. See if you like it.''

The Count leading, they made their way along the corridor and through the wings to the stage. The Count found a switch somewhere and turned on a couple of Edison bulbs. A large vertical platform, built of heavy planks bolted together, was erected at one side of the stage. Ernestine took her place against this.

''Now,'' said the Count, ''there's something else you have to do besides smile. That is not move. Not even a fraction of an inch.''

''I'll certainly try.''

''Hold your arms just a little bit away from your body. And you have to keep your feet together but spread your—limbs just slightly apart.''

''That's not anatomically possible.''

''It's difficult but not impossible.'' The Count opened his wooden case and took out a pair of knives.

''Now let's see that smile.''

Ernestine succeeded brilliantly at this. The smile illuminated the darkened stage, fixing particularly on the Count himself.

The Count's arm made a precise and swift downward motion. One of the knives left his hand and flashed across through the shadows. It struck the planks with a thunk and stood quivering a half-inch from Ernestine's shoulder.

The second knife came to rest exactly opposite, by the other shoulder. ''A shade too high,'' commented the Count. ''It's the horizontal accuracy that matters, not the vertical. Still, I like to be neat.''

Four more knives flashed through the air, landing with four more thunks: two by Ernestine's knees and the other two by the tips of her fingers. She continued to smile just as brilliantly.

''This is the place,'' said the Count, ''where you keep the arms a little way from your body, and the limbs—like I said.''

He took five knives and set them on the top of the opened box. Two of them he took in his two hands. He raised them to the level of his head, held them motionless for a moment, and then the hands snapped. The two knives penetrated the board exactly between Ernestine's elbows.

''Now hold it exactly like that and don't move, honey. This is the one,'' he told Fred, ''that makes them gasp. Especially the ladies.''

He took up the three remaining knives, held two of them loosely on the palm of his left hand, and grasped the blade of the third in his right.

What happened then took place too quickly for the eye to follow. The Count held his left hand with the two knives in it about six inches from his right. In the right hand he lightly grasped the blade of the third knife. Then there was a kind of a flurry, his hands spun together like those of a boxer, and the three knives departed so quickly that they were all in the air at the same time. They struck the board almost with a single sound: thunk-unk-unk. All three of them were between Ernestine's legs. The first stood quivering between her ankles. The second protruded from her slightly parted knees. And the third—could not have struck any higher.

"Bravo," said Fred.

"That's nothing. I haven't yet come to my piece dee resistance."

The Count rubbed his hands together lightly. He removed an object from the box, but it was not a knife. It resembled a pair of miniature railroad wheels joined by an axle, except that in place of wheels there were knife blades without any handles, four on each end, mounted at exactly right angles. The axle joining the two sets of blades was perhaps six inches long. The whole machine was made of the finest polished steel, and the axle was nickel-plated. It gleamed in the dim light.

The Count held it in the air before him, his hands grasping a blade on each side. He tossed it lightly into the air and caught it by another pair of blades.

"Now at this point, honey, you have to raise your chin a little. But keep smiling."

Smiling even more brilliantly, Ernestine raised her chin a fraction of an inch.

"She's pretty good, I'll say that for her," the Count remarked conversationally to Fred. "One of the best I've had."

He raised the wheel of knives and flung it. It sped through the air with a kind of fluttering whistle. When it came to rest it was imbedded in the board on either side of Ernestine's neck, like a kind of odd necklace, its color matching and enhancing that of the silver costume.

The Count turned modestly to Fred, not for applause precisely, but as if to indicate that the performance was over. He rested one hand lightly on his waist. His black shoes were immaculately polished. As artificial as his costume and his demeanor might have seemed on the street outside, on the stage he was the epitome of elegance. His every movement was graceful. It was impossible for him to move a finger, or shift his feet, without displaying the sensuosity of a dancer. His waist was narrow, his hands long and fine in spite of their obvious strength. He had a manner of standing with his arms at his sides and gliding his thumbs over his forefingers, in a lightly sinister way.

"Let's say twenty-five," said Fred. "You'll see she's worth it when the costume's fitted."

"I can see that already. Still, you drive a shrewd bargain."

"She'll make your fortune."

Fred turned to go. Ernestine, framed by the knives, was unable to move. Her chin was raised, and she was still smiling. But she made no effort to turn her head toward Fred, even if this had been possible. Instead her eyes were fixed on the Count. And her smile was no longer totally professional and contrived. There was something knowing in it, a self-assurance. It was connected in some way with the slight creases that had appeared at the corners of her mouth—a Mona Lisa calm, unmistakably sensuous.

Maybe, thought Fred, I have outwitted myself.

16.

At the desk the clerk, with the stony expression he had been wearing for the last few days, slid his key across the mahogany to him, and also a note—a small envelope of expensive creamy paper with his name on the outside in a flowery foreign hand. Fred stood for a moment staring at these elaborate curlicues. But he suppressed his excitement and showed nothing in the presence of the clerk. He slipped the envelope negligently into his pocket, and he didn't open it until he was upstairs in his room with the door locked. His impulse was to rip it open with his fingers. Controlling himself, he went into Herma's room and found a nail file. With this he cut open the top more or less precisely, with only a slight ragged edge here and there.

There were only a dozen or so words on the glossy cream-colored card inside. He hardly bothered to read them, since some prophecy in his blood had accurately foretold him what they would say. Instead his attention was transfixed, like that of some small animal hypnotized by a serpent, by the rococo and elaborate signature that filled the lower half of the card—the name itself with its grandiloquent capitals, and the double looping line underneath with a knot tying it in the middle, as it were, for a final flourish.

Enrico Caruso

He went into the bathroom, cleared his throat, straightened his necktie, and stared for some time with a frown at the image in the mirror. Who should go? He or she? There were advantages to both. And disadvantages. The attraction of sex—a powerful factor and no doubt about it. But she was such a ninny in some ways—flouncing around in her pretty dresses, making friends with everybody, giving herself to this person and that and asking nothing in return. She lacked cynicism. Now if he were she at the moment, the thought occurred to him—he, that is she, would be thinking just the opposite. Fred was persuasive, he was astute, there was his offhand and cogent skill in driving a bargain—but he was such a boor—he lacked subtlety, and he knew nothing about Art. And besides, a couple of men—if left to settle the fate of

some poor female between them, where money was involved—the case
of Ernestine was enough to make the point.

Fred lifted his shoulders, as if to ask the reflection in the mirror,
what can you do? They were all sentimental, at the bottom. (The quite
accidental indecency of the innuendo pleased him; his mouth twitched
a little.) Ernestine—another ninny. Giving her last cent to a slicker,
and then falling in love with a Dago, while knives whistled between her
knees. Così fan tutte—women were like that. They had vapors up
there, moonbeams, instead of brains. He had better take care of the
business himself.

He went into Herma's room and found a piece of paper—why the
Hell was there never any paper in his room?—and scrawled on it with
the stub of a pencil that always rested by the rim of the washbowl.

> A man named Michael Duveen
> Invented a fucking machine
> Concave or convex
> To fit either sex
> But oh what a bastard to clean.

This he stuck into the mirror. Then he found his hat, put it on,
and went out.

At the Grand Opera House he didn't bother to take the note out of
his pocket. He breezed in past the watchman without speaking to him.
He went up the stairway and along the corridor, past the dressing rooms
and the scene dock, to the office. Here he knocked on the door. Inside, the
familiar tenor voice intoned with slight irony, "Entrare." He opened
the door and went in.

Caruso was sitting on the desk, swinging his legs, and behind him
Beckworth was in the chair smoking a cigar. The world-famous im-
presario, the discoverer of Tetrazzini and the introducer of Caruso to
the American public, might have been taken for a businessman except
for the untamed mane of gray hair that suggested something of the
artist. He dressed impeccably, in a gray suit and a white shirt and a
narrow black necktie. The cigar in his fat and soft fingers was a Corona
Corona.

"Ah," he said. "Our friend the boy manager."

Fred ignored him.

"I got your note," he said to Caruso.

Caruso swung around on the desk, crossed his legs, and lowered his
head in the manner of a bull to examine him. "Good afternoon, Signor
Hite. An odd thing has happened. La Moellendorf is not well. This is a
thing that has never occurred before. She has come down with a raging
sore throat and a fever."

"Ah," said Fred.

"The doctor," Caruso went on, "says it's probably quinsy. Or
perhaps bronchitis. Or not exactly quinsy or bronchitis, but something

that is both at once and at the same time neither. The doctor says," he concluded with a direct stare at Fred, "that possibly it is some kind of Oriental disease."

"That doctor is a bum," said Beckworth, chewing his cigar. "If he were any good he wouldn't be here out West. I'm fed up with this gold-miner town. When I think what I've put up with on this trip—Omaha, Salt Lake City, and now this."

"I hope it isn't serious," said Fred.

"For the Moellendorf, no. For us, yes. We have this infernal *Traviata* in rehearsal, it's due to open on the seventeenth, and here it is already the fifteenth."

"And it seems there are no other sopranos in this godforsaken place who can put one note after the other," added Beckworth.

Caruso said, "We tried a creature from the chorus who claims to know the part—poof."

"Who in the world can we find?" said Fred. "Perhaps I can help."

"Why don't we stop our joking, young man? We don't have time."

Beckworth took the cigar out of his mouth and turned to Fred. "Do you think she can do the part?"

"Of course."

"Rico? You said you auditioned her."

"She has a nice litle coloratura voice. She was in some morsel by Victor Herbert at the Larkin. In a couple of weeks she had everybody singing her song."

"Rico, what are you saying? Violetta isn't a coloratura part."

"The first act is a coloratura part. She can learn as she goes along."

Beckworth groaned.

"I believe," said Fred, "that Signor Caruso has also heard her sing "un bel dì vedremo . . . .' "

"I know, I know. 'Mi chiamano Mimì' and the Drinking Song from *Traviata.*"

"She shook the flower in the vase. She can also sing dramatic."

"Victor Herbert! My God."

"She can come over and audition again if you want."

"We don't have time. How much does she want?"

"She doesn't want anything. I'm her manager."

"All right, all right." said Beckworth impatiently. "How much do *you* want?"

"She's getting three hundred a week at the Larkin. But of course the Met—"

"It's only three performances," Beckworth cut in sharply.

"But as Signor Caruso says, Victor Herbert is only cheap spaghetti. This is a much more important vocal responsibility."

"Oh boy," said Beckworth, putting his cigar back in his mouth.

"You see, Beck my old friend," said Caruso, "you have not yet seen the young lady in question with your eyes. She is quite an attractive person. She will please the audience. Your audience of gold miners," he put in. "The Moellendorf," he concluded tactfully, "is a ship that has called at many ports.''

"Yes, but she can sing, when she doesn't have the Chinese Plague. Are we running a beauty contest or an opera?''

Fred didn't care for the direction the conversation was taking. He decided to end it.

"Let's say six hundred. That's two hundred a performance.''

"Don't make me laugh.''

"I happen to know," said Fred, "that Moellendorf once played in a little hick town in Southern California, and got two thousand for a single performance.''

"I'll bet she filled the house too.''

"She cracked up on the 'Dove sono.' ''

"You see Beck, my old friend, I will be there at all times. I can hiss in her ear what to do. Except of course in the 'Dite alla giovine' where she is alone with Germont. That will be the acidic test.''

"I'll say it will. Three hundred for the three.''

"All right," said Fred recklessly. "We'll go back to the Larkin and sing Victor Herbert.''

"Beck, my dear old friend, don't you understand that we have only got two nights until this thing opens? Dio mio. We have not got any choice. Perhaps you would prefer that squeaker from the chorus?''

"A hundred and fifty a night. That would be four fifty for the three.''

"Six hundred.''

Beckworth sighed. "You're some kid. Have a Corona Corona. Well, I hope this frail of yours can strike a note. If not, we're sunk.''

Caruso got up from the desk and began walking around the office rubbing his hands. He grimaced to show his teeth, a mannerism of his when he was impatient.

"We ought to be rehearsing right now. When can she start?''

"She'll be here instantly. I just have to go back to the hotel to— tell her.''

Beckworth struck a match on the desk, and Fred held out the Corona Corona for him to light.

"You ought to work in New York," said Beckworth. "There's nothing for you to do in this gold-miner town. Who else do you manage?''

"Ernestine Lalange, the well-known actress. She has an engagement now at the Larkin.''

"You seem to have good connections at the Larkin.''

"Mr. Larkin is a friend of mine.''

"I thought he was dead," said Beckworth.

There was no need for walking anywhere anymore. Cabs from now on. Fred took the first one standing in line on Mission Street and drove directly to the Palace. There, telling the cabman to wait, he went up to the registration desk in the arcade facing onto the glass-roofed Grand Court.

The clerk, a middle-aged man in a frock coat and white tie, looked up.

"A suite for Miss Herma, please."

"Who?"

"Miss Herma, the opera star. She's singing the lead in *Traviata* at the Grand Opera. She's staying at the Larkin now, but she wishes to change immediately."

"What sort of accommodations does she require?"

"Two rooms, with separate entrances but connecting bath."

"Two rooms?"

"The other's for me." He slipped a card across the polished surface of the desk.

The clerk glanced at it. He seemed less interested in the domestic arrangements of Fred and Herma than in the quality of the card, which was excellent. He checked through his reservation list. "I can give you five twenty and five twenty-two. They both have bay windows on Annie Street. I don't have anything at the moment that faces on Montgomery or Market."

"That's fine. I suppose the bath has a mirror?"

"A mirror? Of course, sir. Will you sign here, please."

"The bags will be coming over from the Larkin."

"Very good." The clerk was still examining the card. "Thank you, Mr. Hite."

Fred deposited the last of the Corona Corona in the cuspidor by the desk and left. Getting into the waiting cab, he drove to the Larkin. The usual clerk, who now seemed very grubby in comparison to his counterpart at the Palace, was behind the desk working away with a toothpick, apparently searching for a remainder of his lunch which he hoped to find there.

"Key please."

The clerk slid the key across the desk. His expression was still stony. "Look here, you've got to clear out this afternoon. You know what the Sheeny said."

"Please don't trouble yourself in the least about the matter. I'll take care of everything. Boy!"

The bellboy stepped forward.

"Now listen carefully," said Fred. "I'm only going to say this once. In exactly twenty minutes, come up to the rooms and get the bags. They will be packed and standing in the doorway. Bring them downstairs and put them in a cab. Send them to the Palace, and pay the fare in advance. Here's twenty dollars. You can keep the change for yourself."

"Golly," said the boy.

"Movin', eh?" said the clerk, taking the toothpick out of his mouth.

"Please forward any correspondence to the Palace."

The clerk put the toothpick back in.

Slipping the key into his pocket, Fred went upstairs. Once in the room, he first flopped open his old horsehide suitcase on top of the bed, took off all of his clothes, and packed them away in it. Shutting the suitcase and latching it, he set it by the door. He checked the ormolu clock on the mantlepiece. It was exactly eight minutes to two. Then he went into the bathroom.

Time passed. The minutes slipped away one by one. The clock in the next room struck two. Herma took a deep breath. She slipped her fingers into the pectoral muscles on each side and lifted them, to see if they could be formed into any sort of protuberances at all. Then she noticed the piece of paper stuck into the frame of the mirror.

Her face flamed. She tore it off, ripped it up, made a tiny ball of it, threw it to the floor, and stamped it underfoot. Thinking better of it, she picked it up from the floor, tore it into even tinier scraps, and flushed them down the toilet.

She found another piece of paper and snatched up the pencil. "I've had enough of your stupid vulgarity," she wrote in a sprawling and angry hand. "Please don't address such things to me again. If you think of any more smut, tell it to your actress friend."

She stuck the note into the mirror. Then, perceiving the futility of this, she pulled it off, tore it into fragments, and flushed them away in the toilet too.

Even if he had come back to read the note, she realized, she would not have wanted to reveal that she was jealous of Ernestine. She flounced into her own room, banged open the tapestry portmanteau, and began dressing.

17.

Herma lived the next two days at breakneck speed. It seemed that day and night she was always at the opera house rehearsing or in her room at the Palace studying the score. She slipped into a kind of trance: the score on the table in her room where she ate, or in her lap in the cabs she took to the opera house, even though it was a ride of only five minutes; fitting her costume; blocking the scenes. Fred was nowhere to be seen. And after the curtain rang down to thunderous applause, Herma in her dressing room looked at herself in the mirror and scarcely knew where she was or how she had got there.

And the frantic pace didn't stop even then. After the performance she went with Caruso and his friends for supper at Delmonico's. The others of the party included Beckworth, the mezzo who had sung Flora, and Lucien Grasse, a veteran hack who could sing anything and in this case had done a creditable job on the baritone part of Germont. The mezzo, Lucì Bonnina, was a small and taciturn thing from Naples, a friend of Caruso's, without particular talent.

Even though it was after midnight the restaurant was crowded.

With great ceremony, clearing the way through the waiters with motions of his hands as though he were shooing birds, the maitre showed them to the table. The party attracted a good deal of attention. Many of the other diners had come from the performance at the Grand Opera House, and heads turned at the sight of the world-famous tenor. There were murmurs of "Caruso," and a single voice could be heard pronouncing the word "Herma" in a low and explanatory tone. Herma was in an elated mood, still feverish from the role she had sung, but she successfully managed to retain her outward calm. She was wearing a Worth gown she had bought that afternoon at the City of Paris, after the final rehearsal. It was silk moiré, so pale a color that it seemed almost silver, and the skirt was pierced with a hundred eyelets so that the strawberry-colored petticoat could be seen under it. The silver brooch she wore at one side, on her shoulder, had a tiny enameled strawberry set into it, scarlet with emerald leaves.

An intoxicated man in evening dress came over and tried to sell Caruso some real estate. The maitre steered him away by the arm. A glossy bill of fare the size of a newspaper was handed round the table. Grasse ordered for all. He was not part of the Met troupe but had only been hired in San Francisco to fill out the cast. He knew the town thoroughly and was a famous bon vivant and a connoisseur of women, wine, and food. First came champagne and oysters. Grasse raised his glass. Herma held her breath, waiting to hear her name, but instead the toast was to Giuseppe Verdi. Never mind, that would be for another time. She took a long sip of champagne with the others and set her glass down. Although the reception of the audience had been tumultuous, with seven or eight curtain calls, no one in the cast had yet said anything about her performance. Beckworth seemed not to be aware she was present. He talked mostly to Caruso, and smiled, although he didn't laugh, at a joke made by Grasse. For the rest he gazed into the middle distance and seemed thoughtful. Perhaps he was counting the evening's house and multiplying it by the price of the tickets.

Lucì Bonnina was seated directly across the table from Herma, next to Grasse. She was short and dark, shaped something like a chicken, although a plump and appetizing one. She said very little, only gazing around at the others out of her large and expressive Neapolitan eyes. She spoke almost no English. Clearly Grasse had designs on her for the evening. He rubbed his hands and signaled the waiter to pour her more champagne. He was full of energy; he bent over her and chinked his glass against hers. She smiled wanly.

"Veuve Cliquot," he said, rolling the champagne around on his tongue. "First rate."

A team of waiters began carrying in Grasse's idea of a light supper. First came a clear turtle broth with saffron, then Sole Marguery— really a Bay halibut masquerading as its cousin from Dover, but excellently done. With the fish, a light Gewürztraminer. The plates were cleared away, and the waiter brought up an enormous joint of beef on a rolling table and sliced off pink slabs for each plate. The wine with this was a Bordeaux, which Grasse sent back because the first bottle was "légèrement pétillant." The Médoc that replaced it was pronounced excellent.

Caruso didn't touch the fish, and he waved the waiter away when he offered the roast. He asked for a little white meat of chicken, which he cut up and ate neatly while sipping the white wine.

"Are you off your appetite, my friend?" asked Grasse.

"I always eat so. In the morning a cup of black coffee, at noon a little white meat of chicken, in the evening perhaps a cutlet. But when the newspapermen write a story about me in the paper, they always say that I eat a lot of spaghetti. What am I? An Italian, a Wop. So it is natural for the newspapermen to say that I eat a lot of spaghetti."

"I thought all Italians ate a lot of spaghetti," said Herma.

"They do, when they are poor," said Caruso. "When they are rich like me they eat a little white meat of chicken."

"But Signor Caruso. How do you have the strength to sing, when you eat so little?"

"In the first place, Alfredo is a light part. Alfredo does not have very much to sing. Violetta and Germont do all the work. In the second place, my strength is in my teeth, as I have told you." He smiled to show them. "In the third place, do not call me Signor Caruso. You may call me Rico."

"Oh, I couldn't call you that."

"You must call me Rico. I will not have you call me Caruso, because we are fellow artists. We are brother and sister. It is true that you have no importance to critics, while I have a great importance to critics. That does not matter. We are artists. You work to sing, and I work to sing. It is the same."

He reached for the bowl of green salad in the middle of the table, searched around in it, found a piece of raw fennel and set it on his plate, and began cutting it up as he had the chicken.

"In Italian this is called *finocchio*, which means a man who likes the boys," he said. He added after a moment, "That is not me." His meal apparently finished, he screwed an Egyptian cigarette into a holder and held it for a waiter to light.

"I also allow myself ten of these, do you say coffin nails, a day. The doctor says it is bad, but it does not prevent me from singing better than anybody in the world." This he said in all modesty, as though there were no point in concealing a fact that was accepted by everyone.

"Smoke eleven, you might sing even better," suggested Grasse.

"You, my friend, are a delightful old cynic, and any day now you are going to fall into decadence."

"Vive la décadence," said Grasse. He reached for the Médoc, holding the bottle by the bottom so that he was able to fill everyone's glasses around the table. As he filled Beckworth's glass his arm brushed against Lucì's breast, causing her eyes to become even more warm and expressive. Caruso held his hand over his glass, which still had a little white wine in it.

"Would anyone like something else?" suggested Grasse. "A millefeuille? An éclair? A mousse au chocolat? A sherbet? The ice cream at Delmonico's is fabulous. It is something from the *Thousand and One Nights*. I particularly recommend the parfait au rhum."

The waiter came and took the dessert orders: the parfait for Grasse and Lucì, sherbert for Beckworth, a bowl of fresh fruit for Caruso.

"Mademoiselle?"

"I would like a Fraise Herma."

"A Fraise—"

"Herma."

"I am sorry, but I don't believe I have ever heard of that."

The maitre came too and the matter was discussed. "Please have the chef come," said Herma.

Mérimée came out, in his immaculate white jacket and toque, wiping his hands on a towel which he handed to a waiter. He looked around the table. "Bonsoir, messieurs et mesdames," he said.

"Now," said the maitre, "if you will explain to Mérimée exactly what it is that you want, we will not only provide you with it, but we will add it to our bill of fare. At Delmonico's, everything is available that is served in any restaurant in the world."

"It's a scoop of lemon-vanilla ice cream, exactly hemispherical," said Herma, "with a strawberry in the middle, and apricot glaze over it."

"Very good," said Mérimée.

The maitre provided a piece of paper and a pencil. "If you could write it down exactly," he said, "so that we could print it correctly in our bill of fare."

Herma wrote it down.

Mérimée looked at it. "The French is incorrect," he said. "There should be an 's' on Fraise."

"No, there is only one strawberry."

"Only one strawberry? But could there not be two strawberries, or three?"

"Of course there couldn't be two strawberries on it, or three. What a monstrosity."

"What a strange creature," murmured Caruso, lifting his dark eyes questioningly at Beckworth. Beckworth shrugged.

The desserts came. The Fraise Herma was exactly as ordered. Herma ate it with her usual technique, starting on the sides and working to the top, while the others watched her curiously. Caruso peeled an apple, inserting a fork into it and twirling it while an even and unbroken ribbon of peeling fell from the knife.

Grasse's hand was always in the air, and a troupe of waiters was always ready to spring to his command. Now he ordered brandy for everyone. Once again Caruso held his hand over the tiny glass as the waiter bent over it with the bottle.

Grasse raised his glass and looked around the table. His eyes stopped on Herma.

"Perhaps we should drink to our impromptu diva."

"Shall we or shall we not?" said Caruso, seeming to consider. He smiled, first at Herma and then, at the others. "Perhaps we might inquire first whether the unfortunate Moellendorf's affliction—"

"The Chinese Plague," put in Beckworth.

"—was really impromptu. Then after that we come to the artistic question."

Lucì was not following. "Cosa dici?"

"Parliamo," explained Caruso, "della voce della nostra piccola Violetta."

"Ma era magnifica."

"Magnificent?" He considered. "In the first act, perhaps. You see, carina," he told Herma, "I do not give other singers the compliments just to make them feel good. Otherwise how would they know when it is not so good, so they can make it better? If a newspaperman asks me how is the voice of Herma, I tell him magnificent. If you ask me, I tell you truthfully how it is."

"And how is it?" asked Herma, quite serious and staring at him directly.

Beckworth lighted a cigarette and watched, saying nothing.

"The first act was magnificent. You have an excellent coloratura. At the end of the opera, everybody clapped and gridavano come dannati—how do you say—they yelled like damned. But that is just because you are pretty, and sing all the music on the correct note. And then, this is San Francisco. It is not Milano or even New York. When you make them yell like damned at La Scala, that will be something."

"Will you please explain to me," said Herma, "how I can make them yell like damned at La Scala?"

He smiled again, and paused for a moment before he spoke. "First, I think, carina, you must live a lot more of life. You do well enough for the little trills in the drinking song. Libiamo, libiamo. That is nothing. But the lyric part, the tragedy, the sob in the voice, the deepness, the self-sacrifice are not quite right in the duet with Germont. Because you are only a child and have not yet lived."

"I started young."

"We all did. I was singing in the streets of Naples when I was ten. But the second act is about something else. It is not about being young and happy. Violetta is a beautiful person but she is not anymore quite so young. Now she has found her love in Alfredo. Now she is pure, she is innalzata, how do you say, uplifted from her former life, and she goes to live with him in the country. But then comes Alfredo's father, Germont. And he says to Violetta, what are you doing to my son? He is in love with you and thinks of nothing else. Yes, says Violetta, he loves me and I too love him. But, says Germont, pardon me, but you are only a courtesan even though reformed. And my daughter, what of her? What of Alfredo's sister? What of this tender young child? Who will marry her if her brother is sunk in dissipation living with a former courtesan?"

"Adesso cosa dici?" said Lucì.

"Dico," said Caruso, "che bisogna vivere molto per cantare Violetta."

Ah," said Lucì. "È vero." She looked at her empty parfait glass, as though she would like another one.

Caruso looked from Grasse to Herma.

"And then the duet. Violetta renounces. She gives up her Alfredo, with her heart breaking, and she says, "Dite alla giovine.' Tell the young girl, so lovely and pure, that I will sacrifice myself for her, so there will be no disgrace in the family and she can get married. And then I will die. Morrà, morrà. And Germont joins in with her and tells her to cry some more, she is not crying enough. Piangi, piangi. The 'Dite alla giovine,' " he said, "is the greatest duet in all opera. It is on account of the sob in Violetta's voice, but she must sob on a very high note. She mounts up, up, and then she comes to her A flat on *sacrifica.*"

"That's not a very high note."

"It is a high note to sob. Mostly sopranos like to sob on low notes. But this is difficult. This is no more coloratura. It is the highest peak of the lyric. A soprano mounting gradually to a high note and then holding it, especially with the little catch of the pathetic, is the most sexy sound it is possible to make by the human voice. And if it is a duet—twice as much."

"There is no such word as sexy," said Beckworth.

"*Sensuale* is sexy, no?"

"No, *sensuale* is sensual."

"Very well, I am saying *sessuale. Sessuale* is sexy. The A flat of the 'Dite alla giovine'—very sexy."

"But Germont isn't Violetta's lover. He is only her lover's father."

"That's because he's a baritone," said Beckworth. "It's always the tenor that gets the girl. The baritone never gets the girl."

"Ah! in the opera," said Grasse. "But in life," he said roguishly, "it's the other way around." He nudged Lucì with his elbow. She shrugged.

"I don't understand why it is," said Herma, "that all the great love duets are between people who can't—you know"—she colored slightly—"get married. Turridu and his mama. Rigoletto and Gilda."

"Germont and Violetta," agreed Caruso. "That is why they are so sexy. Germont and Violetta do not come together in bed, but they come together in the duet, which is better, because it can be done over and over." Here Herma blushed even more. "Da capo, ma più forte!" he went on. "When Violetta mounts to her sacrifica for the second time— che emozione! And Germont follows her with his own A flat an octave lower, until it is resolved in a beautiful harmony, he on G and she on the E flat above."

He attempted to demonstrate.

"che a lei il sacrifica,
   a che morrà, e morrà, e morrà!"

In the middle he abruptly slipped down an octave, without saying anything—since he was singing—but with a little grimace that said clearly, "Falsetto is bad for the voice." Herma helped him. In mezza voce they sang the couplet together.

"che a lei il sacrifica,   "Il nobile cor vincerà.
    e che morrà, e morrà, e morrà."   Sì, il cor vincerà!"

They stopped. People at the other tables were turning to look at them.

"You have not quite got it yet," said Caruso. "In any case, I am afraid we are disturbing."

"No, no!" said Grasse. "You are Caruso! They wish to hear you sing."

"Not for free," said Beckworth.

Herma was entranced. "I didn't know you could sing baritone."

"I can sing anything. Once when I was singing with Chaliapin his voice happened to fail and I sang the basso part. The Victor company asked me to make a record of it. I said no, because it would not be fair to other bassos."

It was never possible to tell whether he was being entirely serious or not. He went on, "We cannot sing here, because we would disturb these people, and besides my friend Beckworth will not let me sing for nothing, as he has told you. But we must go back to the theater, all three of us, and there I will show you how to sing the 'Dite alla giovine.' "

Grasse looked at Lucì, and then at Caruso.

"Me too?"

"Of course, my friend, since you are the baritone."

"You sing it," growled Grasse.

"No, for a trick I can do it, but too much will hurt my voice."

"I have something else to do tonight."

"I am sure you have, but that can be done at any time, and meanwhile we have two more performances of the opera, so we must rehearse the 'Dite alla giovine' more to be sure we have it exactly right."

The bill for the supper came, and Caruso paid it without looking at it.

"Our friend Beck can take Lucì home," he said.

Grasse sighed. Herma was disappointed too, because they never had decided whether to drink the toast to her.

18.

First it was necessary to go and wake up the accompanist, who was staying not at the Palace but at the less expensive Grand across the street. Caruso went up for him while Herma and Grasse waited in the lobby. It was three o'clock in the morning. The lobby was deserted except for a clerk dozing behind the desk. Presently Caruso came down followed by the sleepy-looking pianist, who was wearing an overcoat over his pyjamas and shoes without socks. Since all four of them couldn't fit into the cab, they walked the two short blocks to the Opera House at Third and Mission.

It was a mild spring night with a light breeze from the sea. Herma wore a light velvet cloak, which she left open. The moon, sliding down to the west over Twin Peaks, was visible through a broken curtain of clouds. They passed a policeman who hardly glanced at them, and a drunken woman who shook her fist at them and attempted to speak, but was unable to articulate even a word. They left her clutching the wall of the building in a paroxysm of frustration. Finally, as they turned the corner, Herma looked around to see her sliding to the sidewalk.

At the Opera they walked around to the rear on Jessie Street. There was no one on duty at the stage entrance. Grasse had a key, and they entered. The building was totally dark. They found their way by feeling with their fingers along the walls. The accompanist seemed to be still half asleep. "Have to turn on some lights," he mumbled.

They came out onto the stage. A few dim rays of moonlight penetrated from the clerestory windows at the top of the building. The curtains were open. Out beyond the edge of the stage there was nothing but a great gulf of shadows. It was the somnambulistic pianist who knew where the switches for the lights were. He disappeared off into the wings and presently a pair of bulbs hanging from overhead glowed into incandescence.

The two bulbs illuminated the stage, after a fashion. Some stools were brought up and Grasse and the accompanist pushed out the piano. The gulf out beyond the stage had now turned into a dim ghost of a theater with its pit and its box circles, the gilt on the boxes glowing faintly in the shadowy light. In the middle was the great chandelier of Murano crystal, as large as a barouche. Now, with its lights out, it was only a kind of dim crystalline ghost hanging high in the air on its single chain, seeming to turn an inch or two, now and then, from some breath of air too slight for human beings to detect.

Caruso himself did no work but walked around rubbing his hands, supervising everything. "The piano here. The two stools there. Where is the score?" No one had thought of the score, but luckily a copy was found on the conductor's stand in the pit. "We'll start from the 'Pura siccome un angelo,' a page or two into Act Two. That is a little before the place we want, but you cannot just jump into an aria from cold. You must work up to it first, like making love, with a few cuddles and kisses. Are you there, my friend?''

''M'mm,'' said the pianist. He turned the pages and found the place. Then, blinking sleepily, he stuck his fingers into the keyboard and played the chords of the A flat continuo. Grasse started off.

"Pura siccome un angelo
Iddio mi diè una figlia.''

He sang the aria competently but without any particular enthusiasm. He had done it a thousand times. Oh, Germont and that precious daughter of his! He was so anxious for her to marry that silly goose of a fiancé. Caruso walked around nervously, still rubbing his hands, as though it were a real performance. The accompanist gave the impression that he was a man in an overcoat and pyjamas sitting at a player piano. The notes came out perfectly and in even tempo, without any variations in loudness. Caruso grimaced, showing his teeth. He sang along with the aria—''Deh, non mutate in triboli, le rose dell'amor''— and then stabbed his finger at Herma for her cue—''Ah, comprendo!''

Germont and Violetta went down through their little recitative— sad ultimatums from Germont, and little plaints of grief from Violetta. She would have to give up Alfredo, that was all. It was not enough for her to go away for a few days. She would have to give him up for good. No, Gran Dio! cried Violetta. She would prefer to die. Yet it must be, Germont told her in his gentle rumble. They came to their little pre-duet, a kind of foreshadowing of the ''Dite alla giovine.'' Thus hope is now mute for an unhappy one, she sang. And he: Be the consoling angel of my family. It was not a true duet but a kind of two-part ensemble: he sang a line or two, then she another couplet, then they would join together melodiously for a few lines before separating again.

''Stop,'' said Caruso. ''Basta, basta.''

They stopped and looked to him. The accompanist yawned.

''You are Violetta and you are singing your own death sentence. So how is it that you sing it as though you were riding a horse?''

''I *can* ride a horse.''

''Well, don't do it now. The dramatic voice,'' he said, ''is something else. Here you have been trained by Melba and you do not even understand the dramatic.'' Herma said nothing to this. ''First of all, to sing correctly you must stand correctly. How can I explain. You hold your chest up—so. And pull in your sit-down—so.''

Herma imitated this posture.

''Second, instead of chirping like a pretty bird you must get resonance by making the riso, the smile. Look now.''

He opened his mouth and sang an A in a round tone: ''*Haaa.*''

''That is lyric.''

Then he did the same thing again, except that the mouth spread into a kind of rictus, oval and tight at the edges: ''*Haaa.*''

"That is dramatic. That is the pathos, the voice stretched to the edge of a sob. It is not the head voice, it is still the chest voice, the voix de poitrine. But after coming from the chest it resonates in the head. You do not simply let the sound come out of the mouth from the larynx, you send it into the head and let it vibrate there and gather overtones, before it escapes from the body and is passed to the audience. In French that is called la voix dans le masque. It all depends on the riso. It is not really a smile but a kind of grimace, a stretching of the mouth."

Herma tried it. *"Haaa."*

"Not quite." He came up and stared at her from a range of twelve inches.

"Open your mouth."

She opened her mouth and he peered into it, although she didn't see how he could see anything in the poor light on the stage. Since they were both about the same height, he had to bend slightly at the knees to look into it.

"Excellent. You have a high palate, which makes it easier. Simultaneously with the riso of the mouth, you must raise the palate. There is a thin skin on the roof of the mouth, like a membrane. For the note of pathos it must be lifted."

"Haaa."

"Better. And then we come to the little catch, the sob on *sacrifica*. For this, there is no technique. You must feel. You must be Violetta, sacrificing. Because opera, carina, is partly technique but it is also feeling the part. Always I feel the part. In my *Pagliacci* there comes always, at a certain point, tears in my eyes. And with the tears comes the little catch on *cor*."

He demonstrated.

> "Ridi del duol
> che t'avvelena il *c'or* . . ."

"I have become rich and famous," he said, "through one little catch in my voice. So as you sing, you must remember in your emotions who you are. You are Violetta renouncing her Alfredo, the great love of her life, so that without him she must die. Now we will not bother anymore with these mute hopes and consoling angels, but go directly to the 'Dite.' "

The accompanist struck the dominant, and resolved it. Herma, her chest held up and her sit-down pulled in, her mouth stretched into the riso and the skin of her palate lifted, embarked into her part of the greatest duet in opera.

> "Dite alla giovine
> si bella e pura . . ."

Caruso, rubbing his hands, walked up and down on the stage singing along with her and interrupting himself to shout instructions. *"Now!* The catch on *sacrifica!"*

She came to the bottom and Germont joined in with his "Piangi, piangi!" They went on a few lines into the duet.

"Stop!" said Caruso.

They stopped. He walked up and down, rubbing his hands, and then turned back to her.

"The catch is not right. You are still sobbing on the low note, not the high."

"But *morrà* is sadder than *sacrifica*."

"No, it is not sad that she dies. She dies anyhow. It is sad that she gives up Alfredo. And Germont, this rich man, so fat, with no troubles—" he pointed to Grasse, who turned away scratching his ear— "thinking only about his daughter, joins in telling her to weep. Piangi, piangi! She is not crying enough to suit him! He wants more crying! He sings piangi piangi and you sob. Now try it once more."

Herma clenched her teeth. Singing had been easy until she encountered this terrible Wop! The accompanist played his two chords. She started over again.

> "Dite alla giovine
> si bella e pura . . ."

This time she *felt* like sobbing, somehow. The voice caught slightly on *sacrifica,* like the sleeve of a garment brushing a doorway. She stretched her lips and lifted the skin of her palate. Germont joined in and they came to the end of the stanza.

> "che a lei il sacrifica,   "Il nobile cor vincerà.
> e che morrà, e morrà, e morrà!"   Sì, il cor vincerà!"

"Da capo, ma più forte!" shouted Caruso over the piano chords. "The sob on *sacrifica!* If you will sing it with the right sob, you will bring the house down."

Herma went to the top again.

> "Ah . . . di-te alla gio-vine . . ."

The liquid Italian sounds resonated in her head and then vibrated out into the vast dark theater: "bella . . . pura . . . vittima . . . sventura . . ." And some kind of a miracle happened. The voice became disembodied. It was no longer inside her but about a foot out in front of her, where she could control it effortlessly and do with it what she wanted. She had it—it was easy, easy! ". . . raggio di bene," she sang, exultant and yet with the tremolo of full emotion. This time when she came to the high note of *sacrifica* the sleeve, passing through the door, caught on a nail and tore slightly. "Bene!" shouted Caruso. Herma went on with the warm hurt of sacrifice in her chest, a pain as keen and sweet as the climax of love. Under the voice there was a dull sound in the distance, a rumble as though of tympani. "E che morrà, e morrà, e morrà!" she sang. "Brava!" shouted Caruso while her voice still hung on the note. He whirled around triumphantly and shook his fist in the air. "Carissima, you've done it! That is exactly the catch!"

The note of the tympani grew louder and the floor of the stage shook a little. A few pieces of plaster fell from overhead. The accompanist stopped playing and stood up at the piano. He set his hand protectively over the top of his head. A piece of plaster fell on the piano keys in front of him.

Waves appeared and went rolling across the board floor of the stage. More masonry fell, some of it in chunks as large as a nail keg. The piano moved away to the left across the stage, stopped, and came rolling back again. Herma dodged it.

"Oh dio," said Caruso. "What is this?"

Out in the shadowy gulf of the theater the great chandelier began moving. With great dignity it swayed to one side, paused, and then swung back to the other, in a slow arc of two seconds or more from side to side. Bricks and pieces of plaster fell all around it into the darkness below, but none of them struck it. It swayed more violently, almost to the diagonal, and swung back the other way like a great bell. Then the chain parted. The chandelier seemed to hang poised for an instant, then it moved downward, gathering speed and turning in a slow pirouette. When it struck onto the rows of seats below the sound was like that of a great cymbal struck by a Divine hand: a crash followed by a thousand tinkles, a shock that left the ears ringing and vibrated in the walls of the building. As an anticlimax, an arc lamp fell out of the roof of the theater and struck with a splat of breaking glass. The rumble of tympani continued.

The four on the stage were the audience now, and the drama was taking place out in the darkened theater. As they watched, more things fell: stucco angels, and a large piece of mural from the ceiling, turning end over end in the shadowy air. Then, with a kind of grunt, the first balcony fell. It sagged in the middle like a badly made wedding cake, then simply dropped fifteen feet onto the rows of seats below. An immense cloud of dust arose. Through it the second balcony could be seen falling on top of the first. Then nothing more was visible, because the two lights over the stage went out.

Caruso seemed to have lost his English entirely. "Oh dio dio dio," he said in a strangled tone. "Scappiamo presto."

They groped in the darkness for their coats. Herma's light cloak was draped over a stool. It was some time before Caruso found his overcoat, scarf, and fedora. Then they blundered their way off the stage and down the pitch-black corridor toward the stairs, led by the accompanist, who seemed to have a catlike ability to see in the dark. When they came out onto Jessie Street, they found everything illuminated by a dim and undulating pink glow. It came from several fires, one in a storefront only a little way down Jessie Street and the others around the corner on Mission and Third.

"Oh dio," said Caruso. "I am back in Naples again. It is Vesuvio. Dio dio dio. We had better go back to the hotel."

When they came around the corner onto Mission they found that the entire façade of the Opera House had fallen down into the street, almost blocking it. One of the great caryatids lay stretched on the pavement, the muscular arms reaching almost to the curb on the other side. The lamp she had been holding was flung through the plate-glass window of the restaurant across the street. They skirted around all this rubble. Herma glanced at the downturned stone face: it was Attic, calm, and inscrutable as usual.

They picked their way through the debris in the streets. The rumble of tympani had stopped now and it was silent except for the hiss of escaping gas and an occasional human wail in the distance. Now and then a loose brick fell to the pavement with a thud. One missed them by only a few feet. After that they stayed in the center of the street, keeping cautiously away from the buildings on either side.

On the side street leading down to the rear entrance of the Palace, the drunken woman was still lying in the same place where she had slid to the sidewalk. But now there was an enormous piece of cornice from the building overhead on top of her, with her arms and legs sticking out. A pool of blood had appeared at one side, trickled out through the dust, and then stopped on the cement, where it was beginning to congeal.

"Oh dio," said Caruso. "The voice."

He took off the white woolen scarf and wrapped it carefully around the lower part of his face. They went on down the street. Caruso seemed to be breathing deeply but with his teeth clenched, so that every breath made a kind of seething. In, out, in, out. Herma wondered whether she should tell him to open his mouth and breathe naturally. But he answered for her. "There are millions of people in the world," he hissed through the scarf, "but there is only one voice of Caruso. Dio dio."

"Here's the Palace," said Herma.

The hotel itself was undamaged, but it was almost unrecognizable. The street was filled with rubble from other buildings, and there was an indescribable confusion of half-clad hotel guests, wagons piled with luggage, firemen, and curious onlookers.

The accompanist blinked at all this. He turned to Caruso, scratching his head.

"You all done with me for tonight?"

"Ah dio. But of course."

"Think I'll go back to the Grand and get some sleep."

Caruso stared at him, the lower half of his face still wrapped in the scarf.

"But the hotel is on fire," said Grasse.

"I don't mind. I've got to get some sleep. I'm not used to this."

He went off around the building. No one paid any attention now to the fact that he was wearing pyjamas under his overcoat. A little way down Mission a brick fell near him and he jumped like a cat. That was the last they saw of him.

19.

The lights were still on in the Palace, which had its own dynamos in the basement. There was nothing to worry about, the manager assured them. The building was fireproof and had its own water system. The walls were two feet thick and reinforced by iron rods, and were undamaged by the shock of the earthquake. It was important for everybody to keep calm and obey the instructions of the authorities, which he, the manager, would relay to them when the time came. He was a plump and self-important man in immaculate evening dress, with a white handkerchief showing in his pocket. He spoke to a small crowd of guests, fifty or so, in the Grand Court of the hotel.

The only thing was, he went on, that the authorities had ordered the hotel to be evacuated. There were a number of fires in the neighborhood, and the main line of fire, which had started in the tenements down south of the Slot, was moving toward Market Street and was only a few blocks away. He reiterated that the Palace was fireproof and that nothing would happen to it. Still, the authorities had their rules and they, the guests of the Palace, would have to obey the law just like everybody else. Later, after the authorities had the fire under control, they could come back and reclaim their baggage and other possessions.

Beckworth appeared in the crowd with Lucì in tow.

"Rico, we're moving to the St. Francis. I've made all the arrangements."

"The St. Francis?"

"It's on Union Square. A brand-new hotel. It's perfectly safe. The fire will never reach that far."

"Beck," said Caruso through the scarf, "my voice is gone."

"Well, we'll find it again. You've lost it before. Come on now. I've found a cab. It's waiting outside."

"But can I not take anything? All my possessions! My treasures!" He let the scarf fall and flung up his arms in anguish. "You there! Hotel manager. You great figure of authority. Can I not go to my room and get anything?"

"You can have ten minutes," said the manager. "Only what you can carry in your hands."

"Oh dio. I have a trunk with eighty pairs of shoes. Can I carry them with me in my hands?"

"I don't think so," said the manager.

"Hurry up, Rico. I can't keep the cab waiting."

"Oh dio dio."

Herma took him by the arm and began running with him up the ornate marble stairs. Whether or not the elevators were working, the elevator boys had disappeared somewhere. When they got to the sixth floor Herma was panting a little, but Caruso was still seething at the same rate through his clenched teeth. Evidently for his powerful chest running up six flights of stairs was nothing. He unlocked the door and burst into the suite, leaving the door open behind him. Herma followed.

A thin young Italian in shirt-sleeves and a waistcoat was standing in the bedroom, holding a silver hairbrush in one hand and a pair of shoes in the other. It was Martino, Caruso's valet.

"What are you doing?"

"I am packing, Signore."

"Idiot! We have to leave immediately. We can take nothing."

"Very good, Signore."

He turned away to put the shoes in the trunk and pack the brush in a suitcase. Caruso unwound the scarf from his face and threw it on the floor. "La voce!" he muttered. "When the voice goes, Caruso is nothing." He went into the bathroom, dampened a small towel, and wound it around his mouth in place of the scarf. He attempted to tuck it into place but it fell down. "Never mind! What shall I take?"

"Your money."

"I have only the money in my pocket. Beckworth has the money. I never have the money." Groping through a valise and throwing out neckties and socks onto the floor, he found a small revolver, which he slipped into his coat pocket.

"What's that for?"

"It makes me feel better," said Caruso, still seething through his teeth. "Right at the moment I don't feel good. What else?" His eye fell on the silver-framed photograph of Roosevelt on the table and he took it. A box of Egyptian cigarettes: he slipped it into the other coat pocket.

"Excuse me, Herma. Because I don't feel good, I have to make a call to nature. I will meet you in a minute. Wait at the door."

He disappeared into the bathroom. Herma hesitated for a moment, then she went out the door and raced down the flight of stairs to her own suite. She was carrying a small silver mesh handbag with her handkerchief and cosmetics in it. Into this she slipped her toothbrush and the coins from the locked dresser drawer in Fred's room. There were still a few of the Double Eagles derived from the pawning of Ernestine's brooch. The silver dollars she left behind—too heavy. She didn't possess a revolver, so there was nothing else to take.

She slipped the mesh bag into the pocket of her cloak and started back up the stairs to the sixth floor, but met Caruso coming down. He was still carrying the photograph in its silver frame. The damp towel had fallen down around his neck and looked like a baby's bib.

"Do you feel better?"

"La voce," he gritted as though to himself. "The voice is everything."

They hurried on down the stairs together. The Grand Court was almost deserted now. The manager was waving his arms as though he were herding ducks, trying to get people to leave the building. Grasse, Lucì, and Beckworth were waiting by the registration desk.

Caruso made his grimace at them. He still kept his teeth clenched together. ''Amici,'' he said morosely, ''I've lost my voice.''

''Well, let's go have some breakfast,'' said Grasse. ''You'll feel better then.''

''You are insane! Do you understand what I am saying?''

''Will you please hurry up, everybody? The cab is waiting.''

Somehow Beckworth managed to get them out the door. The cab was standing at the curb on Montgomery Street. It was not really possible for five people to fit into one cab, but they managed it somehow. Lucì sat on Grasse's knees, and Herma with her slim hips fitted into a corner of the seat beside Beckworth.

It was six-thirty now and a ghoulish sort of daylight was beginning to creep over the city. They drove through a scene that might have come from the imagination of a Gustave Doré, all in grays, like an etching. A pall of smoke hung in Market Street at the level of the tops of the buildings. A few fires were burning here and there in shops, and the fire companies were making half-hearted attempts to put them out. But the water mains were broken and there was no water except for what they could bring up in their tank wagons. A short way down Market the Call Building, that indestructible marvel built out of poured concrete and steel, was burning fiercely, with flames coming out of the salt-shaker holes in the dome high at the top. To the left, in the flat expanse of tenements south of the Slot, immense towers of smoke stood in the air, rising to a thousand feet or more and then flattening out into anvils. In places the columns had joined together into a solid wall of smoke, with pink and orange flashes showing now and then at the bottom of it. The fire had advanced considerably in the few minutes they had spent in the hotel. No one seemed to be doing anything about it, or to be particularly concerned. Two men came out of a doorway carrying a large oil painting, set it on the sidewalk, and stood trying to decide what to do with it. Other people stood on housetops, looking at the fire off to the south.

''Dio dio.''

''The fire will never cross Market,'' said Beckworth. ''Calm down, Rico. We're going to the St. Francis and have a nice breakfast.''

''Che dice?'' asked Lucì.

''Che stiamo al sicuro. L'incendio non arriverà fino al St. Francis.''

''Ah bene.''

''I wish I could believe you,'' said Grasse. ''Look, parbleu. There's a curious sight. It's like a stage set.''

At a hotel a short way down Market the entire front wall had fallen away, leaving the rooms intact with all their furniture. Unmade beds, bathrooms with all their fixtures, and neatly furnished but dusty parlors passed by their frame of vision. In one bedroom a man still in his nightshirt was sitting gloomily on the bed with his hands folded, watching the cab as it passed. On the sidewalk in front of the hotel a cat wound delicately through the heaps of rubble, holding its tail in the air. Then it turned, presenting the small and immaculate pink eye under its tail to the watchers in the cab. Herma saw what the cat was looking at: a large gray rat had come out from the rubble and was looking for a chance to scuttle a little way down the sidewalk toward a naked foot protruding from a heap of bricks. Caruso saw it too and pulled the damp towel up over his mouth. The towel was to keep death from his voice, not dust.

They turned the corner onto Powell. From there it was only a few short blocks to Union Square. As promised, the St. Francis was intact and doing business as usual. The cab wheeled up in front of the hotel, where the doorman was still on duty. They all got out except Beckworth.

"The rest of you go in. There are rooms reserved in your names. I've got another piece of business to do."

He went off in the cab in the direction of Market, where the smoke was now looming higher.

They looked at each other. Caruso shrugged. "Beck always says that he does not understand artists. But sometimes I do not understand Beck."

They went in through the door into the almost deserted hotel, and were quickly seated in the restaurant at a table with silver service and immaculate white linen.

"It's Mr. Caruso's party," called the headwaiter. "Step lively there, you others. What is your pleasure, ladies and gentlemen?"

"Breakfast, and lots of it," said Grasse.

"How could anyone eat a mouthful?" said Caruso.

Lucì caught Herma's eye. She seemed uneasy.

"Ma cosa facciamo?"

Herma smiled. "Prendiamo la colazione. Hai fame?"

"Molto. But what is all this?" She waved her arm around her, to indicate everything that was happening.

"Ma è un terremoto."

"Ah. Così." Now that Lucì knew it was an earthquake she seemed relieved. There was no telling what she thought it was before. Perhaps the end of the world.

A platoon of waiters came up with the breakfast. There were eggs sunny-side up, a dozen or so rashers of bacon, a mountain of toast, and a piping hot silver pot of coffee. They devoured all this. Their appetites were incredible, considering the supper they had all had at Delmonico's only a few short hours before. Even Caruso did his share. He ate a piece of toast, cut up a rasher of bacon and delicately ate it with his knife and fork (Herma ate hers with her fingers), and sipped a little black coffee. He still seemed depressed. He said little, and kept glancing out the window as though he expected to see the fire appear any minute behind the glass, or some other Beast of the Apocalypse he had not anticipated.

"Food," said Grasse shrewdly with a sidewise glance at him, "sustains the voice. I always eat a good breakfast."

Caruso took another piece of toast, spread it with butter, and began eating it. When he had finished it to the last crumb he licked the butter from his fingers, and then he held his hand before his face and looked at it. "La voce," he said absently.

Grasse lit a cigar. The waiters were clearing the table. Caruso reached mechanically into his pocket to pay for the breakfast, but at that moment Beckworth arrived.

"Come on, everybody," he said briskly. "We're going to Oakland. The ferries aren't running but I've engaged a launch. I have compartments in the first train leaving for the East."

"I thought we were staying at the St. Francis," said Caruso.

"Not anymore. The plans are changed."

"Have you had your breakfast, Beck?"

"The Devil with my breakfast. Hurry up. The launch won't wait forever."

"Dio dio. Well, let's go. Are Grasse and Herma going too?"

"No, just you and Lucì. Moellendorf will meet us at the Embarcadero."

"Well, Grasse and Herma can come to see us off."

"There's not room in the cab."

"Not room? But we all fitted in the cab before. We can do it again."

Beckworth lifted his shoulders in a helpless gesture. "Well, come on then. But hurry."

No one had paid for the breakfast. The waiters bowed them out, all smiles and ceremony. Outside on Powell Street they all squeezed into the cab as before, Caruso still clutching his photograph in its silver frame.

"Embarcadero," said Beckworth.

"Oh no," said Caruso. "Beck, I have to go back to the Palace."

"Out of the question."

"But all my things."

"Forget it."

"To the Palace!"

"Wait till you see it," said Beckworth.

The Palace was not as fireproof as the manager had contended. As they came down Market they saw that the wall of fire proceeding up from the south had crossed Mission and Jessie and was licking at the rear wall of the hotel. Flames were curling from windows on the lower stories, not only on Jessie Street but around the corner on Montgomery. Jets of water were spouting from hoses on the roof. There was a great clutter of fire engines, wagons, and motorcars around the side entrance on Market.

"To the Embarcadero," Beckworth ordered. "Go on past. Drive around it."

"No, no," said Caruso. Taking advantage of the traffic which caused the cab to stop momentarily, he leaped out and strode across the sidewalk toward the hotel.

"Rico, you madman."

Beckworth got out and followed after him, and Herma came along too. Grasse and Lucì stayed in the cab.

Inside the hotel the Grand Court was filled with smoke. Almost nothing could be seen. An orange glow pulsed from the restaurant down the corridor toward Jessie Street. It was there that most of the smoke was coming from. It billowed out in great clouds, rising up toward the glass roof seven stories overhead.

"Rico!" called Beckworth.

Caruso had disappeared somewhere in the smoke. The Grand Court was piled high with guests' baggage. There were trunks, packing cases, and crates of liquor and wine. There were no guests in sight. The manager was also missing. A crowd of Chinese servants milled about through the piles of baggage, gesticulating and arguing. Now and then a pair of them would pick up a trunk and run off with it toward the entrance onto Market. The scene was Dantesque. Sometimes the Chinese were obscured in the smoke, at other times they could be seen in the pink light of the fire, gibbering at one another and pushing at the baggage.

Caruso reappeared, disheveled and perspiring. "They're stealing my things," he cried. "Al ladro! Thief! There!"

He pointed to a pair of Chinese who were disappearing toward the door with a trunk.

"It is the trunk with my shoes! Ladri! Mascalzoni!"

He followed after them for a few paces, then came to a halt, took the revolver from his pocket, and raised it.

"Stop! I will shoot."

Herma ran up and seized the arm with the revolver. Beckworth was only a few steps behind.

"They're stealing my trunk."

"I see they are, but what are a few shoes compared to a human life?" said Beckworth. "Think of your voice. This building is on fire, Rico."

Caruso pushed the damp towel up over his mouth. "My shoes," he said in a muffled tone.

At that moment the intrepid Martino came down the stairs with flames surrounding him, carrying a small trunk.

"Non vi preoccupate, signore, I have taken care of everything. This is the last of your trunks. The others are being loaded onto a wagon."

"What?"

Martino went off with the trunk. They followed after him. Outside on Market a wagon was in fact waiting, piloted by a phlegmatic driver who did not seem to feel there was anything unusual about the circumstances. He was chewing a toothpick and looking with detachment at the smoke pouring from the upper stories of the Palace. All of Caruso's trunks were piled on the wagon, and Martino was securing a rope around them.

"Where are Lucì and Grasse?" said Caruso. "We must all go on the wagon, otherwise they will steal my things."

He still had the revolver in his hand. Herma decided against an attempt to relieve him of it or persuade him to put it away. Grasse and Lucì were discovered in the cab only a few yards away, hidden in a cloud of smoke.

"Hurry, for the love of God," said Beckworth, in a tone more of exasperation than of alarm.

They all climbed onto the wagon, arranging themselves on the trunks. Grasse helped Lucì on. She smiled, a little dimly. The wagon went off, followed by the cab driver who was explaining that no one had paid him. Beckworth threw him a silver dollar, and then another. He caught them and disappeared in the smoke behind.

They looked back at the Palace. There were flames at almost every window now.

"What happened to the pumps?"

"They're pumping water onto the roof. It's the inside that's on fire."

"Martino, did you bring my cigarettes?" said Caruso. "I only have half a box."

"Oh, Rico," sighed Beckworth.

"They are in a trunk, Signor. Do you want one now?"

"No, I am only allowed ten a day," said Caruso.

The wagon made its way down Market only with difficulty. The pavement was jammed with wagons and motorcars, and abandoned cable cars blocked the way in the center. Here and there a building had collapsed and filled half the street with rubble. At least the fire was well behind them now. A small flame flickered in a storefront here and there, where a gas pipe had broken.

Grasse began looking around under his feet.

"I say, here is Rico's case of champagne. It seems to be Krug Sec. Not the same thing as Veuve Cliquot, but it will do."

Caruso caught sight of another corpse in a pile of bricks across the street. He pulled the damp towel up over his mouth again. He still held the revolver loosely in his hands between his knees.

Grasse managed to pry the case open. He took out a bottle, and then another. "Watch out, everyone. It's warm and it's been agité, jiggled." He unwound the wires of the first bottle and worked the cork loose. It shot out with a sharp report and the wine foamed after it.

"Morbleu. We don't have any glasses."

"Drink it out of the bottle."

"Ah, no. Krug Sec? What an abomination."

He stared at the bottle, which was foaming out over his hands. He handed it to Herma.

"Stop," he told the driver.

He had caught sight of a deserted saloon across the street. The frosted glass windows had fallen out, along with half the front wall. He disappeared into it and came out with five pilsner goblets splayed out in his fingers, two in one hand and three in the other. He handed these up and got back on the wagon.

"I will go crazy," said Beckworth, clutching his brow.

"We never drank to Herma's performance," said Grasse. "Do you remember, Rico? We were going to at Delmonico's, and then we forgot about it."

"We didn't forget. I was still thinking about it."

"Well, what do you think now?"

"Now that you have the dannato stuff open."

He accepted a glass, holding it in one hand and retaining the revolver in the other. "Not every day do I drink at eight in the morning. But this is not every day."

"To Herma."

They all drank, except Herma. She looked at Caruso holding his revolver.

"Are you going to shoot somebody, Rico, you desperado?"

"I may, if they try to steal my things."

She could hardly keep from smiling. Instead she began humming under her breath. They were out of the smoke now. The sun had come out and was shining brightly on the wagon and the street. A quarter of a mile ahead of them the Ferry Building was visible, intact, at the end of Market.

She sang, in an exaggerated Western twang.

> "Goin' up the mountain, goin' out West,
> With a thirty-eight special stickin' out of my vest,
> And it's ride, Railroad Bill."

Caruso smiled faintly.

> "Railroad Bill, Railroad Bill,
> He never worked and he never will,
> And it's ride, Railroad Bill."

"But where did you learn this lingo of cowboy?" he asked her.

"It's my native dialect," Herma laughed. "My Aunt Minnie crossed the plains in a wagon."

She sang the next verse in duet with Grasse, she in cowboy and he in his elegant Parisian accent.

> "A thirty-eight special in a forty-five frame,
> How in the world can I miss him when I'm takin' dead aim,
> And it's ride, Railroad Bill."

Caruso, with a glance at Beckworth, sheepishly put the revolver away in his pocket. "How is it that you too know this, my friend?" he asked Grasse.

"I am very fond of cowboy music. I sing it when I am shaving."

"Ah? Strano. I sing the 'Vesti la giubba.' It makes the hairs stand on their end, so I can shave them easier."

Grasse filled everybody's glasses, and Herma sang another verse. They taught it to Caruso, and he joined in with his Italian accent and rich bel canto.

> "Railroad Bill, he ain't so bad,
> Blew down his Mama, took a shot at his Dad,
> And it's ride, Railroad Bill."

And on to the chorus again :

> "Railroad Bill, Railroad Bill,
> He never worked and he never will,
> And it's ride, Railroad Bill."

"Beck," said Caruso, "I have found my voice again."

"That's nice, Rico. I thought you would. Don't hurt it by singing too much of that garbage."

"And it's ride, Railroad Bill," Caruso sang to himself, a little more cautiously, in mezza voce.

The wagon arrived at the Ferry Building and swung on past it to the left along the Embarcadero. There, at an empty space of wharf, it stopped. The main fire south of Market Street was now far behind them. A little farther along the Embarcadero fireboats from Oakland were spraying great streams of Bay water onto the docks and the buildings beyond. Other firemen were pulling up hoses to wet down the Ferry Building. It looked as though the whole waterfront might be saved from the flames.

They all got out. A steam launch with a tall, spindly funnel was tied to the wharf. In the stern was Madame Moellendorf, holding up a parasol. She didn't speak, since she was still suffering from quinsy if that was what it was, but she stared silently with narrowed eyes at Herma, under the impression that she had encountered her somewhere before.

Martino and the wagon driver began shifting the trunks into the launch. Caruso walked impatiently up and down the wharf, still clutching the photograph. He unwrapped the towel from his neck and threw it away.

"You were a good Violetta, Herma," he said in an offhand way. "It was right that we drink to you. But you still have to learn much. You should remember my sayings about resonance and the voix dans le masque."

"I will."

Out of nowhere two policemen appeared. One of them was stocky and beefy. He seemed to be a sergeant, and did all the talking. The other one swung a club.

"What's going on here?"

Caruso told him, "We are just getting into this launch to leave your beautiful city, which we enjoyed very much, but we are going on to other cities, which have the advantage of not falling down."

"No one to leave the city."

Beckworth stepped forward. "Who says?"

"Mayor's orders. It's to avoid panic. The ferries are stopped. You're not allowed to hire a private boat."

"I am not at all panicked," said Caruso. "I am perfectly calm."

"But we have reservations on a train out of Oakland. We've booked compartments," Beckworth protested.

"You can book the whole train if you like. But you can't leave the city. It's martial law."

"Do you know who this is?" Beckworth asked him.

"He can be the King of Germany for all I care."

There was a moment of awkward silence. Then Caruso bethought himself of the photograph in the silver frame. He handed it to the sergeant.

The sergeant studied the inscription.

> "To my friend
> Enrico Caruso
> from
> Theodore Roosevelt"

He handed back the photograph. "Are you Mr. Caruso?"

"Who else would I be? Would you like me to do the 'Vesti la giubba'?"

"No, it isn't necessary. Who are these other people?"

"My manager. And my wife," he lied blatantly about Lucì.

"Very good, sir." The sergeant saluted. "Have a nice trip. I'm sorry we had an earthquake just when you were visiting our city."

"You are not to blame," said Caruso generously.

The two policemen disappeared. The trunks were all in the launch now, and Lucì had been seated next to the Moellendorf.

Caruso climbed nimbly down into the launch. The pall of smoke over the city was advancing slowly along Market Street.

"A necropolis! I feel I am in the last act of *Aïda*. I must get out of this tomb. Farewell, Herma."

"Goodbye."

"Addìo, Grasse, you bad sensualist."

"The last night of San Francisco, and you had me sing all night, when I could have been—"

"I know. Farewell."

The launch pulled away, turning in a half circle toward Oakland. In the stern the Moellendorf was still staring at Herma. Standing on the edge of the wharf, Herma in her clearest and most dulcet tone sang her the last lines of Cherubino's Canzonetta.

> "Voi che sapete
> che cosa è amor,
> donne, vedete,
> s'io l'ho nel cor."

Then, as the launch dwindled away across the Bay, she turned to Grasse and they walked back together toward the wall of smoke advancing across the city south of Market.

20.

For the next four days and nights Herma did not sleep, except for catnaps in the shelter of a wall, or an hour or two in the corner of somebody's tent. Most of the time she was not really aware whether it was day or night. Now and then the sun shone, but only briefly. For the most part it was obscured by the blanket of smoke drifting slowly eastward with the sea breeze. The gas mains were broken so there were no street lights, and the dynamos that supplied electricity to the houses and shops had come to a stop long ago. The fire burned for two days, devouring a dream city of eternal twilight, now and then lit by the garish flames of the conflagration, then darkened again by the shreds of smoke drifting overhead and sinking down to fill the streets. The smoke filtered the bright scarlet of the flames to mauve, orange, pink, magenta, all the colors in the gelatine array of the theater lighting director. When the moon appeared through a tatter of clouds it was the same pale blood-red as the flames. In this phantasmagoric light the whole population of the city wandered around through the streets, as though fleeing from a plague but uncertain where to go to flee from it, or how to get there.

There were no more cabs to be had, or wagons or other conveyances. The cable-car system of course was totally disabled. Herma and Grasse made their way on foot up Market Street, skirting around the heaps of rubble that had collapsed onto the pavement. Toward them, down Market, poured a crowd of refugees fleeing from the fire south of the Slot, carrying with them everything they had been able to save: clothing, furniture in pushcarts, wheelbarrows piled with crockery, beds rolled on their casters, baby carriages, sewing machines, and pillowcases filled with the family silver. Women carried bundles of clothing, and more than one father of a family staggered along with a piece of furniture on his back, a bureau or a small table. Children dragged mattresses, and Herma and Grasse passed a whole family of five including a grandmother trundling a piano down the street. Not all of the salvaged objects were valuable. It was important to be carrying *something*. These objects were the lares and penates of their lost homes. Even a doorknob, or a window frame with the glass in it, showed that you had once *had* a house. One man had cut down the electric candelabrum—no doubt the pride of the household—and was carrying it in his hand with the dead wire dangling.

A woman sat on the curb of Market wailing, in a monotonous voice, "Oh, my husband is dead, and a young man is dead, and a woman is dead . . ." The litany was repeated over and over again, connected by "ands." No one paid any attention to her. A man wandered around asking everybody where he could get a shave. He had gone to his hotel, he said, and to his surprise it wasn't there anymore. A little farther on there was a small fire in a restaurant and the waiters were using soda siphons to put it out. Everyone stopped to watch this. The fire, extinguished inside the restaurant, reappeared under the eaves out on the sidewalk, and a waiter came out with a stepladder and put this out too. This seemed a purely formal procedure, a gesture of exorcism. From south of the Slot, only a mile or so away, an immense billow of smoke could be seen advancing steadily, vaulting over street after street.

At the corner of Third Street Herma and Grasse stopped. The Grand Opera House was only a block down on Mission. It was afire, but it was emitting only a little smoke and showing almost no flame from the outside. A few yellow tongues darted now and then from the clerestory windows high on the sides. The rear of the building smoked like a hot griddle. Then, instead of bursting into flames as Herma expected, the immense baroque structure simply collapsed. The walls fell inward and the roof came down on top of them in a single slow and graceful motion, accompanied by a prolonged sound like thunder. An instant after the roof struck the ground a million white-hot particles shot up into the air trailing showers of sparks behind them, soaring off in brilliant arcs, like a fabulous and block-long fireworks display for the entertainment of a mad monarch. Once this spectacle was over the remains settled down to burn in a businesslike way, with a loud crackling.

"C'est formidable," Grasse said, but he spoke almost indifferently. "It is always interesting to watch a fire, even when it is your own house that is burning."

She realized that she knew almost nothing about his personal life, except that he was a bachelor.

"Where do you live?"

"South of the Slot. It's gone now. Mrs. Morbihan's boarding house on Howard."

"Funny. Do you know Madame Ernestine, the actress?"

He darted a glance at her. "Ah," he said roguishly. "Everyone knows Ernestine."

"She's only lived there a couple of weeks."

He hesitated for only a moment, then he smiled cryptically. "She makes friends quickly."

He had nothing more to say on this subject. Herma concealed her own little smile. The more fool Fred, she thought, not without a certain satisfaction. They crossed Market and made their way up Stockton toward Union Square.

The images that remained in Herma's memory afterward were fragmentary, and their chronology was curiously twisted. It was hard to recall what had come first and what after, or whether some things had happened at all or had only been part of the strange dream—not unpleasant but simply strange—that seemed superimposed on everything, so that there were two levels of events in that four days of wandering about the city, the real and the fabulous. She clearly remembered, for example, seeing a lion and a pair of leopards slinking through the ruins of the Grand Hotel, although someone told her later that there was no zoo in San Francisco. More real, even though somewhat ghostlike, was the undertaker squatting outside his establishment on Lombard Street completely absorbed in the task of polishing coffin handles, or the well-dressed woman who sat in a cable car on Powell Street waiting for it to start, regardless that the pavement around it was twisted into waves like those of the sea. On Nob Hill, in front of a rococo mansion still untouched by the fire, a man offered a thousand dollars for a team of horses. Behind him was a wagon piled high with a Steinway grand piano, rolls of imported Gobelin tapestries, and crates of fine china and crystal. There were no takers.

But, if there was no zoo, there was a madhouse. Its walls had fallen and the inmates had simply walked out into the city. Creeping along Sutter, trailing their hands on the walls as if they wished to reassure themselves that at least part of the world was still standing, came a procession of sunken-eyed fearful men in pyjamas, some with bare feet. There were seven or eight of them. They glanced about like criminals, and said nothing even to each other, although they kept more or less together in a ragged line, with one straggler, a grossly corpulent old man who could walk only with difficulty, bringing up the rear. One of them, the second in line, was absentmindedly carrying a crowbar, as though he had forgotten he had it. He was a powerfully built man with a pink sunburned neck and arms like tree limbs, and he looked as though he might have been a carpenter. As they passed Herma each of the madmen stared at her, one after the other. A youngish man toward the end, with a soft mustache and anxious guilty eyes, fell out of line and came back to her.

"It's my fault," he told her. "Self-abuse. I tried to stop but I couldn't." His companion told him, "Come on, Willie." He turned away and rejoined the others, still looking back at Herma.

A policeman came along Sutter after them at an unhurried pace. When he caught up with them he first took the crowbar from the hand of the carpenter. Then he said, "All right, boys. Come along. We're going back home." Docilely they turned and followed him. As they disappeared in the distance the young man with the mustache looked back once more at Herma. His soft eyes were fixed on hers for a moment. Then he turned and went on with the others.

It was on the second day. On the steep hill of California Street a crowd had collected, and Herma and Grasse stopped to watch. A house had collapsed and someone was still buried in a bed under the bricks. A bedpost protruded. The passersby began working to throw out the bricks one by one. Two firemen came up and joined in at the work. The others, a score or more of people, simply stood about on the sidewalk watching.

Herma glanced at Grasse. Then she crossed the sidewalk and clambered down, in her gown by Worth of Paris, into the gulf left by the collapse of the building. Grasse followed her. This encouraged some others to join in. They began throwing out bricks. Herma kept at it for a half an hour without stopping to rest. After five minutes her hands were scraped and bleeding. Three of the four bedposts were visible now, and a leg clad in pyjamas was sticking out at one side. But the bed, with the rest of the furniture, had fallen into the cellar below the level of the street, so that Herma, Grasse, and the others were working at the bottom of a steep and shifty pit lined with loose bricks. The bricks had to be flung up in two or three stages, the last workers at the top slinging them out into the street. But no sooner was a part of the bed uncovered than a landslide of bricks occurred at one side, almost burying it again. The dirty pyjama leg was slowly dripping blood. Did people bleed after they were dead, Herma wondered? She began throwing bricks faster. Her hands and face were grimy and her gown was torn in several places.

They freed the bedposts again, then there was another landslide. The two firemen stopped throwing bricks. One of them stood up. He wiped his sweating face with the back of his hand. "Come on, Bill," he said. "There's fires." They left, going off down the hill on California without turning to look back.

The others went on working for a little while longer. Then a red-haired youth stopped and said, "What's the use of digging out people that's dead?" This struck them all as so profoundly true that, without another word, they turned and climbed out into the street. Herma looked back once. The leg was still dripping. Then she went away with Grasse, holding up her hands to look at them. Little dots of blood stood on them, gleaming like rubies through the grime.

He turned and saw what she was doing.

"He was dead."

Herma nodded without meeting his glance.

"A bath would be nice," said Grasse. "No chance of that. Let's see if we can't find some coffee instead."

The fire had crossed Market Street in places now. Columns of smoke could be seen over the rooftops, off beyond the City Hall in the direction of Van Ness. Refugees from south of the Slot were still streaming up Stockton and Powell toward Union Square, carrying Victrolas, furniture, bedding, and kitchen utensils. Herma and Grasse crossed through this procession at right angles, stared at by a solemn child about three who was towing a toy wagon behind him. A patch of sun had come out now and was shining down on a straggling line of hungry and homeless people making their way up Powell Street.

Beyond Powell the refugees thinned out, and there were only a few spectators standing in the street looking at the wall of smoke advancing from the west. It was curiously quiet. There was a chink of masonry as someone dug at the rubble a block or so away, and they could hear a voice from a second-story window talking to someone in the street below. Herma and Grasse didn't say much either. Grasse seemed preoccupied, although not particularly depressed. He even smiled to himself once in a while, in a vacant sort of way. Perhaps, she thought, he was a little bit unhinged.

It was a little farther on, as they were going down O'Farrell toward

Delmonico's, that they saw the first soldiers. They were coming down the street toward them in a long ragged line, with the ruins of St. Mary's Cathedral behind them in the distance. They were wearing campaign hats, tunics carelessly unbuttoned, and narrow trousers with boots. They carried their rifles slung and they had bedrolls over their shoulders. Their uniforms were not very clean and they were various colors of khaki, some faded and some new. There didn't seem to be anybody in charge of them. There were a few officers, but they simply walked along with the rest. They went by one by one. They all wore their hats at different angles, some to one side and some to the other. One red-faced soldier had his hat on exactly square, pulled down over his face, with his eyes glowering underneath. As he went by he stared at Herma and said something to himself, or at least moved his lips as though he were mouthing a word. He was the last for a while. There were more coming along in the distance.

"Here's Delmonico's," said Grasse.

Ahead of them a pair of soldiers turned and went into the restaurant. Three or more followed them. When they got inside Herma and Grasse found a dozen or more soldiers roaming around with their slung rifles through the dim interior. The building was relatively undamaged. A pile of bricks had slid to the floor at one place, and a thin dust hung in the air, drifting slowly back and forth. Except for that the room was exactly as it was when they left it two nights before. The waiters had only partly cleared away the tables. One table was covered with wine glasses with napkins stuck into them. A soldier pulled out a napkin, found the glass still half full of wine, and drank it.

"Where's the coffee, boys?" Grasse asked them.

They stared. None of them spoke. These soldiers were reservists and they looked very young. The one who had drained the wine glass found a bottle of champagne and began unwinding the wires at the neck. When he got them off the cork failed to pop out. Impatiently he banged the bottle on the edge of the table. The neck snapped off, and most of the wine foamed out onto the table and over the soldier's tunic. He drank the rest from the broken neck of the bottle.

"Capn's gonna eat out your ass," one told him.

"Fuck him."

Grasse took Herma by the arm. He led her off toward the kitchen. "They're harmless boys," he said. "It's just the first time they've been away from their mothers."

In the kitchen there were more soldiers. These were better organized, or at least a little more systematic. They had found some firewood and started up the stove, even though the chimney over it had collapsed and the kitchen was littered with bricks. Some of them cleared the bricks off the stove, and others filled the coffeepot from a spigot which miraculously still gave forth a trickle of water.

"Ah. Coffee," said Grasse.

"Who's this?"

"Civilians," said another without turning his head.

The kitchen began to fill with smoke.

"This stove don't draw," said the soldier in charge of the coffeepot.
"Open the damper."

"There ain't no damper. It fell down with the chimney."

"Maybe," said another, "you hadn't ought to light the stove, if there ain't no chimney."

"It just makes a little smoke. What's the difference?"

"You're setting fire to the ceiling," Grasse told them.

"Who is he anyhow?"

"Some kind of Dago. Hey, what are you, Eyetalian?"

"I'm French."

"Says he's a Frog."

"What are you doing in here anyhow?" said the coffeemaker. "You can clear out."

"What right do you have to be here?" said Grasse. "Is it your restaurant?"

"It's martial law, Dad. We've requisitioned this here restaurant and it's a military reservation."

"It's also on fire, as I told you," said Grasse.

The coffeemaker looked up at the ceiling. It was smoking fiercely, and a tongue of flame was visible now in a place where the boards were broken. Some of the soldiers started to drift toward the door. They were met by a pair of policemen rushing in, sweaty and panting. One of them, a sergeant, was hatless.

"Here it is. It's in the kitchen."

"What in Blessed Tarnation do you boys think you're doing?" said the sergeant. "Don't you know better than to light a fire in a place with no chimney?"

"Just makin' some coffee," said one sheepishly.

"All the other fires is still west of Nan Ness. Look at what you've done, you precious idiots. Ain't you heard about the proclamation? No kitchen fires until the building's inspected. You blooming nincompoops are supposed to be enforcing it."

"It was these two civilians done it," said the coffeemaker.

"Clear out, the lot of you. Who's your officer?"

"Tell 'im Capn Andrews. He's a son of a bitch," said a voice in an undertone.

"Capn Andrews."

The sergeant wrote it down.

"Now go on. Get out. You too," he told Herma and Grasse. They all filed out onto the street. As they left the building was burning briskly.

Herma and Grasse went on up O'Farrell toward the wall of smoke in the distance. It was almost nightfall now. A few fires were smoldering in the houses along the street, even though the sergeant had said there were no fires east of Van Ness. Nobody was paying any attention to them. A block ahead were the walls of St. Mary's Cathedral, which were still standing although everything else around it was flattened into a wilderness of bricks. With the blackened church in the background, like the ruins of a medieval French abbey dimly lit in the glow from the fires, the scene resembled an opera set, a Walpurgisnacht for *Faust*.

"Where are we going?" Herma asked him.

"Que voulez-vous, ma petite? We are taking a walk. Perhaps we shall find a restaurant that the soldiers haven't burned down, so we can have a cup of coffee, or perhaps by some miracle we will find a hotel that will provide us with a bed. Two beds," he added quickly. "Ah, here is someone I know. Hallo, Arnold!"

A man about thirty, with a long and equine face, turned and came toward them. He was hatless and wearing a German canvas jacket, an odd coat that came about halfway to his knees.

"Hullo, Lucien."

"It's Arnold Genthe, the well-known photographer," he told Herma. "Arnold, mon vieux! This is Herma, the well-known opera singer. How is it," he asked, "that you are both so well known and you don't know each other? Arnold, my dear friend, how are things with you? What have you been doing with yourself?" he inquired volubly, as though it were a perfectly ordinary meeting between friends on an ordinary day.

"My God, I've been photographing like a madman, until the light failed," said Genthe. "I've used up all my plates. Oh, how I wish I could develop them! But the pipes are broken and there's no water in my laboratory. Lucien, my fortune is made! I've got it all on glass. The burning of the Palace—the City Hall—the crowd in Union Square—the financial district—views of the whole blasted fantastic thing from Nob Hill. A hundred and ten plates and thirty stereoscope slides. Now I've got to figure out how to get them out of town and on a train to the East. The *Times* will buy them. The Chicago *Trib* will buy them, everybody will buy them. And the stereos! I'm exhausted. I've been dragging the two cameras around on my back for two days. Lucien, listen, you bibulous old freak. I've got a bottle of Johannisberger Schloss '68 at home that I've been saving for a special occasion. I think this is it, don't you?"

"If it's a case of drinking something, I say drink it in any case. Where is this precious bottle of Riesling?"

"In my house up on Van Ness. It's just beyond Clay."

"Isn't there fire up that way?"

"No, no. There's no fire that far yet. There may be tomorrow. All the more reason to open the bottle now."

"Alors. En route!" said Grasse.

They went up the street, not exactly arm in arm but crowded together and bumping elbows convivially. Genthe looked at Herma as though noticing her for the first time.

"And who did you say you were?"

"I didn't say. Lucien said I was Herma."

"And what do you do exactly?"

"I sing."

"Ah! delightful." He kept turning to look at her as they walked. He seemed to be quite taken with her. Or perhaps he was just a little delirious from fatigue and from the excitement of the pictures he had taken.

They turned the corner onto Van Ness. Here the advancing wall of fire was only a few blocks away. Yet for some reason there was no one in sight. The first houses across the street were flattened to the ground. After that the row of houses seemed intact. The soldiers—these were regulars from the Presidio—were systematically dynamiting the houses in an effort to stop the fire along the Van Ness Line. As they watched, a pair of soldiers came bolting out of the first standing house. One of them fell to his knees, got up, and began running again. An instant later there was a deafening explosion and the boards, bricks, and furniture of the house flew into the air in a cloud of dust. When the dust settled the house had been converted into a flat layer of rubble like the others on the street.

"Holy Moses!" said Genthe admiringly. "I'd like to get that. But I'm out of plates, and it's too dark now anyhow."

A soldier appeared from nowhere and ordered them to go back the way they had come. He had a rifle in his hands with the bayonet fixed.

"Which way?"

"Any way. Back. You can't go by here."

"Why not?"

"You can see for yerself. They're blowin' up the houses."

"Why?"

"So they won't burn. Have you lost yer wits or what? To make a firebreak."

"Come on," said Genthe.

He led them back a block to Polk, then up the street a short distance to a point where they came back onto a stretch of Van Ness still free of soldiers. From down the street they heard the sharp crack of exploding dynamite again, followed by a kind of crackling sigh as the next house collapsed. From all evidence the dynamiting only made the houses burn better. Already flames were licking in the ruins of the one they had just blown up, perhaps from a broken gas pipe.

A little farther along they found a hastily printed poster nailed to a telegraph pole, and stopped to read it as well as they could make it out in the failing light.

"I don't particularly want to get shot," said Herma.

"We're not looting," said Genthe. "We're only going to my house for a drink."

"It says everyone should stay at home."

"Well, we don't have a home," Grasse pointed out. "Mrs. Morbihan's is burned down, and so is the Palace."

"It's only a little farther," said Genthe. "In the next block."

They crossed Clay and approached the house. A soldier came down the sidewalk toward them, holding his rifle with the fixed bayonet before him in a businesslike way. He was young and had a red face. His hat was cocked to one side and a lock of curly hair stuck out from under it.

"Where do you think you're going?"

PROCLAMATION
BY THE MAYOR

The Federal Troops, the members of the Regular Police Force and all Special Police Officers have been authorized by me to KILL any and all persons found engaged in Looting or in the Commission of Any Other Crime.

I have directed all the Gas and Electric Lighting Co.'s not to turn on Gas or Electricity until I order them to do so. You may therefore expect the city to remain in darkness for an indefinite time.

I request all citizens to remain at home from darkness until daylight every night until order is restored.

I WARN all Citizens of the danger of fire from Damaged or Destroyed Chimneys, Broken or Leaking Gas Pipes or Fixtures, or any like cause.

E. E. SCHMITZ, Mayor

Dated, April 18, 1906.

ALTVATER PRINT. MISSION AND 22D STS.

"This is my house," Genthe said. "I live here. We're just going in to drink a bottle of wine."

"A bottle of wine?"

"To celebrate the occasion."

"What occasion?"

"The earthquake."

"Oh, it's an occasion, is it?"

"Don't you think it's an occasion?"

"You goin' in to drink wine or to have some fun with that girl?"

"Salaud!" cried Grasse. "Mind your tongue, or I'll have a word with your officer."

"My what?"

"Captain Andrews."

"Oh, he's a son of a bitch," said the soldier.

"Then mind your manners, and stand out of the way," said Grasse, still angry.

"You got a key?"

Genthe produced a key and opened the door.

"You can only stay a minute," said the soldier. "I'll go in with you."

They all trooped in, the soldier last, slinging his rifle and bumping the bayonet on the door frame. Genthe lit a lamp. The house was small but tastefully furnished and neat. Genthe's two cameras were standing against the wall on their tripods, the big wooden Eastman for the four-by-six plates and the smaller stereo camera with its twin-goggle lenses. The studio was adjoining, on the other side of the kitchen, and the laboratory was at the rear of the house.

"I'll go get it," said Genthe. "It's in the cellar."

"Don't leave this room," said the soldier.

"I've got to go get the bottle."

He was suspicious. "Where's this cellar?"

"Right here. The door's in the kitchen."

"All right. But I'm watchin' you."

He stood in the kitchen, where he could keep an eye simultaneously on Genthe in the cellar and Herma and Grasse in the parlor.

"Why are you so anxious for people not to enter their own houses?" Herma asked him.

"Looters." After a moment he added, "Anyhow we're blowin' this whole block up."

"If you're going to blow up the house anyhow, what do you care about looters?"

He had nothing to say to this.

Genthe came up the stairs with the bottle. He searched around in the kitchen until he found a corkscrew, then he came out into the parlor carrying the bottle, the corkscrew, and three glasses. The soldier came after him carrying a fourth glass.

"Think I'll join you," he said.

Genthe opened the bottle and filled the four glasses. They drank silently. Genthe picked up the bottle and examined it, regretfully. There was only a little more than a glass left in it. He set it down on the table again, and the soldier picked it up and looked at it.

"Say, this is not bad. What is it?"

"Johannisberger '68."

"Must be one o' them German wines."

"That's right," said Genthe.

The soldier drained the rest of it without bothering with the glass. Then he threw the bottle into the corner.

He said, "Now get out of the house. They're goin' to blow it up."

"*My* house?" Genthe seemed dumbfounded. "Wait a minute. I've got to go into my lab for something."

"Out. Or I'll have to shoot you, see?"

"But what about my plates?"

"You can eat out of your hand." He herded them out of the house onto the sidewalk and away down Van Ness. Genthe didn't bother to lock the door behind him.

It was later; perhaps the same evening. Genthe had disappeared to try to find Mayor Schmitz and get permission to go back to the house for his plates. Herma and Grasse were going up Gough Street, with the fire a few blocks behind them. A line of soldiers was coming down the street toward them, every third or fourth soldier carrying a lantern. They were going systematically into each of the houses on the street; the lanterns could be seen glimmering in the darkened rooms. A pair of soldiers came out of a house leading a thin-faced and grimy man by the arm. Other soldiers came up to him and bound his wrists behind him with a piece of wire. One pushed him roughly. They led him down the street to a place where some householders, forbidden to light fires in their kitchens, had built an impromptu campfire in the street and were cooking soup. In the light of this fire they pushed the grimy man against a wall. He blinked, looking at the fire and then at the soldiers. The soldiers backed away from him and a couple of them raised their rifles. The two sharp reports rang out almost simultaneously. The grimy man slumped and fell on his face, then rolled over on his back.

The soldiers slung their rifles and went on down the street. After a while a man sitting at the campfire got up and went over to look at the body. He stared at the face for some time. Then he came back and sat down at the fire.

"He ain't from this neighborhood," he said.

A little farther down on Gough a crowd had collected. The roof of a house had caught on fire from embers drifting from the main conflagration only a few blocks away, south of Golden Gate Avenue. The fire had eaten down through the ceiling and was now showing at the windows. A pair of soldiers were standing in the small crowd watching it. Herma recognized them as the same two soldiers who had shot the looter.

"Nothin' to do," said one soldier. "This whole block's goin' in a couple of hours anyway."

They all stood for a while watching the flames licking away.

"Ain't ole Missus Parsons still in there?" said someone.

"Not if she has any sense. She'd come out."

"She can't git up, since she had her stroke. She can't do nothin' but lay in bed all day."

"Her daughter takes care of her, I think," said a woman. "Her daughter probably took her out."

"The daughter's kilt," said a man. "A wall fell on her down on Howard."

He hesitated for a moment. Then he moved toward the door which was hanging smoking on its hinges, stuck his head in, and entered.

He came out almost immediately.

"Whole place is on fire in there," he said.

One of the standing soldiers crossed his legs. The other shifted his quid of chewing tobacco from one side of his mouth to the other.

"Canaille!" roared Grasse. He lowered his head and charged into the house like a bull. After a while he came out with an old lady in a nightgown slung over his shoulder like a bag of grain. He laid her down on a mattress in the street, pushing aside a woman who was resting on it.

"Is they anybody else in there, Grandma?" somebody asked her.

"There's the baby," she twittered feebly.

Grasse rushed back into the burning house.

Perhaps that night, perhaps the next night, Herma became separated from Grasse. Not conscious of lack of sleep, but feeling oddly floaty and weightless as though her feet were not quite touching the ground, she went more or less aimlessly through the blackened city. A strange thing had happened that she couldn't quite grasp. By this time the fire had marched across the city like an invading army, burning everything in its path. Somehow she must have passed through this line of fire, and yet she had never noticed when it happened. She was on the blackened side of the city now, no longer on the intact side; in fact there was almost no intact side now that the fire had burned its way through North Beach and all the way to the waterfront. But when had this happened? Perhaps it was when she was asleep, she thought. But she hadn't slept, as far as she could remember. Perhaps she had dreamed.

Another thought occurred to her as she wandered through the streets in her gown by Worth of Paris and her velvet cloak. All her other clothes were burned, and so were Fred's clothes. Worse, there were no more mirrors. Without mirrors, she couldn't . . . it was not that she wished to *become* Fred, but that she wanted a mirror so that she could *say* something important to Fred. She wasn't quite sure what it was. It was about Death. About Death and Love.

A good deal of time had elapsed. She must have slept at some time or another, but she couldn't remember it. As far as she could recall, she hadn't eaten anything either, although this hardly seemed possible. Perhaps the people at the campfire on Gough Street had given her a little of their soup. At any rate, it was the fourth day now and the fires for the most part had burned themselves out. A few columns of smoke could still be seen standing in the sky out beyond Telegraph Hill, but nobody paid very much attention to them. The fire had roared its way in a single angry afternoon through the central business district, leaving the iron skeletons of skyscrapers and a few stone buildings with the glass broken out of their blackened windows.

Herma found herself on Post Street coming out into Union Square. It was a little after dawn on a morning that promised to turn into a beautiful and clear sunny day. The air was crisp, with an acrid but not unpleasant smell of smoke and dampened ashes in the air.

The refugees from south of the Slot, driven away from the Square the day before by the fire, were now beginning to return, bringing their various bundles, now tattered and blackened from being dragged around the city for three days. During the night a ramshackle city of improvised tents and shacks had sprung up on the grass around the Dewey Monument. The Square itself seemed hardly touched by the fire, although the leaves of the trees were singed here and there. A fine gray dust of ashes lay over the grass and everything in the Square, but the people, ignoring this, had spread around their mattresses, their cots, their tents, and their makeshift huts contrived out of boxes and tin signs, with burlap for doors.

There was a carnival quality to the scene, along with a certain air of the lunatic. In the center of the Square an old man was, with great deliberation, trying to decipher the inscription on the Dewey Monument through spectacles from which the lenses had fallen out. Another man, in pink pyjamas and a pink bathrobe, and carrying a pink comforter under his arm, was wandering around barefoot on the gravel path, trying to find a place to put down the comforter so he could go to sleep on it.

The sun had risen enough now to illuminate the blackened hulk of the St. Francis Hotel on Powell Street, but the rest of the Square was still in shadow. The air was chill. A number of people had built open fires and were warming themselves by them. Others had improvised stoves out of rubble, sheet metal, and pieces of stovepipe salvaged from the ruins. Herma stopped to warm herself at one of these rustic kitchens. It belonged to a family of a dozen or more, from babies to an octogenarian great-grandmother, who were somehow managing to live together under a square of canvas stretched on four poles with burlap hanging down for walls.

At one side of the tent Herma caught sight of a basin of warm water and a bar of soap standing on a plank supported on two sawhorses.

"That's what I need."

She hadn't seen a mirror for four days but she could imagine what she looked like. A great lust for soap and water swept over her. People stared as she washed her hands and face in the basin. The water had been used by several persons before and was the color of weak coffee, but it didn't matter, it was warm, and most of the dirt came off her face. A woman, evidently the wife of the family, silently passed her an old blanket end to use as a towel.

Herma said, "That feels good."

The whole family had turned to watch her at these ablutions. They all smiled at one another. Herma felt almost as though she were a member of the family. She passed the improvised towel back to the woman.

"What you had to eat lately, Sister?" asked the woman, not in a kindly voice exactly but in a matter-of-fact monotone.

Herma lifted one eyebrow and made a noncommittal motion of her shoulders.

The woman got out a fork and stuck it into the cauldron seething

on the improvised stove. She came out with a boiled potato, the jacket
still hanging on it in scraps.

Herma took this and sat cross-legged on the grass to eat it. It was
hot and burned her fingers at first. She passed it rapidly from one hand
to the other. This made everybody smile again. Herma smiled too. Then,
her hunger overcoming the pain of the burned fingers, she broke the
potato apart and began eating it. It was delicious. She finished it to the
last scrap, including the jacket, and then licked her fingers. She found
a morsel or two that had fallen into the skirt between her knees, and she
ate these too. Once again there was a round of smiles.

Everyone sat around on boxes, on chunks of rubble, and on the grass
watching Herma eat the potato. It occurred to her that she ought to offer
them some money for it, but she had only the gold pieces in the pocket of
her cloak. She should have brought along some of the silver dollars as
well, she thought.

"Would you like another potato, Dearie?" the wife asked her.

Herma shook her head.

"There's enough potatoes if you want one. We ain't got much else."
She hesitated. "There's a little milk we're savin' for the children. You
could have some of that if you want."

At this suggestion, Herma only glanced at her and then looked away.

The woman seemed very anxious that Herma should have enough
to eat. Perhaps it was because she recognized her as a lady, or perhaps
it was merely her sense of hospitality. This was her home, even though
it was only a canvas on four poles, and Herma was her guest. Or perhaps
it was something about Herma's youthfulness, her slim and virginal
simplicity, her air somehow in spite of her soiled clothing and grime of
having passed through the debacle of the city unscathed, that drew the
woman toward her.

"My husband, he's got a little brandy," she said hopefully. "Warms
you up. I don't hold with it myself. But maybe you'd like a drop."

Herma shook her head again, still smiling. A child perhaps three,
the grimiest and dirtiest child that Herma had ever seen, crawled a little
closer on the grass to get a better look at her. She sat there staring
straight up at Herma's face. Herma was glad she had washed the face,
at least after a fashion.

"What's your name?" she asked the child.

The child stared straight back at her, solemnly, without a word.

"Do you like boiled potatoes?"

This time the child nodded faintly, still watching her out of her
large white eyes in her dirty face.

The husband, a man about thirty who looked as though he might be
a workman or a porter, rummaged around in the box under his feet and
pulled out a small battered accordion. It only had a dozen or so keys,
and a few buttons on the other end, and the bellows in between was
patched with tape. He stuck his hands into the straps on either end and
began playing it softly. He played so badly that for a while it was hard
to tell what he was playing. Herma seemed to recognize it vaguely.

Finally she identified it as the Barcarolle from *Tales of Hoffmann.* He played it very slowly, groping his way from note to note as though he were doing something very difficult, like shoeing a horse.

Herma began humming along softly under her breath.

"Belle nuit, ô nuit d'amour,
Souris à nos ivresses . . ."

The wife stared at her, suddenly transfixed.

"Sing it, Girlie! Go on and sing it out loud!"

A little louder, in mezza voce, Herma continued on to the end.

"Nuit plus douce que le jour,
O belle nuit d'amour!"

"Them ain't the words I know," said the husband.

Everybody smiled at this too. Since the husband knew no French, they seemed to agree, it was natural that he shouldn't recognize the words as the words he knew. In a cracked and off-key voice he sang his version. "Lovely night, oh night of love, oh lovely night of love."

A youth in elegant but filthy clothes—tight-fitting black trousers, a shirt with lace frills, and black polished pumps that were scuffed and stained with ashes—came up and impatiently snatched the accordion out of the husband's hands. He laughed aloud. Facing Herma, he began playing, in galloping tempo and not without a certain expertness:

"Ta ra ra boom-de-ay,
Ta ra ra boom-de-ay."

After a moment everybody was singing it, the various cracked voices and even the piping treble of the little ones, the husband trying to follow along, always a few notes behind, in his scratchy growl.

"Ta ra ra boom-de-ay,
Ta ra ra boom-de-ay.
Ta ta ta boom-de-ay,
Ta ra ra boom-de-ay."

By this time a crowd had collected, some standing around solemnly watching and others grinning. When everyone seemed to have enough of this simpleminded chant, the youth in tight pants set off into *There'll Be a Hot Time in the Old Town Tonight,* which he played even faster, still with his grin.

"*Please, oh, please,* oh do-not-let-me-fall,
You're all mine and I love-you-best-of-all,
And you must *be my man,* or I'll have-no-man-at-all,
There'll be a hot-time, in the old-town, to-ni-i-ite."

This produced a rattle of laughter and some raucous shouts. A voice called out from somewhere in the background. "Hey. Ain't that Herma?"

But it was not the Herma of the triumph at the Opera House that they recognized; it was the Herma of the song that was on everyone's lips.

"Kiss me a-gain!" cried out a voice.

The request was repeated in a clamor of voices, with laughter, and then more clapping. Finally Herma had to get to her feet. The grinning boy gave her a bar or two, and off she went, mounting up from the low G into the clear and sentimental melody in the middle register.

"Sweet summer breeze, whispering trees,
Stars shining softly above;
Roses in bloom, wafted perfume,
Sleepy birds drea-ming of love . . ."

The crowd was utterly silent now, hanging on her every note, some smiling faintly, some expressionless. Almost as though they were in church they listened through the long second verse, and then into the chorus again. The last note swelled to the end with its coda, the last "Kiss me a-gain," and the accordion note died away.

There was a silence. Then a cheer went up from the tattered and hungry people in the Square, waiting for the sunlight to creep slowly over from the burned St. Francis and touch them a little with its warmth. The skeletons of the burned skyscrapers looked down on them. They could be rebuilt, they would be rebuilt. San Francisco was not an old city. There was nothing old in it, nothing that was irreplaceable. It was not like a European city. It was all new, they could build it all over again. They had built it once, and they could build it again.

Herma left the Square on Post Street, turned left on Dupont, and went on up the hill toward Chinatown. After she passed Bush she entered into a kind of wasteland, a level expanse of black and acrid-smelling cinders still smoking in places. The houses and buildings in this part of the city were for the most part flimsily constructed of wood; they had withstood the earthquake but when the fire passed over them they burned like tinder, collapsing into their network of cellars and underground dens. Nothing was left but the checkerboard of streets ascending the hill with squares of ashes and cinders between them, a stove or a burnt-out iron safe sticking up here and there. Only Old St. Mary's Church, with its blackened brick walls and bell tower, was still standing at the corner of California.

A little farther along Dupont she turned down the narrow lane that descended the hill and curved gradually to the left. She had difficulty getting her bearings. All the familiar buildings were gone. Finally she identified the gnarled and blackened limbs of the pine tree that had shaded her once as she rang the bell and stood waiting on this spot. Of the porcelain shop, and the house behind it, there was no sign. The level expanse of cinders and broken rubble stretched off down the hill toward Montgomery Street and the burnt-out business district. Then she saw something sticking up a little: it was the stump of the ancient fig tree that had stood in the garden.

She stood looking at this for a while, then she went back up to Dupont and wandered up and down the street, skirting around the heaps of ashes and cinders, stared at by an occasional Chinese youth or a pair of soldiers with slung rifles. Everything made by human hands had been devoured by the flames. Oddly enough it was the trees, here and there, that had survived. In Portsmouth Square, by some miracle, the straggling elm trees were still standing in the spring sunshine, a little scorched at the edges. The shabby old Chinese gentlemen in black clothes were still sitting around on benches in the sun, exactly as though nothing had happened.

Herma went on slowly across the square on a diagonal gravel path. The square was built on the side of the hill, and she climbed down a short flight of stairs and came out onto the lower part of it toward Kearney Street.

Then she stopped and stood motionless, staring. One of the Chinese gentlemen, seeming as old and shabby as the others and almost indistinguishable from them, was Mr. Ming.

She stood there looking at him for some time. After a while she became aware that he had noticed her too and was looking back at her with a fixed expression, as though he were not at all surprised to see her standing there. It was a look of acceptance—not a smile exactly but a placid look—as though what had happened was in the ordinary manner of events and something that no reasonable man would be surprised at.

He didn't, however, make any gesture or say anything to her, feeling perhaps with his Oriental delicacy that under the circumstances she would prefer not to recognize him.

"Mr. Ming."

He smiled a little and still said nothing. The other Chinese gentlemen, having taken note of the Foreign Devil lady standing in their midst, turned away and went on with their droning and singsong conversations.

Herma took Mr. Ming's elbow and lifted him from the bench. He got reluctantly to his feet.

"Isn't there some place we can go? Just to have a talk," she added smoothly in a matter-of-fact tone.

He still wore his fine gray silk tunic and skirt, in place of the black of the others, but under the dust that covered it the difference was hardly noticeable. His face too seemed gray, whether from the ashes or from some other cause.

He shook his head. "No, there is nothing. As you can see."

With an oddly hieratic gesture, as though it were a ceremony, he pointed around at the level expanse of cinders where Chinatown had been.

With her hand still under his elbow she pulled him gently away. They climbed up the short length of stairs, and at the top of the square they stopped. Here there was a short length of stone wall to sit on, blackened by the fire. Fragments of soot and scraps of burned paper clung in the cracks between the stones.

"Mr. Ming," said Herma.

He looked at her questioning, waiting.

"Your porcelains? All your fine things?"

He looked down and found a flake of gray ash clinging to the silk of his tunic, and flicked it away with his fingernail. It settled to the ground and disintegrated into dust as it touched the pavement.

"Poof." He smiled. "Everything is gone. All the things of this world are cobwebs. A breath can destroy them. Every person of wisdom knows that."

"And what else is there?"

"Nothing."

"And what will become of you now?" she asked.

"Once I had nothing. Now once again I have nothing. That is not important," he told her. "What is important is that a promise I made to you I will now not be able to keep."

"I don't understand."

"I will not be able to marry you. Because now I have nothing. My house, my riches, my fine things, everything that I had to offer you is gone. I am like these other gentlemen, sitting in the sunshine, passing their time in talking about nothing while waiting to die."

Herma didn't explain that she had never intended to hold him to any promise of the sort he described. This wasn't the time to go into that, perhaps. She thought for a moment.

"Do you have friends? Isn't there someone . . ."

"There are the members of my Tong. We are loyal to one another. But they have nothing either, so now we are alike." Here he turned away from her and looked down at the old men sitting in the square. "When all have nothing, it is not so hard to bear. And perhaps they will build another Chinatown. But that," he added, "will be after my time."

Then he turned toward her again. "I have said that I have nothing, dear child. But that is not quite true. I have an inestimable treasure. It is the treasure of what you have given me. A foreigner, and an old man who had ceased to hope for the love of a woman. That memory is more precious to me than all my porcelains."

He still did not quite look at her directly. Sitting on the blackened stone wall with his arms folded, he stared at the square before him, at the knots of dusty old gentlemen in their conversations, then at the hill falling away and the Bay beyond.

Herma stood up. Mr. Ming seemed not to notice. When he said nothing, and did not move, she knelt in the ashes, bent forward, and touched her lips to his forehead. Then, reaching into her cloak, she took out the gold coins and slipped them into his pocket. He seemed about to remonstrate; he turned his head toward her and began to lift his hand. She hurried away up the street, without looking back, before he could follow her.

Turning left on Dupont, Herma went on down the hill through the blackened and leveled remains of the Chinese quarter. There was almost nobody on the street. Here and there a Chinese was scraping in the heaps of cinders, looking for some scrap of treasure in his ruined house. At the corner of California, under the blackened wall of Old St. Mary's, a Chinese boy came up the sidewalk toward her. He was neat and clean, dressed in blue trousers and a tunic she recognized as that of a telegraph boy.

"Missy Helma?"

"Yes."

"Missa Beck Wat, he send launch along you."

"Mr. Beckworth has sent a launch for me?"

He nodded.

She studied him for a moment. He seemed an intelligent boy, calm and with great self-possession. He spoke only when necessary, when she asked him a question.

"But who are you?"

"One time I job boy Nine Stolly House."

"You used to work at the Palace Hotel."

He nodded. "But Nine Stolly House he fall down. Now I job boy teleglaph office, chop chop message in all place city. Teleglaph he fall down," he went on to explain. "Then fella put him up again. Now message come from all place to teleglaph office."

"The wires have been repaired, and now telegrams can be received again."

He nodded.

"Where is the launch?"

"Long watta. You come me, I take you."

He set off through the city, at not too fast a pace so that she could follow him. At Sacramento he turned left, going on down the street through the half-wrecked banks and office buildings of the financial district. During this journey, which took a half an hour or more, he spoke only once. As though a thought had occurred to him, he turned to her and asked curiously, "You flend Missa Ming?"

She smiled at him for a moment. Then she said, "Yes."

He had nothing more to say. They went down Sacramento and came out presently at the waterfront. Here he turned left again and led her a little way down the Embarcadero. At the same wharf where Caruso and the others had left only four days before—it seemed like an eternity —a launch was waiting. Perhaps it was even the same launch, although Herma wasn't sure. It had the same tall, spindly funnel, and the boatman was the one she seemed to remember.

"Miss Herma?" he called up.

"Where's yer bags?"

"I haven't got any."

"Well git in then."

She turned back to the boy and felt down into the pocket of her cloak. It was empty. After a moment's thought she reached up and unpinned the brooch at the shoulder of her dress, silver and green with its tiny design set in enamel.

She held it out to him. "Please take this?"

He shook his head. "Missa Beck Wat, he pay."

Finally she persuaded him to take it. He looked at it, noting the tiny scarlet fruit with its pair of green leaves, the details almost too fine to make out without a magnifying lens, and said without a trace of expression, ''Stlawbelly.''

''Yes,'' she said. ''It's mine. I want you to have it.''

He didn't say anything to this. He didn't thank her. He just stood there holding it somewhat awkwardly in his hand, since there didn't seem to be any pockets in the uniform he was wearing.

Herma, still in her gown by Worth of Paris and her velvet cloak, clambered down a rude wooden ladder into the launch. She took her seat at the stern, exactly where Madame Moellendorf had placed herself four days before. The boatman, ignoring her, busied himself casting off the lines.

''I haven't got any money,'' she told him.

He said nothing for a moment. Then, without turning his head, he said laconically, ''Don't need any. 'Tsall paid.''

Then he went to the small pilot house and pushed open the throttle. The engine began chugging slowly, there was a thrashing under the stern, and the launch turned in a curve and headed out into the Bay. The wharf dwindled away astern with the Chinese boy still standing on it. In only a few minutes the city was receding in the distance and they were out on the open waters of the Bay, calm and yellowish green, with only a slight ripple here and there where the wind ruffled the surface. It was almost noon and warmer now, and the sunlight baked down on the tin roof of the launch. A plume of brownish smoke, filtering from the top of the funnel, was caught by the breeze and drifted on ahead of the launch across the Bay. In the clear sunlit air the Oakland Hills were virginal and green in the distance. Beyond them lay the great capitals of the world with their museums and monuments, their theaters and opera houses, the cities of marble and gold she had dreamed of in her secret reveries and seen only in books. *Da capo, ma più forte!* After the childish awakenings in Santa Ana, after the triumph and exaltation, the suffering and smoky visions of San Francisco, the third great chapter of her life opened before her. *Where's yer bags*, the boatman had asked her. She had nothing, not even a coin in her pocket. Everything was ahead, everything was new. What was behind was only a web of ephemeral shadows, like the blackened city dwindling away on the insubstantial shimmering surface of the Bay. She felt wonderfully free and light, powerful and capable of anything, as though she could fly, or convert herself into a thousand Ariel shapes to enchant the princes and monarchs of the world. She chanted to herself under her breath.

> ''Sì. Mi chiamano Mimì,
> Ma il mio nome è Herma.''

With a final glance at the tower of the Ferry Building behind her, standing like a Venetian campanile in the greenish water, she turned her face to the East.

III. PARIS

1.

And now here she is—it has all happened, just as Mrs. Opdike and Madame Modjeska had prophesied years before—although neither, perhaps, would have imagined the degree of her triumph or the uniqueness of this precise moment that seems to hang, infinitely prolonged, like a drop of water about to fall into some limpid and virginal reflecting pool. She stands in the wings of the Opéra in Paris, waiting for her entrance cue. And it is she who is the prima donna, or rather— and this is the uniqueness of it—she is to sing all three of the leading roles in this complicated pageant of Offenbach which everyone, or almost everyone, said could never in the world be sung by the same soprano. Now she is Herma, but in a moment she will become, one after the other, the three heroines of the *Tales of Hoffmann*. The first is easy : Olympia is only an automaton, a mechanical doll that poet Hoffmann falls in love with because he is deluded by some magical spectacles. Giulietta, the second, is a little more demanding : a Venetian courtesan as cynical as she is enticing, who steals Hoffmann's mirror-reflection under the orders of her sinister master, the magician Dappertutto. And then Antonia, a German maiden for whom to sing is death—driven by her love for Hoffmann, she sings, and dies. And the musical demands of the three parts too are formidable : the first role a tinkly and mechanical coloratura, the second a richer, more intricate lyric part with passages as demanding as the "Dite alla giovine" of *Traviata*, the third the most complex of all, beginning with a simple art song and ending in a dramatic, almost Wagnerian love-death sung in duet with the ghost of the mother. To do these three things in a single evening is like playing concertos successively on the violin, the piano, and the bassoon. Now all Paris, that most exacting and cynical of audiences, sits out there in the great crimson and gold auditorium, waiting to see if she can do it. She is confident. She glances out at the lighted stage and remembers : Herma can do *any thing* that she wants.

She smiles to herself at her doll-like Olympia costume : a short satin skirt with a crinoline and lacy knickers, a bodice covered with large jeweled butterflies, and an improbable golden wig in rolls like German sausages. Bright red lip rouge, two red circles pasted on her cheeks, and false eyebrows of black wire. To top it all, a little golden crown no larger than a teacup. Around her the chorus stands in various negligent attitudes, waiting for their own entrance which will come a little before hers. To her right are the stagehands keeping an eye on the curtain ropes, and high overhead the scene-shifters, in shirt-sleeves, stand looking down from their posts among the pulleys and winches.

Out on the stage, which is set as an opulently furnished scientist's studio, Hoffmann is in the middle of his love song "Ah! laisse éclore ton âme." He has already become enamoured of Olympia in his glimpse of her through the window, not realizing that she is only a mechanical doll. Hoffmann is sung by Wladislaw Czermak, known to everyone from the Director down to the stagehands as Vladi, a veteran workhorse of the Opéra who perhaps doesn't resemble a young German poet very much, but is capable of singing everything from Siegfried to Rodolfo, has a repertory of thirty roles, and never makes a mistake.

Chaliapin appears and introduces himself to Hoffmann in his powerful basso.

> "Je me nomme Coppélius,
> un ami de Monsieur Spalanzani . . ."

He empties out a sack of magic eyeglasses and offers to sell Hoffmann any that he likes. Putting on a pair—they are three ducats—Hoffmann raises a hanging and looks out into the wings, catching sight of the fair Olympia and deluded by the magic glasses into believing that she is real. "Chère ange!" he cries in anguish. "Est-ce bien toi?" (Herma makes a face at him in an effort to make him smile, but to no avail; Vladi is an old hand at such tricks.) Now the chorus, shepherded by an overworked and sweating chorus master, pushes out through the drapes onto the brilliantly lighted stage, leaving Herma alone in the wings. They begin their minuet, while Herma gives a last touch to her sausage-curls and presses the red circles on her cheeks to be sure they are going to stick. The stage manager, watching Spalanzani and Hoffmann, has his hands raised ready to point to her for her cue.

Then the moment comes, the drop falls at last into the waiting pool, and Herma circles out onto the stage in a stiff little pirouette. In his quavering buffo Spalanzani announces, "Mesdames et messieurs, je vous présente ma fille Olympia."

A great "*Ahhhh!*" arises from the chorus of guests on the stage. Still turning, Herma can see nothing. Then, the pirouette ended with a flash of the skirt, she sees before her the great gilded auditorium with its mass of faces—the men in black with white shirtfronts, the ladies in white or pastel—all pointed toward her like upturned flowers. The spectacle is dazzling, even though she can see it only imperfectly over the glare of the footlights. The five tiers of boxes in the ornate Italian manner seem carved of pure gold, heavy with statues, caryatids, and intricately worked friezes. The brilliance of this gilt contrasts luxuriously with the deep wine color, almost a purple, of the velvet hangings and upholstery. The flowerlike faces follow her as she moves across the stage, pirouettes again, and comes to a stiff and graceful little stop facing the orchestra.

So far she has sung nothing. But now a harp is dragged onstage, Spalanzani sits down at it, and—wound up by the servant Cochenille—the Doll does her little trick. Hoffmann stands entranced, watching her through the spectacles provided by the evil Coppélius—for in opera all basso parts are villains. The Doll Song, in truth, doesn't amount to much and could almost be sung by a real mechanical doll, except that the trick is precisely to appear to be mechanical and yet at the same time, somehow, human and charming. She trills it out lightly and jerkingly, to the harp continuo.

> "Les ois-eaux-dans-la-char-mille,
> Dans-les-cieux-l'astre-du-jour,
> Tout-parle-à-la-jeune-fille
> Tout-parle-à-la-jeune fille
> D'a-mour!"

It is a classic coloratura aria in the high register, a frail vibrato waltz. There is a faint note of parody, even when Olympia is singing it properly, but this effect is easy enough too, since Herma privately believes it is a rather silly piece. When Olympia's spring begins to wind down she falls into an exaggerated tremolo in head voice, on the edge of the comic. "A-a-a-h . . . a-a-a-h . . ."

Cochenille, unseen by Hoffman, dexterously winds up the spring in her back. Out of the corner of her eye she sees the prop man, in the wings, spinning a watchman's rattle to make the mechanical creak. Now she again attacks the trills, the succession of little Pekinese-like yips, with her old vitality.

> "Ah! voi-là-la-chan-son-gen-til-le,
> la-chanson-d'Olympia, d'Olympia!"

Building higher and higher in the rapid cadenza of trills, she rises finally to B flat, but sinks like a wounded bird as the spring weakens again. "Ah. Oh. Oooooh . . ."

After being wound up once more by the agile Cochenille, she lilts her way with ease through the rest of it—"voi-là-la-chan-son-mig-non-ne" and so on. Hoffmann is still entranced. The stagehands have stopped what they are doing and are watching from the wings. Even the audience seems a little bewitched; they are perfectly motionless and silent—intent. Probably they are just hoping for her to crack a note. Parisians! The cruelest public in the world, if they catch you in a single weakness, a single false trick. The devil with them! All she has to do is sing the part. In the final coda of trills she goes up to the C, then the E flat in alto, before falling in a long graceful swoop to the A flat four notes below—even that a needle in the chest for some sopranos. The high E flat is perfect—flutelike and effortless, exactly on pitch, held for a long and excruciating moment before the precisely controlled drop to the tonic.

Applause. But it doesn't last for long, the orchestra resumes, Hoffman sings his "Ah! Mon ami! Quelle accent!" and he and Nicklausse exchange their little recitative over the last rattle of clapping. The harp is dragged away and the chorus streams offstage to the waiting supper. It's over. She has done it. Herma, from Santa Ana, has sung a lead aria at the Opéra, before a première audience of the cream of Paris society. The act goes on; she is seated on a divan, and Hoffmann sings his little serenade ("How many things I have to say to you, O my Olympia, let me admire you"). She has nothing to sing now, except an inane "Oui oui" at intervals, which she can do while thinking of something else— especially since the part calls for her to show no expression and simply to gaze into the air with a vacant smile. She feels a triumph—behind the vacant smile there is a real one, which fills her whole body like the warm and fulgent grace that is left after love. Brava Herma!

So this—a lead in the Paris Opéra—is the pinnacle, most would agree, although some would contend that musically speaking La Scala is a touch above Paris, or even perhaps the Staatsoper in Vienna. But for the French repertory—and Offenbach is French of the French, in spite of his slightly comic Rhenish name—no soprano can be said to have arrived until she has stood on this stage, facing out onto the five tiers of gilded boxes, and bent this exacting, jaded, and malicious audience to her will with a perfect performance. Herma had never lost her confidence—she had always known she could do it, even if others had doubted now and then. Yet it had not been easy to arrive at where she was at this instant. To sing Tosca, or the three parts of the *Tales of Hoffmann,* years of study and hard work were necessary—years of squalor and disappointment, of singing coaches hired with a dollar scraped together here and a dollar there, of bad parts in pickup touring companies, of newspaper critics who offered in shabby dressing rooms to go to bed with her in shabby hotels they knew just down the street. "Fred!" she wrote in the note she stuck into the mirror in Cincinnati. "Get that lizard off my back or I'll scratch out his eyes." And Fred, overworked, scrawled back, "What am I supposed to do, go to bed with him myself?"

Then, finally, came the first transatlantic telegram—an offer of a part at the Lyric in London—a minor part, but one she knew perfectly. So, after a quick crossing in the *Saxonia* (tourist class—no bath and no mirror—Herma made the trip alone), there she was, warbling the Canzonetta at the drab English clerks and their pudding-colored wives.

> "Voi che sapete
> che cosa è amor,
> donne, vedete,
> s'io l'ho nel cor."

But by this time Fred knew better how to handle the critics, so that instead of offering to go to bed with Herma they accepted his invitation to dinner at Ciro's, with brandy and a cigar afterward. He was learning his business, she had to admit that. The reviews spoke in passing—since she was not yet the prima donna—of the "California nightingale" who had trilled Cherubino so charmingly.

Still, the Lyric, of course, was not yet Covent Garden. But then came other second leads, on the Continent, and in better and better houses—the San Carlo in Naples, the Châtelet in Paris, and even a bit part at the Opéra; the Théâtre de la Monnaie in Brussels, the Verdi Festival at Parma. It was at Parma, in fact, that there occurred the humiliating little incident that—turned inside out—was perhaps the beginning of the prima donna roles. The humiliating part was that she was obliged to do Flora in *Traviata,* while a plump local sexagenarian, got up to look like the Spanish Armada in full sail, sang the "Dite alla giovine" that she knew so well. If the thing turned inside out, it was that she at least had the satisfaction of reading the next day in the *Corriere della Sera* the no doubt deliberately ambiguous comment, "It is possibly the young American who ought to have done Violetta, and not the familiar Bellancini, of whom it must be said that the best she has to offer is behind." Somehow this clipping must have winged its way like a bird across the Atlantic and found its way to New York, for it was only a month later that the fateful cablegram arrived:

"OFFER TWO THOUSAND DOLLARS THREE PERFORMANCES MIMI APRIL REPLY SOONEST BECKWORTH."

And so on the Mauretania to New York—this time in a double first-class cabin with connecting bath, even though it cost a good part of the two thousand dollars she was to earn. Beckworth, who met her at the pier, was cordial but businesslike—when she thanked him for the launch in San Francisco, he pointed out that he had never paid her for singing Violetta the night of the earthquake and wrote her a check on the spot. And Caruso—a plump and easy-going Rodolfo who sang the part almost with his hands in his pockets, so to speak—treated her precisely as he treated all his opposite leads—helpfully, with courtesy, and absolutely without favoritism, as though she were someone he had sung a single performance with, a number of years ago—which of course was exactly the case. When Fred offered him a cigar he took it, and he treated Herma to a lunch at the Knickerbocker, all with perfect correctness, a Neapolitan charm which was totally professional and at the same time natural and sincere. And he never forgot a voice—he told her, "I hope, carina, that since San Francisco you have learned to sing la voix dans le masque."

It was Caruso himself, pushing aside the director, who drilled her in the pathos, the gentle poignancy, of the final duet with the orchestra playing the love theme softly behind it—"Have they gone? I pretended to be sleeping so that I could be with you. There is so much to say." Mimì coughed and expired, much as in *Traviata,* even though in less elegant surroundings. And Caruso demonstrated again that most sexy of all sounds, a catch of emotion on a high note, in his last broken sob —"Mimì! . . . Mimì! . . . ." Herma, sitting on the rehearsal stool opposite told him, "Be careful. Don't bring down the chandelier." But he didn't smile. Evidently the memory of San Francisco was not a joke for him.

For the opening night, even though it was the tail of the season, the Golden Horseshoe was almost full with its usual brilliant audience of New York's Four Hundred. Only Mrs. Astor's box, the famous number seven, was empty—the Dowager Queen of New York society had died the year before. But all the others—the Vanderbilts and Drexels, the Iselins and Havens—were there, in their starched shirts and diamond stud-pins. And, as Herma waited in the wings for Rodolfo to finish his "Nei cieli bigi," the stage manager whispered to her, "The composer is in the house." Herma said nothing. She only smiled to herself, the composed little fixed smile she had learned from Madame Modjeska. The stage manager waited for the cue, then he raised his arm and pointed at her. Herma knocked on the scenery, or rather a stagehand knocked for her. Opening the prop door, she entered timidly into Rodolfo's garret.

Caruso took her hand. "Che gelida manina!" he sang soulfully, his brown eyes rolling. "Se la lasci riscaldar."

After the Fourth Act was over, after the applause and the curtain calls, after the Diamond Horseshoe was empty and the sweepers began knocking away on the stage with their brooms, an odd silence descended over the Met. The small intermittent sounds that came through the walls only made the building seem emptier. Herma sat before the mirror in her dressing room removing her makeup, or pretending to—in reality she was waiting. Outside the door there were voices, snatches of conversation, as singers in street clothes and musicians carrying their instruments made their way along the corridor toward the stage entrance. Yet she lingered. She *knew* somehow he would come. She took a towel and slowly wiped away the pale deathbed makeup from her face, then dipped her fingers in cold cream and began working it upward from her throat into her cheeks.

Her dresser wanted to go home. "Your street dress, Miss?"

"Not quite yet."

A touch of rouge. As Mama used to do—rubbing it in so there was really no trace of color left, only a faint pinkness left by the friction of the fingers. And a hint of color on the lips, with a tiny brush. She set her hands on her face, lifted her cheeks upward and backward, and gazed into the mirror with its frame of bright electric bulbs. There were two taps on the door.

"Come in."

The door opened. A gentleman entered, not in evening dress but in a dark English sack suit with a neckcloth and pin in place of a cravat. Above this the turned-up points of a white collar were visible. He had a large head, a broad intelligent brow, and a calm, slightly skeptical manner. His mustache and hair were long but neatly trimmed. He had both hands in his pockets and a cigarette in his mouth.

He closed the door, then he took out the cigarette and said in a heavy Italian accent, "Good evening. Pardon me to intrude. I am Puccini."

"Piacere."

"Ah. Parla italiano. Benissimo." From then on they spoke Italian.

"You sing well, Signorina, at least in a light part."

"Grazie tanto," she said with an irony that was evidently not lost on him, to judge from his expression. She turned back to the mirror, took up the towel again, and began carefully wiping her forehead along the hairline.

"Is it true you can ride a horse?"

"A horse?" She laughed. "Of course."

"Have your manager come to me. Signor Ee-tay. I understand that he handles all your affairs. I am staying at the Waldorf."

"Very well."

"Shall we say ten?"

"D'accordo. Alle dieci."

"Buona sera, signorina. A nice Mimì. Not perhaps the finest Mimì I have ever heard, but perfectly adequate. For an American," he added as he politely closed the door.

In the room at the Waldorf, one end of which was dominated by a grand piano with some manuscript paper strewn about on it, he wore the same dark-gray suit and white collar, and his shoes were immaculately polished. He smoked incessantly, lighting a new cigarette from the last half inch of the other before he crushed it out. The saucer by the keyboard of the piano was overflowing with stubs. He got up from the piano, took the cigarette out of his mouth, and examined Fred from across the room.

"Parliamo italiano. Bene?"

"Bene."

They went on in Italian. Fred's accent was not as good as Herma's, but he made fewer mistakes in grammar.

"This little girl of yours . . ." Puccini began. He used the word *fanciulla,* a rather poetic term, which might almost be translated "maiden."

Fred didn't care for the way the conversation was starting. He said nothing and waited for him to go on.

"Rico says she is the only soprano he knows who can ride a horse."

"Ride a horse? Altro! She's a regular cowgirl."

"What is needed is a soprano, not a cowgirl. But she has to ride a horse."

"On stage?"

"Please don't rush me, young man."

Puccini paused again, and seemed to study him for a moment before he went on. He drew at the cigarette and then removed it.

"Have you seen Belasco's play *The Girl of the Golden West?*"

"No. I never go to the theater."

"I first saw it a number of years ago, in 1907. I came to America to see three plays of Belasco—*The Music Master, The Rose of Rancho,* and *The Girl of the Golden West. The Girl of the Golden West* is a beautiful play. It moved me very much. It is like a Sicilian drama of passion and betrayal—an American *Cavalleria Rusticana*. You know, the great American opera has not yet been written. And we are tired of waiting for some American to write it.''

Finding some ashes on the elegant gray waistcoat, he stopped and brushed them away meticulously. ''Excuse me,'' he explained with an air of genuine concern, ''this suit was made in London.'' He went on. ''It is like an American *Cavalleria Rusticana*, except that with the immensity of the land, of the setting, the theme is enlarged from the merely pathetic —even though I have a great respect for my friend Mascagni—to the tragic.''

''Melodramatic, perhaps. It ends happily.''

''I thought you said that you had not seen it.''

''All American stories end happily.''

''Ah, vero? Then perhaps this is why you do not have an opera. You will notice that I always kill my heroines. Manon, Cio-Cio-San, Mimì. Verdi does the same. The mark of a second-rate composer, like Leon-cavallo or Mascagni, is that he kills his heroes instead of his heroines.''

He stopped, lit a new cigarette from the old one, and crushed out the stub.

''The great West of your country interests me. I have never been West, but I have read so much about it, I feel I know it thoroughly. It is a grandiose setting, a setting fit for a great work of art. In 1907 I bought the musical rights of *The Girl of the Golden West* from Belasco. Now''—he pointed to the littered piano—''I am working on a draft of it, from a libretto prepared for me by Zangarini in Italy.'' He puffed at the cigarette and sat down at the piano as though he were about to play. Then he got up again. He strode about the room restlessly.

''I am fed up with these frail heroines and their cose piccole, their little things. *Manon, Bohème, Butterfly* and company. Ce ne sono stufo. I want now a drama of love against a vast and dark background of primitive characters and untrammeled nature. Not an American *Caval-leria* but an American *Tosca*, with a heroine to match the great moun-tains of the West. Could she strike a man to the heart with a knife, do you think, this sopranino of yours?'' He took up a letter opener from the table and stabbed an imaginary Scarpia.

''Ecco il bacio della Tosca!''

he sang in a warm and not unskillful baritone, with a deep note of passion. ''That is a heroine. Could she do that, your little soprano?''

''On stage at least,'' said Fred a little nervously. ''She has sung Tosca, in Naples. And she's not a sopranino, by the way. She can sing mezzo if necessary, and also go to F in alto.''

''Benissimo. Let us call her the fanciulla, then. *La Fanciulla del West*. Have her come and we will go over a little music together. Can she come this afternoon, do you think?''

''Of course.''

''Unless,'' Puccini added quickly, with a concerned air of wishing to be correct in everything, "she is afraid of being in a room alone with me."

"Not unless you are afraid of being in a room alone with her."

Puccini smiled, politely.

In the afternoon he was dressed in exactly the same way—perhaps it was the only suit he had brought to America—except that for some reason he had added a hat, an immaculate pearl-gray fedora. The fastidiousness of his person was in sharp contrast to the confusion and disorder of the hotel room. Containers full of crushed-out cigarettes stood about everywhere; some of the stubs had fallen onto the carpet. The remains of a room-service lunch were resting on the floor in a tray. The piano, with its lid down, was covered with manuscript sheets, in places piled three or four deep. Some of these too had slipped off onto the emerald-green plush carpet.

"Eccomi," said Herma.

Walking about nervously with his cigarette, puffing it now and then, he examined her.

"You are very slim and slight, my dear. Are you sure you get enough to eat?"

"It's because of the lemons. I have five lemons for breakfast, ten more for lunch, and I shampoo my hair with lemons. Everything is lemons. That is the secret of my voice," she told him with a perfectly straight face.

"Ah, vero?" He lifted his eyebrows. "Well, in any case both Rico and your manager Signor Ee-tay assure me you can ride a horse, so evidently you are strong enough for that. Signor Ee-tay says you are a veritable cowgirl."

"I'm a singer, as a matter of fact. It so happens that I can also ride a horse."

"That is exactly the way I put it to him. The singing is first." He ruffled through the heap of manuscript papers on the piano, dropping cigarette ashes all over them. "The heroine, Minnie, is the girl of the camp. However," he added quickly, "she is quite pure. She falls in love with a bandit named Johnson. A fine fellow really."

"I had a real Aunt Minnie. She was a pioneer. She crossed the plains in a wagon and fought the Indians."

"Ah," said Puccini. "Then it's a real western name?"

"She was born in Naples. Her name was really Gelsomina."

"Ah, così." He seemed a little disappointed, or bemused. Plainly he had to do with a queer creature here. "Well, try this, will you. It's only a draft."

He finally found what he was looking for and sat down at the piano with it. Herma looked at the manuscript over his shoulder. It was scrawled over with totally illegible hieroglyphics, the notes huddling together in places like frightened sparrows, at other places soaring off across the page, the lines falling and rising like a sea in storm. The whole manuscript was covered with erasures, ink spots, and smudges from the composer's lunch. The notations seemed to be in a totally un-known language, perhaps Egyptian. One phrase she could make out; a line was crossed out angrily and "merda!" written above it. There were no indications as to who was to sing what.

"This is Minnie's song from the First Act." He set his fingers on the keys and played a few bars. "La, di tum tum tum. *Poesia!*" he roared in a heavy baritone. "That's your cue by Rance, the villain. Then you start in with 'Laggiù nel Soledad.' "

She tried it, while he stared at her face rather than at the music which he knew by heart.

"Laggiù nel Soledad, ero piccini,
Avevo una stanzuccia affumicata,"

and so on. When she came to the "merda!" scrawled above the line she sang it, in place of the "bella" which was crossed out below. "Mamma era merda, aveva un bel piedino."

He stopped. "Are you playing tricks on me?"

"Well, I can't read your writing."

"I don't understand American humor. I believe I have a sense of humor, but the American sense of humor is different. It says, 'Mamma was beautiful and had a pretty foot.' Never mind the merda."

She went through it again. It was a nice little song, ending with a certain touching emotion as it soared up to its high C in the last couplet:

"Si amavan tanto! . . . Anch'io vorrei
Trovare un uomo: e certo l'amerei."

He had nothing much to say. He lit another cigarette and crushed out the old one. He said "Va bene," which was not exactly "That's fine," but simply, "All right, let's go on."

He ruffled through the piles of manuscript looking for something else. "Later in Act One there's your 'I'm only a povera fanciulla' song. I can't find it. Never mind. Later, toward the end, Johnson has an aria in which he tells them, 'Let her believe I am free and far away. Don't tell her how I died.' They're about to hang him. I haven't written that yet. I'm still in the second act. They don't hang him, however, because Minnie comes in galloping on her horse and saves him. She says, 'All you boys love me, and think of all I've done for you, so don't hang him, but let us go off and start a new life.' I haven't written that either. All we have here is a few rough notes. Try this."

He found another sheet and propped it on the piano.

Herma stared at it. "I can't read it. Is that an A flat in alto?"

"No, that is a piece of anchovy." He brushed it away. "This is the duet of Minnie and Johnson, their farewell to the miners before they leave for their new life. It's still very rough. I haven't really written it yet. I'm not sure whether it should be keyed in E flat or in E. Can you sing up to the B natural?"

"Of course."

"Well, try it then. This draft is in E flat. You'll have to transpose

up a half note. Farewell beloved country, farewell my Nevada, mountains of my Sierra, addio!''

''But the gold fields are not in Nevada.''

''Ah vero? Ma dove sono allora?''

''They're in California, of course.''

''I'll have to write to Zangarini.''

She took the sheet from the piano and tried to make out the chicken
scratches. Seizing the pen, she crossed out ''Nevada'' and wrote in
''California.''

''Ahimè, an extra syllable,'' he complained. ''I have to put in a
note.''

''Well, I would think a great composer could put in one little note.''

It was easy enough. He divided a quarter-note into two eighths.
Then she sang it, in a crystal and vibrant tone, even though in mezza
voce.

> ''Addio, mia dolce terra,
>   Addio mia California!''
>   (and there it soared up to the high B natural)
> ''Bei monti della Sierra, o nevi, addio!''

Puccini smiled, his hands still resting on the keys. ''Beautiful,''
he said.

He worked at it all summer and through the fall, while Herma was
vacationing at Stresa and later singing Cherubino at the Scala. The
première, at the Metropolitan in December, was the event of the New
York season. Puccini and Belasco were both present. The cast was a
glittering one, with Herma as Minnie, Caruso as Johnson, and Pasquale
Amato as the Sheriff Rance; the conductor was Toscanini. And when
Herma galloped onstage, on a palomino borrowed from a circus act, and
dismounted to the miners' cries of ''Minnie!'' the house broke up into
a roar that finally brought the audience to its feet. (''Upstaged by a
horse,'' Caruso muttered to Herma as she clung to the noose they were
trying to hang him with.) At the final curtain the shouts of ''Brava!
Bravi tutti!'' (''Bravo cavallo!'' cried some clown) were mingled with
insistent calls for the composer. Puccini, taking the stage for his own
bows, was overwhelmed first by the cast and then by the audience, which
clambered over the footlights to shake his hand and embrace him. ''I
was never so much bekissed in my life,'' he told the press later in the
evening. The papers the next morning, in addition to pointing out that
Puccini was Italy's most eminent composer and had a Rolls Royce, a
villa at Torre del Lago, and another at Viareggio, also praised Herma
with warmth. The *Times* critic gave the impression that he was not
quite sure who she was, but nevertheless commended the Met for presenting this American opera in its première performance on an American stage and with an American prima donna. ''One hopes that Minnie's
Addio in the last act will be only a temporary one,'' he concluded, ''and
that this new diva sprung from our native soil will return to the Met

many times to sing this role so haunting in its Puccinian melodies and yet so American in its optimism, its declaration of independence from the decadence and world-weariness of the European musical theater.''

Yet Herma knew, and Fred knew, and perhaps Puccini himself knew, that the music was not as great as all that. The opera owed its success, or its fad, perhaps, most of all to its setting, and to the figure of its slim and boyish heroine—frail and yet audacious, quintessentially American in the confident and slightly gauche verve of her manner—a cowgirl with a range of three octaves and the faultless tessitura of a Melba. Puccini may have written the music, but it was Herma who caught the imagination of the public. She *was* Minnie, in the popular mind, and it was a long time before anyone else dared to sing the part.

So she sang the *Fanciulla* everywhere in those next two seasons— Genoa, Vienna, Covent Garden (at last), the Fenice in Venice, Aix, La Scala, Toulouse, even Buenos Aires and Melbourne. When she came into Maxim's in Paris the band automatically broke into ''Addio California.'' And the horse (only at Covent Garden would they not allow the horse; there was a clop-clop in the wings, reminding Herma of Mr. Earl Koenig's coconut shells, and she strode onstage stiffly as though she had just dismounted) shared almost equally in her popularity, especially in Argentina, a nation in which there is even more enthusiasm for horses than there is for women.

By the end of the second season Herma was growing more and more weary of the whole business—the stupid libretto in which everyone incessantly shouted ''Hello! Hello!'' on all occasions in the belief that this was the way to speak English, the music in which the only good aria was the tenor's ''Ch'ella mi creda''—and especially the horse, which was a bother to make enter on cue and which frequently misbehaved on stage. (She knew now what Puccini had meant by writing ''merda'' on the score.) It annoyed her that, when she came into Maxim's and the band struck up, people shouted ''Minnie!'' instead of ''Herma!'' Was she going to have to spend her whole life playing this ninny of a cowgirl just because she was an American? Did Melba have to spend her whole career on stage with a kangaroo because she was Australian?

Finally one afternoon in Verona she lost her patience. She sent out for some beautiful glossy writing paper and, when it came, she seized a sheet of it and scrawled, ''Fred, sono stufo di questa Minnie. She makes me throw up. I've had enough!'' She jammed it into the mirror. Then, all this anger having made her hot, she got into the tub and took a cool bath.

''Just chase the buffalo and let the chips fall where they may,'' he wrote her on the mirror the next day. Still, Fred thought, he too was getting fed up (she should have written ''stufa'' instead of ''stufo''— she could never get the grammar right) with all these miners and sweaty horses. More important, it was not getting the girl anywhere. Never was there a famous diva who owed her career to her skill as an equestrian.

Some other feat was needed—equally striking but more musical—something like Caruso singing Chaliapin's basso part. Herma could sing higher than anybody else, but so could every soprano. It had to be something more—some feat of virtuosity, something athletic that no one else could do. Like singing a trio singlehanded (it could be done with phonographs) or playing three parts in the same opera, with lightning costume changes between the acts. It would take some thought. Paris, La Scala, or the Staatsoper? De l'audace, encore de l'audace, et toujours de l'audace! Try for the top first. He went to the post office and sent a telegram.

> "MEYNER OPERA PARIS HERMA AVAILABLE NEXT
> SEASON MAJOR ROLE ONLY FANCIULLA EXCLUDED."

In Paris rumor had it that Pol Lloiseaux, the Artistic Director, had a notion of doing the *Tales of Hoffman* in the coming season, if he could find the sopranos for the three leads. Meyner, the Directeur en Chef, was not very enthusiastic about the idea. Too expensive, the sets were elaborate and you needed three prima donnas, and people were tired of Offenbach. Nothing was settled yet, and even if they did the *Tales* the casting would take place only in September.

Herma, as soon as she was moved back into her apartment in Avenue Kléber and unpacked, went out to the Café de la Paix with Lloiseaux, who was an old friend of hers. As they settled into the table on the terrasse she was annoyed to hear the band break into "Addio California" just as it did at Maxim's. This was Fred's work—he went around bribing Chefs d'Orchestre. Still, it was pleasing that the waiter, without being told, immediately set in front of her a Fraise Herma, perfectly made, with a large and symmetrical strawberry in the middle of it. Heads turned as she poised her spoon over it. She caught a murmur from the next table.

"C'est la Herma."

"Ah, ça c'est formidable. Cette glace! C'est comme la Pêche Melba, tu sais. C'est la nouvelle sensation."

"Ah, mon ami, tu sais, à Paris on a la nouvelle sensation chaque jour."

"Oui, mais quand même . . ."

Lloiseaux, who overheard it too, traded a smile with her. Herma carefully scooped around the edges of the glistening hemisphere with her spoon, to the dying strains of Johnson's and Minnie's duet. "Addio, mia dolce terra, addio, mia California." How she hated that finale with its banal high B. And yet for some reason she felt her eyes brimming. She took the napkin and dabbed at them. Like Madame Modjeska and her "Last Rose of Summer"! It was stupid. She wasn't a Californian, she was a European, an international opera star. The new sensation, as the Monsieur at the next table said. Home was the comfortable apartment in Avenue Kléber, with the view of the Eiffel Tower and the river. She smiled through her tears, *because* of her tears, at Lloiseaux.

"Tu a quelque chose, ma petite?"

She shook her head. Perhaps the tears weren't for the farewell duet at all but for the ice cream, which tasted exactly like Aunt Minnie's lemon vanilla. It was the nostalgia of Mignon's song: Connais-tu le pays où fleurit les citrons? The land where the lemons bloom is California, Herma.

"Oui! oui!" warbles Olympia for the fifth time, in response to Hoffmann's impassioned declarations. The others are gone, off at their supper, and they are alone on the stage with only Hoffmann's friend Nicklausse as their witness. Seated in a Louis Quinze armchair, her arms arranged stiffly at her sides, she listens while Hoffmann sings his aria. "You are mine! Our hearts are forever united. Ah! say, do you comprehend the eternal joy of hearts at peace?"

"Oui! oui!"

The armchair is set slightly at an angle, so that Herma, wearing her bright doll-like smile, is facing directly into the tiers of boxes at the right-hand edge of the stage. For some time she has been aware of a queer-looking party occupying the box in the second tier. They contrast sharply with the occupants of the other boxes—the select society of Paris in their Sholte dinner jackets, their gowns of Paquin and Vionnet, their Cartier jewelry. These are a more raffish bunch. There are four or five of them, all male. One is an elderly man who is a musician or composer if Herma ever saw one, with a mane of unkempt white hair down to his collar, a tobacco-stained mustache, dark bags under his eyes, and a flowing Byronic cravat. The others are all younger, each in his way with a flair of the bohemian. In contrast to the society people, who are chattering and gazing at others across the theater with their opera glasses, they are watching the opera intently. The most striking of them, perhaps, is a pale and curious person like an oriental sorcerer, with a black beard and black-rimmed eyes. Or a Persian prince; there is something refined and exotic, slightly decadent, in the contrast between the pallid face and the eyes so dark they almost seem rimmed with kohl. This person is dressed in an extraordinary costume. Not only is he wearing a fur coat over his evening dress, but he is wrapped in a white shawl and seems to have a blanket or robe over his knees, even though it is a mild evening. Because of the arrangement of the theater, with the tiers of boxes extending to the edge of the stage, he is only a few yards from Herma. Their glances meet for an instant. He smiles faintly, then goes on watching with his intent and skeptical and yet penetrating expression.

Hoffmann, having finished his "Ah! laisse éclore ton âme," seizes Olympia's hand and presses it. She stands up, still with her fixed little smile. Hoffmann, beside himself with delight, follows her as she parades stiffly around the stage in circles. Spalanzani, appearing with the chorus of guests, urges her to dance, and she falls into Hoffmann's arms.

"Oui! oui!"

To the tune of a demented waltz they circle the stage, fly off into the wings, and reappear again dancing at a madder and madder pace.

Hoffmann falls exhausted into the armchair, and Olympia, still whirling, disappears into the wings with the velocity of a cannonball. Behind the flat, in the semidarkness, she stops and turns back toward the stage.

"Whew!"

She exchanges a smile with the stage manager. Her part in the First Act is over. A few yards to her right the prop man, with a little machine turned by a crank, produces an appalling sound of exploding springs. Olympia is no more; the Doll is broken. "Un automate!" cries Hoffmann in anguish from the stage. The chorus sings their mocking little lament. "Ah! ah! ah! ah! ah! ah! It is shattered! shattered! shattered!"

The stage manager watches the chorus. From where he stands he can't see the conductor. He catches the eyes of the two stagehands waiting by their ropes. At the exact moment the chorus finishes he raises his arm and points. Curtain!

2.

The Second Act: Giulietta. Blechmann, the property manager, has provided a real gondola, an eighteenth-century one borrowed from the Ca' Rezzonico in Venice. It rolls on a carriage with noiseless wheels, and is drawn across the rear of the stage by a cord attached to a windlass apparatus. The gondola is a macabre and beautiful thing, a kind of black coffin with dark damask cushions. In it Herma is sitting with Maggie Teyte, who sings the role of Hoffmann's companion Nicklausse. Madame Teyte is dressed in elegant tight-fitting silver breeches, an embroidered coat, and a short wig. Herma is in carnival costume: a black domino and a filmy black and white gown with a bouffant skirt. Her wig—it cost four hundred francs at Bodin's in Avenue de l'Opéra and she paid for it herself—is Titian blond.

The gondola with its occupants waits offstage while the orchestra winds its way through the sinuous overture and into the Barcarolle theme. The full orchestra gives way to a harp continuo, and the stage manager raises two hands, one to Herma and the other to the man waiting at the windlass. The gondola moves forward. Herma stretches her mouth into the voix dans le masque—and now she really is wearing a mask, even though it is only a domino over the eyes.

"Belle nuit, ô nuit d'amour,
Souris à nos ivresses!"

A funny little thought occurs to Herma—something she has forgotten for years—the man with his broken accordion in Union Square, singing, "Lovely night, oh night of love." The Barcarolle, in fact, is about as difficult as a Baptist hymn. In the second chorus Madame Teyte joins in, in a somewhat fuller and more mature voice on the edge of the mezzo. Privately, to tell the truth, Herma and Madame Teyte are not on very good terms at the moment—Herma is jealous of Madame Teyte's tight-fitting breeches, and Madame Teyte is even more annoyed because Herma has been given the lead in this act even though she herself knows the part thoroughly and has sung Giulietta a dozen times. However, as they glide into view on the stage, they gaze soulfully at each other.

Madame Teyte has the easy part of the duet—Herma finds a way to suggest this by the expression on the lower part of her face, as they gaze at each other through the duet. Giulietta has the melody, and Nicklausse only follows along with her a third lower. However, the whole thing is in a low register—the trouble comes in projecting sufficiently on some of the low notes, not the highs. The highest note in the Barcarolle is only an F sharp, more than an octave below Herma's top, while Madame Teyte—here at the end of the duet—croons away a good deal below her. But she has the range for it and can sing a mezzo part as easily as a soprano. When they finish there is a little rattle of applause from the audience, although this isn't customary.

Hoffmann is intrigued by the fair masked courtesan, but is warned of her false charms by Nicklausse. He begs him to flee—for, should he fall in love with her, the sinister Schlemil, her lover of the moment, would strike him down out of jealousy. "I, love a courtesan?" replies Hoffmann contemptuously. "Beware of spells and dreams," Nicklausse tells him. He warns him that the magician Dapertutto, a second incarnation of his evil demon Coppélius, is lurking on the scene. "I'll be damned if he makes me love her," declares Hoffmann recklessly.

Herma for the moment is offstage, and Chaliapin, at her elbow, is about to make his entrance as Dapertutto. He tugs at his demon costume and adjusts his wicked mustache. Although they are almost touching elbows he doesn't smile at her or show any sign that she is there. He smells of cologne and greasepaint. Why is it, Herma thinks, that she is never particularly fond of bassos? Of course all basso parts are villain parts, but surely it can't be that. There is something—sinister—about being able to sing so low. Bassos can make your bowels vibrate, even when you don't want them to. And of course Chaliapin is a terrible egotist. But they are all terrible egotists. She, Herma, is a terrible egotist. And as for Maggie Teyte . . .

Her hand on the curtain, she pushes it aside an inch. The hussy is still out there in her silver breeches, pretending to be a pretty youth. Her masculinity, Herma thinks, is not very convincing. Her breeches not only go all the way up her legs but a little beyond, into the vulva. A clearly visible crease shows when she faces toward the audience. The hypocritical bitch; she pretends to be so cool and English. Herma, waiting in the wings, is having a raging fit of her professional disease. Well, let her play Nicklausse in her circus tights. And to the devil too with Chaliapin, with his Russian-bear manners and his arctic aloofness. She, Herma, is Olympia, Giulietta, and Antonia—one diva in three parts, a Holy Wonder, a thing never before seen at the Opéra and declared

impossible by Meyner the manager. And that was not easy to carry off.
Even with Fred's help, and Lloiseaux's.

When she came back from Verona to Paris that summer it took
Herma a little while to realize that Lloiseaux had had all along the notion of casting a single soprano for the three parts of the *Tales*. And
even, perhaps, that he had secretly thought of Herma for the role—
although it was more likely that it was the timely arrival of Fred's
telegram that had put this idea in his head. She had met Lloiseaux
several seasons before, when she first came to the Continent and had
sung Oscar in *Un Ballo in Maschera* at the Opéra. It was a small part
—just a page who announced people—but Lloiseaux had noticed her,
offered her tactful advice, and took her sometimes for an apéritif in
the afternoon to the Café de la Paix, where he always sat at the same
table at the end of the terrasse, in the winter behind the removable
glass partition.

It was all perfectly innocent—Lloiseaux was a respectable gentleman in his sixties, even though he was a kind of wraith of a man, all
bones and odd angles, with a piercing eye and a shock of electrified hair—
something, in fact, like a character of E. T. A. Hoffmann. His eccentricities were celebrated. He walked in a kind of swoop like a flying
bird, and he said "morbleu" or "ma foi" in every other phrase,
usually at the end of the sentence. He also had characteristic gestures:
one in which he *waved* an idea toward you with both hands as though
he were wafting a spirit through the air, and another in which he stroked
a quite imaginary beard, which seemed to end about six inches below
his chin, to judge from the point where he stopped stroking.

But who wasn't a little eccentric, in this unreal and slightly fabulous world of the opera? At least he seemed harmless—avuncular was
the word, although he made a very queer kind of uncle. The innocence
in their relations persisted even though she once entertained him in her
room at the Hôtel Scribe, where she stayed in those days when she was
in Paris. The circumstances were that there was a piano in her room
and he wanted to show her something about Amelia's part in the *Ballo,*
and not her own little Oscar part. Why not go to the Opéra across the
square, which was full of pianos, and why should he want to tell her
something about Amelia's part? Herma didn't ask. There were many
mysteries about Lloiseaux. Only a few things one could be sure of—
that he had an impeccable ear, a prodigious memory, and the cunning
of a fox; and that when he did something there was always a reason
for it.

It was possible, of course, that he wished or hoped to seduce her.
If so, he seemed to be waiting for her to make the overture—a notion
which made her smile. Or—leaving the crassly physical out of it—that
he had fallen half in love with her, in a sentimental and innocent old
man's way. Perhaps he just liked to be around pretty young girls, and
this was why he had spent his life in the theater. At any rate, even in

the privacy of the hotel room, he seemed to be not fond of her so much as friendly—he behaved with perfect correctness, accepted the cup of tea she offered, and demonstrated in a kind of hummingbird squeak how Amelia should do her love duet with Riccardo. (Herma took the tenor part—it was a circus and finally they broke up laughing.)

But then Lloiseaux, gazing around and sipping the last of his tea, set the cup down and said in a surprised tone, "But my dear, why do you live in a hotel, parbleu?"

"It's very convenient. It's just across the square from the Opéra, and there are two rooms with connecting bath so that—Fred can be close at hand," she concluded awkwardly and coloring a little, as though he were about to ask her why it was necessary to take baths with one's manager.

But he didn't seem interested in her ablutionary habits. "But you can't entertain here, ma foi. And above all, it is not the thing that a prima donna should do. She should live with panache. She should have her own establishment, and it should be in the proper quarter, somewhere around the Étoile, parbleu."

"But I'm not a prima donna yet."

"You can do lead parts. You've just sung Riccardo," he joked. "The point is, you *will* be a prima donna, and it is necessary to prepare for the role. For life is an opera too, in which we play roles, and people will believe in us only if we play them properly, morbleu. People may say, 'Who is Herma? A singer who stays at the Scribe.' Or they may say, 'Who is Herma? Ah, la diva. I've been to her place in the Étoile quarter. A fabulous afternoon.' "

"But I don't have enough money for an apartment."

"How much does the Scribe cost?"

"Two hundred francs a week. And an apartment, at least a thousand."

"Ah," advised the old fox, who knew Paris thoroughly, "but you mustn't rent one, you must buy one. In the end it's cheaper. And, if you pay eight thousand francs down, the payments will be only five hundred a month, which you can easily afford. It's a sound business." He scratched his electric hair. "If there should be a war—and it seems likely, with all these Austrians and Serbians rattling their sabers in the Balkans—property values will rise, and you will surely gain by it."

"But I don't have eight thousand francs."

"I will lend it to you, parbleu."

"But that's ridiculous."

"Life is ridiculous. Take my word for it. I have lived a great deal more of it than you have."

"I know nothing about money," she told him. "You'll have to talk to Fred."

"Why do you want to lend Herma eight thousand francs?" Fred asked him bluntly.

It was the next day and they were in the other room of the suite at the Scribe, across from the connecting bath—where there was no piano, but instead a businesslike-looking desk with papers stuck in the pigeon-holes. Fred leaned back with his feet on the desk. Lloiseaux sat opposite, in a pretentious but slightly shabby armchair of the kind found in hotels.

"Because she has a promising career before her, and I wish to help her in it. In order to be a prima donna—" Lloiseaux waved the idea toward him.

"I know. It is necessary to live with a certain panache. At present, of course, we're only in Paris now and then. We travel all over Europe and live out of suitcases. So we don't need an apartment in Paris. Of course, if she were a sociétaire"—meaning a permanent member of the Opéra company.

But Lloiseaux didn't rise to this bait. In any case it wasn't his decision to make, and he could only advise Meyner in such matters. "All these things will come in time. In the meantime, she needs a base, parbleu." (He spoke of "she" throughout the conversation, while Fred went on saying "we.") "There ought to be some place to which she can return, where she can live between seasons, and where she can acquire friends and become known in society. The only other possible base is Milan. But life is not so pleasant there, it is a more provincial city, and besides she is very well liked here."

"Yes," said Fred. He lit a cigar without offering one to Lloiseaux, who was said to have asthma. After it drew, he said nothing for a moment while he stared at the other man over the tops of his shoes.

"She will need eight thousand to pay down on the apartment," Lloiseaux went on, "and another few francs for furnishings and such things. Say ten thousand, just to be sure she has enough."

"In short," said Fred, "like many others, you wish to set up an opera singer in an apartment. I imagine you will want to pay a visit to her from time to time. Is that it?"

"Ah, ma foi. Everyone will want to come to visit her," said Lloiseaux blandly.

And so Herma acquired the apartment in Avenue Kléber—two bed-rooms with connecting bath, a large salon with a slanting ceiling and a window filling one whole wall—really an artist's studio, except that it faced south and not north—a small kitchenette and a breakfast room, and a nook for the maid if there should ever be one. In the salon there was a Knabe baby grand, a Persian sort of couch with carved feet and an elaborate embroidered spread, a good deal of the art-nouveau furniture that was just coming into fashion, and even a Beardsley print on the wall, just risqué enough to be interesting without offending any-one. Herma had chosen some of these things herself with the help of a decorator, and Lloiseaux the rest. Out through the large window was a view of that tapering and tetrapodal iron monstrosity that dominated the skyline of Paris and was already becoming its landmark—the Awful Tower, those who spoke English called it. The bathtub was carved from a single block of Carrara—like the one in Madame Modjeska's railroad car, Herma remembered. Fred's room, which faced east toward the Bois de Boulogne, had a telescope mounted on a tripod, so in the lack of anything else to do he could spy on the ladies and gentlemen taking the air in their carriages along the Lac Inférieur. Although there were fewer carriages and more motorcars in the streets now—you could hear the rumble even from the apartment, which was on the fourth floor.

There was an electric lift in the building, needless to say—like a sedan chair, or a kind of tiny coffin set upright, made of gilded iron and glass, so small that it would hold only two people, or three if they were very well acquainted. When Herma had her Wednesdays—which soon acquired a certain fame at least in the circle of the Opéra and its followers—the guests had to come up in three or four trips, while the boy who brought the champagne and the other amenities carried them sweating up the rear service stairs.

The Wednesdays caught on. It was just as Lloiseaux had predicted —"Herma? Ah, la diva. I've been to her place in Avenue Kléber. A fabulous afternoon." (Although some of them did say, "Ah, you're Minnie," which made her grind her teeth.) Of course, nobody very famous had come yet—other singers from the Opéra, music students, minor Latin American diplomats, and once the timid Mr. Sienkiewicz, who remembered her from the evening years before at Madame Modjeska's. "It's true that he won the Nobel Prize," Herma told the other guests blithely, "but here he is just our Henry."

Under the circumstances, it was natural that there were plenty of unattached men—that is, admirers. Herma fended them off, adroitly and not without a certain amusement. She didn't care to be courted. She preferred to be the one who chose, and she hadn't found anybody yet that she cared to confer this grace upon. Everyone said that London was the City of Men and Paris the City of Women. There was a good deal to be said for that—the shops, the couturiers, the cafés-dansants and the whole warm, receiving, gay and sun-filled grace of the city were preeminently feminine. Yet there were plenty of men too—otherwise there would have been no point in calling it the City of Women, which implied that it was also the Paradise of Men. Amour—as the French called it in their ambiguous way that muddled the whole matter—hung always heavily in the air. And indeed it was difficult not to be constantly reminded of the subject, with that view out the window of the Tour Eiffel "erected" on the Champs de Mars, "thrusting up," as people said, on the horizon, and seeming to "penetrate" the very heavens. (What brutes men were, Herma thought, as she always had—but now with a complacent little shrug.) Yet she persisted in her "quaint honor" as some poem or other had it. The suitors came, took their glass of champagne and their petits-fours, or the Beluga caviar on English tea biscuits, and departed without ever seeing the riot of pink damask and strawberry-colored velours in the bedroom. The picture in the bedroom was a Fernand Khnopff—a boy scarcely more than a child lying asleep on a fragment of broken Greek temple, while a girl, as naked as he was, bent over curiously to

gaze at him—the strawberry motif of the room caught in the red silken
scarf that hung in the girl's hand. Herma had her secret names for
the two figures in the painting. But she told no one else about them.

In the middle of all this fun for Herma life was not so easy for Fred,
and he was beginning to show the strain. Herma was living as though
she were a prima donna, but she was still getting paid second-lead fees,
and he had to sweat to find the five hundred francs a month for the
payments on the apartment. Dog-tired at the end of the day, he wrote
on the mirror:

> "Twinkle, twinkle, little star,
> Who the Hell do you think you are?"

He was missing in the afternoons when the caviar and the Moët et
Chandon appeared, and meanwhile every morning he was working his
rear off finding her parts and trying to get her name known among
managers, journalists, and critics. When the rumor came that the director of the Théâtre de la Monnaie in Brussels was in town conducting
auditions for a Puccini series, it was necessary for him to bluff his way
past the staff of the Hôtel Lutétia and have a private talk with this
gentleman before the others got to him. She got the job—*Butterfly,
Tosca, Manon,* and *Bohème,* her first leads on the Continent except for
the tiresome *Fanciulla.* He made lightning trips to theaters in the provinces—Strasbourg, Rouen, Bordeaux—and came back the same day, in
time for Herma's performance, perhaps, in *The Magic Flute* at the
Châtelet that evening. He found out how to hire claques and how much
to pay them. Herma toyed with her ice cream in cafés, but he used
cafés to do business in. He made arrangements with the Victor Company
to send over its equipment to Paris so that Herma wouldn't have to go
to New York to do her first records, her "Mi chiamano Mimì," her "Dite
alla giovine," and the Canzonetta from *The Marriage of Figaro.* He
talked Herma, Herma to everybody until every manager in Europe was
sick of the subject and slunk away as soon as he saw Fred approaching.
Yet the name was spreading. Printed on a playbill, it was enough now
to fill a house, at least in Brussels or in Strasbourg.

"The New Melba" was the phrase that came to everybody's lips.
Yet Herma was not quite Melba, even though Fred was careful not to
make any objection when the comparison was made. Melba, Fred admitted, had a sublime voice with a silvery and powerful timbre, and was
superb in certain parts she had made famous and were her acknowledged territory—Juliette in *Roméo et Juliette,* Marguerite in *Faust,*
Ophélia in *Hamlet.* And a large repertory of other things she did—here
he would shrug—well enough. "And of course she's very experienced,"
he would add offhandedly—an adroit reference to the fact that she was
no longer extremely young—which everyone was aware of anyhow.

Herma was not Melba. But she was something else, and in her way
something more. There were many barrel-chested Fräuleins who could
bellow Brünnhilde, many charming birds who could twitter Lakmé, many

specialists like Maggie Teyte who was famous for her Debussy and her French art songs (here Teyte would have gritted her teeth if she had heard him). But Herma could do anything. Name a part and she could sing it, if she had two days' notice, the score, an accompanist, and a répétiteur. She could do coloratura, lyric, and dramatic parts, and sing mezzo for an evening or two if necessary. She had three solid octaves with no strain at bottom or top. Her voice was perhaps not a great voice; still, if greatness might consist of doing many different things fairly well, and even occasionally bringing an audience to its feet in a storm of applause and bravas, then Herma's might be great.

But Herma's voice was not great. Even Herma herself secretly knew this. Did Fred know it? Fred was a promoter, an entrepreneur. His business was to generate enthusiasm. He said many things and ended by believing them himself—"È una diva," or "C'est la nouvelle Melba," all in his confident California twang. So for Fred, Herma's voice was great, when he was talking to somebody else, in a café or in some manager's office. What he thought in his private thoughts—he really didn't have time for private thoughts. He was too busy.

When there was nothing else to do, he went around to cafés passing out the sheet music for the "Addio California" to the orchestra, along with, of course, a small discreet envelope for the Chef d'Orchestre. He used the same techniques, or similar, to disseminate the fame of the Fraise Herma, which was beginning to displace Pêches Melba and Chicken Tetrazzini (and certainly Melba Toast) in the fancy of the public. The large and important cafés—Maxim's, the Café de la Paix, Fouquet's, the Royal—had already added it to their dessert menus. Now it was the turn of the small café in Montparnasse and the outlying boulevards. Fred would come along the sidewalk, glance at the posted menu as though he had an idle quarter of an hour to spend, saunter in with a *Figaro* under his arm, and take a seat on the terrasse.

"A Fraise Herma, please."

"A what?"

(Here an indignant reaction; he took the cigarette from his mouth and looked up from his newspaper.)

"Fraise Herma."

"It's not on the menu."

"Send the dessert chef."

And when he came, the instructions were very simple. "First, a crystal goblet, which must be of the best quality, and without flaw. Then . . ."

Other small and discreet envelopes, of course, had to be passed out to dessert chefs and the like. The goal—which Fred was fast approaching —was a Paris in which the orchestra in every café and hotel would break into the "Addio California" the moment Herma appeared on the scene, and a waiter would come up, immediately and smoothly, to set before her a Fraise Herma constructed to the precise formula. If the strawberry slid off to one side, or if an inferior café tried to palm off caramel syrup in place of apricot glaze—someone would suffer—there would be an uproar.

It was Herma herself who thought of the final touch to add to the now-famous confection. At a late supper at the Ritz with the Brazilian military attaché, after a performance of the *Fanciulla* (bother the stupid thing), she gazed at her apparently perfect Fraise Herma without touching it, and called for Olivier the headwaiter, an old friend of hers by this time.

There was something wrong?

No, she mused thoughtfully, it was that—something was missing. The final touch was lacking somehow. Perhaps if a—what?—a little ring of whipped cream could be added around the rim of the goblet, to hide the place where the ice cream and the glaze melted and blurred together a little . . .

Olivier sent for Clémentin, the dessert chef and the acknowledged master of his trade in all Paris.

Whipped cream?

Yes. That is, beaten cream, so that it becomes solid.

After a little linguistic discussion, Clémentin grasped that what she wished was Crème Chantilly. Herma in her turn explained to him that Crème Chantilly in English was whipped cream, crème fouettée, and Clémentin commented after a moment of thought, with a little smile, "That is a very passionate idea."

So the waiter took the Fraise Herma back to the kitchen, and there Clémentin remodeled it, or rather threw it away, since it was already melting, and made another one, getting out his pastry gun at the end to add a little ring of ruffled Chantilly around the edge of the goblet. This he brought to the table himself. And more—an unprecedented event—he stayed to watch her while she ate it.

The people at nearby tables were looking too, along with the Brazilian military attaché, who had ordered only coffee after the supper but was now thinking of changing his mind. The Fraise Herma was in fact transformed. Now the pale gold hemisphere with its strawberry point emerged modestly and enticingly, as it were, from a lacy lingerie of whipped cream, as though half unwilling to show itself. And when Herma, according to her usual technique, began by daintily lifting away the white frill around the edges of the goblet before attacking the mound in the center, it was almost as though someone were—the Brazilian attaché colored a little and smiled sheepishly. He ordered one for himself.

After this celebrated evening, Herma was shrewd enough to credit Clémentin as the inventor of the confection, and it was so indicated on the menu of the Ritz in its next printing:

Fraise Herma
après la création de M. Clémentin, maître-chef patissier

The casting for the *Tales* took place in September. The production was scheduled for April, toward the end of the season. It was agreed from the beginning that the permanent company would do the minor parts, Chaliapin the basso, and Vladi Czermak the tenor. Meyner insistently held out for three different sopranos to sing Olympia, Giulietta, and

Antonia. His arguments were incisive, knowledgeable, and authoritative. They broke down fundamentally into three points:

1. The first role was coloratura, the second lyric, and the third dramatic, and no one could possibly sing them all.

2. Three divas on a playbill are three times as attractive as one diva. The public gets more for its money, so it believes.

3. If he had one soprano sing all three parts he would have to pay her too much, which would set a bad precedent and damage morale among the other artistes.

Lloiseaux addressed himself solely to the first of these three points, at least in the preliminary stages.

"There is Herma," he said.

"Ah, the famous Minnie. Well, we can do the *Fanciulla* later in the season, if you want."

"She refuses to do the *Fanciulla* anymore, parbleu. She's fed up with it."

(And this was shrewd on Lloiseaux's part, because prima donnas are supposed to be temperamental—as much as managers profess to be annoyed with this—and if they aren't temperamental it sometimes causes doubts as to whether they have any talent.)

Meyner said, "Let her go sing in Milwaukee or somewhere then."

Lloiseaux made his next chess move. He only advanced a pawn, but into a shrewd square.

"At least she could do a magnificent Olympia."

"That I'll concede."

"Of course, to sing Olympia one need only be a walking music box," Lloiseaux went on craftily. "Yet she could do the others too, ma foi. She has an impressive versatility."

"Three sopranos," said Meyner. Lloiseau was crafty, but Meyner was no fool himself, and like everybody else he knew that Lloiseaux had lent Herma money to buy an apartment.

Lloiseaux pretended to surrender ground.

"Giulietta then? And Antonia?"

"Maggie Teyte is available. She will just have finished *Pelléas et Mélisande* at Covent Garden."

"A Debussy specialist. Although a charming woman, I'll admit."

"And we can try Moellendorf for Antonia."

"Ah, ma foi. Is she still around? I thought she had died in the previous century."

"She did a *Tosca* at the Met just last season. And the Countess in *The Marriage of Figaro*."

"Yes, the Countess is what she should always do. There's no singing to the part."

"Pol, I tell you, three divas are three times as many as one diva. And Moellendorf, although I agree she is something of a relic, is indisputably a diva."

"Antonia is not a grandmother," muttered Lloiseaux.

Meyner was hardly listening. He seemed to be gazing at the poster on the Morris column.

"with
WLADISLAW CZERMAK
FEODOR CHALIAPIN
Mlle HERMA
MAGGIE TEYTE
and
ALBERTINA MOELLENDORF
of the Metropolitan Opera Company."

Lloiseaux said, "Well, why don't we try everybody in town, and see who does it best, parbleu." Meyner didn't notice that he said "it" and not "them"—Lloiseaux still had the notion that one soprano was going to do it all.

The upshot was that a kind of audition session took place, more or less as though they were recruiting Conservatory students for parts in the chorus. Meyner sat in the back of the theater with his secretary, who couldn't typewrite but who could answer the telephone in his office and made an excellent Wienerschnitzel—as an Austrian he had a nostalgia for the cooking of his native land. He and Lloiseaux, on the stage, shouted back and forth. The Moellendorf was still in America and didn't attend, even if she had been willing to lower herself to such a demeaning contest, but there was no shortage of sopranos. The wings were crammed with them. Some were in street clothes and some had contrived a makeshift costume or other. Maggie Teyte, in a fur coat and busby, sat in a third-row orchestra seat while waiting for her turn; she refused to mingle with all these second leads and fugitives from the Opéra Comique. There were a half dozen or so contenders for each of the three roles, and in general they all offered the same selections: the Olympias the Doll Song, the Giuliettas the Barcarolle, and the Antonias her "Elle a fui, la tourterelle."

"En avant, tout le monde," said Lloiseaux. "THESE ARE THE OLYMPIAS," he shouted to Meyner at the rear of the theater.

"All right, all right."

They came out one by one and twittered their "Les-ois-eaux-dans-la-char-mille," accompanied by a bored pianist. Teyte didn't compete in this. She sat in the orchestra in her fur hat, buffing her nails with an emery board. As each contender appeared the prompter called out the names from a list. Meyner dictated notes to his secretary. Herma, in her strawberry-colored frock and a bow in her short hair, tossed off the song with élan, almost as though she weren't paying attention. She held the E flat at the end so long that the pianist looked up from his keyboard. Gracefully she curved down to the tonic and ended. Meyner shrugged and made a remark to the secretary. He had expected Herma to do Olympia anyhow.

"Allons, allons, mesdemoiselles. THESE ARE THE GIULIETTAS."

"All right, all right."

Teyte got up, came to the stage with a hand negligently on her waist, and sang a very respectable Barcarolle indeed. It was so beautiful that Lloiseaux across the stage couldn't help humming the Nicklausse part along with her. Without pausing in the song she gave him a meaningful look: Will you shut up? She went on with her "O belle nuit d'amour," but this imprudence of Lloiseaux had thrown her off a little. She stalled slightly on a low note, but got through to the end.

"She probably has a cold," said Meyner. "Are you free afterward?" he asked the secretary.

"Of course."

"Why don't you go on ahead to the apartment. Make some coffee." He glanced at his watch. "Give me the notes. I'll come around after this boring business is over."

"Tina Ferrari!" announced the prompter.

"Who? Ah, the one from La Scala. I didn't know she was in town." He turned to the secretary. "Better, have some champagne sent up."

Ferrari came out onto the stage, in a Titian-blond wig and a well-padded flowing gown. The low notes of her Barcarolle, powerful and vibrant, made the longer strings of the piano thrum slightly. The resonance of her voice gave the impression, almost, that she was singing the Nicklausse harmony part at the same time. Meyner glanced her curiously. "Not bad." He made a note. "Dinner afterward at Larue's, if you like," he suggested to the secretary.

The rest of the Giuliettas were indifferent. They were all competent, but the song was so easy that you could hardly tell them apart.

"THESE ARE THE ANTONIAS," shouted Lloiseaux.

Teyte's "Elle a fui, la tourterelle" was masterful. It was exactly her sort of music: a French art song, melodic but oblique, slightly odd, almost Debussyian. Meyner didn't bother to take a note. Teyte would do Antonia. The last of the contenders was announced as Emma Schweitzer. Meyner had never heard of her. He glanced at his watch again. A quarter after four. Since his position called for him to work at night, he had over many years formed the habit of amour at five in the afternoon. The secretary had already left. He sat alone in the back of the theater, wishing that idiot Lloiseaux would get on with it.

The Schweitzer, a Rhenish-looking Fräulein in a kind of white nightgown and a russet wig, did a surprisingly impressive Antonia. It was almost indistinguishable from Teyte's, but not quite. It was as though she were ingeniously imitating Teyte, or had heard her on a phonograph record. Meyner gave her a four on his scale of one to five. It didn't matter, Teyte would do Antonia.

"THAT'S ALL," shouted Lloiseaux from the stage.

Meyner came forward with his notebook.

"Very well, cher maître. You are the Artistic Director and I wouldn't dream of interfering with your aesthetic judgements. I am only the Dirécteur en Chef, but I will tell you what I think. Herma for Olympia,

Ferrari for Giulietta, and Teyte for Antonia.''

''The decision is of course yours, mon cher ami.'' They were both very polite. They almost exchanged bows. The singers, who were still on stage, stood around in a little crowd listening to this vital exchange.

''Unfortunately,'' Lloiseaux went on, ''the Ferrari was unable to attend, and so Mademoiselle Herma was kind enough to stand in for her.''

Herma, with a bright smile, took off the Germanic nightgown and dropped it on the stage, revealing herself in her strawberry-colored frock. She threw away the russet wig and clapped on Giulietta's wig of Titian blond. Never mind the padded gown. The voice was enough. The pianist, coached in advance, gave her the chord, and she did the song again. ''Belle nuit, ô nuit d'amour,'' she intoned in the lower register, again making the piano strings vibrate a little.

''Pol, is this another of your tricks?''

''Just a quod erat demonstrandum,'' said Lloiseaux smoothly. ''Would you like to hear her do the Tourterelle again?''

''No, don't bother. Very well, you sly scoundrel. Herma can do Olympia and Giulietta. Teyte will do Antonia. It will skew the playbill, to have one do two and the other one. I personally like symmetry. But . . .''

Now Lloiseaux advanced his queen across a board already swept almost bare of opposition.

''But Julian.''

Meyner stared at him suspiciously. ''Yes?''

''You have forgotten about the Nicklausse part.''

''Well, what about it?''

''Maggie Teyte,'' said Lloiseaux simply.

''Teyte is doing Antonia.''

''Yes. Well, Herma could do that too, as she has just demonstrated, ma foi.''

''La Moellendorf could do it.''

''Why not Patti? She's still in her seventies and perfectly healthy.''

''What are you up to, Pol?''

Meyner glanced at his watch again. But Lloiseaux took his time.

''I can give you two good reasons why Teyte should sing Nicklausse,'' he said. ''Her left leg and her right leg.''

Meyner glanced at Teyte. Under the fur coat was a long Paquin gown that came down to her ankles.

''You have beheld these famous limbs?'' Lloiseaux inquired.

''Who hasn't?''

Teyte colored, but Meyner meant only that she had played many breeches parts before and they had all seen her do Cherubino.

''No, it won't do, Pol. We are not hiring legs. She sings the best Antonia.''

Lloiseaux stroked his imaginary beard. ''Julian, an opera company exists to make money, ma foi, exactly like a soap factory. Why should I have to tell you this? It is what you have told to me many times,'' he pointed out with his sly and Hoffmannesque smile. "Imagine—you could advertise Maggie Teyte in breeches in all three acts, and at the same time Herma singing three heroines—an unprecedented feat."

"It's not unprecedented. Gatti-Casazza did it at the Scala."

"Yes, but it was a fiasco, because he tried to do it with his mistress and she made a wreck of all three parts, parbleu. We're going to do it right."

Everybody stood about listening to the discussion. This was the place for Teyte to have a tantrum to show that she had temperament too. It was clear enough what was happening. She bit her lip in the direction of Lloiseaux and seemed about to say something.

"And Madame Teyte of course sings magnificently," put in Lloiseaux quickly. "Nicklausse is an important part. She appears in all three acts and actually, ma foi, sings more lines than the three prima donnas put together. I recommend silver breeches. And very closely fitting. I can even recommend a tailor if you like."

"Our own costume people can do it." Meyner was beginning to feel a little cornered by all this brilliant end game of Lloiseaux, even now after the match was won.

As for Herma, she seethed at the thought of Teyte's shapely calves. With difficulty she retained her bright little smile, playing a doll-like Olympia to Lloiseaux's Coppélius.

"Maggie, my dear," said Meyner tactfully, "how does this strike you?"

Teyte said nothing. She stalked back and sat down in her seat in the orchestra. But she didn't say no.

Meyner turned back to Herma, who had taken off her Giulietta wig and was her slim and adolescent self again. He told her sarcastically, "Why don't you give Monsieur Lloiseaux a great big kiss for what he has just done for you?"

This reminded him of something and he looked at his watch once more. A quarter after five.

And indeed, why didn't she? That is, give Lloiseaux a great big kiss or something. Sometimes this bothered her a little. There was no objection on grounds of—affection. He was sympathique enough. It was, as she always told herself, because it was she who liked to be the one who chose. And in this case it was he who—for some reason—had chosen her as the object of his favor.

And this was where the bother came in. It wasn't his casting her for all three roles of the *Tales* that caused her the twinges of conscience. It was the money he had lent her for the apartment. Because there really were no altruists, were there? There couldn't be. If a person gives you money, it is because he expects something in return—if only the pleasure of an apéritif with you at the Café de la Paix. Which was harmless enough, Herma went on in her helical and constantly ascending coil of feminine logic. And then too, a person might give you money simply

because the act of giving gave *him* pleasure. As you might take pleasure
in giving money to a beggar-child. Herma always gave money to Gypsies
when they came up to her on the street—smiling falsely and pathetically,
the mother kicking the older daughter and hissing under her breath,
''Show the baby! show the baby!'' The Gypsies played out their personal
opera and she played hers—one in which Lloiseaux was her funny uncle,
who sang Amelia in falsetto and gave her coins.

And besides—she told herself, still coiling in her serpentine way
around the subject—Madame Modjeska said you·should always take
money when it's offered you, because it is only for your Art, and Art is
never highly paid enough. And then, Giulietta takes money from men
too, doesn't she?

At the very moment, in fact, Dapertutto is preparing to offer her a
diamond. Alone on the stage, he gazes at the gem. ''Scintille, diamant!
Miroir où se prend l'alouette,'' he booms to himself in his powerful basso.
The lark to be caught with it is Giulietta herself, although she will only
use it to steal Hoffmann's reflection. She watches from the wings, waiting
for her cue. Chaliapin *is* a vain creature. Where a soprano can be vain
about her high notes, a basso has the advantage that he can be vain about
his low *and* his high notes. In this case the low note is the A two octaves
down, at the beginning of the aria, and the high note is the E on ''on
y laisse la vie.'' This is his principal aria of the opera and Chaliapin takes
his time. He lingers over these two feats of the larynx, and does the whole
thing over again from the coda. Then, after a pause, the two chords and
the flourish from the orchestra, Herma's cue.

She slips lightly out from the wings and comes forward, as though
fascinated by the diamond that Dapertutto holds out to her. ''Cher ange,''
he rumbles, slipping it onto her finger.

And what does he require of his servant? she inquires with light
irony.

Only to steal, through the power of the magic gem, the reflection of
Hoffmann.

What! his reflection!

Yes, it amuses him to possess the life and soul of others. He has already done it with Schlemil. ''Je varie mes plaisirs.'' And at that moment Herma understands why Lloiseaux gives her money. Through this
jewel—her voice—he will exert his power over others—he will have his
way with Meyner. For some reason this notion makes her feel even more
affection for Lloiseaux, and even more dislike for Chaliapin.

But now comes something more pleasant—her love duet with Hoffmann, or rather the seduction scene in which he is transported with love
and she is all charm and deceit. Dapertutto slips away and Hoffmann
dashes onstage, having lost everything at the gaming table. Instantly he
falls under the spell of the magic gem. Although she urges him to flee,
warning that his rival Schlemil may ''strike you down in my arms,'' it
is to no avail. She listens, smiling faintly under her domino, while he
embarks passionately into his love aria.

"O Dieu de quelle ivresse embrases-tu mon âme!
Comme un concert divin ta voix m'a pénétré . . ."

Oh, but that Vladi is beautiful! Not for nothing has he sung romantic tenor parts for thirty years. One hand on his breast and the other held out to her, he pours out his heart in a voice flowing with gold and emotion. With an easy legato he soars over the stretches, some of them four or five notes—rising effortlessly to a high E, an octave above Chaliapin's. "Oh! with what rapture you fire my soul!" He has dominated and hypnotized the audience, Herma notices without a trace of jealousy. The coughing and program-rattling stop and every face in the theater is fixed on him. He has even hypnotized *her;* not as Herma, and not even as Giulietta the character, but as Giulietta the singer. For, on the stage, one voice can only enchant another voice, not a person. The character belongs to the librettist, the singer belongs to the composer. (All this Herma thinks behind her mask, in a kind of a trance yet keenly aware of what is going on, while Vladi sings his aria.) Thus the performer, singing and acting, is the creature of both at once and is divided in two. Insofar as she is Giulietta she is the creation of the librettist; insofar as she is a soprano singing, she is the creation of Offenbach. And it is this second creature that is enchanted by the voice of Vladi. "Your glances into mine have poured their flames!" he concludes in his rapture.

Herma waits for the applause to end after the aria. Well, she counters with a sly smile, but Hoffman has lost all his money at the table, and she is—in business. She has a proposal. She enlaces him in her arms and picks up a mirror from the table.

"What I ask from you is your faithful likeness . . . your features, your look, your face . . . this reflection."

"What! My reflection! What madness!"

Yes, she tells him, it can detach itself from the polished glass, to hide itself intact here, in her heart.

"Dans mon coeur! C'est moi,
C'est moi qui t'en supplie!
Hoffmann, comble mes voeux!"

Something has happened, something odd that distracted her. When she came to "Hoffmann" her eye caught a flash from the mirror and she saw—another face—thin, more boyish than Vladi, a shock of hair over the brow, a knowing, somehow ominous smile. A kind of chill passes over her, then she feels hot.

She almost drops the mirror. But she goes on, through the love theme which now becomes a mocking little duet. The reflection! That is her price! It is yours, yours forever, he swears. Herma still feels odd; impulsively she flings the mirror from her and it shatters. This is not in the stage business as planned, but it is a dramatic gesture and there is a little clatter of applause. She and Vladi go on. Now the action accelerates, whipped to a frenzy by the music and by Hoffmann's uncontrollable desire. Hoffmann, going to the large standing mirror at the corner of the

stage, discovers with horror that he has in fact lost his reflection. The
rival Schlemil enters, just as Giulietta has warned, and Hoffmann slays
him in a duel. In the confusion Giulietta has slipped away. The chorus is
heard again in the Barcarolle, now in an ironic tone:

> "Belle nuit! ô nuit d'amour,
> Souris à nos ivresses . . ."

Hoffmann stares. Giulietta glides by in the gondola with the hideous
dwarf Pitichinaccio, smiling mockingly. "Miserable!" cries Hoffmann.

The gondola comes to a stop in the wings and Herma climbs out, adjusting the wig for her curtain calls. "That was a genuine Murano hand
mirror! Where the devil am I going to get another one before tomorrow
night?" complains Blechmann the prop man.

3.

The Third Act: Antonia. The costume is simple, but
charming and a little pathetic: a white négligée, a russet-colored wig with
a soft chignon at the back, and a white ribbon in the hair. Alone at the
harpsichord, Antonia sings a soft fragment of her turtledove song: "Elle
a fuit, la tourterelle." But she must not sing; she is forbidden to sing,
because a secret inward disease lurks waiting in her lungs. For her, to
sing is fatal. Hardly knowing what she is doing, she goes on in mezza
voce. Then, entranced and saddened by the portrait of her mother on the
wall, she breaks into full voice and soars to an A natural on "Tout mon
coeur est à toi!" Will she die of this? No, not yet.

Herma gets a nice round of applause for her Tourterelle. Her father
comes on stage—Councilor Crespel, an old bore. Upbraids her for singing, as he always does. It was the memory of her mother that moved her,
she pleads. He cries out, "That is my torment! Your beloved mother be-
queathed to you her voice!" And also the red spots in her cheeks—the
fatal sign of consumption.

The audience is attentive through all this but a little restive. They
are waiting for Hoffmann to appear. Because, when Antonia sings with
Hoffmann, the motif of the Third Act will emerge in the duet, and the
motif is Death. Nobody but a Doll died in the first act, and only the in-
significant Schlemil in the second. But now it is to be the heroine—that
most melancholy and moving of all spectacles, the death of a beautiful
woman.

Antonia is sent away to her room by her father, and Hoffmann appears, admitted by the comic deaf servant Franz. Hurrying away into
the darkened wings, Herma almost bumps into Madame Teyte in her
Nicklausse costume. Teyte is not in a very good humor. It is true as
Lloiseaux said that Nicklausse appears in all three acts, but in the Third

Act it is virtually a silent part and he only has to peal out "Malheureux!" at the end. For the rest he follows Hoffmann around like a deaf and dumb spaniel. However—since even at the Opéra these little economies must be made—Teyte will also be called upon shortly to simulate the voice of the mother's portrait on the wall. The two of them stand together, only a foot or two apart, in the semi-obscurity of the gallery. Madame Teyte stares at Herma stonily, while Herma only glances meaningfully at the crotch of the silver breeches, which are much too tight to be decent. "Don't miss your cue, my dear," Teyte breathes with a tight smile.

And here it comes. Hoffmann is seated at the harpsichord, strumming the keys and recalling the love song that he and Antonia used to sing together. Herma floats out in her white négligée, and he rises to take her in his arms. Antonia! She pulls him toward the harpsichord, her hand trembling. Accompanying herself, she begins the moving and tender love song, delicate, fragile, yet with its faint suggestion of shadow under the oblique and slightly sinister harmony.

> "C'est une chanson d'amour qui s'envole triste ou folle,
> Qui s'envole triste ou folle tour à tour!"

Triste ou folle! Is it melancholy or madness? "The new Rose smiles at the Spring. Alas, how long will it live?" A moisture blurs in her eyes a little as she thinks of Madame Modjeska's "Last Rose of Summer," and she smiles to herself at this, smiles at the thought of the Rose, smiles at Hoffmann. The tears are really just for the beauty of the music. They don't go deep. She holds the long note at the end of the song, and Hoffmann joins in. "A ray of flame adorns your beauty. Will you see Summer, flower of the soul?" They finish together, Antonia on a beautiful and clear high A.

Silence. Then a disturbing chord from the orchestra. Antonia lifts her hand to her heart and seems about to faint. What is it! Hoffmann starts. Nothing, she reassures him. Hearing her father approaching, she rises and slips offstage.

In the darkened gallery she catches sight of Lloiseaux. He smiles at her and nods. She did the duet beautifully. The ritardando and slight pause on "... tour à tour"—exactly in the manner of Teyte. This phonographic trick probably accounts for part of his smile. As for Madame Teyte herself, she has gone around to the other side of the stage, preparing to simulate the voice of the portrait. The makeup girl appears and quickly repairs the consumptive spots on Herma's cheeks, which are beginning to run a little from perspiration.

Assez! She pushes the girl away to look out onto the brilliantly lighted stage. Hoffmann has hidden himself in the window recess, and Crespel is engaged in a recitative with the sinister and insinuating Dr. Miracle, the third incarnation of Hoffmann's evil antagonist. Chaliapin is wearing the most fantastic of his three costumes: a moth-eaten fur coat, a large beaver hat, and a waistcoat hung all over with medals, watches, bangles, chains, and surgical instruments, like a walking hardware store. The pockets of his coat clank: they are full of necromantic

potions. Crespel shrinks from him. Gravedigger! Assassin! He, a doctor?
Ha! ha! ha! cries out Dr. Miracle, with an evil laugh, and a fanfare
from the orchestra. I have come to cure your daughter.

To kill my daughter, rather, as you killed her mother, rumbles
Crespel. Crespel is also a basso part. The two bassos, Chaliapin and the
hack from the Opéra company whose name has slipped her mind, discuss the matter in the nether region down below middle C. Her father!
The basso whose name she can't even remember. A strange half-forgotten
little pain runs through her at the thought of Papa, dead years ago now
of typhoid, and Mama before him, with her pale and delicate cheerfulness,
her life of sickness and closed rooms. She tries to recall if Papa was a
basso. But to her surprise she can't remember; it is as though he never
had a voice. He couldn't have been a basso, though—he so mild and conciliatory, so tentative, so inept in his gentle bewilderment before the
mystery of Woman, both wife and daughter comprised. And, she thinks,
trying to recall, he couldn't have been a tenor either; he was too old. All
tenors are young, even when they are middle-aged like Vladi. Perhaps
he was a baritone like Germont. Piangi, piangi! And Violetta wept for
Germont, she now knew, and not only for herself and Alfredo. She wept
because Germont—so inflexible in his rectitude and yet so tender and
gallant—was someone she could never love, not even as a daughter loves
a father. It was too late—she had already given herself to Alfredo, and
to her doomed life as a courtesan (her art!). One always weeps for one's
father when it is too late. Now Herma feels real tears welling in her eyes
and seeping down onto the red cheek spots, and this time she doesn't
smile through them. Germont, in her vision, is transformed somehow into
a large blurry shape with a mustache and a derby, who smiles vaguely
and doesn't know what to say to her. Papa at the Summer Social, after
she sang *The Last Rose of Summer*—hanging back at the rear and chewing his mustache, too shy to come forward even though he was a newspaperman, while Madame Modjeska gave her the Double Eagle. And at
the *Marriage of Figaro,* clapping mechanically at the rear of the theater
long after everybody else had stopped—proud and yet bewildered, his
heart full of clumsy male emotion for this prodigal creature he had be-
gotten, gleaming with talent, who was now escaping from his grasp. And
Mama beside him with her proud smile—Mama who was pale and not
well and rested in the afternoon, making her way through life as best
she could with Female Remedies. And then Herma had gone off with
Madame Modjeska and her friends, to enjoy her triumph with the famous
of the world, leaving Papa and Mama to go back alone to the small house
on Ross Street.

Waiting for her cue in the darkened gallery, Herma imagines an
evening at Madame Modjeska's in which Papa and Mama were there too
(but would they have allowed Madame Modjeska to write the note to Mr.
Larkin?), a *Traviata* in San Francisco in which they were present in a
gilded box to hear her sing Violetta (but they might have perished in the
earthquake). She imagines herself telling a reporter with his poised pencil

(this might have been in New York after a performance at the Met), "I owe it all to my Papa and Mama." Papa had paid twenty dollars for the Edison phonograph. It was perhaps a fifth of his salary for the month. And now she makes hundreds, thousands, for a single performance! In francs of course, but it is still a lot of money. The tears well in her eyes again. This is stupid. With an angry toss of her head she shakes them away. Here she is, the star of the Opéra in Paris, dissolving her makeup because she never paid Papa back for the phonograph. It was all Fred's fault anyhow. The very first money she earned he had spent on a bicycle. And then the flying . . . The race in San Francisco! It was a folly. He might have broken his neck. And now Paris . . .

For, just as Herma earned more and more money as she moved from provincial American companies to second-lead roles in Europe to prima-donna parts, so Fred spent more and more on aeroplanes. He quickly found out where they were in Paris—at Issy-les-Moulineaux, just outside the city beyond the Porte de Versailles. There, in a broad grassy field by the banks of the Seine, a pair of corrugated-iron hangars were erected and a half-dozen Farmans and Voisins stood about in the sunshine like lazy insects warming their wings. Fred took the Métro to the end of the line at Place Balard and from there walked the short distance to the field. He now possessed a pair of tailored riding breeches from Lalande in Rue St.-Honoré, Russian-leather cavalry boots, and a leather jacket, and he carried his goggles and helmet in a small kit bag. Along with a thick bundle of francs, which went in the kit bag too, because the riding breeches were too carefully cut to be spoiled with lumps in the pockets.

Not only were the rental fees steep, but a good deal of money went for lessons. He had never really been properly trained, and if he had avoided a serious accident up to now (the pancake landing at the Presidio he didn't consider serious) it had been mainly a matter of luck. Now he settled down to serious training, under the mentorship of Louis Castel-Jaloux, a pioneer flyer who had been a partner of Paulhan but now had a stiff knee from an accident and could no longer fly himself. The Farman trainer, however, was a two-place pusher—it had an odd kind of mono-coque sticking out in front of it, like a canvas boat, and Castel-Jaloux sat behind him with his stiff leg extended along Fred's side, shouting in-structions at him in French with a Provençal accent. Fred began to ac-quire a new vocabulary: *aviation* itself (in America everybody had just called it flying), *empennage, décollage, atterrissage, levier de command* (also called the *manche à balais* or broomstick), *palonnier* (this was the rudder bar), and a number of maneuvers including *virer, faire la boucle, piquer du nez, perte de vitesse,* and *vrille.* This last he had only heard about, never experienced. But he was soon to become acquainted with it.

Castel-Jaloux was a disciplinarian. He began with ground lessons, taught with the aid of a folding blackboard set up near the hangar. Fred was introduced to the mysteries of the Bernoulli effect, wing loading, angle of attack, and lift-drag ratio. The first time they got into the trainer he only allowed Fred to taxi up and down the field, to get the feel of the controls. Before they went in, he told him to give a touch to the throttle and pull back on the stick a little; the Farman rose perhaps a foot off the grass and settled down again, to roll along lurching over the potholes which were almost as bad here at Issy as they had been at the Presidio.

Then the first flight. They always flew in the morning, when there was less risk from the tricky winds that sometimes blew over the field from the river. Fred got in and pulled down his goggles, and Castel-Jaloux arranged himself carefully behind, fitting his stiff leg into place. The mechanic spun the airscrew—once, twice, three times—and there was a ragged roar from behind. The unreliable Antoinette engine had been given up and the Farman now used the vastly superior Gnôme, a rotary which reeked of castor oil and imparted odd gyroscopic qualities to the machine, but was light and powerful and, best of all, always ran, as long as it was supplied with fuel. It made a lot of noise, almost as much as the Curtiss motorcycle engine. Castel-Jaloux had to shout to make himself heard.

"FULL THROTTLE. CONTROLS AT THE CENTER. YOU CAN PULL BACK ON THE STICK NOW."

The Farman rose like a dream, leaving the bumpy grass behind, and all Paris suddenly sprang out and was visible from the open cockpit: the Eiffel Tower to the left, the dome of the Invalides, an excursion boat on the Seine, the two square spires of Notre-Dame, the Panthéon, and the green park of Vincennes beyond. The controls were simple. The broomstick, so-called, was really a light aluminum tubing with a handle at the top like a spade. You pushed it left or right to bank, forward or back to glide or climb. The rudder bar was simply a pivoted board with cutouts for your feet. There was an oil-pressure gauge, a tachometer, and an altimeter calibrated in meters. A piece of doweling with a mark on it at every centimeter floated in the fuel tank; this was the fuel gauge. The last mark on the dowel was red; when it disappeared you had ten minutes to get home. There was no compass. There was no need for a compass, because you only flew when the sun was shining. If the sun wasn't shining, you didn't fly and so you didn't need a compass. The sun, Castel-Jaloux explained to him since he was a foreigner and perhaps didn't understand, rose in the east and set in the west.

"HEAD WEST."

They always took the same route, which carried them first around Paris to the south, skirted along the edge of the Bois de Vincennes, and turned out into the countryside near Joinville. While they went, Castel-Jaloux explained why they flew over the countryside instead of over Paris. "FIRST, IF THE GNÔME SHOULD QUIT. BUT IT NEVER QUITS. THERE WILL BE SOME OPEN COUNTRY TO COME DOWN IN. SECOND, IF YOU MAKE A MISTAKE. BUT DON'T MAKE ANY MISTAKE. YOU WILL KILL AT THE MOST SOME COW INSTEAD OF A PARISIAN."

Fred nodded. It was impossible to turn his head around enough to see Castel-Jaloux, and in any case there was nothing to answer. Fred kept the altimeter at three hundred meters, about a thousand feet. The two rivers below split, the Seine going one way and the Marne the other. He followed along the valley of the Marne to Lagny, about twenty-five kilometers out of Paris. South of Lagny Castel-Jaloux had him bank in a wide curve, with a chateau under his left wing as a marker, and head back to the east. Just after crossing the Marne they turned a little to pass over the tiny hamlet of Bordeaux-sur-Marne, where Castel-Jaloux had a country house. Here he had Fred waggle his wings, and the housekeeper, a middle-aged peasant woman to judge from what you could see at three hundred meters, always ran out and flapped her apron to show that she recognized the Farman. "MADAME MANGE-PETIT," shouted Castel-Jaloux. "THE SALT OF THE EARTH."

Approaching Paris, the first thing you saw of course was the Eiffel Tower sticking up in the Champs de Mars, ahead and to the right. They went over Neuilly and the Bois de Boulogne. Boulogne-Billancourt was ahead, lying in its loop of the Seine; Issy lay under the right wing. "START YOUR BANK HERE," shouted Castel-Jaloux. "HALF THROTTLE. PUSH YOUR STICK DOWN A LITTLE. NOT TOO MUCH." He had an extraordinary way of retaining a commonplace and matter-of-fact tone while shouting at the top of his voice. Of course he had a lot of practice. The Farman floated in over the hangars and the edge of the field and touched down with a waggling sway. It raced along over the grass. "PULL BACK," shouted Castel-Jaloux. Fred saw that on the uneven grass there was danger of a ground loop unless you kept the tail firmly down.

After he had shut off the engine, Castel-Jaloux said, "As soon as you touch the grass, pull the stick all the way back. Lay it right on your pecker."

After Fred was adept enough at these routine turns, banks, and landings, Castel-Jaloux began putting him through more advanced tricks and training him to deal with various kinds of emergencies: dead-engine drills, overshooting or undershooting the field, steering with the stick alone in case the rudder broke, crosswind landings, and stalls. For the stalls they went up to five hundred meters, Fred set the throttle at eighty percent, and then pulled back gradually on the stick. The Gnôme had a lot of power. The Farman, grumbling and creaking, climbed up to five fifty and to six hundred, while the note of the engine gradually grew more labored.

"THAT'S YOUR MAXIMUM CLIMB ANGLE," shouted Castel-Jaloux at a certain point.

Fred held the stick firm, and the controls began to get mushy. The singing of the wind in the wires grew fainter and descended the musical scale. Then the horizon ahead fell out of sight, the wind noise died away, and the Farman seemed to hang poised by its nose for a second.

"DON'T LET IT ROLL OFF TO THE SIDE. CONTROLS DEAD CENTER."

The nose plunged. There was the slightly sickening sensation of a lift dropping. The horizon appeared and shot up into the sky, and the wind began singing in the wires again. The pastures and scattered houses of the Val de Marne rushed up.

"PULL UP. EASY AT FIRST."

The stick was so hard that Fred was afraid he would break something. He set his teeth and pulled back on it, bracing his feet on the rudder bar. But the Farman was well built and sturdy. It came up out of the dive, the wind screaming insanely, and leveled out at perhaps two hundred meters above the winding river.

"THAT'S FINE. USUALLY," yelled Castel-Jaloux, "WE TRY TO PULL OUT A LITTLE HIGHER. BUT IT'S ALL RIGHT AS LONG AS IT'S ABOVE THE GROUND."

On a later stall, he showed Fred how to correct for any tendency to roll off sideways, with a simultaneous touch of the rudder and stick in the other direction. Since the conditions of the lessons didn't encourage conversation in the air, Fred waited until they were on the ground and the engine cut before he asked, "What would happen if we did roll off?"

Castel-Jaloux climbed out stiffly, pulled his cane out after him, and began limping his way over toward the hangar.

"The next time we'll try a vrille," he said.

They went up to five hundred again, this time over the open country a little to the west of Lagny. "CLIMB A LITTLE MORE." Fred watched the altimeter. Five fifty; six hundred. "A LITTLE MORE." When they were at seven hundred meters Castel-Jaloux yelled, "NOW WE'RE GOING TO STALL AGAIN. THROTTLE AT EIGHTY. CONTROLS CENTER. NOW PULL UP."

The ominous descending note of the wind again. The horizon ahead fell out of sight. The Farman slowed, lost its buoyancy, and began to waggle. This time, just as the nose began to fall, Castel-Jaloux shouted, "LEFT BANK. ROLL AND PUSH THE STICK FORWARD. NOW."

Fred did as he was told. The left wing dropped and the Farman rolled over. The horizon came into view again, but this time it shot up on the left and began rotating crazily. The Farman, its tail up and nose pointed at the ground, spiraled down around the tip of its left wing. The pace increased until it was whirling madly like a stone at the end of a string. The ground below rushed up.

Fred tried the controls. They seemed to be locked; the stick was jammed over to the left against his knee. Exerting all his strength, he managed to pull it over an inch, but it shook in his hands until he was afraid something would break. He let it go again and it snapped back to the left. The Farman went on down in a sickening spiral. The horizon spun around in a circle, swooping and plunging. Fred felt a cold sweat springing out.

It was all wrong. Something wrong was happening. The rotation and plunging were so violent that he was whirled around like a fish on a hook, and he could scarcely even keep his wits about him to realize where he was, let alone comprehend what Castel-Jaloux was shouting at him.

I'm going to die, he thought with absolute conviction.

"FORGET THE STICK. THROTTLE BACK. CENTER THE RUDDER."

Castel-Jaloux was telling him to throttle back and center the rudder, he managed to grasp. The rudder! He had forgotten it in his struggle with the stick. He jammed his feet onto the bar and pushed with all his strength against it, and managed to get it straight.

"STICK FORWARD."

Like a marionette he followed the instructions. To his surprise he found that, although he couldn't center the stick by pushing it sideways, it would go forward. The Farman came out of its mad pirouette. But it was still diving steeply and at a terrific speed.

"NOW PULL BACK EASY," came the calm shout from behind him.

The control stick, a moment ago his enemy, became his old friend again. It was still stiff, but it no. longer fluttered and it came back when he pulled it. The Farman, rushing toward the ground, gradually pulled up and curved out into a glide. Fred was covered with sweat and he could feel his heart bumping against the leather jacket. He applied a little throttle and leveled out the wings.

"THAT WAS A VRILLE TO THE LEFT," shouted Castel-Jaloux. "NOW WE'LL TRY A VRILLE TO THE RIGHT."

Fred climbed back up to seven hundred and did this too. Now that he knew what was happening, and what to do about it, it wasn't quite so frightening. But it still made your stomach feel as though it were going to pull loose from your insides and fly up through your mouth. He came out of the right vrille at three hundred, pulled out of the dive, and banked to turn back toward Issy.

"TRÈS BIEN," shouted Castel-Jaloux a little less loudly than usual, as though he were saying it to himself.

Fred, his face still damp from sweat, drifted in over the hangars and came to a slightly bumpy landing. When the engine came to a stop Castel-Jaloux got out with his cane, walked a few feet away from the aeroplane to a patch of grass, and vomited. He came back saying calmly, "I am subject to airsickness."

They walked away toward the hangar, going slowly because of Castel-Jaloux's stiff leg.

"It was an Austrian named Bernstein who found out how to recover from a vrille," he remarked matter-of-factly. "Before that, everybody who went into a spin was killed."

That was the last of the lessons. Fred soloed in the Farman and flew it a half-dozen times, always following the same route out past Vincennes to the valley of the Marne and banking around to turn at Lagny. "Don't fly over the city," Castel-Jaloux told him again. "It's full of valuable monuments." He seemed to have a vision of Fred crashing in through the roof of the Louvre and destroying the Mona Lisa. Fred was getting a little bored with the Farman. It was a very steady aeroplane, ideally suited as a trainer, but it was slow and not very maneuverable. Besides he was getting tired of the Marne valley. He had his own private vision in which he circled the Eiffel Tower in a sleek monoplane, of the kind depicted on the picture postcards sold in Rue de Rivoli, while young women in fashionable pastel gowns looked up admiringly.

"How about the Blériot?"

"The Blériot?"

There were two Blériot monoplanes on the field at Issy, an early model with an Anzani engine, and a new XI-2 powered by an 80-horse-power Gnôme, mounted on the nose of the craft ahead of the pilot. On both machines the fuselage was covered to a point just behind the pilot, and from there an open framework extended to the tail. The linen of the XI-2 was doped a bright silver.

"I personally don't trust monoplanes," said Castel-Jaloux. "It is impossible to brace a single wing properly." It was exactly, Fred remembered, what Kinney had told him in San Francisco. Still, Blériot had crossed the English Channel in the thing, and the XI-2 was an improved model. On top of the wing, just in front of the pilot, was a short stubby mast to hold up the guy wires.

"People always imagine the wings are going to break off upward, because they hold the aeroplane up," said Castel-Jaloux. "But if you hit some turbulence, the wings may break off downward."

Thus the upright strut with the wires extending to the ends of the wings. The thing seemed well designed and was sturdy enough. It would climb to three thousand and do a hundred and twenty kilometers an hour in level flight. However it had a short air time, only a half an hour. Blériot had barely made it across the Channel.

"I'd like to try it," said Fred.

"It's two hundred an hour."

The Farman had only been a hundred and twenty, and this was a smaller and lighter machine. "It's the risk," said Castel-Jaloux.

"That is, a hundred for a half an hour."

"C'est ça."

Fred handed over the hundred. Castel-Jaloux always demanded payment in advance for the solo flights. Before, when they had flown in the two-place Farman, he had allowed Fred to pay afterward.

Castel-Jaloux didn't even hang around to check Fred out in the Blériot. Fred got into the unfamiliar cockpit and strapped himself into place. He identified the instruments, checked the controls, and waggled the stick, looking around to see if the ailerons worked. The mechanic pulled the prop around a couple of times, then Fred switched on and the Gnôme caught. The mechanic pulled away the chocks. He was off.

The Blériot took to the air more quickly than the Farman; it was light and had intoxicating power. It was also far more responsive. In flying the Farman you simply trundled along like an omnibus, and if you wanted to turn it would go where you pointed it. But the light Blériot was more like a bicycle; a moment of inattention and it was doing something on its own. It seemed to *want* to arc, bank, pirouette, and swoop like a lark—so that, where in the Farman you flew for the most part in a straight line, in the Blériot he found himself constantly tempted into acrobatics. On impulse he curved left over the Parc de Vincennes with its grim chateau and continued banking in a climbing circle. When he came out of it, instead of turning back eastward toward the Marne, he continued on north around the edge of the city.

Following the line of the old fortifications, he flew along with two green patches drifting by on his left, the Père Lachaise cemetery and the Parc des Buttes-Chaumont. A little farther on, tempted by the dazzling white domes of the Sacré-Coeur on the horizon, he turned in and flew directly over the city, crossing the Gare du Nord and the Grands Boulevards. When he came up to the Sacré-Coeur he flew around behind it only a hundred meters above the housetops, so that the Butte Montmartre cut off the view of the city to the south. Castel-Jaloux can't see me, he thought with the pleasure of a misbehaving boy.

The Gare St.-Lazare, the Parc Monceau. After the circle over Vincennes he couldn't resist another spiral around the Étoile; the cartwheel of streets with the Arc de Triomphe in the center seemed to be designed exactly to circle an aeroplane around, even though it was conceived by Haussmann who never saw an aeroplane. He leveled out. Ahead was the river, and beyond it the Champs de Mars and the Eiffel Tower.

The Blériot was a joy to bank and turn. Fred pushed the stick and rudder bar back and forth rhythmically, and the machine swung along in a series of graceful swoops like a lark at twilight. The Eiffel Tower rushed up ahead and to the left. Although black from the distance, at close range it had a tawny brownish tinge to it like the limbs of a lion. He was flying at two hundred meters, and the top of the Tower was a hundred meters higher. In the complex upward-arching structure there were platforms at three levels, successively smaller as the Tower tapered. At the top a large tricolor flag floated in the breeze. Below, the four great curved legs were planted in the city like the roots of some Gargantuan tree. The thing was immense, dwarfing the tiny figures of the people on the three observation platforms. He could almost have flown the Blériot through the giant graceful arches of the legs at the bottom, he thought.

When the Tower came abeam on his left he cut in, the stick against his left knee and the rudder bar angled. The Blériot dipped its wing and went into a tight circle. The Tower with its intricate iron fretwork was only a hundred meters or so away. Banking to the left as he was, he could clearly see the white tablecloths set for lunch in the restaurant on the second level. A curious waiter gazed out, a napkin over his arm. Above, at the third-level, a tourist peered at him through a pair of binoculars.

He looked down. All Paris was turning under him in an enormous circle, as precise as though drawn by a geometer's compass. In the middle, turning with it, was the Tower. He had a feeling of dominance, of exultation. It was as though the great iron mast were the axis of the world, which now spun to his command. It was the biggest thing in Paris and he had seized it and made it his own, so to speak, through catching it in the loop of his effortless and agile flight.

He was not sure whether he had gone around only once or completed more than a full circle. Slightly disoriented, he straightened out into level flight again. The Tower dwindled away behind. He looked down onto the pavement where the two avenues crossed under the iron structure. There were no young ladies in pastel gowns, only a nurse with a pram looking up at him. Presumably the baby was looking up too, but it was too tiny for Fred to tell.

Crossing the river, he found himself flying over the Bois de Boulogne. He glanced at his watch. He had been in the air almost a half an hour. He came out over the Seine again where it made its great loop around the suburbs. Here he cut along under the bluff of St.-Cloud, below the level of the houses on top of the escarpment. He still had the feeling he was hiding from Castel-Jaloux. He *was* a bad boy, he thought.

At the Pont de St.-Cloud he banked left and went into his glide. It was a perfect approach. The housetops fled by smoothly under him, the river came up ahead, and beyond it was the green field at Issy. He touched down perfectly on the grass, wheels and tail skid simultaneously. The Blériot waggled and bumped as it slowed. When he applied the power to taxi, however, the engine spluttered and stopped. He was out of gas.

He was at the extreme edge of the field. It was a long walk back to the hangars. As he approached he saw Lefebre, the mechanic, getting out the small Renault truck to tow the Blériot back across the field.

Castel-Jaloux was leaning against the hangar propped on his cane. ''What was the menu?''

''The menu?''

''At the restaurant,'' said Castel-Jaloux, ''on the second level.''

Fred took the Métro back into town and let himself into the apartment with his key. He dropped the kit bag with his goggles and helmet in it, and took off the leather jacket and threw it onto a chair. He glanced at his watch. Twelve forty-five. Herma had a rehearsal at two.

In his own room he stripped off the rest of his clothes and went naked into the bathroom. Who should take the bath, Herma or Fred? This question was always a minor perplex. It hinged in Fred's mind—and he was not particularly fond of baths—on the matter of whether—that part of him that disappeared when he became Herma—had recently been contaminated by any special event. If so, it needed a rinsing off. But this (he realized with a mild surprise) had not taken place for quite some time now. Perhaps he ought to . . . well, he had other things to consider now.

He stood before the mirror concentrating. People develop more will-power—their wills get stronger—as they get older. Besides, he had more practice now. It took only a minute or two. Although with his wristwatch off (it was necessary to take everything off) he had no way of measuring the time precisely. He focused his concentration at the exact center of the image in the mirror.

An inward and upward, slipping, viscous sensation. There it went—it diminished and grew shorter. Bah! And that noise—the little strangled glug at the end—it wasn't really pretty. Still it was a relief to have the ugly thing out of sight. Herma opened the taps to turn the hot and cold water into the tub.

Then all at once something gripped her from inside, a sudden cold clutch. It was like a memory from another life, a previous incarnation.

The sky outside seemed dark, perhaps a thunderstorm. Paris often grayed over in this way, to brighten again in the sunlight only a few moments later. But it was not that.

Still naked, she went into the salon and looked out the window to the south. The sun shone brightly. There were only a few clouds over St.-Cloud, leaving shadows on the greenish bluff. She still felt queer. It was not that the premonition was unpleasant. In fact, the frightening thing about it was that it was—attractive. A shadow, a vague chill inside, a reminder of mortality. It was sexy, as Caruso said. But Art and Life, the great truth suddenly struck her, were not the same. At the Opéra, Death was only a song, a shift to the minor mode, a catch in the voice. In the air, hurtling through the sky in a fragile and fallible machine, it was a sharp reality—something concrete and hard—iron and aluminum, sharp edges, deadly weights that could sever and crush the human flesh that had set them into motion. The little coldness still hung there below her breastbone, a kind of vacuum. She went into her own room for a piece of letter paper and wrote on it.

"Please, for God's sake, Hell take you, will you be careful of yourself? Not only because, if you should cease to exist, I would too, like that Chinese emperor who existed only because a butterfly was dreaming about him. But also because . . ."

She was about to write ". . . because I am fond of you." But that was not what she had meant to say. What had she meant to say anyhow? She tore up the note and threw it into the wastebasket, then she went back into the bathroom. The tub was almost overflowing. She turned the taps off and slipped into the tepid, soothing, and forgetful water—Lethe.

Yet this little hollow feeling under her chest—not a dream so much as a kind of hunger, a temptation to do something that she knew was forbidden (but what?)—persisted, for days and even weeks. In fact, it had been there for a long time, she realized; perhaps it had always been there. She didn't particularly find it unpleasant; in time it grew familiar, a kind of companion. It was possible that, even though Art was not Life, this little dark place inside her enabled her to sing certain parts better, with a deeper resonance—a moving shadow in the voice—that would not have been there otherwise. Caruso sang the betrayed Pagliaccio with deeper feeling, perhaps, after his beloved Ada had left him for another man. "Out of our great sorrows we make little songs." Who said that? Some poet; Lloiseaux had quoted him. Yet what great sorrow did she have? No one had deserted her, her career swept forward and upward with irresistible momentum, and her Wednesdays were constantly more successful. Only now and then did she have the notion that if she looked out the window she might see the little silver monoplane scudding over the rooftops, circling around the Eiffel Tower, and then slipping away under the bluff of St.-Cloud toward Issy. It was a simple hallucination, probably harmless. And anyhow, as she told herself, Fred never flew in the afternoon.

A Viennese dream doctor, the same one who had discovered that love was a sickness, contended that sometimes a person might imagine he were two people inhabiting the same head, arguing with each other, or coming and going successively as though they lived in the same apartment but came there only at different times. But, if it were a madness, it seemed to be a harmless one. And wasn't it an equal madness to be Herma and yet at the same time to imagine you were Antonia—to shed tears, real tears, for a mother who was only a portrait on the wall? And even that not a real portrait of a real mother, but only something contrived by a clever scene painter! Herma, waiting in the wings, feels for the little valve in the center of her emotions that will, in a moment, enable her to well out convincing signs of grief, while at the same time engaging in a difficult and intricate trio. A little moisture appears immediately; the lighted stage blurs. Too soon! She turns the valve back a little and the tears are temporarily stanched.

Dr. Miracle, followed by Crespel, exits into the wings with his bottles clanking. Chaliapin's evil expression disappears and he resumes his normal face. "Your turn to go out and howl a bit," he tells Herma as he brushes past her.

Hoffmann is alone on the stage. "To sing no more!" he laments. "Alas! how can I obtain from her such a sacrifice?"

On "sacrifice" Herma pushes the curtain aside and comes out into the glare of the footlights with a sad little smile. "Well! What did my father say?"

But he will tell her nothing; only begs her not to sing. "Later you will know all . . . love beckons us both!"

Vladi takes her hand. There is a little twist in his smile—a private irony for her, for Herma and not for Antonia. Isn't this ridiculous, the smile says. Antonia promises Hoffmann to sing no more. They part; Hoffmann exits to the left, and the bothersome Dr. Miracle enters again from the right and steals up behind her. He has weighty things to say, in his sinister and measured basso.

> "You will sing no more? Do you know what sacrifice
> you are imposing on your youth?
> Have you measured it?
> Grace, beauty, talent, a sacred gift,
> all these goods that Heaven has shared with you,
> will you now flee from them
> into the shadow . . . ?"

Herma feels all at once the little hollow place in her chest. Almost a panic. She recovers quickly and tells Miracle to go about his business. But this *is* his business; to tempt her into song and destroy her. He stretches an arm and points at the portrait on the wall. "Listen!"

Out of the corner of her eye Herma can see Maggie Teyte, in the wings, standing before a kind of mahogany sounding box intended to give her voice an eerie and ghostlike effect. This contrivance is mounted on a scaffold to reach to the height of her mouth. Since she is a little shorter than the average soprano, however, she has to stand almost on tiptoe to sing into it. "Antonia!" she intones.

ANTONIA: "O Heavens!"
MIRACLE: "Listen!"
VOICE: "Antonia!"
ANTONIA: "O God! My mother! my mother!"

And the trio begins. Herma sings to the portrait, Teyte sings into the wooden box. Antonia grows constantly more hysterical. Miracle urges and eggs her on.

ANTONIA: "Ah! c'est ma mère, c'est elle!
Son âme m'appelle!"
MIRACLE: "C'est sa voix, l'entends-tu!
Sa voix, meilleure conseillère,
qui te legue un talent que le monde a perdu!"
VOICE: "Antonia!"

The music mounts, mounts, and with it the emotion. It is as though Antonia and her mother were winding up a tapered hill of Purgatory, on separate paths but entwined together, with the basso following two octaves below. Now is the time for the little valve; the tears well forth.

VOICE: "Chère enfant! que j'appelle
comme autrefois,
c'est ta mère, c'est elle!
Entends sa voix!"
MIRACLE: "Ecoute!"
ANTONIA: "Son âme, son âme m'appelle!
Ma mère! ma mère! ma mère!"

The trio continues its fatal ascent. Beginning with a B natural in the middle of the register, it climbs, falls back, climbs again, the daughter's voice urged constantly higher by the mother's, both encouraged by Miracle who gets out his violin and begins playing madly, up and up, past the high C sharp which is the top for most sopranos and on into the region of rarefied air, of nothingness, where only the violin can follow and even the mother is left behind—toward that final piercing E natural, that gathering to a last strained point of the larynx, that is Death.

Chaliapin has stalked after her this way now for three acts: first as Coppélius, then as Dapertutto, now as Dr. Miracle. She still doesn't care for him. He is feline, slinky, in spite of his massive chest and the great low voice that shakes the floorboards: a lion. Sing! sing! sing again! he snarls in a low C sharp at the dying Antonia. And then, singing, she remembers: it wasn't Papa who was the basso in Santa Ana, it was Dr. Violet. And he clanked the same way, with his pockets full of medical instruments. No Dr. Violet can save Antonia; it is that other sinister physician, Dr. Miracle, who drives her relentlessly into the shadow.

Crespel hangs anxiously over her. "C'est ma mère, ma mère qui m'appelle!" she sings to him in a voice still piercingly high but wasted away now to a thread. It is almost the end for Antonia. Hoffmann rushes in followed by Nicklausse. She falls onto the couch, her arm dangling. There is silence, then the moving soft strains of the trio begin again from the orchestra. This resolves, through a miracle of harmony as simple and natural as it is unexpected, into the love duet of Hoffmann and Antonia. Lying on the couch with her eyes fixed on Hoffmann, she sings it in mezza voce, breaking out into full voice only on that magnificent single note, with its long tremolo, on the last word.

> "Triste ou folle . . .
> Ah—C'est une chanson d'amour!"

She closes her eyes. As from a great distance she hears Crespel singing his grief, Hoffmann calling for a doctor, Miracle appearing with a mocking cry of "Présent!" and lifting her lifeless wrist, and Hoffmann's final anguished cry of "Antonia . . . !" The orchestra crashes out the finale. There is a moment of silence, then a great roar of applause from the audience. The pink glow through her closed eyelids grows dim; the curtain has fallen.

She gets up quickly and takes Vladi's hand. The stage is suddenly full of people behind the closed curtain. The stage manager is just at one side. "Hoffmann and Antonia first!" he calls out.

The chorus master holds the curtain apart, and Herma slips out onto the forestage pulling Vladi after her. The roar of clapping rises to a din. Smiling, she and Vladi bow, and turn left and right. Then, still hand in hand, they retreat behind the curtain again.

"Nicklausse and Miracle!"

Teyte and Chaliapin go out. The clapping rises a little, but not as much as for Herma and Vladi. There are a few bravos, but no bravas. Even though Teyte is a prima donna in London, tonight she is only Nicklausse and nobody notices her. Probably only a few in the audience know that she sang the voice of the portrait. Chaliapin pulls her back in, smiling broadly.

"Everybody out! All principals!"

They go out in a line, hand in hand: Chaliapin, Teyte, Vladi, Herma, and the Crespel whose name she can never remember. And an unexpected thing happens that shakes Herma at the center of her viscera, like a low note from a basso. The long roar of applause continues, but as she herself passes out through the curtain it rises to a bellow like that of a great animal, to subside again as Crespel comes out behind her and they stand in a line, smiling over the footlights.

"Bravo!" "Brava!" "Bravi tutti!"

After a minute or more of this they retreat. The applause continues. From the other side of the curtain a chant begins, gradually rising until it is clearly audible over the general rattle of clapping.

> *"Her! ma!"*
> *"Her! ma!"*
> *"Her! ma!"*
> *"Her! ma!"*
> *"Her! ma!"*

The stage manager looks around, locates Herma, and stretches out his arm to her. Nodding, he beckons with his uplifted hand. The curtain is held open again, and she slips out before the sea of white faces, black dinner jackets, and pastel gowns of the ladies. A jewel somewhere up in the boxes catches the light and sparkles. Turning to the left, she notices again the quiet person occupying the box in the second tier— the Persian Prince with his short black beard and dark eyes. His fur coat is like Dr. Miracle's, it now occurs to her, except that he is not sinister, only odd and a little fané, as though he were not well. The others in his box are clapping but he is not; he is simply watching with his penetrating expression that somehow has a faint touch of amuse- ment about it. He is looking at *her*—not at Antonia, but at Herma. He turns to say something to the person next to him, and Herma looks away.

A bouquet sails up over the footlights to land on the stage, and then another. There are more bravas. Some of them are shouting "Brava l'Erma!" When Fred hired the claque he could at least have found some who knew how to pronounce an H. After the third and fourth bouquet the Niagara of the applause begins to diminish a little.

"Bien. C'est fini," says the low voice of the stage manager behind her. Still smiling and bowing, she retreats back through the held-open curtain. Chaliapin is making a "Whew!" gesture and rubbing his face. Vladi, as they move away into the shadows of the wings, clasps her neck and kisses her on the cheek.

A few voices out in the theater are still calling "Herma!" but the applause has almost stopped. Herma goes down the iron spiral staircase to the corridor leading to the dressing rooms. Just before the door of her room she encounters Maggie Teyte in the corridor. They exchange a long look. Then Teyte says in English, simply, and without the least trace of malice, "You did beautifully on the trio, my dear."

Herma pushes in through the door of her dressing room. It is jammed full of people. Lloiseaux is there, smiling. He pats her on the head as though she were a child. There are porters carrying flowers, her dresser, the makeup girl, people from the chorus who want to hug her. The cork comes out of a champagne bottle with a pop. Lloiseaux holds out a bubbling glass to her. She shakes her head. All this goes on for five minutes or so.

"Everybody out of here," says Lloiseaux. "Let her change."

He goes out, carrying the bottle of champagne in one hand and his glass in the other. The others follow him out. Even one of the porters has procured a glass of champagne and is carrying it with him as he goes out the door.

It is suddenly quiet. She sits before the mirror while the dresser pulls off her Antonia wig. Teyte, it now occurs to her, congratulated her on the trio but said nothing about the Tourterelle song, which is her own specialty. An invisible little thrust of the needle. Still, she behaved with perfect correctness. Watching as the dresser fluffs out her short hair, Herma thinks, that is what it is to be a professional.

4.

And so it happened. She did it, the thing that everyone said couldn't be done. And they had chanted her name—*her* name—until she had to go out alone and take that last long curtain call. Trampling the others underfoot, trampling over Maggie Teyte, she stood on top of the heap. "My name is Herma and I am going to be an opera star," she had told Madame Modjeska. And what was it like? Was she different, somehow, now that it had happened? What she felt at the moment was only a little twinge of regret. There would never be another evening like this one, she knew. She might do things that were bigger and better, there might be even more curtain calls and more flowers, but this one evening could never take place again. It was tonight that it had happened—and after tonight there would be—tomorrow and . . . other evenings. It was better not to think about time too much. It made you unhappy, it was even a little frightening. Madame Moellendorf . . . Her thoughts strayed, then trailed away entirely until she didn't think at all.

There was a knock on the door. The dresser went on working on her hair. Herma said, "Entrez."

The door opened. A smiling olive-faced young man appeared.

"In the words of the Prologo in *I Pagliacci,* 'Si puo?' Excuse me. I am no baritone . . ."

She looked around, then turned back to her mirror.

"You're Reynaldo Hahn."

"Ah, you know me?"

"You're the music critic of the *Figaro,* I believe."

He made a mock face of disappointment. "I write for several papers. But in my pride I like to believe I am a musician and composer."

She turned and examined him more carefully. He had a neat mustache and a small clipped beard. He was elegantly clad except that he was wearing a kind of velvet smoking jacket instead of evening dress. He held a cigarette which he nervously put to his lips now and then. She recognized him now as one of the four men who had been in the box of the Persian Prince. He had been sitting to the rear, behind the old gentleman with the mane of white hair, and she hadn't been able to make him out clearly from the stage. But at close range she had recognized him immediately. He was a familiar figure in Maxim's and the cafés around the Opéra quarter, and his appearance was unmistakable —he was handsome but not conventionally so. There was something dark and Mediterranean about him—quick dramatic gestures, a slightly flamboyant manner—perhaps he was Spanish or Italian.

"How did you get in?"

"I have a pass from Monsieur Meyner."

He smiled again at this and puffed his cigarette. He seemed perfectly at ease in the dressing room. He settled into a chair and crossed his legs. Obviously he was enjoying himself.

"If you want to write your review, there's no point in your watching the dresser comb my hair. You might as well go back to the *Figaro* and write it."

"Ah! but it's not for that."

"What's it for then?"

"It's on account of Marcel."

"Marcel?"

"You don't know who Marcel is?"

Without turning from the mirror she said, "No." But she had already guessed it was the Persian Prince.

This too delighted him. He seemed pleased at every turn of the conversation. "Ah. Fantastic! Here you are, you live in Paris and you are a prima donna of the Opéra, and you don't know who Marcel is. Well, you must come down and meet him. That's what I've come for."

The dresser had finished her hair now. Herma began removing her makeup with a towel and a little cold cream.

"Why doesn't he come here?"

"Well, he doesn't do that sort of thing, you see. For one thing he can't climb stairs." Hahn took a puff at his cigarette. "Anyhow it's not his custom to come to dressing rooms," he went on. "He's waiting in the car."

"The car?"

"Yes. It's perfectly innocent. The car is parked in Rue Scribe and Marcel is waiting in it."

This was an odd arrangement. Herma went on working with the towel, wiping carefully along her brow near the hairline, while she thought. "If he's so unwell why does he come to operas?"

"Oh, so many questions." He pawed the air with his free hand. He had a number of slightly effeminate gestures. "They will all be answered of themselves, if you'll only come down. How soon will you be finished?"

"Aren't you impatient though." She finished her face and began applying lip rouge with a little brush, removing all but a trace afterward with the towel. "Perhaps he'll kidnap me and take me to his seraglio in Persia."

Hahn wrinkled his brow, still smiling. "Persia?"

It seemed like a very indiscreet sort of escapade. She had no idea who any of these people were, except that Hahn was said to lead a rather free life.

"Who was the elderly gentleman who was in the box with you?"

"Who? Oh, that was just Gaby."

This was getting her nowhere. On impulse she said, "Go on out and shut the door, and I'll put a dress on."

"Triumph!" He threw his cigarette onto the floor, crushed it with his immaculate patent-leather slipper, and went out.

Perhaps they *would* kidnap her into a seraglio, Herma thought. But the old gentleman would serve as duenna, and Hahn seemed more reckless and insouciant than sinister. And it would do no harm (the Fred inside her whispered) to become better acquainted with the *Figaro* critic. She put on a Vionnet gown, a long affair in gray moiré that ended just above her ankles, and threw a cloak around her shoulders. No scent—a faint hint of Fabergé still clung in the gown.

"Mademoiselle's bag," the dresser reminded her. "And—ah." She added a pearl choker around Herma's neck, and a bracelet with a single pearl dangling from it to match. "Have a pleasant evening, Mademoiselle."

"Do *you* know who Marcel is?"

"No, Mademoiselle."

With a last fleeting glance at the mirror she went out.

The car waiting in Rue Scribe was an old Hispano-Suiza tourer, royal blue in color and fitted with window screens even though it was a mild evening. Hahn opened the door on the sidewalk side. Nothing could be seen in the darkness inside the car. "It's Marcel and Gaby. All perfectly innocent," he said, still apparently pondering the remark about the seraglio.

Herma got in. The Persian Prince in his fur coat smiled wanly at her. She sat next to him, and Hahn and the old gentleman were installed on the jump seats facing to the rear. The chauffeur in the front seat had evidently been the fourth person in the box. He was a dark, rather plump young man with a pleasant manner. They *were* an odd lot of people. Herma had imagined that she was to sit in the car for a few moments while the Persian Prince talked to her. But the chauffeur started the motor and drew away along Rue Scribe. The car circled around the Place de l'Opéra and turned off it into Rue de la Paix. No one said anything. Finally the Persian Prince, almost invisible in the darkness, said quietly, "It was nice of you to come."

Herma sat rather stiffly, watching the hotels and shops go by behind the transparent and slightly wavy window screen. Across from her Hahn lit another cigarette. The car had polished brass handles and fittings, and it was upholstered in gray glove leather. She now recognized the old gentleman with the mane of white hair. It was Gabriel Fauré. She had seen his picture in *L'Illustration*. Surely nothing unseemly would happen in the presence of an eminent composer. The street widened out into Place Vendôme. The car drew up in front of the Ritz and stopped.

Identifying someone of importance inside, perhaps M. Fauré, the doorman opened the door of the tourer as though it were the most elegant limousine in Paris. They got out, Hahn extending a hand to help both Fauré and the Persian Prince under the elbow. Herma was left to clamber out for herself. To her surprise the chauffeur went in with them, under the modest white marquée hardly noticeable from the street. The Hispano was abandoned at the curb, steaming and clicking as a motor-car will.

The silver and gold foyer inside was immense. The floor was an expanse of tawny-colored marble, gleaming with wax. A woman with dark red hair appeared from behind a pillar and came straight toward them across the floor: swathed to the neck in furs, rather beyond her best years but still attractive, with a powerful and assertive sexuality. "Mon cher amour!" she burst out at Hahn, extending a hand.

Hahn took the hand. A diamond bracelet glittered on the rather thin wrist. He seemed a little less than pleased. But still he said with his usual good-natured insouciance, "Won't you come and break a crust with us, Liane dear?"

It was Liane de Pougy, who had starred in *Feminissima* years before at the Larkin in San Francisco. Probably she wouldn't remember Herma. At the moment she didn't even deign to notice her. "I'd be enchanted," she told Hahn. She seemed a little cool toward the Persian Prince too. She smiled mechanically at Fauré.

A waiter appeared and led them down the corridor to a gold and cherry private room. According to the songs, as Herma remembered, it was in such places that young girls fell. She smiled brilliantly and said to Pougy, "I sang with you once in San Francisco, years ago."

"Ah?"

"Yes. In *Feminissima*. I sang a song called 'Si tu m'aimes comme je t'aime, tu m'aimes.' It was the stupidest thing I've ever heard in my life."

"I'm sure it was," said Pougy a little distractedly. Her attention was still on Hahn. Perhaps also she didn't care to be reminded of anything that had happened so long ago. The waiter seated them at a table with a linen cloth and embroidered Louis Quinze chairs. An extra chair was brought up for Pougy. With a regal motion of her chin she indicated her fur coat. The waiter removed it. Under it was a rose-colored gown cut so low that the division between her breasts was clearly visible, and even, when she bent forward, a glimpse of roseate nipple. Glancing in her direction, Hahn said with faint irony, "Liane, dear, you are charming this evening."

Although Herma often came to the restaurant at the Ritz she had never been in this part of the hotel before. The room seemed to be permanently maintained for Marcel and his guests. The table was a small one; it was barely large enough for the five of them. There was an oriental carpet on the floor, and across the room a large Pleyel grand with music stands and some extra chairs near it. On the wall was what appeared to be an authentic Vermeer. Under it was a kind of divan scattered with cushions. For ruining young girls. Herma was still enjoying herself and entertained with the whole situation. For other decorations, there was only an archaic bust of Apollo on a pedestal. There were no flowers, she noticed, and the room was shut hermetically tight. Hardly a sound could be heard from the other parts of the hotel. The chauffeur Agostinelli had retreated to a kind of alcove behind the piano where he waited in case he was needed. He could be seen through the open door laying out a game of solitaire.

Olivier came in, without a note pad or anything in his hands. He had a perfect memory and never forgot an order. He bent first over the Persian Prince.

"Monsieur?"

"I haven't eaten anything for two days, Olivier. I've been writing; but first I want very strong black coffee, double strength. So," he put in anxiously, "you mustn't be afraid to charge me double for it on the bill. Afterward," he added pessimistically, "perhaps I will be able to keep something light on my stomach."

Fauré ordered a beefsteak, rare. Leonine was the word for him, Herma decided. For Hahn, a London Grill and fried potatoes. Pougy ordered Crèpes aux Champignons, and Herma—remembering Caruso —a little white meat of chicken with a few blades of asparagus. Olivier seemed impressed by this last; asparagus was out of season and very expensive. He disappeared with a faint bow.

Herma was seated next to Marcel. "So you're a writer?"

"Oh my soul," said Hahn. "I cannot understand how someone has never heard of Marcel Proust. Haven't you read *Les Plaisirs et les Jours?*"

"No. I don't read very much."

"Or *Le Bible d'Amiens?*"

"Why should she read anything, Reynaldo dear?" said Marcel. "It's not her métier. I don't sing opera and she doesn't write books. Anyhow I haven't published my novel yet."

"So you're writing a novel?"

"Ah, my dear. It's an interminable task. I never expect to see the end of it. I write a little every day. I have a pile so high." He indicated, holding his hand a foot or so above the table. "Grasset is going to print some of it, even though I'll have to pay him."

He sighed, and sipped a little of the black coffee. He had taken off the fur coat now and was revealed in an old-fashioned frock coat and striped trousers, like a diplomat, except that the clothes were worn and a little baggy, giving him the slightly touching look of a clown. For some reason he had added a white carnation boutonnière. He turned and looked at her with his penetrating and soft glance. "Your Giulietta was charming."

"Ah. You preferred the Giulietta to the others?"

"Yes. Antonia is too much like myself." He did not offer any explanation of this rather cryptic statement. "And as for Olympia, I'm too old to play with dolls."

"Did you ever, Marcel?" Reynaldo asked.

"Oh yes. As a child I played with dolls. My grandmother gave them to me."

The waiter poured out wine for everybody except Proust—a Saint-Emilion and a Montrachet white. Pougy sent hers away and asked for champagne. It was brought instantly. Hahn was slumped negligently in his chair, and Pougy was sitting opposite him. Evidently their ankles touched, because he sat up abruptly and stared at her with a cat-and-mouse sort of smile.

"Marcel prefers Giulietta," he said, "because she is the most vicious of the three."

"No, it's Reynaldo who is vicious," said Marcel. "Il aime les filles." This was evidently a private joke between them. Pougy didn't seem to be amused.

Marcel turned to Herma again. After a moment he said, "Broken mirrors bring misfortune."

After a moment she grasped that he was talking about the second act of the *Tales*. "Yes, seven years of bad luck, we say in English. But that's only when you break them by accident, not on purpose."

"And why did you break it?"

"It's part of the business."

"No it isn't. I've seen the *Tales* a dozen times, and Giulietta never breaks the mirror."

"You must know a great deal about opera."

"No." He offered his Persian Prince smile. He was charming when he smiled. "It's just that I'm observant. It's the métier of the novelist. I'm an invalid, so I have nothing else to do except observe everything in life very carefully."

Fauré, who had not said a word, went on methodically cutting up and disposing of his beefsteak. Hahn ignored his food for the most part and smoked one cigarette after another. A sandwich and a glass of beer were provided for Agostinelli in his alcove. Proust asked for a plate of noodles, perfectly plain except for a little butter and a touch of garlic. At the end the waiter, following the directions no doubt of the omniscient Olivier, brought Fraise Herma for everybody except Proust and Pougy, who declined on account of her diet. "My régime," she called it in her queenlike way.

Fauré stared at the pale hemisphere in its circle of whipped cream as though he were not sure what he was supposed to do with it. Hahn ate the strawberry first, then scooped up a little of the whipped cream around the edge. He put his spoon down. He really wasn't hungry.

"Sing something for us, Reynaldo," suggested Marcel. "And try not to roll your R's. He has a slight Spanish accent," he explained to Herma. "He was born in Venezuela. We call him our Venezuelan Macaque."

"Marcel is always saying that I have a slight Spanish accent. But this isn't so. The truth is that I have cultivated my voice in French to roll the R's, since to grasseyer the R's in the Parisian manner when singing is vulgar and music hall." He glanced in the direction of Pougy, who showed no expression at all. "And this habit has passed over into my ordinary speech. I sing at all times, so to speak. And so they say I have a slight Spanish accent."

"He has a slight Spanish accent," said Marcel.

Hahn sat down at the Pleyel and sang a song or two of Debussy, without removing the cigarette from his mouth. Like Puccini, he always had a cigarette, but he could do more than Puccini could; he could sing with it dangling from the corner of his mouth. Marcel told Herma to pay no attention. It was only his ''Apache airs,'' as he called them.

''He's really a very gentle fellow, very cultivated, and speaks six languages. Including Macaque,'' he added.

Lifting his hand from the piano, Hahn cheerfully made an obscene gesture in his direction. Then he changed tempos deftly and broke into some Offenbach, not from the *Tales* but from the early operettas, *Orphée aux Enfers* and *La Belle Hélène*. ''When I was little,'' he said from the piano, the cigarette still dangling, ''it was to the strains of Offenbach that my father used to dandle me on his knee. Because of this, Offenbach to me is rhythm. Offenbach is an important influence on my work. I am famous for my mastery of rhythm.''

''The rhythm of a macaque,'' said Marcel. He seemed to be enjoying himself and had thrown off his invalid languor. He bent to tell some private joke to Fauré, who smiled broadly.

To show his versatility, Hahn went on to the Barcarolle from the *Tales*. He had a delicate and pleasing but slightly gravelly tenor; he had perhaps damaged his voice by singing too much or by his continual smoking.

> ''O belle nuit d'amour,
> Giuliette est vicieuse,''

he concluded with a seraphic earnestness.

Marcel smiled. ''Gaby, won't you . . .''

Still without a word, Fauré got up and went to the Pleyel. As a pianist and musician he was obviously a different sort of thing from Hahn. He played seriously and with impeccable form, even though rather negligently. He ran through a part of his piano quartet in C minor, then, at Marcel's request, his *Romance sans paroles*. Hahn, slumped in his chair again, said, ''For lechery and litanies, there is nothing to match our dear Gaby. I have always thought this was the sort of music a pederast might hum while raping a choirboy.''

He glanced at Herma to see if he had succeeded in shocking her. But she only inquired demurely, ''Does the word *violer* in French have anything to do with *violon?*''

Hahn shrugged. ''What an idea.'' But the notion seemed to intrigue Marcel. He murmured to himself, ''Le long sanglot des violons . . .''

Fauré was ready to get up. But Marcel insisted that Herma sing something, and he stayed at the piano to accompany her. Herma sang some Schubert lieder, then her own song or two of Debussy. When she came to the end of the second one Marcel gazed at her with his lazy Persian eyes.

''Won't you sing us a bit of your 'Addio California'?''

''Addio Marcel,'' said Herma, turning as if to go.

Hahn said, "Marcel, my dear, I don't think she cares much for the part. And in fact it's quite a stupid little opera. There's no music in it, and it's full of cowboys and Indians."

"Only one Indian," said Herma.

"Well, excuse me." Marcel applied his charm again. He was exquisite when he wished to please. "It's just that—the first time I saw you it was as Minnie, galloping onto the stage with your American verve. You seemed—half a boy . . . a charming ambiguity." His lazy glance was particularly penetrating here. "And then when I heard that the same person was going to do all three roles of the *Tales*—and such an interesting person—I couldn't resist coming out. Although I never come out."

"They seem to know you well here."

"Ah, I come out to the Ritz. That's different. It's like home here."

"Well, well," said Fauré, getting up rather heavily from the piano. He found his overcoat on a chair.

"Gaby is too eminent to stay up late," apologized Marcel. "Not only is he France's most eminent living composer . . ."

"Come, come. There's Debussy," said the old gentleman.

". . . but he is also the director of the Consérvatoire."

"I shall resign soon," said Fauré. "I'm tired of auditioning the mistresses of politicians. Goodnight, tout le monde. Goodnight, Marcel, you wicked boy."

"Alfred," Proust called softly.

Agostinelli got up from his card table in the alcove and appeared in the doorway.

"Could you be so good as to take M. Fauré home to Place des Victoires?" he asked with elaborate politeness, as though Agostinelli were doing him a favor.

Agostinelli and Fauré went off. The others stayed; the waiter brought coffee.

Hahn slid into the chair next to Herma. "Don't you find yourself flattered that Gabriel Fauré accompanies you?"

"Paderewski has," she said indifferently.

"Oh my soul. The little thing is sure of herself. Perhaps, if I practice hard, I too may be allowed to accompany you someday." He too was charming, in his bantering way, very different from the elaborate politesse of Marcel.

"I'd be *enchanted* if someone asked me to sing," said Pougy.

"Ah, Liane dear," said Hahn gallantly. "We've forgotten you."

He went back to the piano, and Pougy sang her "Moi j'ai vecu bien" in a throaty music-hall contralto.

"Elle a vecu bien. Indeed she has. Even a little too well," murmured Marcel.

"How merciless you are."

He allowed his soft dark eyes to play upon her for a moment before replying. "Not at all. It is life that is merciless. It is Time. I only observe its effects." All this with the same air of elaborate and diplomatic tact, as though he were apologizing for his remarks and yet believed them to be true. "It is Time that is merciless." If this were an unpleasant fact, at least he could say it with extreme politeness, a tone almost of regret. He spoke to everyone, Herma thought, in the way you speak to someone who has had a death in the family.

Pougy went on through the verse, then started the chorus for the second time. When she came to the R's she sang them with deep Parisian grasseyement, practically swallowing them. Hahn raised an eyebrow. His hands flew back and forth along the keyboard; his cigarette dangled. At the end of the chorus he joined in in harmony, a third below her:

> "Je regrette rien,
> désormais c'est fini,
> moi j'ai vecu bien."

Agostinelli reappeared, having taken Fauré back to his apartment. They all got up and searched for their wraps. Marcel donned his fur coat and wrapped the shawl under it, leaving the coat hanging open. Agostinelli was carrying the robe to wrap around his knees in the car.

Now Marcel began emptying his pockets in all directions. He paid the bill and tipped everyone heavily. He called the headwaiter mon cher Olivier, he called the first waiter mon cher Eustache, and he called the second waiter mon cher Hals. In the foyer he gave something to the chasseur, whom he called mon cher Maurice. He seemed worried whether he had given the chasseur enough.

In the middle of the foyer they stopped. It was the crucial point of separation.

Pougy said, "Won't you come up for a little, Reynaldo dear? There's my famous Turkish coffee."

"No, I have to go home and write my review of Herma's performance."

"In that case," she said a little stiffly, "perhaps she should go home with you and help you write it. No doubt it will be highly favorable."

With a little actressy smile she turned and went off toward the lifts.

"Goodnight, Liane dear. Sweet dreams."

There was a silence. They made their way toward the door.

"Poor Liane," said Hahn. "She was waiting for us. She found out somehow we were going to the Opéra, and she knew we would come on here afterward."

The doorman opened the door with a bow. Marcel felt in his pockets and found them empty.

"Jules, mon cher, could you by any chance lend me fifty francs?"

The doorman got out his wallet and produced the banknotes with alacrity.

"No, please keep it," Marcel told him. "It is for you."

5.

Fred came into the Café de la Paix with a *Figaro* under his arm and looked around in a leisurely way. It was about ten o'clock in the morning. He saw Lloiseaux seated alone at his usual table by the angle of the street and nodded to him. He was uncertain whether to go and join him. Then across the terrasse he caught sight of something else: a shock of flame-colored hair, a pale face, and a pair of dark eyes heavy with makeup. Zing! went the harp string in his blood. There was nothing he could do about it. It was too powerful for him. It was pleasant enough, but even if it were unpleasant there would have been nothing he could do to prevent it.

He took a table and unfolded his newspaper. When the waiter came he ordered a Café Crème. While he waited for the coffee to come he got out a calling card from his waistcoat, groped for a stub of pencil, and wrote something on it. Then he turned to his newspaper.

The coffee came. "If you would be so kind as to give this to the lady." He indicated with a motion of his head. He slipped the card into his hand along with a ten-franc piece. The waiter nodded.

He pretended to read the newspaper for a while, watching Pougy over the top of it. She was sitting before an empty glass that had had something greenish and feminine in it, probably a Chartreuse. The waiter went up to the table, bowed, and set the card in front of her in a saucer. She looked interrogatively. The waiter, with his head, indicated Fred.

Pougy focused in his direction. She examined him for some time. Then, while she still looked straight at him, her chin went down a fraction of an inch and came back up again.

In an exaggeratedly leisurely manner, forcing himself to be calm, he folded up the newspaper, abandoned his half-finished coffee, and crossed the terrasse to her table. She was wearing a lacy arabesque sort of gown that fitted tightly to a point below the breasts and then flared out into a flowing skirt. It was the dappled color of an autumn leaf—scarlet here, a reddish brown there. In the plunging décolletage, between the breasts and a little to the left, Fred made out a tiny mole, the same dark flame color as her hair.

"Meester Hite?"

"Yes, but I speak French."

"Ah, bon." She regarded him. "And you are a manager of singers?"

He nodded.

"But," she said hastily, "won't you please sit down? It was thoughtless of me. I beg you. Won't you take something?"

He shook his head. It was a mild spring day and the street was filled with a yellow sunlight. His mouth was dry. Perhaps he should order something after all—a lemonade. He unbuttoned his jacket and sat down at the table.

She was still studying him, a faint smile playing at the corners of her mouth. "And whom else do you manage?"

With difficulty he took his eyes from the tiny mole. "Herma, for example."

"Who?"

"You met her the other night at the Ritz."

"Ah, la petite," she said indifferently. It was funny, he thought, how everyone called Herma "the little one" even though she was taller than the average Frenchman—perhaps because she was so slim and gave the impression of lightness. "We should discuss it," Pougy went on. "It is true that at the moment I have no manager. I have had many managers," she said, "but they have all cheated me. I find that, on the whole, all men are cheaters. Qu'en penses-tu?"

"Yes, on the whole we are a dishonest sex," he agreed.

He was finding his voice again. The trick, he discovered, was to keep his eyes on her face and firmly resist any temptation to look at anything farther down.

"Why are you so silent?"

"It's just that . . ."

"You have heard me sing?"

"Of course. The other night . . ." He almost betrayed himself. ". . . at the Larkin, in San Francisco."

She took his blunder, perhaps, for the grammatical mistake of a foreigner. A little of her smile disappeared. "Ah well. A provincial city. In a barbarian country. But if you were to hear me with a proper audience—a Parisian audience. At the Casino de Paris . . ."

"Is that where you are singing now?"

"No, at the moment I am between engagements." The usual euphemism of unemployed entertainers. "Besides, as you know, one must economize the voice," she said in the throaty contralto broken by the smoke of a thousand music halls. "Perhaps I will go to Buenos Aires," she added through some internal connection in her logic that was not clear.

"Herma was very well received there."

It seemed to be a policy on her part to ignore any reference to Herma. She returned to their own affairs. "Perhaps you could give me advice. But this," she said, "is not the place to discuss it."

He found himself out on the sidewalk with her, in the sun which made him perspire a little. It was only five minutes' walk down the street to Place Vendôme, but she insisted on taking a taxi. "I am an artiste, not an athlete." There were three or four taxis waiting. He helped her into one and climbed in after her. He had never noticed before that taxis were so intimate and shadowy inside. Their bodies touched on the worn leather seat. Pougy's scent mingled with the smell of leather and the faint and musky, not unpleasant odor of perspiration.

She slipped her arm under his. She spoke in a low and coaxing,

intimate tone. "Alors, tu veux vraiment me diriger?" He realized that
she had spoken to him in the familiar second person from the beginning.
He tried to remember whether he had said *tu* or *vous* to her. Neither,
probably; he had hardly opened his mouth yet.

She moved a little closer. Their two bodies were now in contact from
shoulder to ankle. She spoke in an even lower voice.

"Do you really think you could manage me?"

"I could manage you beautifully."

"And would you enjoy managing me?"

"It would be the greatest imaginable pleasure."

What was wrong with this snail of a taxi that it went so slowly!
Would it never get to the Ritz? Besides the conversation was idiotic.
He cast about for something more to say. "And would you enjoy being
managed by me?"

"I'd be enchanted."

At last the car drew up in front of the Ritz. They got out and Fred
paid the taxi. The doorman was the one who was on duty in the morning,
not the Jules of a few nights before. They swept in through the door,
across the foyer, and into the lift with hardly any effort on their own,
as though borne along on a hot wind. As soon as they were in the room
and the door shut she wrapped an arm around him and planted a kiss
in the middle of his brow.

"But if you are to manage me you must see me in costume."

"It isn't necessary," he muttered. But she was already gone. Deft
at quick changes, she reappeared again in only a few moments. The
costume she was wearing might have been intended for a pornographic
Aïda. The lower half was a filmy skirt, through which the russet pubic
triangle was clearly visible. Above it she wore a kind of short-sleeved
gauze chemise, and over this a tight-fitting vest of soft red moroccan
leather. There were circles cut out of the leather for the breasts, leaving
them covered only by the gauze which hid nothing, only softening and
enhancing the contours and subtle contrasts of color. There was an Aïda
helmet partly covering her auburn hair. Her feet were bare.

"Do you like it?"

He nodded. Then he fell, quite literally and in every sense of the
word: as Adam fell to Eve, and also onto a large square couch he
hadn't noticed before, with a satin cover and a pile of velvet pillows.
He was entangled in gauze and warm flesh.

"Manage me! Dirige-moi!" he heard her pleading throatily. But
the managing was taking place all in the other direction.

Coming to himself, he found her parading around the room in the
gauze chemise. Perhaps she had never taken it off. It fastened in the
front only with a pair of flimsy ribbons which she left untied.

Now, for the first time, examining her undistracted by the distorting
lens of desire, he was able to appraise her objectively. She was indeed a
magnificent creature. The ravages of time had confined themselves, as
they often do, to those parts of her that showed when she was dressed:

her hands and her face. Below the neck she might have been a woman of twenty-five. To his American eyes she seemed a little short and stocky, but her proportions were perfect. Above all it was her complexion that struck. It was a pure and translucent alabaster only faintly tinged with pink, and quite evenly; the same clear and pale radiance extended to every part of her body. Pink was not quite it; it was the color of her hair—dark smoldering flame—that faintly tinged the alabaster, so that the shadow under the pale surface had a russet cast, autumnal rather than girlish. She strode around the room restlessly, picking up a magazine and leafing through it, lighting a cigarette and setting it down on a saucer. Each time she turned in Fred's direction she seemed to radiate an electric current. The breasts were magnificent: modest in size and symmetrical as though designed by geometric angels. They were the same pure complexion as the rest of her. No need to fix vision on the little mole now. The two aureoles for which it stood symbol were clearly visible. They too were exactly the color of her hair, the color of flame darkened by smoke.

The gauze chemise covered only the upper part of her arms and her back to a point a little below the waist. She turned away from him and her feet precisely together, bent over the tiny pantry to do something or other. Perhaps she was making coffee. The edge of the gauze lifted a little. From across the room Fred contemplated two moonlike convexities as perfect in proportion as a pair of classic amphorae. Whereas in many women the habit of sitting down left these shapes a little reddened, these were the same perfect paleness as the rest of her, except that a little below the center of each was a reddish dot the size of a pencil eraser. At first the idea struck him that they might be some kind of bizarre cosmetic, an analogy or reminder of the two aureoles on the other side of her body and higher up.

"What's that?"

"What?"

"Those two marks."

She whirled around as though in an effort to catch sight of them herself. Then she said matter-of-factly, "That's where a lover shot me. Twice. Once on each side."

She turned back to making the coffee. Whenever she straightened up the marks disappeared under the gauze; when she bent over they reappeared, like an actress taking curtain calls.

"It was very tiresome, très ennuyant. I had to go to a surgeon to have the bullets removed." She fussed at the pantry for a while, then went on with the story. "I was concerned about the scars, and I asked him if they would show. He was the soul of delicacy. He said, 'Madame, that depends entirely on you.' "

All this with her back turned. Presently she came back to the couch, drew up a little table to it, and set down two cups of Turkish coffee on tiny gilded saucers. Fred had halfway finished dressing. In shirt and trousers, but no shoes, he sipped a little from his cup.

"Well, Frédéric dear. You manage things very well," she said, sitting down beside him on the sofa. But offhandedly; there was a mechanical and indifferent quality to her now as though she had done all these things many times before.

The coffee was thick, strong, and gritty. The sediment was not removed from it, only ground to a fine powder. A greenish iridescence played on the surface of the liquid. There was a taste of some rare chemical, a perfume like patchouli.

"What's in this anyhow?"

"Just a little oil of haschisch."

He got up and spat what was in his mouth into a potted plant.

"What a child you are."

"That's what you like about me, isn't it?"

"Yes, but children are so tiresome. They will never do what one wants them to do."

"It depends I suppose on what you want them to do."

"Youth is wasted on the young. They are unable to appreciate even the youth of others."

This, it seemed to him, was a fairly profound remark, coming from a person of such apparent frivolity. "It's true," he said, "that I prefer more mature women. They have . . ."

"Yes, I know. A knowledge of the world," she said with an edgy sarcasm. "That's what they always tell us when we've been around a bit too long."

"I was thinking more of physical attributes."

"Ah, you like these." Quite simply she curved her two hands under her breasts. "They are quite nice, everyone tells me. Possibly you have what they call a complex. You are only searching for a mother." At this Fred colored a little. "Ah, I see I have struck home. Excuse me. We will talk about something else. Everyone has his little quirks. I, for instance, prefer young men. Perhaps I am searching for a son."

Fred felt the conversation was becoming a little too aberrant for his taste. It skirted the edge of a dark gulf he preferred not to explore. "I'm glad anyhow you like me," he said by way of changing the subject.

"You are very nice," she said detachedly, almost indifferently. And then after a moment, "I have loved the same man for many years."

"Who?"

"Ah?" She turned toward him with a little smile of surprise. "You don't know? But everyone knows. It's Reynaldo. But he—prefers Marcel."

"So—they are lovers?"

"No. They were, a long time ago. Now they are only friends. But Reynaldo still doesn't care very much for the ladies."

"And Marcel?"

"He is a perfect *gentleman*," she said, setting her teeth to give the word the proper English intonation. "He has sometimes tried to fall in love with young ladies, but it was not a success."

She drained her coffee delicately and set the cup down. He saw her eyeing his own half-empty cup, as though she might drink that too, but evidently she decided not to.

"But poor Reynaldo has now received his just deserts," she went on, "because Marcel these days is more interested in the lower orders."

"Agostinelli?"

She nodded, a little mysteriously, although there seemed to be nothing very mysterious about what she was saying. "Marcel is a spoiled child. He had a mother and a grandmother. He was never denied anything he wanted."

"And is he an important writer?"

"My dear, how can I say? I read nothing except *L'Illustration*. He hasn't written very much."

"But the novel he is working on now?"

She seemed impatient at all this talk about Proust. "My dear Frédéric, Marcel is a dilettante. A rich dilettante. A rich Jewish dilettante." She got up again and strode around the room. Yet there was something artificial about her emotion. It was a *Phèdre* part: beautiful and mature femininity, outraged on account of jealousy.

"If Reynaldo doesn't care for you," said Fred, "Reynaldo is making an important mistake."

At this she smiled again. But her smile was like her annoyance somehow: contrived and mechanical, the emotion of an actress. "Bah! the managers don't want me any more. They want silly young things like your Herma, with no sophistication or finesse. No knowledge of the world."

At this Fred took umbrage a little. "She does have a voice."

"Ah well, voice. That isn't what they care about, you know, out there in the theater."

"Not in the music hall, perhaps."

"That's what I'm talking about. They don't want a voice. They want a personality. They want me! They want Pougy!" she declared with an arm uplifted. She struck a pose, legs spread apart and torso thrust forward, like the Spirit of Battle on a victory arch.

At this spectacle Fred in spite of himself felt a stir of desire. For a moment he thought he might almost be ready to start the whole thing over again. Instead he groped for his necktie and began knotting it. Still sitting on the couch, he slipped his feet into his shoes. He stood up.

She looked at him sideways. "Mon cher Frédéric. Aren't you going to make me a little gift before you leave?"

"Gift?"

"Surely you have a little money to spare?"

He looked at her. "Are you serious?"

"Of course."

"But I didn't think . . ."

She shrugged. "What will you?" she said imperturbably. "The managers won't have me anymore. And somehow I must pay the bills. The Ritz isn't cheap, you know."

"What do you think would be appropriate?"

"Appropriate?"

"What do the others . . ."

"Perhaps a thousand francs," she said quickly and in a business-like way.

He gave it to her.

He found his waistcoat and coat and put them on. Before the mirror in the entry he tossed back his hair and smoothed it with his fingers.

"Would you like a comb?"

"No."

"I like you better as a tousled little beast anyhow."

Before he left he asked her, "By the way, why did the lover shoot you?"

"Because, after I had provided him with every delight that the heart of man could hope for, I asked him if he didn't have a little gift to leave me."

Fred smiled faintly.

"But you," she said, "could not be so ungallant."

6.

After the four performances of the *Tales* at the Opéra, Herma was free for a few days and then she had a lead in a *Traviata* at the Châtelet—not the most prominent theater in Paris but a good company, with Etienne Bos as director. Violetta was her favorite part, perhaps because the duet with Germont in the second act always reminded her of Grasse—so jolly and wicked at Delmonico's, stuffing himself and at the same time feeling for Lucì's skirt—and later, dashing into the burning house for the baby. And then too she had been coached in the duet by an expert—"If you will sing it with the right sob, you will bring the house down." There was always a big burst of applause after the duet, and a few bravas. Still she did the finale well too. That plaintive but vibrant "Ah! Ma io ritorno a viver! Oh gioia!" as she fell back on the couch. She took several curtain calls, a bouquet or two, and went off to her dressing room quite blithely, with a little smile.

It was odd, she thought as the dresser brought the towel and the cold cream, that she had become a specialist in death scenes—she who was so carefree and content in her ordinary daily life. But perhaps it was only because so many operas ended with the heroine expiring. Except of course for Minnie, who sang her "Addio California" and then went off to live happily with Johnson—but that was an American story. All the others expired in the last act—Mimì, Aïda, Tosca, Antonia, Butterfly, Violetta . . . Still feeling pleased with herself, she hummed the "Dite alla giovine" as the dresser combed out her hair. "And then die, and then die, and then die!" The face in the mirror smiled back at her.

When she was dressed she got out the small folded note again and looked at it. The mauve notepaper was expensive, the handwriting delicate and precise.

"My dear. Everyone knows of your Wednesdays. But alas! I never go out. And in the afternoon—unthinkable. But you may come here if you wish. However I beg you, not before midnight. Only at night am I alive. And, earlier in the evening, I work."

It was signed only with a stiff and florid little "M." Perhaps he didn't care to give out autographs. Still, he was charming when he wished to please. We women like them, perhaps, she thought, because they are no danger to us, and we can flirt and play with them as we please. Besides, they are interested in the same things we are.

With the trace of the little smile still on her face, she put the note away in her handbag, threw a cape around her shoulders, and went out. She found a taxi in Avenue Victoria, just around the corner from the stage entrance. The taxi went along Rue de Rivoli, up the avenue and past the Opéra with its circle of lamps held up by caryatids, and on into Rue Auber. Another turn, and it came out onto a broad avenue lined with plane trees. It was almost deserted; only a policeman here and there or a couple half hidden in the shadow of the trees. Place St.-Augustin went by, then a little farther on the taxi stopped and she got out. In the glow of the street lamp she made out the gleam of the brass number over the door: 102 Boulevard Haussmann.

The concièrge was still up, even though it was after midnight: an old woman with her gray hair pulled tightly back on both sides. She glanced up at Herma, then went back to her *Petit Parisien*. A dim bulb was burning in the entryway. Herma after some searching found the antiquated lift, opened the iron and glass door, and figured out which buttons to push to make it work. On the first floor she got out. It was very dark on the landing and she groped around trying to find a bell. Finally she knocked gently at the door.

When the door opened there was hardly any more light inside the apartment. An unkempt Marcel, smiling faintly and saying nothing, showed her in. He was swathed in woolen pyjamas and a pair of sweaters. It was warm in the room and a veil of moisture glistened on his face.

He closed the door behind her. They were standing in a large salon which had the air of not being used very much. It was almost bare of furniture; there was only a divan and a pair of chairs, all three with dustcovers over them, and an étagère with a small night-light burning on it. This accounted for the shadowy gloom as you came in. On the wall Herma made out a portrait of Marcel, evidently done a number of years before; it showed him as a young man in his twenties in evening dress and holding a cigarette. By the door was a mysterious object which proved to be an elephant's foot adapted for holding umbrellas.

Still without a word, he led her across the room and through the door beyond. There, in the combined study and bedroom, it was a little lighter. There was a lamp with a glass shade on the writing desk and another smaller one by the bed. The bed was unmade and rumpled. In addition to the desk there was a table covered with stacks of paper, and there were more papers and books piled on the bed. An old-fashioned cabinet, high and narrow with a glass door, was devoted solely to medicines: a collection of bottles, vials, and papers containing powders, some of them torn and empty. On the top of the cabinet a saucer of Legras Powder smoldered, exuding a thread of smoke and a sharp odor of camphor. There were many other odors: the medicines, the not-very-clean bedclothes, the remains of food on various trays and dishes around the room, the chamber pot clearly visible under the bed. The walls, not only in the bedroom but in the salon as well, were lined with cork. Not a sound penetrated into the apartment from the outside.

He seemed perfectly well aware that these conditions under which he lived might seem odd to others. "You see," he explained without asking her to take a seat (and indeed there was no place to sit except for the sofa across the room, which was also piled high with books and papers), "it's the bad season for me. From April on—the pollen from the plane trees alone. If you were to bring a single flower into the apartment, I would be unable to breathe for a week. And the noise—the omnibus goes directly by on the boulevard. And under me on the ground floor there is a terrible doctor who, as far as I can tell, bangs saucepans together. I can't tell you why." If he could hear anything at all through the cork on the walls, Herma thought, he must have extraordinarily sensitive hearing. "And I must work," he went on. "For me"— he waved his hand toward the papers scattered around the room—"it is the only thing of any importance."

Here he smiled apologetically, as if to indicate a faint irony on the importance of the work; or more precisely, she had the impression, on the subject of the egotism of all artists and writers, himself and perhaps even Herma included.

He reached for an electric button at the end of a tangled cord by the bedside. After a few moments a sullen dark-faced young woman appeared in the doorway. Obviously she had been awakened from her sleep.

"Coffee," said Marcel shortly.

In only ten minutes or so she came back with two small cups of black coffee and a bowl of sugar on a tray. She left again, all without having spoken a word.

"That is Anna. She's the wife of Alfred."

"They live here?"

"Yes. They occupy the other bedroom. She's a tiresome creature. But Alfred . . . is necessary to me. He typewrites my manuscripts," he added quickly. This was new information for Herma, who had supposed that Agostinelli was his chauffeur. And he, sensing perhaps that she was skeptical of this detail, went on to explain rather redundantly,

"I've taught him to typewrite."

They had both remained standing from the time they entered the room. She sipped her coffee. He barely touched his to his lips and then set it down. He seemed to be content to look at Herma, to study her in his leisurely, penetrating, and yet not unfriendly way. In his pyjamas, wrapped to the throat in sweaters, he looked even more like an oriental sorcerer, or a swami capable of levitation or long existence without nourishment. The light from the two lamps, illuminating him from below, intensified the orchidaceous quality of the pale face with its short beard and the shaggy hair falling over the brow. He moved slowly about the room, allowing his fingers to glide over this and that.

"But, even though I am not allowed to have flowers, other beautiful creatures come here," he said with a glance and a smile. Suddenly she was aware again of his charm—dark and elaborate and yet somehow childlike. After a silence, and another examining look, he began, "You must find it strange . . ."

"Strange?"

"Not only this room, but . . . everything. Paris. Europe. Our old world." He paused again for a moment, seeming to muse. "Each of us is different for every other. We are all characters in the private novels of those we know. I think of you somehow as a creature out of *Paul et Virginie*, or *Atala*—a farouche innocent child out of the paradise of the New World. The Girl of the Golden West." Here again he showed by his smile that he was aware of her dislike for the part of Minnie.

"Or . . . do you know Fernand Khnopff?"

"I have one on my wall."

". . . One of those fey mysterious creatures in his paintings—half girl, half boy—whose innocence seems to conceal some secret . . . creatures from the other side of the world."

Herma said nothing. He was striking a little too close. He seemed to see everything about her, to see inside her, as though she were made of glass. She turned away, pretending to examine a book on the table, in the hope that he would change the subject. In this she was successful; or perhaps with his own exquisite sensibility he was aware that he was embarrassing her. After a moment he asked in another voice, more casual, "What is it like in California?"

"Have you been to Nice?"

"Yes. Many times."

"Well, it's nothing like that. There are no grand hotels, no Promenade des Anglais. It's hot and dusty. There are rows of orange groves, and towns with white wooden houses. And there are churches. They're wooden and white too, with tall steeples."

"I wouldn't care for that. I like stones. Old stones. Des vieilles pierres . . ."

Here he seemed to fall into a reverie. His voice trailed off. When he resumed it was as though he were talking to himself.

"There is a small town called Illiers, near Chartres. When I was little I used to go there with my family in the summer, to stay with my

aunt Amiot. The colored light of the windows there in the church, falling on certain old stones . . .''

He stopped, picked up one of the long columns of paper on the
table and glanced at it, and set it down again.

Herma perceived. After a moment of silence she encouraged him,
''What is your novel about?''

''How can I explain? It would be like showing you the back of a
tapestry, and you would never understand the picture unless you could
see it from the front.'' He said nothing for a moment, and then he
added, ''It is very complicated.''

''I don't read very many novels.''

''Yes. You told me once. Perhaps not very many people will want
to read it. Only my friends. The N.R.F. doesn't want to publish it. I've
had to pay Grasset to have some of it printed . . .''

Again, drifting around the room with his fingers gliding over things,
he stopped at the table, hesitated, and picked up the long proof sheet
sticky with fresh ink. He held it up to her, like a schoolboy showing his
work, and smiled foolishly. Then he took it over to the bed and sat down
by the lamp.

He read. ''For a long time I used to go to bed early.'' The voice was
curiously unlike his ordinary speaking voice. It was high and scratchy,
theatrical, slightly affected. It was not clear why he fell into this voice
when reading—because of the great importance he attached to his work,
or as a joke—out of irony.

''Sometimes, when I had put out my candle, my eyes would close
so quickly that I had not even time to say, 'I'm going to sleep.'
And a half an hour later the thought that it was time to go to sleep
would awaken me; I would try to put away the book which, I
imagined, was still in my hands, and to blow out the light; I had
been thinking all the time, while I was asleep, of what I had just
been reading, but my thoughts had run into a channel of their own,
until I myself seemed actually to have become the subject of my
book: a church, a quartet, the rivalry between François I and
Charles V . . .''

The scratchy and histrionic voice went on. He read for a long time,
perhaps an hour. At one point Herma thought that she might have fallen
asleep, but it was only that the voice that was telling the story was telling it from the world of sleep, so that the listener too was drawn into
this transformed and transfigured, yet brilliant and detailed world of
somnolence. She didn't understand it very well. It was too hard—the
sentences were too long and complex—but she understood that a voice—
not the voice of Marcel but the voice of the words on the long columns of
paper—was speaking seriously and precisely about itself, about its deep-
est and most profound experience in the dark vale of memory. The
monstrous grammatical constructions were like enormous creatures that
one couldn't see all at once, only a limb here or a staring and uncanny
eye there. Yet she was drawn, somehow, into the world of Combray and

inhabited it, as one might inhabit the world of Fernand Khnopff.

". . . a strange and pitiless mirror with square feet, which stood across one corner of the room, cleared for itself a site I had not looked to find tenanted in the quiet surroundings of my normal field of vision; that room in which my mind, forcing itself for hours on end to leave its moorings, to elongate itself upward so as to take on the exact shape of the room, and to reach the summit of that monstrous funnel, had passed so many anxious nights while my body lay stretched out in bed, my eyes staring upward . . .''

It was the mirror of the house on Ross Street. *Elongate . . . monstrous funnel.* A little prickly feeling seeped through her. Each of the details, the magic lantern, Golo "riding at a jerky trot,'' the walk along Swann's Way through the wheat, the Madeleine dipped in tea and melting on the tongue, happened to *her,* as though they had been drawn out of her own dim and forbidden memory.

She didn't notice when he stopped. She only became aware, at a certain point, that he was no longer reading.

"It's about Time.''

"Yes. Everything is. All novels are about Time. And everything is a novel.''

He seemed different. Perhaps it was only because he was tired. She looked at his invalid paleness, his nervous hands and his unconvincing, somehow frightened smile.

"You told me once that you were like Antonia in the *Tales of Hoffmann.*''

He seemed not to remember. Finally he said, "Yes, it's because I'm not well, and because of my writing. My Art.'' This with his apologetic smile. "It's not really good for me. When I write, it gives me a fever, and that isn't really good for me. Just as singing was not good for Antonia.'' He glanced at the proofs on the table. "And yet, just like Antonia, I must.''

"And . . . Illiers. Do you still go there in the summer?''

"No. There is no one alive there that I know anymore. Now I go to the seaside. To Deauville or Cabourg. And I write about that too. I am writing about it now.'' Putting aside the proofs, he turned to some manuscript sheets on the desk. Then he set them down again. "But perhaps this doesn't interest you.''

"Yes, it does,'' she said quickly. "It's only that it's—so deep. I'm not quite sure I follow it. But I like things that are deep.''

"If things are too deep, one can drown in them.''

She glanced at him. But he was smiling. It was not serious. He was only chiding her for not reading novels. The clock on the desk showed that it was after three in the morning. She got up from the sofa where she had been sitting on a heap of books.

"Please don't leave. It is only now that I come to life.''

"I must. I have to sing again tomorrow night—that is, tonight.''

He rang, and the sullen-faced Anna appeared.

"Please go to St.-Augustin—it's only a few steps—and get a taxi for the young lady."

It wasn't clear why he told Anna that it was only a few steps to St.-Augustin. Surely she must have known that. It was perhaps for *her* benefit—to demonstrate that, although Anna was a dreary creature, he didn't intentionally treat her badly or put her to unnecessary discomfort. Herma could easily have walked to the square herself—more easily than Anna—since she was wide awake. But she said nothing.

"We are both nocturnal creatures," he said. "You because your life is in the theater, and I—because it is the way I am. I can only sleep in the daytime. I have to take veronal and . . . other things." He waved a limp hand at the collection of bottles in the cabinet. "They're bad for me too. Very few things are good for me. One is the sea air."

All this was rather disconnected. She waited for him to go on. After a moment he said, "Perhaps you would like to go to Cabourg with me. I am going next month. Alfred will drive us. He is also a chauffeur," he explained superfluously, forgetting perhaps that it was Alfred who had driven them to the Ritz the night of the *Tales of Hoffmann*. "It will be perfectly proper. Anna will be along." The mild and amused resignation of his lifted eyebrow showed what he thought of this part of the idea. "It's charming at this time of the year. There are many diversions. Do you care for Baccarat?"

"No."

Here he laughed outright at her directness. "Well, come anyhow. I love to be surrounded by young girls. And yet I am . . . not an ogre."

So he knew that she knew.

Anna appeared to say that the taxi was below. Herma took his hand, which was moist and warm and seemed boneless. He stayed in the bedroom and didn't show her to the door; neither did Anna, who disappeared wordlessly off into her part of the apartment. Herma went down in the lift and across the sidewalk to the taxi waiting with its door open.

Instead of telling the driver to take her to Avenue Kléber, she said impulsively, "Place de l'Opéra." The taxi went back along the route she had come by earlier in the evening: Boulevard Haussmann, Place St.-Augustin, Rue Auber. It came out into the broad square illuminated with its ornate street lamps. Here she told the driver to stop.

The grandiose pillared façade of the Opéra, the dome with its patina of green, the caryatids with their lamps, everything was exactly the same. But now in the gray light of predawn it seemed shabby and grimy, somehow insubstantial, as though made from wood and canvas like a theatrical set, contrasted to the images that still lingered in her mind—the glowing and brilliant solidity, like the light of stained-glass windows playing on stone, of the world of Combray.

7.

Marcel meant the invitation seriously; there was nothing
frivolous about him, in spite of his detached and faintly ironic way of
looking at things, and he always meant what he said. But in the end it
was Fred and not Herma who went with him to Cabourg in May. It
was inevitable that Fred and Marcel should meet—Fred in fact called
at Boulevard Haussmann to deliver a pair of complimentary tickets to
the *Traviata* at the Châtelet and found the door opened by the rumpled
Oriental Sorcerer himself, who explained that he was "desolated" that
he couldn't accept the tickets on account of his health, but was "enchanted" that Fred had had the "exquisite courtesy" of thinking of
him. It was inevitable too that Marcel, with his interest in everything
that was different from himself, should be attracted to Fred, with his
American frankness and offhand manner, his slender and yet tough and
assured good looks—even the strain of brash adolescent recklessness,
the bad-boy or voyou quality that made him so attractive to women of
a certain age.

In the month that followed Fred came now and then to Boulevard
Haussmann, although it was difficult because of their badly matched
schedules. There was almost no time of the day when they were both
awake and free, and if Fred went there late at night after one of
Herma's performances he got no sleep at all, and both he and Herma
were cross the next day. The best time was in the late afternoon, when
Marcel woke up and rang for tea, and had an hour or two before he
ate his bizarre supper of buttered noodles, or an omelette with rusks,
and then banished his visitor to set to work on the constantly growing
mountain of manuscript on the desk.

And naturally Fred, like everyone else, was attracted to Marcel—
his elaborate courtesy, his dark oriental beauty, his sensitive and necromantic intelligence that saw instantly through to one's secrets and yet
disarmed the victim with its admixture of compassion and intimacy. Beyond this, he was interested in him because he was a celebrity and there
was never any harm in knowing a celebrity, and also because he was
very odd, and odd people were always interesting.

Yet this was too crass a way to put it. No one was immune to
Marcel's charms, no one who knew him—although he had enemies and
had even once—incredible as it seemed—fought a duel at dawn in the
Bois de Boulogne—and he, Fred, was as charmed as the others. It was
a pleasure to be in the presence of Marcel, under whatever circumstances;
even if his cork-lined room smelled like an Algerian souk—or if he
often chose to make strange, sly, and elaborately courteous remarks that
seemed to reflect on individuals present—or if the three-way relations
among Marcel, Agostinelli, and Anna were too dark and perilous a

subject to be thought about very much. Even so implacable an enemy as Liane de Pougy had to concede Marcel's charm. That was why she disliked him so much; because of the power he exerted over Reynaldo, even now years after their intimacy had turned into an ordinary friendship between two men. "Monsieur Marcel has enemies, but they are wrong, and even they know it," as Agostinelli put it.

Marcel's nocturnal habits having to be taken into account above all, they left from Paris a little before midnight in the Hispano tourer: Agostinelli at the wheel and Anna in front with him, Marcel and Fred almost lost in the large salonlike interior, the baggage on top and strapped to the rear. They arrived at the Grand Hôtel just at dawn. Of all the times of day it was possible to arrive and register at the Grand Hôtel in Cabourg, nobody else had ever arrived at dawn except Marcel.

A drowsy chasseur came out and got their baggage. They were installed in three rooms: a double for Anna and Agostinelli, and large singles for Fred and Marcel. Fred and Marcel went to sleep, Fred because he had been up all night talking in the car and could hardly keep his eyes open, and Marcel because it was his ordinary time to do so. When Fred woke up it was after noon. He went down to the restaurant and had something to eat. Then he looked around a little. In the gray dawn of the arrival he had scarcely noticed anything except the chasseur showing him which way to set his feet. The hotel and the town itself were pleasant, in a late-Victorian and vulgar sort of way. The hotel faced onto a circular park, with the casino adjoining it so that you could go from one to the other without going outdoors. At the rear was a terraced garden, then the beach with the somewhat chilly-looking sea behind it. On the seawall some girls were throwing up a diabolo and catching it on a string with two sticks. At this time of the year most of the guests were women and children. There were plenty of girls, and all of them seemed to be pretty. Fred had coffee on the terrasse, looking down on the beach.

So began a new kind of existence, the life of Cabourg. It was a brief one, lasting only for two weeks. Evidently Marcel didn't work very much during these interludes at the seaside. He made notes, or might write a manuscript page or two and set it aside. But he came chiefly for the sea air, which was good for his asthma, and the society—so he said, although he had hardly anything to do with others and kept to his own private ways, for the most part, observing things rather than taking part in them directly. Once, to Fred's astonishment and even the mild surprise of Agostinelli, he appeared on the golf course in white suede shoes and a long violet cloak like that of an archbishop, along with a friend encountered by chance, the publisher Calmette; but he was unable to master the game because he was convinced that the player who took the most strokes to get around the course was the winner. Perhaps this was only one of his private jokes.

Yet in secret and in his own way he was always working, Fred began to see. Once, when he emerged in the late afternoon, he and Fred had tea on the terrasse of the hotel overlooking the beach. While they were still sitting over their empty cups a little band of girls came through the terrasse, laughing and chattering like pastel birds, on their way down to the beach. When they caught sight of Marcel they waved and smiled—he nodded, with a slightly ironic expression, in a sign of recognition. They wound on down through the paths of the flower garden. The slanting afternoon sun bathed everything in a brilliant yellowish clarity. Marcel went on looking down at the beach for a moment, then he reached for the menu on the table and tore off the corner of it. With a fountain pen he wrote something. Reading upside down, Fred managed to make out, ''The shadows of young girls on flowers.'' Marcel carefully put away the piece of cardboard in the pocket of his vaudeville comedian's frock coat. The waiter came, immediately noticed the torn menu, took it and folded it under his arm, and went away with a bow.

At sunset a ladies' brass band played on the beach, under a spider-web of electric lights that provided illumination as twilight came on. At other times there might be chamber music, or a black American jazz band which Marcel gazed at with the fascination of one observing strange creatures from another planet. He asked Fred if jazz was played in every home in America. Fred had never heard of it until he came to France. In the evening they dined in the excellent hotel restaurant—Marcel seldom left the hotel, even after dark—and then they would usually take their coffee in the lounge—Fred bored, and Marcel leafing idly through English illustrated magazines. ''I know English, you know. I've translated Ruskin.'' ''But you don't speak it?'' ''Ah no. Zat eez too deefeecult.''

Sometimes, later in the evening, Marcel played Baccarat according to an extraordinary system—he stayed in his room, reading or inhaling the fumes from Legras Powders, while Agostinelli sat at the green baize table in the casino and from time to time dispatched notes by waiters to his employer to ask which card to play next, or how to extricate himself from a difficult situation. Sometimes he won by this method, more usually he lost, but not very much. In the daytime of course he slept; Agostinelli was free, and he and Fred were often together.

Fred studied the motoring map of France, which was printed in halves, with the northern half on one side and the southern on the other. He was trying to see if you could get from Cabourg to Le Mans and back again during the day, before Marcel awoke in the late afternoon. You could. It wasn't necessary to go through Paris; you went on a narrow country road to Lisieux and then on the highway through Argentan and Alençon. It was only about a hundred and sixty kilometers. Agostinelli said he could do it in two hours or a little more if there wasn't too much traffic.

They left the next morning about ten. It was a mild day, almost cloudless, and they took off the removable window-screens from the sides of the car. Agostinelli drove with skill down the winding country road to Lisieux, a good deal faster than he drove when he was chauffeuring Marcel. He was enjoying himself. Fred slumped back in the seat with a cigar, watching the Normandy countryside with its hedgerows go by. There were long periods of silence. When they did speak the conversation was mainly about automobiles. Agostinelli told him that he had originally worked for the Taximètres Unic company in Monaco, but the company had sent him to Cabourg where there was a good deal of business in the summer. Monsieur Marcel had engaged the taxi for tours to look at the local old stones—Bayeux, the steeples of Caen, Balleroy, the cathedral at Lisieux. Finding that he was using the car almost every day, and requesting Agostinelli when he telephoned to the agency, he asked his friend Monsieur Bizet, the director of the company, if he couldn't buy the taxi. "They were at the lycée together," he explained. Agostinelli was evidently impressed by the word lycée, even though he wasn't quite sure what went on in such a place. As a special favor Monsieur Bizet allowed him to buy the taxi assigned to Agostinelli, and Monsieur Marcel had it painted royal blue and upholstered in light-blue leather. Agostinelli of course came with the car. From then on he was Monsieur Marcel's employee.

"The Unic was a good machine," said Agostinelli, "but it had the enclosed salon at the rear and the driver sat out in front exposed to the weather. I didn't mind," he smiled, "but it was painful to the mind of Monsieur Marcel to see me sitting out in the rain. And so last year he bought me the Hispano."

"Bought you?"

"Yes. He bought the Hispano. It's a much finer piece of machinery. In fact Monsieur Marcel doesn't know how fine it is. Essentially it is a racing automobile. The chassis is that of the 15-T model which won the 1910 Coupe de l'Auto at Boulogne. It has the bored-out engine—2.6 liters—with the short-stroke crankshaft. The coachwork is by Lefèvrier of Lyon. Monsieur Marcel doesn't really need such a powerful engine. But he told me to select any car I liked."

He related all this in a combination of quiet technical competence and boyish enthusiasm. He was an extremely attractive person, and best of all he was only partly aware of this himself. Everything about him suggested youth and good nature—his slight plumpness, the lock of hair that hung over his forehead so that he brushed it negligently back now and then, his charming smile—not at all complex or oriental like the smile of Marcel, simply that of a small boy who wanted to please. When Marcel wasn't in the car he took off his chauffeur's cap and set it on the seat beside him. He was proud of the rest of his uniform, polishing the brass buttons until they shone like gold and oiling the black leather of the military belt.

He kept his hands in kid-leather gloves in the correct racing position on the wheel. He seldom took his eyes off the road ahead. "Zuccarelli, in

the 15-T, turned the three kilometers at Boulogne in one minute forty,''
he said.

Between Lisieux and Argentan, driving at a hundred kilometers an
hour down the winding road, Agostinelli ran over a chicken. Looking
around, they saw a small tornado of feathers turning in the air, and
behind it a woman flapping her apron angrily and shouting something
incomprehensible over the roar of the engine.

At Argentan, about halfway to Le Mans, Agostinelli drove around
through the streets until he found a paint and varnish shop. There
was a glossy sign over it, ''Huiles et Peintures.'' Leaving the Hispano
running, Agostinelli shouted to the proprietor who came to the door,
''Do you have a little essence?'' The proprietor nodded and came out
in a moment in his spotted canvas apron, lugging two large metal cans
with spouts, containing each one perhaps twenty liters or so. The two
cans were emptied into the fuel tank, which was a large cylinder
mounted at the rear with a filling pipe sticking up from it.

They started off again. The Hispano was a brutish machine to crank
and Agostinelli always left the engine running if possible. They had
lunch at the railroad station buffet at Alençon (Agostinelli had to crank
the beast afterward to start it), then came into Le Mans in the early
afternoon. They drove through the outskirts and around the city to the
former racecourse at Les Hunaudières, where the Wrights had flown
in 1909. Now it was converted to a full-fledged aerodrome, with two
large hangars with arching metal roofs, an office, and a flying school.

There were a number of machines lined up on the grass in front of
the hangars. Fred went into the office and came out with the rental
manager who showed him what was available. Most of the machines
were privately owned. For rental there were some obsolete Farmans, a
Demoiselle monoplane, a pair of Bréguets, and a Deperdussin with the
Antoinette engine that Fred didn't trust. Fred chose a two-place
Bréguet biplane, of the same type the French army had purchased for
some trials for possible military use. The engine was a 60-horsepower
Anzani radial with pushrod-operated overhead valves. The magneto
system was twinned so that if one half of it failed the other part would
still go on providing a spark. There was no oil sump; the castor-oil
lubricant was mixed with the fuel.

Agostinelli examined the engine with interest and asked a number
of questions. He had never seen a radial engine and wanted to know
exactly how the fuel was supplied to the cylinders. And wouldn't the
horizontal cylinders wear oval because of the weight of the pistons?
The rental manager lifted his eyebrow at this. It was a well-known
difficulty with radials. Obviously Agostinelli had an instinct for machinery.

''There's no muffler system.''

''No. It isn't necessary in the air.''

''It must be very noisy.''

"Very."

Fred had his helmet and goggles with him along with the rest of his flying gear. The manager lent Agostinelli a pair of goggles. Fred remembered how the mechanic Kinney had lent him the goggles when he flew at the Presidio, years ago. Like the young man who flew the Wright Flyer in San Francisco, Agostinelli turned his cap around backward so it wouldn't blow off.

They mounted into their places. Fred, looking around, showed Agostinelli how to fasten his safety harness. A mechanic swung the propeller a few times, the engine caught, and they were off.

There was a tall row of elm trees a little beyond the upwind edge of the field. Obviously there were two ways to deal with this. You could try to climb over the trees or you could go into a climbing turn to the right almost as soon as you were off the ground. Fred, trusting his own flying ability more than the power of the unfamiliar engine, decided to do the turn. The elm trees swung around, as though whirled on the end of a string, and dropped away below. The Anzani had a lot of power. Probably he could have cleared the trees easily on a straight takeoff. The aerodrome dropped away behind. He went up to fifteen hundred and settled out on a course to the west, over the rolling farm country of the Sarthe. At this altitude he could catch a glimpse now and then of the valley of the Loire, far away to the south. The small map which the manager had lent him was fastened to the instrument panel with a piece of tape.

The Bréguet had a single long cockpit with two tandem seats in it so that Agostinelli was directly behind him and could watch what he was doing. Whenever he made a maneuver Fred pointed at the control stick or at his feet on the rudder bar to show Agostinelli what he was doing. Agostinelli nodded. He was interested in everything and he seemed to comprehend quickly. Once, without touching his own dual stick, he cupped his hands around it and made motions to the right, to verify that this was what was done in a right turn. Fred, looking around, nodded and yelled, "THAT'S JUST TO BANK. YOU HAVE TO WORK THE RUDDER BAR AT THE SAME TIME." At a certain point, with his hands and feet still on the controls, he turned around and allowed Agostinelli to pretend at least that he was banking the aeroplane in a turn. He gave it a little too much rudder and Fred held the bar stiff with his feet to stop it. "FINE, FINE." He felt like Castel-Jaloux, yelling encouragement at the student who was in imminent danger at every moment of throwing the craft into a spin or breaking off its wings. "TAKE YOUR FEET OFF THE BAR NOW. LEAVE THE STICK ALONE."

Fred made a wide turn over a town—it was called Voivies, he verified from the map—and headed back toward Les Hunaudières, following along the ribbon of a small river which divided around an island and then came back together, thus providing him with a landmark. To the left and below he caught sight of the two large silver hangars. He glanced at his watch; they had been in the air a little less than an hour. From his long habit of renting aeroplanes by the hour Fred had developed an instinct for this unit of time and invariably glided into a landing at fifty-eight or fifty-nine minutes, thus avoiding having to pay for over-time. It was also a good way to avoid running out of fuel. If there were no women aviators, perhaps it was because they had no sense of time. Herma was always late for rehearsals. Probably Marcel couldn't fly an aeroplane either. Fred cut the throttle, banked in a descending curve to the left, and lined up on the field.

The grass rushed up. The field at Le Mans was smoother than the one at Issy, more like a golf course than a pasture. The heavy two-place machine dropped a little faster than he expected, and the skid bounced a little as he touched down. Stick back! Right on your pecker, as Castel-Jaloux always said. Another reason why women couldn't fly.

He taxied the Bréguet up and wheeled to a stop in the line before the hangars. They got out. Agostinelli took off his goggles and turned his cap the right way around. They started to walk away, then Agostinelli turned and went back.

He looked at the Bréguet again. Standing with his hand on the guy wire that supported the two wings, he said, "Monsieur Frédéric, beside this, a motor car is a heavy and clumsy thing."

8.

Agostinelli took a few lessons—once again at Le Mans, before they left Cabourg—and then, after they were back in Paris, at Issy-les-Molineaux, flying the old Farman with Castel-Jaloux's stiff leg stuck out beside him.

But he didn't have much time for flying. Monsieur Marcel was al-ways sending him on errands, and he often stayed up half the night taking Monsieur Marcel or his friends to hear music, to restaurants, or to the Ritz—Monsieur Marcel sometimes lent the car and stayed home himself, if he wasn't feeling well enough to go out. And the next day, after being up half the night, Agostinelli was too sleepy to fly.

Besides, he didn't really have the money for the lessons. Monsieur Marcel paid him adequately but barely so, and he had Anna to support as well as himself. Anna was paid nothing, even though she lived in the apartment and often stayed up half the night herself administering to Monsieur Marcel's various wants. Monsieur Marcel disliked her so much that he preferred to pretend she didn't exist, so he didn't pay her. He, Agostinelli, didn't have any friends in Paris and the only one he could talk to about these things was Monsieur Frédéric.

They met in a café in Rue d'Astorg, just off Boulevard Haussmann, near the pharmacy where Agostinelli pretended he had gone out to buy some drugs. Agostinelli complained that he was practically a prisoner. He had no freedom, he couldn't go and do what he wanted, he was always at Monsieur Marcel's call at any time of the day or night. He was con-

fined to the apartment much of the time, even in the daytime when
Monsieur Marcel was sleeping, because he might wake up and call for
Agostinelli to take a message to Madame de Noailles, Madame Arman de
Caillavet, or some other of his many society-lady friends whom he wished
to please with some charming thought that had struck him, or whose
invitation he wished to accept or decline.

"You see, Monsieur Frédéric, I am still very fond of Monsieur
Marcel. He has always been very nice to me. But a man is entitled to
some life of his own. Even a convict in prison is left alone for a few hours
while he sleeps every night. And Anna. It isn't fair to Anna. Perhaps
you could speak to Monsieur Marcel."

"Why don't you talk to him yourself?"

"When you talk to someone about things that are so delicate, it's
important that you choose exactly the right words. I'm afraid Monsieur
Marcel might be angry, or that he might turn against me and that would
end our friendship. You would know the proper words to choose. You're
an educated man, Monsieur Frédéric. Un homme cultivé. You would know
how to talk to him."

"I don't even speak French very well."

"I don't know what to do, Monsieur Frédéric. I still like Monsieur
Marcel very much."

But Fred didn't talk to Marcel about it. It was really none of his
business, and he too didn't want to offend Marcel by mingling in something that was really a personal matter. He liked Agostinelli, but he also
liked Marcel too. It was intruding between a man and his wife. And of
course Anna . . . Fred himself didn't care very much for Anna.

Fred didn't see very much of Marcel in these days. He himself was
busy, and Marcel was evidently preoccupied with other things, or perhaps
he had found out somehow that Fred had taken Agostinelli to Le Mans
and was cool toward him on account of this. Agostinelli might even have
told him about the trip himself, in his frank and open way. Well, Fred
thought, they would have to settle it between themselves. His own life
was complicated enough as it was.

Agostinelli took only four or five lessons at Issy. He made progress,
but he had the problem that he had so much experience with automobiles
that he regarded the aeroplane as a kind of a car with wings, and tried to
drive it instead of flying it. Still he was full of enthusiasm, his basic instinct for machinery was good, and he learned quickly. He never soloed
at Issy. Evidently Castel-Jaloux wasn't satisfied. Still, Fred remembered,
he himself hadn't soloed until he had had a half-dozen lessons or so with
Castel-Jaloux, and he had a lot of flying experience before he came to
Paris. It was difficult for Agostinelli, because he could only get away for
a lesson once every couple of weeks, sometimes not even that, and sometimes he forgot in between what he had learned before.

Once Fred was out at Issy flying himself and he was still there when
Agostinelli came back with Castel-Jaloux from his lesson. The Farman
wobbled around to line up with the field, but it was far too low when it
straightened out. Evidently Castel-Jaloux took over, because the engine

gunned up to a higher note and the Farman circled around the field again before it came in, this time at the proper altitude. He let Agostinelli land it, however, because even from across the field Fred could tell from his stance that he was gripping the stick and staring out with boyish seriousness through the windscreen.

When he had taxied around and brought the Farman up before the hangar, not quite in line with the others, he and Castel-Jaloux got out. They came slowly in toward the office, Castel-Jaloux helping himself with his cane. Fred heard him telling Agostinelli in his mild tone, "Don't forget. When you turn you lose altitude. It's not like a car; there's no road to hold you up."

It was a little after this that Marcel telephoned to the apartment in Avenue Kléber. He seemed irritated when he heard Herma's voice answer.

"Put Fred on the apparatus."

"He's not here."

"Well, where is he?"

"I can't say."

"Then have him come to me. I must speak to him," said Marcel, and hung up the apparatus abruptly without saying good-bye. Where was his charm now? These were the manners of an Oriental despot, Herma thought, not a friend.

Fred waited until the next day and then he went around to Boulevard Haussmann about five o'clock when he was sure Marcel would be up. He started to knock on the door, but Marcel had evidently heard the lift coming up and had left the door a little ajar. He pushed it open and went in.

Marcel was standing at the other end of the large salon. Perhaps he had left the door open because he didn't want to be standing so close to him when he came in the room, or to be in danger of having to take his offered hand. He was dressed as though to go out, in his frock coat, rumpled trousers, and a collar with stand-up points.

His paleness was accentuated in the gloomy shadows of the room with its closed shutters and its furniture in dust covers. He said immediately, "I don't want Alfred to fly."

"Marcel. I'm sorry. It was I who took him to Le Mans and got him interested in the first place. But it's a natural thing for him to do. He's very much attached to it. He's good with machinery of all kinds."

Marcel's voice became shrill. "I know he's attached to it. But I don't want him doing it anymore. Do you understand?"

"He can do what he likes," said Fred, angry himself. "It's no business of mine. How can I stop him?"

Marcel said nothing to this, and after a moment Fred went on in a somewhat calmer voice. "It's quite safe. The machines are well maintained and the instructors are competent."

Marcel was beside himself. Fred had never seen him in such a state. The face had whitened until it was corpselike. "It's not that," he said in his high and cracked histrionic voice. "It's the people he associates with in such places. The scum of the aerodromes.''

Fred said, ''You don't know what you are talking about.''

After that Marcel, still pale with anger, said nothing. He went off to the other side of the room and coughed into a handkerchief. The quarrel had probably given him a slight fever. Like all hypochondriacs, Fred thought, he used his sickness to impose his will on others.

The next day he sent Fred a bunch of dahlias from Caumartin in Rue St.-Honoré, and a note saying simply, ''We should not quarrel.''

9.

About a week after that, Agostinelli telephoned from Boulevard Haussmann to ask if Fred could meet him again in the café in Rue d'Astorg. He, Agostinelli, didn't like to conduct long conversations by telephone, and besides he couldn't say very much because Monsieur Marcel was asleep in the next room.

Fred went to the café, which was small and dark inside, and almost empty. They sat in the rear; Fred had a coffee and Agostinelli only a mineral water.

Agostinelli began immediately by saying that he had decided to leave the service of Monsieur Marcel. He wanted to devote himself seriously to flying lessons, because he wanted to become a professional aviator. He frowned as he explained this, because being serious was difficult for him. ''A man only has one life. And I have to decide whether I want to live it being Monsieur Marcel's chauffeur, or being someone for myself, doing something I want to do.''

''Have you told Marcel yet?''

He shook his head. ''I'm afraid it will pain him. But what will you, Monsieur Frédéric? There are times in life when people must be hurt. Sometimes there's no other way. As when you are tired of a woman, and you have to tell her you're going to leave her.''

It was only a metaphor. Evidently it didn't occur to him that there was any greater parallel to his relations with Marcel.

''So my mind is made up. And, even if Monsieur Marcel were to agree to the flying lessons, I want to leave Paris. Anna isn't happy in Paris. She doesn't know anybody here and the climate depresses her. I want to go to the south, where I can go on flying even in the winter when the weather is bad.''

Fred considered. There was an instructor he knew from Issy who had gone to set up his own flying school in Antibes. He didn't know what to think about the whole situation. It would be bad for Marcel in any case, but Agostinelli was determined to go, and perhaps the best thing he could do was to help him out in any way he could, otherwise there would only be two unhappy persons instead of one.

"Do you know Antibes?"

"Of course, Monsieur Frédéric. I am from Monaco. All my people live on the Côte d'Azur."

"I know a man who has a flying school at La Grimaudière, near Antibes. His name is Soldati. I could write him a letter for you."

"Is it a good school?"

"I don't know. He used to be at Issy. I think the school is rather small. But he's a good flyer."

Agostinelli was thoughtful. Evidently he still had some doubts about the whole idea. But he was determined to carry through with his plan. He sipped his glass of water. Then he said, "Why don't you come too, Monsieur Frédéric? It would be a little holiday for you. And you could fly too at Antibes."

It was not clear why he suggested this. Perhaps only out of friendliness. Certainly everything about him suggested the friendly and open candor of a large amiable puppy. One could hardly imagine deviousness in him, but it was possible too that it had occurred to him that if Fred went along, then Marcel couldn't so easily accuse him of having run away in order to be with Anna. Probably it would be better, if only for that reason, if Fred went along with them.

He wasn't really deceiving himself. He knew it was a temptation, but Fred had never been very good at resisting temptation. He thought about it. Herma was just finishing Zerlina in *Don Giovanni* at the Opéra, and after that she was free until July when she was to sing in Parma at the annual Verdi Festival. He could go with Agostinelli in the car to Antibes, stay a week or two, and then go on by train to Nice, Genoa, Milan, and Parma.

"For a couple of weeks perhaps."

"We have many friends on the Côte d'Azur. We can easily find you a place to stay."

"I think you ought to tell Marcel before you go."

"Perhaps you could tell him, Monsieur Frédéric."

In the end neither of them told him. Agostinelli and Anna simply showed up with the Hispano in Avenue Kléber at ten o'clock in the morning. Fred knew that Marcel was asleep at that hour of the day. With the help of the concièrge, Fred brought downstairs an astounding assortment of baggage, some of it old and battered but other pieces new, in expensive bright-red leather. Agostinelli had no comment on the baggage. He was used to eccentricities in the moneyed classes. The baggage was all piled in somehow, partly in the rear against the folded-up jump seats and partly strapped on top of the car.

They left the city by the Porte de la Chapelle and the St.-Denis road. It was still good weather, summer was coming on, and the transparent window screens were packed away in the rear. The warm air streamed pleasantly past the side of Fred's head, ruffling his hair. Anna tucked herself away in the rear among the baggage and drowsed. After a while you forgot she was there. They stopped at Fontainebleau for lunch. They ate outdoors on the terrasse of the Aigle Noir and Fred bought a bottle of champagne, after lunch, to toast the new venture. It was turning out to be a pleasant trip. Paris and all its problems were behind. Perhaps it would work out after all.

It was too long a trip for one day, even with the redoubtable Agostinelli at the wheel and without Marcel in the car. They stopped for the night at Lyon and had about another four hours to drive the next day. Agostinelli didn't talk very much; he was concentrating on his driving on the narrow road lined with plane trees, where a bicycle or a peasant with a cart might always appear unexpectedly. Beyond Avignon, where the road came out into the plain and widened a little, it was easier driving.

He looked around to be sure Anna was asleep. He said, "Monsieur Frédéric, have you ever felt an inclination for a person of the same sex?"

Fred felt this was an odd way to put it. After a moment's pause he said, "No."

"Neither have I. Although of course I'm very fond of Monsieur Marcel. But it's not the same thing. You understand, Monsieur Frédéric."

"Yes."

"Not as one is fond of a woman."

"I understand," said Fred.

"But you have to eat. Il faut vivre. Life is like that. Still, I am very fond of Monsieur Marcel."

After that the conversation lapsed for a while. The Hispano raced down the road to the south, through Aix and Brignoles, hardly slowing for the villages. They came out onto the sea at St.-Raphaël. Fred stared out through the windshield at the long hood and the gleaming radiator ornament.

"Are you sure this is your car, Alfred?"

"Certainly, Monsieur Frédéric. It is signed in my name. Monsieur Marcel wanted me to have it."

This evidently reminded him again of the subject of the relations of the sexes, because after a moment he turned and asked bluntly, in his open and friendly way, "You are not romantic toward Mademoiselle Herma?"

Fred wasn't sure how to answer this; or rather he wasn't sure why he felt confused after having said "No."

"You know," he told Agostinelli, "you are one of the few Frenchmen" (he meant Frenchmen of the uneducated class, although he didn't put it this way) "you are one of the few Frenchmen who can pronounce the letter *H*."

"That is because I learned to pronounce Hispano, Monsieur Frédéric," said Agostinelli.

With the help of their friends, Agostinelli and Anna found a small villa with flowers growing over the doorway on the road a kilometer or so out of Antibes. It was the first real home they had ever had. Always before they had lived with relatives, or with Monsieur Marcel. Fred took a room at the Beau Rivage at Port Vauban, which was near enough to the airfield at La Grimaudière that he could walk to it in a quarter of an hour. There was also a motorbus that went down the coast road every so often, but it wasn't very reliable. The first day or two Agostinelli came by in the car to take him to the field, but after that he sold the Hispano to pay for the flying lessons.

The first time they all went out to the field—it was really too modest to call an aerodrome—Fred found that the flying school was a somewhat shaky enterprise. Emile Soldati, the instructor he had known in Paris, was an excellent flyer whose experience went back to the pioneer days with Paulhan and Blériot. But he ran the school practically single-handed, with the help of his brother who took care of the business side of it, and didn't even have a mechanic—he hired a mechanic by the hour when he needed one and did the minor servicing and repairs himself. He had only two aeroplanes—a Farman trainer similar to the one Fred and Agostinelli had flown at Issy, and a small Voisin monoplane for students to fly after they had soloed. The Farman appeared to be in fairly good condition. In fact, it turned out that it was one of the Farmans from the Castel-Jaloux school at Issy, and Soldati had bought it and flown it down to Antibes when he started his own school about a year ago. But the Voisin was old—a design imitated from the Blériots of five years ago—and it had the Antoinette engine that was no longer manufactured and was hard to find parts for. Fred inspected the Voisin dubiously. In spite of its age it seemed to be in good repair. The engine was clean and seemed to have been recently worked on. A small crack in the propeller was patched neatly with a piece of tin. He reached up to the stubby mast and tested the tension of the guy wires. He remembered Kinney: ''No way you can brace just one wing.''

Agostinelli could hardly wait to get into the air. Anna had never seen him fly. It was funny and a little touching to watch him; he behaved exactly like a boy of eighteen showing off for his girl. He put on his helmet and buckled it seriously, leaving his goggles up on his forehead like an old-time flyer. He clambered into the Farman and Soldati got in behind him. Agostinelli pulled his goggles down and waved to Anna. The engine started with a clatter and off they went. Anna watched entranced as the heavy biplane lumbered to the edge of the field, turned around, and roared louder as it lurched into motion. It gathered speed, the skid came up off the grass, and almost at the same moment the Farman rose up and soared past them in the air. Soldati climbed out straight for a kilometer or two, then banked and turned left over the sea.

It was a beautiful setting. The field was almost at the edge of the Mediterranean; there was only the coast road and a narrow stretch of sand and then the sea. The broad curve of the Baie des Anges dwindled away to the north where Nice was lost in the haze. To the south was the promontory of the Cap d'Antibes with a lighthouse on it, and dotted along the cape were the luxury villas of Antibes and Juan-les-Pins.

In the warm sunshine of the south Anna seemed a different person. She seemed to glow, her sullenness left her—or turned into a kind of heavy languor that was unexpectedly attractive—and she was like a creature who had come back to her own place at last after a life of exile. She paid no attention to Fred. She kept her eyes fixed on the dot of the Farman as it crept slowly along the coast, turned over the cape, and began coming back over the sea.

While he waited Fred looked around at the other planes on the field. There were only four or five. Two of them were available for rent: a Morane-Saulnier midwing monoplane, and a Caudron B-II biplane with a 40-horsepower Anzani engine. The Caudron was the better machine, but it was expensive to rent and it burned up a lot of fuel. He looked at the Morane-Saulnier. The midwing design was a big improvement over the Blériot and the Voisin with their wing on top of the fuselage. The stub-mast was still necessary for upward bracing, but the wires had a better angle with the wing mounted lower, and the long struts that went down to the landing gear looked unbreakable. He thought he might try the Morane-Saulnier. The Caudron was probably safer but not as interesting. He climbed up and looked into the cockpit of the small monoplane. The instruments were neatly laid out: oil pressure and temperature gauges, compass, fuel gauge, rev counter, and an airspeed indicator. The instrument panel was polished aluminum and there was a padded leather coaming around the cockpit. He began to itch to fly it.

The Farman came back in, with Agostinelli evidently at the controls. He turned into his approach a little too low, or perhaps he had failed again to allow for the aeroplane squashing down a little in a turn. But there was plenty of room on the field and he landed only a little too short. He taxied to a stop and climbed out, and he and Anna exchanged a big kiss. He was smiling all over.

As it happened Fred didn't fly very much at Antibes. He went up in the Morane-Saulnier once, but the next day somebody else banged it down too hard and damaged the landing gear. The Caudron, as he had expected, was not very interesting. It had been developed for the military and was heavily built to carry an observer and, perhaps, armament or bombs. It was hard to get off the ground, climbed slowly, and steered like a straw hat. Fred lost interest after a flight or two, especially since the rental agency wanted two hundred francs an hour for it.

Besides the weather wasn't as good after the first couple of days. Clouds with dark bottoms drifted over and there were light rain showers. Once in a while a dark line squall would come in from over the sea, leaving a tropic downpour as it passed, and afterward the wind would blow fitfully in savage little gusts for the rest of the day. Since it was a crosswind it made it impossible to fly. "This is nothing," said Soldati. "You should see the way the mistral blows in the winter." Because of these summer squalls, Agostinelli took his lessons early in the morning when it was calm and clear even though the grass was damp. Anna didn't like to get up so early in the morning; she stayed in the villa and slept.

Fred began to get a little bored. Perhaps, he thought, he ought to go back to Paris, or go directly on to Milan and stay there for a few days before he went on to Parma. Still, it was pleasant enough in Antibes. The

Beau Rivage was an éxpensive hotel and the room was large and comfortable. Naturally there was a mirror in the bath. Once he turned himself
into Herma and had lunch in the hotel restaurant, followed by a walk
on the esplanade under the palm trees. But she was pursued by a serious
gentleman in blue spectacles, who pressed her so relentlessly that she
flounced her way back into the hotel and never tried the experiment again.

At La Grimaudière, under the direction of Soldati, Agostinelli
learned fast and soloed in less than two weeks. He and Anna came to the
hotel to tell Fred about it. Agostinelli was full of enthusiasm and wanted
Fred and Anna to go with him the next day to the field to watch him do
it again.

They went out in the afternoon, since Anna still felt herself unable
to get up before ten or so in the morning. The usual squall had gone
through and left a stiff wind behind it. There were whitecaps out over
the Baie des Anges, and the flag at the edge of the field was flapping and
shredded at the edges. But the angle of the wind wasn't as bad as it had
been after the other storms, and the field was broad enough that Agostinelli could take off at a diagonal, almost into the wind. The steel-colored
clouds were still drifting in from the west; the air over the field was gray.

The Voisin was out on the line and fueled. Agostinelli climbed in,
buckled his helmet, and pulled down his goggles. He nodded to Soldati
to indicate that the gas valve was open. Soldati spun the propeller a half-
dozen times and then Agostinelli switched on. The Antoinette didn't
catch at first. Only at the third spin did it cough, bang out a puff or two
of blue smoke, and rise to its barking roar. Agostinelli didn't look at
Anna. Very serious, his face inert, he opened the throttle and bumped
away over the grass. Behind the goggles nothing showed in his expression.

He crossed to the far corner of the field so that he could take off
diagonally into the wind. It was a little bumpier this way, since this part
of the field wasn't used very much. He raced by over the grass only a
short distance from the hangars, still not turning his head to look at
them. Because of the stiff wind the Voisin took to the air all at once, the
skid and the two wheels rising together. This sent him up in a steep
climb, and he overcorrected and came down when he leveled, settling out
only twenty feet or so above the grass.

They watched the Voisin go off across the coast road and the beach
and dwindle away to the south over the Baie des Anges. It still didn't
have much altitude; it slipped out to sea just above the level of the whitecaps. Evidently, after his abrupt takeoff into the stiff wind, Agostinelli
was cautious about pulling back the stick. He was about two kilometers
out when he decided to turn and come back in toward the land. At that
distance the Voisin was only a small dot with the thin line of the wing
on either side, and the landing gear dangling below. As Fred watched
he saw the right wing tip lift up a little. Something clutched at his heart.
Don't bank so close to the water, Alfred! It makes the aeroplane lose
altitude when you bank. Just at that moment the Voisin hesitated, and
sank to merge with the horizon. The left wing tip caught the water, sending up a plume of spray. For an instant they saw the tail go up, like a

pointing finger, and settle again. The Voisin sank almost immediately.

Anna gave a stifled scream and stuffed her fist in her mouth. Soldati turned and ran toward the office to telephone for the harbor police at Antibes.

At the hotel Fred, still feeling numb and light, as though something were missing on the inside of him, stopped at the desk and asked for a telegram form. He filled this out, and then stood for a moment looking vacantly at the words he had written, as though he had forgotten where he was or what he was doing. Finally, noticing that the clerk was looking at him curiously, he pushed the telegram across the desk along with a ten-franc note and walked away without a word.

At the telephone in the hotel foyer he also called the station and reserved a first-class seat in the night train to Paris. He glanced at his watch. It was a couple of hours. He phoned to La Grimaudière to see if the body had been recovered yet. It hadn't. He went upstairs to pack.

A taxi, stopping under the white Moorish porch of the hotel just at dusk, collected him and his voluminous baggage and took him to the station. There he checked the baggage directly through to the apartment in Avenue Kléber, keeping only a small handbag for the train.

After he was in the compartment and the train had started it occurred to him that he could have taken a Wagon-Lit, but he hadn't. He wasn't sleepy anyhow; he had been bored and without much to do in the past few days and he had slept more than enough. He shared the compartment with a nun, who must have been a Mother Superior since she traveled in a first-class seat, a businessman who was immaculately neat if somewhat portly, and a French army major in dress uniform with a red képi. None of these people spoke to each other or to Fred. This was because it was a first-class compartment. What you were paying for was the right not to be spoken to by your fellow passengers. If it were third class, everyone would be chattering away, cutting up bread and cheese and sharing it and passing around a wine bottle. It was a good thing he had gone first class. He didn't feel like trading bread and cheese with people and drinking wine. About ten o'clock he went to the dining car and took a table, but when he looked at the menu he realized that all he wanted was a cup of black coffee. He was nervous and edgy and still felt light and floaty.

He went back to his compartment. The Mother Superior had fallen asleep, the businessman was reading a newspaper, and the major stared at him stonily with his hands on his knees. Fred tried to fall asleep too but it wasn't any good. He leaned back with his head on the seat and his eyes closed. When he opened his eyes he saw the ceiling of the car, made out of an odd kind of embossed and gilded tin, and in the middle of it a squat milky-colored electric light. All at once the powerful sensation struck him that beyond the ceiling was the sky. The sky was dark and deep. It extended to infinity. It went on through the stars—past them—past the galaxies—into frightening spaces where no one had ever been and no one could even think about. If the world should turn upside down, you could fall into that and go on falling forever. That was what the sky was. It was Nothing. He didn't care to go on pursuing this line of thought and he looked around to see if by chance the businessman had discarded his newspaper, or if there was anything else to read. There wasn't.

During the night the major got up from his seat and came across the compartment and tried to violate him. He was unable to speak or make any noise. He looked to the others for help, but found that the businessman and the Mother Superior were locked in a passionate embrace, kissing feverishly. He woke up. They were all in their proper places, asleep except for the major who had turned sideways in his seat and was staring out the window into the darkness.

After that he stayed awake, watching the blackness whirl by and the lights of an occasional village or town slamming past at high speed as the express train went up the main line toward the capital. He couldn't see his watch in the dim light of the lamp overhead but they were getting closer. He was tired and wished that he had been able to sleep. Fontainebleau, Melun, Corbeil. A trace of gray light was showing now through the window. The train went across the river and it was in Charenton with the Bois de Vincennes dimly visible to the right. The brakes gripped underneath and it slowed gradually. Then it went on slowly past an orange light, past a trainman standing by the track with an oil pot in his hand, and under the gloomy roof of the station. It came to a stop with a lurch and a hiss of steam. "Gare de Lyon!" the voice of a trainman called out, echoing under the immense glass and steel roof.

The Mother Superior stood up and collected her belongings, and so did the two others. Fred didn't feel like getting up from his seat. It was the way you felt when you didn't want to get up in the morning, or you didn't want to jump into the cold water when you were swimming. He just wanted to stay where he was. He didn't want to go out and do what he had to do.

He sat there for perhaps two or three minutes and then realized this was stupid. He got up and looked around for his handbag. It wasn't there. He looked on the floor of the compartment and in the woven nets over the seats. But the compartment was empty. He opened the door and stepped down onto the platform, and saw the businessman at the far end of the station making rapidly away with the handbag in his hand. Fred didn't even bother to pursue him. There was nothing in the bag anyhow except a change of underwear and socks, his flying helmet and goggles, and his shaving gear. It had the key to the apartment in it too, but the concièrge could let him in.

Out in front there weren't any taxis. He waited until one drew up, pushed in front of another gentleman who was trying to catch it, and got in. He gave the driver the address in Boulevard Haussmann. The trip across Paris seemed to take a long time, but he realized that he didn't care how long it took and wanted it to be even longer; he didn't want to get there. Place de la République, Boulevard Montmartre, Boulevard Haussmann. The taxi drew up in front of the apartment.

He pushed through the polished glass door and crossed the entryway toward the lift, then changed his mind and went back to the concièrge sitting as usual at her table in the loge. She was already up, with a tiny cup of coffee in front of her, or had been up all night.

"Is he alone?"

"Of course he is alone. Who else would there be?" she snapped. "There's only me to take care of him." She added, "He hasn't slept for two weeks."

Fred said nothing, turned away, and went up in the lift. When he knocked it was quite a time before the door opened. He didn't knock again. At last it opened and he went in.

Marcel was standing by the door in his rumpled pyjamas and sweaters. He didn't move and Fred had to shut the door himself. He crossed the room slowly and slipped his fingers over the sofa in its dust cover, then he turned. They stood and looked at each other from across the room. The telegram and its torn blue envelope lay on the étagère by the night light. Marcel's face had a grayish cast, almost violet, from the effects of veronal. It seemed deeply sunken in on the bones of his skull, although this was only perhaps the effect of the shadows in the room. Neither of them spoke. Fred found that his eyes were brimming with tears, and so were Marcel's. It was a long time that they stood there. Time, in fact, was suspended, as it is in Art, or in those crucial moments in the turning of human life when mortality is stripped bare and nothing can be said or done. They were both conscious of the unseen presence between them, both in tears, unable to speak, unable to touch as their emotion called for them to do, separated by the immense dark gulf of the Taboo older than civilization, older than temples and gods, perhaps older than mankind itself.

10.

It was later that summer that the war began. The weather was hot, and Paris was dusty and a little stifling. On the afternoon of August first Herma had gone to a tea dance with a friend, the dancer Bella Pontsis, at Armenonville, the rendezvous of the haut monde in the Bois de Boulogne. Afterward she remembered the moment precisely: they were sitting at their table under the trees with tea and pastries in front of them, chatting and watching the dancers. The orchestra was working away at a trivial and sentimental little waltz with words in English.

> "Nights are long
> Since you went away,
> I think about you
> All through the day,
> My Buddy . . ."

People hummed as they danced. English things and speaking English were fashionable that year. The waltz came to an end and the musicians rearranged the music on their stands. They were about to begin again when the manager, a small and self-important bald man with a mustache, stepped forward and stopped them. He said, "Mesdames et Messieurs, mobilization has been ordered. It begins at midnight. All those who are registered for mobilization are instructed to report to their points of assembly."

He ordered the orchestra to play the *Marseillaise*. Everybody stood up for the music, then sat down again. Some people were dazed, others were smiling. A middle-aged businessman at the next table began speaking confidentially to his companion. The men of military age were for the most part silent. A few people went back out onto the dance floor and danced around without the orchestra, still humming the waltz to themselves. Little by little people left, coming out from underneath the arbor over the dance floor into a late afternoon sunshine sparkling with tiny gold particles.

Because of the excitement Herma and Bella couldn't find a taxi and decided to walk back through the Bois and along the Champs-Elysées. Here and there people were standing in clusters on the sidewalk, talking animatedly about the news. Except for that nothing was changed; Paris was exactly as before, the shops were open, full of expensive merchandise, and the cafés were crowded. News vendors went by shouting "Mobilization!" in the same mechanical way they had shouted "Forty Die in Train Accident!" or "Actress Shoots Lover!" the day before. About halfway down the Champs-Elysées a taxi came along crammed with young men who were perhaps Sorbonne students. In any case they had been drinking. "To Berlin! To Berlin!" they shouted. One of them waved a pistol out of the taxi, laughing. No one paid any attention to them.

And in fact very little changed during those first weeks. The men of mobilization age left, and soldiers in uniform appeared in the streets. The Opéra of course was closed for the summer, but the performances went on at the Châtelet, the Opéra Comique, and the music halls of Montmartre. Herma's last engagement had been the festival at Parma in July, and now she was free until September when she was to begin rehearsing *La Forza del Destino* at the Opéra. She sang at a private recital or two, and went on giving her Wednesdays—she even persuaded the old Gabriel Fauré to come to one, and he seemed to enjoy himself, humming along with the Debussy as Herma sang it but refusing to go to the piano himself. He drank sherry and told some anecdotes about the Consérvatoire, where the daughter of a cabinet minister had once attempted to sing "Vissi d'arte" for an audition but failed miserably because he, Fauré, had instructed the accompanist to play it two notes high, in C natural instead of A flat. No one spoke about the war.

The theaters and music halls were still full. There were more people in Paris than usual in the summer because many people had canceled their holidays. Yet there was a strange quality to the city. A Paris from which all the men of military age were removed—or so it seemed, although probably there were a good many of them left—was a Paris somehow altered, not only a feminine city but a city populated by women alone. The few soldiers who had been seen in the streets got their orders and left, and none of them had been on duty long enough to come back to the city on leave. The men in the theaters were schoolboys with their mothers or men over forty. At the tea dances in the Bois you saw girls dancing together. There was a sudden new informality in the theaters and at other social events. Men wore sack suits instead of evening dress, and tailored suits were fashionable for the ladies instead of gowns. Imitations of military uniforms were popular. Women's suits had leather belts and epaulets, and horizon blue and khaki were the favorite colors. There were signs offering ''Costumes en khaki'' in the window of every modiste. In the restaurants there were shortages of beef and pâté, and other things that came from the war zone in eastern France, but people were good-natured about it, taking ''whatever there was,'' a trout in aspic or a mixed grill of steak and sausages. A new dance came in: the tango. You saw suave young men with pomaded hair, perhaps Argentines, teaching it to girls at Armenonville. It became chic in society to use soldier slang. The dinner wine, whatever the rare vintage, was referred to as pinard: ''Voudriez-vous bien, cher monsieur, me verser un peu de pinard, je vous prie?'' The troops were referred to as ''the poilus'' not ''the soldiers.'' And if you admired something you said, ''Il n'y a rien de si coco.'' The rest of August it remained hot. For some reason the water supply failed now and then, and only a trickle came out of the faucets. ''What will you?'' people said. ''It's the war.'' There was no complaining and people seemed to enjoy these small discomforts. It gave them the feeling they were sacrificing something, just like the poilus in the trenches. Perhaps this was why the government arranged for the water supply to fail.

Herma's friend Bella Pontsis had been the prima ballerina of the Opéra in the nineties. Now she was somewhat past her best years, but still vigorous and in good condition. She operated a dancing school in Rue Godot de Mauroy, and now and then she did a choreography for the Opéra. Herma was often with her, since she didn't care for schoolboys or middle-aged businessmen, and didn't know any Argentines. They went to tea dances—but didn't dance together—to the Odéon to see the aged Bernhardt do *Phèdre,* and for picnics in the country, to Barbizon or Rambouillet.

Bella was Greek, dark and passionate, with exaggerated gestures and an impulsive way of speaking. She had come to France as a child but still spoke with a slight accent. She wore her hair loose, often with a jeweled band around it, and sometimes scandalized the Parisians by going barefoot to cafés in the Champs-Elysées. More commonly she wore sandals with thongs tied around the ankles. She was very beautiful in her way— a little fanée in a way that gave her an attractive kind of decadence— eyes set in shadows, a slightly beaky nose, but a beautiful complexion, a soft sensitive mouth, and a trim dancer's figure with a narrow waist and strong wrists and ankles. She was moody and sometimes fell into silence for hours on end, at other times talked endlessly until neither she nor anybody else understood any longer what she was talking about. But in either case she was animated: constantly in motion, moving about the room, picking up this and that, impulsively embracing friends both male and female and kissing them on the cheeks in the French manner, affectionate to animals and unable to pass a poodle on the Champs-Elysées without picking it up, waving to half the girls in the cafés because they were either her students or dancers she had known in the corps de ballet of the Opéra.

She sometimes came to Herma's Wednesdays. But only once did Herma go to Bella's apartment, a large and elaborately furnished set of rooms over her studio in Rue Godot de Mauroy, just off the boulevards. They had been to Barbizon and came back in the train, tired and dusty, and Bella suggested they go to her apartment and bathe before they went out to dinner at Maxim's. As they went up in the tiny lift Bella smiled, gazed at her, and impulsively kissed her. Still with her little smile, she let her into the apartment.

It was full of Persian rugs, oriental hangings, divans, and pillows. There were large brass vases from Samarkand, a scimitar hanging on a velvet cord, and a large white-enameled cage with a macaw in it. A faint odor of incense lingered in the air. Herma took her bath first. An amusing notion struck her—a trick to play on Bella—but there was no mirror in the bath, or anywhere else in the apartment, it now occurred to her. Perhaps as you got older you didn't care to have them around you. The bath, like the rest of the apartment, was an oriental kind of thing—a square sunken pool, large enough to float a small boat, into which you sank, voluptuously, in warm green-tinted water that smelled of mint. Everything in the bathroom was marble, even the bidet. The towel, when she got out, was a violet affair the size of a bedspread and deliciously soft. Along the marble counter were scents of every description. Herma rejected the more exotic ones, chose a little lavender, and touched it behind her ears and inside her elbows. She put on the things that Bella had left her in place of the dusty tailored suit: a narrow clinging silken robe with a slit skirt, enameled bracelets, and matching earrings. The robe fitted her perfectly even though she was taller than Bella. Evidently Bella kept clothing of various sizes in the apartment to lend to friends. Herma was not sure she was going to wear all this to Maxim's. Perhaps the khaki suit could be dusted off and put back on.

She came out, and Bella, with a theatrical gesture, showed her into the large salon and invited her to seat herself on the divan. Then she disappeared for her own bath. Herma waited. On the low table before her were multicolored liqueurs in elaborate bottles, bonbons and creamy pastel candies with perfumelike flavors, and crisp wafers speckled with paprika. She helped herself to a tiny glass of raki. The bonbons she didn't care for, and the paprika wafers were so spicy that after she ate one she had to go off to the kitchen for a glass of water. She came back and arranged herself on the divan again.

Bella appeared suddenly, on tiptoe and with a pirouette, as if making an entrance. She came down from her toes and smiled. "I have put on my costumes for you." It was not quite clear why costumes was in the plural. Perhaps it was her imperfect French. In any case, what she was wearing was striking indeed. It was a wide flowing gown with enormous sleeves, so broad they almost touched the floor when she lowered her arms. The stuff was a pale gold silk with a good deal of embroidery, in silver and scarlet. When she moved, her bare feet could be seen. There were brass rings on her ankles and wrists. Her loose hair streamed out from a turban which was deftly wrapped from a scarf of the same silk as the gown.

She swung around again, making the sleeves fly and the skirt swirl over the floor. She took to the air, her feet apart and both off the floor at once, with a jingle of brass. She alighted on one foot, the other knee bent and the ankle in front of her body. This particular maneuver ended with her settling gracefully, like a bird, onto the divan next to Herma. She radiated a heavy odor of patchouli, along with a little perspiration.

"What are you drinking? Ah, raki." She poured some Crème de Menthe for herself. "To our careers. To your career, my dear. Ah, mine is finished."

"Surely not."

"I can dance, dance. Ah yes, for my friends I can dance. For you. But not for the grand publique. They would make laughs. They are pitiless. Believe me. I have known. They will be pitiless to you too, when your time comes."

"They're not pitiless to Bernhardt."

This made her furious. "Ah, merde. That cow. She has to do nothing. She doesn't have to move. She only has to stand on the stage, leaning on her cane, and recite what she has recited for forty years." Lowering her voice an octave, and infusing it with an exaggerated dramatic pathos, she declaimed a fragment of Racine.

". . . Tu connais ce fils de l'Amazone,
Ce prince si longtemps par moi-même opprimé?"

"Bah. Any female impersonator from Montmartre could do it. Do you know Félix Mayol? 'Viens Poupoule,' " she sang throatily in another imitation, this time of the well-known transvestite entertainer. She was certainly adept at parody, and the flexibility of her voice was remarkable for one who was not a trained singer. "Sublime. He is a good friend of mine. Although not in the way you might imagine. And you, my dear." She turned suddenly to Herma, as though she had been reciting to an audience and noticed only for the first time that she was with a single person. "You've never told me. Do you have a petit ami?"

"No. Not now."

"Have you ever?"

Herma smiled and said nothing.

"Oh, I know them. I've known men—so many . . ." Here she made a gesture of astonishing obscenity. Herma could scarcely believe it. "They all want the same thing. They wish to humiliate us, above all. First we must be knocked flat and spread out like a frog. Then they fall on top of us. The quicker over the better. Their sweaty odor. Their pride of peacocks. And their precious accessories, of which they're so proud. Dangling like two prunes and a banana in a shopping net . . . or sticking up at you like a hat rack. Je m'en fiche de leurs appartenances, ma chère.'' She got up and leaped around the room, to liberate the energy generated by her anger. "But now we forget such a boring subject. I dance for you. I dance only for my friends. You are honored.''

Herma was prepared to be honored. But it was odd of her to say so— to *order* her to be honored, so to speak. Bella went to the Victrola—which also gave the appearance of having been manufactured in Bagdad, although this was hardly possible—and put on a record. It was an atonal sort of reverie, probably something by Saint-Saëns. Then she began dancing. Although she had spent her career as a prima ballerina in the classic tradition, she danced now in a more personal and exotic style, something like Isadora Duncan, between the athletic and the oriental. She retained, however, the leaps and entrechats of her classical training. It was the arms, mainly, that were used in a way different from that of the classical ballet. While the legs danced, the arms gestured more in the manner of an actress than the manner of a dancer. The fluttering hands moved up and down the body as though caressing it, they flattened onto her face and parted to reveal it detail by detail; they spread in the wide flowing sleeves and pointed like two arrows at her body. Dance, Herma thought as she watched, is only an elaborate set of gestures calling attention to one's self.

The Saint-Saëns ended. Bella threw away the record without putting it into its envelope and fitted on another one. It was the "Dance of the Seven Veils" from *Salomé*. Once again she swirled around the room. The flowing silk gown came off and sailed into a corner. As she danced she unwound the turban too; it turned into a long pale-gold scarf that streamed behind her, around her body in coils, over her head like a cowboy's lariat. It too flew off lightly into the corner, taking some time to settle down into a soft mass indistinguishable from the gown.

Under the gown was a more closely fitting garment, and one of even more fragile stuff. It was a kind of sleeveless tunic, ending at the knees, perhaps of lace, although the work was too fine to be seen from across the room. In any case it was translucent enough that a third garment, a kind of dark net or reticulation, could be seen through it. Now that her arms were bare, Bella skillfully worked the brass rings on her wrists so that their tinkling exactly accompanied the sinuous strains of the Strauss. The tunic came off—it went to the opposite corner of the room rather than on top of the gown and the veil. Hardly pausing in her dance, almost as though it were part of the choreography, Bella turned the record over and began the other side.

The layers of costume seemed endless. No doubt, thought Herma, there were seven of them. The tight-fitting net of knotted cords was attached at the top to a wide golden collar in the Egyptian style which had not been visible before. At the bottom, just above her thighs, it disappeared into a mass of gauze veils of various pastel colors. Through the net it could be seen that her breasts were enclosed in brass hemispheres. The veils came off one by one—this was where the number seven came in, probably—and Bella was clad only in the net, a brief cache-sexe, and the shiny brass cups on her breasts. Herma looked at the needle crawling across the Victrola with a rhythmic lurch. It was almost at the end of the record.

The net came off—Bella swung it out with a flourish like a gladiator. The net was attached to the Egyptian collar, and when the collar came off the net did too, with the collar serving as a handle. It was possible that Bella planned to snare her, gladiator fashion, with this contrivance. Her gestures mimicked this action, in fact. But after a few more bars of Strauss the net was flung into the corner with the rest.

Bella extended her arms around behind her back. She had the flexibility of a contortionist; without effort and without bending her trunk she reached behind and unfastened the chain that held the two elaborately embossed hemispheres. They came off too, with a jingle matching that of the brass rings. The music came to an end and Bella stood before her like an exultant Lysistrata, her legs apart and the two brass cups dangling high in the air. The lower part of her costume was only a triangle in front and a string behind. Higher up there was an affair of beads, perhaps an inch wide, draped around her firm and unsagging breasts. The brass rings remained on her wrists and ankles.

The Victrola needle, having come to the end of its path, was jerking back and forth in the inane manner of such contrivances. Bella rather impatiently pushed the lever to stop it. Then she looked pointedly at Herma.

"Tu veux?"

Well, did she want or didn't she? In principle there was nothing against it. Except that . . .

"You see," Herma began to explain tactfully. "How can I put it? I agree with you in some respects about men. It's just that"—it was very awkward to explain—"that part of me is inside me, so I like something to be inside it." When Bella said nothing she added, perhaps superfluously, "That's the reason we're made that way, isn't it? Otherwise I don't see any point to it."

Whereupon Bella, looking cryptically at her, went off and came back with an extraordinary object. It was fashioned out of ivory, perhaps a foot long, and curved, with a handle at one end like a dagger. In color it was pale as milk, with a slight yellowish cast. It was elaborately carved, with inscriptions and wavy decorations along the curving shaft. It resembled a serpent, even to the head on the end with a tiny mouth. The thing was evidently of Arabic work, for it was circumsized—it would hardly have been Jewish.

With her chin held high, she offered it with a theatrical gesture, thrusting it out bolt upright.

Herma began to laugh. "Oh, Bella. If I chose, I could show you a much better one than that."

11.

At the end of the summer, as the hot days of August drew to a close, the war took a turn for the worse. The Germans had swept through Belgium in only a few days—they raped nuns and cut off the hands of little children, the papers said, although perhaps this was only propaganda. The French offensive in Lorraine came to a halt; two German armies advanced through Toul and Epinal and closed their jaws around Verdun. The French fell back, abandoning one line of trenches after another. The English were cut off in Flanders and the Pas de Calais. The newspapers spoke of "withdrawal to previously prepared positions." But you only had to look at the map to see that the capital was in danger. By the first week in September the Germans were along the Marne, and on still nights when there was no wind the sound of guns could be heard in Paris.

General Gallieni, the military commander of Paris, decided to throw his last reserves into the battle to the east, leaving the capital unprotected. Six thousand troops of the Fourth Corps were just detraining in Paris to serve as a defence garrison for the city, and he ordered them to the Marne the same day in requisitioned taxicabs, which had to disgorge their passengers. The taxis took them to the Ourcq, only sixty kilometers from the capital, and made two trips a day. That morning Herma and Bella were shopping in the St.-Honoré quarter, and a policeman stepped out into the street in front of their taxi and stopped it with a white-gloved hand.

"Allez," he told the driver. "To the Ministry of War, at the Invalides."

"But my fares?"

"Out."

The driver, a small shy man with a wispy mustache, opened the door for them, explaining with a little smile of pride, "We have to go to battle." He got back in and drove away. The taxi disappeared down the street in the direction of the Pont Alexandre III.

Herma and Bella—still good friends, although not yet, or ever, lovers—decided to walk over to the Left Bank and see what was happening. But when they came out into Place de la Concorde they found it had already been converted into an assembly point for the troops. The immense square was full of taxicabs, mostly Renaults with their shovel noses, along with a few old Unics. Backing and filling, they milled around trying to arrange themselves in rows. Meanwhile a long column of troops, not yet provided with battle uniforms and still in horizon blue, came down the quay from the Gare de Lyon with their rifles slung and mess kits clanking. Each man had a knapsack, a bedroll, and a bandolier of ammunition. In the square, between the rows of taxis, they began forming up raggedly into companies.

The crowd watching them was somber at first. But as the square filled up with taxis, soldiers, and spectators a festive spirit began to spread. From the balcony of the Hôtel Crillon facing the square an enormous tricolor tumbled down. People went up Rue Royale to pastry shops and brought back éclairs and cognac for the soldiers. Girls impulsively kissed them. One midinette, who was probably no better than she ought to be, was passed along hand to hand to forty or more soldiers. There were shouts of "To Berlin!" and "Vive la France!"

Herma and Bella caught a glimpse of General Gallieni himself, who had come down to Concorde to see if his orders were being carried out. He was a crusty old bird, lean and wrinkled, with a braided képi pulled down over his eyes, small round glasses with gold frames, and a straggly gray mustache. He was surrounded by his staff officers in black tunics and scarlet breeches. They stood under the porch of the Ministry of the Marine for a while, then Gallieni strode out into the square followed by his officers.

"Allez-y, mes enfants!" he screeched like a bird. "Go get them. The fate of France depends on you."

The soldiers crammed into the taxicabs, as many of them as would fit. The rest of them would have to wait for the second trip of the day. A girl who had been surreptitiously inserted into a taxi was put out. As the taxis started their engines and began rolling more bottles of cognac were pushed in through their windows. "Vive la France!" cried the crowd. "Hang the Kaiser!" The taxis circled the square, their engines rumbling and their horns blaring like Roland's oliphant at Roncevalles, then they set off up the avenue toward the Porte de Pantin. A few people who had not been able to get their bottles of cognac into the taxis drew out the corks and began drinking them. There were a few more cries of "Vive la France!" Across the square, under the statue of the Spirit of Strasbourg, a woman put her face into her hands and began weeping.

This First Battle of the Marne, as it was later called, was terrible. After only a day or two the wounded began streaming back into Paris in ambulances, in trains, and even in boxcars. The hospitals were full. The government forbade people to drape mourning in their windows; there would be too many of them and it was bad for morale. At the Opéra the rehearsals of the *Forza del Destino* stopped and the rest of the season was canceled. The Châtelet and the Comédie Française were closed too, except for benefit performances for the troops.

Now people began to take the war seriously. The crowds in the cafés were somber, studying their newspapers. A German aeroplane came over and dropped a bomb in Maisons-Alfort, killing three people. There were shortages in the shops; one day there would be no meat and the next day no bread. It "went to the troops," people said. For entertainment there were the cinemas, which were still open and sometimes showed newsreels of the troops in the trenches, and the music halls in Montmartre, which broke out into a patriotic vein with the dancers clad in tricolor. Every performance—even the transvestite Félix Mayol prancing and singing in his squeaky soprano—ended with the *Marseillaise.*

Fred had to scour about and find something for Herma to do. It wasn't a matter of money; she had long since paid off Lloiseaux his ten thousand francs for the apartment and there was a comfortable balance in the bank. But a performer had to remain in the public eye, otherwise they would forget you. There were benefits for the troops: Herma sang at the Châtelet and helped to raise enough money to send a trainload of bandages to the front. She sang the *Marseillaise* at a ceremony under the Arc de Triomphe, honoring the dead of the Marne. In November Fred got her an engagement to take part in a benefit performance at the Val-de-Grace, the old abbey near Montparnasse which had been converted into a military hospital and was now full of wounded soldiers from the Marne.

The large chapel of the abbey was crammed full of wounded, some in wheelchairs, some rolled in by nurses in their beds, some able to walk. A few of them were officers. The officers were treated in a separate part of the hospital, but evidently they were allowed to come to the entertainment in the chapel with the others. In addition to Herma, who was announced as "the celebrated American prima donna from the Opéra," there was an entertainer from a music hall who sang comic songs, a juggler, a magician, and a Hungarian czardas-violinist.

Herma didn't know what to sing. She began with a French art song or two, a trifle of Debussy, and the Canzonetta from *The Marriage of Figaro.* There was polite applause after each selection. But obviously it was not what they were accustomed to. She tried some Stephen Foster songs—which were warmly applauded, with grins—and then *The Last Rose of Summer.* After conferring with the pianist, she finished with *Ta Ra Ra Boom-de-ay,* and succeeded in getting most of them to sing it along with her, in growls and grunts, in the second chorus. There was more clapping, from those who could use their arms, and laughter.

Herma sat down, and the Hungarian began playing his czardas. She had a good view of the audience from her position on the improvised platform. They were French of all kinds—Provençals, blond-headed Normans, dark fiery Corsicans, stolid and round-headed Auvergnats, even a few Senegalese with ebony skins and long powerful limbs. Some, the more badly wounded, could only lie propped in bed and stare out of hollow eyes. Others, in wheelchairs, were amputees, or had head wounds or limbs in casts.

From her vantage point on the platform her eye was caught by a very young soldier in the front row who had a bandage around his head and never took his eyes from Herma's face, then by an officer leaning negligently against a column on the left—the only man in the chapel who wasn't seated or in bed. His left arm was in a sling. He too had watched Herma attentively while she sang, with a little smile playing on his lips. He hadn't joined in the singing, she noticed, but his smile became broader during the Stephen Foster songs, and he began to laugh when the others roared away at *Ta Ra Ra Boom-de-ay*. He had a small neat mustache and his uniform was immaculate. He looked as though he had just stepped in off the boulevard to watch the entertainment, and had put his arm in a sling to be polite to the others. Next to him was another officer with a deep frown, sitting in a chair with his leg propped on another chair. The first officer—the one with the sling—caught her eye once. But this made him blush and he turned away.

After the performance, the entertainers were to "mingle with the troops to cheer them" as the instructions had it. Nurses came around serving a kind of tea-time snack or casse-croûte. There was strong army pinard in tin cups, along with chocolates in silver wrappers and fruit-cake donated by some American charitable organization or other. This combination didn't seem to strike the French soldiers as odd. They filled their pockets with the chocolates. As for the fruitcake, it was foreign and no doubt in America people ate fruitcake with red wine. They were anxious to be agreeable, since Herma was American. They ate the chocolates and fruitcake and the performers went around, stopping to talk to one group or another.

Herma wound her way through the chapel cluttered with its beds and wheelchairs. A number of soldiers trailed after her hoping to speak to her, but she was pitiless. She had already decided with whom she wanted to talk. She went straight to the officer with his arm in the sling standing by the column. "What do you expect?" she heard a voice behind her. "They go for the officers."

The officer by the column was a captain, she now saw by the stripes on his sleeve, and so was his scowling friend in the chair. The one who was standing up was well built even though he was not very tall. He had a powerful chest and his wrists were strong and supple, the wrists of a wrestler. His complexion was a pale and even bronze, the color of sherry.

"I'm Herma."

"I'm called Tancrède," he said, still smiling but coloring a little. "And this silent fellow is Blanchot."

The standard opening for a conversation, it seemed, was "How were you wounded?"

He smiled a little more broadly. "You see," he explained, "Blanchot and I are friends, so we arranged to be both hit by the same bullet so we could be in the hospital together."

"The same bullet?"

The two captains exchanged a look.

Tancrède said, "Well, Blanchot doesn't like to talk about it, because we were shot in a retreat, and that's damaging to his sense of honor."

"But the whole army was retreating."

"That doesn't make any difference. If Blanchot is to be wounded, he wants to be wounded gloriously. You see, it was this way. We were at a regimental staff meeting in a farmhouse, and when we came out there were no more troops. Our companies had disappeared, because the Boches were advancing more quickly than expected. While we were in our meeting the platoon commanders made the decision to withdraw. It wasn't their fault. It was just the result of confusion."

"Stop chattering about it," growled Blanchot, frowning more deeply.

"So Blanchot and I began setting off across the countryside trying to find our companies. We came to a stone wall, and I climbed over it and turned around waiting for him to come after. He had just climbed onto the wall when a bullet—not aimed particularly at us and coming from a long distance—went through the calf of his leg and then lodged in my chest. So we were both hit by the same bullet."

"Your chest?"

"Yes. You see, my arm is in a sling so I won't hurt the chest muscles by swinging it around and doing violent exercises with it. There's nothing wrong with the arm."

"They ought to put your mouth in a sling," said Blanchot.

"Why is your friend so fierce?"

"Well you see, soldiers have to be fierce to the enemy. And to do this, they have to practice being fierce all the time."

"But what about you?"

"Ah, I'm not a real soldier. I'm only a chocolate soldier," he laughed. "Have a chocolate." He took one out of his pocket and offered it to her.

There was something Bacchic about him, something powerful and wily. Perhaps it was only the tufts of hair at his temples, his catlike green eyes, and his constant air of amusement, as though he knew something that ordinary mortals didn't.

"Besides," he said, "I'm a graduate of St.-Cyr, whereas he was promoted up through the ranks. Therefore he has to be more fierce in order to make it clear to everybody that he's an officer."

"Shut your face, why don't you," said Blanchot.

Herma unwrapped the chocolate and ate it. She looked around her. "It's so somber here." There was a depressing-looking crucifix on the wall. The blood was depicted with great realism; the Sufferer looked as though He needed some medical attention too. "Can you ever go out?"

"Oh yes, we can go out, since we're officers, provided some way can be found to transport us."

"What are you talking about?" said Blanchot angrily. "We can transport ourselves. I can limp." He in fact had a cane by his side, an odd contrivance with a T-shaped handle at the top. "And you don't walk on your arm. Or your chest either."

"Well, I was only thinking about Blanchot. I can walk well enough."

"Think about yourself," growled Blanchot.

"Well, suppose I come by tomorrow afternoon then and take you both to a café."

"Fine," said Tancrède. "Even a restaurant. The things they give you to eat here are terrible."

Herma said goodbye to them and left. Her hearing was excellent, like her other senses. "She hasn't got much chest," she heard Blanchot say to his friend as she moved away through the chapel.

Herma took them to the places she knew best: first to the Café de la Paix for an apéritif, then to Larue's. She ordered her usual white meat of chicken with a little asparagus, and Tancrède a broiled salmon with madeira sauce. Blanchot ordered a steak and fries. The waiter wrote down the orders imperturbably.

The fried potatoes came in a sterling-silver hot dish, the cover of which the waiter removed with a flourish. Handling the serving spoon and fork deftly with one hand, he set the neat heap of frites on Blanchot's plate. He showed no sign that this was not one of Larue's most refined specialties, his famous blanquette de veau or his squab en papillote.

Herma chose the wines, a Saint-Emilion for Blanchot and a Mersault for herself and Tancrède. The waiter poured the wine, and Tancrède began to explain in detail how a light mortar worked—its range, explosive power, and rate of fire. This was his specialty; he had been to a technical school and was qualified to lecture to troops on the subject. "I can get five shells into the air at once. At a range of two kilometers, the circle of error is only fifty meters."

"What happens to the people when the shells hit them?"

"Oh, it kills them. You see," he explained, arranging the salt and pepper and other objects on the table, and rumpling the tablecloth so as to make trenches, "a rifle or an ordinary artillery weapon has a flat trajectory. So it's impossible to use them to dislodge troops who are properly entrenched. But a mortar has a high firing angle and comes down almost vertically, and falls directly into the trenches. The trick is to get it aimed accurately enough. At a range of two kilometers, a change in elevation of the barrel of only one degree causes a deflection of a hundred meters."

Herma was sure this was true. She tried to imagine Tancrède in a trench, making an adjustment of one degree in the elevation of a mortar barrel, while Blanchot looked on glowering.

"How does it feel to be in a battle? Are you angry at the enemy?"

"Who?"

"The Germans."

He shrugged. "No, I'm not angry at the Boches. It's my métier. For civilians, perhaps, it's all right to be angry at the enemy. But for me it's a métier. Getting angry will only interfere with your aim. If you are trying to shoot somebody and you are all trembling with anger, you will probably miss him. It's like getting angry at the target in a shooting gallery. It is bad for the aim.''

''Then the German who shot you was not angry at you?''

He considered.

''Probably not. The bullet came from a long way off. It was a spent bullet. But perhaps he was angry—he was trying to hit somebody else, and because he was angry he missed.'' He reflected on this, as though he had grasped for the first time how it was that he had managed to get wounded.

Blanchot had finished his steak and fries and drunk the bottle of wine. He laid down his knife and fork. ''When will America come into the war?'' he asked abruptly.

Tancrède too turned to her.

''I don't know. Not for a while perhaps. I don't think people are ready for it. Maybe they won't come at all.''

Blanchot said coldly, ''Then we will win without them.''

''Blanchot, don't be such a pig,'' said Tancrède. ''The Americans will come and help us. Just give them a little time.''

Blanchot said, ''They'll come at the very end.'' He added, ''Besides, a lot of Americans are Germans. Your President Roosevelt was a German.''

''He was Dutch,'' said Tancrède.

''Oh, for heaven's sake. Don't let's quarrel,'' said Herma. ''Your General Lafayette came over and helped us in some previous century or other, when we were fighting the English, so I'm sure we will come over and help you.''

''You aren't very strong on history.''

''Well, wasn't that the way it was?''

''Pretty much.''

''Lafayette, c'était un aristo,'' said Blanchot. ''He had class, a type like that. They don't have any aristos in America. That's the trouble with them. Too much democracy.'' It was his longest speech of the evening.

Herma took a breath. To smooth over the argument she asked, ''Does anybody like ice cream?''

Blanchot didn't care for any dessert. She ordered two Fraises Hermas. When the waiter brought them he wasn't sure which of the three they were for, so he set them together in the center of the table. Larue's too now made them in the manner of the Ritz, with a frothy little ring of whipped cream around the edge of the goblet. The lemon-vanilla ice cream was formed into perfect hemispheres, and the glaze too was exactly the right shade of amber. Since it was winter, the strawberries were hothouse fruit and rather small. The two goblets sat together on the table about eight inches apart. Tancrède looked at them, then he caught Herma's eye and blushed.

They were both from the Touraine—Tancrède from Chinon and Blanchot from Amboise—and they didn't know much about Paris. Herma, in a succession of taxis all no doubt veterans of the Battle of the Marne, conducted touristic tours for them in the afternoons. Blanchot limped along with his T-shaped cane. They went up in the Eiffel Tower, and she showed them the city from the Butte Montmartre. What else? Would they like to see the Panthéon, the Nôtre-Dame, the Sainte-Chapelle?

"The Opéra," said Tancrède.

It was closed, of course, but Herma took them around to the stage entrance in Rue Gluck, where the old doorkeeper Monsieur Dupetit was on duty as usual. For some reason she had a slight pudeur about showing them her dressing room, although dozens of men had been in it before. Instead they went, the three of them, out onto the wide stage—the curtain was open and the vast auditorium out beyond it, shadowy and silent, was like an empty gulf. Tancrède looked out at the countless rows of crimson plush seats, at the five tiers of empty boxes. "Oh, I'd be afraid of so many people," he joked.

Stepping forward to the dead footlights, Herma clasped her hands and trilled a bit of coloratura:

> "Les ois-eaux-dans-la-char-mille,
> Dans-les-cieux-l'astre-du-jour . . ."

Her voice echoed strangely in the vast emptiness out before her; it was as though she were singing in outer space—in a universe without matter —a disembodied voice. She had sung in empty theaters before, at auditions or rehearsals, but this was different. It was that *no one was listening*. She felt a little chill inside, just under the place where her ribs ended. "Let's go," she said.

She took them up the narrow spiral staircase to show them the great mechanical skeleton of the theater above the stage. There were ropes and cables, heavy steel beams, great machines for hoisting the scenery, vast cogwheels like those in clocks but as high as a standing man. Tancrède examined all this with interest, and even Blanchot looked about at things and frowned a little less than usual.

"And all this," said Tancrède, "is so that you can sing your little—" he squeaked up into a falsetto—" 'Les-ois-eaux-dans-la-char-mille.' "

His imitation of a coloratura soprano was enough, almost, to make Blanchot smile. "You had better stay with your trench mortars and leave singing to me," Herma advised.

They went down the iron stairs again—the two officers with perfect correctness following after her, just as they had proceeded her up the stairs, so that there was no question of anyone looking up her skirt—and led them around a circular corridor, through a door, and out onto a balcony overlooking the great entrance hall of the Opéra, itself as large as a church or a provincial theater. Everything was marble: the broad marble staircase ascended, divided into two before a pair of immense marble caryatids, and then turned and continued along a pair of matching corridors lined with marble columns. Only two of the countless crystal chandeliers were lighted; the vaulted ceiling overhead was hardly visible in the gloom. Tancrède ran his hand over the polished marble balustrade before him, yellowish with a smoky dark pattern in the surface, as though under glass. Blanchot too seemed inspired to an unusual loquacity by the Opéra and by the staircase in particular.

"French civilization. It is for this that we are fighting," he said sternly.

Tancrède shrugged. "It's for the rich."

"Well, you're rich. You're a count."

"Are you a count?" asked Herma in surprise. "You never told me that."

"Well, he doesn't like to mention it," said Blanchot.

Tancrède said, "Just because you're a count, that doesn't mean you're rich. There are plenty of poor counts."

"Well, you're a rich one."

"Anyhow," said Tancrède, "we don't have counts anymore since the Revolution. It's an honorary title. As they say, that and a franc will get you a ride on the Métro."

As in all cases where you are involved with two men who are friends —or two women if it is the other way around—the difficulty was in getting Tancrède separated from Blanchot. They seemed inseparable. It was as though—even though they were soldiers and had been tested in battle —they were afraid of going about the city alone. Even with Herma as a guide. Or perhaps it was precisely being alone with Herma that they were afraid of. There was a bashful or boyish quality about both of them, especially where women were involved.

By discreet questioning of the nurses she found that even the patient-officers in the hospital had guard nights when they had to remain on duty in the enlisted men's wards, in order to prevent them, perhaps, from cutting their throats, or making advances to the nurses. Blanchot's guard night was Wednesday, so she rang up Tancrède from her apartment and asked him to go to dinner on Wednesday. There was a telephone in the officers' ward; the trouble was that you had to talk with everyone else in the ward listening. She was still saying "vous" to both of them, so her "can you come to dinner" could have been either singular or plural.

"We can't," he said. "It's Blanchot's duty night."

"I didn't mean Blanchot."

"Yes, but he's my friend. I go everywhere with him."

"That's nonsense," said Herma. "I have something to tell you that I don't necessarily want Blanchot to listen to." She said "toi" now to make it perfectly clear.

"What would that be?"

"Perhaps I want to discuss the shape of Blanchot's ears, or tell you something personal," said Herma rather impatiently. Men! Oh, but they were dense.

"Well, I suppose," he said in a voice that sounded rather dubious. "I'll explain it to him."

"What is there to explain? I'll come by for you at six. We'll go to the Café de la Paix for an apéritif first."

"Alors. Bien," he said finally. Herma hung up and started deciding what she would wear.

She took him to a small Hungarian restaurant, where they dined by candlelight while a violinist played gypsy melodies. It was the same one, she recognized, who had played czardas at the benefit at the Val-de-Grace; he caught her eye and smiled.

Tancrède had never seen her in anything but the tailored khaki suit. Now she had changed it for a simple white gown with a red ribbon in the hem, and a matching ribbon in her hair. But he seemed not to notice, or at least gave no sign. In spite of her best efforts, the conversation fell onto Blanchot. There was some discussion as to whether they shouldn't find a girl for him, so they could go out together as a foursome. (A quadrille, as it was called in French.) Herma knew lots of girls at the Opéra, and they were all pretty.

Tancrède said, "He is a virgin. He's saving himself for his wife."

"Is he engaged then?"

"No, he has not found anyone worthy of him. Or as he puts it, he has not found anyone he is worthy of."

Herma said, "When he marries, do you think he will be fierce to his wife?"

"Oh no. He may *look* fierce to her, but he will behave tenderly."

"That would be interesting to see."

"Blanchot is very complex. We are all very complex. He once found a rabbit with a broken leg in the trenches, and fixed it with a splint he made from a tongue depressor he got from the medical orderly. He took care of it until it got well. Frowning all the while, of course. I don't know how the rabbit got into the trenches."

"With soldiers like Blanchot, I'm sure France will win the war."

"Of course it will. Who else would win?" said Tancrède with mild surprise, as though the idea had never occurred to him. Perhaps he couldn't remember the names of the various countries France was fighting at the moment, or thought they were of no importance. They were just the enemy.

"Perhaps Hungary will. This is a Hungarian restaurant. Look how strong the waiters are."

"Gypsies," said Tancrède contemptuously.

When she led him out of the lift and through the door he looked around without curiosity at the apartment. He seemed perfectly content to be here or someplace else; it didn't matter to him. The curtains were open in the large window facing to the north. Only a small lamp with a rose-colored shade glowed on the table. Paris, darkened for the war, sprawled out before them in a semicircle, from the hills of St.-Cloud on the right to the Panthéon on the left, with the Eiffel Tower etched against the gray sky in the middle distance. Tancrède's eye passed over the art-nouveau furniture, the Beardsley print, the fashionable baby grand piano, but he had nothing to say. If he's a count, she thought, perhaps he doesn't like all these modern things.

"Would you like something to drink?"

"All right."

"A cognac?"

"Very good."

She gave him a splash of Courvoisier in a balloon glass, and took a little Grand Marnier herself. She liked it because the faint flavor of oranges reminded her of California. She sipped it, regarding him gravely over the rim of the glass. He walked around the room with his cognac, looked at everything, and then stood in a soldierly way with his feet apart, staring out the window at the panorama of Paris.

He was a stoic creature. Probably he would have preferred to be on the battlefield, but he was too polite to say so. But, after the exasperating task of separating him from Blanchot, it was no trick at all to get him from the salon into the bedroom.

"If you don't like Beardsley," she said, "perhaps you'd prefer Fernand Khnopff."

"I beg your pardon?"

"It's in the bedroom."

"All right."

After that it was easier. He hardly glanced at the Khnopff. Of course he had no way of knowing that he was the first man other than the decorator (and Fred if you counted him) ever to behold this work of art. As he turned from the painting she heard him murmur something like "A pair of sissies." Then, bumping up against her, he embraced her and took her face in his hands. He was not an idiot after all and he had perfectly normal desires. It was just his military dignity.

Once the uniform was off he seemed to change into another person. He wore only a light bandage around his chest now to protect the wound from the friction of his clothing. He removed this and Herma caught a glimpse of a small scar, exactly where a medal would have been if he had been wearing his uniform. When he took off his shoes there were tiny tufts of hair growing on the top of each foot, giving him a quite innocent and yet goatlike quality, as though this small trace of the Dionysian sprang out of him in spite of his best efforts to repress it. The sherry-colored body gave off a faint sheen, almost silvery. Even though he was stocky and powerfully built there was not an ounce of fat on him. His abdomen was concave and the bones of his pelvis showed clearly through the skin. The small tuft of hair at the bottom of his stomach was as neat as his mustache. Perhaps he trimmed it too with the same scissors. Herma had spread the bedclothes back in advance, before she went out to meet him for dinner, but if he noticed this he gave no sign.

In the throes of love, Tancrède managed to retain to the end his two incompatible qualities, his slight amusement and his embarrassment at anything personal. Perhaps he really is a god, thought Herma, and he is afraid we mortals will discover his secret. Then she didn't think anything at all for a while, because he was not only passionate and considerate but very skillful—he was one of those gentle and taciturn men who knew how to *do* things—the sort of man that Herma had been drawn to and desired ever since she was a child. Their keen and sweet common desire mounted gradually in steps like an aria, fell back and mounted again, and finally swept them both away in a high tremolo, so to speak, with crashing chords from the orchestra. Then Tancrède, drawing away from her and looking at her with his little smile, as though taking a curtain call, was persuaded to do an encore, repeating the same aria with equal warmth and no perceptible diminution of vigor in the finale.

Separating herself at last from him, content and exhausted, Herma turned over and pressed her face into the pillow. After a moment she said, "Wow."

"What does that mean?"

"That's American for 'C'est formidable.' "

She got up. They sat cross-legged on the bed then, he at one end and she at the other, and looked at each other. It was only at such times that you really noticed the other person; before the thing happened your vision was blurred by desire. With his usual air of grave amusement he examined her boyish young American body, apricot over lemon. Her attention centered mainly on his scar. In the center was a red rosette, the size of a pencil eraser, and radiating from it were the four arms of a cross, thin red lines as though traced with a fine pen.

"They had to go looking for the bullet with a knife. That's when they made the star."

"It isn't a star, it's a cross."

"Well, please don't attribute stigmata to me. It was an accident. If you get in the way of a bullet that's a misfortune, not an honor."

"May I touch it?"

He had no objection. She set her fingers lightly on the place. There was only a small depression, as though something had made a dent in the skin. Nothing at all could be felt along the crossed red lines. The surgeon was very skillful.

"But your heart is all right?"

"Yes. You may be misinformed as to where the heart is. It's not where you lay your hand when you're declaring something. It's closer to the center."

"Let me listen."

"What a curious creature you are."

But she laid her head against his chest—at the place indicated, not far from the center of his body—and listened. She heard a steady muffled bump, like a regimental drummer playing through a sheet of felt.

"It's very slow."

"To have a slow pulse, you must be in good physical condition. You know, if you go on brushing my chest with your hair that way, the whole thing is going to start over again."

She drew away and went back to her cross-legged position on the bed.

He asked her, "How is it that you know so much?"

"I know so much?"

"You seem to know—what a man wants."

"Don't all women?"

"I haven't met all women," he said, coloring a little, but still smiling. He was silent for a moment, and then after a thought he asked, "Are all American girls like this?"

"No," said Herma a little crossly, "and I'm not like this either except with you."

"I have the impression that—you chose me."

"How impressionable you are."

He thought for a moment. "According to old-fashioned morality, that's not quite correct. However, it's quite pleasant."

"It's the way of the future. Wait until you see how your grandchildren behave."

"Ah, I don't expect to have any grandchildren."

"What do you mean by that?"

But he wouldn't say anything more about it. He changed the subject. "Do you remember that conversation we had with Blanchot?"

"About what?"

"About America, and the war. You've paid us back yourself for General Lafayette."

"That's probably not necessary. I imagine the American girls paid off General Lafayette on the spot."

"Ah, mon dieu. What a creature. You're very nice. It's too bad. We're leaving tomorrow. We're going to rejoin our regiment on the Somme."

"Tomorrow?"

"Yes."

"Why . . . didn't you tell me?"

"Oh, that sort of thing always involves a lot of sentiment."

"Then I won't see you anymore."

"No, I'm afraid not."

"Then perhaps we'd better get back in bed one last time," said Herma.

12.

The rest of that winter Herma was very busy. In December she went on a tour of the provinces, singing at benefits in Toulouse, Bordeaux, and Pau. At Christmas she was back in Paris again—she and Lloiseaux celebrated at Larue's with an austere wartime dinner, a simple filet of sole with haricots, and a bottle of 1913 Moët et Chandon from Larue's last case—there wasn't anymore champagne after that because the country it came from was now a battleground and Reims was in ruins. Then she went away again, to entertain the troops in the training barracks at Orléans, and came back to prepare for a concert performance at the Salle Pleyel of *La Forza del Destino*—the same opera that had been scheduled for the autumn when the war began, but now without costumes and sets. The government evidently believed now that it was better to keep people entertained and pretend that everything was normal. Tancrède wrote once or twice. Once he sent a photograph showing the two of them—himself laughing, Blanchot frowning—in front of a house that had been blasted flat by shells and consisted only of a window held up by a few stones. She stuck this into the edge of the mirror in the bathroom. Then, for some reason, she took it down and hid it away in the top drawer of her bureau, under the underclothing. It was stupid. It was that—she didn't want Fred to see it.

It was evident now that the war was not going to be a short one. "Out of the trenches by Christmas"—nobody thought about that now. The newspapers were not very pleasant reading, even though they tried to gloss over the facts and you had to read them twice and then study the maps to see what was happening. The Central Powers and the Allies were locked in a death grip on the Western Front, from the Swiss border to the Pas de Calais. The British were deployed on the left, along the Channel coast, and the French on the center and right, from Gambrai to the Swiss border near Basel. The Germans were well dug in and well supplied. Neither side could gain the initiative. Sometimes a thousand lives were paid for a scrap of land the size of a cemetery, and the next day the territory would be lost again. The fighting was particularly savage in the Somme sector and on the Meuse, around Verdun. It was a bitterly cold winter. Rains filled the trenches with water and vehicles bogged down in the mud. The poilus, living in a mixture of mud, excrement, and corpses, caught typhoid and died. There were rumors of gas, used only by the Boches of course.

In Paris there were real shortages now. When Herma went out she saw long lines in front of the butcher shops, and stray cats began to disappear from the streets. Almost every night the electricity was cut off for an hour to two, trapping people underground in the Métro and causing a new shortage, that of candles. Coal was in short supply too and houses and apartments were cold; people wore their overcoats indoors. The music halls in Montmartre were still full, and the cafés around the Opéra and on the Champs-Elysées were crowded, mostly because cafés were warmer than apartments. In St.-Denis a pervert murdered a little girl and cut her body into pieces. People were horrified by this and discussed it for days, in order not to talk about the greater horrors that were taking place on the Western Front.

It was early February. Herma came home from her rehearsal at the Salle Pleyel about four o'clock and was crossing the entryway toward the lift when the concièrge came after her and gave her a telegram. She got a lot of telegrams, offering her engagements or discussing arrangements for tours, and usually she left them for Fred to take care of. She went up to the apartment, took off her fur cap and cloak and threw

them onto a chair, and lifted her hair with her hands. Then she slit open
the blue envelope with her fingernail.

"OUR FRIEND DIED GLORIOUSLY FOR THE FATHERLAND LEADING ATTACK
ON BOCHE MACHINE GUN NEST FONTAINE-LES-CROISELLES SOMME SECTOR
0600 HOURS TUESDAY X COMMANDING GENERAL HAS RECOMMENDED CROIX
DE GUERRE X VIVE LA FRANCE X BLANCHOT."

She had not expected it. He was so full of vitality and so cheerful,
he seemed life itself. But he had known. "I don't expect to have any
grandchildren." She went into the bedroom and lay down fully clothed
on the bed, her face in the pillow. A kind of spasm formed inside her and
wanted to break loose, but she held it back. I will not cry, she told herself.
A man would not cry and so I will not. And she didn't; she only felt
dry and broken. Instead she lay there for a long time, until the gray
light of afternoon turned to twilight and, on the hill on the other side
of Paris, the lights came on one by one against the dark sky.

Then she got up and went into the salon to look out the large window, her eyes blurry and her lower lip held tightly in her teeth. The
lights on the hill above St.-Cloud might have been stars. The city was
deserted, its inhabitants invisible. There was no one she could call on or
go to. Lloiseaux, Bella, Marcel, a few friends at the Opéra—no, there
was nobody. She felt all at once surrounded by infinite space, infinite
darkness. Surely everyone is not so alone, she thought. Surely there was
someone. And then it came to her who it was that she wanted above all to
be with her, to comfort her—an American like her, with his boyish
enthusiasm, his brashness, his cheerfulness, his optimism—someone she
could talk to like herself. They would trade insults, throw pillows at
each other, and finally he would make her smile a little. But he was on
the other side of the mirror. Unlike Alice in the story, she couldn't go
there. "I have the impression that you chose me," said Tancrède. But
there was one who was forbidden to her.

13.

It was the next fall, a year and a half after the death of
Agostinelli, before she saw Marcel again or heard anything from him.
Then he telephoned unexpectedly and asked her to dinner at the Ritz.
"Reynaldo will be along. It's perfectly correct," said his reedy, slightly
affected voice over the wire. There would be music afterward; he didn't
specify what. "We will come by for you. It's in Avenue Wagram,
isn't it?"

"No, 78 Avenue Kléber."

"Ah, Avenue Kléber." He hung up.

The taxi was an ordinary rented one; evidently he hadn't acquired another Agostinelli. No one discussed Agostinelli or mentioned him during the entire evening. Marcel seemed emaciated; the rings around his eyes were darker, and when he laughed—which he still did now and then, unexpectedly—it came out as a harsh helpless cackle. In the taxi he imitated Clémenceau, Diaghilev, and Oscar Wilde. He was witty in a new and artificial, rather macabre way. Reynaldo was in uniform and was about to join his regiment. He seemed his usual self, although he didn't say much. He hummed, drummed his fingers, and looked out the window, not laughing at Marcel's imitations.

It had rained earlier in the evening and the streets were wet. The taxi went on through the almost deserted city, its lights glittering yellowishly on the pavement. At the Ritz they were shown into the private room and Marcel sat down, a pale bearded fur-coated figure on a little gilt chair. He didn't seem to recognize the waiters and didn't call them by their first names anymore.

The Ritz was exactly as always, except that they too were short of coal and the rooms were a little chilly. They still had some 1913 Moët et Chandon; evidently they had had a better stock than Larue's, or they had paid illegal prices for it. They dined splendidly, except for the cold room. As usual Marcel took no wine but drank endless cups of black coffee. Now and then he took out his handkerchief and coughed into it, in a rather unconvincing and theatrical way.

Reynaldo took up the cue. "I don't think this cold room is good for you."

"No it isn't."

"We ought to leave."

It was eleven o'clock. Marcel paid for the dinner and tipped everybody with his usual carelessness. The doorman found them another taxi and they got into it. Reynaldo gave the driver an address that Herma didn't recognize. Marcel, in the dark corner of the taxi, murmured to himself, "Ah! quand refleuriront les roses de septembre!" He seemed to have turned into a parody, a vaudeville satire on his old self. Then he sat up, smiled at Herma, and said in a perfectly normal tone, "And now for the music."

"Music?"

"The Poulet-Quartet."

"Ah, they're playing this evening?"

"Yes."

It was after eleven now. "But where?"

"Chez moi. Boulevard Haussmann."

"You mean they're waiting for us there?"

"No. We have to go to collect them."

They went first to get the viola player, Amable Massis, who lived far out in the Plaisance quarter beyond Montparnasse. His mother, who answered the door, was indignant. A sleepy Massis in pyjamas appeared behind her. "I have come to recall you to your awful promise," intoned Marcel in his sepulchral voice.

Massis reappeared after a few minutes, wrapped in his overcoat and hatless, his hair ruffled, carrying his instrument case and portfolio. They went on to collect the young Gaston Poulet, the first violinist and organizer of the quartet, and then the second violin Victor Gentil and the cellist Louis Ruyssen. Ruyssen was difficult to persuade. He was a bachelor who lived a mysterious life and perhaps he had someone with him in the apartment. At last he came out, sulking, carrying his large instrument in its canvas bag. Somehow they all crammed into the taxi, Poulet and the instruments up in front with the driver, Gentil and Ruyssen on the jump seats, and the other four jammed shoulder to shoulder in the rear. Ruyssen, who was directly opposite Marcel, sat staring at him without a word.

"It *was* agreed," said Marcel.

Ruyssen only growled. "It isn't good for a cello to take it out on such a damp night."

Arriving at the apartment in Boulevard Haussmann, everyone cheered up a little. The cork-lined rooms were warmer than most apartments in Paris. Marcel had a small charcoal stove in the bedroom, which was so small that they were almost as crowded in it as they had been in the taxi. Marcel got onto the bed, still in his fur coat, and pulled the spread up over his knees. He had now found a housekeeper, a tall foxy-faced woman named Céleste who seemed thoroughly in charge of things. She brought coffee and reproached Marcel for having gone out in such unsuitable weather. He said nothing and appeared not to notice that she was there. She disappeared, not at all put out by his impoliteness.

The program, it transpired, was to be the late Beethoven quartets. The four musicians set up their stands and began tuning their instruments, still a little sulky. Poulet, when the instruments were tuned, turned to Marcel.

"Monsieur, we have all the quartets. Which did you wish?"

"Shall we say the E flat. The one with the scherzo."

"Opus 127," said Poulet.

They arranged the music on the stands and lifted their instruments. Then, with a nod from Poulet, they began. The vigorous play of the two violins, the slightly heavier and resonant voice of the viola, the baritone of the cello filled the small room. The first movement was a spare and clean skeletal statement, without decoration and utterly devoid of emotion. It was rather somber, and so was the adagio movement that followed it. Marcel watched intently, his eyes burning in their dark sockets and the coffee untouched by his side. In the middle of the adagio there was a strange set of birdlike cries from the violins, accompanied by a strumming cello continuo. Then—after this outburst, as it were—the four instruments returned to their abstruse and complex development of the theme. The two violins wove in and out, sometimes one climbing over the other for a few bars and then returning to the normal harmonic stance a third below. It was a difficult music—highly intellectual—not at all like the sentimental and lachrymose Verdi that Herma was used to, or the light-hearted and elegant, harmonious Mozart. The theme was distorted, inverted, abandoned for a few bars, and then reintroduced again. It was as though the music were unwilling to give way to silence, or unable to find its way to a conclusion; then finally it came to an end in a very gentle, almost reluctant chord in the middle register.

The scherzo movement that followed was falsely light. It was a parody of gay and light string music—as if to say with a mocking little smile, you see what goes by the name of pleasure with ordinary men. But we who know . . .

It was this scherzo that Marcel had been waiting for. He listened intently, his fingers in his beard, his dark Persian eyes fixed on the musicians. The harmonies were not quite right. Yet the correct harmonies were implied, behind the notes. The music said: you see, this is the way the harmonies ought to be. But they are not. The universe is awry. Herma turned to look at Marcel. There was nothing affected or theatrical about him now. His attention was fixed on the quartet, aware of nothing in the room but the music. He was as intent and calm as though watching the execution of an enemy, or the slow wilting and decay of a flower. His eyes met hers briefly; there was no expression and he turned away again. Reynaldo, too, sitting stiffly in his uniform with his képi on his knees, was listening intently. He was facing not toward the musicians, but toward the odd figure of Marcel on the bed across the room. Now and then he smiled, as though some inward thought had struck him.

The finale was slightly frenetic. The instruments gave the impression of trying to escape from one another—from their common fourness—and yet they were bound together in the prison of their form. They struggled, but in vain. At last they came to a resolution of sorts— a kind of truce. The chords that ended the movement were slightly dissonant.

When it ended no one spoke. There was silence, broken only by a little goatlike cough from Marcel. Poulet waited, his face turned questioningly to Marcel. Then Marcel said, "The C sharp minor."

"Opus 131."

They arranged their music again, and began. The quartet was very long; it had seven movements. It began very slowly and gently with a single violin voice, joined after a measure or two by the second violin, then by the deeper voice of the viola. Finally the cello joined them from below, and together they worked gradually into the complex texture of the fugue. In some way the music suggested intimations of a recollected suffering, now exalted and purified. The single theme of the fugue was developed in infinite parallel progressions and variations; a strangely spare, somber statement.

There followed two short allegros. The fourth movement, an andante, also seemed to be searching, but now it was as though the four voices were searching together, and for the same thing—like four hunters scouting over low hills, separated now and then, and then rejoining, but their eyes always forward in the same direction. What were they hunting for? None of them dared to speak its name.

Herma, sitting in a rather stiff and uncomfortable chair with hardly room on the floor for her feet, followed the andante only with difficulty. She was not really trained to follow antiphonies with four voices—when you sang the Sextet from *Lucia* you just sang your own part and let the others worry about the rest—and she had to focus her attention with effort in order to follow the thread of the thematic development. She lost track of the movements. There was a presto, and then an adagio. It began with great dignity, taking its time. A lyrical note crept in, almost imperceptibly, but was soon submerged in the purely mathematical development of the theme. The four voices tested against each other warily—formed chords and dissolved—regrouped, and proceeded stealthily across the midnight landscape of the quartet. Now and then the cello broke out angrily in a strident note, but this indignation was soon lost, and the voices fell back into their contrapuntal lacework of harmony.

Without any particular transition, led by a sudden impetus from the cello, this adagio broke rhythm and began rushing on more quickly toward the end. After that it was an odd kind of music that didn't seem to be scored in any particular tempo. It was a kind of light ethereal fugue in which only the three smaller instruments engaged and the cello remained below, as though softly chiding or guiding, in its even baritone. Now and then the cello joined in for a bar or two, as if to show the others how fugues were done. It was clear that the cello, which had seemed so reticent and had remained below and in the background, was the master and had been all along. It was this deeper voice that had underlain the others and sustained them, otherwise they would have lost their way in this dark countryside they were exploring. This Herma understood, or half understood, but there were many things she did not understand. She tried to follow, but was distracted by the abrupt shifts of tempo, by the constant dissonances in the complex harmony. It was nothing like Verdi or anything in the opera. It was music of the mind. When he wrote these last quartets, Beethoven had been burned clean by suffering and was no longer the slave of emotions. The histrionics of the Eroica were behind, the moving lyricism of the Pastoral, the bombast and exaltation of the Ninth. He was deaf and could not hear what he had written, only see the motions of the bows on the instruments. This was pure music, made not for human emotions, or for humans, but for the abstract Mind.

The fugue resolved at last into a set of short sharp declarative statements, like the codas in the symphonies, only written in grotesque miniature for the tiny orchestra—in parody, as it were. There were three abrupt identical chords in C sharp, chords of absolute simplicity, chords that anyone might have written. Then there was silence.

For a long moment no one spoke. Poulet sat with his instrument resting on his knees. Then Marcel said quietly, in his ordinary matter-of-fact tone, "Thank you, my friends."

The four put the music away in their portfolios. "It's late," said

Ruyssen, still a little surly, already pulling the cover onto his cello.

"It was good of you to come. We will take you home now. I am sorry if there was any inconvenience. You see, I am not well enough to go to concerts."

He charmed them all. In the end even Ruyssen shook his hand. Rather awkwardly Marcel opened the drawer of the bedside table, took out an envelope bulging with bank notes, and gave it to Poulet. Poulet stuck this into his coat pocket. Laden with their instruments, their folded stands, and their music, they bumped their way out of the apartment, followed by Herma, Reynaldo, and Marcel.

Céleste had telephoned for a taxi. It was late at night now and it was some time before the taxi came. It was cold in the entryway and Marcel took shelter in the loge, wrapping his scarf around his mouth and the lower part of his face. The taxi came and they got in, according to the same crammed and uncomfortable arrangement as before.

"Extra charge for more than four. And—baggage," said the driver, watching as the instrument cases were passed in one by one.

"Very good, my friend," said Marcel, still calm.

They delivered the quartet to their homes, Massis last to his apartment far out beyond the Montparnasse cemetery. The driver, who seemed unfriendly, tolerated all this circus with contempt, only because the fare would be very large. He turned around to the three passengers remaining.

"And now?"

Marcel looked at Reynaldo. He smiled faintly.

"Should we go, do you think?"

"Why not?"

"And shall Herma come too?"

Reynaldo considered. "It's hardly suitable."

"No. You're right. Seventy-eight Avenue Kléber," Marcel told the driver.

The taxi went off down Rue de la Convention in the direction of the river. There was silence for a while. Then Marcel said craftily, to no one in particular, "But perhaps Fred could come."

Herma looked at him. It was dark in the taxi. Now and then a street lamp went past and the pale oval of his face could be seen.

"Come where?"

"I know that Fred is free tonight," he said, gazing at her fixedly.

"That's up to him."

"We'll take you home. It was good of you to come. Sometimes one hungers for the company of a charming young woman. Simply to look upon—to be with. And music." In the dark corner of the taxi he sighed, in his slightly affected way. "It is my only consolation now. My only diversion. Music enables us to have experiences in the soul that we are no longer able to have in the body."

Reynoldo smiled a little at this. They crossed the river on the Pont Mirabeau and went on up the quays past the Trocadéro. There was no traffic and in only a few minutes the taxi stopped in front of the apartment in Avenue Kléber. Herma got out, and Reynaldo gallantly climbed out after her to escort her across the sidewalk to the door.

"Send Fred down," came Marcel's imperious histrionic voice from inside the taxi.

Herma went up while Marcel and Reynaldo waited in the taxi. After a quarter of an hour or so Fred appeared, in the winter costume which he now affected in order to identify himself as an American and radiate a slight aura of legend: a Stetson and a fleece-lined leather coat that came down to his knees. On the sidewalk, before the dark shape of the taxi with its invisible occupants, he stopped. It occurred to him that Marcel perhaps still bore him some resentment over the matter of Agostinelli. He was not sure what was happening or whether it was a good idea.

Marcel's voice from inside the taxi was friendly and intimate, almost cajoling. "Get in, Fred."

"Where are you going?"

"To a certain place. Come along. You'll find it interesting."

He got in, rather gingerly, and the taxi went off. He was sitting on the jump seat with Reynaldo and Marcel opposite him. No one said anything. The taxi went up the avenue, around the circle of the Etoile, and along the boulevards to a small narrow street near the Madeleine. There it drew up before an elegant eighteenth-century mansion. The shutters were tightly closed. The building was dark on the outside and there was no sign or other identifying mark on the door. From every appearance it was a private residence.

They got out. Marcel paid the driver, after considerable negotiations of a peculiar sort: the driver kept adding on charges for extra passengers, for the musical instruments, and so on, and Marcel insisted on paying him even more. Finally it was settled. Marcel, holding the scarf over his mouth, pulled the old-fashioned bell cord under the marquée.

The door was opened by a valet and they entered. The large vestibule was lighted only dimly, by lamps with colored glass shades. Beyond was a long and narrow salon with a bronze chandelier hanging from the ceiling. There were a dozen or so men lounging around on the divans or standing in pairs smoking cigarettes, all of them young. It was an odd assortment. Some were genteel and refined, Swinburnish, with pale languid faces and expensive, rather old-fashioned clothing. Others seemed to be genuine toughs from the Halles or the barge docks. One was a powerful young man in skin-tight trousers and a sleeveless singlet, his bare shoulders gleaming. The salon, and the rooms beyond it as well as they could be glimpsed, were furnished in ornate Louis XV style. There were screens, divans, étagères, period clocks, veneer Boulle marquetry, Sèvres figurines, a small Renaissance bronze of a naked youth extracting a thorn from his foot. Over the chimneypiece was a portrait by Nattier, and a large Fragonard occupied the opposite wall.

All this seemed to suggest, perhaps, the town house of a Parisian aristocrat, opulent and slightly old-fashioned. But in other respects the establishment was like a hotel. There was a reception desk with a small blue-shaded lamp on it, and behind it was the owner and proprietor, Julien Lecouvreur. Marcel introduced him ceremoniously to Fred.

Lecouvreur was a person—not precisely a young man, he appeared to be in his mid-thirties—of great elegance and suavity. He had an olive skin and a pencil-thin mustache which he touched now and then with his finger before he spoke. He was coatless, dressed in striped formal trousers, a cravat and a waistcoat. His shirt cuffs were fastened with large gold links. He took Fred's hand politely.

"It is a pleasure to make the acquaintance of Monsieur."

Marcel, his fingers playing in his beard, explained in a gentle voice, "Julien is someone I . . . knew . . . many years ago. When he decided to go into business for himself, it was I who lent him the money to set himself up here. Isn't that so, Julien?"

"That is exactly so."

Marcel smiled a ghost of his old smile. "I'm afraid that some of my grandmother's furniture is here too," he said with a mock sigh. "Certain pieces are priceless."

"Monsieur is very kind," said Julien.

"But now he is independent. He has paid me back, and the establishment is entirely his. And it's very profitable, is it not, Julien?"

"My clients are the cream of Paris society. For them, expense is no object."

Reynaldo, paying no attention to the conversation, was looking around at the young men in the room. "There's someone new," he said.

"Ah?"

With a discreet motion of his head Reynaldo indicated the youth in the sleeveless singlet.

"Ah yes. That's Maurice. He's from an excellent family, but he prefers to affect that costume. It pleases—certain persons."

Marcel's smile had disappeared. He evidently didn't care for this turn in the conversation. He suggested to Julien, "Perhaps you might care to show the gentleman your library and other beautiful things."

Julien bowed. He came out from behind the desk and caught the eye of a young man with curly hair and a flowing Byronic collar, who took his place at the desk. Then he led the way up an ornate staircase that curved about in a half circle as it rose to the balcony above.

"Originally," Marcel explained as they went, "this was the town house of the Marignys. They lost it at the time of the Revolution, and then it passed into the hands of various bourgeois. More recently it belonged to the wealthy entrepreneur M. Plaghki, whom I know, so I was able to arrange for Julien to purchase it."

All this he delivered in his artificial affected voice, which now turned into a kind of parody of the manner of a tourist guide.

"Very little of the furniture, however, is original. It had to be replaced at considerable cost. However, if one knows how to go about such things, favorable opportunities can be found." It was clear that he had helped Julien also with the furnishings, in addition to his grandmother's furniture which he had given or lent him.

Fred had a notion what the ''library'' and the ''beautiful things'' upstairs might be like. But he was mistaken. The beautiful things were paintings and objets-d'art, most of the eighteenth century. There was another Fragonard a little smaller than the one in the salon but still priceless, a Boucher, a pair of twinned Watteaus, and a small bust of Madame de Pompadour by Houdon. In glass cases there were rare and expensive bibelots, figurines, Chinese porcelains. The library, occupying a large room which evidently had originally been the master bedroom, specialized mainly in books on heraldry, genealogy, and history of the nobility, all in fine leather bindings. Some were incunabula, others were illuminated manuscripts on vellum. For ten minutes or so Julien showed Fred the books, while Marcel stood by offering a comment now and then, stroking his beard with a complacent air. It struck Fred that, compared to the elegance of the Hôtel Marigny, Marcel's own apartment in Boulevard Haussmann seemed small and cramped, even a little squalid. Boulevard Haussmann was the center of his more important world, the world of his novel, the world of Art. This was another world, the world of his secret pleasure, of his vice. For it was clear that Julien did not really own the Hôtel Marigny. It was the creature of Marcel's imagination, made concrete and realized in its every detail through the working of his own highly refined taste and will.

''You see,'' Marcel explained, ''Julien was for many years footman in a number of the most aristocratic houses of Europe. I need only mention the Prince d'Essling, the Count Orloff, and the Duc de Rohan.'' Julien smiled in his careful feline way. He seemed not at all disconcerted that Marcel revealed his past as a servant. ''It was then that he began his interest in the genealogies of the European nobility. If I have a question regarding custom, or the correctness of a social procedure, I always bring it to Julien. Now suppose, Julien,'' he asked him, ''that a lady were giving a dinner party and invited both a general and a bishop. Which would take precedence?''

''The bishop would take precedence,'' said Julien immediately, ''and would be seated on the lady's right.''

''These are only games,'' said Marcel with a sideways smile at Fred. ''But Julien, I have a real question for you, for a page in my book. Let us take the Duchesse de Guermantes, who does not exist. Suppose she invited the Duchesse d'Uzès, who is the first duchess of France, and the Princesse Murat, who is higher in rank but of a more recent family.''

Julien said imperturbably, ''The Duchesse de Guermantes would never ask the Duchesse d'Uzès and the Princesse Murat on the same evening.''

''He is my walking *Almanach de Gotha*,'' said Marcel. ''He is indispensable for the information he gives me. He can tell you immediately whether a Montesquieu or a De Bréyoures is of the Bonapartist or Orléanist line, or whether a cabinet minister takes precedence over a

Spanish count. Without him I couldn't write my book. Allow me to give you something, Julien, for your professional advice.'' He got out his checkbook. "Let's say fifty francs.''

Julien demurred; he wouldn't hear of it.

"Very well, let's say a hundred.'' Finally Julien had to accept the check, to prevent the figure from going even higher.

They left the library and went back down the long hall toward the stairway. There were several rooms along the hall, and others on the corridor that led along the rear of the building. In one room Fred caught a glimpse of chains and shackles through a half-open door, and in another a tube of vaseline was clearly visible on the bedside table. The other two didn't seem to notice these things. They went downstairs again to rejoin Reynaldo, who had not gone up with them but had stayed in the salon talking to the young men. Julien took up his position behind the desk. He looked at Fred and then at Marcel. "Monsieur is one of us?'' he inquired politely.

Marcel lifted his shoulders, with a faint smile.

"In addition to the persons you see here,'' said Julien, seeming to address himself to Fred but without looking at him directly, "I have a large selection of others who are available on call. There are many tastes. Some ask me for a footman, or a choirboy, or a colored chauffeur. There is one man who will have no one but a butcher. I have no butcher, but I have a young man who comes in a butcher's apron, with real bloodstains. We spare no expense to have each detail right. Just now Scotsmen are at a premium, I don't know why. Perhaps on account of their kilts.''

"Perhaps it's because of the war,'' said Reynaldo. "There are a lot of Scotsmen in Paris.''

"Ah, the war. What a terrible thing. And here you, Monsieur Reynaldo, are in uniform. They shouldn't make fine gentlemen like you go to war,'' he said in a concerned tone and without apparent irony. "With one of us, it's different. But if a person like Monsieur should be killed, what a loss. It would be an atrocity. Every last one of the Boches should be killed. And think of what they did at Louvain, cutting off the children's hands.''

"That's all propaganda,'' said Reynaldo.

"Do you think so, Monsieur?'' said Julien, still polite.

Marcel, sensing a quarrel, changed the subject again. "Perhaps you would like to meet some of these persons,'' he suggested to Fred.

They moved over to the carpet between the divans, in the center of the room. Several young men clustered around. Sherry was served and the conversation became general. The boy with the Byronic collar stared with admiration at Reynaldo. "Ah, what a fine uniform,'' he said. Reynaldo wore an elegant black tunic with lieutenant's stripes, tailored riding breeches, and cavalry boots. He had taken off his braided képi and set it on the table when he entered. "And you are going off to fight?'' asked the boy.

Reynaldo made an indifferent gesture.

"Alas, if they ever come for me," sighed Marcel.

"I hope they put you in the shock troops," Reynaldo told him.

The young men were all very polite, even the toughs from the Halles and the dockworkers, who were perhaps not real either but only well-brought-up young men wearing costumes. They were particularly interested in Fred, who was still wearing his leather coat and had not taken off his Stetson.

"Are you a cowboy, Monsieur?" one asked respectfully.

"No."

"But you are from the Far West?"

"Yes."

"I am interested in cowboys and things of the Far West. I have some books in my room if you would like to see them."

"No, thanks," said Fred.

"You have other preferences?" inquired Julien politely.

"I have no preferences at all."

"It's late," said Marcel. "We ought to be going. I have what I came for, Julien, your information about the Duchesse de Guermantes. I am infinitely grateful to you. And so, good evening."

"If you would like to see my western books some other time," said the young man.

"Yes, some other time," said Fred.

"Good evening, Messieurs," said Julien. "I am pleased to have been of service. And I am happy to have made your acquaintance, Monsieur Frédéric. Whomever Monsieur Marcel brings, anything in the house is his for the asking. Monsieur Marcel is a real gentleman, of the old-fashioned kind. There are not so many like him any more."

"Good night, Julien."

Outside in the street it seemed unusually dark. After a moment Fred grasped that it was because the street lamps were out, perhaps because of one of the usual electricity shortages. They stood under the marquée for a moment waiting for their eyes to adjust to the darkness. On the wall by the doorway, dimly visible in the starlight, someone had chalked in crude letters "Sodome." Marcel saw that Fred had noticed it and smiled faintly.

They left the doorway and groped their way along the sidewalk toward the boulevard. When they came to the first cross street they saw far over to the east, in the direction of Vincennes, a searchlight beam stabbing up into the sky and then moving along the undersurface of a cloud.

"A Zeppelin raid," said Reynaldo.

"Ah, they say they're exquisite," said Marcel. "You know, I've never seen one. There was one the other night but I was working and didn't notice. Now I've given Céleste explicit orders to call me if there's another one."

"You're welcome," said Reynaldo. "I'm going to bed. I've got to report at ten in the morning." He glanced at his watch, which was invisible in the darkness. "This morning," he corrected.

There were no taxis, even after they reached the boulevard, and Reynaldo left them and set off on foot. He lived nearby in Rue de Provence, only five minutes away. Marcel wrapped his shawl around his mouth and he and Fred set out in search of a taxi. "There's sure to be one at the Madeleine," came Marcel's muffled voice through the shawl.

They found one, parked at the curb in the dark shadow of the church, but the driver explained that it was against regulations to take passengers during an air raid. Only if he picked them up before the alarm sounded could he continue to take them to their destination. And the alarm had sounded an hour ago. So if they were stopped by the police, Marcel and Fred would have to swear that they had been driving around in the taxi already an hour or more. "But doing what?" said the driver. "That's the hard part of the question. You gentlemen had better make up your minds."

Marcel cocked an eye at Fred.

"Looking for girls," said Fred.

Marcel smiled at this. They got in and shut the door.

The driver, as well as could be seen in the dim starlight and the glow from his instrument panel, was a good-looking young man with dark hair. He had a slight accent, perhaps Italian. "Where to?"

Marcel looked questioningly at Fred. "To the Sacré-Coeur, to watch the Zeppelins."

"Ah, that's out of the question. I have the police to think of, gentlemen. If I break the regulations I can lose my license."

"Ah, if it's only the police, don't trouble yourself," said Marcel. "I'm a personal friend of the Prefect of Paris. Here's my card."

He passed a fifty-franc bill forward through the opening in the glass.

"It's easy enough for you gentlemen," said the driver, putting the car in gear and setting it into motion. "You're rich. If a chauffeur loses his license, he's out of luck."

"I've known many chauffeurs," said Marcel. "If you lose your license, I'll . . ."

Then he stopped, in mid-sentence, and looked out the window into the darkness. Fred knew what he had been about to say. ". . . I'll hire you myself."

The car went on slowly through the pitch-black streets. There were more searchlights now, some from the Left Bank, perhaps in the Luxembourg Gardens. The streets were deserted. Now and then a spectator could be seen on a rooftop, silhouetted in the starlight or dimly illuminated in the loom of a searchlight beam. Rue d'Amsterdam, Boulevard de Clichy, Rue de Clignancourt. The taxi wound up the hill toward the white mosquelike church with its collection of domes, one large and four small, glowing in the starlight. It came to a stop not far from the balustrade under the church. Marcel told the driver to wait, with a ghostly little smile promising more fifty-franc bills.

They looked out over the vast city stretched out before them in the starlight. The spectacle was impressive and rather unearthly. The landmarks of the city were difficult to make out in the darkness. The outline of the Eiffel Tower was unmistakable against the sky, and a little to the left of it the dome of the Invalides. Except for that there were only unidentified shapes and lumps scattered out in the darkness before them, with the silver thread of the river dividing the city in two. The Ile de la Cité with the Notre-Dame on it could be made out because the river divided around it and then came back together again at the Vert-Galant.

There were perhaps two dozen or more searchlights now playing in the sky. The beams from the Luxembourg Gardens, splaying out and then coming together in an apex again, wandered slowly over the clouds. Then one found its mark, and the others followed it. A surprisingly narrow and graceful silver cigar, with four vanes at its tapering rear, was caught in the converging shafts of light somewhere to the left of the Luxembourg, perhaps near the Jardin des Plantes. There were others; a single searchlight beam followed a Zeppelin drifting slowly along the curve of the river near Boulogne.

"It is as beautiful as they said," murmured Marcel. "These are machines that have never been seen before. And perhaps in a few years they will be obsolete; they will never be seen again." He had forgotten his shawl now; it fell down revealing his pale face with its dark intent eyes in the starlight. "They appear only at night, and only to the elect —those who watch at night. It is as though they were odd gods from an unknown mythology. From another planet."

There were flashes of light from the Left Bank near the Panthéon, and others along the quays, but whether they were bombs falling or guns firing at the Zeppelins was not clear.

Fred imagined the men high overhead in fur-lined leather clothing, moving about in the dimly lit interior of the gondola, adjusting the controls, watching the instruments of the engines, checking the apparatus that released the bombs.

"You poetize things a little too much," he said. "They're simply German machines to kill people."

"Yes, they are death gods," said Marcel quite calmly.

As they watched, a searchlight beam much closer than the others, perhaps in the Parc Monceau or the Montmartre Cemetery, found its own Zeppelin, this one so near that the gondola underneath and the small engine nacelles could be clearly made out. The stabbing beam played across the airship, lost it for a moment, and then swung across the sky and found it again. The Zeppelin was moving across the city from east to west, and the searchlight was now behind it. The beam struck its underquarters at the rear just forward of the tail and bored upward relentlessly, as if in an effort to penetrate it and destroy it. The Zeppelin seemed to sway a little, but the shaft of light stuck to it doggedly, following its every movement. Fred allowed himself a sideways glance at Marcel. But if Marcel noticed the analogy he said nothing.

14.

Herma woke up late. It was a rainy Sunday morning. She had no engagements and nothing to do with herself all day except do exactly what she wanted. She yawned, stretched sensuously in the bed, turned over, and dozed again for a few moments.

But she really wasn't sleepy anymore. She got out of bed, lazily turned on the lamp (it was ten o'clock in the morning, but the autumn gray outside was depressing and she preferred to keep the curtains drawn even in the daytime), and went into the tiny kitchen for her breakfast: a single large Spanish orange, thick-skinned and pungent, more reddish and wild than the pale California oranges of her childhood. Standing before the sink in her nightgown, she cut the spongy skin into neat segments and removed them. Then she divided the orange into sections and ate them one by one, leaning over the sink so that the juice wouldn't drip onto her gown.

It was always Herma who ate breakfast and never Fred, just as it was always Herma who slept at night and not Fred (unless he was with one of his lady friends, the promiscuous pig, and then precious little sleeping took place). Fred had a voracious appetite in the morning and if he had eaten breakfast it would have been croissants with butter and jam, scrambled eggs, sausage, fried chicken livers and heaven knows what, and then where would her famous slimness go. No, Fred, she thought complacently, you are not allowed to have breakfast. You lack self-control. You are charming in your boyish impulsiveness, your reckless and insouciant surrender to all the temptations of life, but you are not going to ruin my figure. She put the slices of orange peel away in the receptacle provided, wiped off the kitchen counter, held the tips of her fingers under the water tap, and dried them. She went into the bathroom, slipped out of her nightgown, and hung it carefully on a hook.

The Sunday morning bath was one of her secret indulgences. Everything about the bathroom pleased her: the gold-plated fittings, the tub of magenta-colored Carrara, the imported Italian tile on the floor, the warm fleece of the bath mat under her toes, the delicate scent of lavendar and rosemary. She turned on both taps and added a handful of scented salts. Then when the tub was full of water so hot that it steamed (this was very wasteful in wartime), she got in and sank into a luxury of violet-colored foam.

She didn't mind it hot. The hotter the better. Now and then she disappeared entirely under the surface of the foam, emerging after a moment to gaze lazily at her toe arising from the violet lace at the other end of the tub. She squeezed a sponge over the top of her head. She didn't bother to shampoo her hair or wash anything in particular. It wasn't so much an ablutionary bath as a ritualistic one. She usually came out clean enough. A hot soaking for half an hour removed every-thing extraneous, and her short hair was as easy to wash as a boy's. She stood up, waited a moment to allow the violet foam to slither off her, and stepped out onto the mat.

She dried herself with an enormous soft Turkish towel, threw the towel into the corner, and then stood with her chin lifted and her arms hanging straight down, examining herself in the mirror. She was a pretty thing, no doubt about that. Tall and slender, narrow-shouldered, finely modeled, still with an attractive combination of adolescent grace and slight gawkishness—even though she was not so young as all that anymore—she had the kind of body that was not destined, ever, to be old. (A little shadow—she dismissed this thought.) Her short hair, with one lock falling over the brow, was now in style and exactly the way everyone else was doing their hair in the new atmosphere of wartime casualness and economy. Stimulated by the bath, her smooth apricot-over-lemon complexion showed just a faint flush of blood at the corners of the cheeks. Her hands and feet were a little large for the rest of her, but this went with the adolescent awkwardness—all young animals had large feet. It was the grace of a young colt. Her face was a perfect oval, her glance steady-eyed with a trace of a smile playing on her lips. Just above the mouth there was a kind of peach-down that showed only when the light struck it in a certain way to make a shadow—as it did now, in the diffuse pink glow from the fixture overhead. Still staring fixedly at the image in the mirror, she raised her hands and placed them, thumbs and forefingers stretched in an arc, at the sides of her chest. She pushed upward. There was no mistake about it anymore. When she did this there was a slight suggestion now of little twin swellings around the roseate buds on either side—a phenomenon that appeared when she was Herma, only when she stood in a certain light, and only when she assisted things a little by raising the soft flesh with her hands. Yet it pleased her. It made her feel feminine, complacent, and faintly mysteri-ous—magical was perhaps the word. She went on looking at herself for some time. Then she noticed something stuck into the side of the mirror —a polished glossy card, partly printed and partly in handwriting.

THIS CERTIFIES THAT

Herma

IS A MEMBER OF THE
ITTY BITTY TITTY COMMITTEE

She tore it off and flung it into the wastebasket. She looked around for something to smash, but she didn't want to break the mirror and everything else in the bathroom was solid marble. The conceited, vain, heartless, cocky, sarcastic, selfish, vulgar brat! She stamped her foot, hurting herself a little. He and his obsession with the bovine—there were plenty of people who liked her *just the way she was.* She was fed up with these little billets-doux in the mirror. She had been getting them for years now. It wasn't funny. He could take his glossy card, his sense of humor, and the whole business and stick it—he even made *her* vulgar, that was the worst of it.

She started to go into her bedroom to dress, then changed her mind. Opening her dresser drawer, she found a large safety pin and went back through the bath into Fred's room. She jerked open the top drawer of his dresser where he kept his underwear, handkerchiefs, and neckties, all in a jumble. She found a pair of underpants and stuck the pin into them, point inward, leaving it unfastened. She craftily set the underpants on top of the other garments in the drawer, rumpled them a little to make them look as though they had been dropped casually, and shut the drawer. Then she flounced away into her own room to get dressed.

This wicked and ingenious trap remained in the drawer until the next day. Fred had things to do on that Monday morning, all of them business for Herma, of course. He was preoccupied with thinking about them and planning his day. He came out of the bathroom naked, found a pair of socks on the floor and put them on first (they had only been worn once), and solemnly put on a soft felt hat and then knotted a cravat around his naked neck. He couldn't resist going into the bathroom to look at himself in this rig. Great. Any number of his lady friends would swoon with desire. He went back into his room, took off the hat, necktie, and socks (they did smell a little and he was meeting somebody important at noon), and opened the dresser for a pair of underpants.

Sitting on the bed, he pulled the underpants up over his legs, still thinking about something else. When he stood up and hoisted them the last inch he felt a sharp and excruciating pain. He doubled up and stifled a cry.

Gingerly he lowered the underpants and looked at himself. There was a drop of blood on the thing all right. Right near the end too, the most sensitive part. He gritted his teeth. There was blood on the underpants too. He took them off, removed the open safety pin, and threw them both into the corner of the room. He sat down on the bed again. He felt moisture welling into his eyes and he took a corner of the sheet and wiped them. He felt funny. He didn't know what it was exactly. It wasn't the pain, it was something else. It was a sense of prickling and shrinking—of nebulous anxiety, of loss. Looking down and opening his legs again, he found that what he vaguely feared was happening—the thing was gone, disappeared, drawn up inside—in indignation, or fear of the vagina dentata, the great male-devouring monster of femaleness that hung over the world like an incubus, the all-seeing, all-punishing Mother-Beast who threatened in an awful voice to "cut it off if you go on playing with yourself." And now she had done it. It still hurt like the devil. But the hurt was inside now, along with the rest of it. He (now she), her eyes still brimming with tears, went into her own room, put on her nightgown, and lay face down on the bed. After a while she noticed she was sobbing softly.

She had to get up. Fred had an appointment at noon. She lay there perhaps an hour. Then she pushed herself up from the bed, dried her eyes on the corner of her own bedsheet, and went to the escritoire across the room. Sitting down, she took a piece of pink notepaper and a fountain pen.

"*To My Buddy,*" she wrote. "*The world is full of pain. There is too much of it. Why should we hurt each other? I am sorry if I hurt you. But you hurt me too, in my mind. That's what you can't understand. But I forgive you, we must forgive each other, and somehow we must reach across the mirror to each other and be friends, instead of seeking over the world like two lost and lorn creatures looking for something we can never find, suspicious of each other and always fighting. Fred, je t'aime. You are my brother, you are Myself. What is to become of us? Why must Male and Female always hate? We cannot be saved, Fred, unless we love each other as we love ourselves. We both know a great deal about love. You know how to love women, and I know how to love men. Why then can't we love each other? If not, we are lost. You have made me feel very sad. And I have hurt you in a delicate place. I am sorry. And I wish you too could be sorry for me once in a while.*"

She read this over. Then she took it into the bathroom and slipped it into the frame at the side of the mirror. She glanced back through the open door at the ormolu clock in her bedroom. It was after eleven-thirty. Backing away from the mirror, she lowered her arms to her sides and began the exercise of will that had become so familiar now that it was almost a reflex—to force out of her that magic organ of transformation that made her self into two selves, her world into two worlds, her consciousness into a battleground where the two most primitive forces in the universe were pitted against each other—one conscious and waking, the other lurking furtively in the shadows. At the very last moment, as an afterthought, she applied a little lavender perfume to the tip of her finger and touched it to the note on the mirror.

15.

Fred's engagement was a lunch with a journalist who proposed to write an article on Herma for *L'Illustration*, except that he wanted to be bribed to do it—the way he put it was that the editor had to be bribed to accept the article, since it was not really news but advertising—"and in wartime," he added, the son of a bitch. And he, the writer, was only passing along the sum in question to the real culprit, that unprincipled thief of an editor. After taking his cut, no doubt. Never mind, an article in *L'Illustration* was worth the money. They agreed on two hundred francs, and Fred would supply some photographs. Would Fred care for a drink? No, he wouldn't. He wasn't in a very good mood. He wasn't sure exactly what was wrong with him.

He left the restaurant and after walking aimlessly for a while found himself in Place St.-Augustin. It had started to rain again. He wasn't far from the café in Rue d'Astorg where he used to meet Agostinelli. He found it after a little searching, went in, and ordered a cup of coffee. He had never noticed before but it was called the Café des Américains, perhaps because of the many shops for tourists in the Grands Boulevards nearby. When the coffee came he left it untouched, lit a cigarette, and sat there for some time looking out through the steamy window at the people passing in the street. There was an odor in the place, as in all cafés in the winter, of stale beer, fried potatoes, and cigarette smoke. It wasn't unpleasant. After a while he became aware of another faint scent, and it was only after a time that he identified it. He crushed out his cigarette, took the pink notepaper out of his pocket, and read it again.

She had the style of a sentimental schoolgirl. Yet she got to him somehow, damn her. "Fred, je t'aime. You are my brother, you are Myself. What is to become of us?" He felt a little twinge as though his eyes were going to film over and start blurring again. It was stupid. Who was he having this fight with anyhow? After all, he was only one person. Just as some people are happy one day and sad the next, he was a man one day and a woman the next. It was a simple enough matter, no more than a glove turned inside out. A lot of people would think it was queer, but there was no need to let them know about it. To believe that you are two people is only a dream, the kind of a dream where you are at a funeral and you walk up to the coffin and look in and the corpse is yourself. That was sick. He was not interested in dreams, he was wide awake, and he knew who he was. When she asked him to feel sorry for her, she was only asking him to feel sorry for himself. And that wasn't his game. He was the American go-getter, the boy who could do anything, the confidence kid. He could handle his own affairs—he always had—his and hers too. That was what manager meant. He was the one who ran things. So no more of this stupid sentimentalism.

He started to crumple up the note, then he decided he didn't want to leave it on the café table or in the ashtray. He straightened it out, folded it again, and put it back in his pocket. What was to become of them? she wanted to know. There was no need for anything to *become* of them. They had already arrived. They were here. They were in Paris and Herma's name was on every poster column. Next week she would be in *L'Illustration*. He was good at what he did. She would have to admit that. (There he was again, thinking about himself as two people.) There was a slang term for it, for all this talking people up, persuading restaurants to serve Fraise Herma, bribing journalists, getting articles in *L'Illustration,* and buying drinks for critics. It was called puffing. That was his life. Puffing in the daytime, fornication at night. And sometimes in the afternoon.

A pair of soldiers went by the window, one glum and the other laughing at something and punching the glum one on the shoulder. They were on leave probably and in a week they would be back in the trenches. He remembered the Zeppelins. The war for him, as it was for Marcel, was a spectator sport. He chased skirts, ate lunch with journalists, and visited Sodomite brothels, while what was perhaps the greatest drama of European history was being played out only a short distance away, so near that on still nights you could hear the faint sound of guns in the distance. He hadn't flown for almost two years. It was the spring before the war began, he remembered, when he flew at Antibes with Agostinelli. The whole business of Agostinelli left him in an unsettled state of mind. It was like an unfinished story, or a song that stuck in your head because you couldn't remember the last line. There was still something to happen about Agostinelli, something final. He lit another cigarette but he didn't smoke it either; he set it in the ashtray and watched it. It was odd that Marcel, after it was all over, had never resented the business of Agostinelli—he had never shown any sign that he, Fred, was guilty of anything or responsible for what had happened. And he wasn't, of course. Agostinelli wasn't a child. He was a man, a free agent. Flying was dangerous. Everybody knew that.

Perhaps, after the war was over, he could go back to flying again. That was his life—it was their life. She made the money, and he spent it on aeroplanes. *Fred, je t'aime. You are my brother, you are Myself. What is to become of us?* It was a funny way for her to put it, he thought. There was no question what was to become of her. She would be an international prima donna; she already was. He saw that what she had meant was: *what is going to become of you?* He looked at what he had done, and what he would go on doing the rest of his life. Sitting around in cafés, and flying on weekends. It wasn't enough. In the end you had to do something for yourself—that wasn't it exactly—something for someone besides yourself. Something that—Herma would admire. Like Tancrède, Herma's soldier-boy. What was he supposed to do, go out in the trenches and bayonet a Boche? He wasn't really strong enough for that. He wasn't in good enough shape; he smoked too many cigarettes and didn't get enough sleep. Besides it was their war, the French. And then he remembered something he had read in the *Figaro* a few days before. Something about Americans. He sat bolt upright in his chair and stared out into the street. Another pair of Frenchmen went by the café window in uniform. One of them was an aviator; he had wings in gold embroidery sewn onto his leather coat.

He got up, went to the cashier's desk, set a franc in the saucer by her elbow, and picked up the telephone. When the operator came on he gave her the number of Lucienne de Mainboche's apartment. The maid answered, and after a moment Lucienne came on the wire. He asked her if she would like to go to the tea dance at Maxim's. She would.

"I'll come by for you at five."

"No, dear boy, I'll be out shopping. I'll meet you there."

"Au revoir."

"Ta ta, chéri."

He glanced at his watch. He still had a couple of hours. He had
planned to go around to the photographer's and make a selection of
pictures for the *L'Illustration* article. Instead he went to the address he
had jotted down on a slip of paper in his pocket. It was in the Hôtel
Palais d'Orsay on the quay, not far from the Foreign Ministry. After
checking with the porter, he went up to the second floor where an office
had been installed in a suite overlooking the river. There was a low glass
partition in the anteroom and behind it a spectacled girl was sitting
typing.

"Escadrille Américaine?"

"Yes, but I'm American."

He saw now she was wearing the uniform of the Norton-Harjes
Ambulance Corps.

"I want to join the Lafayette Escadrille."

She put a piece of paper in her machine, lined it up, looked at it
through her glasses, and began typing. "Are you a flyer?"

"Yes."

"Do you have a license?" She stopped typing with a look of vex-
ation, got out her eraser, and corrected something.

"No."

"Do you have a diploma or a certificate or something from a flying
school?"

"No, but I have a lot of experience."

A Frenchman stuck his head out of the inner office. "Qu'est-ce que
c'est?"

"Rien. Je m'en occuperai."

Her accent was perfect. Perhaps, he thought, he could break his
engagement with Lucienne. She wasn't very pretty, but perhaps she
would be prettier with her glasses off.

"If you don't have a license, and you don't have a school certificate," she said, "then you can sign up, and if you pass the physical"—
she glanced at his thin frame and his immature, rather intent face—"I
can send you to the training school at Pau."

"Training school?"

"Yes, it's a basic five-week course in flying."

"But I already know how to fly."

"That's what a lot of people say, but if you don't have the papers
you have to go to the training school."

"I'm trying to tell you that I'm an experienced flyer. I've flown
Blériots, Farmans, Bréguets, everything there is."

"If you're really good, you can go through the school in less
time."

"Can I see Mr. Prince?"

"No, he's with the squadron."

"Where is the squadron now?"

"At Luxeuil-les-Bains, in the Vosges."

"Well, I want to be sent there directly."

"That's out of the question." She made another mistake, said "Damn!" and got out her eraser again.

The Frenchman opened the door again. "Qu'est-ce que c'est?"

"Alain, occupe-toi de tes oignons." The door shut again.

"Isn't there any way . . ."

"Not unless you have a license. Do you have a hearing defect, or what is your problem?"

Fred decided to try another tack. He crossed his legs and leaned on the counter. He put on his most boyish and winning manner. He made an offhand American-to-American smile.

"It would take a while to explain it. Are you free later this afternoon?"

"No, I'm not."

"What about this evening?"

"I'm having dinner with my fiancé."

"I suppose that's Alain?"

"That's none of your business."

He turned away and stamped off. "Well then the hell with the whole thing. You can stuff it."

"Thank you. I am glad we've been able to be of assistance." She went back to her typing.

Lucienne was late at Maxim's. Women always were. Actually Fred was a little early; he had nothing to do for the rest of the afternoon and the taxi from the Quai d'Orsay had taken only a quarter of an hour. He would have walked except that it was still raining a little. It was so dark that the street lights had come on at four, their yellowish glow making the gray air seem slightly sickly.

Inside Maxim's the tables had been cleared away at one end of the main room and a small string orchestra was playing Strauss, Delibes, and Lehar. A few couples were dancing. Most of the men were French officers or foreigners. Fred ordered tea and sat with his feet on the chair opposite reading a *Figaro*. He estimated that she would arrive, perhaps, about a quarter after five.

He had met Lucienne de Mainboche through his negotiations with a committee of wives of government officials who were arranging for a benefit performance at the Odéon. It was the usual affair to buy bandages or provide hot cocoa for the poilus in the trenches, he had forgotten what. The committee met in a room at the Ecole des Beaux-Arts. Most of the government wives were middle-aged. Lucienne was about forty perhaps. She reminded him somewhat of Ernestine in San Francisco; the same magnificent bosom, the same wise and penetrating, lightly ironic manner. But there was a vein of the aristocratic in her, exactly opposite to Ernestine's healthy strain of the vulgar. She was more sedate and queenlike—something perhaps like a younger Madame Modjeska. She even wore her hair in the same diademlike coil, and held her chin slightly high, with a trace of hauteur, yet with a smile always lurking just under the surface of her expression. Twang! went the harp string inside Fred. It was not long before he was calling her Lucienne and they were saying tu and toi to each other.

Her husband, Evry de Mainboche, was something important in the Ministry of War. Perhaps he was an underminister. He was a thin active man about Lucienne's age, with a frown and a hawklike nose. Fred had met him once or twice. He was very busy at the Ministry, often working late at night, and he seemed to have no objection to Fred taking Lucienne to tea dances or concerts or meeting her in cafés. Many of her friends had young men who took them places, some of them officers on leave, some diplomatic people or other foreigners. The English word flirt was fashionable just then. People said, ''C'est son flirt de la semaine.'' His flirt with Lucienne had lasted a little longer than a week now, although he had not yet succeeded in obtaining the heartfelt object of his desire. Lucienne was always in motion, always talking, always wanting to go to different places, always with her friends so that it was difficult to be with her alone.

Maxim's was a kind of headquarters for her set. There were sure to be at least two or three of her friends here at teatime. He lowered his *Figaro* cautiously and looked around the room. He caught sight of only one of them, a middle-aged woman named Madame de Bruyvres. She was with a colonel of cavalry in red breeches who had set his practically solid gold képi on the table in front of him. Fred was planning out the whole thing in his mind. The danger was in getting involved with a group of people and not being able to extricate Lucienne from them so he could talk to her alone. Madame de Bruyvres turned in his direction and he ducked back behind his *Figaro*. Apparently she had not noticed him. Fred sipped his tea and glanced at his watch. It was a quarter after five.

''I'm sorry I'm late.''

It was Lucienne, exactly on schedule. She was in furs with a diamond bracelet glittering inside the right sleeve.

''It doesn't matter.'' He got up quickly, came around the table, and helped her into her chair.

''So solicitous today.''

''It's because you're so charming.''

She was. Once she was seated and had thrown back her fur over the chair he could scarcely take his eyes from her. She was wearing a satin frock with darts—he thought they were called—at the waist so that it fitted her snugly, like a blouse. The twin moonlike swellings in the front of it were perfect geometric hemispheres, except that when she turned to one side or the other—as she did just then—a very faint shadow the size of a grape would appear in the center of one but not the other.

''Don't stare, chéri, it's not polite. Ah, there's Ary.'' She waved across the room to Madame de Bruyvres. ''She's with Colonel Mangepré.

He's in Intelligence, but if there's no one more intelligent than him in the Army I'm afraid the Boches may win. Shall we go and join them? No, I can see you don't want to."

"Tea?"

"Oh, I'm a bundle of nerves. I haven't had a minute to stop all day. A fine à l'eau."

All the better. Fred sipped his own tea and admired the finely boned line of her cheek, the queenly way she held her head, the coiled coronet of hair. Unfortunately she was still looking around the room to see if there was anyone else she knew. When her brandy came she sipped only a little of it.

"Shall we dance?"

They tangoed around the floor a half-dozen times to the strain of some Argentine confection. Only their fingertips touched, with now and then a discreet bump of the hips. When the music stopped she started to go back to the table, but he held her hand. The next set was a waltz; he slipped his arm behind her back, took her right hand in his left, and started off in a skillful half turn. His arm pressed her back, and her breasts touched lightly against his chest.

"Wicked."

"You waltz divinely."

"Look, there's Ary dancing with the Colonel. He doesn't waltz very well."

"He thinks he's riding his horse."

"Why is he wearing spurs if he works in an office?"

"Perhaps to spur on his subordinates."

The waltz ended. In the final dip backward, which lifted one of her slippers from the floor, he managed to insert his leg between her knees.

"You waltz even too well, Frédéric," she said with a somewhat sibylline smile.

At the table she sipped a little more of her brandy. She looked around the room. Another of her friends had come in, a well-known society butterfly named Coco de Levy-Souza. If you didn't have a *de* in your name you just put one in. No one seemed to care. When the music recommenced they got up and danced again, with some further touches of Fred's celebrated skill. Lucienne's face was slightly flushed. Everything was going splendidly. Still, when they came back to the table again he saw that the thing was wavering on a razor edge. It was six o'clock now and too many of her friends were arriving. First Ary, now Coco, and next it would be somebody else.

"Do you want another drink?"

"Not really."

"Shall we go somewhere else?"

"All right. Where?"

"Somewhere."

"Evry," she said distantly, "is working this evening. He won't be home until midnight."

"Shall we go to your apartment?"

"Oh no. There are the servants."

Better and better. He helped her into her furs and paid the check. Outside he helped her into a taxi.

"You are the perfect *gentleman* this afternoon."

She said it in English, with exactly the same intonation that Liane de Pougy had; lightly ironic, perhaps.

"Seventy-eight Avenue Kléber."

The taxi went off. Lucienne said nothing. It was dark now and only a few pedestrians hurried along huddled in the light rain. When the car stopped in front of the building the driver unfurled an enormous black umbrella and escorted them both to the door.

"And what is this?"

"This is 78 Avenue Kléber."

In the apartment she allowed him to remove the furs once more, and looked about her curiously.

"But this is Herma's place."

It was uncertain how she knew this, or what she meant by it. Perhaps because the decorations seemed to have been chosen by a woman. And because of the piano.

"Yes."

"But she's not here now?"

"No."

"You're sure she won't come?"

"Absolutely."

"It's a charming little place." She went to the window and looked out over the dark city. "The view."

"Yes, the Eiffel Tower."

She swung around to face him, her hips twisting sensuously.

"Ah, but you are subtle. One would never think that a child like you, an American . . ."

"All Americans are children. That's why you like us."

"Although you are a perverse child."

More than she knew. He went to the mantlepiece and removed the single long-stemmed rosebud from the crystal vase. The cursed thing was dripping wet. He managed inconspicuously to dry it on his coat sleeve. She sat down on the divan, and he slipped down beside her, half sideways, sitting on one hip.

"Would you care for something?"

"Something?"

"Another fine à l'eau?"

"Oh, no."

He touched the rosebud lightly to her lips. Then, as she smiled in slight bafflement, he bent forward and kissed her. She was one of those who closed her eyes when kissed, he noticed. The side of the rosebud in his careful fingers slipped down her cheek, across her jaw, and along her throat to the place where the neckline of her frock began. In order to have it go any farther it was going to be necessary to make a change in the arrangements. He imagined the rosebud touching lightly at the tip of her breast and then proceeding on down along her magnificently modeled flank to that pink secret, its concave other self.

"Wouldn't we . . ."

"Chéri?"

"Be more . . ."

"Comfortable in the bedroom," she finished for him.

Here she emitted a peal of laughter, quite unexpected. He had never heard her laugh before. "Oh, you are all alike. I think you learn these phrases from some book." Extricating herself from his embrace, she sat up on the divan and began repairing the damage to her coiffure.

"But what's the matter?"

"The matter?"

"I thought you . . . cared something for me, Lucienne."

"But I do," she said lightly. "I just don't think that such things are important, or that—one should surrender herself to every passing impulse in this way."

Fred slid toward her again on the divan, the rosebud still in his left hand. She took the flower from him and stood up.

Fred stood up too and faced her whitely.

"I don't understand."

"Oh, you poor thing. Now I've hurt your feelings. You're all so vain. It's like Don Giovanni and his catalogue. How many is it? I always forget. Six hundred and forty in Italy, a hundred in France, and in Spain, one thousand and three."

She seemed playful now, not hostile at all. She gave the impression that she was enjoying herself.

"It's not a question of a thousand and three in Spain. It's a question of you and me."

"That's just what Don Giovanni told them, each and every one."

"Lucienne . . ."

"And besides," she said, turning away across the room, "I am a married woman. I have made vows to my husband. Did you ever think of that?"

He stared at her. "Tu blagues."

"No, I am not joking. Why should I joke about a thing like that? And when you make a vow to a person," she went on, "and then you break it, you are telling that person a lie."

"But Evry . . ."

Here she stopped and faced him. She was still smiling, but it was a serious and earnest smile now, a smile as if she wanted to tell him something.

"You see, Frédéric, it is all very well for Evry to allow me my flirt of the week. That's what is done in our circle. But it's only a game. And the game has its little rules. One of the rules is that I tell Evry everything. So I imagine I'll have to hand you back your little flower, and say au revoir."

"Lucienne."

"What?"

"Let's talk seriously."

"All right." She waited expectantly, still facing him from across the room.

"Let's sit down first."

"Will you be a good boy?"

"Yes. And will you stop referring to me as a child. I'm getting tired of it."

"Very well." She was quite serious herself now.

They sat down on opposite ends of the divan, facing each other. She waited for him to speak.

"I want to join the aviation. I'm a flyer and I want to get into the war."

"Bravo."

"But I want you to help me. Evry is in the War Ministry, isn't he?"

"Ahah. Now I see the whole thing." She still showed no sign of resentment; she was only amused.

He went on staring at her stonily. "Well?"

"Yes. As a matter of fact he's the Underminister for Aviation."

"I want to join the Lafayette Escadrille."

"The Escadrille Américaine?"

"Yes."

"But chéri, Evry has nothing to do with Americans."

"But they wear French uniforms. They're in the French service. I think it's technically a part of the Foreign Legion."

"I'm not sure that's in Evry's department."

"If it's aviation it is."

"But not if it's Foreign Legion." She got up and drifted away across the room. "I think," she said, "that the Americans who are in charge of it are the ones who decide who can join."

"Still, will you speak to Evry about it?"

She smiled faintly, still twirling the rose. "But you see, chéri, that is exactly what I cannot do. Because, if I asked Evry to do a favor for you, that would make it clear to everyone that . . . don't you see? And of course we haven't."

"No, we haven't," said Fred, staring at her steadily and not smiling. It was the first time in his life, he realized, that he had ever failed to succeed with a woman when he had really tried. He analyzed his emotions. She was right. It was just vanity. He felt anger and damaged self-esteem, but no desire.

"I'll take you home," he said curtly.

"It isn't necessary. I'm quite capable of taking a taxi by myself."

"But it's raining."

"Your concièrge will phone for the taxi, and the driver will be sure to have one of those enormous black umbrellas."

He came forward to kiss her again, but instead she applied her lips delicately to the tip of the rosebud. Then she handed it to him, and he put it back into the crystal vase.

"Au revoir, chéri," She glanced at the print on the wall. "That Beardsley is wicked."

"You should see the Khnopff in the bedroom."

"You'd like me to."

She was gone.

In the end it was Herma who had to explain it to Lloiseaux, over lunch at Larue's. Lloiseaux was exactly as he had always been—sly, spry, and not quite vertical—seeming to float through rooms without moving his feet. He was ageless; he gave the impression that he had been born a wily old man with a shock of electric hair. If anything he grew thinner and more immaterial as he grew older. From behind, now, he looked like an empty overcoat; from the front he looked like one of E. T. A. Hoffmann's more improbable inventions, perhaps Dr. Spalanzani. He left his overcoat on during lunch, since the heating in Larue's was inadequate.

"You see, Fred isn't happy," she explained to him. "He's restless. The war is going on and he doesn't have any part in it. He wants to join the aviation."

He scarcely seemed to follow what she was saying. He was preoccupied with shelling a bowl of tiny crayfish one by one and dipping them in sauce.

"The aviation?"

"Yes."

"Why the aviation?"

"Because he's a flyer."

"But he's American."

"He wants to join the Lafayette Escadrille."

"Ah," said Lloiseaux. He thought for a moment. "I think that's a splendid idea," he concluded.

He was very slow in responding. It was impossible to tell whether he was senile or only wily.

"But they want to send him to a stupid training school first for five weeks, to learn how to fly. But he already knows how to fly. He doesn't want to wait for five weeks."

"Yes, I've noticed he's very impatient, parbleu."

Did he grasp anything at all of what she was trying to say? "I thought that you . . . ."

But he seemed to be following her all right, in his way. "I don't know what to advise you. I don't know very much about aeroplanes," he said vaguely.

"Perhaps you know somebody in the Ministry."

"The Ministry?"

"Yes, you have so many friends."

"I do?"

"Or you could simply write a letter, as Artistic Director of the Opéra, explaining that you know Fred and . . ."

"I don't think that would do any good."

He searched around on the table for his glass of white wine, took a sip, and went back to shelling écrivisses.

"I do know a young American music lover. A splendid young fellow, a graduate of Harvard University. He has a rich father too. Perhaps he could help."

"A music lover?"

"Yes. His name is Mr. Norman Prince."

"But he's the one who is organizing the Lafayette Escadrille!"

"Of course he is, my dear," said Lloiseaux.

Herma went to see Marcel in Boulevard Haussmann one last time. She hadn't intended to tell him it was the last time; but in his sorcerer's way, studying her with his dark eyes, he seemed to seek out and find everything.

"I came to tell you . . ."

"That you're going away."

"Fred is joining the aviation. He's leaving in a week."

"And you?"

"I . . ."

Here she stopped. She didn't know what to say.

Marcel had not been well; he had had spasms, Céleste said, and he seemed to have lost weight. The room was shut up tightly, with the close and fuggy atmosphere of a sickroom, and the aromatic powders were smoldering in a saucer by the bedside. Marcel was propped on the pillow in his usual pyjamas with several sweaters over them, a shawl around his shoulders. He reached for a camphor cigarette, lit it, and set it in a saucer after drawing a little of the pungent vapor into his lungs. His pale face seemed stretched on its bones; his eyes burned even more intensely than usual. Yet he seemed quite calm. He drew on the medicinal cigarette again and set it aside. For a long moment neither of them spoke. He lay motionless on the bed, his knees propped up under the covers, never taking his eyes from her.

Finally he smiled. "You're afraid that I've caught you out. But it was long ago that I caught you out. You see, I am the only one who knows your secret. It is because of this that we are friends. Both you and I, and Fred too."

"Secret?"

He seemed to turn away from this for the moment. "Even the wily Ulysses didn't recognize Athena at first. That was because he was mortal. But the gods are immediately perceptible to each other, as like to like. So we in the world, even in a theater, even before we have spoken, recognize each other as kindred."

"I saw you too, before I was five minutes into the Olympia act."

"Of course you did. Believe me, it is not in order to invite prima donnas to supper at the Ritz that I go, so very rarely, to the Opéra. And I imagine that you too are not in the habit of accepting invitations from every music lover in the audience who takes a fancy to you."

"No I'm not."

"Then why did you accept?"

She had no answer to this, because she didn't know.

His formerly charming smile had a slight cadaverlike quality to it now, a kind of rictus. It was as though he made it only with difficulty. Yet it was still charming, perhaps because one *saw* that it was difficult for him to make it.

"Do you know the Myth of the Androgynes in Plato?"

"I don't read very much, as you know."

"It's in the *Symposium*. Once mankind was one, Plato tells us, and there was only a single sex. The two that we have now were joined together in a single being, in perpetual bliss. But, not content with their mortal happiness, these creatures attempted to climb into Heaven and lay hands on the gods. As a punishment, Zeus had them cut in two and banished to the opposite corners of the earth. Since then the halves have been separated, each wandering over the earth looking for the other.

" 'And when one of them meets with his other half,' " he went on, falling into his theatrical reading voice and evidently quoting from memory, " 'the actual half of himself, whether he be a youth or a lover of another sort, the pair are lost in amazement of love and friendship and intimacy, and will not be out of the other's sight even for a moment; these are the people who pass their whole lives together, yet they could not explain what they desire of the other.' "

He paused to see if she had some comment, but she said nothing.

"I have looked high for my other half, and I have looked low," he went on in his ordinary voice. "But I have not found him." (The French was ambiguous—"Je ne l'ai pas trouvé"—it could be either him or her.) "Once I almost found him but he slipped away. Now I've despaired of finding him. And so I am as you see me. J'en suis malade—I am sick of this disease."

"You have asthma. That can happen to anybody."

"No. I am not speaking of that. The disease I am speaking of is love. I mean even in the purest of its forms, the love of the mind. The other thing—more concupiscence—may be an evil. But love is a disease, and that is far worse."

He had kept his eyes intently on her all along. But here he paused and seemed to stare at her even more fixedly, a restrained smile at the corners of his mouth. "As I told you once, I am very observant. That is my métier. And I have observed something about you that no one else has noticed."

She waited.

"It is that no one has ever seen you together."

"Marcel . . ."

"So I have guessed your secret. No, it is not that the two are one. It is that it is this *other* that you love—the other that is yourself. An other who will always elude you, even though you may go seeking him eternally over the face of the earth. Because you are reaching for a person who can never be grasped, who will always elude you. And who will reach for you too in vain, in just the same way."

She looked back at him quite calmly, still saying nothing.

"In general, people should beware of telling their secrets to novelists. Because the novelists will always reveal them, even though they swear not to. In most cases, this is why people tell the secrets—because they secretly want them to be revealed."

"I don't."

"I know. And you needn't worry, I will never reveal yours, because it is too strange for any story. No one would believe it. Even when I tell my own secret in my book, it will be carefully concealed so that no one will recognize it."

"So it is not asthma then. You are sick of your secret."

He nodded.

"But I am not."

"Are you so sure?" He waited, and when she said nothing he went on. "We are more alike than you think. We have committed the Sin Against the Holy Ghost, the sin for which there is no forgiveness—that of loving no one but one's own self. And the punishment for that is first loneliness and then death."

"I am not lonely, and I . . ."

She stopped. For a long moment they regarded each other.

"Let me embrace you, my dear. It is a long time since I have embraced a young girl."

She went forward to the bed and bent down. The arms in their layers of damp clothing, thin but surprisingly strong, held and pressed her. And she too clasped the thin torso in her own arms. The untidy black beard, surprisingly soft, brushed against her cheek. There was a strong odor of camphor, of perspiration, and of the sickroom. Then he released her and she stood before the bed.

"Good-bye, Marcel."

"Usually, in French, when we part we say au revoir."

"Yes, you do," said Herma. "But now I am saying good-bye."

She turned and fled, while he watched—a pale, dark-eyed, faintly smiling sibyl.

16.

To get from Paris to Luxeuil-les-Bains you took the night train from the Gare de l'Est to Lure in the Franche-Comté, only about fifty kilometers from the point where the French, Swiss, and German borders came together at Basel. The train ran only at night because beyond Belfort some trains had been attacked in the daytime by German aviation. Ordinarily the trip would have taken only about five hours, but because of the long delays for troop trains and the general confusion of the war it was noon the next day before Fred got off at Lure with his baggage. He had a sandwich and a glass of beer in the station buffet, and then he looked around for the car that was supposed to take him to Luxeuil.

He found it waiting in the mall of leafless elm trees on the other side of the station. It was a smart Packard touring car, painted khaki but except for that in excellent civilian condition, with everything polished and the leather seats glowing. The driver, limping around the car, helped him pile the bags into the rear seat. There were quite a few of them but the driver made no comment.

"You've 'ad a bite to eat, sir?"

"Yes."

Fred took another look at him. He was a small man with a red face, dressed in civilian clothing except for a French army tunic that was too large for him and a military fatigue cap without insignia.

"You're British?"

"Yes sir." He was very loquacious. He volunteered everything in a cheerful voice without being asked. "You see, I was 'it up on the Somme. A Blighty wound they call it. That's one good enough to 'ave you sent back to merry old England. Wot everybody's looking, you know sir. But first they sent me 'ere to the hospital at Looxul, and when I was well enough to travel, I decided to stay put. I've got no one at 'ome, you see sir. It's a pleasant spot at Luxool and I can 'elp out a bit with the war, even with my leg. So they made me steward and batman for the Yanks. Splendid chaps they are. Full of fun. I never knew much about Yanks. But these chaps are the salt of the earth. They know 'ow to 'ave a good time, I can tell you. Eat well too, better than us. A cushy berth I've got. I don't ask for better. And I'm 'elping out with the war too, you see sir."

"Yes," said Fred. "What did you say your name was?"

"They call me Tiffin, they do, cause that's not my name. They're full of jokes. And you're Leftenant 'Ite."

"That's right."

"Pleasure to meet you, sir."

Fred looked out through the windshield at the long khaki hood with a nickle-plated hinge running along the center of it. "This is quite a car."

"This 'ere is Leftenant Prince's car, sir. They send it to Lure for the new chaps, cause it's more elegant than them Fiat lorries we 'ave."

It was eighteen kilometers to Luxeuil. The big touring car ran smoothly along a paved road between rows of poplars. There was no sign of the war here, even though the front was only fifty kilometers away. It was not an active front, at least not on the ground. Tiffin slowed down for an occasional village, or a herd of dairy cows being shooed along by a boy with a stick. It was a pleasant pastoral landscape. The weather was still uncertain, with rain clouds lurking along the horizon to the west, but the sun was shining down thinly on the damp fields.

"Going to join the squadron, are you sir?"

"Yes."

"Salt of the earth, those chaps are." He glanced sideways at Fred. "Flyer, are you sir?"

"Yes."

"Younger than most." He looked at him again, a little more carefully this time.

"I'm twenty-eight."

"Wouldn't 'ave thought it."

He had nothing more to say for a while. They went through a town called St.-Sauveur and Fred could see a big aerodrome over on the left. He didn't have a map but they weren't very far from Luxeuil. There were a few houses scattered along the road now. A mile or so out of town Tiffin pulled the Packard over to the side of the road with its engine idling.

A company of troops in column of four was coming toward them along the road ahead. The road was narrow and the car had to pull over to let them by. They were good-looking troops, well equipped and evidently in good shape, although perhaps a little thin and pale. Some of them seemed very young. Their dish-shaped helmets were tipped at various angles, and they carried their rifles slung with their thumbs in the slings. Their boots thudded rhythmically on the paved road. They had all sorts of gear—canteens, bayonets, bedrolls, trenching tools, musette bags, gas masks, bandoliers—draped on them and hanging from all sides. A lieutenant who seemed hardly more than a boy followed along in the ditch by the side. On the other side was a corporal yelling "Hep!" at every fourth pace. A heavy odor of sweat came up from the marching column. As they passed the Packard some of them broke out into a ragged song. They didn't sing very well and most of them couldn't strike a note. They yelled out the tune in a way that seemed to be their custom, leaving a pause of eight paces between the lines.

"Mademoiselle from Armenteers, parlee voo . . ."

The eight paces were marked off by the corporal's even "Hep! . . . hep . . ."

"Mademoiselle from Armenteers, parlee voo . . ."

Another pause. As they passed the Packard some of them looked to the side and grinned. The boy lieutenant went by without turning his head.

"Mademoiselle from Armenteers,
    She asn't been fucked in forty years,
    Inky dinky par-lee voo."

The last of them went by. Tiffin started the Packard again. "East Surrey Regiment. Them chaps 'as been in the rest camp 'ere at Luxool. Now they're going back in the line." The company, with full gear, was marching the eighteen kilometers to Lure to be loaded onto trains.

"They seem cheerful enough."

"Most of them lads will never see 'ome again. The average survival in the trenches is three weeks, they say."

After that he had nothing much more to say. He went back to his driving. The Surrey company had almost disappeared down the curve of the road. Behind him Fred heard a distant yell.

> "She won the Palm and the Croix de Guerre
> For washing soldiers' underwear . . .
> Inky dinky par-lee voo."

Tiffin drove the Packard up and stopped it in the grass by the hangar. "You want to talk to Captain Theenel, you do, sir. We'll leave the bags in the car for the time."

Fred got out and looked around. The field was a big grassy meadow with only a few bumps and low swellings. The prevailing wind was from the west. There were some trees to the east, but they were not very high and there was a gap in them you could land through. Down the field, in front of a row of newly erected hangars, were a number of Sopwith bombers, big blue machines with red, white, and blue British roundels on the fuselages. Nearer, lined up in a ragged row by the Escadrille hangar, were the Nieuport 17's with Indian-head cockades on the sides and French roundels on the wings. The Indian heads were rather crudely painted and were imitated, he recognized, from the trademark on the Savage Ammunition crate. At the end of the line a Nieuport was being wheeled around on the field with four or five mechanics holding up the tail. From somewhere in the distance, probably from the British hangars down the field, there was the ragged blat of an engine being tuned.

He went into the Escadrille hangar. It was a large one, dim and shadowy inside, and at first he couldn't see much. There were several of the older Nieuport 11's in various stages of dismemberment, and a single Nieuport 17 with the tail propped up on a dolly and the engine pulled, the disassembled engine lying on a platform in front of it. Two officers were standing in front of the platform discussing the engine with a mechanic. They turned and glanced at Fred briefly and then went back to their conversation. Their clothing was a little bizarre. One was wearing a fur coat over a smartly tailored French uniform, and the other a faded Foreign Legion uniform with flared breeches, although he had replaced the puttees with hunting boots. Fred asked a mechanic for Captain Thénault. The man pointed to a small dusty office off in one corner of the hangar.

Thénault was about Fred's age. He was a St.-Cyr graduate and a military professional, and he took the war seriously as he did everything else. He was slightly smaller than the average man, quiet and compactly built. He wore a neatly pressed cavalry uniform and a blue képi without insignia of rank. He stood up and shook hands stiffly in the French manner. Then he sat down behind the table again and motioned to the chair for Fred.

"They said in Paris to report to you. I thought the Escadrille were all Americans."

"They are," said Thénault, "but someone has to be in charge of this menagerie, and unfortunately I have the job."

"Yes, I saw some rather odd uniforms out in the hangar."

Thénault smiled. "You mean Prince's fur coat. At first I tried to enforce a little discipline. But then I threw up the job and now I just let them fly. Most of them are from well-to-do families and they're used to doing as they please. Americans are different anyhow. They don't like discipline. They're excellent flyers, most of them. If they aren't they don't last long. It's a good squadron."

He spoke English perfectly with only a slight accent. He was the only Frenchman Fred had ever met who could pronounce the *th*.

"I'm happy to be a part of it."

"You're not a member of the squadron yet, you know."

"I thought . . ."

"Let's go outside."

Thénault got up and took an officer's baton from the table. He led the way through the hangar and out into the sunshine, slapping the baton against his riding breeches.

"You're the one who hasn't been to the school at Pau?"

"That's right."

"Yes. Lieutenant Prince said you were to be treated specially."

This with a slight edge to the tone, although he was not unfriendly. They went up to the first Nieuport on the line. It seemed to be brand new. It was a beautiful aeroplane. It had the new 110-horsepower Le Rhône, and the Vickers gun mounted on the cowl was synchronized to fire through the propeller. The fuselage was short and stubby and the wings braced with a strong vee-strut; it had a businesslike look to it. The landing gear with its disk wheels was at the very front, almost under the engine.

Thénault beckoned to a mechanic, who came out at a half run.

"This machine is fueled?"

"C'est plein, mon capitaine."

"Good."

He bent down under the Nieuport and set his baton on the grass exactly between the wheels.

He said to Fred, "Go up and do a slow roll over the field, then climb to twelve hundred, and do a vrille to the left and a vrille to the right and recover. When you come back in, bring it up and stop it right where it is now, with the baton between the wheels."

Fred nodded. The two officers, he noticed, had come out of the hangar and were standing by the big open doorway watching. The mechanics who had been wheeling around the Nieuport had stopped too to watch. One of them came up with a fur-lined combination and flying boots, and Fred took off his coat and put them on. The mechanic handed him the helmet and goggles. The leather shock helmet went on over the goggles. It took him a while to get this straight because usually the helmet went on first and then the goggles. The shock helmet looked

something like a leather football helmet with a padded ring around the
rim of it. He didn't like it because it was tight and it made his head
feel heavy. He got it on, and the mechanic showed him how to arrange
the strap to push the goggles up on the helmet.

He set his boot into the step cut into the side of the fuselage, pulled
himself up, and dropped into the cockpit. There was a smell of gasoline,
castor oil, and fresh dope. He fastened his harness and looked around at
the unfamiliar instruments. There was a compass, an altimeter, a rev
counter, an oil pulsator to show that oil was flowing, and a small clock.
The stick had a handle like a shovel on top of it, with a small button
in the middle marked M.G. He kept his thumb carefully away from this,
even though the gun wasn't charged. He waggled the controls and looked
around to see if the surfaces were responding. Then he gestured with his
thumb up to the mechanic standing out in front of the propeller.

"Plein gaz," the mechanic called.

Fred found the fuel cock just under the panel on the right-hand side
and opened it. He pulled the goggles down over his face and adjusted
them with both hands.

The mechanic swung the prop around while the Le Rhône wheezed
and coughed. There was a stronger smell of raw gasoline.

"Contact."

He flipped up the magneto switch. "Contact."

It started on the second swing. After that nothing could be heard
above the brassy barking roar of the Le Rhône. He pushed forward on
the throttle and at the same time kicked the rudder bar. The Nieuport
moved out from the line and turned onto the pasture, kicking up leaves
and dust behind it.

As he taxied out, Fred noticed a shallow depression in the center of
the field, a few yards long and perhaps a foot deep. It was almost invisible from the distance because the grass was growing in it. He made
a mental note of this. There was no trouble in taking off a little to one
side of it, but when you came back in you would have to touch down
almost on the hole because of the gap in the trees to the east. Thénault
hadn't mentioned this. Perhaps he was waiting for him to find it for himself. At the end of the field he saw that the small cluster of figures in
front of the hangar was still watching him.

He kicked the Nieuport around with the skid tearing up grass. He
glanced at the rev counter; it was steady, indicating that the engine
was warm. He pushed the throttle wide open.

With the skid on the ground he could see almost nothing to the
front. He had to crane his head around the cowl to see what was going
on in front of the aeroplane. But when the skid came up there was a
quick and rising sense of exhilaration. Everything was clear, he could
see in all directions, the cumbersome machine acquired sensitivity and
became an extension of his body. The Nieuport gathered speed rapidly,
pulled by the powerful and reliable Le Rhône. He pulled back slightly
on the stick. The bumping underneath stopped and the Nieuport rose
gracefully, tilted only a little to the right. He corrected, crossed the end

of the field, and went into a climbing turn to the east.

At five hundred meters he looked around. The town of Luxeuil lay under his wing, a kilometer or two from the field. The rain clouds were still piled up along the horizon to the west. To the south the rolling country ran away toward Lure and the plain of the Franche-Comté. Ahead, to the east, the convoluted slopes of the Vosges rose away toward Mulhouse, the German border, and the Rhine. He banked into a turn again and settled back on the approach to the field.

In a down-angling power glide the Nieuport picked up speed rapidly. The wind sang in the wires and the farmland below flashed by with increasing speed. The field—the Escadrille hangar to the left and the others at the far end—staggered up rapidly ahead. A glance at the altimeter—three hundred. He nudged the throttle a little and pulled the stick back as he went into the roll, so that he rolled up and not down and came back out almost on the same level where he had started. As he went over, everything below him—the mountains to the east, the hangars, the rain clouds on the horizon—revolved slowly, hung sideways, and then turned upside down. At the top he was looking straight down at the hangar and the little cluster of men standing in front of it watching him. The horizon swung on rapidly around, wobbled, and came to a stop. He was out of it and flying flat, only a little dizzied from hanging upside down for a second or two.

He set the throttle at about three-quarters and began the climb up to twelve hundred. Thirty-nine hundred feet; he still converted mentally to the altitudes he had learned to fly on in America. He pulled up into a slow stall and kicked the rudder over.

The Nieuport spun beautifully. Seeming to pivot on the tip of the left wing, it sank in a tight spiral. Fred kept his eyes on the altimeter. The strap of the shock helmet cut into his throat and irritated him; he jerked the snap free. At three hundred—only about a thousand feet—he centered the controls and then carefully pulled back the stick. He had no idea whether the thing was going to come out of it, but it was the easiest machine to handle he had ever flown. It leveled out flat with the wires screaming a hundred meters above the hangars, and he banked it around to climb up for the spin to the other side.

The right vrille was the same. The torque effect of the Le Rhône rotary, in fact, made it even easier to recover from the spin to the right. As the wings leveled and he started pulling out of the dive he stuck his head out from behind the cowl to line up on the horizon and his helmet came off with a single snap, the metal fitting on the flap dealing him a nasty thwack over the eye. The wind flogged at his hair, slapping it against the side of his head. The hell with the bloody thing anyhow. It was no good and it was uncomfortable. He permitted himself a glance behind. A tiny dot like a dead bird sank down in the air far below him: the lost helmet.

He banked around and turned into his approach over the main street of Luxeuil with its double row of stone houses. Two hundred meters, half throttle. A little crosswind from the left. He corrected with a touch of stick and rudder. As he went over the gap in the trees, a little before the field, he cut back the throttle and the note of the Le Rhône dropped to a sputtering bark. The fence at the edge of the field went by. As the grass rushed up at him he deliberately touched down a little hard, so that the Nieuport bounced up and floated along with its wheels just brushing the tops of the grass, across the depression and down onto the solid ground beyond.

He taxied back with his skid bumping. When he came to his place in the line he gave it a burst of throttle and kicked the Nieuport around with the skid digging up grass and dirt. He came to a stop and cut the engine with the baton exactly between the wheels. He climbed out without a word, while the others watched.

"Where's your helmet?" said Thénault.

"I forgot to snap it."

Thénault had nothing to say to this.

In the office Thénault spread out a map on the table.

"We came here originally to fly escorts for the British." With a motion of his head he indicated the Sopwiths at the other end of the field. "They're Canadians actually. They're from the Third Wing Royal Naval Air Service. They came here from the Dardanelles. But they're holding the Sopwiths for a big raid on Oberndorf that's to take place in a little while. In the meantime we've been flying mainly defensive missions."

He stopped and turned to the map.

"The Germans have Albatros bombers based here at Habsheim, near Mulhouse. The Albatros is not a very good machine. It's heavy and it tends to fall apart when it is stressed. But it will carry a heavy load of bombs. They come over usually at dawn, to raid our own fields west of Belfort. We're stationed here at Luxeuil, near the border, in a good position to cut them off without using unnecessary fuel for a long flight."

Fred looked at the map. The distances were greater than he thought: it was forty kilometers from Belfort to Mulhouse and about seventy from Mulhouse back to Luxeuil.

"At first they were escorting them with Fokker III monoplanes. But they weren't much good and we could outfly them easily. Now they've started escorting them with two-seater Aviatik scouts. This is another matter. The observer in the rear of the Aviatik has got a heavy-caliber Parabellum gun with a hundred-and-sixty-degree firing arc. It's very dangerous to come up at him from the rear. There are two theories on how to deal with them. They come out of the east at dawn, so one tactic is to attack them from behind, so that you will come at them out of the sun. The trouble with this is that the Aviatik's guns are ranged to the rear. So some people think it's better to wait until they've made their bombing run and are on their way home. Then you can come at them head on, still from the east, but out of the way of the guns on the Aviatiks."

Fred studied the triangle on the map: Mulhouse-Belfort-Luxeuil.

He could see that to chase the Albatrosses back to the Rhine and return would take the maximum two-hour endurance of the Nieuports.

''Why let them bomb the fields? I would think you could take them right away.''

''Because that way you have to come at them from the rear,'' said Thénault.

He opened the drawer of the table and took out, one by one, three small mahogany boxes. He lined them up on the table.

''I have here three Croix de Guerre which were awarded last week to aviators of this group.'' He said, ''I have to wrap them up and send them to their families.''

He put the boxes back in the drawer and got up from the table. ''It was the rear gunners on the Aviatiks that did that. Wait till they turn back to the east. Otherwise it's suicide.''

In Luxeuil the Escadrille was quartered in a villa adjoining the old Roman baths. The whole situation was luxurious. The spa town was almost deserted because of the war and, along with the Canadians who were quartered in the Centre Hôpital nearby, they had the place to themselves. Except for breakfast they ate their meals at the Hôtel de la Pomme d'Or, the best hotel in town, whose proprietor was an excellent chef.

It was a two-story villa with a bathroom on each floor. Fred's room, which he shared with an officer named Raoul Lufbery, was on the ground floor, and the bathroom was a curious arrangement with an entrance in the hall and another separate entrance outside in the garden. There was a large mirror, not over the washbowl but over the bathtub. If you wanted to see anything of yourself below your waist you had to stand in the bathtub, but perhaps whoever planned it hadn't considered that.

In the central room—it was an old stone house, built in the eighteenth century, and you could hardly call it a salon—the phonograph was kept wound up incessantly. Fritz Kreisler was playing the *Chanson sans paroles,* and this was followed by *Oh Movin' Man, Don't Take Ma Baby Grand.* When Fred came out in his riding breeches and leather jacket it was playing *Poor Butterfly.* The room was full of officers in various bizarre costumes—fur-lined jackets, motheaten sweaters, parts of French, English, and Foreign Legion uniforms, Prince in his fur coat. Some of them wore their hats indoors: flowing berets, Foreign Legion pillboxes, long elfin stocking caps. A cognac bottle was going around. Thénault looked up and said nothing. ''This is Fred Hite,'' shouted Prince over the racket.

Just at that moment the record ended and somebody lifted off the arm. There was a silence.

''Where's your mustache, Freddy?'' said someone.

It was a tall, broad, red-faced man who had evidently drunk quite a little cognac. His hair was combed in a pompadour, with a strand that stuck out over his ear.

''That's just Roy Willkie,'' said Prince. ''Don't pay any attention to him.''

Fred looked around. It was true that almost everybody else had a mustache. Some were bushy like Theodore Roosevelt's, some were long and drooping, others like Thénault's neatly clipped.

"My old lady," said Willkie not to Fred but to the others, "that's my Paris old lady, says kissing a guy without a mustache is like eating an egg without salt."

"He does have a little peach-down there," said somebody else.

"There's no way you can fly a Nieuport without a mustache," said Willkie.

"I saw him fly this afternoon," said Prince quietly.

"How did he do?"

"His shock helmet fell off."

"Those fucking things are no good anyhow."

"What happened to the music?"

Somebody put on *Minnie the Mermaid.*

"Have a drink, Freddy," said Willkie.

The tinny voice sang:

> "She lost her morals
> Down among the corals
> Gee but she was good to me . . ."

It was only five minutes' walk down the main street of the small resort town to the Pomme d'Or, but Prince insisted on taking his car. He and Fred got in, along with Lufbery and another officer named Bill Thaw who was carrying a half-grown lion cub with him. This was Whiskey, the squadron mascot, who, as Prince explained, was born on a transatlantic liner, acquired in some fashion by a Brazilian dentist, and bought by a syndicate of a half dozen of them when the squadron was on leave in Paris. But as he got bigger the only one who could handle him was Bill Thaw. If anyone else approached him he was likely to take a piece out of your hand. Thaw was a large, rather heavy man with a gentle smile and a wisp of a mustache, and perhaps Whiskey thought he was his mother. Thaw got into the back seat with Whiskey and prevented him from eating the leather upholstery. The Packard started and they went off down the narrow cobbled street.

Prince parked on the wrong side of the street in front of the hotel. There was no other traffic and everybody knew the American car anyhow. They got out. The others were coming along down the street.

Prince wrinkled his nose and looked into the back seat.

"Oh, balls."

"What is it, Norman?"

"This animal has shitted in my beautiful car."

"Well, tell Bill," said Lufbery. "Bill should have housebroken him. It's his fault."

"But what am I going to do?"

"You're going to come in to dinner."

"It's only lion dung," said Thaw. "In Africa they eat it. It's said to make you brave."

"The ill-mannered beast," said Prince.

They went in. Whiskey was tied to a hat rack in the foyer, where he couldn't attack anyone. Monsieur Groscolas himself, in his white apron, came out of the kitchen to greet them. He and his wife ran the hotel themselves, along with a female cousin from the country and a boy to serve as waiter. In the dining room the table was set with a white cloth and antique sterling silver. Every piece of furniture in the room, according to Monsieur Groscolas, was an heirloom and had been in the family since before the Revolution. There was an enormous sideboard, grotesque and intricately carved, that might have been used for a set of *Tales of Hoffman*. Through the door at the other end Fred caught a glimpse of a billiard room. The billiard table too was in the same style.

Madame Groscolas appeared, moist-faced and smiling, and referred to them all as "mes enfants." She could never get their American names straight. They all sat down at the long table. There was an empty chair near the head of the table, an odd-looking one with elaborately carved hardwood arms. Fred moved toward it, but Prince said, "Don't sit there."

Everyone had fallen silent. Fred took another chair. He was between Prince and Lufbery, a wiry compact man with his hair clipped short like a tight helmet. He was reserved and didn't say very much. He had an unconscious habit of tightening his jaw muscles every two seconds or so, as though some slow and even pulse were working in his head. He didn't seem very friendly, but he was correct toward Fred and he hadn't joined in the jibes about the mustache.

As Madame Groscolas was opening the wine Prince told Fred in an offhand tone, "That's where Rockwell always sat. We ought to get rid of that chair."

The dinner was Lucullan. There was trout, then a baked hare, and roasted grouse en casserole. The wine was a good Médoc, better wine than you could get in Paris during the war. At the end you could have café filtre or American coffee. Fred elected for American coffee and it was passed to him in a large crockery cup without a handle.

He looked around the table. "Sugar?"

There was a delay of perhaps three seconds. Then Willkie reached behind him and took a sugar dispenser from the sideboard. Amid a certain amount of groping and fumbling this was passed down the table to Fred. Willkie was watching him with a sly rustic smile. Fred put the sugar in, stirred it, and took a sip.

It was all he could do not to choke. It was horribly salty; it was like drinking brine. Everybody was watching him. Lufbery, stone-faced, with the little shadow working at the corner of his jaw.

Without showing any sign that there was anything wrong with it, he drank the whole cup, sip by sip. Then he set the cup down and took a spoon from the table.

"Excuse me."

He went out through the front door of the hotel and crossed the sidewalk to the car. There was no street lighting of course and it was pitch dark inside the back seat. He had to find what he was looking for mainly by odor. Finally he got a piece of it in the spoon and, balancing it carefully, took it back into the hotel.

The others hardly seemed to have missed him and had gone back to talking. Only one or two looked up as he came back in. Fred went around the table to Willkie's place and carefully dropped the lump of lion dung into his coffee. Then, handing the spoon to Madame Groscolas to be washed, he went back to his own chair and sat down.

Now everyone was looking at Willkie. His face reddened. He started to get up and then changed his mind.

Prince said, "Go ahead and drink it, Roy."

17.

Herma went down the road in the starlight, a canvas musette bag slung over her shoulder, feeling a feminine satisfaction even in the darkness with her smartly cut Norton-Harjes Ambulance Corps uniform with the American-flag patch on the shoulder. The road led out past the Roman baths and around a public park to a cluster of Nissen huts erected on what was formerly a polo field. She was not sure where to turn off the road. Then in the starlight she made out the sign on the fence: "B.E.F. Rest Camp Luxeuil-les-Bains." There was no one in sight in the area around the temporary corrugated-iron buildings. She had to wander around in the darkness for some time before she found the rec hut. Finally she noticed some noise coming from one of the larger huts, and glimmers of light through scratches in the painted-over windows. She pushed open the door and went in.

Inside the air was thick with cigarette smoke and the odor of beer and fried food. There were perhaps a hundred men crowded into a room only thirty feet or so long and half as wide. At the other end of the room an Anzac soldier was inexpertly playing a piano. Three or four soldiers were leaning on the piano singing. Most of the others were sitting at table with tin cups of tea or glasses of beer before them, talking, leafing through old copies of *Punch,* or slapping down Solitaire games.

"Smokes, boys?"

A soldier at the nearest table looked up.

"Hi, it's the cigarette miss."

"But it's not the same one."

"Of course it's not the same one, you bloody idiot. This one's a Yank."

"When's America coming in, Miss?"

The others at the table grinned at this.

"In a while. But in the meantime, have a smoke."

Others in the room had noticed her now and were getting up, a little sheepishly, to come her way. She opened the musette and began passing out blue packs of Caporals. But there were too many hands and finally she was flinging the packs out to the small crowd that gathered around her. In only a few minutes the cigarettes were gone.

They all tried to talk at once. She could hardly make sense out of it, since some of them were speaking Cockney and others some north-country accent or other that was practically incomprehensible. A soldier who had broken open a pack of Caporals passed her one and lit it. She drew on it and then looked around the room again.

There were men from almost every regiment on the Somme and Meuse fronts. She didn't know all the badges but she recognized the Cheshire Regiment and Royal Fusiliers. At first the men pressing around her seemed animated. But when you looked more carefully there was fatigue and strain in almost every face. Most of them were hollow-eyed and underweight, and here and there the white of an old fear showed in a pair of eyes, a hag-ridden face out of an Edvard Munch painting. A good many wore bandages or supported themselves on canes. One of them, a boy not more than eighteen, simply stared at her out of eyes sunk deep in shadows. Finally he spoke.

"Wot part of the Stytes are you from, Miss?"

"California."

"I'm from Bermondsey. Dje know where that is?"

"No."

"Well, I don't know where California is."

The others laughed at this. There was a slight edge to these jibes. They hadn't quite accepted her yet. She hadn't been where they had. They didn't trust anybody who hadn't been in the trenches. You couldn't talk to people. They just wanted to make encouraging speeches to urge you to go back. The generals, the newspapers, the Red Cross girls, all of them.

You could tell this from the song they were singing at the other end of the room, in a mock-sentimental tone, to the tune of *When You Wore a Tulip*.

> "I wore a tunic,
> A dirty khaki tunic,
> And you wore civilian clothes.
> We fought and fled at Loos
> While you were on the booze
> The booze that no one here knows.
>
> Oh, you were with the wenches
> While we were in the trenches
> Facing the German foe.
> Oh, you were a-slacking

While we were attacking
Down the Menin road.''

Herma pushed her way through the crowd to the piano. The Anzac piano player was doing his best. Somebody had stuck one of Herma's Caporals in his mouth and lighted it. He had to play everything in C natural where there weren't too many black notes, and even then he got lost in the more complex harmonies. They made room at the piano for Herma and she leaned on it too, drawing on her cigarette.

"*Wash Me In the Water,*" called somebody.

He groped into it as best he could, while the others sang raucously.

"Wash me in the water
That you washed your dirty daughter
And I shall be whiter
Than the whitewash on the wall.''

"That's not a very nice one to sing while the Miss is 'ere,'' said someone over the din.

"It's all right.''

The Anzac finished *Wash Me In the Water,* after his fashion, and then he stopped and turned to her.

"Can you play this thing?''

She shook her head.

He gave her another look, more searching.

"I'll bet you can sing though.''

Herma smiled. Setting her cigarette in a tin pan on the piano, she tried *There'll Be a Hot Time in the Old Town Tonight.* But this was far too fast for the Anzac. He gave up and threw up his hands. Someone encouraged him, "Come on, Alfie.'' Several others punched him. But it was beyond his powers.

"How about *Tipperary?*'' she asked.

"No, we're fed up to here with *Tipperary.* No one's Irish anyhow.''

"Who the bloody hell wants to go to Tipperary? It's me old Croydon girl I want to see.''

"How about this then.''

After a conference with the Anzac, she sang the one in soldier-French that they all knew.

"Après la guerre finie,
Soldat anglais parti;
Mam'selle Fransay boko pleuray
Après la guerre finie.''

Most of them sang this along with her, although one of them substituted "Mam'selle Fransay can go to hell'' for the third line. Perhaps it was the one who wanted his old Croydon girl. There was some applause at the end.

She told them, "Here's one I'll bet you know.''

In a mock-pathetic voice, as though she didn't have a friend in the world and wished someone to take pity on her, she began to the tune of *Since I Lost You:*

> "I've lost my rifle and bayonet,
> I've lost my pull-through too,
> I've lost my disk and my puttees,
> I've lost my four-by-two.
> I've lost my sew-kit and my gas-mask,
> I've lost my bedroll too;
> I've lost my rations and my greatcoat . . ."
> (The last line in a tone of plaintive lament)
> "Oh Sergeant, what shall I do?"

This was greeted with laughter, and more applause. Most of the men in the room had stopped what they were doing now and turned around toward the piano. The Anzac had gained confidence with *I've Lost My Rifle,* which was a slow tune without too many complexities and one he could keep up with fairly capably.

He looked up at her and put down his cigarette too. He was a man about her own age with an odd complexion, the lower part of his face raw and red and the forehead white. He had evidently been wounded in the head because there was still an oval dressing the size of an egg pasted to the side of his temple.

"Dje know this then. It's a Yank song."

He played a few bars and stopped.

Herma nodded and began it, in a soft half-voice at first, to the absolutely silent room. She sang slowly, pausing between the phrases so that her voice lingered in the smoky air.

> "Nights . . .
> are long . . .
> since you went away . . ."

The Anzac followed her easily, not taking his eyes from her face. His fingers planted in the keys moved from chord to slow chord. Every eye in the room was fixed on her. Her silver-edged soprano, still restrained and soft, moved through the lines of the banal and sentimental popular waltz.

> "I think . . .
> about you . . .
> all through the day,
> my Buddy . . .
> my Buddy . . .
> nobody quite so true . . ."

He was playing it in the wrong key, and she had to start on a high G and slide up to an A on "no-*body*" in the last line. But this was nothing; she had an octave above that she could use if she wanted. In the second stanza she opened into a slightly stronger timbre, but still with a music-hall fragility, a thin tone of sentiment, rather than the full power of the opera voice.

> "Miss . . .
> your voice . . .
> the touch of your hand . . .
> just long . . .
> to know . . .
> that you understand . . .
> my Buddy . . .
> my Buddy . . ."

She went up to the A again and held it for an instant in a clinging tremolo on the last "Buddy . . ."

> "your Buddy . . .
> misses you."

When she finished on the C there was silence for a moment, and then the applause broke out. But it was a different sort of applause from the clapping and laughter she had evoked with the comic songs. No one was smiling now and every face in the room was turned to her. One young soldier, thin and pale, couldn't clap because his arm was in a cast and only nodded, as though he wanted somehow to communicate to her. She caught his eye for an instant. When the applause finally died out the Anzac looked at her. Nobody in the room was playing cards or reading *Punch* anymore. They were waiting—for something—something that she had to give. They didn't know what it was but they knew there was more and they were waiting for it. There was a clumsy and unspoken appeal, a pull of desire or longing, in the faces turned toward her. The boy with his arm in a cast was staring at her fixedly, biting his lip.

"What next?"

The Anzac said, "Sing one that you like, Miss."

She conferred with him, setting her own fingers on the opening chord on the piano.

He nodded. "We all know that, Miss."

She began slowly, lingering over each note with precision, pitching her voice as carefully and clearly as though she were singing Verdi before the cream of Paris society at the Opéra. All her years of craft and skill went into the voice, the long hours of practice, the rehearsals hammered out line by line in empty theaters, the pure timbre, the professional tricks and precision. It was an opera voice, the voice of an international prima donna, a Melba or a Tetrazzini; but the flattened and slightly pathetic tone, the lingering glide from one note to the next, was that of the sentimental music-hall tradition they knew from their half-forgotten civilian past, from their London leaves.

> "There's a long, long trail a-winding
> Into the land of my dreams;
> Where the nightingales are singing
> And a white moon beams . . ."

The Anzac had a little trouble getting from the D seventh chord to the G seventh at the end of the stanza. But it didn't matter, no one was paying any attention to him.

> "There's a long, long night of waiting,
> Until my dreams all . . . come true . . ."

Slow tempo, she told herself. Keep it slow. She moved on through the second stanza with a lingering clarity, as though the voice were reluctant, almost, to move from note to note. And for *them,* the listeners, each note was in fact something they did not wish her to leave; they hung on it, savoring every last particle of the emotion it evoked, as if by magic, as she transformed and exalted the banal campfire song that all of them knew. Into·this last stanza— she knew it was to be the last—she put all the skill and wisdom of her whole young lifetime from the moment when, sitting on Mama's lap, she had felt the talent in her and chimed in with the Baptist choir. The voice was hardly more than a whisper, but it was a whisper with a timbre that penetrated to every corner of the room and suffused with its flowerlike clarity even the odor of cigarette smoke and stale beer that clung in the air—a voice that spoke to each man intimately as though the others in the crowded room were not there. The listeners were as silent and expectant as the expensively dressed audience of the Opéra on the brink of Violetta's death scene. The notes clung in the air, shimmered, and followed one after the other.

> "Till the day . . .
> When I'll be go-ing . . .
> Down that *lo-ong* . . . *lo-ong* . . . trail with you."

There was a moment of churchlike silence. It was as though they were rapt; no one moved. Then one man clapped, and another, and the hut was filled with a deafening roar of applause that went on for a long time. The pale boy with the cast still had his eyes fixed on her. The applause continued as though it would never stop. Here and there was a face with moisture-filled eyes, and she saw an old soldier furtively lift his arm and dab at his cheek with his shirt cuff. *Tonight you have made Modjeska get out her handkerchief,* she remembered, *and that is not easy to do.* It was that little lingering catch in the voice on *lo-ong* in the last line, she knew—as though a tear in the voice was being suppressed only with difficulty. She had learned that from Caruso—"the sexiest sound in the world." It was technique. That was technique. But there was feeling in it too; the moisture had welled in her own eyes. When there was feeling, and when there was technique, and they joined together like two lovers embraced, that was Art.

At last the clapping died out. She took her musette bag from the piano and started for the door. *Most of them lads will never see 'ome again,* said Tiffin. "Good luck, boys," she called over her shoulder. No one moved. Just as she reached the door, the old soldier who had touched his eye with his shirt cuff got up and came after her. She caught a glimpse of the badge and chevrons; he was a sergeant of the Royal Fusiliers. He followed her outside and came up to her in the darkness, and she turned.

He seemed uncertain what to say.

"God bless you, Miss."

She smiled. Then she turned and went out, through the compound and past the fence, and turned onto the road. It was dark and there were ragged clouds overhead; only a little starlight showed through the rifts. With the musette over her shoulder she went down the hard stone road, guiding herself by the line of leafless poplars on the right. She had never been happier. An exultation sprang up in her and filled her breast, as though it would burst out in a flood of luminous brilliance. For the last time she looked up at the stars with her girl's eyes. She was at peace with herself, and with the dark sky and the world. "J'ai vecu!" she thought. "I have lived! I have lived!" A great warmth and bliss spread through her; she was one with the dark earth, the stars, and the vast void of empty space beyond them. Like a gentle thunder, a promise of rain, she heard the rumble of distant gunfire from the trenches forty kilometers to the east.

18.

"It's time, sir."

Fred opened his eyes to see Tiffin with a lighted candle, bending over him with his hand on his arm. Lufbery was already up, pulling on the hunting boots he wore over his Foreign Legion trousers.

"What time is it?"

"Four o'clock, sir."

"The weather?"

"Good weather, sir. Broken clouds."

He got out of bed and dressed rapidly, then went to the W.C. off the hall. When he came out Lufbery and the others were already gathered around the table in the main room, where there were brioches and a pot of steaming coffee. The room was lighted with a single kerosene lamp. It was still pitch dark outside. The phonograph glittered in the gloom at the end of the room. Fred poured himself some coffee, then took the sugar dispenser and tasted a little on his finger to be sure it was really sugar. Thénault noticed him and smiled in his quiet way.

The coffee was pretty bad. It was neither French coffee nor American coffee and after a while Fred realized it was English coffee: Tiffin had made it. Everybody was drinking it. It was part of the suffering of war.

"Everybody finished?" Thénault glanced at his watch. "I want everybody at the field by four-thirty."

"Okay, General," said Thaw, still sitting with his feet on the table. Roy Willkie, hatless, saluted him gravely.

It was cold outside in the dark street. The fur-lined combinations were kept at the field and they were wearing their usual odd-lot costumes, some of them summer uniforms. They stamped their feet on the pavement to warm them. Only Prince in his fur coat looked comfortable. There were about eighteen of them when they were loaded into the transport. For some reason Fred, privileged again, rode in the Packard touring car with Prince, Thaw, and Lufbery. The others came on behind in two Fiat trucks with canvas tops and a double row of benches in the rear. The Fiat trucks blatted and backfired down the narrow street out of town.

At the field the three vehicles stopped on the grass by the hangar and they all got out. Then it was hurry up and wait, as it always is in a war. The mechanics were loading the Vickers guns and checking them. One Nieuport had a gun that had jammed the day before and they wanted to test it. A half dozen of them got around to the rear, picked up the skid, and pointed the aeroplane north toward the foothills of the Vosges. Then a mechanic got in, armed the gun, and pushed the button on the stick. There was an ear-splitting clatter as eight or ten rounds went out. The gun smoked and there was a smell of hot oil. The rounds went out over the Luxeuil-Ormoiche road, but with the skid on the ground the rounds went high and fell into the unpopulated hills a kilometer or two away. The mechanic pulled out the belt and loaded it with a fresh one. It was Thaw's Nieuport. "That marches now, mon lieutenant," the mechanic told him.

They pulled on the combinations and collected their helmets and goggles. The heavy fur-lined garment warmed Fred up a little; it had been very cold standing in the street. Luxeuil was almost in the mountains and it was colder than it was in Paris. Then they sat around at tables in the hangar, smoking cigarettes and talking about the girls in Luxeuil or the last leave in Paris when they had bought the lion and taken it around to bars in taxis and the barman at the Chatham had mistaken it for a dog at first, until Thaw told him it was a chien-lion. After that the barman went into the back room and refused to come out and they had to mix their own drinks. Apparently they had spent most of the three-day leave at the Chatham or at Harry's just a few doors away in Rue Daunou. For some reason Lufbery had gone to Chartres and got into a fight with a railway employee because his papers weren't in order, and spent the night in jail.

"I just went to Chartres to see my marraine," he explained to Fred. A marraine was a godmother. Women, some of them young and pretty and some old trouts, would agree to adopt a soldier or a flyer and write him letters and send him knitted scarves and cognac and so on. You always went to see your marraine when you went on leave. "It was worth it," Lufbery said. "I knocked out one of the railway guy's teeth.'' He didn't say what happened with the marraine.

There was another pot of coffee but no one drank very much of it. It wasn't a good idea to drink too much liquid, because a couple of hours later you had to get rid of it, especially if you were keyed-up and tense, and that was hard to do when you were flying a Nieuport. Norman Prince kept going to the office to use the telephone. The third or fourth time he came out walking quickly but not running, carrying his helmet by the strap. He said ''Albatrosses have crossed the Rhine at Mulhouse.''

They got up and went out, putting on their helmets and fastening them as they went. It was almost light now. The mechanics were already running down the line of Nieuports. Fred was struck with the hurrying of the mechanics and the apparent leisure of the pilots. But this was because they knew it took the mechanics thirty seconds or so to get to the Nieuports and pull the canvases off the engines, and there was no point wearing yourself out running down the line when you had to wait anyhow. At Fred's side was Lufbery, the muscle tightening rhythmically in his cheek. ''These broken clouds at about three thousand are good,'' he said quietly. ''You stay above them and you can spot the Albatrosses through the holes. They can't fly that high with bombs.''

Lufbery's Nieuport and Fred's were the first two in the line. Fred climbed in and settled into the cockpit, and the mechanic was turning over the prop almost before he had his harness buckled. Three or four engines started almost at once. To his right he saw Lufbery's Nieuport moving out, throwing up dust and leaves. He opened the throttle and kicked the rudder around to the right to follow him.

They bumped down along the taxi strip at the side. Lufbery and Fred were halfway down the field before the others began to move out of the line. When Lufbery swung around at the end to take off, Fred turned a little short of him so that the two aeroplanes were parallel and a few yards apart. Lufbery was off almost immediately. He accelerated down the field, his skid came up, the Nieuport skimmed along with one wheel on the grass for a second or two and then lifted. Fred waited impatiently for a few seconds until the rev counter steadied, showing that the engine was warm, then he followed him, rushing down the grass and feeling the sense of exhilaration as the skid came up and then the wheels left the ground and the bumping turned into an even soft lifting, and the hangars and the field and the other Nieuports taxiing fell away behind.

They broke out of the cover at about twenty-eight hundred meters and went on up to three. It was very cold at that altitude. The wind battered around the cowl and cut like a knife at Fred's exposed cheeks. After a while he couldn't feel anything in his face, as though it were anesthetized. Even through the goggles the cold stung his eyes and made them water, and he blinked to clear his vision. Lufbery was on his right and a little ahead. There was no sign of the others. They had settled on a course a little to the south of east; the compass in front of Fred read 110. Evidently Lufbery knew where he was going. Fred could see him clearly only fifty yards or so away, his compact body bent over the stick and his head hunched in to keep it out of the cold. Now and then he turned his head, as if to see if Fred were still there. You couldn't tell anything about his expression through the goggles.

They were flying above broken cumulo-nimbus that were dark on their lower sides. A little silver from the east was beginning to tinge the upper edges of the clouds now, lightening the sky above them. Fred felt his fingers getting stiff from the cold and worked them inside the fur-lined gloves. The icy air battering around the cowl cut even through the heavy fur-lined combination. Down below, under the clouds, the land was still dark. He caught a glimpse of a meandering pewter-colored thread in the valley below, the Rhône-Rhine Canal. Crossing it just under him was a set of parallel jagged scratches, as faint as the lines in a hand: the trenches. He didn't have much chance to study the map in its roller case in front of him because he was flying so close to Lufbery and intent on keeping formation.

Then Lufbery waggled his wings to attract his attention. Lifting his left arm in its heavy clothing, he pointed ahead and to the left. Below, through a rift in the clouds, Fred made out a cluster of buglike black shapes, a dozen or so Albatrosses in vees of three. They were barely visible against the countryside which, under the clouds, was a green so dark it was almost black. At one side and a little behind them was a formation of Aviatiks, recognizable by their narrower, slightly slanted wings and their small tail assemblies. They were moving west toward Belfort with the sun behind them. Over the steady roar of the engine Thénault's words thudded in his ears. *Wait till they turn back to the east. Otherwise it's suicide.*

He nodded, facing Lufbery and moving his head up and down in exaggerated motions. Lufbery's wings tottered a little again. It was not clear whether it was another signal or whether he was getting ready to roll over and go down. Then unexpectedly they both went into a patch of cloud and everything was white for a few seconds. Fred was afraid of sliding into Lufbery over on his right and drifted a little the other way.

When he came out he was alone. There was no sign of Lufbery. There were more clouds ahead but they were higher and he raced along under them, the gray wisps and tatters fleeting by only a few yards overhead. He banked around to the right to see if he could clear the clouds and see better where he was. Then out of the corner of his eye he was aware of another racing shadow, above him and a little behind. At first he thought it was Lufbery, or a Fokker chasseur from Habsheim. Stretched and wobbling like a shape seen under water, unsteady in the stiff air, it seemed insubstantial and flimsy. In an effort to elude it, or at least to catch a better glimpse of it, he kicked the rudder bar and slid over to the left again. Then he looked around. It was hard to concentrate with the roar of the engine and the high whine of the wind in the wires, and it was a bad idea to turn your head when you were flying at high altitude and couldn't see the horizon. But in the instant he looked he knew what it was. His mind spun back to that distant and half-forgotten time when he had first stood before the mirror in the house on Ross Street, the old and tarnished one with many gray splotches in it as though it were the map of an unknown continent. There had been something lurking there, under the surface of the glass. And that dark thing had followed him, it had followed both of them waiting for its moment, it had always been there; he knew that now.

An instant later he flashed out into the diagonal sunlight again. It was crazy! He gritted his teeth and smiled. What he had seen was only the shadow of his own Nieuport racing over the underside of a cloud. He felt quite calm now. It had not really frightened him. A kind of knowledge, the answer to a secret, spread through him and he felt good. He knew now what he was doing, and it was what he wanted to do. It was what she would have wanted too. He was sure of that. He glanced around again but the sky was empty. You couldn't grasp it; it was only a shadow that fled over the clouds. At the speed of the Nieuport it was gone in a second or two.

He banked left again and came back onto his course. Putting his head out gingerly into the icy blast, he looked down and to the left. Through a larger gap in the clouds he could see them below more clearly. They were almost under him now, in perfect formation in vees of three: twelve Albatrosses and nine Aviatiks. He reached forward and pulled the cocking handle of the Vickers. The Albatrosses had disappeared again, then he caught another glimpse of them through a rift. He rolled over on one side and went down toward them, into the shadow.

In a work of historical fiction founded on fact, a number of biographical and historical sources must necessarily be utilized. I am particularly indebted to George Painter's *Proust: The Later Years*, to Frances Alda's *Men, Women, and Tenors*, to Herbert Molloy Mason's *The Lafayette Escadrille*, and to Stanley Jackson's *Caruso*. The other books consulted are too numerous to mention, and in any case this is not a work of scholarship; it is a fiction into which the events of the real world have been incorporated when necessary, yet invariably altered and transformed. In particular, the discerning reader will notice certain distortions of time, as in the novel of Proust.

Thanks are also due to John Joss for advice on early aviation, and to Alexis Walker for information on vocal technique.

McD.H.

MacDonald Harris is the author of eight novels before this one, including *The Treasure of Sainte Foy, The Balloonist,* which was nominated for the National Book Award in fiction, *Yukiko,* and *Pandora's Galley.* His award-winning short fiction has appeared in *Harper's, Atlantic Monthly,* and many other magazines. He has taught in the Writing Program at the University of California, Irvine. Except for frequent stays in Europe, he lives in Southern California.